## PAN'S GARDEN

*Pan's Garden* is a thematic collection of stories which, in the words of the author, "illustrates that characteristic belief, present in all my work, that there exists a definite relationship between Human Beings and Nature." From the opening novella, "The Man Whom the Trees Loved"—in which Nature welcomes and absorbs the soul of a man—to the concluding "The Temptation of the Clay"—in which Nature rejects the spirit of the man who tries to profit from it—we are transported into a natural world where the elements hold sway. Mike Ashley, in his introduction, calls *Pan's Garden* "the definitive volume of Blackwood's short stories... because it defines the true nature of Blackwood's writing."

## INCREDIBLE ADVENTURES

*Incredible Adventures* represents what biographer Mike Ashley calls "the last outburst of his golden period" and is comprised of three novellas and two short stories. Here, nature is a living force, truth is the only religion and the past holds sway over the present. At times almost surreal in their intensity, these tales exert a strange power over the reader, opening our eyes to a larger world around us. From the rugged mountains of Eastern Europe in "The Regeneration of Lord Ernie" to the vast deserts of Egypt in "A Descent Into Egypt," Blackwood takes us to other places—and other worlds.

# ALSO BY ALGERNON BLACKWOOD

NOVELS:
Jimbo: A Fantasy (1909)
The Education of Uncle Paul (1909)
The Human Chord (1910)
The Centaur (1911)
A Prisoner in Fairyland (1913)
The Extra Day (1916)
Julius Le Vallon: An Episode (1916)
The Wave: An Egyptian Aftermath (1916)
The Promise of Air (1918)
The Garden of Survival (1918)
The Bright Messenger (1921)

CHILDREN'S BOOKS:
Sambo and Snitch (1927)
Mr. Cupboard (1928)
Dudley and Gilderoy: A Nonsense (1929)
By Underground (1930)
The Parrot and the - Cat (1931)
The Italian Conjuror (1932)
Maria (of England) in the Rain (1933)
Sergeant Poppett and Policeman James (1934)
The Fruit Stoners (1934)
How the Circus Came to Tea (1936)
The Adventures of Dudley and Gilderoy (1941)

AUTOBIOGRAPHY:
Episodes Before Thirty (1923)

ORIGINAL SHORT STORY COLLECTIONS:
The Empty House and Other Ghost Stories (1906)
The Listener and Other Stories (1907)
John Silence —
    Physician Extraordinary (1908)
The Lost Valley and Other Stories (1910)
Pan's Garden: A Volume of Nature Stories (1912)
Incredible Adventures (1914)
Ten Minute Stories (1914)
Day and Night Stories (1917)
The Wolves of God and Other Fey Stories, w/Wildred Wilson (1921)
Tongues of Fire and Other Sketches (1924)
Full Circle (1929) [single story]
Shocks (1935)
The Doll and One Other (1946)
The Mysterious House (1987) [single story]
The Magic Mirror: Lost Supernatural and Mystery Stories (1989)

PLAYS:
Karma: A Reincarnation Play, w/Violet Pearn (1918)
Through the Crack w/Violet Pearn (1925)

# PAN'S GARDEN
# INCREDIBLE ADVENTURES
## TWO CLASSIC COLLECTIONS BY
# ALGERNON BLACKWOOD

**Stark House Press • Eureka California**
www.StarkHousePress.com

PAN'S GARDEN / INCREDIBLE ADVENTURES

Published by Stark House Press
1315 H Street
Eureka, CA 95501, USA
griffinskye3@sbcglobal.net
www.starkhousepress.com

PAN'S GARDEN
Originally published in 1912 by Macmillan, London and New York;
copyright © 1912 by The Macmillan Company.
Reprinted with permission from the 2000 hardback edition by Tartarus Press.

True Inspiration copyright © 2000 by Mike Ashley

INCREDIBLE ADVENTURES
Originally published in 1914 by Macmillan, London; copyright © 1914
by The Macmillan Company.

Nothing Happening Here copyright © 2002 by Tim Lebbon

All rights reserved

ISBN: 1-933586-15-x
ISBN 13: 978-1-933586-15-1

Cover design and layout by Mark Shepard, www.shepgraphics.com
Cover illustration by Cynthia Bryn Williams based on
a drawing by W. Graham Robertson
Proofread by Joanne Applen

*Publisher's Note: Rather than tamper with Blackwood's prose, we have kept in all cases to the spelling from the original hardback editions. The publisher would personally like to thank Mike Ashley for all his help in bringing these Algernon Blackwood books back into print; and Tim Lebbon for his insightful contribution.*

PUBLISHER'S NOTE
This is a work of fiction. Names, characters, places and incidents are either the products of the author's imagination or used fictitiously, and any resemblance to actual persons, living or dead, events or locales, is entirely coincidental.
Without limiting the rights under copyright reserved above, no part of this publication may be reproduced, stored, or introduced into a retrieval system or transmitted in any form or by any means (electronic, mechanical, photocopying, recording or otherwise) without the prior written permission of both the copyright owner and the above publisher of this book.

First Stark House Press Edition: March 2007

REPRINT EDITION

# CONTENTS

## Pan's Garden

True Inspiration *by Mike Ashley* .................... 8
Man Whom the Trees Loved .................... 13
The South Wind ............................. 62
The Sea Fit ................................. 65
The Attic .................................. 75
The Heath Fire .............................. 80
The Messenger .............................. 86
The Glamour of the Snow. .................... 89
The Return ................................ 104
Sand ..................................... 108
The Transfer ............................... 165
Clairvoyance ............................... 173
The Golden Fly ............................. 177
Special Delivery ............................ 181
The Destruction of Smith .................... 188
The Temptation of the Clay .................. 193

## Incredible Adventures

'Nothing Happening Here' *an Introduction
to Incredible Adventures by Tim Lebbon* ............. 250
The Regeneration of Lord Ernie ................ 253
The Sacrifice ............................... 300
The Damned ............................... 318
A Descent into Egypt ........................ 375
Wayfarers ................................. 425

# Pan's Garden

## A Volume of Nature Stories

by Algernon Blackwood

TO
M. S.—K.
WHO MADE WITH ME THESE LITTLE PATHS
ACROSS PAN'S TANGLED GARDEN.

## True Inspiration

An Introduction
by Mike Ashley

On October 16th 1911, while resident at his *pension* in Bôle in Switzerland, Algernon Blackwood wrote to the publisher, Frederick Macmillan, with the following proposal.

In the course of a short time I shall have ready the MS of a book I want to bring out, if possible, in the Spring. Although composed of separate pieces, varying from 26,000 words to 2,000 words, it is a coherent whole, the same idea running throughout, and it illustrates that characteristic belief, present in all my work, that there exists a definite relationship between Human Beings and Nature.

Thus was the birth of what became *Pan's Garden*, though at the outset Blackwood named the collection after its lead story, "The Man Whom the Trees Loved." It was even promoted under that name in early catalogues.

*Pan's Garden* remains for me the definitive volume of Blackwood's short stories: not because it necessarily contains all of his best work in the genre, although it certainly includes several stories that I consider to be his greatest, but because it defines the true nature of Blackwood's writing. It is at the heart of his most creative and inspired productions and, because of that, it is worth spending some time exploring the contents of the book and placing the stories in the context of Blackwood's other writings at this time.

*Pan's Garden* was compiled at the end of what was indisputably Blackwood's single most creative period. A little over a year earlier he had encountered a form of writer's block. He was so full of inspiration that he just could not write. During May and June of 1910 Blackwood had travelled through the Caucasus. He wrote about this forty years later in an article for the *London Mystery Magazine*, "The Birth of an Idea".

After an extended tour I came home charged with a thousand storms of beauty and wonder, only to find that I could not write a line about it all. Stunned and bewildered by what I had seen, the mind was speechless, incapable of expressing anything beyond a few superficial travel sketches. Indeed, a year passed without even a desire to write about it until suddenly, one night in a filthy London fog, I caught a sound which seemed to me ravishing, yes, it was intoxicating music.

Outside Blackwood's rooms was a street urchin playing a penny whistle. Somehow that music unlocked Blackwood's imagination.

I rushed back into my room and to my writing-table. A flood had been let loose in me, its origin apparently the trivial detail of a wheezy penny whistle. It all stormed up out of the subconscious, and I began a book, a book that, good or bad, released the dramatized emotions of my journey a year before through the Caucasus.

That book was *The Centaur*, and the inspiration did not stop there. During the winter of 1910-1911, as Blackwood struggled with the immensity of *The Centaur*, he was also working on another novel. This was the story of an elemental trapped in the body of a child. He had been at a loss as to how to finish the novel but, somehow, the inspiration that brought *The Centaur* back to life, also revived what became *Julius LeVallon*. If Blackwood had written nothing else, these two books alone would stand testament to a unique and gifted writer.

Yet still the inspiration flowed. Having finished *Julius LeVallon*, he laid aside *The Centaur* for a while and wrote "The Man Whom the Trees Loved", the story that opens *Pan's Garden*. In fact, almost all of the stories in this collection were written during the summer of 1911, in and around the completion of *Julius LeVallon* and *The Centaur*. The staggering intensity of inspiration that fired those two remarkable books flowed over into *Pan's Garden*, making them a trilogy which stand at the pinnacle of Blackwood's creativity. That inspiration ran its course for perhaps another year, sufficient for him to dig out and rework his early unsold novel, *Jimbo*, and to write the stories for his later volume *Incredible Adventures*. By the outbreak of the First World War, Blackwood's most creative period was over.

When advising Macmillan of the volume, Blackwood explained that "I have been steadily adding to this book for some years, taking in turn different aspects of Nature—sea, mountains, snow, fire, etc." It is not clear how long a period Blackwood meant by "some years". The earliest story in the book (at least in terms of publication date) is "The South Wind" which appeared in the *Westminster Gazette* of January 29th 1910 and was almost certainly written only a week or two earlier. The last story to be finished was "Sand", completed even as the book had reached proof stage in March 1912. There is evidence, however, as we shall see, that some of these stories had been begun long before.

I have also wondered whether Blackwood had originally considered other stories for the book. Certainly there were similar stories written at this time which were used in other collections. These include "Dream Trespass", with its strange vision of the past and association of place, which was written between "Clairvoyance" and "The Glamour of the Snow". This eventually appeared in *Ten Minute Stories*. (1914) Then there is "Perspective", written just before "The South Wind" and squeezed at the last minute into *The Lost Valley* (1910), in which a human being is used as a pawn of Nature. Both of these stories would have been at home in *Pan's Garden*.

The title is wonderfully appropriate for Blackwood's work—Pan was the Greek god who personified Nature and the wild world around us. *Pan's Gar-*

*den* celebrates the wild parts of the Earth, those which had not been cultivated or spoiled by man. Pan was the nickname by which Blackwood was known to his close friends. Perhaps of greater import, Blackwood was in many ways a Nature spirit himself. He hated towns and cities or anywhere where civilisation had robbed the Earth of its soul. He wrote about this passion for Nature in his autobiography, *Episodes Before Thirty* (1923).

> By far the strongest influence in my life, however, was Nature; it betrayed itself early, growing in intensity with every year. Bringing comfort, companionship, inspiration, joy, the spell of Nature has remained dominant, a truly magical spell. Always immense and potent, the years have strengthened it. The early feeling that everything was alive, a dim sense that some kind of consciousness struggled through every form, even that a sort of inarticulate communication with this 'other life' was possible, could I but discover the way—these moods coloured its opening wonder.

It was in Nature that Blackwood sought solace.

> In times of trouble, as equally in times of joy, it was to Nature I ever turned instinctively. In those moments of deepest feeling when individuals must necessarily be alone, yet stand at the same time in most urgent need of understanding companionship, it was Nature and Nature only that could comfort me.

It was to the wild and unconquered parts of the world that Blackwood was most attracted. From the vast forests of the Canadian north, to the mountains of the Caucasus and the deserts of Egypt—this was Blackwood's world and, by association, Pan's Garden. The inspiration of Nature is what makes Blackwood's world unique. He applies the word supernatural in its strictest sense. Whereas the word now tends to encompass ghosts or anything spooky, Blackwood regarded the supernatural as a higher level of consciousness within Nature. He believed that by a close association with the natural world, the mind and spirit could, if not exactly commune with Nature, at least gain an insight into this greater world.

It is this relationship which he had begun to explore in his earlier stories. Blackwood disliked the epithet 'Ghost Man', with which he was so readily dubbed by the media as a result of his popularity on radio and television in the late 1930s and 40s. For the most part Blackwood's tales are not straightforward ghost stories. His very best, those which come from the heart and are closest to his philosophy of life, are far removed from the classic ghost story and yet remain firmly within the tradition of supernatural fiction.

The earliest published stories are the most traditional, probably because they were regarded as more commercially viable, but also because Blackwood was writing the dark horrors of his early life out of his system. The collapse of his first business venture, his near-fatal illness, his experiences as a victim of grand larceny, his fears of arrest because of an innocent involvement in an insurance scam, his experiences with drugs and, above all, the belief that he had lost the love of his father who died before they could be reconciled - all these factors cast a depression over Blackwood's early days. Most of these themes emerged in standard ghost stories at first, such as "The Empty House" and "A Case of Eavesdropping." Yet even in his first two collections, *The Empty House and Other Ghost Stories* (1906) and *The Listener and Other Stories* (1907), there are some stories which show clear signs of what was to come. "A Haunted Island" might, on the surface, be the story of a haunted house, but at its heart it is about the spiritual resonance of living in a remote and savagely beautiful part of the world. "The Wood of the Dead" is another story in which the remoteness of the location inspires visions.

Amongst these early stories two stand out as major signposts pointing toward *Pan's Garden*. The first was "The Willows", where two men camping on a remote island in the River Danube witness the power of inter-dimensional forces. The other is "The Wendigo", undoubtedly amongst Blackwood's most incredible pieces of writing, where he seeks to capture a personification of the Call of the Wild. In a later radio talk Blackwood explained that he wrote "The Wendigo" whilst sheltering in a hut in the mountains of Switzerland during a raging snow storm when the wind seemed to talk to him.

Every story which makes up *Pan's Garden* is inspired by a particular *genius loci*. At the end of each story Blackwood notes the place with which it is associated. These range from Helouan in Egypt for "Sand", to Sandhills, in Surrey (the home of the book's illustrator, W. Graham Robertson), for "The Heath Fire" and "The Transfer". Others are set in the French Jura or the Swiss Alps, where Blackwood spent every winter, or in Britain, wherever his travels took him. The Haven Hotel, of "The Sea Fit", is in Poole, Dorset, overlooking the Isle of Purbeck, where Blackwood watched the wild sea battering the shore. I have sat in the lounge where Blackwood wrote this story and watched the wind and rain assault the coast. This was, incidentally, the hotel from which Marconi sent his first transatlantic radio message. The location of Hank's Camp for "The Destruction of Smith" is odd because it suggests that this is an early story which Blackwood was only able to finish just before the book went to press, in January 1912. Hank was a guide and tracker who took Blackwood and his colleagues on expeditions into the Canadian forests. Since this story has an American setting, I suspect it somehow grew from discussions and fireside tales during Blackwood's travels in North America in the 1890s. I confess I have yet to identify The Lavender Room of "Clairvoyance", but believe it may be situated in one of the London clubs that Blackwood frequented.

All of the stories appeared first in magazines or newspapers, except for "The Temptation of the Clay" and "Sand". They were, in any case, perhaps too long for magazine publication and neither is appropriate for serialisation. Not that there would have been time for this. "The Temptation of the Clay" was finished in October 1911, specifically for the book. In, January 1912, Blackwood paid his first visit to Egypt, staying in a hotel and health resort run by his friend Baroness de Knoop in Helouan, south of Cairo. Blackwood's encounter with the immensity of Egypt's past would inspire several stories, of which "Sand" was the first. "Though I had begun it long ago," he told Frederick Macmillan in March 1912, "I could not finish it faithfully until I had seen and felt the Desert first hand." Although most of the stories in *Pan's Garden* later resurfaced in other, retrospective compilations of Blackwood's work, neither "Sand" nor "Temptation of the Clay" were ever reprinted, almost certainly because of their length. This edition of *Pan's Garden* therefore marks their first appearance for almost ninety years.

One final word. These stories are potent. They are the quintessence of some of the most inspired creativity you will find anywhere in the world of supernatural fiction. Like fine wines or beautiful food, they are best taken of sparingly. Do not try and read this book all at once. Savour it. Choose a single story now and again. Keep it there on your shelf of favourite reading and dip into it. This book may open the channel between you and Nature. Do not treat it lightly.

# The Man Whom the Trees Loved

I

HE painted trees as by some special divining instinct of their essential qualities. He understood them. He knew why in an oak forest, for instance, each individual was utterly distinct from its fellows, and why no two beeches in the whole world were alike. People asked him down to paint a favourite lime or silver birch, for he caught the individuality of a tree as some catch the individuality of a horse. How he managed it was something of a puzzle, for he never had painting lessons, his drawing was often wildly inaccurate, and, while his perception of a Tree Personality was true and vivid, his rendering of it might almost approach the ludicrous. Yet the character and personality of that particular tree stood there alive beneath his brush—shining, frowning, dreaming, as the case might be, friendly or hostile, good or evil. It emerged.

There was nothing else in the wide world that he could paint; flowers and landscapes he only muddled away into a smudge; with people he was helpless and hopeless; also with animals. Skies he could sometimes manage, or effects of wind in foliage, but as a rule he left these all severely alone. He kept to trees, wisely following an instinct that was guided by love. It was quite arresting, this way he had of making a tree look almost like a being—alive. It approached the uncanny.

"Yes, Sanderson knows what he's doing when he paints a tree!" thought old David Bittacy, C.B., late of the Woods and Forests. "Why, you can almost hear it rustle. You can smell the thing. You can hear the rain drip through its leaves. You can almost see the branches move. It grows." For in this way somewhat he expressed his satisfaction, half to persuade himself that the twenty guineas were well spent (since his wife thought otherwise), and half to explain this uncanny reality of life that lay in the fine old cedar framed above his study table.

Yet in the general view the mind of Mr Bittacy was held to be austere, not to say morose. Few divined in him the secretly tenacious love of nature that had been fostered by years spent in the forests and jungles of the eastern world. It was odd for an Englishman, due possibly to that Eurasian ancestor. Surreptitiously, as though half ashamed of it, he had kept alive a sense of beauty that hardly belonged to his type, and was unusual for its vitality. Trees, in particular, nourished it. He, also, understood trees, felt a subtle sense of communion with them, born perhaps of those years he had lived in caring for them, guarding, protecting, nursing, years of solitude among their great shadowy presences. He kept it largely to himself, of course, because he knew the world he lived in. He also kept it from his wife—to some extent. He knew it came between them, knew that she feared it, was opposed. But what he did not know, or realise at any rate, was the extent to which she grasped the power which they wielded over his life. Her fear, he judged, was simply due to those years in India, when for weeks at a time his calling took him away from her into the jungle forests, while she remained at home dreading all manner of evils that might befall him. This, of course, explained her instinctive opposition to the passion for woods that still influenced and clung to him. It was a natural survival of those anxious days of waiting in solitude for his safe return.

For Mrs Bittacy, daughter of an evangelical clergyman, was a self-sacrificing woman, who in most things found a happy duty in sharing her husband's joys and sorrows to the point of self-obliteration. Only in this matter of the trees she was less successful than in others. It remained a problem difficult of compromise.

He knew, for instance, that what she objected to in this portrait of the cedar on their lawn was really not the price he had given for it, but the unpleasant way in which the transaction emphasised this breach between their common interests—the only one they had, but deep.

Sanderson, the artist, earned little enough money by his strange talent; such cheques were few and far between. The owners of fine or interesting trees who cared to have them painted singly were rare indeed and the "studies" that he made for his own delight he also kept for his own delight. Even were there buyers, he would not sell them. Only a few, and these peculiarly intimate friends, might even see them, for he disliked to hear the undiscerning criticisms of those who did not understand. Not that he minded laughter at his craftmanship—he admitted it with scorn—but that remarks about the personality of the tree itself could easily wound or anger him. He resented slighting observations concerning them, as though insults offered to personal friends who could not answer for themselves. He was instantly up in arms.

"It really *is* extraordinary," said a Woman who Understood, "that you can make that cypress seem an individual, when in reality all cypresses are so *exactly* alike."

And though the bit of calculated flattery had come so near to saying the right, true thing, Sanderson flushed as though she had slighted a friend beneath his very nose. Abruptly he passed in front of her and turned the picture to the wall.

"Almost as queer," he answered rudely, copying her silly emphasis, "as that *you* should have imagined individuality in your husband, Madame, when in reality all men are so *exactly* alike!"

Since the only thing that differentiated her husband from the mob was the money for which she had married him, Sanderson's relations with that particular family terminated on the spot, chance of prospective "orders" with it. His sensitiveness, perhaps, was morbid. At any rate the way to reach his heart lay through his trees. He might be said to love trees. He certainly drew a splendid inspiration from them, and the source of a man's inspiration, be it music, religion, or a woman, is never a safe thing to criticise.

"I do think, perhaps, it was just a little extravagant, dear," said Mrs Bittacy, referring to the cedar cheque, "when we want a lawn-mower so badly too. But, as it gives you such pleasure—"

"It reminds me of a certain day, Sophia," replied the old gentleman, looking first proudly at herself, then fondly at the picture, "now long gone by. It reminds me of another tree—that Kentish lawn in the spring, birds singing in the lilacs, and someone in a muslin frock waiting patiently beneath a certain cedar—not the one in the picture, I know, but—"

"I was not waiting," she said indignantly, "I was picking fir-cones for the schoolroom fire—"

"Fir-cones, my dear, do not grow on cedars, and schoolroom fires were not made in June in my young days."

"And anyhow it isn't the same cedar."

"It has made me fond of all cedars for its sake," he answered, "and it reminds me that you are the same young girl still—"

She crossed the room to his side, and together they looked out of the window where, upon the lawn of their Hampshire cottage, a ragged Lebanon stood in solitary state.

"You're as full of dreams as ever," she said gently, "and I don't regret the cheque a bit—really. Only it would have been more real if it had been the original tree, wouldn't it?"

"That was blown down long ago. I passed the place last year, and there's not a sign of it left," he replied tenderly. And presently, when he released her from his side, she went up to the wall and carefully dusted the picture Sanderson had made of the cedar on their present lawn. She went all round the frame with her tiny handkerchief, standing on tiptoe to reach the top rim.

"What I like about it," said the old fellow to himself when his wife had left the room, "is the way he has made it live. All trees have it, of course, but a cedar taught it to me first—the 'something' trees possess that make them know I'm there when I stand close and watch. I suppose I felt it then because I was in love, and love reveals life everywhere." He glanced a moment at the Lebanon looming gaunt and sombre through the gathering dusk. A curious wistful expression danced a moment through his eyes. "Yes, Sanderson has seen it as it is," he murmured, "solemnly dreaming there its dim hidden life against the Forest edge, and as different from that other tree in Kent as I am from—from the vicar, say. It's quite a stranger, too. I don't know anything about it really. That other cedar I loved; this old fellow I respect. Friendly though—yes, on the whole quite friendly. He's painted the friendliness right enough. He saw that. I'd like to know that man better," he added. "I'd like to ask him how he saw so clearly that it stands there between this cottage and the Forest—yet somehow more in sympathy with us than with the mass of woods behind—a sort of go-between. *That* I never noticed before. I see it now—through his eyes. It stands there like a sentinel—protective rather."

He turned away abruptly to look through the window. He saw the great encircling mass of gloom that was the Forest, fringing their little lawn. It pressed up closer in the darkness. The prim garden with its formal beds of flowers seemed an impertinence almost—some little coloured insect that sought to settle on a sleeping monster—some gaudy fly that danced impudently down the edge of a great river that could engulf it with a toss of its smallest wave. That Forest with its thousand years of growth and its deep spreading being was some such slumbering monster, yes. Their cottage and garden stood too near its running lip. When the winds were strong and lifted its shadowy skirts of black and purple... He loved this feeling of the Forest Personality; he had always loved it.

"Queer," he reflected, "awfully queer, that trees should bring me such a sense of dim, vast living! I used to feel it particularly, I remember, in India; in Canadian woods as well; but never in little English woods till here. And Sanderson's the only man I ever knew who felt it too. He's never said so, but there's the proof," and he turned again to the picture that he loved. A thrill of unaccustomed life ran through him as he looked. "I wonder, by Jove, I wonder," his thoughts ran on, "whether a tree—er—in any lawful meaning of the term can be—alive. I remember some writing fellow telling me long ago that trees had once been moving things, animal organisms of some sort, that had stood so long feeding, sleeping, dreaming, or something, in the same place, that they had lost the power to get away... !"

Fancies flew pell-mell about his mind, and, lighting a cheroot, he dropped into an armchair beside the open window and let them play. Outside the blackbirds whistled in the shrubberies across the lawn. He smelt the earth and trees and flowers, the perfume of mown grass, and the bits of open heathland far away in the heart of the woods. The summer wind stirred very faintly through the leaves. But the great New Forest hardly raised her sweeping skirts of black and purple shadow.

Mr Bittacy, however, knew intimately every detail of that wilderness of trees within. He knew all the purple coombs splashed with yellow waves of gorse sweet with juniper and myrtle, and gleaming with clear and dark-eyed pools that watched the sky. There hawks hovered, circling hour by hour, and the flicker of the peewit's flight with its melancholy, petulant cry, deepened the sense of stillness. He knew the solitary pines, dwarfed, tufted, vigorous, that sang to every lost wind, travellers like the gipsies who pitched their bush-like tents beneath them; he knew the shaggy ponies, with foals like baby centaurs; the chattering jays, the milky call of cuckoos in the spring, and the boom of the bittern from the lonely marshes. The undergrowth of watching hollies, he knew too, strange and mysterious, with their dark, suggestive beauty, and the yellow shimmer of their pale dropped leaves.

Here all the Forest lived and breathed in safety, secure from mutilation. No terror of the axe could haunt the peace of its vast subconscious life, no terror of devastating Man afflict it with the dread of premature death. It knew itself supreme; it spread and preened itself without concealment. It set no spires to carry warnings, for no wind brought messages of alarm as it bulged outwards to the sun and stars.

But, once its leafy portals left behind, the trees of the countryside were otherwise. The houses threatened them; they knew themselves in danger. The roads were no longer glades of silent turf, but noisy, cruel ways by which men came to attack them. They were civilised, cared for—but cared for in order that some day they might be put to death. Even in the villages, where the solemn and immemorial repose of giant chestnuts aped security, the tossing of a silver birch against their mass, impatient in the littlest wind, brought warning. Dust clogged their leaves. The inner humming of their quiet life became inaudible beneath the scream and shriek of clattering traffic. They longed and prayed to enter the great Peace of the Forest yonder, but they could not move. They knew, moreover, that the Forest with its august, deep splendour despised and pitied them. They were a thing of artificial gardens, and belonged to beds of flowers all forced to grow one way...

"I'd like to know that artist fellow better," was the thought upon which he returned at length to the things of practical life. "I wonder if Sophia would mind him here for a bit—?" He rose with the sound of the gong, brushing the ashes from his speckled waistcoat. He pulled the waistcoat down. He was slim and spare in figure, active in his movements. In the dim light, but for that silvery moustache, he might easily have passed for a man of forty. "I'll suggest it to her anyhow," he decided on his way upstairs to dress. His thought really was that Sanderson could probably explain this world of things he had always felt about—trees. A man who could paint the soul of a cedar in that way must know it all.

"Why not?" she gave her verdict later over the bread-and-butter pudding "unless you think he'd find it dull without companions."

"He would paint all day in the Forest, dear. I'd like to pick his brains a bit, too, if I could manage it."

"You can manage anything, David," was what she answered, for this elderly childless couple used an affectionate politeness long since deemed old-fashioned. The remark, however, displeased her, making her feel uneasy, and she did not notice his rejoinder, smiling his pleasure and content—"Except yourself and our bank account, my dear." This passion of his for trees was of old a bone of contention, though very mild contention. It frightened her. That was the truth. The Bible, her Baedeker for earth and heaven, did not mention it. Her husband, while humouring her, could never alter that instinctive dread she had. He soothed, but never changed her. She liked the woods, perhaps as spots for shade and picnics, but she could not, as he did, love them.

And after dinner, with a lamp beside the open window, he read aloud from *The Times* the evening post had brought, such fragments as he thought might interest her. The custom was invariable, except on Sundays, when, to please his wife, he dozed over Tennyson or Farrar as their mood might be. She knitted while he read, asked gentle questions, told him his voice was a "lovely reading voice," and enjoyed the little discussions that occasions prompted because he always let her win them with "Ah, Sophia, I had never thought of it quite in *that* way before but now you mention it I must say I think there's something in it..."

For David Bittacy was wise. It was long after marriage, during his months of loneliness spent with trees and forests in India, his wife waiting at home in the Bungalow, that his other, deeper side had developed the strange passion that she could not understand. And after one or two serious attempts to let her share it with him, he had given up and learned to hide it from her. He learned, that is, to speak of it only casually for since she knew it was there, to keep silence altogether would only increase her pain. So from time to time he skimmed the surface just to let her show him where he was wrong and think she won the day. It remained a debatable land of compromise. He listened with patience to her criticisms, her excursions and alarms, knowing that while it gave her satisfaction, it could not change himself. The thing lay in him too deep and true for change. But, for peace' sake, some meeting-place was desirable, and he found it thus.

It was her one fault in his eyes, this religious mania carried over from her upbringing, and it did no serious harm. Great emotion could shake it sometimes out of her. She clung to it because her father taught it her and not because she had thought it out for herself. Indeed, like many women, she never really *thought* at all, but merely reflected the images of others' thinking which she had learned to see. So, wise in his knowledge of human nature, old David Bittacy accepted the pain of being obliged to keep a portion of his inner life shut off from the woman he deeply loved. He regarded her little biblical phrases as oddities that still clung to a rather fine, big soul—like horns and little useless things some animals have not yet lost in the course of evolution while they have outgrown their use.

"My dear, what is it? You frightened me!" She asked it suddenly, sitting up so abruptly that her cap dropped sideways almost to her ear. For David Bittacy behind his crackling paper had uttered a sharp exclamation of surprise. He had lowered the sheet and was staring at her over the tops of his gold glasses.

"Listen to this, if you please," he said, a note of eagerness in his voice, "listen to this, my dear Sophia. It's from an address by Francis Darwin before the Royal Society. He is president, you know, and son of the great Darwin. Listen carefully, I beg you. It is *most* significant."

"I *am* listening, David," she said with some astonishment, looking up. She stopped her knitting.

For a second she glanced behind her. Something had suddenly changed in the room, and it made her feel wide awake, though before she had been almost dozing. Her husband's voice and manner had introduced this new thing. Her instincts rose in warning. "*Do* read it, dear." He took a deep breath, looking first again over the rims of his glasses to make quite sure of her attention. He had evidently come across something of genuine interest, although herself she often found the passages from these "Addresses" somewhat heavy.

In a deep, emphatic voice he read aloud

"'It is impossible to know whether or not plants are conscious but it is consistent with the doctrine of continuity that in all living things there is something psychic, and if we accept this point of view—'"

"If," she interrupted, scenting danger.

He ignored the interruption as a thing of slight value he was accustomed to.

"'If we accept this point of view,'" he continued, "'we must believe that in plants there exists a faint copy of *what we know as consciousness in ourselves*.'"

He laid the paper down and steadily stared at her. Their eyes met. He had italicised the last phrase.

For a minute or two his wife made no reply or comment. They stared at one another in silence. He waited for the meaning of the words to reach her understanding with full import. Then he turned and read them again in part, while she, released from that curious driving look in his eyes, instinctively again glanced over her shoulder round the room. It was almost as if she felt someone had come in to them unnoticed.

"We must believe that in plants there exists a faint copy of what we know as consciousness in ourselves."

"*If,*" she repeated lamely, feeling before the stare of those questioning eyes she must say something, but not yet having gathered her wits together quite.

"*Consciousness*," he rejoined. And then he added gravely: "That, my dear, is the statement of a scientific man of the Twentieth Century."

Mrs Bittacy sat forward in her chair so that her silk flounces crackled louder than the newspaper. She made a characteristic little sound between sniffing and snorting. She put her shoes closely together, with her hands upon her knees.

"David," she said quietly, "I think these scientific men are simply losing their heads. There is nothing in the Bible that I can remember about any such thing whatsoever."

"Nothing, Sophia, that I can remember either," he answered patiently. Then, after a pause, he added, half to himself perhaps more than to her: "And, now that I come to think about it, it seems that Sanderson once said something to me that was similar."

"Then Mr Sanderson is a wise and thoughtful man, and a safe man," she quickly took him up, "if he said that."

For she thought her husband referred to her remark about the Bible, and not to her judgment of the scientific men. And he did not correct her mistake.

"And plants, you see, dear, are not the same thing as trees," she drove her advantage home, "not quite, that is."

"I agree," said David quietly "but both belong to the great vegetable kingdom."

There was a moment's pause before she answered.

"Pah! the vegetable kingdom, indeed!" She tossed her pretty old head. And into the words she put a degree of contempt that, could the vegetable kingdom have heard it, might have made it feel ashamed for covering a third of the world with its wonderful tangled network of roots and branches, delicate shaking leaves, and its millions of spires that caught the sun and wind and rain. Its very right to existence seemed in question.

## II

SANDERSON accordingly came down, and on the whole his short visit was a success. Why he came at all was a mystery to those who heard of it, for he never paid visits and was certainly not the kind of man to court a customer. There must have been something in Bittacy he liked.

Mrs Bittacy was glad when he left. He brought no dress-suit for one thing, not even a dinner-jacket, and he wore very low collars with big balloon ties like a Frenchman, and let his hair grow longer than was nice, she felt. Not that these things were important, but that she considered them symptoms of something a little disordered. The ties were unnecessarily flowing.

For all that he was an interesting man, and, in spite of his eccentricities of dress and so forth, a gentleman. "Perhaps," she reflected in her genuinely charitable heart, "he had other uses for the twenty guineas, an invalid sister or an old mother to support!" She had no notion of the cost of brushes, frames, paints, and canvases. Also she forgave him much for the sake of his beautiful eyes and his eager enthusiasm of manner. So many men of thirty were already blasé.

Still, when the visit was over, she felt relieved. She said nothing about his coming a second time, and her husband, she was glad to notice, had likewise made no suggestion. For, truth to tell, the way the younger man engrossed the older, keeping him out for hours in the Forest, talking on the lawn in the blazing sun, and in the evenings when the damp of dusk came creeping out from the surrounding woods, all regardless of his age and usual habits, was not quite to her taste. Of course, Mr Sanderson did not know how easily those attacks of Indian fever came back, but David surely might have told him.

They talked trees from morning till night. It stirred in her the old subconscious trail of dread, a trail that led ever into the darkness of big woods and such feelings, as her early evangelical training taught her, were temptings. To regard them in any other way was to play with danger.

Her mind, as she watched these two, was charged with curious thoughts of dread she could not understand, yet feared the more on that account. The way they studied that old mangy cedar was a trifle unnecessary, unwise, she felt. It was disregarding the sense of proportion which deity had set upon the world for men's safe guidance.

Even after dinner they smoked their cigars upon the low branches that swept down and touched the lawn, until at length she insisted on their coming in. Cedars, she had somewhere heard, were not safe after sundown; it was not wholesome to be too near them; to sleep beneath them was even dangerous, though what the precise danger was she had forgotten. The upas was the tree she really meant.

At any rate she summoned David in, and Sanderson came presently after him.

For a long time, before deciding on this peremptory step, she had watched them surreptitiously from the drawing-room window—her husband and her guest. The dusk enveloped them with its damp veil of gauze. She saw the glowing tips of their cigars, and heard the drone of voices. Bats flitted overhead, and big, silent moths whirred softly over the rhododendron blossoms. And it came suddenly to her, while she watched, that her husband had somehow altered these last few days— since Mr Sanderson's arrival in fact. A change had come over him, though what it was she could not say. She hesitated, indeed, to search. That was the instinctive dread operating in her. Provided it passed she would rather not know. Small things, of course, she noticed small outward signs. He had neglected *The Times* for one thing, left off his speckled waistcoats for another. He was absent-minded sometimes; showed vagueness in practical details where hitherto he showed decision. And—he had begun to talk in his sleep again.

These and a dozen other small peculiarities came suddenly upon her with the rush of a combined attack. They brought with them a faint distress that made her shiver. Momentarily her mind was startled, then confused, as her eyes picked out the shadowy figures in the dusk, the cedar covering them, the Forest close at their backs. And then, before she could think, or seek internal guidance as her habit was, this whisper, muffled and very hurried, ran across her brain: "It's Mr Sanderson. Call David in at once!"

And she had done so. Her shrill voice crossed the lawn and died away into the Forest, quickly smothered. No echo followed it. The sound fell dead against the rampart of a thousand listening trees.

"The damp is so very penetrating, even in summer," she murmured when they came obediently. She was half surprised at her own audacity, half repentant. They came so meekly at her call. "And my husband is sensitive to fever from the East. No, *please* do not throw away your cigars. We can sit by the open window and enjoy the evening while you smoke."

She was very talkative for a moment; subconscious excitement was the cause.

"It is so still—so wonderfully still," she went on, as no one spoke, "so peaceful, and the air so very sweet... and God is always near to those who need His aid." The words slipped out before she realised quite what she was saying, yet fortunately, in time to lower her voice, for no one heard them. They were, perhaps, an instinctive expression of relief. It flustered her that she could have said the thing at all.

Sanderson brought her shawl and helped to arrange the chairs she thanked him in her old-fashioned, gentle way, declining the lamps which he had offered to light. "They attract the moths and insects so, I think!"

The three of them sat there in the gloaming, Mr Bittacy's white moustache and his wife's yellow shawl gleaming at either end of the little horseshoe,

Sanderson with his wild black hair and shining eyes midway between them. The painter went on talking softly, continuing evidently the conversation begun with his host beneath the cedar. Mrs Bittacy, on her guard, listened— uneasily.

"For trees, you see, rather conceal themselves in daylight. They reveal themselves fully only after sunset. I never *know* a tree," he bowed here slightly towards the lady as though to apologise for something he felt she would not quite understand or like, "until I've seen it in the night. Your cedar, for instance," looking towards her husband again so that Mrs Bittacy caught the gleaming of his turned eyes, "I failed with badly at first, because I did it in the morning. You shall see tomorrow what I mean—that first sketch is upstairs in my portfolio; it's quite another tree to the one you bought. That view"— he leaned forward, lowering his voice—"I caught one morning about two o'clock in very faint moonlight and the stars. I saw the naked being of the thing—"

"You mean that you went out, Mr Sanderson, at that hour?" the old lady asked with astonishment and mild rebuke. She did not care particularly for his choice of adjectives either.

"I fear it was rather a liberty to take in another's house, perhaps," he answered courteously. "But, having chanced to wake, I saw the tree from my window, and made my way downstairs."

"It's a wonder Boxer didn't bite you; he sleeps loose in the hall," she said.

"On the contrary. The dog came out with me. I hope," he added, "the noise didn't disturb you, though it's rather late to say so. I feel quite guilty." His white teeth showed in the dusk as he smiled. A smell of earth and flowers stole in through the window on a breath of wandering air.

Mrs Bittacy said nothing at the moment. "We both sleep like tops," put in her husband, laughing. "You're a courageous man, though, Sanderson and, by Jove, the picture justifies you. Few artists would have taken so much trouble, though I read once that Holman Hunt, Rossetti, or someone of that lot, painted all night in his orchard to get an effect of moonlight that he wanted."

He chattered on. His wife was glad to hear his voice; it made her feel more easy in her mind. But presently the other held the floor again, and her thoughts grew darkened and afraid. Instinctively she feared the influence on her husband. The mystery and wonder that lie in woods, in forests, in great gatherings of trees everywhere, seemed so real and present while he talked.

"The Night transfigures all things in a way," he was saying "but nothing so searchingly as trees. From behind a veil that sunlight hangs before them in the day they emerge and show themselves. Even buildings do that—in a measure—but trees particularly. In the daytime they sleep; at night they wake, they manifest, turn active—live. You remember," turning politely again in the direction of his hostess, "how clearly Henley understood that?"

"That socialist person, you mean?" asked the lady. Her tone and accent made the substantive sound criminal. It almost hissed, the way she uttered it.

"The poet, yes," replied the artist tactfully, "the friend of Stevenson, you remember, Stevenson who wrote those charming children's verses."

He quoted in a low voice the lines he meant. It was, for once, the time, the place, and the setting all together. The words floated out across the lawn towards the wall of blue darkness where the big Forest swept the little garden with its league-long curve that was like the shore-line of a sea. A wave of distant sound that was like surf accompanied his voice, as though the wind was fain to listen too:

Not to the staring Day,
For all the importunate questionings he pursues
In his big, violent voice,
Shall those mild things of bulk and multitude,
The trees—God's sentinels...
Yield of their huge, unutterable selves.

\* \* \*

But at the word
Of the ancient, sacerdotal Night,
Night of the many secrets, whose effect—
Transfiguring, hierophantic, dread—
Themselves alone may fully apprehend,
They tremble and are changed:
In each the uncouth, individual soul
Looms forth and glooms
Essential, and, their bodily presences
Touched with inordinate significance,
Wearing the darkness like a livery
Of some mysterious and tremendous guild,
They brood—they menace—they appal.

The voice of Mrs Bittacy presently broke the silence that followed.

"I like that part about God's sentinels," she murmured. There was no sharpness in her tone; it was hushed and quiet. The truth, so musically uttered, muted her shrill objections though it had not lessened her alarm. Her husband made no comment; his cigar, she noticed, had gone out.

"And old trees in particular," continued the artist, as though to himself, "have very definite personalities. You can offend, wound, please them; the moment you stand within their shade you feel whether they come out to you, or whether they withdraw." He turned abruptly towards his host. "You know that singular essay of Prentice Mulford's, no doubt, 'God in the Trees'—extravagant perhaps, but yet with a fine true beauty in it? You've never read it, no?" he asked.

But it was Mrs Bittacy who answered; her husband keeping his curious deep silence.

"I never did!" It fell like a drip of cold water from the face muffled in the yellow shawl; even a child could have supplied the remainder of the unspoken thought.

"Ah," said Sanderson gently, "but there is 'God' in the trees, God in a very subtle aspect and sometimes—I have known the trees express it too—that which is *not* God—dark and terrible. Have you ever noticed, too, how clearly trees show what they want—choose their companions, at least? How beeches, for instance, allow no life too near them—birds or squirrels in their boughs, nor any growth beneath? The silence in the beech wood is quite terrifying often! And how pines like bilberry bushes at their feet and sometimes little oaks—all trees making a clear, deliberate choice, and holding firmly to it? Some trees obviously—it's very strange and marked—seem to prefer the human."

The old lady sat up crackling, for this was more than she could permit. Her stiff silk dress emitted little sharp reports.

"We know," she answered, "that He was said to have walked in the garden in the cool of the evening"—the gulp betrayed the effort that it cost her—"but we are nowhere told that He hid in the trees, or anything like that. Trees, after all, we must remember, are only large vegetables."

"True," was the soft answer, "but in everything that grows, has life, that is, there's mystery past all finding out. The wonder that lies hidden in our own souls lies also hidden, I venture to assert, in the stupidity and silence of a mere potato."

The observation was not meant to be amusing. It was *not* amusing. No one laughed. On the contrary, the words conveyed in too literal a sense the feeling that haunted all that conversation. Each one in his own way realised—with beauty, with wonder, with alarm—that the talk had somehow brought the whole vegetable kingdom nearer to that of man. Some link had been established between the two. It was not wise, with that great Forest listening at their very doors, to speak so plainly. The Forest edged up closer while they did so.

And Mrs Bittacy, anxious to interrupt the horrid spell, broke suddenly in upon it with a matter-of-fact suggestion. She did not like her husband's prolonged silence, stillness. He seemed so negative—so changed.

"David," she said, raising her voice, "I think you're feeling the dampness. It's grown chilly. The fever comes so suddenly, you know, and it might be wise to take the tincture. I'll go and get it, dear, at once. It's better." And before he could object she had left the room to bring the homoeopathic dose that she believed in, and that, to please her, he swallowed by the tumblerful from week to week.

And the moment the door closed behind her, Sanderson began again, though now in quite a different tone. Mr Bittacy sat up in his chair. The two men obviously resumed the conversation—the real conversation interrupted beneath the cedar—and left aside the sham one which was so much dust merely thrown in the old lady's eyes.

"Trees love you, that's the fact," he said earnestly. "Your service to them all these years abroad has made them know you."

"Know me?"

"Made them, yes,"—he paused a moment, then added,—"made them *aware of your presence;* aware of a force outside themselves that deliberately seeks their welfare, don't you see?"

"By Jove, Sanderson—!" This put into plain language actual sensations he had felt, yet had never dared to phrase in words before. "They get into touch with me, as it were?" he ventured, laughing at his own sentence, yet laughing only with his lips.

"Exactly," was the quick, emphatic reply. "They seek to blend with something they feel instinctively to be good for them, helpful to their essential beings, encouraging to their best expression—their life."

"Good Lord, Sir!" Bittacy heard himself saying, "but you're putting my own thoughts into words. D'you know, I've felt something like that for years. As though—" he looked round to make sure his wife was not there, then finished the sentence—"as though the trees were after me—"

"'Amalgamate' seems the best word, perhaps," said Sanderson slowly. "They would draw you to themselves. Good forces, you see, always seek to merge; evil to separate; that's why Good in the end must always win the day—everywhere. The accumulation in the long run becomes overwhelming. Evil tends to separation, dissolution, death. The comradeship of trees, their instinct to run together, is a vital symbol. Trees in a mass are good; alone, you may take it generally, are—well, dangerous. Look at a monkey-puzzler, or better still, a holly. Look at it, watch it, understand it. Did you ever see more plainly an evil thought made visible? They're wicked. Beautiful too, oh yes! There's a strange, miscalculated beauty often in evil—"

"That cedar, then—?"

"Not evil, no but alien, rather. Cedars grow in forests all together. The poor thing has drifted, that is all."

They were getting rather deep. Sanderson, talking against time, spoke so fast. It was too condensed. Bittacy hardly followed that last bit. His mind floundered among his own less definite, less sorted thoughts, till presently another sentence from the artist startled him into attention again.

"That cedar will protect you here, though, because you both have humanised it by your thinking so lovingly of its presence. The others can't get past it, as it were."

"Protect me!" he exclaimed. "Protect me from their love?"

Sanderson laughed. "We're getting rather mixed," he said "we're talking of one thing in the terms of another really. But what I mean is—you see—that their love for you, their 'awareness' of your personality and presence involves the idea of winning you—across the border—into themselves—into their world of living. It means, in a way, taking you over."

The ideas the artist started in his mind ran furious wild races to and fro. It was like a maze sprung suddenly into movement. The whirling of the intricate lines bewildered him. They went so fast, leaving but half an explanation of their goal. He followed first one, then another, but a new one always dashed across to intercept before he could get anywhere.

"But India," he said, presently in a lower voice, "India is so far away—from this little English forest. The trees, too, are utterly different for one thing?"

The rustle of skirts warned of Mrs Bittacy's approach. This was a sentence he could turn round another way in case she came up and pressed for explanation.

"There is communion among trees all the world over," was the strange quick reply. "They always know."

"They always know! You think then—"

"The winds, you see—the great, swift carriers! They have their ancient rights of way about the world. An easterly wind, for instance, carrying on stage by stage as it were—linking dropped messages and meanings from land to land like the birds—an easterly wind—"

Mrs Bittacy swept in upon them with the tumbler—

"There, David," she said, "that will ward off any beginnings of attack. Just a spoonful, dear. Oh, oh! not *all*!" for he had swallowed half the contents at a single gulp as usual "another dose before you go to bed, and the balance in the morning, first thing when you wake."

She turned to her guest, who put the tumbler down for her upon a table at his elbow. She had heard them speak of the east wind. She emphasised the warning she had misinterpreted. The private part of the conversation came to an abrupt end.

"It is the one thing that upsets him more than any other—an east wind," she said, "and I am glad, Mr Sanderson,to hear you think so too."

### III

A DEEP hush followed, in the middle of which an owl was heard calling its muffled note in the forest. A big moth whirred with a soft collision against one of the windows. Mrs Bittacy started slightly, but no one spoke. Above the trees the stars were faintly visible. From the distance came the barking of a dog.

Bittacy, relighting his cigar, broke the little spell of silence that had caught all three.

"It's rather a comforting thought," he said, throwing the match out of the window, "that life is about us everywhere, and that there is really no dividing line between what we call organic and inorganic."

"The universe, yes," said Sanderson, "is all one, really. We're puzzled by the gaps we cannot see across, but as a fact, I suppose, there are no gaps at all."

Mrs Bittacy rustled ominously, holding her peace meanwhile. She feared long words she did not understand. Beelzebub lay hid among too many syllables.

"In trees and plants especially, there dreams an exquisite life that no one yet has proved unconscious."

"Or conscious either, Mr Sanderson," she neatly interjected. "It's only man that was made after His image, not shrubberies and things..."

Her husband interposed without delay.

"It is not necessary," he explained suavely, "to say that they're alive in the sense that we are alive. At the same time," with an eye to his wife, "I see no harm in holding, dear, that all created things contain some measure of His life Who made them. It's only beautiful to hold that He created nothing dead. We are not pantheists for all that!" he added soothingly.

"Oh, no! Not that, I hope!" The word alarmed her. It was worse than pope. Through her puzzled mind stole a stealthy, dangerous thing... like a panther.

"I like to think that even in decay there's life," the painter murmured. "The falling apart of rotten wood breeds sentiency; there's force and motion in the falling of a dying leaf, in the breaking up and crumbling of everything indeed. And take an inert stone: it's crammed with heat and weight and potencies of all sorts. What holds its particles together indeed? We understand it as little as gravity or why a needle always turns to the 'North.' Both things may be a mode of life."

"You think a compass has a soul, Mr Sanderson?" exclaimed the lady with a crackling of her silk flounces that conveyed a sense of outrage even more plainly than her tone. The artist smiled to himself in the darkness, but it was Bittacy who hastened to reply.

"Our friend merely suggests that these mysterious agencies," he said quietly, "may be due to some kind of life we cannot understand. Why should water only run downhill? Why should trees grow at right angles to the surface of the ground and towards the sun? Why should the worlds spin for ever on their axes? Why should fire change the form of everything it touches without really destroying them? To say these things follow the law of their being explains nothing. Mr Sanderson merely suggests—poetically, my dear, of course—that these may be manifestations of life, though life at a different stage to ours."

"The '*breath* of life,' we read, 'He breathed into them.' These things do not breathe." She said it with triumph.

Then Sanderson put in a word. But he spoke rather to himself or to his host than by way of serious rejoinder to the ruffled lady.

"But plants do breathe too, you know," he said. "They breathe, they eat, they digest, they move about, and they adapt themselves to their environment as men and animals do. They have a nervous system too... at least a complex system of nuclei which have some of the qualities of nerve cells. They may have memory too. Certainly, they know definite action in response to stimulus. And though this may be physiological, no one has proved that it is only that, and not —psychological."

He did not notice, apparently, the little gasp that was audible behind the yellow shawl. Bittacy cleared his throat, threw his extinguished cigar upon the lawn, crossed and recrossed his legs.

"And in trees," continued the other, "behind a great forest, for instance," pointing towards the woods, "may stand a rather splendid Entity that manifests through all the thousand individual trees—some huge collective life, quite as minutely and delicately organised as our own. It might merge and blend with ours under certain conditions, so that we could understand it by *being* it, for a time at least. It might even engulf human vitality into the immense whirlpool of its own vast dreaming life. The pull of a big forest on a man can be tremendous and utterly overwhelming."

The mouth of Mrs Bittacy was heard to close with a snap. Her shawl, and particularly her crackling dress, exhaled the protest that burned within her like a pain. She was too distressed to be overawed, but at the same time too confused 'mid the litter of words and meanings half understood, to find immediate phrases she could use. Whatever the actual meaning of his language might be, however, and whatever subtle dangers lay concealed behind them meanwhile, they certainly wove a kind of gentle spell with the glimmering darkness that held all three delicately enmeshed there by that open window. The odours of dewy lawn, flowers, trees, and earth formed part of it.

"The moods," he continued, "that people waken in us are due to their hidden life affecting our own. Deep calls to deep. A person, for instance, joins you in an empty room you both instantly change. The new arrival, though in silence, has caused a change of mood. May not the moods of Nature touch and stir us in virtue of a similar prerogative? The sea, the hills, the desert, wake passion, joy, terror, as the case may be for a few, perhaps," he glanced significantly at his host so that Mrs Bittacy again caught the turning of his eyes, "emotions of a curious, flaming splendour that are quite nameless. Well... whence come these powers? Surely from nothing that is... dead! Does not the influence of a forest, its sway and strange ascendancy over certain minds, betray a direct manifestation of life? It lies otherwise beyond all explanation, this mysterious emanation of big woods. Some natures, of course, deliberately invite it. The authority of a host of trees,"—his voice grew almost solemn as he said the words—"is something not to be denied. One feels it here, I think, particularly."

There was considerable tension in the air as he ceased speaking. Mr Bittacy had not intended that the talk should go so far. They had drifted. He did not wish to see his wife unhappy or afraid, and he was aware—acutely so—that her feelings were stirred to a point he did not care about. Something in her, as he put it, was "working up" towards explosion.

He sought to generalise the conversation, diluting this accumulated emotion by spreading it.

"The sea is His and He made it," he suggested vaguely, hoping Sanderson would take the hint, "and with the trees it is the same..."

"The whole gigantic vegetable kingdom, yes," the artist took him up, "all at the service of man, for food, for shelter and for a thousand purposes of his daily life. Is it not striking what a lot of the globe they cover... exquisitely organised life, yet stationary, always ready to our hand when we want them, never running away? But the taking them, for all that, not so easy. One man shrinks from picking flowers, another from cutting down trees. And, it's curious that most of the forest tales and legends are dark, mysterious, and somewhat ill-omened. The forest-beings are rarely gay and harmless. The forest life was felt as terrible. Tree-worship still survives today. Wood-cutters... those who take the life of trees... you see, a race of haunted men..."

He stopped abruptly, a singular catch in his voice Bittacy felt something even before the sentences were over. His wife, he knew, felt it still more strongly. For it was in the middle of the heavy silence following upon these last remarks, that Mrs Bittacy, rising with a violent abruptness from her chair, drew the attention of the others to something moving towards them across the lawn. It came silently. In outline it was large and curiously spread. It rose high, too, for the sky above the shrubberies, still pale gold from the sunset, was dimmed by its passage. She declared afterwards that it moved in "looping circles," but what she perhaps meant to convey was "spirals."

She screamed faintly. "It's come at last! And it's you that brought it!"

She turned excitedly, half afraid, half angry, to Sanderson. With a breathless sort of gasp she said it, politeness all forgotten. "I knew it... if you went on. I knew it. Oh! Oh!" And she cried again, "Your talking has brought it out!" The terror that shook her voice was rather dreadful.

But the confusion of her vehement words passed unnoticed in the first surprise they caused. For a moment nothing happened.

"What is it you think you see, my dear?" asked her husband, startled. Sanderson said nothing. All three leaned forward, the men still sitting, but Mrs Bittacy had rushed hurriedly to the window, placing herself of a purpose, as it seemed, between her husband and the lawn. She pointed. Her little hand made a silhouette against the sky, the yellow shawl hanging from the arm like a cloud.

"Beyond the cedar—between it and the lilacs." The voice had lost its shrillness; it was thin and hushed. "There... now you see it going round upon itself again—going back, thank God!... going back to the Forest." It sank to a whisper, shaking. She repeated, with a great dropping sigh of relief—"Thank God! I thought... at first... it was coming here... to us!... David to *you*!"

She stepped back from the window, her movements confused, feeling in the darkness for the support of a chair, and finding her husband's outstretched hand instead. "Hold me, dear, hold me, please ... tight. Do not let me go." She was in what he called afterwards "a regular state." He drew her firmly down upon her chair again.

"Smoke, Sophie, my dear," he said quickly, trying to make his voice calm and natural. "I see it, yes. It's smoke blowing over from the gardener's cottage..."

"But, David,"—and there was new horror in her whisper now—"it made a noise. It makes it still. I hear it swishing." Some such word she used—swishing, sishing, rushing, or something of the kind. "David, I'm very frightened. It's something awful! That man has called it out... !"

"Hush, hush," whispered her husband. He stroked her trembling hand beside him.

"It is in the wind," said Sanderson, speaking for the first time, very quietly. The expression on his face was not visible in the gloom, but his voice was soft and unafraid. At the sound of it, Mrs Bittacy started violently again. Bittacy drew his chair a little forward to obstruct her view of him. He felt bewildered himself, a little, hardly knowing quite what to say or do. It was all so very curious and sudden.

But Mrs Bittacy was badly frightened. It seemed to her that what she saw came from the enveloping forest just beyond their little garden. It emerged in a sort of secret way, moving towards them as with a purpose, stealthily, difficultly. Then something stopped it. It could not advance beyond the cedar. The cedar—this impression remained with her afterwards, too—prevented, kept it back. Like a rising sea the Forest had surged a moment in their direction through the covering darkness, and this visible movement was its first wave. Thus to her mind it seemed... like that mysterious turn of the tide that used to frighten and mystify her in childhood on the sands. The outward surge of some enormous Power was what she felt... something to which every instinct in her being rose in opposition because it threatened her and hers. In that moment she realised the Personality of the Forest... menacing.

In the stumbling movement that she made away from the window and towards the bell she barely caught the sentence Sanderson—or was it her husband?—murmured to himself: "It came because we talked of it; our thinking made it aware of us and brought it out. But the cedar stops it. It cannot cross the lawn, you see..."

All three were standing now, and her husband's voice broke in with authority while his wife's fingers touched the bell.

"My dear, I should *not* say anything to Thompson." The anxiety he felt was manifest in his voice, but his outward composure had returned. "The gardener can go..."

Then Sanderson cut him short. "Allow me," he said quickly. "I'll see if anything's wrong." And before either of them could answer or object, he was gone, leaping out by the open window. They saw his figure vanish with a run across the lawn into the darkness.

A moment later the maid entered, in answer to the bell, and with her came the loud barking of the terrier from the hall.

"The lamps," said her master shortly, and as she softly closed the door behind her, they heard the wind pass with a mournful sound of singing round the outer walls. A rustle of foliage from the distance passed within it.

"You see, the wind is rising. It was the wind!" He put a comforting arm about her, distressed to feel that she was trembling. But he knew that he was trembling too, though with a kind of odd elation rather than alarm. "And it was smoke that you saw coming from Stride's cottage, or from the rubbish heaps he's been burning in the kitchen garden. The noise we heard was the branches rustling in the wind. Why should you be so nervous?"

A thin whispering voice answered him:

"I was afraid for *you*, dear. Something frightened me for *you*. That man makes me feel so uneasy and uncomfortable for his influence upon you. It's very foolish, I know. I think... I'm tired; I feel so overwrought and restless." The words poured out in a hurried jumble and she kept turning to the window while she spoke.

"The strain of having a visitor," he said soothingly, "has taxed you. We're so unused to having people in the house. He goes tomorrow." He warmed her cold hands between his own, stroking them tenderly. More, for the life of him, he could not say or do. The joy of a strange, internal excitement made his heart beat faster. He knew not what it was. He knew only, perhaps, whence it came.

She peered close into his face through the gloom, and said a curious thing. "I thought, David, for a moment... you seemed... different. My nerves are all on edge tonight." She made no further reference to her husband's visitor.

A sound of footsteps from the lawn warned of Sanderson's return, as he answered quickly in a lowered tone—"There's no need to be afraid on my account, dear girl. There's nothing wrong with me, I assure you I never felt so well and happy in my life."

Thompson came in with the lamps and brightness, and scarcely had she gone again when Sanderson in turn was seen climbing through the window.

"There's nothing," he said lightly, as he closed it behind him. "Somebody's been burning leaves, and the smoke is drifting a little through the trees. The wind," he added, glancing at his host a moment significantly, but in so discreet a way that Mrs Bittacy did not observe it, "the wind, too, has begun to roar... in the Forest... further out."

But Mrs Bittacy noticed about him two things which increased her uneasiness. She noticed the shining of his eyes, because a similar light had suddenly come into her husband's and she noticed, too, the apparent depth of meaning he put into those simple words that "the wind had begun to roar in the Forest... further out." Her mind retained the disagreeable impression that he meant more than he said. In his tone lay quite another implication. It was not actually "wind" he spoke of, and it would not remain "further out"... rather, it was coming in. Another impression she got too—still more unwelcome— was that her husband understood his hidden meaning.

### IV

"DAVID, dear," she observed gently as soon as they were alone upstairs, "I have a horrible uneasy, feeling about that man. I cannot get rid of it." The tremor in her voice caught all his tenderness.

He turned to look at her. "Of what kind, my dear? You're so imaginative sometimes, aren't you?"

"I think," she hesitated, stammering a little, confused, still frightened, "I mean—isn't he a hypnotist, or full of those theofosical ideas, or something of the sort? You know what I mean—"

He was too accustomed to her little confused alarms to explain them away seriously as a rule, or to correct her verbal inaccuracies, but tonight he felt she needed careful, tender treatment. He soothed her as best he could.

"But there's no harm in that, even if he is," he answered quietly. "Those are only new names for very old ideas, you know, dear." There was no trace of impatience in his voice.

"That's what I mean," she replied, the texts he dreaded rising in an unuttered crowd behind the words. "He's one of those things that we are warned would come—one of those Latter-Day things." For her mind still bristled with the bogeys of Antichrist and Prophecy, and she had only escaped the Number of the Beast, as it were, by the skin of her teeth. The Pope drew most of her fire usually, because she could understand him; the target was plain and she could shoot. But this tree-and-forest business was so vague and horrible. It terrified her. "He makes me think," she went on, "of Principalities and Powers in high places, and of things that walk in darkness. I did *not* like the way he spoke of trees getting alive in the night, and all that it made me think of wolves in sheep's clothing. And when I saw that awful thing in the sky above the lawn—"

But he interrupted her at once, for that was something he had decided it was best to leave unmentioned. Certainly it was better not discussed.

"He only meant, I think, Sophie," he put in gravely, yet with a little smile, "that trees may have a measure of conscious life—rather a nice idea on the whole, surely,—something like that bit we read in the *Times* the other night, you remember—and that a big forest may possess a sort of Collective Personality. Remember, he's an artist, and poetical."

"It's dangerous," she said emphatically. "I feel it's playing with fire, unwise, unsafe—"

"Yet all to the glory of God," he urged gently. "We must not shut our ears and eyes to knowledge—of any kind, must we?"

"With you, David, the wish is always farther than the thought," she rejoined. For, like the child who thought that "suffered under Pontius Pilate" was "suffered under a bunch of violets," she heard her proverbs phonetically and reproduced them thus. She hoped to convey her warning in the quotation. "And we must always try the spirits whether they be of God," she added tentatively.

"Certainly, dear, we can always do that," he assented, getting into bed.

But, after a little pause, during which she blew the light out, David Bittacy settling down to sleep with an excitement in his blood that was new and bewilderingly delightful, realised that perhaps he had not said quite enough to comfort her. She was lying awake by his side, still frightened. He put his head up in the darkness.

"Sophie," he said softly, "you must remember, too, that in any case between us and—and all that sort of thing—there is a great gulf fixed, a gulf that cannot be crossed—er—while we are still in the body."

And hearing no reply, he satisfied himself that she was already asleep and happy. But Mrs Bittacy was not asleep. She heard the sentence, only she said nothing because she felt her thought was better unexpressed. She was afraid to hear the words in the darkness. The Forest outside was listening and might hear them too—the Forest that was "roaring further out."

And the thought was this: That gulf, of course, existed, but Sanderson had somehow bridged it.

It was much later that night when she awoke out of troubled, uneasy dreams and heard a sound that twisted her very nerves with fear. It passed immediately with full waking, for, listen as she might, there was nothing audible but the inarticulate murmur of the night. It was in her dreams she heard it, and the dreams had vanished with it. But the sound was recognisable, for it was that rushing noise that had come across the lawn only this time closer. Just above her face while she slept had passed this murmur as of rustling branches in the very room, a sound of foliage whispering. "A going in the tops of the mulberry trees," ran through her mind. She had dreamed that she lay beneath a spreading tree somewhere, a tree that whispered with ten thousand soft lips of green and the dream continued for a moment even after waking.

She sat up in bed and stared about her. The window was open at the top; she saw the stars; the door, she remembered, was locked as usual; the room, of course, was empty. The deep hush of the summer night lay over all, broken only by another sound that now issued from the shadows close beside the bed, a human sound, yet unnatural, a sound that seized the fear with which she had waked and instantly increased it. And, although it was one she recognised as familiar, at first she could not name it. Some seconds certainly passed—and, they were very long ones—before she understood that it was her husband talking in his sleep.

The direction of the voice confused and puzzled her, moreover, for it was not, as she first supposed, beside her. There was distance in it. The next minute, by the light of the sinking candle flame, she saw his white figure standing out in the middle of the room, half-way towards the window. The candlelight slowly grew. She saw him move then nearer to the window, with arms outstretched. His speech was low and mumbled, the words running together too much to be distinguishable.

And she shivered. To her, sleep-talking was uncanny to the point of horror; it was like the talking of the dead, mere parody of a living voice, unnatural.

"David!" she whispered, dreading the sound of her own voice, and half afraid to interrupt him and see his face. She could not bear the sight of the wide-opened eyes. "David, you're walking in your sleep. Do—come back to bed, dear, *please!*"

Her whisper seemed so dreadfully loud in the still darkness. At the sound of her voice he paused, then turned slowly round to face her. His widely-opened eyes stared into her own without recognition; they looked through her into something beyond; it was as though he knew the direction of the sound, yet could not see her. They were shining, she noticed, as the eyes of Sanderson had shone several hours ago and his face was flushed, distraught. Anxiety was written upon every feature. And, instantly, recognising that the fever was upon him, she forgot her terror temporarily in practical considerations. He came back to bed without waking. She closed his eyelids. Presently he composed himself quietly to sleep, or rather to deeper sleep. She contrived to make him swallow something from the tumbler beside the bed.

Then she rose very quietly to close the window, feeling the night air blow in too fresh and keen. She put the candle where it could not reach him. The sight of the big Baxter Bible beside it comforted her a little, but all through her under-being ran the warnings of a curious alarm. And it was while in the act of fastening the catch with one hand and pulling the string of the blind with the other, that her husband sat up again in bed and spoke in words this time that were distinctly audible. The eyes had opened wide again. He pointed. She stood stock still and listened, her shadow distorted on the blind. He did not come out towards her as at first she feared.

The whispering voice was very clear, horrible, too, beyond all she had ever known.

"They are roaring in the Forest further out... and I... must go and see." He stared beyond her as he said it, to the woods. "They are needing me. They sent for me..." Then his eyes wandering back again to things within the room, he lay down, his purpose suddenly changed. And that change was horrible as well, more horrible, perhaps, because of its revelation of another detailed world he moved in far away from her.

The singular phrase chilled her blood; for a moment she was utterly terrified. That tone of the somnambulist, differing so slightly yet so distressingly from normal, waking speech, seemed to her somehow wicked. Evil and danger lay waiting thick behind it. She leaned against the window-sill, shaking in every limb. She had an awful feeling for a moment that something was coming in to fetch him.

"Not yet, then," she heard in a much lower voice from the bed, "but later. It will be better so... I shall go later..."

The words expressed some fringe of these alarms that had haunted her so long, and that the arrival and presence of Sanderson seemed to have brought to the very edge of a climax she could not even dare to think about. They gave it form they brought it closer; they sent her thoughts to her Deity in a wild, deep prayer for help and guidance. For here was a direct, unconscious betrayal of a world of inner purposes and claims her husband recognised while he kept them almost wholly to himself.

By the time she reached his side and knew the comfort of his touch, the eyes had closed again, this time of their own accord, and the head lay calmly back upon the pillows. She gently straightened the bed clothes. She watched him for some minutes, shading the candle carefully with one hand. There was a smile of strangest peace upon the face.

Then, blowing out the candle, she knelt down and prayed before getting back into bed. But no sleep came to her. She lay awake all night thinking, wondering, praying, until at length with the chorus of the birds and the glimmer of the dawn upon the green blind, she fell into a slumber of complete exhaustion.

But while she slept the wind continued roaring in the Forest further out. The sound came closer—sometimes very close indeed.

## V

WITH the departure of Sanderson the significance of the curious incidents waned, because the moods that had produced them passed away. Mrs Bittacy soon afterwards came to regard them as some growth of disproportion that had been very largely, perhaps, in her own mind. It did not strike her that this change was sudden, for it came about quite naturally. For one thing her husband never spoke of the matter, and for another she remembered how many things in life that had seemed inexplicable and singular at the time turned out later to have been quite commonplace.

Most of it, certainly, she put down to the presence of the artist and to his wild, suggestive talk. With his welcome removal, the world turned ordinary again and safe. The fever, though it lasted as usual a short time only, had not allowed of her husband's getting up to say good-bye, and she had conveyed his regrets and adieux. In the morning Mr Sanderson had seemed ordinary enough. In his town hat and gloves, as she saw him go, he seemed tame and unalarming.

"After all," she thought as she watched the pony-cart bear him off, "he's only an artist!" What she had thought he might be otherwise her slim imagination did not venture to disclose. Her change of feeling was wholesome and refreshing. She felt a little ashamed of her behaviour. She gave him a smile—genuine because the relief she felt was genuine—as he bent over her hand and kissed it, but she did not suggest a second visit, and her husband, she noted with satisfaction and relief had said nothing either.

The little household fell again into the normal and sleepy routine to which it was accustomed. The name of Arthur Sanderson was rarely if ever mentioned. Nor, for her part, did she mention to her husband the incident of his walking in his sleep and the wild words he used. But to forget it was equally impossible. Thus it lay buried deep within her like a centre of some unknown disease of which it was a mysterious symptom, waiting to spread at the first favourable opportunity. She prayed against it every night and morning: prayed that she might forget it—that God would keep her husband safe from harm.

For in spite of much surface foolishness that many might have read as weakness, Mrs Bittacy had balance, sanity, and a fine deep faith. She was greater than she knew. Her love for her husband and her God were somehow one, an achievement only possible to a single-hearted nobility of soul.

There followed a summer of great violence and beauty; of beauty, because the refreshing rains at night prolonged the glory of the spring and spread it all across July, keeping the foliage young and sweet of violence, because the winds that tore about the south of England brushed the whole country into dancing movement. They swept the woods magnificently, and kept them roaring with a perpetual grand voice. Their deepest notes seemed never to leave the sky. They sang and shouted, and torn leaves raced and fluttered through the air long before their usually appointed time. Many a tree, after days of this roaring and dancing, fell exhausted to the ground. The cedar on the lawn gave up two limbs that fell upon successive days, at the same hour too—just before dusk. The wind often makes its most boisterous effort at that time, before it drops with the sun, and these two huge branches lay in dark ruin covering half the lawn. They spread across it and towards the house. They left an ugly gaping space upon the tree, so that the Lebanon looked unfinished, half destroyed, a monster shorn of its old-time comeliness and splendour. Far more of the Forest was now visible than before; it peered through the breach of the broken defences. They could see from the windows of the house now—especially from the drawing-room and bed-room windows—straight out into the glades and depths beyond.

Mrs Bittacy's niece and nephew, who were staying on a visit at the time, enjoyed themselves immensely helping the gardeners carry off the fragments. It took two days to do this, for Mr Bittacy insisted on the branches being moved entire. He would not allow them to be chopped also, he would not consent to their use as firewood. Under his superintendence the unwieldy masses were dragged to the edge of the garden and arranged upon the frontier line between the Forest and the lawn. The children were delighted with the scheme. They entered into it with enthusiasm. At all costs this defence against the inroads of the Forest must be made secure. They caught their uncle's earnestness, felt even something of a hidden motive that he had, and the visit, usually rather dreaded, became the visit of their lives instead. It was Aunt Sophia this time who seemed discouraging and dull.

"She's got so old and funny," opined Stephen.

But Alice, who felt in the silent displeasure of her aunt some secret thing that half alarmed her, said:

"I think she's afraid of the woods. She never comes into them with us, you see."

"All the more reason then for making this wall impreg— all fat and thick and solid," he concluded, unable to manage the longer word. "Then nothing—simply *nothing*—can get through. Can't it, Uncle David?"

And Mr Bittacy, jacket discarded and working in his speckled waistcoat, went puffing to their aid, arranging the massive limb of the cedar like a hedge.

"Come on," he said, "whatever happens, you know, we must finish before it's dark. Already the wind is roaring in the Forest further out." And Alice caught the phrase and instantly echoed it. "Stevie," she cried below her breath, "look sharp, you lazy lump. Didn't you hear what Uncle David said? It'll come in and catch us before we've done!"

They worked like Trojans, and, sitting beneath the wistaria tree that climbed the southern wall of the cottage, Mrs Bittacy with her knitting watched them calling from time to time insignificant messages of counsel and advice. The messages passed, of course, unheeded. Mostly, indeed, they were unheard, for the workers were too absorbed. She warned her husband not to get too hot, Alice not to tear her dress, Stephen not to strain his back with pulling. Her mind hovered between the homoeopathic medicine-chest upstairs and her anxiety to see the business finished.

For this breaking up of the cedar had stirred again her slumbering alarms. It revived memories of the visit of Mr Sanderson that had been sinking into oblivion; she recalled his queer and odious way of talking, and many things she hoped forgotten drew their heads up from that subconscious region to which all forgetting is impossible. They looked at her and nodded. They were full of life; they had no intention of being pushed aside and buried permanently. "Now look!" they whispered, "didn't we tell you so?" They had been merely waiting the right moment to assert their presence. And all her former vague distress crept over her. Anxiety, uneasiness returned. That dreadful sinking of the heart came too.

This incident of the cedar's breaking up was actually so unimportant, and yet her husband's attitude towards it made it so significant. There was nothing that he said in particular, or did, or left undone that frightened her, but his general air of earnestness seemed so unwarranted. She felt that he deemed the thing important. He was so exercised about it. This evidence of sudden concern and interest, buried all the summer from her sight and knowledge, she realised now had been buried purposely; he had kept it intentionally concealed. Deeply submerged in him there ran this tide of other thoughts, desires, hopes. What were they? Whither did they lead? The accident to the tree betrayed it most unpleasantly and, doubtless, more than he was aware.

She watched his grave and serious face as he worked there with the children, and as she watched she felt afraid. It vexed her that the children worked so eagerly. They unconsciously supported him. The thing she feared she would not even name. But it was waiting.

Moreover, as far as her puzzled mind could deal with a dread so vague and incoherent, the collapse of the cedar somehow brought it nearer. The fact that, all so ill-explained and formless, the thing yet lay in her consciousness, out of reach but moving and alive, filled her with a kind of puzzled, dreadful wonder. Its presence was so very real, its power so gripping, its partial concealment so abominable. Then, out of the dim confusion, she grasped one thought and saw it stand quite clear before her eyes. She found difficulty in clothing it in words, but its meaning perhaps was this: That cedar stood in their life for something friendly; its downfall meant disaster; a sense of some protective influence about the cottage, and about her husband in particular, was thereby weakened.

"Why do you fear the big winds so?" he had asked her several days before, after a particularly boisterous day and the answer she gave surprised her while she gave it. One of those heads poked up unconsciously, and let slip the truth:

"Because, David, I feel they—bring the Forest with them," she faltered. "They blow something from the trees—into the mind—into the house."

He looked at her keenly for a moment.

"That must be why I love them then," he answered. "They blow the souls of the trees about the sky like clouds."

The conversation dropped. She had never heard him talk in quite that way before.

And another time, when he had coaxed her to go with him down one of the nearer glades, she asked why he took the small hand-axe with him, and what he wanted it for.

"To cut the ivy that clings to the trunks and takes their life away," he said.

"But can't the verdurers do that?" she asked. "That's what they're paid for, isn't it?"

Whereupon he explained that ivy was a parasite the trees knew not how to fight alone, and that the verdurers were careless and did not do it thoroughly. They gave a chop here and there, leaving the tree to do the rest for itself if it could.

"Besides, I like to do it for them. I love to help them and protect," he added, the foliage rustling all about his quiet words as they went.

And these stray remarks, as his attitude towards the broken cedar, betrayed this curious, subtle change that was going forward in his personality. Slowly and surely all the summer it had increased.

It was growing—the thought startled her horribly—just as a tree grows, the outer evidence from day to day so slight as to be unnoticeable, yet the rising tide so deep and irresistible. The alteration spread all through and over him, was in both mind and actions, sometimes almost in his face as well. Occasionally, thus, it stood up straight outside himself and frightened her. His life was somehow becoming linked so intimately with trees, and with all that trees signified. His interests became more and more their interests, his activity combined with theirs, his thoughts and feelings theirs, his purpose, hope, desire, his fate—

His fate! The darkness of some vague, enormous terror dropped its shadow on her when she thought of it. Some instinct in her heart she dreaded infinitely more than death—for death meant sweet translation for his soul—came gradually to associate the thought of him with the thought of trees, in particular with these Forest trees. Sometimes, before she could face the thing, argue it away, or pray it into silence, she found the thought of him running swiftly through her mind like a thought of the Forest itself, the two most intimately linked and joined together, each a part and complement of the other, one being.

The idea was too dim for her to see it face to face. Its mere possibility dissolved the instant she focussed it to get the truth behind it. It was too utterly elusive, mad, protæan. Under the attack of even a minute's concentration the very meaning of it vanished, melted away. The idea lay really behind any words that she could ever find, beyond the touch of definite thought. Her mind was unable to grapple with it. But, while it vanished, the trail of its approach and disappearance flickered a moment before her shaking vision. The horror certainly remained.

Reduced to the simple human statement that her temperament sought instinctively it stood perhaps at this: Her husband loved her, and he loved the trees as well but the trees came first, claimed parts of him she did not know. *She* loved her God and him. *He* loved the trees and her.

Thus, in guise of some faint, distressing compromise, the matter shaped itself for her perplexed mind in the terms of conflict. A silent, hidden battle raged, but as yet raged far away. The breaking of the cedar was a visible outward fragment of a distant and mysterious encounter that was coming daily closer to them both. The wind, instead of roaring in the Forest further out, now came nearer, booming in fitful gusts about its edge and frontiers.

Meanwhile the summer dimmed. The autumn winds went sighing through the woods; leaves turned to golden red, and the evenings were drawing in with cosy shadows before the first sign of anything seriously untoward made its appearance. It came then with a flat, decided kind of violence that indicated mature preparation beforehand. It was not impulsive nor ill-considered. In a fashion it seemed expected, and indeed inevitable. For within a fortnight of their annual change to the little village of Seillans above St Raphael—a change so regular for the past ten years that it was not even discussed between them—David Bittacy abruptly refused to go.

Thompson had laid the tea-table, prepared the spirit lamp beneath the urn, pulled down the blinds in that swift and silent way she had, and left the room. The lamps were still unlit. The fire-light shone on the chintz armchairs, and Boxer lay asleep on the black horse-hair rug. Upon the walls the gilt picture frames gleamed faintly, the pictures themselves indistinguishable. Mrs Bittacy had warmed the teapot and was in the act of pouring the water in to heat the cups when her husband, looking up from his chair across the hearth, made the abrupt announcement:

"My dear," he said, as though following a train of thought of which she only heard this final phrase, "it's really quite impossible for me to go."

And so abrupt, inconsequent, it sounded that she at first misunderstood. She thought he meant go out into the garden or the woods. But her heart leaped all the same. The tone of his voice was ominous.

"Of course not," she answered, "it would be *most* unwise. Why should you—?" She referred to the mist that always spread on autumn nights upon the lawn but before she finished the sentence she knew that *he* referred to something else. And her heart then gave its second horrible leap.

"David! You mean abroad?" she gasped.

"I mean abroad, dear, yes."

It reminded her of the tone he used when saying good-bye years ago before one of those jungle expeditions she dreaded. His voice then was so serious, so final. It was serious and final now. For several moments she could think of nothing to say. She busied herself with the teapot. She had filled one cup with hot water till it overflowed, and she emptied it slowly into the slop-basin, trying with all her might not to let him see the trembling of her hand. The firelight and the dimness of the room both helped her. But in any case he would hardly have noticed it. His thoughts were far away...

## VI

MRS BITTACY had never liked their present home. She preferred a flat, more open country that left approaches clear. She liked to see things coming. This cottage on the very edge of the old hunting grounds of William the Conqueror had never satisfied her ideal of a safe and pleasant place to settle down in. The sea-coast, with treeless downs behind and a clear horizon in front, as at Eastbourne, say, was her ideal of a proper home.

It was curious, this instinctive aversion she felt to being shut in—by trees especially; a kind of claustrophobia almost probably due, as has been said, to the days in India when the trees took her husband off and surrounded him with dangers. In those weeks of solitude the feeling had matured. She had fought it in her fashion, but never conquered it. Apparently routed, it had a way of creeping back in other forms. In this particular case, yielding to his strong desire, she thought the battle won, but the terror of the trees came back before the first month had passed. They laughed in her face.

She never lost knowledge of the fact that the leagues of forest lay about their cottage like a mighty wall, a crowding, watching, listening presence that shut them in from freedom and escape. Far from morbid naturally, she did her best to deny the thought, and so simple and unartificial was her type of mind that for weeks together she would wholly lose it. Then, suddenly it would return upon her with a rush of bleak reality. It was not only in her mind; it existed apart from any mere mood; a separate fear that walked alone; it came and went, yet when it went—went only to watch her from another point of view. It was in abeyance—hidden round the corner.

The Forest never let her go completely. It was ever ready to encroach. All the branches, she sometimes fancied, stretched one way—towards their tiny cottage and garden, as though it sought to draw them in and merge them in itself. Its great, deep-breathing soul resented the mockery, the insolence, the irritation of the prim garden at its very gates. It would absorb and smother them if it could. And every wind that blew its thundering message over the huge sounding-board of the million, shaking trees conveyed the purpose that it had. They had angered its great soul. At its heart was this deep, incessant roaring.

All this she never framed in words; the subtleties of language lay far beyond her reach. But instinctively she felt it and more besides. It troubled her profoundly. Chiefly, moreover, for her husband. Merely for herself, the nightmare might have left her cold. It was David's peculiar interest in the trees that gave the special invitation.

Jealousy, then, in its most subtle aspect came to strengthen this aversion and dislike, for it came in a form that no reasonable wife could possibly object to. Her husband's passion, she reflected, was natural and inborn. It had decided his vocation, fed his ambition, nourished his dreams, desires, hopes. All his best years of active life had been spent in the care and guardianship of trees. He knew them, understood their secret life and nature, "managed" them intuitively as other men "managed" dogs and horses. He could not live for long away from them without a strange, acute nostalgia that stole his peace of mind and consequently his strength of body. A forest made him happy and at peace; it nursed and fed and soothed his deepest moods. Trees influenced the sources of his life, lowered or raised the very heart-beat in him. Cut off from them he languished as a lover of the sea can droop inland, or a mountaineer may pine in the flat monotony of the plains.

This she could understand, in a fashion at least, and make allowances for. She had yielded gently, even sweetly, to his choice of their English home for in the little island there is nothing that suggests the woods of wilder countries so nearly as the New Forest. It has the genuine air and mystery, the depth and splendour, the loneliness, and here and there the strong, untamable quality of old-time forests as Bittacy of the Department knew them.

In a single detail only had he yielded to her wishes. He consented to a cottage on the edge, instead of in the heart of it. And for a dozen years now they had dwelt in peace and happiness at the lips of this great spreading thing that covered so many leagues with its tangle of swamps and moors and splendid ancient trees.

Only with the last two years or so—with his own increasing age, and physical decline perhaps—had come this marked growth of passionate interest in the welfare of the Forest. She had watched it grow, at first had laughed at it, then talked sympathetically so far as sincerity permitted, then had argued mildly, and finally come to realise that its treatment lay altogether beyond her powers, and so had come to fear it with all her heart.

The six weeks they annually spent away from their English home, each regarded very differently of course. For her husband it meant a painful exile that did his health no good; he yearned for his trees—the sight and sound and smell of them; but for herself it meant release from a haunting dread—escape. To renounce those six weeks by the sea on the sunny, shining coast of France, was almost more than this little woman, even with her unselfishness, could face.

After the first shock of the announcement, she reflected as deeply as her nature permitted, prayed, wept in secret—and made up her mind. Duty, she felt clearly, pointed to renouncement. The discipline would certainly be severe—she did not dream at the moment how severe!—but this fine, consistent little Christian saw it plain; she accepted it, too, without any sighing of the martyr, though the courage she showed was of the martyr order. Her husband should never know the cost. In all but this one passion his unselfishness was ever as great as her own. The love she had borne him all these years, like the love she bore her anthropomorphic deity, was deep and real. She loved to suffer for them both. Besides, the way her husband had put it to her was singular. It did not take the form of a mere selfish predilection. Something higher than two wills in conflict seeking compromise was in it from the beginning.

"I feel, Sophia, it would be really more than I could manage," he said slowly, gazing into the fire over the tops of his stretched-out muddy boots. "My duty and my happiness lie here with the Forest and with you. My life is deeply rooted in this place. Something I can't define connects my inner being with these trees, and separation would make me ill—might even kill me. My hold on life would weaken; here is my source of supply. I cannot explain it better than that." He looked up steadily into her face across the table so that she saw the gravity of his expression and the shining of his steady eyes.

"David, you feel it as strongly as that!" she said, forgetting the tea things altogether.

"Yes," he replied, "I do. And it's not of the body only; I feel it in my soul."

The reality of what he hinted at crept into that shadow-covered room like an actual Presence and stood beside them. It came not by the windows or the door, but it filled the entire space between the walls and ceiling. It took the heat from the fire before her face. She felt suddenly cold, confused a little, frightened. She almost felt the rush of foliage in the wind. It stood between them.

"There are things—some things," she faltered, "we are not intended to know, I think." The words expressed her general attitude to life, not alone to this particular incident.

And after a pause of several minutes, disregarding the criticism as though he had not heard it—"I cannot explain it better than that, you see," his grave voice answered. "There *is* this deep, tremendous link,—some secret power they emanate that keeps me well and happy and—alive. If you cannot understand, I feel at least you may be able to—forgive." His tone grew tender, gentle, soft. "My selfishness, I know, must seem quite unforgivable. I cannot help it; somehow these trees, this ancient Forest, both seem knitted into all that makes me live, and if I go—"

There was a little sound of collapse in his voice. He stopped abruptly, and sank back in his chair. And, at that, a distinct lump came up into her throat which she had great difficulty in managing while she went over and put her arms about him.

"My dear," she murmured, "God will direct. We will accept His guidance. He has always shown the way before."

"My selfishness afflicts me—" he began, but she would not let him finish.

"David, He will direct. Nothing shall harm you. You've never once been selfish, and I cannot bear to hear you say such things. The way will open that is best for you—for both of us." She kissed him; she would not let him speak; her heart was in her throat, and she felt for him far more than for herself.

And then he had suggested that she should go alone perhaps for a shorter time, and stay in her brother's villa with the children, Alice and Stephen. It was always open to her as she well knew.

"You need the change," he said, when the lamps had been lit and the servant had gone out again "you need it as much as I dread it. I could manage somehow till you returned, and should feel happier that way if you went. I cannot leave this Forest that I love so well. I even feel, Sophie dear"—he sat up straight and faced her as he half whispered it—"that I can *never* leave it again. My life and happiness lie here together."

And even while scorning the idea that she could leave him alone with the Influence of the Forest all about him to have its unimpeded way, she felt the pangs of that subtle jealousy bite keen and close. He loved the Forest better than herself, for he placed it first. Behind the words, moreover, hid the unuttered thought that made her so uneasy. The terror Sanderson had brought revived and shook its wings before her very eyes. For the whole conversation, of which this was a fragment, conveyed the unutterable implication that while he could not spare the trees, they equally could not spare him. The vividness with which he managed to conceal and yet betray the fact brought a profound distress that crossed the border between presentiment and warning into positive alarm.

He clearly felt that the trees would miss him—the trees he tended, guarded, watched over, loved.

"David, I shall stay here with you. I think you need me really, —don't you?" Eagerly, with a touch of heart-felt passion, the words poured out.

"Now more than ever, dear. God bless you for your sweet unselfishness. And your sacrifice," he added, "is all the greater because you cannot understand the thing that makes it necessary for me to stay."

"Perhaps in the spring instead—" she said, with a tremor in the voice.

"In the spring—perhaps," he answered gently, almost beneath his breath. "For they will not need me then. All the world can love them in the spring. It's in the winter that they're lonely and neglected. I wish to stay with them particularly then. I even feel I ought to—and I must."

And in this way, without further speech, the decision was made. Mrs Bittacy, at least, asked no more questions. Yet she could not bring herself to show more sympathy than was necessary. She felt, for one thing, that if she did, it might lead him to speak freely, and to tell her things she could not possibly bear to know. And she dared not take the risk of that.

### VII

THIS was at the end of summer, but the autumn followed close. The conversation really marked the threshold between the two seasons, and marked at the same time the line between her husband's negative and aggressive state. She almost felt she had done wrong to yield; he grew so bold, concealment all discarded. He went, that is, quite openly to the woods, forgetting all his duties, all his former occupations. He even sought to coax her to go with him. The hidden thing blazed out without disguise. And, while she trembled at his energy, she admired the virile passion he displayed. Her jealousy had long ago retired before her fear, accepting the second place. Her one desire now was to protect. The wife turned wholly mother.

He said so little, but—he hated to come in. From morning to night he wandered in the Forest; often he went out after dinner; his mind was charged with trees—their foliage, growth, development their wonder, beauty, strength their loneliness in isolation, their power in a herded mass. He knew the effect of every wind upon them; the danger from the boisterous north, the glory from the west, the eastern dryness, and the soft, moist tenderness that a south wind left upon their thinning boughs. He spoke all day of their sensations: how they drank the fading sunshine, dreamed in the moonlight, thrilled to the kiss of stars. The dew could bring them half the passion of the night, but frost sent them plunging beneath the ground to dwell with hopes of a later coming softness in their roots. They nursed the life they carried— insects, larvae, chrysalis—and when the skies above them melted, he spoke of them standing "motionless in an ecstasy of rain," or in the noon of sunshine "self-poised upon their prodigy of shade."

And once in the middle of the night she woke at the sound of his voice, and heard him—wide awake, not talking in his sleep—but talking towards the window where the shadow of the cedar fell at noon:

O art thou sighing for Lebanon
In the long breeze that streams to thy delicious East?
Sighing for Lebanon, Dark cedar

and, when, half charmed, half terrified, she turned and called to him by name, he merely said—

"My dear, I felt the loneliness—suddenly realised it—the alien desolation of that tree, set here upon our little lawn in England when all her Eastern brothers call to her in sleep." And the answer seemed so queer, so "unevangelical," that she waited in silence till he slept again. The poetry passed her by. It seemed unnecessary and out of place. It made her ache with suspicion, fear, jealousy.

The fear, however, seemed somehow all lapped up and banished soon afterwards by her unwilling admiration of the rushing splendour of her husband's state. Her anxiety, at any rate, shifted from the religious to the medical. She thought he might be losing his steadiness of mind a little. How often in her prayers she offered thanks for the guidance that had made her stay with him to help and watch is impossible to say. It certainly was twice a day.

She even went so far once, when Mr Mortimer, the vicar, called, and brought with him a more or less distinguished doctor—as to tell the professional man privately some symptoms of her husband's queerness. And his answer that there was "nothing he could prescribe for" added not a little to her sense of unholy bewilderment. No doubt Sir James had never been "consulted" under such unorthodox conditions before. His sense of what was becoming naturally overrode his acquired instincts as a skilled instrument that might help the race.

"No fever, you think?" she asked insistently with hurry, determined to get something from him.

"Nothing that *I* can deal with, as I told you, Madam," replied the offended allopathic Knight.

Evidently he did not care about being invited to examine patients in this surreptitious way before a teapot on the lawn, chance of a fee most problematical. He liked to see a tongue and feel a thumping pulse to know the pedigree and bank account of his questioner as well. It was most unusual, in abominable taste besides. Of course it was. But the drowning woman seized the only straw she could.

For now the aggressive attitude of her husband overcame her to the point where she found it difficult even to question him. Yet in the house he was so kind and gentle, doing all he could to make her sacrifice as easy as possible.

"David, you really *are* unwise to go out now. The night is damp and very chilly. The ground is soaked in dew. You'll catch your death of cold."

His face lightened. "Won't you come with me, dear,—just for once? I'm only going to the corner of the hollies to see the beech that stands so lonely by itself."

She had been out with him in the short dark afternoon, and they had passed that evil group of hollies where the gipsies camped. Nothing else would grow there, but the hollies throve upon the stony soil.

"David, the beech is all right and safe." She had learned his phraseology a little, made clever out of due season by her love. "There's no wind tonight."

"But it's rising," he answered, "rising in the east. I heard it in the bare and hungry larches. They need the sun and dew, and always cry out when the wind's upon them from the east."

She sent a short unspoken prayer most swiftly to her deity as she heard him say it. For every time now, when he spoke in this familiar, intimate way of the life of the trees, she felt a sheet of cold fasten tight against her very skin and flesh. She shivered. How *could* he possibly know such things?

Yet, in all else, and in the relations of his daily life, he was sane and reasonable, loving, kind and tender. It was only on the subject of the trees he seemed unhinged and queer. Most curiously it seemed that, since the collapse of the cedar they both loved, though in different fashion, his departure from the normal had increased. Why else did he watch them as a man might watch a sickly child? Why did he linger especially in the dusk to catch their "mood of night" as he called it? Why think so carefully upon them when the frost was threatening or the wind appeared to rise?

As she put it so frequently now to herself—How could he possibly *know* such things?

He went. As she closed the front door after him she heard the distant roaring in the Forest...

And then it suddenly struck her: How could she know them too?

It dropped upon her like a blow that she felt at once all over, upon body, heart and mind. The discovery rushed out from its ambush to overwhelm. The truth of it, making all arguing futile, numbed her faculties. But though at first it deadened her, she soon revived, and her being rose into aggressive opposition. A wild yet calculated courage like that which animates the leaders of splendid forlorn hopes flamed in her little person—flamed grandly, and invincible. While knowing herself insignificant and weak, she knew at the same time that power at her back which moves the worlds. The faith that filled her was the weapon in her hands, and the right by which she claimed it but the spirit of utter, selfless sacrifice that characterised her life was the means by which she mastered its immediate use. For a kind of white and faultless intuition guided her to the attack. Behind her stood her Bible and her God.

How so magnificent a divination came to her at all may well be a matter for astonishment, though some clue of explanation lies, perhaps, in the very simpleness of her nature. At any rate, she saw quite clearly certain things; saw them in moments only—after prayer, in the still silence of the night, or when left alone those long hours in the house with her knitting and her thoughts—and the guidance which then flashed into her remained, even after the manner of its coming was forgotten.

They came to her, these things she saw, formless, wordless; she could not put them into any kind of language but by the very fact of being uncaught in sentences they retained their original clear vigour.

Hours of patient waiting brought the first, and the others followed easily afterwards, by degrees, on subsequent days, a little and a little. Her husband had been gone since early morning, and had taken his luncheon with him. She was sitting by the tea things, the cups and teapot warmed, the muffins in the fender keeping hot, all ready for his return, when she realised quite abruptly that this thing which took him off which kept him out so many hours day after day, this thing that was against her own little will and instincts—was enormous as the sea. It was no mere prettiness of single Trees, but something massed and mountainous. About her rose the wall of its huge opposition to the sky, its scale gigantic, its power utterly prodigious. What she knew of it hitherto as green and delicate forms waving and rustling in the winds was but, as it were, the spray of foam that broke into sight upon the nearer edge of viewless depths far, far away. The trees, indeed, were sentinels set visibly about the limits of a camp that itself remained invisible. The awful hum and murmur of the main body in the distance passed into that still room about her with the firelight and hissing kettle. Out yonder—in the Forest further out—the thing that was ever roaring at the centre was dreadfully increasing.

The sense of definite battle, too—battle between herself and the Forest for his soul—came with it. Its presentment was as clear as though Thompson had come into the room and quietly told her that the cottage was surrounded. "Please, ma'am, there are trees come up about the house," she might have suddenly announced. And equally might have heard her own answer: "It's all right, Thompson. The main body is still far away."

Immediately upon its heels, then, came another truth, with a close reality that shocked her. She saw that jealousy was not confined to the human and animal world alone, but ran through all creation. The Vegetable Kingdom knew it too. So-called inanimate nature shared it with the rest. Trees felt it. This Forest just beyond the window— standing there in the silence of the autumn evening across the little lawn—this Forest understood it equally. The remorseless, branching power that sought to keep exclusively for itself the thing it loved and needed, spread like a running desire through all its million leaves and stems and roots. In humans, of course, it was consciously directed; in animals it acted with frank instinctiveness; but in trees this jealousy rose in some blind tide of impersonal and unconscious wrath that would sweep opposition from its path as the wind sweeps powdered snow from the surface of the ice. Their number was a host with endless reinforcements, and once it realised its passion was returned the power increased... Her husband loved the trees... They had become aware of it... They would take him from her in the end...

Then, while she heard his footsteps in the hall and the closing of the front door, she saw a third thing clearly —realised the widening of the gap between herself and him. This other love had made it. All these weeks of the summer when she felt so close to him, now especially when she had made the biggest sacrifice of her life to stay by his side and help him, he had been slowly, surely—drawing away. The estrangement was here and now—a fact accomplished. It had been all this time maturing there yawned this broad deep space between them. Across the empty distance she saw the change in merciless perspective. It revealed his face and figure, dearly-loved, once fondly worshipped, far on the other side in shadowy distance, small, the back turned from her, and moving while she watched—moving away from her.

They had their tea in silence then. She asked no questions, he volunteered no information of his day. The heart was big within her, and the terrible loneliness of age spread through her like a rising icy mist. She watched him, filling all his wants. His hair was untidy and his boots were caked with blackish mud. He moved with a restless, swaying motion that somehow blanched her cheek and sent a miserable shivering down her back. It reminded her of trees. His eyes were very bright.

He brought in with him an odour of the earth and forest that seemed to choke her and make it difficult to breathe and—what she noticed with a climax of almost uncontrollable alarm—upon his face beneath the lamplight shone traces of a mild, faint glory that made her think of moonlight falling upon a wood through speckled shadows. It was his new-found happiness that shone there, a happiness uncaused by her and in which she had no part.

In his coat was a spray of faded yellow beech leaves. "I brought this from the Forest for you," he said, with all the air that belonged to his little acts of devotion long ago. And she took the spray of leaves mechanically with a smile and a murmured "thank you, dear," as though he had unknowingly put into her hands the weapon for her own destruction and she had accepted it.

And when the tea was over and he left the room, he did not go to his study, or to change his clothes. She heard the front door softly shut behind him as he again went out towards the Forest.

A moment later she was in her room upstairs, kneeling beside the bed—the side he slept on—and praying wildly through a flood of tears that God would save and keep him to her. Wind brushed the window panes behind her while she knelt.

## VIII

ONE sunny November morning, when the strain had reached a pitch that made repression almost unmanageable, she came to an impulsive decision, and obeyed it. Her husband had again gone out with luncheon for the day. She took adventure in her hands and followed him. The power of seeing-clear was strong upon her, forcing her up to some unnatural level of understanding. To stay indoors and wait inactive for his return seemed suddenly impossible. She meant to know what he knew, feel what he felt, put herself in his place. She would dare the fascination of the Forest—share it with him. It was greatly daring but it would give her greater understanding how to help and save him and therefore greater Power. She went upstairs a moment first to pray.

In a thick, warm skirt, and wearing heavy boots—those walking boots she used with him upon the mountains about Seillans—she left the cottage by the back way and turned towards the Forest. She could not actually follow him, for he had started off an hour before and she knew not exactly his direction. What was so urgent in her was the wish to be with him in the woods, to walk beneath the leafless branches just as he did: to be there when he was there, even though not together. For it had come to her that she might thus share with him for once this horrible mighty life and breathing of the trees he loved. In winter, he had said, they needed him particularly and winter now was coming. Her love *must* bring her something of what he felt himself—the huge attraction, the suction and the pull of all the trees. Thus, in some vicarious fashion, she might share, though unknown to himself, this very thing that was taking him away from her. She might thus even lessen its attack upon himself.

The impulse came to her clairvoyantly, and she obeyed without a sign of hesitation. Deeper comprehension would come to her of the whole awful puzzle. And come it did, yet not in the way she imagined and expected.

The air was very still, the sky a cold pale blue, but cloudless. The entire Forest stood silent, at attention. It knew perfectly well that she had come. It knew the moment when she entered; watched and followed her and behind her something dropped without a sound and shut her in. Her feet upon the glades of mossy grass fell silently, as the oaks and beeches shifted past in rows and took up their positions at her back. It was not pleasant, this way they grew so dense behind her the instant she had passed. She realised that they gathered in an ever-growing army, massed, herded, trooped, between her and the cottage, shutting off escape. They let her pass so easily, but to get out again she would know them differently—thick, crowded, branches all drawn and hostile. Already their increasing numbers bewildered her. In front, they looked so sparse and scattered, with open spaces where the sunshine fell but when she turned it seemed they stood so close together, a serried army, darkening the sunlight. They blocked the day, collected all the shadows, stood with their leafless and forbidding rampart like the night. They swallowed down into themselves the very glade by which she came. For when she glanced behind her—rarely—the way she had come was shadowy and lost.

Yet the morning sparkled overhead, and a glance of excitement ran quivering through the entire day. It was what she always knew as "children's weather," so clear and harmless, without a sign of danger, nothing ominous to threaten or alarm. Steadfast in her purpose, looking back as little as she dared, Sophia Bittacy marched slowly and deliberately into the heart of the silent woods, deeper, ever deeper...

And then, abruptly, in an open space where the sunshine fell unhindered, she stopped. It was one of the breathing-places of the forest. Dead, withered bracken lay in patches of unsightly grey. There were bits of heather too. All round the trees stood looking on—oak, beech, holly, ash, pine, larch, with here and there small groups of juniper. On the lips of this breathing-space of the woods she stopped to rest, disobeying her instinct for the first time. For the other instinct in her was to go on. She did not really want to rest.

This was the little act that brought it to her—the wireless message from a vast Emitter.

"I've been stopped," she thought to herself with a horrid qualm.

She looked about her in this quiet, ancient place. Nothing stirred. There was no life nor sign of life no birds sang no rabbits scuttled off at her approach. The stillness was bewildering, and gravity hung down upon it like a heavy curtain. It hushed the heart in her. Could this be part of what her husband felt—this sense of thick entanglement with stems, boughs, roots, and foliage?

"This has always been as it is now," she thought, yet not knowing why she thought it. "Ever since the Forest grew it has been still and secret here. It has never changed." The curtain of silence drew closer while she said it, thickening round her. "For a thousand years—I'm here with a thousand years. And behind this place stand all the forests of the world!"

So foreign to her temperament were such thoughts, and so alien to all she had been taught to look for in Nature, that she strove against them. She made an effort to oppose. But they clung and haunted just the same; they refused to be dispersed. The curtain hung dense and heavy as though its texture thickened. The air with difficulty came through.

And then she thought that curtain stirred. There was movement somewhere. That obscure dim thing which ever broods behind the visible appearances of trees came nearer to her. She caught her breath and stared about her, listening intently. The trees, perhaps because she saw them more in detail now, it seemed to her had changed. A vague, faint alteration spread over them, at first so slight she scarcely would admit it, then growing steadily, though still obscurely, outwards. "They tremble and are changed," flashed through her mind; the horrid line that Sanderson had quoted. Yet the change was graceful for all the uncouthness attendant upon the size of so vast a movement. They had turned in her direction. That was it. *They saw her.*

In this way the change expressed itself in her groping, terrified thought. Till now it had been otherwise: she had looked at them from her own point of view; now they looked at her from theirs. They stared her in the face and eyes; they stared at her all over. In some unkind, resentful, hostile way, they watched her. Hitherto in life she had watched them variously, in superficial ways, reading into them what her own mind suggested. Now they read into her the things they actually *were*, and not merely another's interpretation of them.

They seemed in their motionless silence there instinct with life, a life, moreover, that breathed about her a species of terrible soft enchantment that bewitched. It branched all through her, climbing to the brain. The Forest held her with its huge and giant fascination. In this secluded breathing-spot that the centuries had left untouched, she had stepped close against the hidden pulse of the whole collective mass of them. They were aware of her and had turned to gaze with their myriad, vast sight upon the intruder. They shouted at her in the silence. For she wanted to look back at them, but it was like staring at a crowd, and her glance merely shifted from one tree to another, hurriedly, finding in none the one she sought. They saw her so easily, each and all. The rows that stood behind her also stared. But she could not return the gaze. Her husband, she realised, could. And their steady stare shocked her as though in some sense she knew that she was naked. They saw so much of her: she saw of them—so little.

Her efforts to return their gaze were pitiful. The constant shifting increased her bewilderment. Conscious of this awful and enormous sight all over her, she let her eyes first rest upon the ground and then she closed them altogether. She kept the lids as tight together as ever they would go.

But the sight of the trees came even into that inner darkness behind the fastened lids, for there was no escaping it. Outside, in the light, she still knew that the leaves of the hollies glittered smoothly, that the dead foliage of the oaks hung crisp in the air above her, that the needles of the little junipers were pointing all one way. The spread perception of the Forest was focussed on herself, and no mere shutting of the eyes could hide its scattered yet concentrated stare—the all-inclusive vision of great woods.

There was no wind, yet here and there a single leaf hanging by its dried-up stalk shook all alone with great rapidity—rattling. It was the sentry drawing attention to her presence. And then, again, as once long weeks before, she felt their Being as a tide about her. The tide had turned. That memory of her childhood sands came back, when the nurse said, "The tide has turned now we must go in," and she saw the mass of piled-up waters, green and heaped to the horizon, and realised that it was slowly coming in. The gigantic mass of it, too vast for hurry, loaded with massive purpose, she used to feel, was moving towards herself. The fluid body of the sea was creeping along beneath the sky to the very spot upon the yellow sands where she stood and played. The sight and thought of it had always overwhelmed her with a sense of awe—as though her puny self were the object of the whole sea's advance. "The tide has turned; we had better now go in."

This was happening now about her—the same thing was happening in the woods—slow, sure, and steady, and its motion as little discernible as the sea's. The tide had turned. The small human presence that had ventured among its green and mountainous depths, moreover, was its objective.

That all was clear within her while she sat and waited with tight-shut lids. But the next moment she opened her eyes with a sudden realization of something more. The presence that it sought was after all not hers. It was the presence of someone other than herself. And then she understood. Her eyes had opened with a click, it seemed but the sound, in reality, was outside herself. Across the clearing where the sunshine lay so calm and still, she saw the figure of her husband moving among the trees—a man, like a tree, walking.

With hands behind his back, and head uplifted, he moved quite slowly, as though absorbed in his own thoughts. Hardly fifty paces separated them, hut he had no inkling of her presence there so near. With mind intent and senses all turned inwards, he marched past her like a figure in a dream, and like a figure in a dream she saw him go. Love, yearning, pity rose in a storm within her, but as in nightmare she found no words or movement possible. She sat and watched him go—go from her—go into the deeper reaches of the green enveloping woods. Desire to save, to bid him stop and turn, ran in a passion through her being, but there was nothing she could do. She saw him go away from her, go of his own accord and willingly beyond her she saw the branches drop about his steps and hide him. His figure faded out among the speckled shade and sunlight. The trees covered him. The tide just took him, all unresisting and content to go. Upon the bosom of the green soft sea he floated away beyond her reach of vision. Her eyes could follow him no longer. He was gone.

And then for the first time she realised, even at that distance, that the look upon his face was one of peace and happiness—rapt, and caught away in joy, a look of youth. That expression now he never showed to her. But she *had* known it. Years ago, in the early days of their married life, she had seen it on his face. Now it no longer obeyed the summons of her presence and her love. The woods alone could call it forth; it answered to the trees; the Forest had taken every part of him—from her—his very heart and soul...

Her sight that had plunged inwards to the fields of faded memory now came back to outer things again. She looked about her, and her love, returning empty-handed and unsatisfied, left her open to the invading of the bleakest terror she had ever known. That such things could be real and happen found her helpless utterly. Terror invaded the quietest corners of her heart, that had never yet known quailing. She could not—for moments at any rate—reach either her Bible or her God. Desolate in an empty world of fear she sat with eyes too dry and hot for tears, yet with a coldness as of ice upon her very flesh. She stared, unseeing, about her. That horror which stalks in the stillness of the noonday, when the glare of an artificial sunshine lights up the motionless trees, moved all about her. In front and behind she was aware of it. Beyond this stealthy silence, just within the edge of it, the things of another world were passing. But she could not know them. Her husband knew them, knew their beauty and their awe, yes, but for her they were out of reach. She might not share with him the very least of them. It seemed that behind and through the glare of this wintry noonday in the heart of the woods there brooded another universe of life and passion, for her all unexpressed. The silence veiled it, the stillness hid it but he moved with it all and understood. His love interpreted it.

She rose to her feet, tottered feebly, and collapsed again upon the moss. Yet for herself she felt no terror; no little personal fear could touch her whose anguish and deep longing streamed all out to him whom she so bravely loved. In this time of utter self-forgetfulness, when she realised that the battle was hopeless, thinking she had lost even her God, she found Him again quite close beside her like a little Presence in this terrible heart of the hostile Forest. But at first she did not recognise that He was there; she did not know Him in that strangely unacceptable guise. For He stood so very close, so very intimate, so very sweet and comforting, and yet so hard to understand—as Resignation.

Once more she struggled to her feet, and this time turned successfully and slowly made her way along the mossy glade by which she came. And at first she marvelled, though only for a moment, at the ease with which she found the path. For a moment only, because almost at once she saw the truth. The trees were glad that she should go. They helped her on her way. The Forest did not want her.

The tide was coming in, indeed, yet not for her.

And so, in another of those flashes of clear-vision that of late had lifted life above the normal level, she saw and understood the whole terrible thing complete.

Till now, though unexpressed in thought or language, her fear had been that the woods her husband loved would somehow take him from her—to merge his life in theirs—even to kill him in some mysterious way. This time she saw her deep mistake, and so seeing, let in upon herself the fuller agony of horror. For their jealousy was not the petty jealousy of animals or humans. They wanted him because they loved him, but they did not want him dead. Full charged with his splendid life and enthusiasm they wanted him. They wanted him—alive.

It was she who stood in their way, and it was she whom they intended to remove.

This was what brought the sense of abject helplessness. She stood upon the sands against an entire ocean slowly rolling in against her. For, as all the forces of a human being combine unconsciously to eject a grain of sand that has crept beneath the skin to cause discomfort, so the entire mass of what Sanderson had called the Collective Consciousness of the Forest strove to eject this human atom that stood across the path of its desire. Loving her husband, she had crept beneath its skin. It was her they would eject and take away; it was her they would destroy, not him. Him, whom they loved and needed, they would keep alive. They meant to take him living.

She reached the house in safety, though she never remembered how she found her way. It was made all simple for her. The branches almost urged her out.

But behind her, as she left the shadowed precincts, she felt as though some towering Angel of the Woods let fall across the threshold the flaming sword of a countless multitude of leaves that formed behind her a barrier, green, shimmering, and impassable. Into the Forest she never walked again.

*       *       *

And she went about her daily duties with a calm and quietness that was a perpetual astonishment even to herself, for it hardly seemed of this world at all. She talked to her husband when he came in for tea—after dark. Resignation brings a curious large courage—when there is nothing more to lose. The soul takes risks, and dares. Is it a curious short-cut sometimes to the heights?

"David, I went into the Forest, too, this morning; soon after you I went. I saw you there."

"Wasn't it wonderful?" he answered simply, inclining his head a little. There was no surprise or annoyance in his look; a mild and gentle *ennui* rather. He asked no real question. She thought of some garden tree the wind attacks too suddenly, bending it over when it does not want to bend—the mild unwillingness with which it yields. She often saw him this way now, in the terms of trees.

"It was very wonderful indeed, dear, yes," she replied low, her voice not faltering though indistinct. "But for me it was too—too strange and big."

The passion of tears lay just below the quiet voice all unbetrayed. Somehow she kept them back.

There was a pause, and then he added

"I find it more and more so every day." His voice passed through the lamp-lit room like a murmur of the wind in branches. The look of youth and happiness she had caught upon his face out there had wholly gone, and an expression of weariness was in its place, as of a man distressed vaguely at finding himself in uncongenial surroundings where he is slightly ill at ease. It was the house he hated—coming back to rooms and walls and furniture. The ceilings and closed windows confined him. Yet, in it, no suggestion that he found *her* irksome. Her presence seemed of no account at all indeed, he hardly noticed her. For whole long periods he lost her, did not know that she was there. He had no need of her. He lived alone. Each lived alone.

The outward signs by which she recognised that the awful battle was against her and the terms of surrender accepted were pathetic. She put the medicine-chest away upon the shelf; she gave the orders for his pocket-luncheon before he asked; she went to bed alone and early, leaving the front door unlocked, with milk and bread and butter in the hall beside the lamp—all concessions that she felt impelled to make. For more and more, unless the weather was too violent, he went out after dinner even, staying for hours in the woods. But she never slept until she heard the front door close below, and knew soon afterwards his careful step come creeping up the stairs and into the room so softly. Until she heard his regular deep breathing close beside her, she lay awake. All strength or desire to resist had gone for good. The thing against her was too huge and powerful. Capitulation was complete, a fact accomplished. She dated it from the day she followed him to the Forest.

Moreover, the time for evacuation—her own evacuation—seemed approaching. It came stealthily ever nearer, surely and slowly as the rising tide she used to dread. At the high-water mark she stood waiting calmly—waiting to be swept away. Across the lawn all those terrible days of early winter, the encircling Forest watched it come, guiding its silent swell and currents towards her feet. Only she never once gave up her Bible or her praying. This complete resignation, moreover, had somehow brought to her a strange great understanding, and if she could not share her husband's horrible abandonment to powers outside himself, she could, and did, in some half-groping way grasp at shadowy meanings that might make such abandonment—possible, yes, but more than merely possible—in some extraordinary sense not evil.

Hitherto she had divided the beyond-world into two sharp halves—spirits good or spirits evil. But thoughts came to her now, on soft and very tentative feet, like the footsteps of the gods which are on wool, that besides these definite classes, there might be other Powers as well, belonging definitely to neither one nor other. Her thought stopped dead at that. But the big idea found lodgment in her little mind, and, owing to the largeness of her heart, remained there unejected. It even brought a certain solace with it.

The failure—or unwillingness, as she preferred to state it—of her God to interfere and help, that also she came in a measure to understand. For here, she found it more and more possible to imagine, was perhaps no positive evil at work, but only something that usually stands away from humankind, something alien and not commonly recognised. There *was* a gulf fixed between the two, and Mr Sanderson *had* bridged it, by his talk, his explanations, his attitude of mind. Through these her husband had found the way into it. His temperament and natural passion for the woods had prepared the soul in him, and the moment he saw the way to go he took it—the line of least resistance. Life was, of course, open to all, and her husband had the right to choose it where he would. He had chosen it—away from her, away from other men, but not necessarily away from God. This was an enormous concession that she skirted, never really faced; it was too revolutionary to face. But its possibility peeped into her bewildered mind. It might delay his progress, or it might advance it. Who could know? And why should God, who ordered all things with such magnificent detail, from the pathway of a sun to the falling of a sparrow, object to his free choice, or interfere to hinder him and stop?

She came to realise resignation, that is, in another aspect. It gave her comfort, if not peace. She fought against all belittling of her God. It was, perhaps, enough that He—knew.

"You are not alone, dear, in the trees out there?" she ventured one night, as he crept on tiptoe into the room not far from midnight. "God is with you?"

"Magnificently," was the immediate answer, given with enthusiasm, "for He is everywhere. And I only wish that you—"

But she stuffed the clothes against her ears. That invitation on his lips was more than she could bear to hear. It seemed like asking her to hurry to her own execution. She buried her face among the sheets and blankets, shaking all over like a leaf.

## IX

AND so the thought that she was the one to go remained and grew. It was, perhaps, first sign of that weakening of the mind which indicated the singular manner of her going. For it was her mental opposition, the trees felt, that stood in their way. Once that was overcome, obliterated, her physical presence did not matter. She would be harmless.

Having accepted defeat, because she had come to feel that his obsession was not actually evil, she accepted at the same time the conditions of an atrocious loneliness. She stood now from her husband farther than from the moon. They had no visitors. Callers were few and far between, and less encouraged than before. The empty dark of winter was before them. Among the neighbours was none in whom, without disloyalty to her husband, she could confide. Mr Mortimer, had he been single, might have helped her in this desert of solitude that preyed upon her mind, but his wife was there the obstacle for Mrs Mortimer wore sandals, believed that nuts were the complete food of man, and indulged in other idiosyncrasies that classed her inevitably among the "latter signs" which Mrs Bittacy had been taught to dread as dangerous. She stood most desolately alone.

Solitude, therefore, in which the mind unhindered feeds upon its own delusions, was the assignable cause of her gradual mental disruption and collapse.

With the definite arrival of the colder weather her husband gave up his rambles after dark; evenings were spent together over the fire; he read *The Times;* they even talked about their postponed visit abroad in the coming spring. No restlessness was on him at the change; he seemed content and easy in his mind; spoke little of the trees and woods; enjoyed far better health than if there had been change of scene, and to herself was tender, kind, solicitous over trifles, as in the distant days of their first honeymoon.

But this deep calm could not deceive her; it meant, she fully understood, that he felt sure of himself, sure of her, and sure of the trees as well. It all lay buried in the depths of him, too secure and deep, too intimately established in his central being to permit of those surface fluctuations which betray disharmony within. His life was hid with trees. Even the fever, so dreaded in the damp of winter, left him free. She now knew why. The fever was due to their efforts to obtain him, his efforts to respond and go—physical results of a fierce unrest he had never understood till Sanderson came with his wicked explanations. Now it was otherwise. The bridge was made. And—he had gone.

And she, brave, loyal, and consistent soul, found herself utterly alone, even trying to make his passage easy. It seemed that she stood at the bottom of some huge ravine that opened in her mind, the walls whereof instead of rock were trees that reached enormous to the sky, engulfing her. God alone knew that she was there. He watched, permitted, even perhaps approved. At any rate—He knew.

During those quiet evenings in the house, moreover, while they sat over the fire listening to the roaming winds about the house, her husband knew continual access to the world his alien love had furnished for him. Never for a single instant was he cut off from it. She gazed at the newspaper spread before his face and knees, saw the smoke of his cheroot curl up above the edge, noticed the little hole in his evening socks, and listened to the paragraphs he read aloud as of old. But this was all a veil he spread about himself of purpose. Behind it—he escaped. It was the conjurer's trick to divert the sight to unimportant details while the essential thing went forward unobserved. He managed wonderfully; she loved him for the pains he took to spare her distress; but all the while she knew that the body lolling in that armchair before her eyes contained the merest fragment of his actual self. It was little better than a corpse. It was an empty shell. The essential soul of him was out yonder with the Forest—farther out near that ever-roaring heart of it.

And, with the dark, the Forest came up boldly and pressed against the very walls and windows, peering in upon them, joining hands above the slates and chimneys. The winds were always walking on the lawn and gravel paths; steps came and went and came again; someone seemed always talking in the woods, someone was in the building too. She passed them on the stairs, or running soft and muffled, very large and gentle, down the passages and landings after dusk, as though loose fragments of the Day had broken off and stayed there caught among the shadows, trying to get out. They blundered silently all about the house. They waited till she passed, then made a run for it. And her husband always knew. She saw him more than once deliberately avoid them—because *she* was there. More than once, too, she saw him stand and listen when he thought she was not near, then heard herself the long bounding stride of their approach across the silent garden. Already *he* had heard them in the windy distance of the night, far, far away.

They sped, she well knew, along that glade of mossy turf by which she last came out; it cushioned their tread exactly as it had cushioned her own.

It seemed to her the trees were always in the house with him, and in their very bedroom. He welcomed them, unaware that she also knew, and trembled.

One night in their bedroom it caught her unawares. She woke out of deep sleep and it came upon her before she could gather her forces for control.

The day had been wildly boisterous, but now the wind had dropped; only its rags went fluttering through the night. The rays of the full moon fell in a shower between the branches. Overhead still raced the scud and wrack, shaped like hurrying monsters but below the earth was quiet. Still and dripping stood the hosts of trees. Their trunks gleamed wet and sparkling where the moon caught them. There was a strong smell of mould and fallen leaves. The air was sharp—heavy with odour.

And she knew all this the instant that she woke for it seemed to her that she had been elsewhere—following her husband—as though she had been *out*! There was no dream at all, merely this definite, haunting certainty. It dived away, lost, buried in the night. She sat upright in bed. She had come back.

The room shone pale in the moonlight reflected through the windows, for the blinds were up, and she saw her husband's form beside her, motionless in deep sleep. But what caught her unawares was the horrid thing that by this fact of sudden, unexpected waking she had surprised; these other things in the room, beside the very bed, gathered close about him while he slept. It was their dreadful boldness—herself of no account as it were—that terrified her into screaming before she could collect her powers to prevent. She screamed before she realised what she did—a long, high shriek of terror that filled the room, yet made so little actual sound. For wet and shimmering presences stood grouped all round that bed. She saw their outline underneath the ceiling, the green, spread bulk of them, their vague extension over walls and furniture. They shifted to and fro, massed yet translucent, mild yet thick, moving and turning within themselves to a hushed noise of multitudinous soft rustling. In their sound was something very sweet and winning that fell into her with a spell of horrible enchantment. They were so mild, each one alone, yet so terrific in their combination. Cold seized her. The sheets against her body turned to ice.

She screamed a second time, though the sound hardly issued from her throat. The spell sank deeper, reaching to the heart for it softened all the currents of her blood and took life from her in a stream— towards themselves. Resistance in that moment seemed impossible.

Her husband then stirred in his sleep, and woke. And, instantly, the forms drew up, erect, and gathered themselves in some amazing way together. They lessened in extent—then scattered through the air like an effect of light when shadows seek to smother it. It was tremendous, yet most exquisite. A sheet of pale-green shadow that yet had form and substance filled the room. There was a rush of silent movement, as the Presences drew past her through the air,—and they were gone.

But, clearest of all, she saw the manner of their going for she recognised in their tumult of escape by the window open at the top, the same wide "looping circles"—spirals it seemed—that she had seen upon the lawn those weeks ago when Sanderson had talked. The room once more was empty.

In the collapse that followed, she heard her husband's voice, as though coming from some great distance. Her own replies she heard as well. Both were so strange and unlike their normal speech, the very words unnatural

"What is it, dear? Why do you wake me *now*?" And his voice whispered it with a sighing sound, like wind in pine boughs.

"A moment since something went past me through the air of the room. Back to the night outside it went." Her voice, too, held the same note as of wind entangled among too many leaves.

"My dear, it *was* the wind."

"But it called, David. It was calling *you*—by name!"

"The stir of the branches, dear, was what you heard. Now, sleep again, I beg you, sleep."

"It had a crowd of eyes all through and over it—before and behind—" Her voice grew louder. But his own in reply sank lower, far away, and oddly hushed.

"The moonlight, dear, upon the sea of twigs and boughs in the rain, was what you saw."

"But it frightened me. I've lost my God—and you—I'm cold as death!"

"My dear, it is the cold of the early morning hours. The whole world sleeps. Now sleep again yourself."

He whispered close to her ear. She felt his hand stroking her. His voice was soft and very soothing. But only a part of him was there; only a part of him was speaking; it was a half-emptied body that lay beside her and uttered these strange sentences, even forcing her own singular choice of words. The horrible, dim enchantment of the trees was close about them in the room—gnarled, ancient, lonely trees of winter, whispering round the human life they loved.

"And let me sleep again," she heard him murmur as he settled down among the clothes, "sleep back into that deep, delicious peace from which you called me..."

His dreamy, happy tone, and that look of youth and joy she discerned upon his features even in the filtered moonlight, touched her again as with the spell of those shining, mild green presences. It sank down into her. She felt sleep grope for her. On the threshold of slumber one of those strange vagrant voices that loss of consciousness lets loose cried faintly in her heart—

"There is joy in the Forest over one sinner that—"

Then sleep took her before she had time to realise even that she was vilely parodying one of her most precious texts, and that the irreverence was ghastly...

And though she quickly slept again, her sleep was not as usual, dreamless. It was not woods and trees she dreamed of, but a small and curious dream that kept coming again and again upon her: that she stood upon a wee, bare rock in the sea, and that the tide was rising. The water first came to her feet, then to her knees, then to her waist. Each time the dream returned, the tide seemed higher. Once it rose to her neck, once even to her mouth, covering her lips for a moment so that she could not breathe. She did not wake between the dreams; a period of drab and dreamless slumber intervened. But, finally, the water rose above her eyes and face, completely covering her head.

And then came explanation—the sort of explanation dreams bring. She understood. For, beneath the water, she had seen the world of seaweed rising from the bottom of the sea like a forest of dense green—long, sinuous stems, immense thick branches, millions of feelers spreading through the darkened watery depths the power of their ocean foliage. The Vegetable Kingdom was even in the sea. It was everywhere. Earth, air, and water helped it, way of escape there was none.

And even underneath the sea she heard that terrible sound of roaring— was it surf or wind or voices?—further out, yet coming steadily towards her.

And so, in the loneliness of that drab English winter, the mind of Mrs Bittacy, preying upon itself, and fed by constant dread, went lost in disproportion. Dreariness filled the weeks with dismal, sunless skies and a clinging moisture that knew no wholesome tonic of keen frosts. Alone with her thoughts, both her husband and her God withdrawn into distance, she counted the days to Spring. She groped her way, stumbling down the long dark tunnel. Through the arch at the far end lay a brilliant picture of the violet sea sparkling on the coast of France. There lay safety and escape for both of them, could she but hold on. Behind her the trees blocked up the other entrance. She never once looked back.

She drooped. Vitality passed from her, drawn out and away as by some steady suction. Immense and incessant was this sensation of her powers draining off. The taps were all turned on. Her personality, as it were, streamed steadily away, coaxed outwards by this Power that never wearied and seemed inexhaustible. It won her as the full moon wins the tide. She waned; she faded; she obeyed.

At first she watched the process, and recognised exactly what was going on. Her physical life, and that balance of the mind which depends on physical well-being, were being slowly undermined. She saw that clearly. Only the soul, dwelling like a star apart from these and independent of them, lay safe somewhere—with her distant God. That she knew—tranquilly. The spiritual love that linked her to her husband was safe from all attack. Later, in His good time, they would merge together again because of it. But, meanwhile, all of her that had kinship with the earth was slowly going. This separation was being remorselessly accomplished. Every part of her the trees could touch was being steadily drained from her. She was being—removed.

After a time, however, even this power of realisation went, so that she no longer "watched the process" or knew exactly what was going on. The one satisfaction she had known—the feeling that it was sweet to suffer for his sake—went with it. She stood utterly alone with this terror of the trees... mid the ruins of her broken and disordered mind.

She slept badly; woke in the morning with hot and tired eyes; her head ached dully; she grew confused in thought and lost the clues of daily life in the most feeble fashion. At the same time she lost sight, too, of that brilliant picture at the exit of the tunnel; it faded away into a tiny semicircle of pale light, the violet sea and the sunshine the merest point of white, remote as a star and equally inaccessible. She knew now that she could never reach it. And through the darkness that stretched behind, the power of the trees came close and caught her, twining about her feet and arms, climbing to her very lips. She woke at night, finding it difficult to breathe. There seemed wet leaves pressed against her mouth, and soft green tendrils clinging to her neck. Her feet were heavy, half rooted, as it were, in deep, thick earth. Huge creepers stretched along the whole of that black tunnel, feeling about her person for points where they might fasten well, as ivy or the giant parasites of the Vegetable Kingdom settle down on the trees themselves to sap their life and kill them.

Slowly and surely the morbid growth possessed her life and held her. She feared those very winds that ran about the wintry forest. They were in league with it. They helped it everywhere.

"Why don't you sleep, dear?" It was her husband now who played the rôle of nurse, tending her little wants with an honest care that at least aped the services of love. He was so utterly unconscious of the raging battle he had caused. "What is it keeps you so wide awake and restless?"

"The winds," she whispered in the dark. For hours she had lain watching the tossing of the trees through the blindless windows. "They go walking and talking everywhere tonight, keeping me awake. And all the time they call so loudly to you."

And his strange whispered answer appalled her for a moment until the meaning of it faded and left her in a dark confusion of the mind that was now becoming almost permanent.

"The trees excite them in the night. The winds are the great swift carriers. Go with them, dear—and not against. You'll find sleep that way if you do."

"The storm is rising," she began, hardly knowing what she said.

"All the more then—go with them. Don't resist. They'll take you to the trees, that's all."

Resist! The word touched on the button of some text that once had helped her.

"Resist the devil and he will flee from you," she heard her whispered answer, and the same second had buried her face beneath the clothes in a flood of hysterical weeping.

But her husband did not seem disturbed. Perhaps he did not hear it, for the wind ran just then against the windows with a booming shout, and the roaring of the Forest farther out came behind the blow, surging into the room. Perhaps, too, he was already asleep again. She slowly regained a sort of dull composure. Her face emerged from the tangle of sheets and blankets. With a growing terror over her—she listened. The storm was rising. It came with a sudden and impetuous rush that made all further sleep for her impossible.

Alone in a shaking world, it seemed, she lay and listened. That storm interpreted for her mind the climax. The Forest bellowed out its victory to the winds; the winds in turn proclaimed it to the Night. The whole world knew of her complete defeat, her loss, her little human pain. This was the roar and shout of victory that she listened to.

For, unmistakably, the trees were shouting in the dark. There were sounds, too, like the flapping of great sails, a thousand at a time, and sometimes reports that resembled more than anything else the distant booming of enormous drums. The trees stood up—the whole beleaguering host of them stood up—and with the uproar of their million branches drummed the thundering message out across the night. It seemed as if they all had broken loose. Their roots swept trailing over field and hedge and roof. They tossed their bushy heads beneath the clouds with a wild, delighted shuffling of great boughs. With trunks upright they raced leaping through the sky. There was upheaval and adventure in the awful sound they made, and their cry was like the cry of a sea that has broken through its gates and poured loose upon the world...

Through it all her husband slept peacefully as though he heard it not. It was, as she well knew, the sleep of the semi-dead. For he was out with all that clamouring turmoil. The part of him that she had lost was there. The form that slept so calmly at her side was but the shell, half emptied...

And when the winter's morning stole upon the scene at length, with a pale, washed sunshine that followed the departing tempest, the first thing she saw, as she crept to the window and looked out, was the ruined cedar lying on the lawn. Only the gaunt and crippled trunk of it remained. The single giant bough that had been left to it lay dark upon the grass, sucked endways towards the Forest by a great wind eddy. It lay there like a mass of drift-wood from a wreck, left by the ebbing of a high springtide upon the sands—remnant of some friendly, splendid vessel that once had sheltered men.

And in the distance she heard the roaring of the Forest further out. Her husband's voice was in it.

HOLMESLY.

## The South Wind

IT is impossible to say through which sense, or combination of senses, I knew that Someone was approaching—was already near; but most probably it was the deep underlying "mother-sense" including them all that conveyed the delicate warning. At any rate, the scene-shifters of my moods knew it too, for very swiftly they prepared the stage then, ever soft-footed and invisible, stood aside to wait.

As I went down the village street on my way to bed after midnight, the high Alpine valley lay silent in its frozen stillness. For days it had now lain thus, even the mouths of its cataracts stopped with ice; and for days, too, the dry, tight cold had drawn up the nerves of the humans in it to a sharp, thin pitch of exhilaration that at last began to call for the gentler comfort of relaxation. The key had been a little too high, the inner tautness too prolonged. The tension of that implacable north east wind, the *bise noire*, had drawn its twisted wires too long through our very entrails. We all sighed for some loosening of the bands—the comforting touch of something damp, soft, less penetratingly acute.

And now, as I turned, midway in the little journey from the inn to my room above La Poste, this sudden warning that Someone was approaching repeated its silent wireless message, and I paused to listen and to watch.

Yet at first I searched in vain. The village street lay empty—a white ribbon between the black walls of the big-roofed châlets; there were no lights in any of the houses; the hotels stood gaunt and ugly with their myriad shuttered windows; and the church, topped by the Crown of Savoy in stone, was so engulfed by the shadows of the mountains that it seemed almost a part of them.

Beyond, reared the immense buttresses of the Dent du Midi, terrible and stalwart against the sky, their feet resting among the crowding pines, their streaked precipices tilting up at violent angles towards the stars. The bands of snow, belting their enormous flanks, stretched for miles, faintly gleaming, like Saturn's rings. To the right I could just make out the pinnacles of the Dents Blanches, cruelly pointed and, still farther, the Dent de Bonnaveau, as of iron and crystal, running up its gaunt and dreadful pyramid into relentless depths of night. Everywhere in the hard, black-sparkling air was the rigid spell of winter. It seemed as if this valley could never melt again, never know currents of warm wind, never taste the sun, nor yield its million flowers.

And now, dipping down behind me out of the reaches of the darkness, the New Comer moved close, heralded by this subtle yet compelling admonition that had arrested me in my very tracks. For, just as I turned in at the door, kicking the crunched snow from my boots against the granite step, I knew that, from the heart of all this tightly frozen winter's night, the "Someone" whose message had travelled so delicately in advance was now, quite suddenly, at my very heels. And while my eyes lifted to sift their way between the darkness and the snow I became aware that It was already coming down the village street. It ran on feathered feet, pressing close against the enclosing walls, yet at the same time spreading from side to side, brushing the window-panes, rustling against the doors, and even including the shingled roofs in its enveloping advent. It came, too— *against the wind*...

It flew up close and passed me, very faintly singing, running down between the châlets and the church, very swift, very soft, neither man nor animal, neither woman, girl, nor child, turning the corner of the snowy road beyond the *Curé's* house with a rushing, cantering motion, that made me think of a Body of water—something of fluid and generous shape, too mighty to be confined in common forms. And, as it passed, it touched me— touched me through all skin and flesh upon the naked nerves, loosening, relieving, setting free the congealed sources of life which the *bise* so long had mercilessly bound, so that magic currents, flowing and released, washed down all the secret byways of the spirit and flooded again with full tide into a thousand dried-up cisterns of the heart.

The thrill I experienced is quite incommunicable in words. I ran upstairs and opened all my windows wide, knowing that soon the Messenger would return with a million others—only to find that already it had been there before me. Its taste was in the air, fragrant and alive in my very mouth—and all the currents of the inner life ran sweet again, and full. Nothing in the whole village was quite the same as it had been before. The deeply slumbering peasants, even behind their shuttered windows and barred doors; the *Curé*, the servants at the inn, the consumptive man opposite, the children in the house behind the church, the horde of tourists in the caravanserai—all knew—more or less, according to the delicacy of their receiving apparatus— that Something charged with fresh and living force had swept on viewless feet down the village street, passed noiselessly between the cracks of doors and windows, touched nerves and eyelids, and—set them free. In response to the great Order of Release that the messenger had left everywhere behind her, even the dreams of the sleepers had shifted into softer and more flowing keys...

And the Valley—the Valley also knew! For, as I watched from my window, something loosened about the trees and stones and boulders; about the massed snows on the great slopes; about the roots of the hanging icicles that fringed and sheeted the dark cliffs; and down in the deepest beds of the killed and silent streams. Far overhead, across those desolate bleak shoulders of the mountains, ran some sudden softness like the rush of awakening life... and was gone. A touch, lithe yet dewy, as of silk and water mixed, dropped softly over all... and, silently, without resistance, the *bise noire*, utterly routed, went back to the icy caverns of the north and east, where it sleeps, hated of men, and dreams its keen black dreams of death and desolation...

... And some five hours later, when I woke and looked towards the sunrise, I saw those strips of pearly grey, just tinged with red, the Messenger had been to summon... charged with the warm moisture that brings relief. On the wings of a rising South Wind they came down hurriedly to cap the mountains and to unbind the captive forces of life; then moved with flying streamers up our own valley, sponging from the thirsty woods their richest perfume...

And farther down, in soft, wet fields, stood the leafless poplars, with little pools of water gemming the grass between and pouring their musical overflow through runnels of dark and sodden leaves to join the rapidly increasing torrents descending from the mountains. For across the entire valley ran magically that sweet and welcome message of relief which Job knew when he put the whole delicious tenderness and passion of it into less than a dozen words: "*He comforteth the earth with the south wind.*"

CHAMPÉRY.

## The Sea Fit

THE sea that night sang rather than chanted; all along the far-running shore a rising tide dropped thick foam, and the waves, white-crested, came steadily in with the swing of a deliberate purpose. Overhead, in a cloudless sky, that ancient Enchantress, the full moon, watched their dance across the sheeted sands, guiding them carefully while she drew them up. For through that moonlight, through that roar of surf, there penetrated a singular note of earnestness and meaning—almost as though these common processes of Nature were instinct with the flush of an unusual activity that sought audaciously to cross the borderland into some subtle degree of conscious life. A gauze of light vapour clung upon the surface of the sea, far out—a transparent carpet through which the rollers drove shorewards in a moving pattern.

In the low-roofed bungalow among the sand-dunes the three men sat. Foregathered for Easter, they spent the day fishing and sailing, and at night told yarns of the days when life was younger. It was fortunate that there were three—and later four—because in the mouths of several witnesses an extraordinary thing shall be established—when they agree. And although whisky stood upon the rough table made of planks nailed to barrels, it is childish to pretend that a few drinks invalidate evidence, for alcohol, up to a certain point, intensifies the consciousness, focuses the intellectual powers, sharpens observation and two healthy men, certainly three, must have imbibed an absurd amount before they all see, or omit to see, the same things.

The other bungalows still awaited their summer occupants. Only the lonely tufted sand-dunes watched the sea, shaking their hair of coarse white grass to the winds. The men had the whole spit to themselves—with the wind, the spray, the flying gusts of sand, and that great Easter full moon. There was Major Reese of the Gunners and his half-brother, Dr Malcolm Reese, and Captain Erricson, their host, all men whom the kaleidoscope of life had jostled together a decade ago in many adventures, then flung for years apart about the globe. There was also Erricson's body-servant, "Sinbad," sailor of big seas, and a man who had shared on many a ship all the lust of strange adventure that distinguished his great blonde-haired owner—an ideal servant and dog-faithful, divining his master's moods almost before they were born. On the present occasion, besides crew of the fishing-smack, he was cook, valet, and steward of the bungalow smoking-room as well.

"Big Erricson," Norwegian by extraction, student by adoption, wanderer by blood, a Viking reincarnated if ever there was one, belonged to that type of primitive man in whom burns an inborn love and passion for the sea that amounts to positive worship—devouring tide, a lust and fever in the soul. "All genuine votaries of the old sea-gods have it," he used to say, by way of explaining his carelessness of worldly ambitions. "We're never at our best away from salt water— never quite right. I've got it bang in the heart myself. I'd do a bit before the mast sooner than make a million on shore. Simply can't help it, you see, and never could! It's our gods calling us to worship." And he had never tried to "help it," which explains why he owned nothing in the world on land except this tumble-down, one storey bungalow—more like a ship's cabin than anything else, to which he sometimes asked his bravest and most faithful friends—and a store of curious reading gathered in long, becalmed days at the ends of the world. Heart and mind, that is, carried a queer cargo. "I'm sorry if you poor devils are uncomfortable in her. You must ask Sinbad for anything you want and don't see, remember." As though Sinbad could have supplied comforts that were miles away, or converted a draughty wreck into a snug, taut, brand-new vessel.

Neither of the Reeses had cause for grumbling on the score of comfort, however, for they knew the keen joys of roughing it, and both weather and sport besides had been glorious. It was on another score this particular evening that they found cause for uneasiness, if not for actual grumbling. Erricson had one of his queer sea fits on—the Doctor was responsible for the term—and was in the thick of it, plunging like a straining boat at anchor, talking in a way that made them both feel vaguely uncomfortable and distressed. Neither of them knew exactly perhaps why he should have felt this growing *malaise*, and each was secretly vexed with the other for confirming his own unholy instinct that something uncommon was astir. The loneliness of the sandspit and that melancholy singing of the sea before their very door may have had something to do with it, seeing that both were landsmen; for Imagination is ever Lord of the Lonely Places, and adventurous men remain children to the last. But, whatever it was that affected both men in different fashion, Malcolm Reese, the doctor, had not thought it necessary to mention to his brother that Sinbad had tugged his sleeve on entering and whispered in his ear significantly: "Full moon, sir, please, and he's better without too much! These high spring tides get him all caught off his feet sometimes—clean sea-crazy"; and the man had contrived to let the doctor see the hilt of a small pistol he carried in his hip-pocket.

For Erricson had got upon his old subject: that the gods were not dead, but merely withdrawn, and that even a single true worshipper was enough to draw them down again into touch with the world, into the sphere of humanity, even into active and visible manifestation. He spoke of queer things he had seen in queerer places. He was serious, vehement, voluble and the others had let it pour out unchecked, hoping thereby for its speedier exhaustion. They puffed their pipes in comparative silence, nodding from time to time, shrugging their shoulders, the soldier mystified and bewildered, the doctor alert and keenly watchful.

"And I like the old idea," he had been saying, speaking of these departed pagan deities, "that sacrifice and ritual feed their great beings, and that death is only the final sacrifice by which the worshipper becomes absorbed into them. The devout worshipper"—and there was a singular drive and power behind the words—"should go to his death singing, as to a wedding—the wedding of his soul with the particular deity he has loved and served all his life." He swept his tow-coloured beard with one hand, turning his shaggy head towards the window, where the moonlight lay upon the procession of shaking waves. "It's playing the whole game, I always think, man-fashion. I remember once, some years ago, down there off the coast by Yucatan—"

And then, before they could interfere, he told an extraordinary tale of something he had seen years ago, but told it with such a horrid earnestness of conviction—for it was dreadful, though fine, this adventure—that his listeners shifted in their wicker chairs, struck matches unnecessarily, pulled at their long glasses, and exchanged glances that attempted a smile yet did not quite achieve it. For the tale had to do with sacrifice of human life and a rather haunting pagan ceremonial of the sea, and at its close the room had changed in some indefinable manner—was not exactly as it had been before perhaps—as though the savage earnestness of the language had introduced some new element that made it less cosy, less cheerful, even less warm. A secret lust in the man's heart, born of the sea, and of his intense admiration of the pagan gods called a light into his eye not altogether pleasant.

"They were great Powers, at any rate, those ancient fellows," Erricson went on, refilling his huge pipe bowl; "too great to disappear altogether, though today they may walk the earth in another manner. I swear they're still going it—especially the—" (he hesitated for a mere second) "the old water Powers—the Sea Gods. Terrific beggars, every one of 'em."

"Still move the tides and raise the winds, eh?" from the Doctor.

Erricson spoke again after a moment's silence, with impressive dignity. "And I like, too, the way they manage to keep their names before us," he went on, with a curious eagerness that did not escape the Doctor's observation, while it clearly puzzled the soldier. "There's old Hu, the Druid god of justice, still alive in 'Hue and Cry' there's Typhon hammering his way against us in the typhoon; there's the mighty Hurakar, serpent god of the winds, you know, shouting to us in hurricane and *ouragan* and there's—"

"Venus still at it as hard as ever," interrupted the Major, facetiously, though his brother did not laugh because of their host's almost sacred earnestness of manner and uncanny grimness of face. Exactly how he managed to introduce that element of gravity—of conviction—into such talk neither of his listeners quite understood, for in discussing the affair later they were unable to pitch upon any definite detail that betrayed it. Yet there it was, alive and haunting, even distressingly so. All day he had been silent and morose, but since dusk, with the turn of the tide, in fact, these queer sentences, half mystical, half unintelligible, had begun to pour from him, till now that cabin-like room among the sand-dunes fairly vibrated with the man's emotion. And at last Major Reese, with blundering good intention, tried to shift the key from this portentous subject of sacrifice to something that might eventually lead towards comedy and laughter, and so relieve this growing pressure of melancholy and incredible things. The Viking fellow had just spoken of the possibility of the old gods manifesting themselves visibly, audibly, physically, and so the Major caught him up and made light mention of spiritualism and the so-called "materialisation séances," where physical bodies were alleged to be built up out of the emanations of the medium and the sitters. This crude aspect of the Supernatural was the only possible link the soldier's mind could manage. He caught his brother's eye too late, it seems, for Malcolm Reese realised by this time that something untoward was afoot, and no longer needed the memory of Sinbad's warning to keep him sharply on the look-out. It was not the first time he had seen Erricson "caught" by the sea but he had never known him quite so bad, nor seen his face so flushed and white alternately, nor his eyes so oddly shining. So that Major Reese's well-intentioned allusion only brought wind to fire.

The man of the sea, once Viking, roared with a rush of boisterous laughter at the comic suggestion, then dropped his voice to a sudden hard whisper, awfully earnest, awfully intense. Any one must have started at the abrupt change and the life-and-death manner of the big man. His listeners undeniably both did.

"Bunkum!" he shouted, "bunkum, and be damned to it all! There's only one real materialisation of these immense Outer Beings possible, and that's when the great embodied emotions, which are their sphere of action"—his words became wildly incoherent, painfully struggling to get out—"derived, you see, from their honest worshippers the world over—constituting their Bodies, in fact—come down into matter and get condensed, crystallised into form—to claim that final sacrifice I spoke about just now, and to which any man might feel himself proud and honoured to be summoned... No dying in bed or fading out from old age, but to plunge full-blooded and alive into the great Body of the god who has deigned to descend and fetch you—"

The actual speech may have been even more rambling and incoherent than that. It came out in a torrent of white heat. Dr Reese kicked his brother beneath the table, just in time. The soldier looked thoroughly uncomfortable and amazed, utterly at a loss to know how he had produced the storm. It rather frightened him.

"I know it because I've seen it," went on the sea man, his mind and speech slightly more under control. "Seen the ceremonies that brought these whopping old Nature gods down into form—seen 'em carry off a worshipper into themselves—seen that worshipper, too, go off singing and happy to his death, proud and honoured to be chosen."

"Have you really—by George!" the Major exclaimed. "You tell us a queer thing, Erricson" and it was then for the fifth time that Sinbad cautiously opened the door, peeped in and silently withdrew after giving a swiftly comprehensive glance round the room.

The night outside was windless and serene, only the growing thunder of the tide near the full woke muffled echoes among the sand-dunes.

"Rites and ceremonies," continued the other, his voice booming with a singular enthusiasm, but ignoring the interruption, "are simply means of losing one's self by temporary ecstasy in the God of one's choice—the God one has worshipped all one's life—of being partially absorbed into his being. And sacrifice completes the process—"

"At death, you said?" asked Malcolm Reese, watching him keenly.

"Or voluntary," was the reply that came flash-like. "The devotee becomes wedded to his Deity—goes bang into him, you see, by fire or water or air—as by a drop from a height—according to the nature of the particular God at-one-ment, of course. A man's death that! Fine, you know!"

The man's inner soul was on fire now. He was talking at a fearful pace, his eyes alight, his voice turned somehow into a kind of sing-song that chimed well, singularly well, with the booming of waves outside, and from time to time he turned to the window to stare at the sea and the moon-blanched sands. And then a look of triumph would come into his face—that giant face framed by slow-moving wreaths of pipe smoke.

Sinbad entered for the sixth time without any obvious purpose, busied himself unnecessarily with the glasses and went out again, lingeringly. In the room he kept his eye hard upon his master. This time he contrived to push a chair and a heap of netting between him and the window. No one but Dr Reese observed the manoeuvre. And he took the hint.

"The port-holes fit badly, Erricson," he laughed, but with a touch of authority. "There's a five-knot breeze coming through the cracks worse than an old wreck!" And he moved up to secure the fastening better.

"The room *is* confoundedly cold," Major Reese put in "has been for the last half-hour, too." The soldier looked what he felt—cold—distressed—creepy. "But there's no wind really, you know," he added.

Captain Erricson turned his great bearded visage from one to the other before he answered; there was a gleam of sudden suspicion in his blue eyes. "The beggar's got that back door open again. If he's sent for any one, as he did once before, I swear I'll drown him in fresh water for his impudence—or perhaps—can it be already that he expects—?" He left the sentence incomplete and rang the bell, laughing with a boisterousness that was clearly feigned. "Sinbad, what's this cold in the place? You've got the back door open. Not expecting any one, are you—?"

"Everything's shut tight, Captain. There's a bit of a breeze coming up from the east. And the tide's drawing in at a raging pace—"

"We can all hear *that*. But are you expecting any one? I asked," repeated his master, suspiciously, yet still laughing. One might have said he was trying to give the idea that the man had some land flirtation on hand. They looked one another square in the eye for a moment, these two. It was the straight stare of equals who understood each other well.

"Someone—might be—on the way, as it were, Captain. Couldn't say for certain."

The voice almost trembled. By a sharp twist of the eye, Sinbad managed to shoot a lightning and significant look at the Doctor.

"But this cold—this freezing, damp cold in the place? Are you sure no one's come—by the back ways?" insisted the master. He whispered it. "Across the dunes, for instance?" His voice conveyed awe and delight, both kept hard under.

"It's all over the house, Captain, already," replied the man, and moved across to put more sea-logs on the blazing fire. Even the soldier noticed then that their language was tight with allusion of another kind. To relieve the growing tension and uneasiness in his own mind he took up the word "house" and made fun of it.

"As though it were a mansion," he observed, with a forced chuckle, "instead of a mere sea-shell!" Then, looking about him, he added: "But, all the same, you know, there is a kind of fog getting into the room—from the sea, I suppose coming up with the tide, or something, eh?" The air had certainly in the last twenty minutes turned thickish; it was not all tobacco smoke, and there was a moisture that began to precipitate on the objects in tiny, fine globules. The cold, too, fairly bit.

"I'll take a look round," said Sinbad, significantly, and went out. Only the Doctor perhaps noticed that the man shook, and was white down to the gills. He said nothing, but moved his chair nearer to the window and to his host. It was really a little bit beyond comprehension how the wild words of this old sea-dog in the full sway of his "sea fit" had altered the very air of the room as well as the personal equations of its occupants, for an extraordinary atmosphere of enthusiasm that was almost splendour pulsed about him, yet vilely close to something that suggested terror! Through the armour of every-day common sense that normally clothed the minds of these other two, had crept the faint wedges of a mood that made them vaguely wonder whether the incredible could perhaps sometimes—by way of bewildering exceptions—actually come to pass. The moods of their deepest life, that is to say, were already affected. An inner, and thoroughly unwelcome, change was in progress. And such psychic disturbances once started are hard to arrest. In this case it was well on the way before either the Army or Medicine had been willing to recognise the fact. There was something coming—coming from the sand-dunes or the sea. And it was invited, welcomed at any rate, by Ericson. His deep, volcanic enthusiasm and belief provided the channel. In lesser degree they, too, were caught in it. Moreover, it was terrific, irresistible.

And it was at this point—as the comparing of notes afterwards established—that Father Norden came in, Norden, the big man's nephew, having bicycled over from some point beyond Corfe Castle and raced along the hard Studland sand in the moonlight, and then hullood till a boat had ferried him across the narrow channel of Poole Harbour. Sinbad simply brought him in without any preliminary question or announcement. He could not resist the splendid night and the spring air, explained Norden. He felt sure his uncle could "find a hammock" for him somewhere aft, as he put it. He did not add that Sinbad had telegraphed for him just before sundown from the coast-guard hut. Dr Reese already knew him, but he was introduced to the Major. Norden was a member of the Society of Jesus, an ardent, not clever, and unselfish soul.

Ericson greeted him with obviously mixed feelings, and with an extraordinary sentence: "It doesn't really matter," he exclaimed, after a few commonplaces of talk, "for all religions are the same if you go deep enough. All teach sacrifice, and, without exception, all seek final union by absorption into their Deity." And then, under his breath, turning sideways to peer out of the window, he added a swift rush of half-smothered words that only Dr Reese caught "The Army, the Church, the Medical Profession, and Labour— if they would only all come! What a fine result, what a grand offering! Alone—I seem so unworthy—insignificant... !"

But meanwhile young Norden was speaking before any one could stop him, although the Major did make one or two blundering attempts. For once the Jesuit's tact was at fault. He evidently hoped to introduce a new mood— to shift the current already established by the single force of his own personality. And he was not quite man enough to carry it off.

It was an error of judgment on his part. For the forces he found established in the room were too heavy to lift and alter, their impetus being already acquired. He did his best, anyhow. He began moving with the current—it was not the first sea fit he had combated in this extraordinary personality— then found, too late, that he was carried along with it himself like the rest of them.

"Odd—but couldn't find the bungalow at first," he laughed, somewhat hardly. "It's got a bit of sea-fog all to itself that hides it. I thought perhaps my pagan uncle—"

The Doctor interrupted him hastily, with great energy. "The fog *does* lie caught in these sand hollows—like steam in a cup, you know," he put in. But the other, intent on his own procedure, missed the cue.

"—thought it was smoke at first, and that you were up to some heathen ceremony or other," laughing in Ericson's face "sacrificing to the full moon or the sea, or the spirits of the desolate places that haunt sand-dunes, eh?"

No one spoke for a second, but Ericson's face turned quite radiant.

"My uncle's such a pagan, you know," continued the priest, "that as I flew along those deserted sands from Studland I almost expected to hear old Triton blow his wreathèd horn... or see fair Thetis's tinsel-slippered feet..."

Ericson, suppressing violent gestures, highly excited, face happy as a boy's, was combing his great yellow beard with both hands, and the other two men had begun to speak at once, intent on stopping the flow of unwise allusion. Norden, swallowing a mouthful of cold soda-water, had put the glass down, spluttering over its bubbles, when the sound was first heard at the window. And in the back room the manservant ran, calling something aloud that sounded like "It's coming, God save us, it's coming in... !" Though the Major swears some name was mentioned that he afterwards forgot— Glaucus—Proteus—Pontus—or some such word. The sound itself, however, was plain enough— a kind of imperious tapping on the window-panes as of a multitude of objects. Blown sand it might have been or heavy spray or, as Norden suggested later, a great water-soaked branch of giant seaweed. Every one started up, but Ericson was first upon his feet, and had the window wide open in a twinkling. His voice roared forth over those moonlit sand-dunes and out towards the line of heavy surf ten yards below.

"All along the shore of the Ægean," he bellowed, with a kind of hoarse triumph that shook the heart, "that ancient cry once rang. But it was a lie, a thumping and audacious lie. And He is not the only one. Another still lives—and, by Poseidon, He comes! He knows His own and His own know Him—and His own shall go to meet Him... !"

That reference to the Ægean "cry"! It was so wonderful. Every one, of course, except the soldier, seized the allusion. It was a comprehensive, yet subtle, way of suggesting the idea. And meanwhile all spoke at once, shouted rather, for the Invasion was somehow— monstrous.

"Damn it—that's a bit too much. Something's caught my throat!" The Major, like a man drowning, fought with the furniture in his amazement and dismay. Fighting was his first instinct, of course. "Hurts so infernally— takes the breath," he cried, by way of explaining the extraordinarily violent impetus that moved him, yet half ashamed of himself for seeing nothing he could strike. But Malcolm Reese struggled to get between his host and the open window, saying in tense voice something like "Don't let him get out! Don't let him get out!" While the shouts of warning from Sinbad in the little cramped back offices added to the general confusion. Only Father Norden stood quiet—watching with a kind of admiring wonder the expression of magnificence that had flamed into the visage of Erricson.

"Hark, you fools! Hark!" boomed the Viking figure, standing erect and splendid.

And through that open window, along the far-drawn line of shore from Canford Cliffs to the chalk bluffs of Studland Bay, there certainly ran a sound that was no common roar of surf. It was articulate—a message from the sea—an announcement—a thunderous warning of approach. No mere surf breaking on sand could have compassed so deep and multitudinous a voice of dreadful roaring—far out over the entering tide, yet at the same time close in along the entire sweep of shore, shaking all the ocean, both depth and surface, with its deep vibrations. Into the bungalow chamber came—the SEA!

Out of the night, from the moonlit spaces where it had been steadily accumulating, into that little cabined room so full of humanity and tobacco smoke, came invisibly—the Power of the Sea. Invisible, yes, but mighty, pressed forward by the huge draw of the moon, soft-coated with brine and moisture—the great Sea. And with it, into the minds of those three other men, leaped instantaneously, not to be denied, overwhelming suggestions of water-power, the tear and strain of thousand-mile currents, the irresistible pull and rush of tides, the suction of giant whirlpools—more, the massed and awful impetus of whole driven oceans. The air turned salt and briny, and a welter of seaweed clamped their very skins.

"Glaucus! I come to Thee, great God of the deep Waterways... Father and Master!" Erricson cried aloud in a voice that most marvellously conveyed supreme joy.

The little bungalow trembled as from a blow at the foundations, and the same second the big man was through the window and running down the moonlit sands towards the foam.

"God in Heaven! Did you all see *that*?" shouted Major Reese, for the manner in which the great body slipped through the tiny window-frame was incredible. And then, first tottering with a sudden weakness, he recovered himself and rushed round by the door, followed by his brother. Sinbad, invisible, but not inaudible, was calling aloud from the passage at the back. Father Norden, slimmer than the others—well controlled, too—was through the little window before either of them reached the fringe of beach beyond the sand-dunes. They joined forces halfway down to the water's edge. The figure of Erricson, towering in the moonlight, flew before them, coasting rapidly along the wave-line.

No one of them said a word; they tore along side by side, Norden a trifle in advance. In front of them, head turned seawards, bounded Erricson in great flying leaps, singing as he ran, impossible to overtake.

Then, what they witnessed all three witnessed; the weird grandeur of it in the moonshine was too splendid to allow the smaller emotions of personal alarm, it seems. At any rate, the divergence of opinion afterwards was unaccountably insignificant. For, on a sudden, that heavy roaring sound far out at sea came close in with a swift plunge of speed, followed simultaneously—accompanied, rather—by a dark line that was no mere wave moving: enormously, up and across, between the sea and sky it swept close in to shore. The moonlight caught it for a second as it passed, in a cliff of her bright silver.

And Erricson slowed down, bowed his great head and shoulders, spread his arms out and...

And what? For no one of those amazed witnesses could swear exactly what then came to pass. Upon this impossibility of telling it in language they all three agreed. Only those eyeless dunes of sand that watched, only the white and silent moon overhead, only that long, curved beach of empty and deserted shore retain the complete record, to be revealed some day perhaps when a later Science shall have learned to develop the photographs that Nature takes incessantly upon her secret plates. For Erricson's rough suit of tweed went out in ribbons across the air; his figure somehow turned dark like strips of tide-sucked seaweed; something enveloped and overcame him, half shrouding him from view. He stood for one instant upright, his hair wild in the moonshine, towering, with arms again outstretched; then bent forward, turned, drew out most curiously sideways, uttering the singing sound of tumbling waters. The next instant, curving over like a falling wave, he swept along the glistening surface of the sands—and was gone. In fluid form, wave-like, his being slipped away into the Being of the Sea. A violent tumult convulsed the surface of the tide near in, but at once, and with amazing speed, passed careering away into the deeper water— far out. To his singular death, as to a wedding, Erricson had gone, singing, and well content.

"May God, who holds the sea and all its powers in the hollow of His mighty hand, take them both into Himself!" Norden was on his knees, praying fervently.

The body was never recovered... and the most curious thing of all was that the interior of the cabin, where they found Sinbad shaking with terror when they at length returned, was splashed and sprayed, almost soaked, with salt water. Up into the bigger dunes beside the bungalow, and far beyond the reach of normal tides, lay, too, a great streak and furrow as of a large invading wave, caking the dry sand. A hundred tufts of the coarse grass tussocks had been torn away.

The high tide that night, drawn by the Easter full moon, of course, was known to have been exceptional, for it fairly flooded Poole Harbour, flushing all the coves and bays towards the mouth of the Frome. And the natives up at Arne Bay and Wych always declare that the noise of the sea was heard far inland even up to the nine Barrows of the Purbeck Hills—triumphantly singing.

HAVEN HOTEL

## The Attic

THE forest-girdled village upon the Jura slopes slept soundly, although it was not yet many minutes after ten o'clock. The clang of the *couvre-feu* had indeed just ceased, its notes swept far into the woods by a wind that shook the mountains. This wind now rushed down the deserted street. It howled about the old rambling building called La Citadelle, whose roof towered gaunt and humped above the smaller houses—Château left unfinished long ago by Lord Wemyss, the exiled Jacobite. The families who occupied the various apartments listened to the storm and felt the building tremble. "It's the mountain wind. It will bring the snow," the mother said, without looking up from her knitting. "And how sad it sounds."

But it was not the wind that brought sadness as we sat round the open fire of peat. It was the wind of memories. The lamplight slanted along the narrow room towards the table where breakfast things lay ready for the morning. The double windows were fastened. At the far end stood a door ajar, and on the other side of it the two elder children lay asleep in the big bed. But beside the window was a smaller unused bed, that had been empty now a year. And tonight was the anniversary...

And so the wind brought sadness and long thoughts. The little chap that used to lie there was already twelve months gone, far, far beyond the Hole where the Winds came from, as he called it; yet it seemed only yesterday that I went to tell him a tuck-up story, to stroke Riquette, the old motherly cat that cuddled against his back and laid a paw beside his pillow like a human being, and to hear his funny little earnest whisper say, "*Oncle, tu sais, j'ai prié pour* Petavel." For La Citadelle had its unhappy ghost—of Petavel, the usurer, who had hanged himself in the attic a century gone by, and was known to walk its dreary corridors in search of peace—and this wise Irish mother, calming the boy's fears with wisdom, had told him, "If you pray for Petavel, you'll save his soul and make him happy, and he'll only love you." And, thereafter, this little imaginative boy had done so every night. With a passionate seriousness he did it. He had wonderful, delicate ways like that. In all our hearts he made his fairy nests of wonder. In my own, I know, he lay closer than any joy imaginable, with his big blue eyes, his queer soft questionings, and his splendid child's unselfishness—a sun-kissed flower of innocence that, had he lived, might have sweetened half a world.

"Let's put more peat on," the mother said, as a handful of rain like stones came flinging against the windows "that must be hail." And she went on tiptoe to the inner room. "They're sleeping like two puddings," she whispered, coming presently back. But it struck me she had taken longer than to notice merely that and her face wore an odd expression that made me uncomfortable. I thought she was somehow just about to laugh or cry. By the table a second she hesitated. I caught the flash of indecision as it passed. "Pan," she said suddenly—it was a nickname, stolen from my tuck-up stories, *he* had given me—"I wonder how Riquette got in." She looked hard at me. "It wasn't you, was it?" For we never let her come at night since he had gone. It was too poignant. The beastie always went cuddling and nestling into that empty bed. But this time it was not my doing, and I offered plausible explanations. "But—she's on the bed. Pan, *would* you be so kind—" She left the sentence unfinished, but I easily understood, for a lump had somehow risen in my own throat too, and I remembered now that she had come out from the inner room so quickly—with a kind of hurried rush almost. I put *"mère Riquette"* out into the corridor. A lamp stood on the chair outside the door of another occupant further down, and I urged her gently towards it. She turned and looked at me—straight up into my face but, instead of going down as I suggested, she went slowly in the opposite direction. She stepped softly towards a door in the wall that led up broken stairs into the attics. There she sat down and waited. And so I left her, and came back hastily to the peat fire and companionship. The wind rushed in behind me and slammed the door.

And we talked then somewhat busily of cheerful things of the children's future, the excellence of the cheap Swiss schools, of Christmas presents, skiing, snow, tobogganing. I led the talk away from mournfulness and when these subjects were exhausted I told stories of my own adventures in distant parts of the world. But "mother" listened the whole time—not to me. Her thoughts were all elsewhere. And her air of intently, secretly listening, bordered, I felt, upon the uncanny. For she often stopped her knitting and sat with her eyes fixed upon the air before her, she stared blankly at the wall, her head slightly on one side, her figure tense, attention strained— elsewhere. Or, when my talk positively demanded it, her nod was oddly mechanical and her eyes looked through and past me. The wind continued very loud and roaring but the fire glowed, the room was warm and cosy. Yet she shivered, and when I drew attention to it, her reply, "I do feel cold, but I didn't know I shivered," was given as though she spoke across the air to someone else. But what impressed me even more uncomfortably were her repeated questions about Riquette. When a pause in my tales permitted, she would look up with "I wonder where Riquette went?" or, thinking of the inclement night, "I hope mère Riquette's not out of doors. Perhaps Madame Favre has taken her in?" I offered to go and see. Indeed I was already half-way across the room when there came the heavy bang at the door that rooted me to the ground where I stood. It was not wind. It was something alive that made it rattle. There was a second blow. A thud on the corridor boards followed, and then a high, odd voice that at first was as human as the cry of a child.

It is undeniable that we both started, and for myself I can answer truthfully that a chill ran down my spine but what frightened me more than the sudden noise and the eerie cry was the way "mother" supplied the immediate explanation. For behind the words "It's only Riquette; she sometimes springs at the door like that; perhaps we'd better let her in," was a certain touch of uncanny quiet that made me feel she had known the cat would come, and knew also *why* she came. One cannot explain such impressions further. They leave their vital touch, then go their way. Into the little room, however, in that moment there came between us this uncomfortable sense that the night held other purposes than our own—and that my companion was aware of them. There was something going on far, far removed from the routine of life as we were accustomed to it. Moreover, our usual routine was the eddy, while this was the main stream. It felt big, I mean.

And so it was that the entrance of the familiar, friendly creature brought this thing both itself and "mother" *knew*, but whereof I as yet was ignorant. I held the door wide. The draught rushed through behind her, and sent a shower of sparks about the fireplace. The lamp flickered and gave a little gulp. And Riquette marched slowly past, with all the impressive dignity of her kind, towards the other door that stood ajar. Turning the corner like a shadow, she disappeared into the room where the two children slept. We heard the soft thud with which she leaped upon the bed. Then, in a lull of the wind, she came back again and sat on the oilcloth, staring into "mother's" face. She mewed and put a paw out, drawing the black dress softly with half-opened claws. And it was all so horribly suggestive and pathetic, it revived such poignant memories, that I got up impulsively—I think I had actually said the words, "We'd better put her out, mother, after all"—when my companion rose to her feet and forestalled me. She said another thing instead. It took my breath away to hear it. "She wants us to go with her. Pan, will you come too?" The surprise on my face must have asked the question, for I do not remember saying anything. "To the attic," she said quietly.

She stood there by the table, a tall, grave figure dressed in black, and her face above the lamp-shade caught the full glare of light. Its expression positively stiffened me. She seemed so secure in her singular purpose. And her familiar appearance had so oddly given place to something wholly strange to me. She looked like another person—almost with the unwelcome transformation of the sleep-walker about her. Cold came over me as I watched her, for I remembered suddenly her Irish second-sight, her story years ago of meeting a figure on the attic stairs, the figure of Petavel. And the idea of this motherly, sedate, and wholesome woman, absorbed day and night in prosaic domestic duties, and yet "seeing" things, touched the incongruous almost to the point of alarm. It was so distressingly convincing.

Yet she knew quite well that I would come. Indeed, following the excited animal, she was already by the door, and a moment later, still without answering or protesting, I was with them in the draughty corridor. There was something inevitable in her manner that made it impossible to refuse. She took the lamp from its nail on the wall, and following our four-footed guide, who ran with obvious pleasure just in front, she opened the door into the courtyard. The wind nearly put the lamp out, but a minute later we were safe inside the passage that led up flights of creaky wooden stairs towards the world of tenantless attics overhead.

And I shall never forget the way the excited Riquette first stood up and put her paws upon the various doors, trotted ahead, turned back to watch us coming, and then finally sat down and waited on the threshold of the empty, raftered space that occupied the entire length of the building underneath the roof. For her manner was more that of an intelligent dog than of a cat, and sometimes more like that of a human mind than either.

We had come up without a single word. The howling of the wind as we rose higher was like the roar of artillery. There were many broken stairs, and the narrow way was full of twists and turnings. It was a dreadful journey. I felt eyes watching us from all the yawning spaces of the darkness, and the noise of the storm smothered footsteps everywhere. Troops of shadows kept us company. But it was on the threshold of this big, chief attic, when "mother" stopped abruptly to put down the lamp, that real fear took hold of me. For Riquette marched steadily forward into the middle of the dusty flooring, picking her way among the fallen tiles and mortar, as though she went towards—someone. She purred loudly and uttered little cries of excited pleasure. Her tail went up into the air, and she lowered her head with the unmistakable intention of being stroked. Her lips opened and shut. Her green eyes smiled. She *was* being stroked.

It was an unforgettable performance. I would rather have witnessed an execution or a murder than watch that mysterious creature twist and turn about in the way she did. Her magnified shadow was as large as a pony on the floor and rafters. I wanted to hide the whole thing by extinguishing the lamp. For, even before the mysterious action began, I experienced the sudden rush of conviction that others besides ourselves were in this attic—and standing very close to us indeed. And, although there was ice in my blood, there was also a strange swelling of the heart that only love and tenderness could bring.

But, whatever it was, my human companion, still silent, knew and understood. She saw. And her soft whisper that ran with the wind among the rafters, "*Il a prié pour* Petavel *et le hon Dieu l'a entendu,*" did not amaze me one quarter as much as the expression I then caught upon her radiant face. Tears ran down the cheeks, but they were tears of happiness. Her whole figure seemed lit up. She opened her arms—picture of great Motherhood, proud, blessed, and tender beyond words. I thought she was going to fall, for she took quick steps forward but when I moved to catch her, she drew me aside instead with a sudden gesture that brought fear back in the place of wonder.

"Let them pass," she whispered grandly. "Pan, don't you see... He's leading him into peace and safety... by the hand!" And her joy seemed to kill the shadows and fill the entire attic with white light. Then, almost simultaneously with her words, she swayed. I was in time to catch her, but as I did so, across the very spot where we had just been standing—two figures, I swear, went past us like a flood of light.

There was a moment next of such confusion that I did not see what happened to Riquette, for the sight of my companion kneeling on the dusty boards and praying with a curious sort of passionate happiness, while tears pressed between her covering fingers—the strange wonder of this made me utterly oblivious to minor details...

We were sitting round the peat fire again, and "mother" was saying to me in the gentlest, tenderest whisper I ever heard from human lips—"Pan, I think perhaps that's why God took him..."
And when a little later we went in to make Riquette cosy in the empty bed, ever since kept sacred to her use, the mournfulness had lifted and in the place of resignation was proud peace and joy that knew no longer sad or selfish questionings.

BÔLE.

## The Heath Fire

THE men at luncheon in Rennie's Surrey cottage that September day were discussing, of course, the heat. All agreed it had been exceptional. But nothing unusual was said until O'Hara spoke of the heath fires. They had been rather terrific, several in a single day, devouring trees and bushes, endangering human life, and spreading with remarkable rapidity. The flames, too, had been extraordinarily high and vehement for heath fires. And O'Hara's tone had introduced into the commonplace talk something new—the element of mystery; it was nothing definite he said, but manner, eyes, hushed voice and the rest conveyed it. And it was genuine. What he *felt* reached the others rather than what he said. The atmosphere in the little room, with the honeysuckle trailing sweetly across the open windows, changed; the talk became of a sudden less casual, frank, familiar; and the men glanced at one another across the table, laughing still, yet with an odd touch of constraint marking little awkward, unfilled pauses. Being a group of normal Englishmen, they disliked mystery; it made them feel uncomfortable; for the things O'Hara hinted at had touched that kind of elemental terror that lurks secretly in all human beings. Guarded by "culture," but never wholly concealed, the unwelcome thing made its presence known—the hint of primitive dread that, for instance, great thunder-storms, tidal waves, or violent conflagrations rouse.

And instinctively they fell at once to discussing the obvious causes of the fires. The stockbroker, scenting imagination, edged mentally away, sniffing. But the journalist was full of brisk information, "simply given."

"The sun starts them in Canada, using a dewdrop as a lens," he said, "and an engine's spark, remember, carries an immense distance without losing its heat."

"But hardly miles," said another, who had not been really listening.

"It's my belief," put in the critic keenly, "that a lot were done on purpose. Bits of live coal wrapped in cloth were found, you know." He was a little, weasel-faced iconoclast, dropping the acid of doubt and disbelief wherever he went, but offering nothing in the place of what he destroyed. His head was turret-shaped, lips tight and thin, nose and chin running to points like gimlets, with which he bored into the unremunerative clays of life.

"The general unrest, yes," the journalist supported him, and tried to draw the conversation on to labour questions. But their host preferred the fire talk. "I must say," he put in gravely, "that some of the blazes hereabouts were uncommonly—er—queer. They started, I mean, so oddly. You remember, O'Hara, only last week that suspicious one over Kettlebury way—?"

It seemed he wished to draw the artist out, and that the artist, feeling the general opposition, declined.

"Why seek an unusual explanation at all?" the critic said at length, impatiently. "It's all natural enough, if you ask me."

"Natural! Oh yes!" broke in O'Hara, with a sudden vehemence that betrayed feeling none had as yet suspected; "provided you don't limit the word to mean only what we understand. There's nothing anywhere—unnatural."

A laugh cut short the threatened tirade, and the journalist expressed the general feeling with "Oh *you*, Jim! You'd see a devil in a dust-storm, or a fairy in the tea-leaves of your cup!"

"And why not, pray? Devils and fairies are every bit as true as formulæ."

Someone tactfully guided them away from a profitless discussion, and they talked glibly of the damage done, the hideousness of the destroyed moors, the gaunt, black, ugly slopes, fifty-foot flames, roaring noises, and the splendour of the enormous smoke-clouds that had filled the skies. And Rennie, still hoping to coax O'Hara, repeated tales the beaters had brought in that crying, as though living things were caught, had been heard in places, and that some had seen tall shapes of fire passing headlong through the choking smoke. For the note O'Hara had struck refused to be ignored. It went on sounding underneath the commonest remark and the atmosphere to the end retained that curious tinge that he had given to it—of the strange, the ominous, the mysterious and unexplained. Until, at last, the artist, having added nothing further to the talk, got up with some abruptness and left the room. He complained briefly that the fever he had suffered from still bothered him and he would go and lie down a bit. The heat, he said, oppressed him.

A silence followed his departure. The broker drew a sigh as though the market had gone up. But Rennie, old, comprehending friend, looked anxious. "Excitement," he said, "not oppression, is the word he meant. He's always a bit strung up when that Black Sea fever gets him. He brought it with him from Batoum." And another brief silence followed.

"Been with you most of the summer, hasn't he?" enquired the journalist, on the trail of a "par," "painting those wild things of his that no one understands." And their host, weighing a moment how much he might in fairness tell, replied—among friends it was—"Yes and this summer they have been more—er—wild and wonderful than usual—an extraordinary rush of colour—splendid schemes, 'conceptions,' I believe you critics call 'em, of fire, as though, in a way, the unusual heat had possessed him for interpretation."

The group expressed its desultory interest by uninspired interjections.

"That was what he meant just now when he said the fires had been mysterious, required explanation, or something—the way they started, rather," concluded Rennie.

Then he hesitated. He laughed a moment, and it was an uneasy, apologetic little laugh. How to continue he hardly knew. Also, he wished to protect his friend from the cheap jeering of miscomprehension. "He is very imaginative, you know," he went on, quietly, as no one spoke. "You remember that glorious mad thing he did of the Fallen Lucifer—driving a star across the heavens till the heat of the descent set a light to half the planets, scorched the old moon to the white cinder that she now is, and passed close enough to earth to send our oceans up in a single jet of steam? Well, this time—he's been at something every bit as wild, only truer—finer. And what is it? Briefly, then, he's got the idea, it seems, that the unusual heat from the sun this year has penetrated deep enough—in places—especially on these unprotected heaths that retain their heat so cleverly—to reach another kindred expression—to waken a response—in sympathy, you see—from the central fires of the earth."

He paused again a moment awkwardly, conscious how clumsily he expressed it. "The parent getting into touch again with its lost child, eh? See the idea? Return of the Fire Prodigal, as it were?"

His listeners stared in silence, the broker looking his obvious relief that O'Hara was not on 'Change, the critic's eyes glancing sharply down that pointed, boring nose of his.

"And the central fires have felt it and risen in response," continued Rennie in a lower voice. "You see the idea? It's big, to say the least. The volcanoes have answered too—there's old Etna, the giant of 'em all, breaking out in fifty new mouths of flame. Heat is latent in everything, only waiting to be called out That match you're striking, this coffee-pot, the warmth in our bodies, and so on—their heat comes first from the sun, and is therefore an actual part of the sun, the origin of all heat and life. And so O'Hara, you know, who sees the universe as a single homogeneous *One* and—and—well, I give it up. Can't explain it, you see. You must get him to do that. But somehow this year— cloudless—the protecting armour of water all gone too—the sun's rays managed to sink in and reach their kind buried deep below. Perhaps, later, we may get him to show us the studies that he's made—whew!— the most—er—amazing things you ever saw!"

The "superiority" of unimaginative minds was inevitable, making Rennie regret that he had told so much. It was almost as if he had been untrue to his friend. But at length the group broke up for the afternoon. They left messages for O'Hara. Two motored, and the journalist took the train. The critic followed his sharp nose to London, where he might ferret out the failures that his mind delighted in. And when they were gone the host slipped quickly upstairs to find his friend. The heat was unbearable to suffocation, the little bedroom like an oven. But Jim O'Hara was not in it.

For, instead of lying down as he had said, a fierce revolt, stirred by the talk of those unvisioned minds below, had wakened, and the deep, sensitive, poet's soul in him had leaped suddenly to the acceptance of an impossible thing. He had escaped, driven forth by the secret call of wonder. He made full speed for the destroyed moors. Fever or no fever, he must see for himself. Did no one understand? Was he the only one?... Walking quickly, he passed the Frensham Ponds, came through that spot of loneliness and beauty, the Lion's Mouth, noting that even there the pool of water had dried up and the rushes waved in the hot air over a bed of hard, caked mud, and so reached within the hour the wide expanse of Thursley Common. On every side the world stretched dark and burnt, a cemetery of cinders. Great thrills rushed through his heart and with the power of a tide that yet came at flashing speed the truth rose up in him... Half running now, he plunged forward another mile or two, and found himself, the only living thing, amid the great waste of heather-land. The blazing sunlight drenched it. It lay, a sheet of weird dark beauty, spreading like a black, enormous garden as far as the eye could reach.

Then, breathless, he paused and looked about him. Within his heart something, long smouldering, ran into sudden flame. Light blazed upon his inner world. For as the scorch of vehement passion may quicken tracts of human consciousness that lie ordinarily inert and unproductive, so here the surface of the earth had turned alive. He knew; he saw; he understood.

Here, in these open sun-traps that gathered and retained the heat, the fire of the Universe had dropped and lain, increasing week by week. These parched, dry months, the soil, free from rejecting and protective moisture, had let it all accumulate till at length it had sunk downwards, inwards, and the sister fires below, responding to the touch of their ancient parent source, too long unfelt, had answered with a swift uprising roar. They had come up with answering joy, and here and there had actually reached the surface, and had leaped out with dancing cry, wild to escape from an age-long prison back to their huge, eternal origin.

This sunshine, ah! what was it? These farthing dips of heat men complained about in their tiny, cage-like houses! It scorched the grass and fields, yes but the surface never held it long enough to let it sink to union with its kindred of the darker fires beneath! These cried for it, but union was ever denied and stifled by the weight of cooled and cooling rock. And the ages of separation had almost cooled remembrance too—fire—the kiss and strength of fire—the flaming embrace and burning lips of the father sun himself... He could have cried with the fierce delight of it all, and the picture he would paint rose there before him, burnt gloriously into the canvas of the entire heavens. Was not his own heat and life also from the sun?...

He stared about him in the deep silence of the afternoon. The world was still. It basked in the windless heat. No living thing stirred, for the common forms of life had fled away. Earth waited. He, too, waited. And then some touch of intuition, blown to white heat, supplied the link the pedestrian intellect missed, and he knew that what he waited for was on the way. For he would *see*. The message he should paint would come before his outer eye as well, though not, as he had first stupidly expected, on some grand, enormous scale. Rather would it be the equivalent of that still, small voice that once had inspired an entire nation...

The wind passed very softly across the unburnt patch of heather where he lay; he heard it rustling in the skeletons of scorched birch trees, and in the gorse and furze bushes that the flame had left so ghostly pale. Farther off it sang in the isolated pines, dying away like surf upon some far-off reef. He smelt the bitter perfume of burnt soil, the pungent, acrid odour of beaten ashes. The purple-black of the moors yawned like openings in the side of the earth. In all directions for miles stretched the deep emptiness of the heatherlands, an immense, dark, magic garden, still black with the feet of wonder that had flown across it and left it so beautifully scarred. The shadow of the terrible embrace still trailed and lingered as though Midnight had screened a time of passion with this curtain of her softest plumes.

And *they* had called it ugly, had spoken of its marred beauty, its hideousness! He laughed exultantly as he drank it in, for the weird and savage splendour everywhere broke loose and spread, passing from the earth into the receptive substance of his own mind. Even the roots of gorse and heather, like petrified, shadow-eating snakes, charged with the mystery of that eternal underworld whence they had risen, lay waiting for the return of the night of sleep whence Fire had wakened them. Lost ghosts of a salamander army that the flame had swept above the ground, they lay anguished and frightened in the glare of the unaccustomed sun...

And waiting, he stared about him in the deep silence of the afternoon. Hazy with distance he saw the peak of Crooksbury, dim in its sheet of pines, waving a blue-plumed crest into the sky for signal and close about him rose the more sombre glory of the lesser knolls and boulders, still cloaked in the swarthy magic of the smoke. Amid pools of ashes in the nearer hollows he saw the blue beauty of the fire-weed that rushes instantly into life behind all conflagrations. It was blowing softly in the wind. And here and there, set like emeralds upon some dusky bosom, lay the brilliant spires of young bracken that rose to clap a thousand tiny hands in the heart of exquisite desolation. In a cloud of green they rustled in the wind above the sea of black... And so within himself O'Hara realised the huge excitement of the flame this fragment of the earth had felt. For Fire, mysterious symbol of universal life, spirit that prodigally gives itself without itself diminishing, had passed in power across this ancient heather-land, leaving the soul of it all naked and unashamed. The sun had loved it. The fires below had risen up and answered. They had known that union with their source which some call death.

And the fires were rising still. The poet's heart in him became suddenly and awfully aware. Ye stars of fire! This patch of unburnt heather where he lay had been untouched as yet, but now the flame in his soul had brought the little needed link and he would *see*. The thing of wonder that the Universe should teach him how to paint was already on the way. Called by the sun, tremendous, splendid parent, the central fires were still rising.

And he turned, weakness and exultation racing for possession of him. The wind passed softly over his face, and with it came a faint, dry sound. It was distant and yet close beside him. At the stir of it there rose also in himself a strange vast thing that was bigger than the bulk of the moon and wide as the extension of swept forests, yet small and gentle as a blade of grass that pricks the lawn in spring. And he realised then that "within" and "without" had turned one, and that over the entire moorland arrived this thing that was happening too in a white-hot point of his own heart. He was linked with the sun and the farthest star, and in his little finger glowed the heat and fire of the universe itself. In sympathy *his own fires were rising too*.

The sound was born—a faint, light noise of crackling in the heather at his feet. He bent his head and searched, and among the obscure and tiny underways of the roots he saw a tip of curling smoke rise slowly upwards. It moved in a thin, blue spiral past his face. Then terror took him that was like a terror of the mountains, yet with it at the same time a realisation of beauty that made the heart leap within him into dazzling radiance. For the incense of this fairy column of thin smoke drew his soul out with it—upwards towards its source. He rose to his feet, trembling...

He watched the line rise slowly to the sky and vanish into blue. The whole expanse of blackened heather-land watched too. Wind sank away; the sunshine dropped to meet it. A sense of deep expectancy, profound and reverent, lay over all that sun-baked moor and the entire sweep of burnt world about him knew with joy that what was taking place in that wee, isolated patch of Surrey heather was the thing the Hebrew mystic knew when the Soul of the Universe became manifest in the bush that burned, yet never was consumed. In that faint sound of crackling, as he stood aside to listen and to watch, O'Hara knew a form of the eternal Voice of Ages. There was no flame, but it seemed to him that all his inner being passed in fiery heat outwards towards its source... He saw the little patch of dried-up heather sink to the level of the black surface all about it—a sifted pile of delicate, pale-blue ashes. The tiny spiral vanished; he watched it disappear, winding upwards out of sight in a little ghostly trail of beauty. So small and soft and simple was this wonder of the world. It was gone. And something in himself had broken, dropped in ashes, and passed also outwards like a tiny mounting flame.

But the picture O'Hara had thought himself designed to paint was never done. It was not even begun. The great canvas of "The Fire Worshipper" stood empty on the easel, for the artist had not strength to lift a brush. Within two days the final breath passed slowly from his lips. The strange fever that so perplexed the doctor by its rapid development and its fury took him so easily. His temperature was extraordinary. The heat, as of an internal fire, fairly devoured him, and the smile upon his face at the last—so Rennie declared—was the most perplexingly wonderful thing he had ever seen. "It was like a great, white flame," he said.

SANDHILLS.

## The Messenger

I HAVE never been afraid of ghostly things, attracted rather with a curious live interest, though it is always out of doors that strange Presences get nearest to me, and in Nature I have encountered warnings, messages, presentiments, and the like, that, by way of help or guidance, have later justified themselves. I have, therefore, welcomed them. But in the little rooms of houses things of much value rarely come, for the thick air chokes the wires, as it were, and distorts or mutilates the clear delivery.

But the other night, here in the carpenter's house, where my attic windows beckon to the mountains and the woods, I woke with the uncomfortably strong suggestion that something was on the way, and that I was not ready. It came along the by-ways of deep sleep. I woke abruptly, alarmed before I was even properly awake. Something was approaching with great swiftness—and I was unprepared.

Across the lake there were faint signs of colour behind the distant Alps, but terraces of mist still lay grey above the vineyards, and the slim poplar, whose tip was level with my face, no more than rustled in the wind of dawn. A shiver, not brought to me by any wind, ran through my nerves, for I knew with a certainty no arguing could lessen nor dispel that something from immensely far away was deliberately now approaching me. The touch of wonder in advance of it was truly awful; its splendour, size, and grandeur belonged to conditions I had surely never known. It came through empty spaces—from another world. While I lay asleep it had been already on the way.

I stood there a moment, seeking for some outward sign that might betray its nature. The last stars were fading in the northern sky, and blue and dim lay the whole long line of the Jura, cloaked beneath still slumbering forests. There was a rumbling of a distant train. Now and then a dog barked in some outlying farm. The Night was up and walking, though as yet she moved but slowly from the sky. Shadows still draped the world. And the warning that had reached me first in sleep rushed through my tingling nerves once more with a certainty not far removed from shock. Something from another world was drawing every minute nearer, with a speed that made me tremble and half-breathless. It would presently arrive. It would stand close beside me and look straight into my face. Into these very eyes that searched the mist and shadow for an outward sign it would gaze intimately with a Message brought for me alone. But into these narrow walls it could only come with difficulty. The message would be maimed. There still was time for preparation. And I hurried into clothes and made my way downstairs and out into the open air.

Thus, at first, by climbing fast, I kept ahead of it, and soon the village lay beneath me in its nest of shadow, and the limestone ridges far above dropped nearer. But the awe and terrible deep wonder did not go. Along these mountain paths, whose every inch was so intimate that I could follow them even in the dark, this sense of breaking grandeur clung to my footsteps, keeping close. Nothing upon the earth—familiar, friendly, well-known, little earth—could have brought this sense that pressed upon the edges of true reverence. It was the awareness that some speeding messenger from spaces far, far beyond the world would presently stand close and touch me, would gaze into my little human eyes, would leave its message as of life or death, and then depart upon its fearful way again—it was this that conveyed the feeling of apprehension that went with me.

And instinctively, while rising higher and higher, I chose the darkest and most sheltered way. I sought the protection of the trees, and ran into the deepest vaults of the forest. The moss was soaking wet beneath my feet, and the thousand tapering spires of the pines dipped upwards into a sky already brightening with palest gold and crimson. There was a whispering and a rustling overhead as the trees, who know everything before it comes, announced to one another that the thing I sought to hide from was already very, very near. Plunging deeper into the woods to hide, this detail of sure knowledge followed me and laughed that the speed of this august arrival was one which made the greatest speed I ever dreamed of a mere standing still...

I hid myself where possible in the darkness that was growing every minute more rare. The air was sharp and exquisitely fresh. I heard birds calling. The low, wet branches kissed my face and hair. A sense of glad relief came over me that I had left the closeness of the little attic chamber, and that I should eventually meet this huge New-comer in the wide, free spaces of the mountains. There must be room where I could hold myself unmanacled to meet it. The village lay far beneath me, a patch of smoke and mist and soft red-brown roofs among the vineyards. And then my gaze turned upwards, and through a rift in the close-wrought ceiling of the trees I saw the clearness of the open sky. A strip of cloud ran through it, carrying off the Night's last little dream... and down into my heart dropped instantly that cold breath of awe I have known but once in life, when staring through the stupendous mouth within the Milky Way—that opening into the outer spaces of eternal darkness, unlit by any single star, men call the Coal Hole.

The futility of escape then took me bodily, and I renounced all further flight. From this speeding Messenger there was no hiding possible. His splendid shoulders already brushed the sky. I heard the rushing of his awful wings... yet in that deep, significant silence with which light steps upon the clouds of morning.

And simultaneously I left the woods behind me and stood upon a naked ridge of rock that all night long had watched the stars.

Then terror passed away like magic. Cool winds from the valleys bore me up. I heard the tinkling of a thousand cowbells from pastures far below in a score of hidden valleys. The cold departed, and with it every trace of little fears. My eyes seemed for an instant blinded, and I knew that deep sense of joy which seems so "unearthly" that it almost stains the sight with the veil of tears. The soul sank to her knees in prayer and worship.

For the messenger from another world had come. He stood beside me on that dizzy ledge. Warmth clothed me, and I knew myself akin to deity. He stood there, gazing straight into my little human eyes. He touched me everywhere. Above the distant Alps the sun came up. His eye looked close into my own.

BÔLE.

# The Glamour of the Snow

I

HIBBERT, always conscious of two worlds, was in this mountain village conscious of three. It lay on the slopes of the Valais Alps, and he had taken a room in the little post office, where he could be at peace to write his book, yet at the same time enjoy the winter sports and find companionship in the hotels when he wanted it.

The three worlds that met and mingled here seemed to his imaginative temperament very obvious, though it is doubtful if another mind less intuitively equipped would have seen them so well-defined. There was the world of tourist English, civilised, quasi-educated, to which he belonged by birth, at any rate; there was the world of peasants to which he felt himself drawn by sympathy—for he loved and admired their toiling, simple life; and there was this other—which he could only call the world of Nature. To this last, however, in virtue of a vehement poetic imagination, and a tumultuous pagan instinct fed by his very blood, he felt that most of him belonged. The others borrowed from it, as it were, for visits. Here, with the soul of Nature, hid his central life.

Between all three was conflict—potential conflict. On the skating-rink each Sunday the tourists regarded the natives as intruders; in the church the peasants plainly questioned: "Why do you come? We are here to worship; you to stare and whisper!" For neither of these two worlds accepted the other. And neither did Nature accept the tourists, for it took advantage of their least mistakes, and indeed, even of the peasant-world "accepted" only those who were strong and bold enough to invade her savage domain with sufficient skill to protect themselves from several forms of—death.

Now Hibbert was keenly aware of this potential conflict and want of harmony; he felt outside, yet caught by it—torn in the three directions because he was partly of each world, but wholly in only one. There grew in him a constant, subtle effort—or, at least, desire—to unify them and decide positively to which he should belong and live in. The attempt, of course, was largely subconscious. It was the natural instinct of a richly imaginative nature seeking the point of equilibrium, so that the mind could feel at peace and his brain be free to do good work.

Among the guests no one especially claimed his interest. The men were nice but undistinguished—athletic schoolmasters, doctors snatching a holiday, good fellows all; the women, equally various—the clever, the would-be-fast, the dare-to-be-dull, the women "who understood," and the usual pack of jolly dancing girls and "flappers." And Hibbert, with his forty odd years of thick experience behind him, got on well with the lot; he understood them all; they belonged to definite, predigested types that are the same the world over, and that he had met the world over long ago.

But to none of them did he belong. His nature was too "multiple" to subscribe to the set of shibboleths of any one class. And, since all liked him, and felt that somehow he seemed outside of them—spectator, looker-on—all sought to claim him.

In a sense, therefore, the three worlds fought for him: natives, tourists, Nature...

It was thus began the singular conflict for the soul of Hibbert. *In* his own soul, however, it took place. Neither the peasants nor the tourists were conscious that they fought for anything. And Nature, they say, is merely blind and automatic.

The assault upon him of the peasants may be left out of account, for it is obvious that they stood no chance of success. The tourist world, however, made a gallant effort to subdue him to themselves. But the evenings in the hotel, when dancing was not in order, were— English. The provincial imagination was set upon a throne and worshipped heavily through incense of the stupidest conventions possible. Hibbert used to go back early to his room in the post office to work.

"It is a mistake on my part to have *realised* that there is any conflict at all," he thought, as he crunched home over the snow at midnight after one of the dances. "It would have been better to have kept outside it all and done my work. Better," he added, looking back down the silent village street to the church tower, "and—safer."

The adjective slipped from his mind before he was aware of it. He turned with an involuntary start and looked about him. He knew perfectly well what it meant—this thought that had thrust its head up from the instinctive region. He understood, without being able to express it fully, the meaning that betrayed itself in the choice of the adjective. For if he had ignored the existence of this conflict he would at the same time have remained outside the arena. Whereas now he had entered the lists. Now this battle for his soul must have issue. And he knew that the spell of Nature was greater for him than all other spells in the world combined—greater than love, revelry, pleasure, greater even than study. He had always been afraid to let himself go. His pagan soul dreaded her terrific powers of witchery even while he worshipped.

The little village already slept. The world lay smothered in snow. The châlet roofs shone white beneath the moon, and pitch-black shadows gathered against the walls of the church. His eye rested a moment on the square stone tower with its frosted cross that pointed to the sky: then travelled with a leap of many thousand feet to the enormous mountains that brushed the brilliant stars. Like a forest rose the huge peaks above the slumbering village, measuring the night and heavens. They beckoned him. And something born of the snowy desolation, born of the midnight and the silent grandeur, born of the great listening hollows of the night, something that lay 'twixt terror and wonder, dropped from the vast wintry spaces down into his heart—and called him. Very softly, unrecorded in any word or thought his brain could compass, it laid its spell upon him. Fingers of snow brushed the surface of his heart. The power and quiet majesty of the winter's night appalled him...

Fumbling a moment with the big unwieldy key, he let himself in and went upstairs to bed. Two thoughts went with him—apparently quite ordinary and sensible ones:

"What fools these peasants are to sleep through such a night!" And the other:

"Those dances tire me. I'll never go again. My work only suffers in the morning." The claims of peasants and tourists upon him seemed thus in a single instant weakened.

The clash of battle troubled half his dreams. Nature had sent her Beauty of the Night and won the first assault. The others, routed and dismayed, fled far away.

## II

"DON'T go back to your dreary old post office. We're going to have supper in my room—something hot. Come and join us. Hurry up!"

There had been an ice carnival, and the last party, tailing up the snow-slope to the hotel, called him. The Chinese lanterns smoked and sputtered on the wires; the band had long since gone. The cold was bitter and the moon came only momentarily between high, driving clouds. From the shed where the people changed from skates to snow-boots he shouted something to the effect that he was "following"; but no answer came; the moving shadows of those who had called were already merged high up against the village darkness. The voices died away. Doors slammed. Hibbert found himself alone on the deserted rink.

And it was then, quite suddenly, the impulse came to—stay and skate alone. The thought of the stuffy hotel room, and of those noisy people with their obvious jokes and laughter, oppressed him. He felt a longing to be alone with the night, to taste her wonder all by himself there beneath the stars, gliding over the ice. It was not yet midnight, and he could skate for half an hour. That supper party, if they noticed his absence at all, would merely think he had changed his mind and gone to bed.

It was an impulse, yes, and not an unnatural one; yet even at the time it struck him that something more than impulse lay concealed behind it. More than invitation, yet certainly less than command, there was a vague queer feeling that he stayed because he had to, almost as though there was something he had forgotten, overlooked, left undone. Imaginative temperaments are often thus; and impulse is ever weakness. For with such ill-considered opening of the doors to hasty action may come an invasion of other forces at the same time—forces merely waiting their opportunity perhaps!

He caught the fugitive warning even while he dismissed it as absurd, and the next minute he was whirling over the smooth ice in delightful curves and loops beneath the moon. There was no fear of collision. He could take his own speed and space as he willed. The shadows of the towering mountains fell across the rink, and a wind of ice came from the forests, where the snow lay ten feet deep. The hotel lights winked and went out. The village slept. The high wire netting could not keep out the wonder of the winter night that grew about him like a presence. He skated on and on, keen exhilarating pleasure in his tingling blood, and weariness all forgotten.

And then, midway in the delight of rushing movement, he saw a figure gliding behind the wire netting, watching him. With a start that almost made him lose his balance—for the abruptness of the new arrival was so unlooked for—he paused and stared. Although the light was dim he made out that it was the figure of a woman and that she was feeling her way along the netting, trying to get in. Against the white background of the snow-field he watched her rather stealthy efforts as she passed with a silent step over the banked-up snow. She was tall and slim and graceful; he could see that even in the dark. And then, of course, he understood. It was another adventurous skater like himself, stolen down unawares from hotel or châlet, and searching for the opening. At once, making a sign and pointing with one hand, he turned swiftly and skated over to the little entrance on the other side.

But, even before he got there, there was a sound on the ice behind him and, with an exclamation of amazement he could not suppress, he turned to see her swerving up to his side across the width of the rink. She had somehow found another way in.

Hibbert, as a rule, was punctilious, and in these free-and-easy places, perhaps, especially so. If only for his own protection he did not seek to make advances unless some kind of introduction paved the way. But for these two to skate together in the semi-darkness without speech, often of necessity brushing shoulders almost, was too absurd to think of. Accordingly he raised his cap and spoke. His actual words he seems unable to recall, nor what the girl said in reply, except that she answered him in accented English with some commonplace about doing figures at midnight on an empty rink. Quite natural it was, and right. She wore grey clothes of some kind, though not the customary long gloves or sweater, for indeed her hands were bare, and presently when he skated with her, he wondered with something like astonishment at their dry and icy coldness.

And she was delicious to skate with—supple, sure, and light, fast as a man yet with the freedom of a child, sinuous and steady at the same time. Her flexibility made him wonder, and when he asked where she had learned she murmured—he caught the breath against his ear and recalled later that it was singularly cold—that she could hardly tell, for she had been accustomed to the ice ever since she could remember.

But her face he never properly saw. A muffler of white fur buried her neck to the ears, and her cap came over the eyes. He only saw that she was young. Nor could he gather her hotel or châlet, for she pointed vaguely, when he asked her, up the slopes. "Just over there—" she said, quickly taking his hand again. He did not press her; no doubt she wished to hide her escapade. And the touch of her hand thrilled him more than anything he could remember; even through his thick glove he felt the softness of that cold and delicate softness.

The clouds thickened over the mountains. It grew darker. They talked very little, and did not always skate together. Often they separated, curving about in corners by themselves, but always coming together again in the centre of the rink; and when she left him thus Hibbert was conscious of—yes, of missing her. He found a peculiar satisfaction, almost a fascination, in skating by her side. It was quite an adventure—these two strangers with the ice and snow and night!

Midnight had long since sounded from the old church tower before they parted. She gave the sign, and he skated quickly to the shed, meaning to find a seat and help her take her skates off. Yet when he turned—she had already gone. He saw her slim figure gliding away across the snow... and hurrying for the last time round the rink alone he searched in vain for the opening she had twice used in this curious way.

"How very queer!" he thought, referring to the wire netting. "She must have lifted it and wriggled under... !"

Wondering how in the world she managed it, what in the world had possessed him to be so free with her, and who in the world she was, he went up the steep slope to the post office and so to bed, her promise to come again another night still ringing delightfully in his ears. And curious were the thoughts and sensations that accompanied him. Most of all, perhaps, was the half suggestion of some dim memory that he had known this girl before, had met her somewhere, more—that she knew him. For in her voice—a low, soft, windy little voice it was, tender and soothing for all its quiet coldness—there lay some faint reminder of two others he had known, both long since gone: the voice of the woman he had loved, and—the voice of his mother.

But this time through his dreams there ran no clash of battle. He was conscious, rather, of something cold and clinging that made him think of sifting snowflakes climbing slowly with entangling touch and thickness round his feet. The snow, coming without noise, each flake so light and tiny none can mark the spot whereon it settles, yet the mass of it able to smother whole villages, wove through the very texture of his mind—cold, bewildering, deadening effort with its clinging network of ten million feathery touches.

### III

IN the morning Hibbert realised he had done, perhaps, a foolish thing. The brilliant sunshine that drenched the valley made him see this, and the sight of his work-table with its typewriter, books, papers, and the rest, brought additional conviction. To have skated with a girl alone at midnight, no matter how innocently the thing had come about, was unwise—unfair, especially to her. Gossip in these little winter resorts was worse than in a provincial town. He hoped no one had seen them. Luckily the night had been dark. Most likely none had heard the ring of skates.

Deciding that in future he would be more careful, he plunged into work, and sought to dismiss the matter from his mind.

But in his times of leisure the memory returned persistently to haunt him. When he "ski-d," "luged," or danced in the evenings, and especially when he skated on the little rink, he was aware that the eyes of his mind forever sought this strange companion of the night. A hundred times he fancied that he saw her, but always sight deceived him. Her face he might not know, but he could hardly fail to recognise her figure. Yet nowhere among the others did he catch a glimpse of that slim young creature he had skated with alone beneath the clouded stars. He searched in vain. Even his inquiries as to the occupants of the private chalets brought no results. He had lost her. But the queer thing was that he felt as though she were somewhere close; he knew she had not really gone. While people came and left with every day, it never once occurred to him that she had left. On the contrary, he felt assured that they would meet again.

This thought he never quite acknowledged. Perhaps it was the wish that fathered it only. And, even when he did meet her, it was a question how he would speak and claim acquaintance, or whether *she* would recognise himself. It might be awkward. He almost came to dread a meeting, though "dread," of course, was far too strong a word to describe an emotion that was half delight, half wondering anticipation.

Meanwhile the season was in full swing. Hibbert felt in perfect health, worked hard, ski-d, skated, luged, and at night danced fairly often—in spite of his decision. This dancing was, however, an act of subconscious surrender; it really meant he hoped to find her among the whirling couples. He was searching for her without quite acknowledging it to himself; and the hotel-world, meanwhile, thinking it had won him over, teased and chaffed him. He made excuses in a similar vein; but all the time he watched and searched and—waited.

For several days the sky held clear and bright and frosty, bitterly cold, everything crisp and sparkling in the sun; but there was no sign of fresh snow, and the ski-ers began to grumble. On the mountains was an icy crust that made "running" dangerous; they wanted the frozen, dry, and powdery snow that makes for speed, renders steering easier and falling less severe. But the keen east wind showed no signs of changing for a whole ten days. Then, suddenly, there came a touch of softer air and the weather-wise began to prophesy.

Hibbert, who was delicately sensitive to the least change in earth or sky, was perhaps the first to feel it.     Only he did not prophesy. He knew through every nerve in his body that moisture had crept into the air, was accumulating, and that presently a fall would come. For he responded to the moods of Nature like a fine barometer.

And the knowledge, this time, brought into his heart a strange little wayward emotion that was hard to account for—a feeling of unexplained uneasiness and disquieting joy. For behind it, woven through it rather, ran a faint exhilaration that connected remotely somewhere with that touch of delicious alarm, that tiny anticipating "dread," that so puzzled him when he thought of his next meeting with his skating companion of the night. It lay beyond all words, all telling, this queer relationship between the two; but somehow the girl and snow ran in a pair across his mind.

Perhaps for imaginative writing-men, more than for other workers, the smallest change of mood betrays itself at once. His work at any rate revealed this slight shifting of emotional values in his soul. Not that his writing suffered, but that it altered, subtly as those changes of sky or sea or landscape that come with the passing of afternoon into evening—imperceptibly. A subconscious excitement sought to push outwards and express itself... and, knowing the uneven effect such moods produced in his work, he laid his pen aside and took instead to reading that he had to do.

Meanwhile the brilliance passed from the sunshine, the sky grew slowly overcast; by dusk the mountain tops came singularly close and sharp; the distant valley rose into absurdly near perspective. The moisture increased, rapidly approaching saturation point, when it must fall in snow. Hibbert watched and waited.

And in the morning the world lay smothered beneath its fresh white carpet. It snowed heavily till noon, thickly, incessantly, chokingly, a foot or more; then the sky cleared, the sun came out in splendour, the wind shifted back to the east, and frost came down upon the mountains with its keenest and most biting tooth. The drop in the temperature was tremendous, but the ski-ers were jubilant. Next day the "running" would be fast and perfect. Already the mass was settling, and the surface freezing into those moss-like, powdery crystals that make the skis run almost of their own accord with the faint "sishing" as of a bird's wings through the air.

## IV

THAT night there was excitement in the little hotel-world, first because there was a *bal costumé*, but chiefly because the new snow had come. And Hibbert went—felt drawn to go; he did not go in costume, but he wanted to talk about the slopes and ski-ing with the other men, and at the same time...

Ah, there was the truth, the deeper necessity that called. For the singular connection between the stranger and the snow again betrayed itself, utterly beyond explanation as before, but vital and insistent. Some hidden instinct in his pagan soul—heaven knows how he phrased it even to himself, if he phrased it at all—whispered that with the snow the girl would be somewhere about, would emerge from her hiding place, would even look for him.

Absolutely unwarranted it was. He laughed while he stood before the little glass and trimmed his moustache, tried to make his black tie sit straight, and shook down his dinner jacket so that it should lie upon the shoulders without a crease. His brown eyes were very bright. "I look younger than I usually do," he thought. It was unusual, even significant, in a man who had no vanity about his appearance and certainly never questioned his age or tried to look younger than he was. Affairs of the heart, with one tumultuous exception that left no fuel for lesser subsequent fires, had never troubled him. The forces of his soul and mind not called upon for "work" and obvious duties, all went to Nature. The desolate, wild places of the earth were what he loved; night, and the beauty of the stars and snow. And this evening he felt their claims upon him mightily stirring. A rising wildness caught his blood, quickened his pulse, woke longing and passion too. But chiefly snow. The snow whirred softly through his thoughts like white, seductive dreams... For the snow had come; and She, it seemed, had somehow come with it—into his mind.

And yet he stood before that twisted mirror and pulled his tie and coat askew a dozen times, as though it mattered. "What in the world is up with me?" he thought. Then, laughing a little, he turned before leaving the room to put his private papers in order. The green morocco desk that held them he took down from the shelf and laid upon the table. Tied to the lid was the visiting card with his brother's London address "in case of accident." On the way down to the hotel he wondered why he had done this, for though imaginative, he was not the kind of man who dealt in presentiments. Moods with him were strong, but ever held in leash.

"It's almost like a warning," he thought, smiling. He drew his thick coat tightly round the throat as the freezing air bit at him. "Those warnings one reads of in stories sometimes... !"

A delicious happiness was in his blood. Over the edge of the hills across the valley rose the moon. He saw her silver sheet the world of snow. Snow covered all. It smothered sound and distance. It smothered houses, streets, and human beings. It smothered—life.

### V

IN the hall there was light and bustle; people were already arriving from the other hotels and châlets, their costumes hidden beneath many wraps. Groups of men in evening dress stood about smoking, talking "snow" and "ski-ing." The band was tuning up. The claims of the hotel-world clashed about him faintly as of old. At the big glass windows of the verandah, peasants stopped a moment on their way home from the *café* to peer. Hibbert thought laughingly of that conflict he used to imagine. He laughed because it suddenly seemed so unreal. He belonged so utterly to Nature and the mountains, and especially to those desolate slopes where now the snow lay thick and fresh and sweet, that there was no question of a conflict at all. The power of the newly fallen snow had caught him, proving it without effort. Out there, upon those lonely reaches of the moonlit ridges, the snow lay ready—masses and masses of it—cool, soft, inviting. He longed for it. It awaited him. He thought of the intoxicating delight of ski-ing in the moonlight...

Thus, somehow, in vivid flashing vision, he thought of it while he stood there smoking with the other men and talking all the "shop" of ski-ing.

And, ever mysteriously blended with this power of the snow, poured also through his inner being the power of the girl. He could not disabuse his mind of the insinuating presence of the two together. He remembered that queer skating-impulse of ten days ago, the impulse that had let her in. That any mind, even an imaginative one, could pass beneath the sway of such a fancy was strange enough; and Hibbert, while fully aware of the disorder, yet found a curious joy in yielding to it. This insubordinate centre that drew him towards old pagan beliefs had assumed command. With a kind of sensuous pleasure he let himself be conquered.

And snow that night seemed in everybody's thoughts. The dancing couples talked of it; the hotel proprietors congratulated one another; it meant good sport and satisfied their guests; every one was planning trips and expeditions, talking of slopes and telemarks, of flying speed and distance, of drifts and crust and frost. Vitality and enthusiasm pulsed in the very air; all were alert and active, positive, radiating currents of creative life even into the stuffy atmosphere of that crowded ball-room. And the snow had caused it, the snow had brought it; all this discharge of eager sparkling energy was due primarily to the— Snow.

But in the mind of Hibbert, by some swift alchemy of his pagan yearnings, this energy became transmuted. It rarefied itself, gleaming in white and crystal currents of passionate anticipation, which he transferred, as by a species of electrical imagination, into the personality of the girl—the Girl of the Snow. She somewhere was waiting for him, expecting him, calling to him softly from those leagues of moonlit mountain. He remembered the touch of that cool, dry hand; the soft and icy breath against his cheek; the hush and softness of her presence in the way she came and the way she had gone again—like a flurry of snow the wind sent gliding up the slopes. She, like himself, belonged out there. He fancied that he heard her little windy voice come sifting to him through the snowy branches of the trees, calling his name... that haunting little voice that dived straight to the centre of his life as once, long years ago, two other voices used to do...

But nowhere among the costumed dancers did he see her slender figure. He danced with one and all, *distrait* and absent, a stupid partner as each girl discovered, his eyes ever turning towards the door and windows, hoping to catch the luring face, the vision that did not come ... and at length, hoping even against hope. For the ballroom thinned; groups left one by one, going home to their hotels and châlets; the band tired obviously; people sat drinking lemon-squashes at the little tables, the men mopping their foreheads, everybody ready for bed.

It was close on midnight. As Hibbert passed through the hall to get his overcoat and snow-boots he saw men in the passage by the "sport-room," greasing their skis against an early start. Knapsack luncheons were being ordered by the kitchen swing doors. He sighed. Lighting a cigarette a friend offered him, he returned a confused reply to some question as to whether he could join their party in the morning. It seemed he did not hear it properly. He passed through the outer vestibule between the double glass doors, and went into the night.

The man who asked the question watched him go, an expression of anxiety momentarily in his eyes.

"Don't think he heard you," said another, laughing. "You've got to shout to Hibbert, his mind's so full of his work."

"He works too hard," suggested the first, "full of queer ideas and dreams."

But Hibbert's silence was not rudeness. He had not caught the invitation, that was all. The call of the hotel world had faded. He no longer heard it. Another wilder call was sounding in his ears.

For up the street he had seen a little figure moving. Close against the shadows of the baker's shop it glided—white, slim, enticing.

## VI

AND at once into his mind passed the hush and softness of the snow—yet with it a searching, crying wildness for the heights. He knew by some incalculable, swift instinct she would not meet him in the village street. It was not there, amid crowding houses, she would speak to him. Indeed, already she had disappeared, melted from view up the white vista of the moonlit road. Yonder, he divined, she waited where the highway narrowed abruptly into the mountain path beyond the châlets.

It did not even occur to him to hesitate; mad though it seemed, and was—this sudden craving for the heights with her, at least for open spaces where the snow lay thick and fresh—it was too imperious to be denied. He does not remember going up to his room, putting the sweater over his evening clothes, and getting into the fur gauntlet gloves and the helmet cap of wool. Most certainly he has no recollection of fastening on his skis; he must have done it automatically. Some faculty of normal observation was in abeyance, as it were. His mind was out beyond the village—out with the snowy mountains and the moon.

Henri Défago, putting up the shutters over his *café* windows, saw him pass, and wondered mildly "*Un monsieur qui fait du ski à cette heure! Il est Anglais, donc...* !" He shrugged his shoulders, as though a man had the right to choose his own way of death. And Marthe Perotti, the hunchback wife of the shoemaker, looking by chance from her window, caught his figure moving swiftly up the road. She had other thoughts, for she knew and believed the old traditions of the witches and snow-beings that steal the souls of men. She had even heard, 'twas said, the dreaded "synagogue" pass roaring down the street at night, and now, as then, she hid her eyes. "They've called to him... and he must go," she murmured, making the sign of the cross.

But no one sought to stop him. Hibbert recalls only a single incident until he found himself beyond the houses, searching for her along the fringe of forest where the moonlight met the snow in a bewildering frieze of fantastic shadows. And the incident was simply this—that he remembered passing the church. Catching the outline of its tower against the stars, he was aware of a faint sense of hesitation. A vague uneasiness came and went—jarred unpleasantly across the flow of his excited feelings, chilling exhilaration. He caught the instant's discord, dismissed it, and—passed on. The seduction of the snow smothered the hint before he realised that it had brushed the skirts of warning.

And then he saw her. She stood there waiting in a little clear space of shining snow, dressed all in white, part of the moonlight and the glistening background, her slender figure just discernible.

"I waited, for I knew you would come," the silvery little voice of windy beauty floated down to him. "You *had* to come."

"I'm ready," he answered, "I knew it too."

The world of Nature caught him to its heart in those few words—the wonder and the glory of the night and snow. Life leaped within him. The passion of his pagan soul exulted, rose in joy, flowed out to her. He neither reflected nor considered, but let himself go like the veriest schoolboy in the wildness of first love.

"Give me your hand," he cried, "I'm coming... !"

"A little farther on, a little higher," came her delicious answer. "Here it is too near the village—and the church."

And the words seemed wholly right and natural; he did not dream of questioning them; he understood that, with this little touch of civilisation in sight, the familiarity he suggested was impossible. Once out upon the open mountains, 'mid the freedom of huge slopes and towering peaks, the stars and moon to witness and the wilderness of snow to watch, they could taste an innocence of happy intercourse free from the dead conventions that imprison literal minds.

He urged his pace, yet did not quite overtake her. The girl kept always just a little bit ahead of his best efforts... And soon they left the trees behind and passed on to the enormous slopes of the sea of snow that rolled in mountainous terror and beauty to the stars. The wonder of the white world caught him away. Under the steady moon-light it was more than haunting. It was a living, white, bewildering power that deliciously confused the senses and laid a spell of wild perplexity upon the heart. It was a personality that cloaked, and yet revealed, itself through all this sheeted whiteness of snow. It rose, went with him, fled before, and followed after. Slowly it dropped lithe, gleaming arms about his neck, gathering him in...

Certainly some soft persuasion coaxed his very soul, urging him ever forwards, upwards, on towards the higher icy slopes. Judgment and reason left their throne, it seemed, completely, as in the madness of intoxication. The girl, slim and seductive, kept always just ahead, so that he never quite came up with her. He saw the white enchantment of her face and figure, something that streamed about her neck flying like a wreath of snow in the wind, and heard the alluring accents of her whispering voice that called from time to time: "A little farther on, a little higher... Then we'll run home together!"

Sometimes he saw her hand stretched out to find his own, but each time, just as he came up with her, he saw her still in front, the hand and arm withdrawn. They took a gentle angle of ascent. The toil seemed nothing. In this crystal, wine-like air fatigue vanished. The sishing of the ski through the powdery surface of the snow was the only sound that broke the stillness; this, with his breathing and the rustle of her skirts, was all he heard. Cold moonshine, snow, and silence held the world. The sky was black, and the peaks beyond cut into it like frosted wedges of iron and steel. Far below the valley slept, the village long since hidden out of sight. He felt that he could never tire... The sound of the church clock rose from time to time faintly through the air—more and more distant.

"Give me your hand. It's time now to turn back."

"Just one more slope," she laughed. "That ridge above us. Then we'll make for home." And her low voice mingled pleasantly with the purring of their skis. His own seemed harsh and ugly by comparison.

"But I have never come so high before. It's glorious! This world of silent snow and moonlight—and *you*. You're a child of the snow, I swear. Let me come up—closer—to see your face—and touch your little hand."

Her laughter answered him.

"Come on! A little higher. Here we're quite alone together."

"It's magnificent," he cried. "But why did you hide away so long? I've looked and searched for you in vain ever since we skated—" he was going to say "ten days ago," but the accurate memory of time had gone from him; he was not sure whether it was days or years or minutes. His thoughts of earth were scattered and confused.

"You looked for me in the wrong places," he heard her murmur just above him. "You looked in places where I never go. Hotels and houses kill me. I avoid them." She laughed—a fine, shrill, windy little laugh.

"I loathe them too—"

He stopped. The girl had suddenly come quite close. A breath of ice passed through his very soul. She had touched him.

"But this awful cold!" he cried out, sharply, "this freezing cold that takes me. The wind is rising; it's a wind of ice. Come, let us turn...!"

But when he plunged forward to hold her, or at least to look, the girl was gone again. And something in the way she stood there a few feet beyond, and stared down into his eyes so steadfastly in silence, made him shiver. The moonlight was behind her, but in some odd way he could not focus sight upon her face, although so close. The gleam of eyes he caught, but all the rest seemed white and snowy as though he looked beyond her—out into space...

The sound of the church bell came up faintly from the valley far below, and he counted the strokes—five. A sudden, curious weakness seized him as he listened. Deep within it was, deadly yet somehow sweet, and hard to resist. He felt like sinking down upon the snow and lying there... They had been climbing for five hours... It was, of course, the warning of complete exhaustion.

With a great effort he fought and overcame it. It passed away as suddenly as it came.

"We'll turn," he said with a decision he hardly felt. "It will be dawn before we reach the village again. Come at once. It's time for home."

The sense of exhilaration had utterly left him. An emotion that was akin to fear swept coldly through him. But her whispering answer turned it instantly to terror—a terror that gripped him horribly and turned him weak and unresisting.

"Our home is—*here*!" A burst of wild, high laughter, loud and shrill, accompanied the words. It was like a whistling wind. The wind *had* risen, and clouds obscured the moon. "A little higher—where we cannot hear the wicked bells," she cried, and for the first time seized him deliberately by the hand. She moved, was suddenly close against his face. Again she touched him.

And Hibbert tried to turn away in escape, and so trying, found for the first time that the power of the snow—that other power which does not exhilarate but deadens effort—was upon him. The suffocating weakness that it brings to exhausted men, luring them to the sleep of death in her clinging soft embrace, lulling the will and conquering all desire for life—this was awfully upon him. His feet were heavy and entangled. He could not turn or move.

The girl stood in front of him, very near; he felt her chilly breath upon his cheeks; her hair passed blindingly across his eyes; and that icy wind came with her. He saw her whiteness close; again, it seemed, his sight passed through her into space as though she had no face. Her arms were round his neck. She drew him softly downwards to his knees. He sank; he yielded utterly; he obeyed. Her weight was upon him, smothering, delicious. The snow was to his waist... She kissed him softly on the lips, the eyes, all over his face. And then she spoke his name in that voice of love and wonder, the voice that held the accent of two others—both taken over long ago by Death—the voice of his mother, and of the woman he had loved.

He made one more feeble effort to resist. Then, realising even while he struggled that this soft weight about his heart was sweeter than anything life could ever bring, he let his muscles relax, and sank back into the soft oblivion of the covering snow. Her wintry kisses bore him into sleep.

## VII

THEY say that men who know the sleep of exhaustion in the snow find no awakening on the hither side of death... The hours passed and the moon sank down below the white world's rim. Then, suddenly, there came a little crash upon his breast and neck, and Hibbert—woke.

He slowly turned bewildered, heavy eyes upon the desolate mountains, stared dizzily about him, tried to rise. At first his muscles would not act; a numbing, aching pain possessed him. He uttered a long, thin cry for help, and heard its faintness swallowed by the wind. And then he understood vaguely why he was only warm—not dead. For this very wind that took his cry had built up a sheltering mound of driven snow against his body while he slept. Like a curving wave it ran beside him. It was the breaking of its over-toppling edge that caused the crash, and the coldness of the mass against his neck that woke him.

Dawn kissed the eastern sky; pale gleams of gold shot every peak with splendour; but ice was in the air, and the dry and frozen snow blew like powder from the surface of the slopes. He saw the points of his skis projecting just below him. Then he—remembered. It seems he had just strength enough to realise that, could he but rise and stand, he might fly with terrific impetus towards the woods and village far beneath. The skis would carry him. But if he failed and fell... !

How he contrived it Hibbert never knew; this fear of death somehow called out his whole available reserve force. He rose slowly, balanced a moment, then, taking the angle of an immense zigzag, started down the awful slopes like an arrow from a bow. And automatically the splendid muscles of the practised ski-er and athlete saved and guided him, for he was hardly conscious of controlling either speed or direction. The snow stung face and eyes like fine steel shot; ridge after ridge flew past; the summits raced across the sky; the valley leaped up with bounds to meet him. He scarcely felt the ground beneath his feet as the huge slopes and distance melted before the lightning speed of that descent from death to life.

He took it in four mile-long zigzags, and it was the turning at each corner that nearly finished him, for then the strain of balancing taxed to the verge of collapse the remnants of his strength.

Slopes that have taken hours to climb can be descended in a short half-hour on skis, but Hibbert had lost all count of time. Quite other thoughts and feelings mastered him in that wild, swift dropping through the air that was like the flight of a bird. For ever close upon his heels came following forms and voices with the whirling snow-dust. He heard that little silvery voice of death and laughter at his back. Shrill and wild, with the whistling of the wind past his ears, he caught its pursuing tones; but in anger now, no longer soft and coaxing. And it was accompanied; she did not follow alone. It seemed a host of these flying figures of the snow chased madly just behind him. He felt them furiously smite his neck and cheeks, snatch at his hands and try to entangle his feet and skis in drifts. His eyes they blinded, and they caught his breath away.

The terror of the heights and snow and winter desolation urged him forward in the maddest race with death a human being ever knew; and so terrific was the speed that before the gold and crimson had left the summits to touch the ice-lips of the lower glaciers, he saw the friendly forest far beneath swing up and welcome him.

And it was then, moving slowly along the edge of the woods, he saw a light. A man was carrying it. A procession of human figures was passing in a dark line laboriously through the snow. And—he heard the sound of chanting.

Instinctively, without a second's hesitation, he changed his course. No longer flying at an angle as before, he pointed his ski straight down the mountain-side. The dreadful steepness did not frighten him. He knew full well it meant a crashing tumble at the bottom, but he also knew it meant a doubling of his speed—with safety at the end. For, though no definite thought passed through his mind, he understood that it was the village *curé* who carried that little gleaming lantern in the dawn, and that he was taking the Host to a châlet on the lower slopes—to some peasant *in extremis*. He remembered her terror of the church and bells. She feared the holy symbols.

There was one last wild cry in his ears as he started, a shriek of the wind before his face, and a rush of stinging snow against closed eyelids—and then he dropped through empty space. Speed took sight from him. It seemed he flew off the surface of the world.

\* \* \*

Indistinctly he recalls the murmur of men's voices, the touch of strong arms that lifted him, and the shooting pains as the ski were unfastened from the twisted ankle... for when he opened his eyes again to normal life he found himself lying in his bed at the post office with the doctor at his side. But for years to come the story of "mad Hibbert's" ski-ing at night is recounted in that mountain village. He went, it seems, up slopes, and to a height that no man in his senses ever tried before. The tourists were agog about it for the rest of the season, and the very same day two of the bolder men went over the actual ground and photographed the slopes. Later Hibbert saw these photographs. He noticed one curious thing about them—though he did not mention it to any one:

There was only a single track.

CHAMPÉRY.

## The Return

IT was curious—that sense of dull uneasiness that came over him so suddenly, so stealthily at first he scarcely noticed it, but with such marked increase after a time that he presently got up and left the theatre. His seat was on the gangway of the dress circle, and he slipped out awkwardly in the middle of what seemed to be the best and jolliest song of the piece. The full house was shaking with laughter; so infectious was the gaiety that even strangers turned to one another as much as to say: "Now, isn't *that* funny—?"

It was curious, too, the way the feeling first got into him at all, here in the full swing of laughter, music, light-heartedness, for it came as a vague suggestion: "I've forgotten something—something I meant to do—something of importance. What in the world was it, now?" And he thought hard, searching vainly through his mind; then dismissed it as the dancing caught his attention. It came back a little later again, during a passage of long-winded talk that bored him and set his attention free once more, but came more strongly this time, insisting on an answer. What could it have been that he had overlooked, left undone, omitted to see to? It went on nibbling at the subconscious part of him. Several times this happened, this dismissal and return, till at last the thing declared itself more plainly—and he felt bothered, troubled, distinctly uneasy.

He was wanted somewhere. There was somewhere else he ought to be. That describes it best, perhaps. Some engagement of moment had entirely slipped his memory—an engagement that involved another person, too. But where, what, with whom? And, at length, this vague uneasiness amounted to positive discomfort, so that he felt unable to enjoy the piece—and left abruptly. Like a man to whom comes suddenly the horrible idea that the match he lit his cigarette with and flung into the waste-paper basket on leaving was not really out—a sort of panic distress—he jumped into a taxi-cab and hurried to his flat: to find everything in order, of course; no smoke, no fire, no smell of burning.

But his evening was spoilt. He sat smoking in his armchair at home—this businessman of forty, practical in mind, of character some called stolid—cursing himself for an imaginative fool. It was now too late to go back to the theatre; the club bored him; he spent an hour with the evening papers, dipping into books, sipping a long cool drink; doing odds and ends about the flat; "I'll go to bed early for a change," he laughed, but really all the time fighting—yes, deliberately fighting—this strange attack of uneasiness that so insidiously grew upwards, outwards from the buried depths of him that sought so strenuously to deny it. It never occurred to him that he was ill. He was *not* ill. His health was thunderingly good. He was robust as a coal-heaver.

The flat was roomy, high up on the top floor, yet in a busy part of town, so that the roar of traffic mounted round it like a sea. Through the open windows came the fresh night air of June. He had never noticed before how sweet the London night air could be, and that not all the smoke and dust could smother a certain touch of wild fragrance that tinctured it with perfume—yes, almost perfume—as of the country. He swallowed a draught of it as he stood there, staring out across the tangled world of roofs and chimney-pots. He saw the procession of the clouds; he saw the stars; he saw the moonlight falling in a shower of silver spears upon the slates and wires and steeples. And something in him quickened—something that had never stirred before.

He turned with a horrid start, for the uneasiness had of a sudden leaped within him like an animal. There was someone in the flat.

Instantly, with action, even this slight action, the fancy vanished; but, all the same, he switched on the electric lights and made a search. For it seemed to him that someone had crept up close behind him while he stood there watching the Night—someone, moreover, whose silent presence fingered with unerring touch both this new thing that had quickened in his heart *and* that sense of original deep uneasiness. He was amazed at himself, angry; indignant that he could be thus foolishly upset over nothing, yet at the same time profoundly distressed at this vehement growth of a new thing in his well-ordered personality. Growth? He dismissed the word the moment it occurred to him. But it had occurred to him. It stayed. While he searched the empty flat, the long passages, the gloomy bedroom at the end, the little hall where he kept his overcoats and golf sticks—it stayed. Growth! It was oddly disquieting. Growth, to him, involved—though he neither acknowledged nor recognised the truth perhaps—some kind of undesirable changeableness, instability, unbalance.

Yet, singular as it all was, he realised that the uneasiness and the sudden appreciation of Beauty that was so new to him had both entered by the same door into his being. When he came back to the front room he noticed that he was perspiring. There were little drops of moisture on his forehead. And down his spine ran positively chills—little, faint quivers of cold. He was shivering.

He lit his big meerschaum pipe, and left the lights all burning. The feeling that there was something he had overlooked, forgotten, left undone, had vanished. Whatever the original cause of this absurd uneasiness might be— he called it absurd on purpose, because he now realised in the depths of him that it was really more vital than he cared about—it was much nearer to discovery than before. It dodged about just below the threshold of discovery. It was as close as that. Any moment he would know what it was: he would *remember*. Yes, he would remember. Meanwhile, he was in the right place. No desire to go elsewhere afflicted him, as in the theatre. Here was the place, here in the flat.

And then it was, with a kind of sudden burst and rush—it seemed to him the only way to phrase it—memory gave up her dead.

At first he only caught her peeping round the corner at him, drawing aside a corner of an enormous curtain, as it were; striving for more complete entrance as though the mass of it were difficult to move. But he understood; he knew; he recognised. It was enough for that. An entrance into his being—heart, mind, soul—was being attempted, and the entrance, because of his stolid temperament, was difficult of accomplishment. There was effort, strain. Something in him had first to be opened up, widened, made soft and ready as by an operation, before full entrance could be effected. This much he grasped, though for the life of him he could not have put it into words. Also, he knew *who* it was that sought an entrance. Deliberately from himself he withheld the name. But he knew, as surely as though Straughan stood in the room and faced him with a knife, saying, "Let me in, let me in. I wish you to know I'm here. I'm clearing a way... ! You recall our promise... ?"

He rose from his chair and went to the open window again, the strange fear slowly passing. The cool air fanned his cheeks. Beauty, till now, had scarcely ever brushed the surface of his soul. He had never troubled his head about it. It passed him by, indifferent; and he had ever loathed the mouthy prating of it on others' lips. He was practical; beauty was for dreamers, for women, for men who had means and leisure. He had not exactly scorned it; rather it had never touched his life, to sweeten, cheer, uplift. Artists for him were like monks—another sex almost, useless beings who never helped the world go round. He was for action always, work, activity, achievement—as he saw them. He remembered Straughan vaguely—Straughan, the ever impecunious, friend of his youth, always talking of colour, sound—mysterious, ineffective things. He even forgot what they had quarrelled about, if they *had* quarrelled at all even; or why they had gone apart all these years ago. And, certainly, he had forgotten any promise. Memory, as yet, only peeped round the corner of that huge curtain at him, tentatively, suggestively, yet—he was obliged to admit it—somewhat winningly. He was conscious of this gentle, sweet seductiveness that now replaced his fear.

And, as he stood now at the open window, peering over huge London, Beauty came close and smote him between the eyes. She came blindingly, with her train of stars and clouds and perfumes. Night, mysterious, myriad-eyed, and flaming across her sea of haunted shadows, invaded his heart and shook him with her immemorial wonder and delight. He found no words, of course, to clothe the new, unwonted sensations. He only knew that all his former dread, uneasiness, distress, and with them this idea of "growth" that had seemed so repugnant to him, were merged, swept up, and gathered magnificently home into a wave of Beauty that enveloped him. "See it ... and understand," ran a secret inner whisper across his mind. He saw. He understood...

He went back and turned the lights out. Then he took his place again at that open window, drinking in the night. He saw a new world; a species of intoxication held him. He sighed... as his thoughts blundered for expression among words and sentences that knew him not. But the delight was there, the wonder, the mystery. He watched, with heart alternately tightening and expanding, the transfiguring play of moon and shadow over the sea of buildings. He saw the dance of the hurrying clouds, the open patches into outer space, the veiling and unveiling of that ancient silvery face; and he caught strange whispers of the hierophantic, sacerdotal Power that has echoed down the world since Time began and dropped strange magic phrases into every poet's heart since first "God dawned on Chaos"—the Beauty of the Night...

A long time passed—it may have been one hour, it may have been three—when at length he turned away and went slowly to his bedroom. A deep peace lay over him. Something quite new and blessed had crept into his life and thought. He could not quite understand it all. He only knew that it uplifted. There was no longer the least sign of affliction or distress. Even the inevitable reaction that, of course, set in could not destroy that.

And then, as he lay in bed, nearing the borderland of sleep, suddenly and without any obvious suggestion to bring it, he remembered another thing. He remembered the promise. Memory got past the big curtain for an instant, and showed her face. She looked into his eyes. It must have been a dozen years ago when Straughan and he had made that foolish, solemn promise that whoever died first should show himself, if possible, to the other.

He had utterly forgotten it—till now. But Straughan had not forgotten it. The letter came three weeks later, from India. That very evening Straughan had died—at nine o'clock. And he had come back— in the Beauty that he loved.

CHARING CROSS ROAD.

# Sand

I

As Felix Henriot came through the streets that January night the fog was stifling, but when he reached his little flat upon the top floor there came a sound of wind. Wind was stirring about the world. It blew against his windows, but at first so faintly that he hardly noticed it. Then, with an abrupt rise and fall like a wailing voice that sought to claim attention, it called him. He peered through the window into the blurred darkness, listening.

There is no cry in the world like that of the homeless wind. A vague excitement, scarcely to be analysed, ran through his blood. The curtain of fog waved momentarily aside. Henriot fancied a star peeped down at him.

"It will change things a bit—at last," he sighed, settling back into his chair. "It will bring movement!"

Already something in himself had changed. A restlessness, as of that wandering wind, woke in his heart—the desire to be off and away. Other things could rouse this wildness too: falling water, the singing of a bird, an odour of wood-fire, a glimpse of winding road. But the cry of wind, always searching, questioning, travelling the world's great routes, remained ever the master-touch. High longing took his mood in hand. Mid seven millions he felt suddenly—lonely.

"I will arise and go now, for always night and day
I hear lake water lapping with low sounds by the shore;
While I stand on the roadway, or on the pavements gray,
I hear it in the deep heart's core."

He murmured the words over softly to himself. The emotion that produced *Innisfree* passed strongly through him. He too would be over the hills and far away. He craved movement, change, adventure— somewhere far from shops and crowds and motor-'busses. For a week the fog had stifled London. This wind brought life.

Where should he go? Desire was long; his purse was short.

He glanced at his books, letters, newspapers. They had no interest now. Instead he listened. The panorama of other journeys rolled in colour through the little room, flying on one another's heels. Henriot enjoyed this remembered essence of his travels more than the travels themselves. The crying wind brought so many voices, all of them seductive

There was a soft crashing of waves upon the Black Sea shores, where the huge Caucasus beckoned in the sky beyond; a rustling in the umbrella pines and cactus at Marseilles, whence magic steamers start about the world like flying dreams. He heard the plash of fountains upon Mount Ida's slopes, and the whisper of the tamarisk on Marathon. It was dawn once more upon the

Ionian Sea, and he smelt the perfume of the Cyclades. Blue-veiled islands melted in the sunshine, and across the dewy lawns of Tempe, moistened by the spray of many waterfalls, he saw—Great Heavens above—the dancing of white forms... or was it only mist the sunshine painted against Pelion?...
"Methought, among the lawns together, we wandered underneath the young grey dawn. And multitudes of dense white fleecy clouds shepherded by the slow, unwilling wind..."

And then, into his stuffy room, slipped the singing perfume of a wallflower on a ruined tower, and with it the sweetness of hot ivy. He heard the "yellow bees in the ivy bloom." Wind whipped over the open hills—this very wind that laboured drearily through the London fog.

And—he was caught. The darkness melted from the city. The fog whisked off into an azure sky. The roar of traffic turned into booming of the sea. There was a whistling among cordage, and the floor swayed to and fro. He saw a sailor touch his cap and pocket the two-franc piece. The siren hooted—ominous sound that had started him on many a journey of adventure—and the roar of London became mere insignificant clatter of a child's toy carriages.

He loved that siren's call; there was something deep and pitiless in it. It drew the wanderers forth from cities everywhere: "Leave your known world behind you, and come with me for better or for worse! The anchor is up; it is too late to change. Only—beware! You shall know curious things—and alone!"

Henriot stirred uneasily in his chair. He turned with sudden energy to the shelf of guide-books, maps and timetables—possessions he most valued in the whole room. He was a happy-go-lucky, adventure-loving soul, careless of common standards, athirst ever for the new and strange.

"That's the best of having a cheap flat," he laughed, "and no ties in the world. I can turn the key and disappear. No one cares or knows —no one but the thieving caretaker. And he's long ago found out that there's nothing here worth taking!"

There followed then no lengthy indecision. Preparation was even shorter still. He was always ready for a move, and his sojourn in cities was but breathing-space while he gathered pennies for further wanderings. An enormous kit-bag—sack-shaped, very worn and dirty— emerged speedily from the bottom of a cupboard in the wall. It was of limitless capacity. The key and padlock rattled in its depths. Cigarette ashes covered everything while he stuffed it full of ancient, indescribable garments. And his voice, singing of those "yellow bees in the ivy bloom," mingled with the crying of the rising wind about his windows. His restlessness had disappeared by magic.

This time, however, there could be no haunted Pelion, nor shady groves of Tempe, for he lived in sophisticated times when money markets regulated movement sternly. Travelling was only for the rich; mere wanderers must pig it. He remembered instead an opportune invitation to the Desert. "Objective" invitation, his genial hosts had called it, knowing his hatred of convention. And Hebuan danced into letters of brilliance upon the inner map of his mind. For Egypt had ever held his spirit in thrall, though as yet he had tried in vain to touch the great buried soul of her. The excavators, the Egyptologists, the archaeologists most of all, plastered her grey ancient face with labels like hotel advertisements on travellers' portmanteaux. They told where she had come from last, but nothing of what she dreamed and thought and loved. The heart of Egypt lay beneath the sand, and the trifling robbery of little details that poked forth from tombs and temples brought no true revelation of her stupendous spiritual splendour. Henriot, in his youth, had searched and dived among what material he could find, believing once—or half believing—that the ceremonial of that ancient system veiled a weight of symbol that was reflected from genuine supersensual knowledge. The rituals, now taken literally, and so pityingly explained away, had once been genuine pathways of approach. But never yet, and least of all in his previous visits to Egypt itself, had he discovered one single person, worthy of speech, who caught at his idea. "Curious," they said, then turned away—to go on digging in the sand. Sand smothered her world today. Excavators discovered skeletons. Museums everywhere stored them—grinning, literal relics that told nothing.

But now, while he packed and sang, these hopes of enthusiastic younger days stirred again—because the emotion that gave them birth was real and true in him. Through the morning mists upon the Nile an old pyramid bowed hugely at him across London roofs: "Come," he heard its awful whisper beneath the ceiling, "I have things to show you, and to tell." He saw the flock of them sailing the Desert like weird grey solemn ships that make no earthly port. And he imagined them as one: multiple expressions of some single unearthly portent they adumbrated in mighty form—dead symbols of some spiritual conception long vanished from the world.

"I mustn't dream like this," he laughed, "or I shall get absent-minded and pack fire-tongs instead of boots. It looks like a jumble sale already!" And he stood on a heap of things to wedge them down still tighter.

But the pictures would not cease. He saw the kites circling high in the blue air. A couple of white vultures flapped lazily away over shining miles. Felucca sails, like giant wings emerging from the ground, curved towards him from the Nile. The palm-trees dropped long shadows over Memphis. He felt the delicious, drenching heat, and the Khamasin, that over-wind from Nubia, brushed his very cheeks. In the little gardens the mish-mish was in bloom... He smelt the Desert... grey sepulchre of cancelled cycles... The stillness of her interminable reaches dropped down upon old London...

The magic of the sand stole round him in its silent-footed tempest.

And while he struggled with that strange, capacious sack, the piles of clothing ran into shapes of gleaming Bedouin faces; London garments settled down with the mournful sound of camels' feet, half dropping wind, half water flowing underground—sound that old Time has brought over into modern life and left a moment for our wonder and perhaps our tears.

He rose at length with the excitement of some deep enchantment in his eyes. The thought of Egypt plunged ever so deeply into him, carrying him into depths where he found it difficult to breathe, so strangely far away it seemed, yet indefinably familiar. He lost his way. A touch of fear came with it.

"A sack like that is the wonder of the world," he laughed again, kicking the unwieldy, sausage-shaped monster into a corner of the room, and sitting down to write the thrilling labels: "Felix Henriot, Alexandria *via* Marseilles." But his pen blotted the letters; there was sand in it. He rewrote the words. Then he remembered a dozen things he had left out. Impatiently, yet with confusion somewhere, he stuffed them in. They ran away into shifting heaps; they disappeared; they emerged suddenly again. It was like packing hot, dry, flowing sand. From the pockets of a coat—he had worn it last summer down Dorset way—out trickled sand. There was sand in his mind and thoughts.

And his dreams that night were full of winds, the old sad winds of Egypt, and of moving, sifting sand. Arabs and Afreets danced amazingly together across dunes he could never reach. For he could not follow fast enough. Something infinitely older than these ever caught his feet and held him back. A million tiny fingers stung and pricked him. Something flung a veil before his eyes. Once it touched him—his face and hands and neck. "Stay here with us," he heard a host of muffled voices crying, but their sound was smothered, buried, rising through the ground. A myriad throats were choked. Till, at last, with a violent effort he turned and seized it. And then the thing he grasped at slipped between his fingers and ran easily away. It had a grey and yellow face, and it moved through all its parts. It flowed as water flows, and yet was solid. It was centuries old.

He cried out to it. "Who are you? What is your name? I surely know you... but I have forgotten... ?"

And it stopped, turning from far away its great uncovered countenance of nameless colouring. He caught a voice. It rolled and boomed and whispered like the wind. And then he woke, with a curious shaking in his heart, and a little touch of chilly perspiration on the skin.

But the voice seemed in the room still—close beside him:

"I am the Sand," he heard, before it died away.

And next he realised that the glitter of Paris lay behind him, and a steamer was taking him with much unnecessary motion across a sparkling sea towards Alexandria. Gladly he saw the Riviera fade below the horizon, with its hard bright sunshine, treacherous winds, and its smear of rich, conventional English. All restlessness now had left him. True vagabond still at forty, he only felt the unrest and discomfort of life when caught in the network of routine and rigid streets, no chance of breaking loose. He was off again at last, money scarce enough indeed, but the joy of wandering expressing itself in happy emotions of release. Every warning of calculation was stifled. He thought of the American woman who walked out of her Long Island house one summer's day to look at a passing sail—and was gone eight years before she walked in again. Eight years of roving travel. He had always felt respect and admiration for that woman.

For Felix Henriot, with his admixture of foreign blood, was philosopher as well as vagabond, a strong poetic and religious strain sometimes breaking out through fissures in his complex nature. He had seen much life; had read many books. The passionate desire of youth to solve the world's big riddles had given place to a resignation filled to the brim with wonder. Anything *might* be true. Nothing surprised him. The most outlandish beliefs, for all he knew, might fringe truth somewhere. He had escaped that cheap cynicism with which disappointed men soothe their vanity when they realise that an intelligible explanation of the universe lies beyond their powers. He no longer expected final answers.

For him, even the smallest journeys held the spice of some adventure; all minutes were loaded with enticing potentialities. And they shaped for themselves somehow a dramatic form. "It's like a story," his friends said when he told his travels. It always was a story.

But the adventure that lay waiting for him where the silent streets of little Hebuan kiss the great Desert's lips, was of a different kind to any Henriot had yet encountered. Looking back, he has often asked himself "How in the world can I accept it ?"

And, perhaps, he never yet has accepted it. It was sand that brought it. For the Desert, the stupendous thing that mothers little Hebuan, produced it.

## II

HE slipped through Cairo with the same relief that he left the Riviera, resenting its social vulgarity so close to the imperial aristocracy of the Desert; he settled down into the peace of soft and silent little Hebuan. The hotel in which he had a room on the top floor had been formerly a Khedivial Palace. It had the air of a palace still. He felt himself in a country-house, with lofty ceilings, cool and airy corridors, spacious halls. Soft-footed Arabs attended to his wants; white walls let in light and air without a sign of heat; there was a feeling of a large, spread tent pitched on the very sand; and the wind that stirred the oleanders in the shady gardens also crept in to rustle the palm leaves of his favourite corner seat. Through the large windows where once the Khedive held high court, the sunshine blazed upon vistaed leagues of Desert.

And from his bedroom windows he watched the sun dip into gold and crimson behind the swelling Libyan sands. This side of the pyramids he saw the Nile meander among palm groves and tilled fields. Across his balcony railings the Egyptian stars trooped down beside his very bed, shaping old constellations for his dreams; while, to the south, he looked out upon the vast untamable Body of the sands that carpeted the world for thousands of miles towards Upper Egypt, Nubia, and the dread Sahara itself. He wondered again why people thought it necessary to go so far afield to know the

Desert. Here, within half an hour of Cairo, it lay breathing solemnly at his very doors.

For little Hebuan, caught thus between the shoulders of the Libyan and Arabian Deserts, is utterly sand-haunted. The Desert lies all round it like a sea. Henriot felt he never could escape from it, as he moved about the island whose coasts are washed with sand. Down each broad and shining street the two end houses framed a vista of its dim immensity—glimpses of shimmering blue, or flame-touched purple. There were stretches of deep sea-green as well, far off upon its bosom. The streets were open channels of approach, and the eye ran down them as along the tube of a telescope laid to catch incredible distance out of space. Through them the Desert reached in with long, thin feelers towards the village. Its Being flooded into Hebuan, and over it. Past walls and houses, churches and hotels, the sea of Desert pressed in silently with its myriad soft feet of sand. It poured in everywhere, through crack and slit and crannie. These were reminders of possession and ownership. And every passing wind that lifted eddies of dust at the street corners were messages from the quiet, powerful Thing that permitted Hebuan to lie and dream so peacefully in the sunshine. Mere artificial oasis, its existence was temporary, held on lease, just for ninety-nine centuries or so.

This sea idea became insistent. For, in certain lights, and especially in the brief, bewildering dusk, the Desert rose—swaying towards the small white houses. The waves of it ran for fifty miles without a break. It was too deep for foam or surface agitation, yet it knew the swell of tides. And underneath flowed resolute currents, linking distance to the centre. These many deserts were really one. A storm, just retreated, had tossed Hebuan upon the shore and left it there to dry; but any morning he would wake to find it had been carried off again into the depths. Some fragment, at least, would disappear. The grim Mokattam Hills were rollers that ever threatened to topple down and submerge the sandy bar that men called Hebuan.

Being soundless, and devoid of perfume, the Desert's message reached him through two senses only—sight and touch; chiefly, of course, the former. Its invasion was concentrated through the eyes. And vision, thus uncorrected, went what pace it pleased. The Desert played with him. Sand stole into his being—through the eyes.

And so obsessing was this majesty of its close presence, that Henriot sometimes wondered how people dared their little social activities within its very sight and hearing; how they played golf and tennis upon reclaimed edges of its face, picnicked so blithely hard upon its frontiers, and danced at night while this stern, unfathomable Thing lay breathing just beyond the trumpery walls that kept it out. The challenge of their shallow admiration seemed presumptuous, almost provocative. Their pursuit of pleasure suggested insolent indifference. They ran fool-hardy hazards, he felt; for there was no worship in their vulgar hearts. With a mental shudder, sometimes he watched the cheap tourist horde go laughing, chattering past within view of its ancient, half-closed eyes. It was like defying deity.

For, to his stirred imagination the sublimity of the Desert dwarfed humanity. These people had been wiser to choose another place for the flaunting of their tawdry insignificance. Any minute this Wilderness, "huddled in grey annihilation," might awake and notice them...!

In his own hotel were several "smart," so-called "Society" people who emphasised the protest in him to the point of definite contempt. Overdressed, the latest worldly novel under their arms, they strutted the narrow pavements of their tiny world, immensely pleased with themselves. Their vacuous minds expressed themselves in the slang of their exclusive circle— value being the element excluded. The pettiness of their outlook hardly distressed him—he was too familiar with it at home—but their essential vulgarity, their innate ugliness, seemed more than usually offensive in the grandeur of its present setting. Into the mighty sands they took the latest London scandal, gabbling it over even among the Tombs and Temples. And "it was to laugh," the pains they spent wondering whom they might condescend to know, never dreaming that they themselves were not worth knowing. Against the background of the noble Desert their titles seemed the cap and bells of clowns.

And Henriot, knowing some of them personally, could not always escape their insipid company. Yet he was the gainer. They little guessed how their commonness heightened contrast, set mercilessly thus beside the strange, eternal beauty of the sand.

Occasionally the protest in his soul betrayed itself in words, which of course they did not understand. "He is so clever, isn't he?" And then, having relieved his feelings, he would comfort himself characteristically:

"The Desert has not noticed them. The Sand is not aware of their existence. How should the sea take note of rubbish that lies above its tide-line?"

For Henriot drew near to its great shifting altars in an attitude of worship. The wilderness made him kneel in heart. Its shining reaches led to the oldest Temple in the world, and every journey that he made was like a sacrament. For him the Desert was a consecrated place. It was sacred.

And his tactful hosts, knowing his peculiarities, left their house open to him when he cared to come—they lived upon the northern edge of the oasis—and he was as free as though he were absolutely alone. He blessed them; he rejoiced that he had come. Little Hebuan accepted him. The Desert knew that he was there.

From his corner of the big dining-room he could see the other guests, but his roving eye always returned to the figure of a solitary man who sat at an adjoining table, and whose personality stirred his interest. While affecting to look elsewhere, he studied him as closely as might be. There was something about the stranger that touched his curiosity—a certain air of expectation that he wore. But it was more than that: it was anticipation, apprehension in it somewhere. The man was nervous, uneasy. His restless way of suddenly looking about him proved it. Henriot tried every one else in the room as well but, though his thought settled on others too, he always came back to the figure of this solitary being opposite, who ate his dinner as if afraid of being seen, and glanced up sometimes as if fearful of being watched. Henriot's curiosity, before he knew it, became suspicion. There was mystery here. The table, he noticed, was laid for two.

"Is he an actor, a priest of some strange religion, an enquiry agent, or just—a crank?" was the thought that first occurred to him. And the question suggested itself without amusement. The impression of subterfuge and caution he conveyed left his observer unsatisfied.

The face was clean shaven, dark, and strong thick hair, straight yet bushy, was slightly unkempt; it was streaked with grey; and an unexpected mobility when he smiled ran over the features that he seemed to hold rigid by deliberate effort. The man was cut to no quite common measure. Henriot jumped to an intuitive conclusion: "He's not here for pleasure or merely sight-seeing. Something serious has brought him out to Egypt." For the face combined too ill-assorted qualities: an obstinate tenacity that might even mean brutality, and was certainly repulsive, yet, with it, an undecipherable dreaminess betrayed by lines of the mouth, but above all in the very light blue eyes, so rarely raised. Those eyes, he felt, had looked upon unusual things; "dreaminess" was not an adequate description "searching" conveyed it better. The true source of the queer impression remained elusive. And hence, perhaps, the incongruous marriage in the face—mobility laid upon a matter-of-fact foundation underneath. The face showed conflict.

And Henriot, watching him, felt decidedly intrigued. "I'd like to know that man, and all about him." His name, he learned later, was Richard Vance; from Birmingham; a businessman. But it was not the Birmingham he wished to know; it was the—other: cause of the elusive, dreamy searching. Though facing one another at so short a distance, their eyes, however, did not meet. And this, Henriot well knew, was a sure sign that he himself was also under observation. Richard Vance, from Birmingham, was equally taking careful note of Felix Henriot, from London.

Thus, he could wait his time. They would come together later. An opportunity would certainly present itself. The first links in a curious chain had already caught; soon the chain would tighten, pull as though by chance, and bring their lives into one and the same circle. Wondering in particular for what kind of a companion the second cover was laid, Henriot felt certain that their eventual coming together was inevitable. He possessed this kind of divination from first impressions, and not uncommonly it proved correct.

Following instinct, therefore, he took no steps towards acquaintance, and for several days, owing to the fact that he dined frequently with his hosts, he saw nothing more of Richard Vance, the businessman from Birmingham. Then, one night, coming home late from his friend's house, he had passed along the great corridor, and was actually a step or so into his bedroom, when a drawling voice sounded close behind him. It was an unpleasant sound. It was very near him too—

"I beg your pardon, but have you, by any chance, such a thing as a compass you could lend me?"

The voice was so close that he started. Vance stood within touching distance of his body. He had stolen up like a ghostly Arab, must have followed him, too, some little distance, for further down the passage the light of an open door—he had passed it on his way—showed where he came from.

"Eh? I beg your pardon? A—compass, did you say?" He felt disconcerted for a moment. How short the man was, now that he saw him standing. Broad and powerful too. Henriot looked down upon his thick head of hair. The personality and voice repelled him. Possibly his face, caught unawares, betrayed this.

"Forgive my startling you," said the other apologetically, while the softer expression danced in for a moment and disorganised the rigid set of the face. "The soft carpet, you know. I'm afraid you didn't hear my tread. I wondered"—he smiled again slightly at the nature of the request—"if—by any chance—you had a pocket compass you could lend me?"

"Ah, a compass, yes! Please don't apologise. I believe I have one— if you'll wait a moment. Come in, won't you? I'll have a look."

The other thanked him but waited in the passage. Henriot, it so happened, had a compass, and produced it after a moment's search.

"I am greatly indebted to you—if I may return it in the morning. You will forgive my disturbing you at such an hour. My own is broken, and I wanted—er—to find the true north."

Henriot stammered some reply, and the man was gone. It was all over in a minute. He locked his door and sat down in his chair to think. The little incident had upset him, though for the life of him he could not imagine why. It ought by rights to have been almost ludicrous, yet instead it was the exact reverse—half threatening. Why should not a man want a compass? But, again, why should he? And at midnight? The voice, the eyes, the near presence—what did they bring that set his nerves thus asking unusual questions? This strange impression that something grave was happening, something unearthly— how was it born exactly? The man's proximity came like a shock. It had made him start. He brought—thus the idea came unbidden to his mind—something with him that galvanised him quite absurdly, as fear does, or delight, or great wonder. There was a music in his voice too— a certain—well, he could only call it lilt, that reminded him of plainsong, intoning, chanting. Drawling was *not* the word at all.

He tried to dismiss it as imagination, but it would not be dismissed. The disturbance in himself was caused by something not imaginary, but real. And then, for the first time, he discovered that the man had brought a faint, elusive suggestion of perfume with him, an aromatic odour, that made him think of priests and churches. The ghost of it still lingered in the air. Ah, here then was the origin of the notion that his voice had chanted: it was surely the suggestion of incense. But incense, intoning, a compass to find the true north—at midnight in a Desert hotel!

A touch of uneasiness ran through the curiosity and excitement that he felt.

And he undressed for bed. "Confound my old imagination," he thought, "what tricks it plays me! It'll keep me awake!"

But the questions, once started in his mind, continued. He must find explanation of one kind or another before he could lie down and sleep, and he found it at length in—the stars. The man was an astronomer of sorts; possibly an astrologer into the bargain! Why not? The stars were wonderful above Hebuan. Was there not an observatory on the Mokattam Hills, too, where tourists could use the telescopes on privileged days? He had it at last. He even stole out on to his balcony to see if the stranger perhaps was looking through some wonderful apparatus at the heavens. Their rooms were on the same side. But the shuttered windows revealed no stooping figure with eyes glued to a telescope. The stars blinked in their many thousands down upon the silent desert. The night held neither sound nor movement. There was a cool breeze blowing across the Nile from the Lybian Sands. It nipped; and he stepped back quickly into the room again. Drawing the mosquito curtains carefully about the bed, he put the light out and turned over to sleep.

And sleep came quickly, contrary to his expectations, though it was a light and surface sleep. That last glimpse of the darkened Desert lying beneath the Egyptian stars had touched him with some hand of awful power that ousted the first, lesser excitement. It calmed and soothed him in one sense, yet in another, a sense he could not understand, it caught him in a net of deep, deep feelings whose mesh, while infinitely delicate, was utterly stupendous. His nerves this deeper emotion left alone: it reached instead to something infinite in him that mere nerves could neither deal with nor interpret. The soul awoke and whispered in him while his body slept.

And the little, foolish dreams that ran to and fro across this veil of surface sleep brought oddly tangled pictures of things quite tiny and at the same time of others that were mighty beyond words. With these two counters Nightmare played. They interwove. There was the figure of this dark-faced man with the compass, measuring the sky to find the true north, and there were hints of giant Presences that hovered just outside some curious outline that he traced upon the ground, copied in some nightmare fashion from the heavens. The excitement caused by his visitor's singular request mingled with the profounder sensations his final look at the stars and Desert stirred. The two were somehow interrelated.

Some hours later, before this surface sleep passed into genuine slumber, Henriot woke—with an appalling feeling that the Desert had come creeping into his room and now stared down upon him where he lay in bed. The wind was crying audibly about the walls outside. A faint, sharp tapping came against the window panes.

He sprang instantly out of bed, not yet awake enough to feel actual alarm, yet with the nightmare touch still close enough to cause a sort of feverish, loose bewilderment. He switched the lights on. A moment later he knew the meaning of that curious tapping, for the rising wind was flinging tiny specks of sand against the glass. The idea that they had summoned him belonged, of course, to dream.

He opened the window, and stepped out on to the balcony. The stone was very cold under his bare feet. There was a wash of wind all over him. He saw the sheet of glimmering, pale desert near and far; and something stung his skin below the eyes.

"The sand," he whispered, "again the sand; always the sand. Waking or sleeping, the sand is everywhere—nothing but sand, sand, Sand..."

He rubbed his eyes. It was like talking in his sleep, talking to someone who had questioned him just before he woke. But was he really properly awake? It seemed next day that he had dreamed it. Something enormous, with rustling skirts of sand, had just retreated far into the Desert. Sand went with it—flowing, trailing, smothering the world. The wind died down.

And Henriot went back to sleep, caught instantly away into unconsciousness; covered, blinded, swept over by this spreading thing of reddish brown with the great, grey face, whose Being was colossal yet quite tiny, and whose fingers, wings and eyes were countless as the stars.

But all night long it watched and waited, rising to peer above the little balcony, and sometimes entering the room and piling up beside his very pillow. He dreamed of Sand.

### III

For some days Henriot saw little of the man who came from Birmingham and pushed curiosity to a climax by asking for a compass in the middle of the night. For one thing, he was a good deal with his friends upon the other side of Hebuan, and for another, he slept several nights in the Desert.

He loved the gigantic peace the Desert gave him. The world was forgotten there; and not the world merely, but all memory of it. Everything faded out. The soul turned inwards upon itself.

An Arab boy and donkey took out sleeping-bag, food and water to the Wadi Hof, a desolate gorge about an hour eastwards. It winds between cliffs whose summits rise some thousand feet above the sea. It opens suddenly, cut deep into the swaying world of level plateaux and undulating hills. It moves about too; he never found it in the same place twice—like an arm of the Desert that shifted with the changing lights. Here he watched dawns and sunsets, slept through the midday heat, and enjoyed the unearthly colouring that swept Day and Night across the huge horizons. In solitude the Desert soaked down into him. At night the jackals cried in the darkness round his cautiously-fed camp fire—small, because wood had to be carried—and in the daytime kites circled overhead to inspect him, and an occasional white vulture flapped across the blue. The weird desolation of this rocky valley, he thought, was like the scenery of the moon. He took no watch with him, and the arrival of the donkey boy an hour after sunrise came almost from another planet, bringing things of time and common life out of some distant gulf where they had lain forgotten among lost ages.

The short hour of twilight brought, too, a bewitchment into the silence that was a little less than comfortable. Full light or darkness he could manage, but this time of half things made him want to shut his eyes and hide. Its effect stepped over imagination. The mind got lost. He could not understand it. For the cliffs and boulders of discoloured limestone shone then with an inward glow that signalled to the Desert with veiled lanterns. The misshappen hills, carved by wind and rain into ominous outlines, stirred and nodded. In the morning light they retired into themselves, asleep. But at dusk the tide retreated. They rose from the sea, emerging naked, threatening. They ran together and joined shoulders, the entire army of them. And the glow of their sandy bodies, self-luminous, continued even beneath the stars. Only the moonlight drowned it. For the moonrise over the Mokattam Hills brought a white, grand loveliness that drenched the entire Desert. It drew a marvellous sweetness from the sand. It shone across a world as yet unfinished, whereon no life might show itself for ages yet to come. He was alone then upon an empty star, before the creation of things that breathed and moved.

What impressed him, however, more than everything else was the enormous vitality that rose out of all this apparent death. There was no hint of the melancholy that belongs commonly to flatness; the sadness of wide, monotonous landscape was not here. The endless repetition of sweeping vale and plateau brought infinity within measurable comprehension. He grasped a definite meaning in the phrase "world without end": the Desert had no end and no beginning. It gave him a sense of eternal peace, the silent peace that star-fields know. Instead of subduing the soul with bewilderment, it inspired with courage, confidence, hope. Through this sand which was the wreck of countless geological ages, rushed life that was terrific and uplifting, too huge to include melancholy, too deep to betray itself in movement. Here was the stillness of eternity. Behind the spread grey masque of apparent death lay stores of accumulated life, ready to break forth at any point. In the Desert he felt himself absolutely royal.

And this contrast of Life, veiling itself in Death, was a contradiction that somehow intoxicated. The Desert exhilaration never left him. He was never alone. A companionship of millions went with him, and he *felt* the Desert close, as stars are close to one another, or grains of sand.

It was the Khamasin, the hot wind bringing sand, that drove him in—with the feeling that these few days and nights had been immeasurable, and that he had been away a thousand years. He came back with the magic of the Desert in his blood, hotel-life tasteless and insipid by comparison. To human impressions thus he was fresh and vividly sensitive. His being, cleaned and sensitized by pure grandeur, "felt" people—for a time at any rate—with an uncommon sharpness of receptive judgment. He returned to a life somehow mean and meagre, resuming insignificance with his dinner jacket. Out with the sand he had been regal; now, like a slave, he strutted self-conscious and reduced.

But this imperial standard of the Desert stayed a little time beside him, its purity focussing judgment like a lens. The specks of smaller emotions left it clear at first, and as his eye wandered vaguely over the people assembled in the dining-room, it was arrested with a vivid shock upon two figures at the little table facing him.

He had forgotten Vance, the Birmingham man who sought the North at midnight with a pocket compass. He now saw him again, with an intuitive discernment entirely fresh. Before memory brought up her clouding associations, some brilliance flashed a light upon him. "That man," Henriot thought, "might have come with me. He would have understood and loved it!" But the thought was really this—a moment's reflection spread it, rather "He belongs somewhere to the Desert; the Desert brought him out here." And, again, hidden swiftly behind it like a movement running below water—"What does he want with it? What is the deeper motive he conceals? For there *is* a deeper motive; and it *is* concealed."

But it was the woman seated next him who absorbed his attention really, even while this thought flashed and went its way. The empty chair was occupied at last. Unlike his first encounter with the man, she looked straight at him. Their eyes met fully. For several seconds there was steady mutual inspection, while her penetrating stare, intent without being rude, passed searchingly all over his face. It was disconcerting. Crumbling his bread, he looked equally hard at her, unable to turn away, determined not to be the first to shift his gaze. And when at length she lowered her eyes he felt that many things had happened, as in a long period of intimate conversation. Her mind had judged him through and through. Questions and answers flashed. They were no longer strangers. For the rest of dinner, though he was careful to avoid direct inspection, he was aware that she felt his presence and was secretly speaking with him. She asked questions beneath her breath. The answers rose with the quickened pulses in his blood. Moreover, she explained Richard Vance. It was this woman's power that shone reflected in the man. She was the one who knew the big, unusual things. Vance merely echoed the rush of her vital personality.

This was the first impression that he got—from the most striking, curious face he had ever seen in a woman. It remained very near him all through the meal: she had moved to his table, it seemed she sat beside him. Their minds certainly knew contact from that moment.

It is never difficult to credit strangers with the qualities and knowledge that oneself craves for, and no doubt Henriot's active fancy went busily to work. But, none the less, this thing remained and grew: that this woman was aware of the hidden things of Egypt he had always longed to know. There was knowledge and guidance she could impart. Her soul was searching among ancient things. Her face brought the Desert back into his thoughts. And with it came—the sand.

Here was the flash. The sight of her restored the peace and splendour he had left behind him in his Desert camps. The rest, of course, was what his imagination constructed upon this slender basis. Only,—not all of it was imagination.

Now, Henriot knew little enough of women, and had no pose of "understanding" them. His experience was of the slightest; the love and veneration felt for his own mother had set the entire sex upon the heights. His affairs with women, if so they may be called, had been transient—all but those of early youth, which having never known the devastating test of fulfilment, still remained ideal and superb. There was unconscious humour in his attitude—from a distance; for he regarded women with wonder and respect, as puzzles that sweetened but complicated life, might even endanger it. He certainly was not a marrying man! But now, as he felt the presence of this woman so deliberately possess him, there came over him two clear, strong messages, each vivid with certainty. One was that banal suggestion of familiarity claimed by lovers and the like—he had often heard of it—"I have known that woman before; I have met her ages ago somewhere; she is strangely familiar to me"; and the other, growing out of it almost: "Have nothing to do with her; she will bring you trouble and confusion; avoid her, and be warned";—in fact, a distinct presentiment.

Yet, although Henriot dismissed both impressions as having no shred of evidence to justify them, the original clear judgment, as he studied her extraordinary countenance, persisted through all denials. The familiarity, and the presentiment, remained. There also remained this other—an enormous imaginative leap!—that she could teach him "Egypt."

He watched her carefully, in a sense fascinated. He could only describe the face as black, so dark it was with the darkness of great age. Elderly was the obvious, natural word; but elderly described the features only. The expression of the face wore centuries. Nor was it merely the coal-black eyes that betrayed an ancient, age-travelled soul behind them. The entire presentment mysteriously conveyed it. This woman's heart knew long-forgotten things— the thought kept beating up against him. There were cheek-bones, oddly high, that made him think involuntarily of the well-advertised Pharaoh, Ramases; a square, deep jaw; and an aquiline nose that gave the final touch of power. For the power undeniably was there, and while the general effect had grimness in it, there was neither harshness nor any forbidding touch about it. There was an implacable sternness in the set of lips and jaw, and, most curious of all, the eyelids over the steady eyes of black were level as a ruler. This level framing made the woman's stare remarkable beyond description. Henriot thought of an idol carved in stone, stone hard and black, with eyes that stared across the sand into a world of things non-human, very far away, forgotten of men. The face was finely ugly. This strange dark beauty flashed flame about it.

And, as the way ever was with him, Henriot next fell to constructing the possible lives of herself and her companion, though without much success. Imagination soon stopped dead. She was not old enough to be Vance's mother, and assuredly she was not his wife. His interest was more than merely piqued—it was puzzled uncommonly. What was the contrast that made the man seem beside her—vile? Whence came, too, the impression that she exercised some strong authority, though never directly exercised, that held him at her mercy? How did he guess that the man resented it, yet did not dare oppose, and that, apparently acquiescing goodhumouredly, his will was deliberately held in abeyance, and that he waited sulkily, biding his time? There was furtiveness in every gesture and expression. A hidden motive lurked in him; unworthiness somewhere; he was determined yet ashamed. He watched her ceaselessly and with such uncanny closeness.

Henriot imagined he divined all this. He leaped to the guess that his expenses were being paid. A good deal more was being paid besides. She was a rich relation, from whom he had expectations; he was serving his seven years, ashamed of his servitude, ever calculating escape—but, perhaps, no ordinary escape. A faint shudder ran over him. He drew in the reins of imagination.

Of course, the probabilities were that he was hopelessly astray— one usually is on such occasions—but this time, it so happened, he was singularly right. Before one thing only his ready invention stopped every time. This vileness, this notion of unworthiness in Vance, could not be negative merely. A man with that face was no inactive weakling. The motive he was at such pains to conceal, betraying its existence by that very fact, moved, surely, towards aggressive action. Disguised, it never slept. Vance was sharply on the alert. He had a plan deep out of sight. And Henriot remembered how the man's soft approach along the carpeted corridor had made him start. He recalled the quasi shock it gave him. He thought again of the feeling of discomfort he had experienced.

Next, his eager fancy sought to plumb the business these two had together in Egypt—in the Desert. For the Desert, he felt convinced, had brought them out. But here, though he constructed numerous explanations, another barrier stopped him. Because he *knew*. This woman was in touch with that aspect of ancient Egypt he himself had ever sought in vain; and not merely with stones the sand had buried so deep, but with the meanings they once represented, buried so utterly by the sands of later thought.

And here, being ignorant, he found no clue that could lead to any satisfactory result, for he possessed no knowledge that might guide him. He floundered—until Fate helped him. And the instant Fate helped him, the warning and presentiment he had dismissed as fanciful, became real again. He hesitated. Caution acted. He would think twice before taking steps to form acquaintance. "Better not," thought whispered. "Better leave them alone, this queer couple. They're after things that won't do you any good." This idea of mischief, almost of danger, in their purposes was oddly insistent for what could possibly convey it? But, while he hesitated, Fate, who sent the warning, pushed him at the same time into the circle of their lives: at first tentatively—he might still have escaped; but soon urgently—curiosity led him inexorably towards the end.

## IV

IT was so simple a manoeuvre by which Fate began the innocent game. The woman left a couple of books behind her on the table one night, and Henriot, after a moment's hesitation, took them out after her. He knew the titles—*The House of the Master*, and *The House of the Hidden Places*, both singular interpretations of the Pyramids that once had held his own mind spellbound. Their ideas had been since disproved, if he remembered rightly, yet the titles were a clue—a clue to that imaginative part of his mind that was so busy constructing theories and had found its stride. Loose sheets of paper, covered with notes in a minute handwriting, lay between the pages; but these, of course, he did not read, noticing only that they were written round designs of various kinds—intricate designs.

He discovered Vance in a corner of the smoking-lounge. The woman had disappeared.

Vance thanked him politely. "My aunt is so forgetful sometimes," he said, and took them with a covert eagerness that did not escape the other's observation. He folded up the sheets and put them carefully in his pocket. On one there was an inksketched map, crammed with detail, that might well have referred to some portion of the Desert. The points of the compass stood out boldly at the bottom. There were involved geometrical designs again. Henriot saw them. They exchanged, then, the commonplaces of conversation, but these led to nothing further. Vance was nervous and betrayed impatience. He presently excused himself and left the lounge. Ten minutes later he passed through the outer hall, the woman beside him, and the pair of them, wrapped up in cloak and ulster, went out into the night. At the door, Vance turned and threw a quick, investigating glance in his direction. There seemed a hint of questioning in that glance; it might almost have been a tentative invitation. But, also, he wanted to see if their exit had been particularly noticed—and by whom.

This, briefly told, was the first manoeuvre by which Fate introduced them. There was nothing in it. The details were so insignificant, so slight the conversation, so meagre the pieces thus added to Henriot's imaginative structure. Yet they somehow built it up and made it solid; the outline in his mind began to stand foursquare. That writing, those designs, the manner of the man, their going out together, the final curious look—each and all betrayed points of a hidden thing. Subconsciously he was excavating their buried purposes. The sand was shifting. The concentration of his mind incessantly upon them removed it grain by grain and speck by speck. Tips of the smothered thing emerged. Presently a subsidence would follow with a rush and light would blaze upon its skeleton. He felt it stirring underneath his feet—this flowing movement of light, dry, heaped-up sand. It was always— sand.

Then other incidents of a similar kind came about, clearing the way to a natural acquaintanceship. Henriot watched the process with amusement, yet with another feeling too that was only a little less than anxiety. A keen observer, no detail escaped him; he saw the forces of their lives draw closer. It made him think of the devices of young people who desire to know one another, yet cannot get a proper introduction. Fate condescended to such little tricks. They wanted a third person, he began to feel. A third was necessary to some plan they had on hand, and—they waited to see if he could fill the place. This woman, with whom he had yet exchanged no single word, seemed so familiar to him, well known for years. They weighed and watched him, wondering if he would do.

None of the devices were too obviously used, but at length Henriot picked up so many forgotten articles, and heard so many significant phrases, casually let fall, that he began to feel like the villain in a machine-made play, where the hero for ever drops clues his enemy is intended to discover.

Introduction followed inevitably. "My aunt can tell you; she knows Arabic perfectly." He had been discussing the meaning of some local name or other with a neighbour after dinner, and Vance had joined them. The neighbour moved away; these two were left standing alone, and he accepted a cigarette from the other's case. There was a rustle of skirts behind them. "Here she comes," said Vance; "you will let me introduce you." He did not ask for Henriot's name; he had already taken the trouble to find it out—another little betrayal, and another clue.

It was in a secluded corner of the great hall, and Henriot turned to see the woman's stately figure coming towards them across the thick carpet that deadened her footsteps. She came sailing up, her black eyes fixed upon his face. Very erect, head upright, shoulders almost squared, she moved wonderfully well; there was dignity and power in her walk. She was dressed in black, and her face was like the night. He found it impossible to say what lent her this air of impressiveness and solemnity that was almost majestic. But there was this touch of darkness and of power in the way she came that made him think of some sphinx-like figure of stone, some idol motionless in all its parts but moving as a whole, and gliding across—sand. Beneath those level lids her eyes stared hard at him. And a faint sensation of distress stirred in him deep, deep down. Where had he seen those eyes before?

He bowed, as she joined them, and Vance led the way to the armchairs in a corner of the lounge. The meeting, as the talk that followed, he felt, were all part of a preconceived plan. It had happened before. The woman, that is, was familiar to him—to some part of his being that had dropped stitches of old, old memory.

Lady Statham! At first the name had disappointed him. So many folk wear titles, as syllables in certain tongues wear accents—without them being mute, unnoticed, unpronounced. Nonentities, born to names, so often claim attention for their insignificance in this way. But this woman, had she been Jemima Jones, would have made the name distinguished and select. She was a big and sombre personality. Why was it, he wondered afterwards, that for a moment something in him shrank, and that his mind, metaphorically speaking, flung up an arm in self-protection? The instinct flashed and passed. But it seemed to him born of an automatic feeling that he must protect—not himself, but the woman from the man. There was confusion in it all; links were missing. He studied her intently. She was a woman who had none of the external feminine signals in either dress or manner, no graces, no little womanly hesitations and alarms, no daintiness, yet neither anything distinctly masculine. Her charm was strong, possessing; only he kept forgetting that he was talking to a—woman; and the thing she inspired in him included, with respect and wonder, somewhere also this curious hint of dread. This instinct to protect her fled as soon as it was born, for the interest of the conversation in which she so quickly plunged him obliterated all minor emotions whatsoever. Here, for the first time, he drew close to Egypt, the Egypt he had sought so long. It was not to be explained. He *felt* it.

Beginning with commonplaces, such as "You like Egypt? You find here what you expected?" she led him into better regions with "One finds here what one brings." He knew the delightful experience of talking fluently on subjects he was at home in, and to some one who understood. The feeling at first that to this woman he could not say mere anythings, slipped into its opposite—that he could say everything. Strangers ten minutes ago, they were at once in deep and intimate talk together. He found his ideas readily followed, agreed with up to a point—the point which permits discussion to start from a basis of general accord towards speculation. In the excitement of ideas he neglected the uncomfortable note that had stirred his caution, forgot the warning too. Her mind, moreover, seemed known to him; he was often aware of what she was going to say before he actually heard it; the current of her thoughts struck a familiar gait, and more than once he experienced vividly again the odd sensation that it all had happened before. The very sentences and phrases with which she pointed the turns of her unusual ideas were never wholly unexpected.

For her ideas were decidedly unusual, in the sense that she accepted without question speculations not commonly deemed worth consideration at all, indeed not ordinarily even known. Henriot knew them, because he had read in many fields. It was the strength of her belief that fascinated him. She offered no apologies. She knew. And while he talked, she listening with folded arms and her black eyes fixed upon his own, Richard Vance watched with vigilant eyes and listened too, ceaselessly alert. Vance joined in little enough, however, gave no opinions, his attitude one of general acquiescence. Twice, when pauses of slackening interest made it possible, Henriot fancied he surprised another quality in this negative attitude. Interpreting it each time differently, he yet dismissed both interpretations with a smile. His imagination leaped so absurdly to violent conclusions. They were not tenable: Vance was neither her keeper, nor was he in some fashion a detective. Yet in his manner was sometimes this suggestion of the detective order. He watched with such deep attention, and he concealed it so clumsily with an affectation of careless indifference.

There is nothing more dangerous than that impulsive intimacy strangers sometimes adopt when an atmosphere of mutual sympathy takes them by surprise, for it is akin to the false frankness friends affect when telling "candidly" one another's faults. The mood is invariably regretted later. Henriot, however, yielded to it now with something like abandon. The pleasure of talking with this woman was so unexpected, and so keen.

For Lady Statham believed apparently in some Egypt of her dreams. Her interest was neither historical, archaeological, nor political. It was religious—yet hardly of this earth at all. The conversation turned upon the knowledge of the ancient Egyptians from an unearthly point of view, and even while he talked he was vaguely aware that it was *her* mind talking through his own. She drew out his ideas and made him say them. But this he was properly aware of only afterwards—that she had cleverly, mercilessly pumped him of all he had ever known or read upon the subject. Moreover, what Vance watched so intently was himself, and the reactions in himself this remarkable woman produced. That also he realised later.

His first impression that these two belonged to what may be called the "crank" order was justified by the conversation. But, at least, it was interesting crankiness, and the belief behind it made it even fascinating. Long before the end he surprised in her a more vital form of his own attitude that anything *may* be true, since knowledge has never yet found final answers to any of the biggest questions.

He understood, from sentences dropped early in the talk, that she was among those few "superstitious" folk who think that the old Egyptians came closer to reading the eternal riddles of the world than any others, and that their knowledge was a remnant of that ancient Wisdom Religion which existed in the superb, dark civilization of the sunken Atlantis, lost continent that once joined Africa to Mexico. Eighty thousand years ago the dim sands of Poseidonis, great island adjoining the main continent which itself had vanished a vast period before, sank down beneath the waves, and the entire known world today was descended from its survivors. Hence the significant fact that all religions and "mythological" systems begin with a story of a flood— some cataclysmic upheaval that destroyed the world. Egypt itself was colonised by a group of Atlantean priests who brought their curious, deep knowledge with them. They had foreseen the cataclysm.

Lady Statham talked well, bringing into her great dream this strong, insistent quality of belief and fact. She knew, from Plato to Donelly, all that the minds of men have ever speculated upon the gorgeous legend. The evidence for such a sunken continent—Henriot had skimmed it too in years gone by—she made bewilderingly complete. He had heard Baconians demolish Shakespeare with an array of evidence equally overwhelming. It catches the imagination though not the mind. Yet out of her facts, as she presented them, grew a strange likelihood. The force of this woman's personality, and her calm and quiet way of believing all she talked about, took her listener to some extent—further than ever before, certainly—into the great dream after her. And the dream, to say the least, was a picturesque one, laden with wonderful possibilities. For as she talked the spirit of old Egypt moved up, staring down upon him out of eyes lidded so curiously level. Hitherto all had prated to him of the Arabs, their ancient faith and customs, and the splendour of the Bedouins, those Princes of the Desert. But what he sought, barely confessed in words even to himself, was something older far than this. And this strange, dark woman brought it close. Deeps in his soul, long slumbering, awoke. He heard forgotten questions.

Only in this brief way could he attempt to sum up the storm she roused in him.

She carried him far beyond mere outline, however, though afterwards he recalled the details with difficulty. So much more was suggested than actually expressed. She contrived to make the general modern scepticism an evidence of cheap mentality. It was so easy; the depth it affects to conceal, mere emptiness. "We have tried all things, and found all wanting"—the mind, as measuring instrument, merely confessed inadequate. Various shrewd judgments of this kind increased his respect, although her acceptance went so far beyond his own. And, while the label of credulity refused to stick to her, her sense of imaginative wonder enabled her to escape that dreadful compromise, a man's mind in a woman's temperament. She fascinated him.

The spiritual worship of the ancient Egyptians, she held, was a symbolical explanation of things generally alluded to as the secrets of life and death; their knowledge was a remnant of the wisdom of Atlantis. Material relics, equally misunderstood, still stood today at Karnac, Stonehenge, and in the mysterious writings on buried Mexican temples and cities, so significantly akin to the hieroglyphics upon the Egyptian tombs.

"The one misinterpreted as literally as the other," she suggested, "yet both fragments of an advanced knowledge that found its grave in the sea. The Wisdom of that old spiritual system has vanished from the world, only a degraded literalism left of its undecipherable language. The jewel has been lost, and the casket is filled with sand, sand, sand."

How keenly her black eyes searched his own as she said it, and how oddly she made the little word resound. The syllable drew out almost into chanting. Echoes answered from the depths within him, carrying it on and on across some desert of forgotten belief. Veils of sand flew everywhere about his mind. Curtains lifted. Whole hills of sand went shifting into level surfaces whence gardens of dim outline emerged to meet the sunlight.

"But the sand may be removed." It was her nephew, speaking almost for the first time, and the interruption had an odd effect, introducing a sharply practical element. For the tone expressed, so far as he dared express it, disapproval. It was a baited observation, an invitation to opinion.

"We are not sand-diggers, Mr Henriot," put in Lady Statham, before he decided to respond. "Our object is quite another one; and I believe—I have a feeling," she added almost questioningly, "that you might be interested enough to help us perhaps."

He only wondered the direct attack had not come sooner. Its bluntness hardly surprised him. He felt himself leap forward to accept it. A sudden subsidence had freed his feet.

Then the warning operated suddenly—for an instant. Henriot was interested; more, he was half seduced; but, as yet, he did not mean to be included in their purposes, whatever these might be. That shrinking dread came back a moment, and was gone again before he could question it. His eyes looked full at Lady Statham. "What is it that you know?" they asked her. "Tell me the things we once knew together, you and I. These words are merely trifling. And why does another man now stand in my place? For the sands heaped upon my memory are shifting, and it is *you* who are moving them away."

His soul whispered it; his voice said quite another thing, although the words he used seemed oddly chosen:

"There is much in the ideas of ancient Egypt that has attracted me ever since I can remember, though I have never caught up with anything definite enough to follow. There was majesty somewhere in their conceptions—a large, calm majesty of spiritual dominion, one might call it perhaps. I am interested."

Her face remained expressionless as she listened, but there was grave conviction in the eyes that held him like a spell. He saw through them into dim, faint pictures whose background was always sand. He forgot that he was speaking with a woman, a woman who half an hour ago had been a stranger to him. He followed these faded mental pictures, though he never caught them up... It was like his dream in London.

Lady Statham was talking—he had not noticed the means by which she effected the abrupt transition—of familiar beliefs of old Egypt; of the Ka, or Double, by whose existence the survival of the soul was possible, even its return into manifested, physical life; of the astrology, or influence of the heavenly bodies upon all sublunar activities; of terrific forms of other life, known to the ancient worship of Atlantis, great Potencies that might be invoked by ritual and ceremonial, and of their lesser influence as recognised in certain lower forms, hence treated with veneration as the "Sacred Animal" branch of this dim religion. And she spoke lightly of the modern learning which so glibly imagined it was the animals themselves that were looked upon as "gods"—the bull, the bird, the crocodile, the cat. "It's there they all go so absurdly wrong," she said, "taking the symbol for the power symbolised. Yet natural enough. The mind today wears blinkers, studies only the details seen directly before it. Had none of us experienced love, we should think the first lover mad. Few today know the Powers *they* knew, hence deny them. If the world were deaf it would stand with mockery before a hearing group swayed by an orchestra, pitying both listeners and performers. It would deem our admiration of a great swinging bell mere foolish worship of form and movement. Similarly, with high Powers that once expressed themselves in common forms— where best they could—being themselves bodiless. The learned men classify the forms with painstaking detail. But deity has gone out of life. The Powers symbolised are no longer experienced."

"These Powers, you suggest, then—their Kas, as it were—may still—"

But she waved aside the interruption. "They are satisfied, as the common people were, with a degraded literalism," she went on. "Nut was the Heavens, who spread herself across the earth in the form of a woman; Shu, the vastness of space; the ibis typified Thoth, and Hathor was the Patron of the Western Hills; Khonsu, the moon, was personified, as was the deity of the Nile. But the high priest of Ra, the sun, you notice, remained ever the Great One of Visions."

The High Priest, the Great One of Visions!—How wonderfully again she made the sentence sing. She put splendour into it. The pictures shifted suddenly closer in his mind. He saw the grandeur of Memphis and Heliopolis rise against the stars and shake the sand of ages from their stern old temples.

"You think it possible, then, to get into touch with these High Powers you speak of, Powers once manifested in common forms?"

Henriot asked the question with a degree of conviction and solemnity that surprised himself. The scenery changed about him as he listened. The spacious halls of this former khedivial Palace melted into Desert spaces. He smelt the open wilderness, the sand that haunted Hebuan. The soft-footed Arab servants moved across the hall in their white sheets like eddies of dust the wind stirred from the Libyan dunes. And over these two strangers close beside him stole a queer, indefinite alteration. Moods and emotions, nameless as unknown stars, rose through his soul, trailing dark mists of memory from unfathomable distances.

Lady Statham answered him indirectly. He found himself wishing that those steady eyes would sometimes close.

"Love is known only by feeling it," she said, her voice deepening a little. "Behind the form you feel the person loved. The process is an evocation, pure and simple. An arduous ceremonial, involving worship and devotional preparation, is the means. It is a difficult ritual—the only one acknowledged by the world as still effectual. Ritual is the passageway of the soul into the Infinite."

He might have said the words himself. The thought lay in him while she uttered it. Evocation everywhere in life was as true as assimilation. Nevertheless, he stared his companion full in the eyes with a touch of almost rude amazement. But no further questions prompted themselves; or, rather, he declined to ask them. He recalled, somehow uneasily, that in ceremonial the points of the compass have significance, standing for forces and activities that sleep there until invoked, and a passing light fell upon that curious midnight request in the corridor upstairs. These two were on the track of undesirable experiments, he thought... They wished to include him too.

"You go at night sometimes into the Desert?" he heard himself saying. It was impulsive and miscalculated. His feeling that it would be wise to change the conversation resulted in giving it fresh impetus instead.

"We saw you there—in the Wadi Hof," put in Vance, suddenly breaking his long silence; "you too sleep out, then? It means, you know, the Valley of Fear."

"We wondered—" It was Lady Statham's voice, and she leaned forward eagerly as she said it, then abruptly left the sentence incomplete. Henriot started; a sense of momentary acute discomfort again ran over him. The same second she continued, though obviously changing the phrase—"we wondered how you spent your day there, during the heat. But you paint, don't you? You draw, I mean?"

The commonplace question, he realised in every fibre of his being, meant something *they* deemed significant. Was it his talent for drawing that they sought to use him for? Even as he answered with a simple affirmative, he had a flash of intuition that might be fanciful, yet that might be true: that this extraordinary pair were intent upon some ceremony of evocation that should summon into actual physical expression some Power—some type of life—known long ago to ancient worship, and that they even sought to fix its bodily outline with the pencil—his pencil.

A gateway of incredible adventure opened at his feet. He balanced on the edge of knowing unutterable things. Here was a clue that might lead him towards the hidden Egypt he had ever craved to know. An awful hand was beckoning. The sands were shifting. He saw the million eyes of the Desert watching him from beneath the level lids of centuries. Speck by speck, and grain by grain, the sand that smothered memory lifted the countless wrappings that embalmed it.

And he was willing, yet afraid. Why in the world did he hesitate and shrink? Why was it that the presence of this silent, watching personality in the chair beside him kept caution still alive, with warning close behind? The pictures in his mind were gorgeously coloured. It was Richard Vance who somehow streaked them through with black. A thing of darkness, born of this man's unassertive presence, flitted ever across the scenery, marring its grandeur with something evil, petty, dreadful. He held a horrible thought alive. His mind was thinking venal purposes.

In Henriot himself imagination had grown curiously heated, fed by what had been suggested rather than actually said. Ideas of immensity crowded his brain, yet never assumed definite shape. They were familiar, even as this strange woman was familiar. Once, long ago, he had known them well; had even practised them beneath these bright Egyptian stars. Whence came this prodigious glad excitement in his heart, this sense of mighty Powers coaxed down to influence the very details of daily life? Behind them, for all their vagueness, lay an archetypal splendour, fraught with forgotten meanings. He had always been aware of it in this mysterious land, but it had ever hitherto eluded him. It hovered everywhere. He had felt it brooding behind the towering Colossi at Thebes, in the skeletons of wasted temples, in the uncouth comeliness of the Sphinx, and in the crude terror of the Pyramids even. Over the whole of Egypt hung its invisible wings. These were but isolated fragments of the Body that might express it. And the Desert remained its cleanest, truest symbol. Sand knew it closest. Sand might even give it bodily form and outline.

But, while it escaped description in his mind, as equally it eluded visualisation in his soul, he felt that it combined with its vastness something infinitely small as well. Of such wee particles is the giant Desert born...

Henriot started nervously in his chair, convicted once more of unconscionable staring; and at the same moment a group of hotel people, returning from a dance, passed through the hall and nodded him good-night. The scent of the women reached him; and with it the sound of their voices discussing personalities just left behind. A London atmosphere came with them. He caught trivial phrases, uttered in a drawling tone, and followed by the shrill laughter of a girl. They passed upstairs, discussing their little things, like marionettes upon a tiny stage.

But their passage brought him back to things of modern life, and to some standard of familiar measurement. The pictures that his soul had gazed at so deep within, he realised, were a pictorial transfer caught incompletely from this woman's vivid mind. He had seen the Desert as the grey, enormous Tomb where hovered still the Ka of ancient Egypt. Sand screened her visage with the veil of centuries. But She was there, and She was living. Egypt herself had pitched a temporary camp in him, and then moved on.

There was a momentary break, a sense of abruptness and dislocation. And then he became aware that Lady Statham had been speaking for some time before he caught her actual words, and that a certain change had come into her voice as also into her manner.

## V

SHE was leaning closer to him, her face suddenly glowing and alive. Through the stone figure coursed the fires of a passion that deepened the coal-black eyes and communicated a hint of light—of exaltation—to her whole person. It was incredibly moving. To this deep passion was due the power he had felt. It was her entire life; she lived for it, she would die for it. Her calmness of manner enhanced its effect. Hence the strength of those first impressions that had stormed him. The woman had belief; however wild and strange, it was sacred to her. The secret of her influence was—conviction.

His attitude shifted several points then. The wonder in him passed over into awe. The things she knew were real. They were not merely imaginative speculations.

"I knew I was not wrong in thinking you in sympathy with this line of thought," she was saying in lower voice, steady with earnestness, and as though she had read his mind. "You, too, know, though perhaps you hardly realise that you know. It lies so deep in you that you only get vague feelings of it—intimations of memory. Isn't that the case?"

Henriot gave assent with his eyes; it was the truth.

"What we know instinctively," she continued, "is simply what we are trying to remember. Knowledge is memory." She paused a moment watching his face closely. "At least, you are free from that cheap scepticism which labels these old beliefs as superstition." It was not even a question.

"I—worship real belief—of any kind," he stammered, for her words and the close proximity of her atmosphere caused a strange upheaval in his heart that he could not account for. He faltered in his speech. "It is the most vital quality in life—rarer than deity." He was using her own phrases even. "It is creative. It constructs the world anew—"

"And may reconstruct the old."

She said it, lifting her face above him a little, so that her eyes looked down into his own. It grew big and somehow masculine. It was the face of a priest, spiritual power in it. Where, oh where in the echoing Past had he known this woman's soul? He saw her in another setting, a forest of columns dim about her, towering above giant aisles. Again he felt the Desert had come close. Into this tent-like hall of the hotel came the sifting of tiny sand. It heaped softly about the very furniture against his feet, blocking the exits of door and window. It shrouded the little present. The wind that brought it stirred a veil that had hung for ages motionless...

She had been saying many things that he had missed while his mind went searching. "There were types of life the Atlantean system knew it might revive—life unmanifested today in any bodily form," was the sentence he caught with his return to the actual present.

"A type of life?" he whispered, looking about him, as though to see who it was had joined them; "you mean a—soul? Some kind of soul, alien to humanity, or to—to any forms of living thing in the world today?" What she had been saying reached him somehow, it seemed, though he had not heard the words themselves. Still hesitating, he was yet so eager to hear. Already he felt she meant to include him in her purposes, and that in the end he must go willingly. So strong was her persuasion on his mind.

And he felt as if he knew vaguely what was coming. Before she answered his curious question—prompting it indeed—rose in his mind that strange idea of the Group-Soul: the theory that big souls cannot express themselves in a single individual, but need an entire group for their full manifestation.

He listened intently. The reflection that this sudden intimacy was unnatural, he rejected, for many conversations were really gathered into one. Long watching and preparation on both sides had cleared the way for the ripening of acquaintance into confidence—how long he dimly wondered? But if this conception of the Group-Soul was not new, the suggestion Lady Statham developed out of it was both new and startling—and yet always so curiously familiar. Its value for him lay, not in far-fetched evidence that supported it, but in the deep belief which made it a vital asset in an honest inner life.

"An individual," she said quietly, "one soul expressed completely in a single person, I mean, is exceedingly rare. Not often is a physical instrument found perfect enough to provide it with adequate expression. In the lower ranges of humanity—certainly in animal and insect life—one soul is shared by many. Behind a tribe of savages stands one Savage. A flock of birds is a single Bird, scattered through the consciousness of all. They wheel in mid-air, they migrate, they obey the deep intelligence called instinct—all as one. The life of any one lion is the life of all—the lion group-soul that manifests itself in the entire genus. An ant-heap is a single Ant; through the bees spreads the consciousness of a single Bee."

Henriot knew what she was working up to. In his eagerness to hasten disclosure he interrupted—

"And there may be types of life that have no corresponding bodily expression at all, then?" he asked as though the question were forced out of him. "They exist as Powers—unmanifested on the earth today?"

"Powers," she answered, watching him closely with unswerving stare, "that need a group to provide their body—their physical expression—if they came back."

"Came back!" he repeated below his breath.

But she heard him. "They once had expression. Egypt, Atlantis knew them—spiritual Powers that never visit the world today."

"Bodies," he whispered softly, "actual bodies?"

"Their sphere of action, you see, would be their body. And it might be physical outline. So potent a descent of spiritual life would select materials for its body where it could find them. Our conventional notion of a body—what is it? A single outline moving altogether in one direction. For little human souls, or fragments, this is sufficient. But for vaster types of soul an entire host would be required."

"A church?" he ventured. "Some Body of belief, you surely mean?"

She bowed her head a moment in assent. She was determined he should seize her meaning fully.

"A wave of spiritual awakening—a descent of spiritual life upon a nation," she answered slowly, "forms itself a church, and the body of true believers are its sphere of action. They are literally its bodily expression. Each individual believer is a corpuscle in that Body. The Power has provided itself with a vehicle of manifestation. Otherwise we could not know it. And the more real the belief of each individual, the more perfect the expression of the spiritual life behind them all. A Group-soul walks the earth. Moreover, a nation naturally devout could attract a type of soul unknown to a nation that denies all faith. Faith brings back the gods... But today belief is dead, and Deity has left the world."

She talked on and on, developing this main idea that in days of older faiths there were deific types of life upon the earth, evoked by worship and beneficial to humanity. They had long ago withdrawn because the worship which brought them down had died the death. The world had grown pettier. These vast centres of Spiritual Power found no "Body" in which they now could express themselves or manifest... Her thoughts and phrases poured over him like sand. It was always sand he felt—burying the Present and uncovering the Past...

He tried to steady his mind upon familiar objects, but wherever he looked Sand stared him in the face. Outside these trivial walls the Desert lay listening. It lay waiting too. Vance himself had dropped out of recognition. He belonged to the world of things today. But this woman and himself stood thousands of years away, beneath the columns of a Temple in the sands. And the sands were moving. His feet went shifting with them... running down vistas of ageless memory that woke terror by their sheer immensity of distance...

Like a muffled voice that called to him through many veils and wrappings, he heard her describe the stupendous Powers that evocation might coax down again among the world of men.

"To what useful end?" he asked at length, amazed at his own temerity, and because he knew instinctively the answer in advance. It rose through these layers of coiling memory in his soul.

"The extension of spiritual knowledge and the widening of life," she answered. "The link with the 'unearthly kingdom' wherein this ancient system went forever searching, would be re-established. Complete rehabilitation might follow. Portions—little portions of these Powers—expressed themselves naturally once in certain animal types, instinctive life that did not deny or reject them. The worship of sacred animals was the relic of a once gigantic system of evocation—not of monsters," and she smiled sadly, "but of Powers that were willing and ready to descend when worship summoned them."

Again, beneath his breath, Henriot heard himself murmur—his own voice startled him as he whispered it "Actual bodily shape and outline?"

"Material for bodies is everywhere," she answered, equally low; "dust to which we all return; sand, if you prefer it, fine, fine sand. Life moulds it easily enough, when that life is potent."

A certain confusion spread slowly through his mind as he heard her. He lit a cigarette and smoked some minutes in silence. Lady Statham and her nephew waited for him to speak. At length, after some inner battling and hesitation, he put the question that he knew they waited for. It was impossible to resist any longer.

"It would be interesting to know the method," he said, "and to revive, perhaps, by experiment—"

Before he could complete his thought, she took him up:

"There are some who claim to know it," she said gravely—her eyes a moment masterful. "A clue, thus followed, might lead to the entire reconstruction I spoke of"

"And the method?" he repeated faintly.

"Evoke the Power by ceremonial evocation—the ritual is obtainable—and note the form it assumes. Then establish it. This shape or outline once secured, could then be made permanent—a mould for its return at will—its natural physical expression here on earth."

"Idol!" he exclaimed.

"Image," she replied at once. "Life, before we can know it must have a body. Our souls, in order to manifest here, need a material vehicle."

"And—to obtain this form or outline?" he began; "to fix it, rather?"

"Would be required the clever pencil of a fearless looker-on—some one not engaged in the actual evocation. This form, accurately made permanent in solid matter, say in stone, would provide a channel always open. Experiment, properly speaking, might then begin. The cisterns of Power behind would be accessible."

"An amazing proposition!" Henriot exclaimed. What surprised him was that he felt no desire to laugh, and little even to doubt.

"Yet known to every religion that ever deserved the name," put in Vance like a voice from a distance. Blackness came somehow with his interruption—a touch of darkness. He spoke eagerly.

To all the talk that followed, and there was much of it, Henriot listened with but half an ear. This one idea stormed through him with an uproar that killed attention. Judgment was held utterly in abeyance. He carried away from it some vague suggestion that this woman had hinted at previous lives she half remembered, and that every year she came to Egypt, haunting the sands and temples in the effort to recover lost clues. And he recalled afterwards that she said, "This all came to me as a child, just as though it was something half remembered." There was the further suggestion that he himself was not unknown to her; that they, too, had met before. But this, compared to the grave certainty of the rest, was merest fantasy that did not hold his attention. He answered, hardly knowing what he said. His preoccupation with other thoughts deep down was so intense, that he was probably barely polite, uttering empty phrases, with his mind elsewhere. His one desire was to escape and be alone, and it was with genuine relief that he presently excused himself and went upstairs to bed. The halls, he noticed, were empty; an Arab servant waited to put the lights out. He walked up, for the lift had long ceased running.

And the magic of old Egypt stalked beside him. The studies that had fascinated his mind in earlier youth returned with the power that had subdued his mind in boyhood. The cult of Osiris woke in his blood again; Horus and Nephthys stirred in their long-forgotten centres. There revived in him, too long buried, the awful glamour of those liturgal rites and vast body of observances, those spells and formulae of incantation of the oldest known rescension that years ago had captured his imagination and belief—the Book of the Dead. Trumpet voices called to his heart again across the desert of some dim past. There were forms of life—impulses from the Creative Power which is the Universe—other than the soul of man. They could be known. A spiritual exaltation, roused by the words and presence of this singular woman, shouted to him as he went.

Then, as he closed his bedroom door, carefully locking it, there stood beside him—Vance. The forgotten figure of Vance came up close—the watching eyes, the simulated interest, the feigned belief, the detective mental attitude, these broke through the grandiose panorama, bringing darkness. Vance, strong personality that hid behind assumed nonentity for some purpose of his own, intruded with sudden violence, demanding an explanation of his presence.

And, with an equal suddenness, explanation offered itself then and there. It came unsought, its horror of certainty utterly unjustified; and it came in this unexpected fashion

Behind the interest and acquiescence of the man ran—fear: but behind the vivid fear ran another thing that Henriot now perceived was vile. For the first time in his life, Henriot knew it at close quarters, actual, ready to operate. Though familiar enough in daily life to be of common occurrence, Henriot had never realised it as he did now, so close and terrible. In the same way he had never *realised* that he would die—vanish from the busy world of men and women, forgotten as though he had never existed, an eddy of wind-blown dust. And in the man named Richard Vance this thing was close upon blossom. Henriot could not name it to himself. Even in thought it appalled him.

He undressed hurriedly, almost with the child's idea of finding safety between the sheets. His mind undressed itself as well. The business of the day laid itself automatically aside; the will sank down; desire grew inactive. Henriot was exhausted. But, in that stage towards slumber when thinking stops, and only fugitive pictures pass across the mind in shadowy dance, his brain ceased shouting its mechanical explanations, and his soul unveiled a peering eye. Great limbs of memory, smothered by the activities of the Present, stirred their stiffened lengths through the sands of long ago—sands this woman had begun to excavate from some far-off pre-existence they had surely known together. Vagueness and certainty ran hand in hand. Details were unrecoverable, but the emotions in which they were embedded moved.

He turned restlessly in his bed, striving to seize the amazing clues and follow them. But deliberate effort hid them instantly again; they retired instantly into the subconsciousness. With the brain of this body he now occupied they had nothing to do. The brain stored memories of each life only. This ancient script was graven in his soul. Subconsciousness alone could interpret and reveal. And it was his subconscious memory that Lady Statham had been so busily excavating.

Dimly it stirred and moved about the depths within him, never clearly seen, indefinite, felt as a yearning after unrecoverable knowledge. Against the darker background of Vance's fear and sinister purpose—both of this present life, and recent—he saw the grandeur of this woman's impossible dream, and *knew*, beyond argument or reason, that it was true. Judgment and will asleep, he left the impossibility aside, and took the grandeur. The Belief of Lady Statham was not credulity and superstition; it was Memory. Still to this day, over the sands of Egypt, hovered immense spiritual potencies, so vast that they could only know physical expression in a group—in many. Their sphere of bodily manifestation must be a host, each individual unit in that host a corpuscle in the whole.

The wind, rising from the Lybian wastes across the Nile, swept up against the exposed side of the hotel, and made his windows rattle—the old, sad winds of Egypt. Henriot got out of bed to fasten the outside shutters. He stood a moment and watched the moon floating down behind the Sakkara Pyramids. The Pleiades and Orion's Belt hung brilliantly; the Great Bear was close to the horizon. In the sky above the Desert swung ten thousand stars. No sounds rose from the streets of Hebuan. The tide of sand was coming slowly in.

And a flock of enormous thoughts swooped past him from fields of this unbelievable, lost memory. The Desert, pale in the moon, was coextensive with the night, too huge for comfort or understanding, yet charged to the brim with infinite peace. Behind its majesty of silence lay whispers of a vanished language that once could call with power upon mighty spiritual Agencies. Its skirts were folded now, but, slowly across the leagues of sand, they began to stir and rearrange themselves. He grew suddenly aware of this enveloping shroud of sand—as the raw material of bodily expression: Form.

The sand was in his imagination and his mind. Shaking loosely the folds of its gigantic skirts, it rose; it moved a little towards him. He saw the eternal countenance of the Desert watching him—immobile and unchanging behind these shifting veils the winds laid so carefully over it. Egypt, the ancient Egypt, turned in her vast sarcophagus of Desert, wakening from her sleep of ages at the Belief of approaching worshippers.

Only in this insignificant manner could he express a letter of the terrific language that crowded to seek expression through his soul... He closed the shutters and carefully fastened them. He turned to go back to bed, curiously trembling. Then, as he did so, the whole singular delusion caught him with a shock that held him motionless. Up rose the stupendous apparition of the entire Desert and stood behind him on that balcony. Swift as thought, in silence, the Desert stood on end against his very face. It towered across the sky, hiding Orion and the moon; it dipped below the horizons. The whole grey sheet of it rose up before his eyes and stood. Through its unfolding skirts ran ten thousand eddies of swirling sand as the creases of its graveclothes smoothed themselves out in moonlight. And a bleak, scarred countenance, huge as a planet, gazed down into his own...

Through his dreamless sleep that night two things lay active and awake... in the subconscious part that knows no slumber. They were incongruous. One was evil, small and human; the other unearthly and sublime. For the memory of the fear that haunted Vance, and the sinister cause of it, pricked at him all night long. But behind, beyond this common, intelligible emotion, lay the crowding wonder that caught his soul with glory:

The Sand was stirring, the Desert was awake. Ready to mate with them in material form, brooded close the Ka of that colossal Entity that once expressed itself through the myriad life of ancient Egypt.

## VI

NEXT day, and for several days following, Henriot kept out of the path of Lady Statham and her nephew. The acquaintanceship had grown too rapidly to be quite comfortable. It was easy to pretend that he took people at their face value, but it was a pose; one liked to know something of antecedents. It was otherwise difficult to "place" them. And Henriot, for the life of him, could not "place" these two. His Subconsciousness brought explanation when it came—but the Subconsciousness is only temporarily active. When it retired he floundered without a rudder, in confusion.

With the flood of morning sunshine the value of much she had said evaporated. Her presence alone had supplied the key to the cipher. But while the indigestible portions he rejected, there remained a good deal he had already assimilated. The discomfort remained; and with it the grave, unholy reality of it all. It was something more than theory. Results would follow—if he joined them. He would witness curious things.

The force with which it drew him brought hesitation. It operated in him like a shock that numbs at first by its abrupt arrival, and needs time to realise in the right proportions to the rest of life. These right proportions, however, did not come readily, and his emotions ranged between sceptical laughter and complete acceptance. The one detail he felt certain of was this dreadful thing he had divined in Vance. Trying hard to disbelieve it, he found he could not. It was true. Though without a shred of real evidence to support it, the horror of it remained. He knew it in his very bones.

And this, perhaps, was what drove him to seek the comforting companionship of folk he understood and felt at home with. He told his host and hostess about the strangers, though omitting the actual conversation because they would merely smile in blank miscomprehension. But the moment he described the strong black eyes beneath the level eyelids, his hostess turned with a start, her interest deeply, roused: "Why, it's that awful Statham woman," she exclaimed, "that must be Lady Statham, and the man she calls her nephew."

"Sounds like it, certainly," her husband added. "Felix, you'd better clear out. They'll bewitch you too."

And Henriot bridled, yet wondering why he did so. He drew into his shell a little, giving the merest sketch of what had happened. But he listened closely while these two practical old friends supplied him with information in the gossiping way that human nature loves. No doubt there was much embroidery, and more perversion, exaggeration too, but the account evidently rested upon some basis of solid foundation for all that. Smoke and fire go together always.

"He *is* her nephew right enough," Mansfield corrected his wife, before proceeding to his own man's form of elaboration; "no question about that, I believe. He's her favourite nephew, and she's as rich as a pig. He follows her out here every year, waiting for her empty shoes. But they *are* an unsavoury couple. I've met 'em in various parts, all over Egypt, but they always come back to Hebuan in the end. And the stories about them are simply legion. You remember—" he turned hesitatingly to his wife—"some people, I heard," he changed his sentence, "were made quite ill by her."

"I'm sure Felix ought to know, yes," his wife boldly took him up, "my niece, Fanny, had the most extraordinary experience." She turned to Henriot. "Her room was next to Lady Statham in some hotel or other at Assouan or Edfu, and one night she woke and heard a kind of mysterious chanting or intoning next her. Hotel doors are so dreadfully thin. There was a funny smell too, like incense of something sickly, and a man's voice kept chiming in. It went on for hours, while she lay terrified in bed—"

"Frightened, you say?" asked Henriot.

"Out of her skin, yes; she said it was so uncanny—made her feel icy. She wanted to ring the bell, but was afraid to leave her bed. The room was full of—of things, yet she could see nothing. She *felt* them, you see. And after a bit the sound of this sing-song voice so got on her nerves, it half dazed her— a kind of enchantment—she felt choked and suffocated. And then—" It was her turn to hesitate.

"Tell it all," her husband said, quite gravely too.

"Well—something came in. At least, she describes it oddly, rather; she said it made the door bulge inwards from the next room, but not the door alone; the walls bulged or swayed as if a huge thing pressed against them from the other side. And at the same moment her windows—she had two big balconies, and the venetian shutters were fastened—both her windows *darkened*—though it was two in the morning and pitch dark outside. She said it was all one thing—trying to get in; just as water, you see, would rush in through every hole and opening it could find, and all at once. And in spite of her terror—that's the odd part of it—she says she felt a kind of splendour in her—a sort of elation."

"She saw nothing?"

"She says she doesn't remember. Her senses left her, I believe— though she won't admit it."

"Fainted for a minute, probably," said Mansfield.

"So there it is," his wife concluded, after a silence. "And that's true. It happened to my niece, didn't it, John?"

Stories and legendary accounts of strange things that the presence of these two brought poured out then. They were obviously somewhat mixed, one account borrowing picturesque details from another, and all in disproportion, as when people tell stories in a language they are little familiar with. But, listening with avidity, yet also with uneasiness, somehow, Henriot put two and two together. Truth stood behind them somewhere. These two held traffic with the powers that ancient Egypt knew.

"Tell Felix, dear, about the time you met the nephew—horrid creature—in the Valley of the Kings," he heard his wife say presently. And Mansfield told it plainly enough, evidently glad to get it done, though.

"It was some years ago now, and I didn't know who he was then, or anything about him. I don't know much more now—except that he's a dangerous sort of charlatan-devil, I think. But I came across him one night up there by Thebes in the Valley of the Kings—you know, where they buried all their Johnnies with so much magnificence and processions and masses, and all the rest. It's the most astounding, the most haunted place you ever saw, gloomy, silent, full of gorgeous lights and shadows that seem alive—terribly impressive; it makes you creep and shudder. You feel old Egypt watching you."

"Get on, dear," said his wife.

"Well, I was coming home late on a blasted lazy donkey, dog-tired into the bargain, when my donkey boy suddenly ran for his life and left me alone. It was after sunset. The sand was red and shining, and the big cliffs sort of fiery. And my donkey stuck its four feet in the ground and wouldn't budge. Then, about fifty yards away, I saw a fellow— European apparently—doing something—Heaven knows what, for I can't describe it—among the boulders that lie all over the ground there. Ceremony, I suppose you'd call it. I was so interested that at first I watched. Then I saw he wasn't alone. There were a lot of moving things round him, towering big things, that came and went like shadows. That twilight is fearfully bewildering; perspective changes, and distance gets all confused. It's fearfully hard to see properly. I only remember that I got off my donkey and went up closer, and when I was within a dozen yards of him—well, it sounds such rot, you know, but I swear the things suddenly rushed off and left him there alone. They went with a roaring noise like wind; shadowy but tremendously big, they were, and they vanished up against the fiery precipices as though they slipped bang into the stone itself. The only thing I can think of to describe 'em is—well, those sand-storms the Khamasin raises—the hot winds, you know."

"They probably *were* sand," his wife suggested, burning to tell another story of her own.

"Possibly, only there wasn't a breath of wind, and it was hot as blazes—and—I had such extraordinary sensations—never felt anything like it before—wild and exhilarated—drunk, I tell you, drunk."

"You saw them?" asked Henriot. "You made out their shape at all, or outline?"

"Sphinx," he replied at once, "for all the world like sphinxes. You know the kind of face and head these limestone strata in the Desert take—great visages with square Egyptian head-dresses where the driven sand has eaten away the softer stuff beneath? You see it everywhere— enormous idols they seem, with faces and eyes and lips awfully like the sphinx—well, that's the nearest I can get to it." He puffed his pipe hard. But there was no sign of levity in him. He told the actual truth as far as in him lay, yet half ashamed of what he told. And a good deal he left out, too.

"She's got a face of the same sort, that Statham horror," his wife said with a shiver. "Reduce the size, and paint in awful black eyes, and you've got her exactly—a living idol." And all three laughed, yet a laughter without merriment in it.

"And you spoke to the man?"

"I did," the Englishman answered, "though I confess I'm a bit ashamed of the way I spoke. Fact is, I was excited, thunderingly excited, and felt a kind of anger. I wanted to kick the beggar for practising such bally rubbish, and in such a place too. Yet all the time—well, well, I believe it was sheer funk now," he laughed; "for I felt uncommonly queer out there in the dusk, alone with—with that kind of business; and I was angry with myself for feeling it. Anyhow, I went up—I'd lost my donkey boy as well, remember—and slated him like a dog. I can't remember what I said exactly—only that he stood and stared at me in silence. That made it worse—seemed twice as real then. The beggar said no single word the whole time. He signed to me with one hand to clear out. And then, suddenly out of nothing—she—that woman—appeared and stood beside him. I never saw her come. She must have been behind some boulder or other, for she simply rose out of the ground. She stood there and stared at me too—bang in the face. She was turned towards the sunset—what was left of it in the west—and her black eyes shone like—ugh I can't describe it—it was shocking."

"She spoke?"

"She said five words—and her voice—it'll make you laugh—it was metallic like a gong: 'You are in danger here.' That's all she said. I simply turned and cleared out as fast as ever I could. But I had to go on foot. My donkey had followed its boy long before. I tell you—smile as you may—my blood was all curdled for an hour afterwards."

Then he explained that he felt some kind of explanation or apology was due, since the couple lodged in his own hotel, and how he approached the man in the smoking-room after dinner. A conversation resulted—the man was quite intelligent after all—of which only one sentence had remained in his mind.

"Perhaps you can explain it, Felix. I wrote it down, as well as I could remember. The rest confused me beyond words or memory; though I must confess it did not seem—well, not utter rot exactly. It was about astrology and rituals and the worship of the old Egyptians, and I don't know what else besides. Only, he made it intelligible and almost sensible, if only I could have got the hang of the thing enough to remember it. You know," he added, as though believing in spite of himself, "there *is* a lot of that wonderful old Egyptian religious business still hanging about in the atmosphere of this place, say what you like."

"But this sentence?" Henriot asked. And the other went off to get a note-book where he had written it down.

"He was jawing, you see," he continued when he came back, Henriot and his wife having kept silence meanwhile, "about direction being of importance in religious ceremonies, West and North symbolising certain powers, or something of the kind, why people turn to the East and all that sort of thing, and speaking of the whole Universe as if it had living forces tucked away in it that expressed themselves somehow when roused up. That's how I remember it anyhow. And then he said this thing—in answer to some fool question probably that I put." And he read out of the note-book:

"'You were in danger because you came through the Gateway of the West, and the Powers from the Gateway of the East were at that moment rising, and therefore in direct opposition to you.'"

Then came the following, apparently a simile offered by way of explanation. Mansfield read it in a shamefaced tone, evidently prepared for laughter:

"'Whether I strike you on the back or in the face determines what kind of answering force I rouse in you. Direction is significant.' And he said it was the period called the Night of Power—time when the Desert encroaches and spirits are close."

And tossing the book aside, he lit his pipe again and waited a moment to hear what might be said. "Can you explain such gibberish?" he asked at length, as neither of his listeners spoke. But Henriot said he couldn't. And the wife then took up her own tale of stories that had grown about this singular couple.

These were less detailed, and therefore less impressive, but all contributed something towards the atmosphere of reality that framed the entire picture. They belonged to the type one hears at every dinner party in Egypt—stories of the vengeance mummies seem to take on those who robbed them, desecrating their peace of centuries; of a woman wearing a necklace of scarabs taken from a princess's tomb, who felt hands about her throat to strangle her; of little Ka figures, Pasht goddesses, amulets and the rest, that brought curious disaster to those who kept them. They are many and various, astonishingly circumstantial often, and vouched for by persons the reverse of credulous. The modern superstition that haunts the desert gullies with Afreets has nothing in common with them. They rest upon a basis of indubitable experience; and they remain—inexplicable. And about the personalities of Lady Statham and her nephew they crowded like flies attracted by a dish of fruit. The Arabs, too, were afraid of her. She had difficulty in getting guides and dragomen.

"My dear chap," concluded Mansfield, "take my advice and have nothing to do with 'em. There *is* a lot of queer business knocking about in this old country, and people like that know ways of reviving it somehow. It's upset you already; you looked scared, I thought, the moment you came in." They laughed, but the Englishman was in earnest. "I tell you what," he added, "we'll go off for a bit of shooting together. The fields along the Delta are packed with birds now: they're home early this year on their way to the North. What d'ye say, eh?"

But Henriot did not care about the quail shooting. He felt more inclined to be alone and think things out by himself. He had come to his friends for comfort, and instead they had made him uneasy and excited. His interest had suddenly doubled. Though half afraid, he longed to know what these two were up to—to follow the adventure to the bitter end. He disregarded the warning of his host as well as the premonition in his own heart. The sand had caught his feet.

There were moments when he laughed in utter disbelief, but these were optimistic moods that did not last. He always returned to the feeling that truth lurked somewhere in the whole strange business, and that if he joined forces with them, as they seemed to wish, he would witness—well, he hardly knew what—but it enticed him as danger does the reckless man, or death the suicide. The sand had caught his mind.

He decided to offer himself to all they wanted—his pencil too. He would see—a shiver ran through him at the thought—what they saw, and know some eddy of that vanished tide of power and splendour the ancient Egyptian priesthood knew, and that perhaps was even common experience in the far-off days of dim Atlantis. The sand had caught his imagination too. He was utterly sand-haunted.

## VII

AND so he took pains, though without making definite suggestion, to place himself in the way of this woman and her nephew—only to find that his hints were disregarded. They left him alone, if they did not actually avoid him. Moreover, he rarely came across them now. Only at night, or in the queer dusk hours, he caught glimpses of them moving hurriedly off from the hotel, and always desert-wards. And their disregard, well calculated, enflamed his desire to the point when he almost decided to propose himself. Quite suddenly, then, the idea flashed through him—how do they come, these odd revelations, when the mind lies receptive like a plate sensitised by anticipation?—that they were waiting for a certain date, and, with the notion, came Mansfield's remark about "the Night of Power," believed in by the old Egyptian Calendar as a time when the supersensuous world moves close against the minds of men with all its troop of possibilities. And the thought, once lodged in its corner of imagination, grew strong. He looked it up. Ten days from now, he found, Leyel-el-Sud would be upon him, with a moon, too, at the full. And this strange hint of guidance he accepted. In his present mood, as he admitted, smiling to himself, he could accept anything. It was part of it, it belonged to the adventure. But, even while he persuaded himself that it was play, the solemn reality of what lay ahead increased amazingly, sketched darkly in his very soul.

These intervening days he spent as best he could—impatiently, a prey to quite opposite emotions. In the blazing sunshine he thought of it and laughed; but at night he lay often sleepless, calculating chances of escape. He never did escape, however. The Desert that watched little Hebuan with great, unwinking eyes watched also every turn and twist he made. Like this oasis, he basked in the sun of older time, and dreamed beneath forgotten moons. The sand at last had crept into his inmost heart. It sifted over him.

Seeking a reaction from normal, everyday things, he made tourist trips; yet, while recognising the comedy in his attitude, he never could lose sight of the grandeur that banked it up so hauntingly. These two contrary emotions grafted themselves on all he did and saw. He crossed the Nile at Bedrashem, and went again to the Tomb-World of Sakkara; but through all the chatter of veiled and helmeted tourists, the *bandar-log* of our modern Jungle, ran this dark under-stream of awe their monkey methods could not turn aside. One world lay upon another, but this modern layer was a shallow crust that, like the phenomenon of the "desert-film," a mere angle of falling light could instantly obliterate. Beneath the sand, deep down, he passed along the Street of Tombs, as he had often passed before, moved then merely by historical curiosity and admiration, but now by emotions for which he found no name. He saw the enormous sarcophagi of granite in their gloomy chambers where the sacred bulls once lay, swathed and embalmed like human beings, and, in the flickering candle light, the mood of ancient rites surged round him, menacing his doubts and laughter. The least human whisper in these subterraneans, dug out first four thousand years ago, revived ominous Powers that stalked beside him, forbidding and premonitive. He gazed at the spots where Mariette, unearthing them forty years ago, found fresh as of yesterday the marks of fingers and naked feet—of those who set the sixty-five ton slabs in position. And when he came up again into the sunshine he met the eternal questions of the pyramids, over-topping all his mental horizons. Sand blocked all the avenues of younger emotion, leaving the channels of something in him incalculably older, open and clean swept.

He slipped homewards, uncomfortable and followed, glad to be with a crowd—because he was otherwise alone with more than he could dare to think about. Keeping just ahead of his companions, he crossed the desert edge where the ghost of Memphis walks under rustling palm trees that screen no stone left upon another of all its mile-long populous splendours. For here was a vista his imagination could realise; here he could know the comfort of solid ground his feet could touch. Gigantic Ramases, lying on his back beneath their shade and staring at the sky, similarly helped to steady his swaying thoughts. Imagination could deal with these.

And daily thus he watched the busy world go to and fro to its scale of tips and bargaining, and gladly mingled with it, trying to laugh and study guidebooks, and listen to half-fledged explanations, but always seeing the comedy of his poor attempts. Not all those little donkeys, bells tinkling, beads shining, trotting beneath their comical burdens to the tune of shouting and belabouring, could stem this tide of deeper things the woman had let loose in the subconscious part of him. Everywhere he saw the mysterious camels go slouching through the sand, gurgling the water in their skinny, extended throats. Centuries passed between the enormous knee-stroke of their stride. And, every night, the sunsets restored the forbidding, graver mood, with their crimson, golden splendour, their strange green shafts of light, then—sudden twilight that brought the Past upon him with an awful leap. Upon the stage then stepped the figures of this pair of human beings, chanting their ancient plain-song of incantation in the moonlit desert, and working their rites of unholy evocation as the priests had worked them centuries before in the sands that now buried Sakkara fathoms deep.

Then one morning he woke with a question in his mind, as though it had been asked of him in sleep and he had waked just before the answer came. "Why do I spend my time sight-seeing, instead of going alone into the Desert as before? What has made me change?"

This latest mood now asked for explanation. And the answer, coming up automatically, startled him. It was so clear and sure—had been lying in the background all along. One word contained it:

Vance.

The sinister intentions of this man, forgotten in the rush of other emotions, asserted themselves again convincingly. The human horror, so easily comprehensible, had been smothered for the time by the hint of unearthly revelations. But it had operated all the time. Now it took the lead. He dreaded to be alone in the Desert with this dark picture in his mind of what Vance meant to bring there to completion. This abomination of a selfish human will returned to fix its terror in him. To be alone in the Desert meant to be alone with the imaginative picture of what Vance—he knew it with such strange certainty—hoped to bring about there.

There was absolutely no evidence to justify the grim suspicion. It seemed indeed far fetched enough, this connection between the sand and the purpose of an evil-minded, violent man. But Henriot saw it true. He could argue it away in a few minutes—easily. Yet the instant thought ceased, it returned, led up by intuition. It possessed him, filled his mind with horrible possibilities. He feared the Desert as he might have feared the scene of some atrocious crime. And, for the time, this dread of a merely human thing corrected the big seduction of the other—the suggested "supernatural."

Side by side with it, his desire to join himself to the purposes of the woman increased steadily. They kept out of his way apparently; the offer seemed withdrawn; he grew restless, unable to settle to anything for long, and once he asked the porter casually if they were leaving the hotel. Lady Statham had been invisible for days, and Vance was somehow never within speaking distance. He heard with relief that they had not gone—but with dread as well. Keen excitement worked in him underground. He slept badly. Like a schoolboy, he waited for the summons to an important examination that involved portentous issues, and contradictory emotions disturbed his peace of mind abominably.

## VIII

BUT it was not until the end of the week, when Vance approached him with purpose in his eyes and manner, that Henriot knew his fears unfounded, and caught himself trembling with sudden anticipation— because the invitation, so desired yet so dreaded, was actually at hand. Firmly determined to keep caution uppermost, yet he went unresistingly to a secluded corner by the palms where they could talk in privacy. For prudence is of the mind, but desire is of the soul, and while his brain of today whispered wariness, voices in his heart of long ago shouted commands that he knew he must obey with joy.

It was evening and the stars were out. Hebuan, with her fairy twinkling lights, lay silent against the Desert edge. The sand was at the flood. The period of the Encroaching of the Desert was at hand, and the deeps were all astir with movement. But in the windless air was a great peace. A calm of infinite stillness breathed everywhere. The flow of Time, before it rushed away backwards, stopped somewhere between the dust of stars and Desert. The mystery of sand touched every street with its unutterable softness.

And Vance began without the smallest circumlocution. His voice was low, in keeping with the scene, but the words dropped with a sharp distinctness into the other's heart like grains of sand that pricked the skin before they smothered him. Caution they smothered instantly; resistance too.

"I have a message for you from my aunt," he said, as though he brought an invitation to a picnic. Henriot sat in shadow, but his companion's face was in a patch of light that followed them from the windows of the central hall. There was a shining in the light blue eyes that betrayed the excitement his quiet manner concealed. "We are going—the day after tomorrow—to spend the night in the Desert; she wondered if, perhaps, you would care to join us?"

"For your experiment?" asked Henriot bluntly.

Vance smiled with his lips, holding his eyes steady, though unable to suppress the gleam that flashed in them and was gone so swiftly. There was a hint of shrugging his shoulders.

"It is the Night of Power—in the old Egyptian Calendar, you know," he answered with assumed lightness almost, "the final moment of Leyel-el-Sud, the period of Black Nights when the Desert was held to encroach with—with various possibilities of a supernatural order. She wishes to revive a certain practice of the old Egyptians. There *may* be curious results. At any rate, the occasion is a picturesque one—better than this cheap imitation of London life." And he indicated the lights, the signs of people in the hall dressed for gaieties and dances, the hotel orchestra that played after dinner.

Henriot at the moment answered nothing, so great was the rush of conflicting emotions that came he knew not whence. Vance went calmly on. He spoke with a simple frankness that was meant to be disarming. Henriot never took his eyes off him. The two men stared steadily at one another.

"She wants to know if you will come and help too—in a certain way only: not in the experiment itself precisely, but by watching merely and—" He hesitated an instant, half lowering his eyes.

"Drawing the picture," Henriot helped him deliberately.

"Drawing what you see, yes," Vance replied, the voice turned graver in spite of himself. "She wants—she hopes to catch the outlines of anything that happens—"

"Comes."

"Exactly. Determine the shape of anything that comes. You may remember your conversation of the other night with her. She is very certain of success."

This was direct enough at any rate. It was as formal as an invitation to a dinner, and as guileless. The thing he thought he wanted lay within his reach. He had merely to say yes. He did say yes; but first he looked about him instinctively, as for guidance. He looked at the stars twinkling high above the distant Libyan Plateau; at the long arms of the Desert, gleaming weirdly white in the moonlight, and reaching towards him down every opening between the houses; at the heavy mass of the Mokattam Hills, guarding the Arabian Wilderness with strange, peaked barriers, their sand-carved ridges dark and still above the Wadi Hof.

These questionings attracted no response. The Desert watched him, but it did not answer. There was only the shrill whistling cry of the lizards, and the sing-song of a white-robed Arab gliding down the sandy street. And through these sounds he heard his own voice answer: "I will come—yes. But how can I help? Tell me what you propose— your plan?"

And the face of Vance, seen plainly in the electric glare, betrayed his satisfaction. The opposing things in the fellow's mind of darkness fought visibly in his eyes and skin. The sordid motive, planning a dreadful act, leaped to his face, and with it a flash of this other yearning that sought unearthly knowledge, perhaps believed it too. No wonder there was conflict written on his features.

Then all expression vanished again; he leaned forward, lowering his voice.

"You remember our conversation about there being types of life too vast to manifest in a single body, and my aunt's belief that these were known to certain of the older religious systems of the world?"

"Perfectly."

"Her experiment, then, is to bring one of these great Powers back—we possess the sympathetic ritual that can rouse some among them to activity—and win it down into the sphere of our minds, our minds heightened, you see, by ceremonial to that stage of clairvoyant vision which can perceive them."

"And then?" They might have been discussing the building of a house, so naturally followed answer upon question. But the whole body of meaning in the old Egyptian symbolism rushed over him with a force that shook his heart. Memory came so marvellously with it.

"If the Power floods down into our minds with sufficient strength for actual form, to note the outline of such form, and from your drawing model it later in permanent substance. Then we should have means of evoking it at will, for we should have its natural Body—the form it built itself, its signature, image, pattern. A starting-point, you see, for more—leading, she hopes, to a complete reconstruction."

"It might take actual shape—assume a bodily form visible to the eye?" repeated Henriot, amazed as before that doubt and laughter did not break through his mind.

"We are on the earth," was the reply, spoken unnecessarily low since no living thing was within earshot, "we are in physical conditions, are we not? Even a human soul we do not recognise unless we see it in a body—parents provide the outline, the signature, the sigil of the returning soul. This," and he tapped himself upon the breast, "is the physical signature of that type of life we call a soul. Unless there is life of a certain strength behind it, no body forms. And, without a body, we are helpless to control or manage it—deal with it in any way. We could not know it, though being possibly *aware* of it."

"To be aware, you mean, is not sufficient?" For he noticed the italics Vance made use of.

"Too vague, of no value for future use," was the reply. "But once obtain the form, and we have the natural symbol of that particular Power. And a symbol is more than image, it is a direct and concentrated expression of the life it typifies—possibly terrific."

"It may be a body, then, this symbol you speak of."

"Accurate vehicle of manifestation; but 'body' seems the simplest word."

Vance answered very slowly and deliberately, as though weighing how much he would tell. His language was admirably evasive. Few perhaps would have detected the profound significance the curious words he next used unquestionably concealed. Henriot's mind rejected them, but his heart accepted. For the ancient soul in him was listening and aware.

"Life, using matter to express itself in bodily shape, first traces a geometrical pattern. From the lowest form in crystals, upwards to more complicated patterns in the higher organisations—there is always first this geometrical pattern as skeleton. For geometry lies at the root of all possible phenomena and is the mind's interpretation of a living movement towards shape that shall express it.' He brought his eyes closer to the other, lowering his voice again. "Hence," he said softly, "the signs in all the old magical systems—skeleton forms into which the Powers evoked descended; outlines those Powers automatically built up when using matter to express themselves. Such signs are material symbols of their bodiless existence. They attract the life they represent and interpret. Obtain the correct, true symbol, and the Power corresponding to it can approach—once roused and made aware. It has, you see, a ready-made mould into which it can come down."

"Once roused and made aware?" repeated Henriot questioningly, while this man went stammering the letters of a language that he himself had used too long ago to recapture fully.

"Because they have left the world. They sleep, unmanifested. Their forms are no longer known to men. No forms exist on earth today that could contain them. But they may be awakened," he added darkly. "They are bound to answer to the summons, if such summons be accurately made."

"Evocation?" whispered Henriot, more distressed than he cared to admit.

Vance nodded. Leaning still closer to his companion's face, he thrust his lips forward, speaking eagerly, earnestly, yet somehow at the same time, horribly: "And we want—my aunt would ask—your draughtsman's skill, or at any rate your memory afterwards, to establish the outline of anything that comes."

He waited for the answer, still keeping his face uncomfortably close.

Henriot drew back a little. But his mind was fully made up now. He had known from the beginning that he would consent, for the desire in him was stronger than all the caution in the world. The Past inexorably drew him into the circle of these other lives, and the little human dread Vance woke in him seemed just then insignificant by comparison. It was merely of Today.

"You two," he said, trying to bring judgment into it, "engaged in evocation, will be in a state of clairvoyant vision. Granted. But shall I, as an outsider, observing with unexcited mind, see anything, know anything, be aware of anything at all, let alone the drawing of it?"

"Unless," the reply came instantly with decision, "the descent of Power is strong enough to take actual material shape, the experiment is a failure. Anybody can induce subjective vision. Such fantasies have no value though. They are born of an overwrought imagination." And then he added quickly, as though to clinch the matter before caution and hesitation could take effect: "You must watch from the heights above. We shall be in the valley—the Wadi Hof is the place. You must not be too close—"

"Why not too close?" asked Henriot, springing forward like a flash before he could prevent the sudden impulse.

With a quickness equal to his own, Vance answered. There was no faintest sign that he was surprised. His self-control was perfect. Only the glare passed darkly through his eyes and went back again into the sombre soul that bore it.

"For your own safety," he answered low. "The Power, the type of life, she would waken is stupendous. And if roused enough to be attracted by the patterned symbol into which she would decoy it down, it will take actual, physical expression. But how? Where is the Body of Worshippers through whom it can manifest? There is none. It will, therefore, press inanimate matter into the service. The terrific impulse to form itself a means of expression will force all loose matter at hand towards it—sand, stones, all it can compel to yield—everything must rush into the sphere of action in which it operates. Alone, we at the centre, and you, upon the outer fringe, will be safe. Only—you must not come too close."

But Henriot was no longer listening. His soul had turned to ice. For here, in this unguarded moment, the cloven hoof had plainly shown itself. In that suggestion of a particular kind of danger Vance had lifted a corner of the curtain behind which crouched his horrible intention. Vance desired a witness of the extraordinary experiment, but he desired this witness, not merely for the purpose of sketching possible shapes that might present themselves to excited vision. He desired a witness for another reason too. Why had Vance put that idea into his mind, this idea of so peculiar danger? It might well have lost him the very assistance he seemed so anxious to obtain.

Henriot could not fathom it quite. Only one thing was clear to him. He, Henriot, was not the only one in danger.

They talked for long after that—far into the night. The lights went out, and the armed patrol, pacing to and fro outside the iron railings that kept the desert back, eyed them curiously. But the only other thing he gathered of importance was the ledge upon the cliff-top where he was to stand and watch; that he was expected to reach there before sunset and wait till the moon concealed all glimmer in the western sky, and—that the woman, who had been engaged for days in secret preparation of soul and body for the awful rite, would not be visible again until he saw her in the depths of the black valley far below, busy with this man upon audacious, ancient purposes.

## IX

AN hour before sunset Henriot put his rugs and food upon a donkey, and gave the boy directions where to meet him—a considerable distance from the appointed spot. He went himself on foot. He slipped in the heat along the sandy street, where strings of camels still go slouching, shuffling with their loads from the quarries that built the pyramids, and he felt that little friendly Hebuan tried to keep him back. But desire now was far too strong for caution. The desert tide was rising. It easily swept him down the long white street towards the enormous deeps beyond. He felt the pull of a thousand miles before him; and twice a thousand years drove at his back.

Everything still basked in the sunshine. He passed Al Hayat, the stately hotel that dominates the village like a palace built against the sky; and in its pillared colonnades and terraces he saw the throngs of people having late afternoon tea and listening to the music of a regimental band. Men in flannels were playing tennis, parties were climbing off donkeys after long excursions; there was laughter, talking, a babel of many voices. The gaiety called to him; the everyday spirit whispered to stay and join the crowd of lively human beings. Soon there would be merry dinner-parties, dancing, voices of pretty women, sweet white dresses, singing, and the rest. Soft eyes would question and turn dark. He picked out several girls he knew among the palms. But it was all many, oh so many leagues away; centuries lay between him and this modern world. An indescribable loneliness was in his heart. He went searching through the sands of forgotten ages, and wandering among the ruins of a vanished time. He hurried. Already the deeper water caught his breath.

He climbed the steep rise towards the plateau where the Observatory stands, and saw two of the officials whom he knew taking a siesta after their long day's work. He felt that his mind, too, had dived and searched among the heavenly bodies that live in silent, changeless peace remote from the world of men. They recognised him, these two whose eyes also knew tremendous distance close. They beckoned, waving the straws through which they sipped their drinks from tall glasses. Their voices floated down to him as from the starfields. He saw the sun gleam upon the glasses, and heard the clink of the ice against the sides. The stillness was amazing. He waved an answer, and passed quickly on. He could not stop this sliding current of the years.

The tide moved faster, the draw of piled-up cycles urging it. He emerged upon the plateau, and met the cooler Desert air. His feet went crunching on the "desert-film" that spread its curious dark shiny carpet as far as the eye could reach; it lay everywhere, unswept and smooth as when the feet of vanished civilizations trod its burning surface, then dipped behind the curtains Time pins against the stars. And here the body of the tide set all one way. There was a greater strength of current, draught and suction. He felt the powerful undertow. Deeper masses drew his feet sideways, and he felt the rushing of the central body of the sand. The sands were moving, from their foundation upwards. He went unresistingly with them.

Turning a moment, he looked back at shining little Hebuan in the blaze of evening light. The voices reached him very faintly, merged now in a general murmur. Beyond lay the strip of Delta vivid green, the palms, the roofs of Bedrashein, the blue laughter of the Nile with its flocks of curved felucca sails. Further still, rising above the yellow Lybian horizon, gloomed the vast triangles of a dozen Pyramids, cutting their wedge-shaped clefts out of a sky fast crimsoning through a sea of gold. Seen thus, their dignity imposed upon the entire landscape. They towered darkly, symbolic signatures of the ancient Powers that now watched him taking these little steps across their damaged territory.

He gazed a minute, then went on. He saw the big pale face of the moon in the east. Above the ever-silent Thing these giant symbols once interpreted, she rose, grand, effortless, half-terrible as themselves. And, with her, she lifted up this tide of the Desert that drew his feet across the sand to Wadi Hof. A moment later he dipped below the ridge that buried Hebuan and Nile and Pyramids from sight. He entered the ancient waters. Time then, in an instant, flowed back behind his footsteps, obliterating every trace. And with it his mind went too. He stepped across the gulf of centuries, moving into the Past. The Desert lay before him—an open tomb wherein his soul should read presently of things long vanished.

The strange half-lights of sunset began to play their witchery then upon the landscape. A purple glow came down upon the Mokattam Hills. Perspective danced its tricks of false, incredible deception. The soaring kites that were a mile away seemed suddenly close, passing in a moment from the size of gnats to birds with a fabulous stretch of wing. Ridges and cliffs rushed close without a hint of warning, and level places sank into declivities and basins that made him trip and stumble. That indescriable quality of the Desert, which makes timid souls avoid the hour of dusk, emerged; it spread everywhere, undisguised. And the bewilderment it brings is no vain, imagined thing, for it distorts vision utterly, and the effect upon the mind when familiar sight goes floundering is the simplest way in the world of dragging the anchor that grips reality. At the hour of sunset this bewilderment comes upon a man with a disconcerting swiftness. It rose now with all this weird rapidity. Henriot found himself enveloped at a moment's notice.

But, knowing well its effect, he tried to judge it and pass on. The other matters, the object of his journey chief of all, he refused to dwell upon with any imagination. Wisely, his mind, while never losing sight of it, declined to admit the exaggeration that over-elaborate thinking brings. "I'm going to witness an incredible experiment in which two enthusiastic religious dreamers believe firmly," he repeated to himself. "I have agreed to draw—anything I see. There may be truth in it, or they may be merely self-suggested vision due to an artificial exaltation of their minds. I'm interested—perhaps against my better judgment. Yet I'll see the adventure out—because I *must*."

This was the attitude he told himself to take. Whether it was the real one, or merely adopted to warm a cooling courage, he could not tell. The emotions were so complex and warring. His mind, automatically, kept repeating this comforting formula. Deeper than that he could not see to judge. For a man who knew the full content of his thought at such a time would solve some of the oldest psychological problems in the world. Sand had already buried judgment, and with it all attempt to explain the adventure by the standards acceptable to his brain of today. He steered subconsciously through a world of dim, huge, half-remembered wonders.

The sun, with that abrupt Egyptian suddenness, was below the horizon now. The pyramid field had swallowed it. Ra, in his golden boat, sailed distant seas beyond the Lybian wilderness. Henriot walked on and on, aware of utter loneliness. He was walking fields of dream, too remote from modern life to recall companionship he once had surely known. How dim it was, how deep and distant, how lost in this sea of an incalculable Past! He walked into the places that are soundless. The soundlessness of ocean, miles below the surface, was about him. He was with One only—this unfathomable, silent thing where nothing breathes or stirs—no thing but sunshine, shadow and the wind-borne sand. Slowly, in front, the moon climbed up the eastern sky, hanging above the silence—silence that ran unbroken across the horizons to where Suez gleamed upon the waters of a sister sea in motion. That moon was glinting now upon the Arabian Mountains by its desolate shores. Southwards stretched the wastes of Upper Egypt a thousand miles to meet the Nubian wilderness. But over all these separate Deserts stirred the soft whisper of the moving sand—deep murmuring message that Life was on the way to unwind Death. The Ka of Egypt, swathed in centuries of sand, hovered beneath the moon towards her ancient tenement.

For the transformation of the Desert now began in earnest. It grew apace. Before he had gone the first two miles of his hour's journey, the twilight caught the rocky hills and twisted them into those monstrous revelations of physiognomies they barely take the trouble to conceal even in the daytime. And, while he well understood the eroding agencies that have produced them, there yet rose in his mind a deeper interpretation lurking just behind their literal meanings. Here, through the motionless surfaces, that nameless thing the Desert ill conceals urged outwards into embryonic form and shape, akin, he almost felt, to those immense deific symbols of Other Life the Egyptians knew and worshipped. Hence, from the Desert, had first come, he felt, the unearthly life they typified in their monstrous figures of granite, evoked in their stately temples, and communed with in the ritual of their Mystery ceremonials.

This "watching" aspect of the Lybian Desert is really natural enough; but it is just the natural, Henriot knew, that brings the deepest revelations. The surface limestones, resisting the erosion, block themselves ominously against the sky, while the softer sand beneath sets them on altared pedestals that define their isolation splendidly. Blunt and unconquerable, these masses now watched him pass between them. The Desert surface formed them, gave them birth. They rose, they saw, they sank down again—waves upon a sea that carried forgotten life up from the depths below. Of forbidding, even menacing type, they somewhere mated with genuine grandeur. Unformed, according to any standard of human or of animal faces, they achieved an air of giant physiognomy which made them terrible. The unwinking stare of eyes—lidless eyes that yet ever succeed in hiding—looked out under well-marked, level eyebrows, suggesting a vision that included the motives and purposes of his very heart. They looked up grandly, understood why he was there, and then—slowly withdrew their mysterious, penetrating gaze.

The strata built them so marvellously up; the heavy, threatening brows; thick lips, curved by the ages into a semblance of cold smiles; jowls drooping into sandy heaps that climbed against the cheeks; protruding jaws, and the suggestion of shoulders just about to lift the entire bodies out of the sandy beds—this host of countenances conveyed a solemnity of expression that seemed everlasting, implacable as Death. Of human signature they bore no trace, nor was comparison possible between their kind and any animal life. They peopled the Desert here. And their smiles, concealed yet just discernible, went broadening with the darkness into a Desert laughter. The silence bore it underground. But Henriot was aware of it. The troop of faces slipped into that single, enormous countenance which is the visage of the Sand. And he saw it everywhere, yet nowhere.

Thus with the darkness grew his imaginative Interpretation of the Desert. Yet there was construction in it, a construction, moreover, that was *not* entirely his own. Powers, he felt, were rising, stirring, wakening from sleep. Behind the natural faces that he saw, these other things peered gravely at him as he passed. They used, as it were, materials that lay ready to their hand. Imagination furnished these hints of outline, yet the Powers themselves were real. There *was* this amazing movement of the sand. By no other manner could his mind have conceived of such a thing, nor dreamed of this simple, yet dreadful method of approach.

Approach! that was the word that first stood out and startled him. There was approach; something was drawing nearer. The Desert rose and walked beside him. For not alone these ribs of gleaming limestone contributed towards the elemental visages, but the entire hills, of which they were an outcrop, ran to assist in the formation, and were a necessary part of them. He was watched and stared at from behind, in front, on either side, and even from below. The sand that swept him on, kept even pace with him. It turned luminous too, with a patchwork of glimmering effect that was indescribably weird; lanterns glowed within its substance, and by their light he stumbled on, glad of the Arab boy he would presently meet at the appointed place.

The last torch of the sunset had flickered out, melting into the wilderness, when, suddenly opening at his feet, gaped the deep, wide gully known as Wadi Hof. Its curve swept past him.

This first impression came upon him with a certain violence: that the desolate valley rushed. He saw but a section of its curve and sweep, but through its entire length of several miles the Wadi fled away. The moon whitened it like snow, piling black shadows very close against the cliffs. In the flood of moonlight it went rushing past. It was emptying itself.

For a moment the stream of movement seemed to pause and look up into his face, then instantly went on again upon its swift career. It was like the procession of a river to the sea. The valley emptied itself to make way for what was coming. The approach, moreover, had already begun.

Conscious that he was trembling, he stood and gazed into the depths, seeking to steady his mind by the repetition of the little formula he had used before. He said it half aloud. But, while he did so, his heart whispered quite other things. Thoughts the woman and the man had sown rose up in a flock and fell upon him like a storm of sand. Their impetus drove off all support of ordinary ideas. They shook him where he stood, staring down into this river of strange invisible movement that was hundreds of feet in depth and a quarter of a mile across.

He sought to realise himself as he actually was today—mere visitor to Hebuan, tempted into this wild adventure with two strangers. But in vain. That seemed a dream, unreal, a transient detail picked out from the enormous Past that now engulfed him, heart and mind and soul. *This* was the reality.

The shapes and faces that the hills of sand built round him were the play of excited fancy only. By sheer force he pinned his thought against this fact: but further he could not get. There *were* Powers at work; they were being stirred, wakened somewhere into activity. Evocation had already begun. That sense of their approach as he had walked along from Hebuan was not imaginary. A descent of some type of life, vanished from the world too long for recollection, was on the way,—so vast that it would manifest itself in a group of forms, a troop, a host, an army. These two were near him somewhere at this very moment, already long at work, their minds driving beyond this little world. The valley was emptying itself—for the descent of life their ritual invited.

And the movement in the sand was likewise true. He recalled the sentences the woman had used. "My body," he reflected, "like the bodies life makes use of everywhere, is mere upright heap of earth and dust and—sand. Here in the Desert is the raw material, the greatest store of it in the world."

And on the heels of it came sharply that other thing: that this descending Life would press into its service all loose matter within its reach—to form that sphere of action which would be in a literal sense its Body.

In the first few seconds, as he stood there, he realised all this, and realised it with an overwhelming conviction it was futile to deny. The fast-emptying valley would later brim with an unaccustomed and terrific life. Yet Death hid there too—a little, ugly, insignificant death. With the name of Vance it flashed upon his mind and vanished, too tiny to be thought about in this torrent of grander messages that shook the depths within his soul. He bowed his head a moment, hardly knowing what he did. He could have waited thus a thousand years it seemed. He was conscious of a wild desire to run away, to hide, to efface himself utterly, his terror, his curiosity, his little wonder, and not be seen of anything. But it was all vain and foolish. The Desert saw him. The Gigantic knew that he was there. No escape was possible any longer. Caught by the sand, he stood amid eternal things. The river of movement swept him too.

These hills, now motionless as statues, would presently glide forward into the cavalcade, sway like vessels, and go past with the procession. At present only the contents, not the frame, of the Wadi moved. An immense soft brush of moonlight swept it empty for what was on the way... But presently the entire Desert would stand up and also go.

Then, making a sideways movement, his feet kicked against something soft and yielding that lay heaped upon the Desert floor, and Henriot discovered the rugs the Arab boy had carefully set down before he made full speed for the friendly lights of Hebuan. The sound of his departing footsteps had long since died away. He was alone.

The detail restored to him his consciousness of the immediate present, and, stooping, he gathered up the rugs and overcoat and began to make preparations for the night. But the appointed spot, whence he was to watch, lay upon the summit of the opposite cliffs. He must cross the Wadi bed and climb. Slowly and with labour he made his way down a steep cleft into the depth of the Wadi Hof, sliding and stumbling often, till at length he stood upon the floor of shining moonlight. It was very smooth; windless utterly; still as space; each particle of sand lay in its ancient place asleep. The movement, it seemed, had ceased.

He clambered next up the eastern side, through pitch-black shadows, and within the hour reached the ledge upon the top whence he could see below him, like a silvered map, the sweep of the valley bed. The wind nipped keenly here again, coming over the leagues of cooling sand. Loose boulders of splintered rock, started by his climbing, crashed and boomed into the depths. He banked the rugs behind him, wrapped himself in his overcoat, and lay down to wait. Behind him was a two-foot crumbling wall against which he leaned; in front a drop of several hundred feet through space. He lay upon a platform, therefore, invisible from the Desert at his back. Below, the curving Wadi formed a natural amphitheatre in which each separate boulder fallen from the cliffs, and even the little *silla* shrubs the camels eat, were plainly visible. He noted all the bigger ones among them. He counted them over half aloud.

And the moving stream he had been unaware of when crossing the bed itself, now began again. The Wadi went rushing past before the broom of moon-light. Again, the enormous and the tiny combined in one single strange impression. For, through this conception of great movement, stirred also a roving, delicate touch that his imagination felt as bird-like. Behind the solid mass of the Desert's immobility flashed something swift and light and airy. Bizarre pictures interpreted it to him, like rapid snap-shots of a huge flying panorama: he thought of darting dragon-flies seen at Hebuan, of children's little dancing feet, of twinkling butterflies—of birds. Chiefly, yes, of a flock of birds in flight, whose separate units formed a single entity. The idea of the Group-Soul possessed his mind once more. But it came with a sense of more than curiosity or wonder. Veneration lay behind it, a veneration touched with awe. It rose in his deepest thought that here was the first hint of a symbolical representation. A symbol, sacred and inviolable, belonging to some ancient worship that he half remembered in his soul, stirred towards interpretation through all his being.

He lay there waiting, wondering vaguely where his two companions were, yet fear all vanished because he felt attuned to a scale of things too big to mate with definite dread. There was high anticipation in him, but not anxiety. Of himself, as Felix Henriot, indeed, he hardly seemed aware. He was someone else. Or, rather, he was himself at a stage he had known once far, far away in a remote preexistence. He watched himself from dim summits of a Past, of which no further details were as yet recoverable.

Pencil and sketching-block lay ready to his hand. The moon rose higher, tucking the shadows ever more closely against the precipices. The silver passed into a sheet of snowy whiteness, that made every boulder clearly visible. Solemnity deepened everywhere into awe. The Wadi fled silently down the stream of hours. It was almost empty now. And then, abruptly, he was aware of change. The motion altered somewhere. It moved more quietly; pace slackened; the end of the procession that evacuated the depth and length of it went trailing past and turned the distant bend.

"It's slowing up," he whispered, as sure of it as though he had watched a regiment of soldiers filing by. The wind took off his voice like a flying feather of sound.

And there *was* a change. It had begun. Night and the moon stood still to watch and listen. The wind dropped utterly away. The sand ceased its shifting movement. The Desert everywhere stopped still, and turned.

Some curtain, then, that for centuries had veiled the world, drew softly up, leaving a shaded vista down which the eyes of his soul peered towards long-forgotten pictures. Still buried by the sands too deep for full recovery, he yet perceived dim portions of them—things once honoured and loved passionately. For once they had surely been to him the whole of life, not merely a fragment for cheap wonder to inspect. And they were curiously familiar, even as the person of this woman who now evoked them was familiar. Henriot made no pretence to more definite remembrance; but the haunting certainty rushed over him, deeper than doubt or denial, and with such force that he felt no effort to destroy it. Some lost sweetness of spiritual ambitions, lived for with this passionate devotion, and passionately worshipped as men today worship fame and money, revived in him with a tempest of high glory. Centres of memory stirred from an age-long sleep, so that he could have wept at their so complete obliteration hitherto. That such majesty had departed from the world as though it never had existed, was a thought for desolation and for tears. And though the little fragment he was about to witness might be crude in itself and incomplete, yet it was part of a vast system that once explored the richest realms of deity. The reverence in him contained a holiness of the night and of the stars; great, gentle awe lay in it too; for he stood, aflame with anticipation and humility, at the gateway of sacred things.

And this was the mood, no thrill of cheap excitement or alarm to weaken in, in which he first became aware that two spots of darkness he had taken all along for boulders on the snowy valley bed, were actually something very different. They were living figures. They moved. It was not the shadows slowly following the moonlight, but the stir of human beings who all these hours had been motionless as stone. He must have passed them unnoticed within a dozen yards when he crossed the Wadi bed, and a hundred times from this very ledge his eyes had surely rested on them without recognition. Their minds, he knew full well, had not been inactive as their bodies. The important part of the ancient ritual lay, he remembered, in the powers of the evoking mind.

Here, indeed, was no effective nor theatrical approach of the principal figures. It had nothing in common with the cheap external ceremonial of modern days. In forgotten powers of the soul its grandeur lay, potent, splendid, true. Long before he came, perhaps all through the day, these two had laboured with their arduous preparations. They were there, part of the Desert, when hours ago he had crossed the plateau in the twilight. To them—this woman's potent working of old ceremonial—had been due that singular rush of imagination he had felt. He had interpreted the Desert as alive. Here was the explanation. It *was* alive. Life was on the way. Long latent, her intense desire summoned it back to physical expression and the effect upon him had steadily increased as he drew nearer to the centre where she would focus its revival and return. Those singular impressions of being watched and accompanied were explained. A priest of this old-world worship performed a genuine evocation; a Great One of Vision revived the cosmic Powers.

Henriot watched the small figures far below him with a sense of dramatic splendour that only this association of far-off Memory could account for. It was their rising now, and the lifting of their arms to form a slow revolving outline, that marked the abrupt cessation of the larger river of movement; for the sweeping of the Wadi sank into sudden stillness, and these two, with motions not unlike some dance of deliberate solemnity, passed slowly through the moonlight to and fro. His attention fixed upon them both. All other movement ceased. They fastened the flow of Time against the Desert's body.

What happened then? How could his mind interpret an experience so long denied that the power of expression, as of comprehension, has ceased to exist? How translate this symbolical representation, small detail though it was, of a transcendent worship entombed for most so utterly beyond recovery? Its splendour could never lodge in minds that conceive Deity perched upon a cloud within telephoning distance of fashionable churches. How should he phrase it even to himself, whose memory drew up pictures from so dim a past that the language fit to frame them lay unreachable and lost?

Henriot did not know. Perhaps he never yet has known. Certainly, at the time, he did not even try to think. His sensations remain his own—untranslatable; and even that instinctive description the mind gropes for automatically, floundered, halted, and stopped dead. Yet there rose within him somewhere, from depths long drowned in slumber, a reviving power by which he saw, divined and recollected— remembered seemed too literal a word—

these elements of a worship he once had personally known. He, too, had worshipped thus. His soul had moved amid similar evocations in some aconian past, whence now the sand was being cleared away. Symbols of stupendous meaning flashed and went their way across the lifting mists. He hardly caught their meaning, so long it was since he had known them; yet they were familiar as the faces seen in dreams, and some hint of their spiritual significance left faint traces in his heart by means of which their grandeur reached towards interpretation. And all were symbols of a cosmic, deific nature; of Powers that only symbols can express— prayer-books and sacraments used in the Wisdom Religion of an older time, but today known only in the decrepit, literal shell which is their degradation.

Grandly the figures moved across the valley bed. The powers of the heavenly bodies once more joined them. They moved to the measure of a cosmic dance, whose rhythm was creative. The Universe partnered them.

There was this transfiguration of all common, external things. He realised that appearances were visible letters of a soundless language, a language he once had known. The powers of night and moon and desert sand married with points in the fluid stream of his inmost spiritual being that knew and welcomed them. He understood.

Old Egypt herself stooped down from her uncovered throne. The stars sent messengers. There was commotion in the secret, sandy places of the desert. For the Desert had grown Temple. Columns reared against the sky. There rose, from leagues away, the chanting of the sand.

The temples, where once this came to pass, were gone, their ruin questioned by alien hearts that knew not their spiritual meaning. But here the entire Desert swept in to form a shrine, and the Majesty that once was Egypt stepped grandly back across ages of denial and neglect. The sand was altar, and the stars were altar lights. The moon lit up the vast recesses of the ceiling, and the wind from a thousand miles brought in the perfume of her incense. For with that faith which shifts mountains from their sandy bed, two passionate, believing souls invoked the Ka of Egypt.

And the motions that they made, he saw, were definite harmonious patterns their dark figures traced upon the shining valley floor. Like the points of compasses, with stems invisible, and directed from the sky, their movements marked the outlines of great signatures of power—the sigils of the type of life they would evoke. It would come as a Procession. No individual outline could contain it. It needed for its visible expression—many. The descent of a group-soul, known to the worship of this mighty system, rose from its lair of centuries and moved hugely down upon them. The Ka, answering to the summons, would mate with sand. The Desert was its Body.

Yet it was not this that he had come to fix with block and pencil. Not yet was the moment when his skill might be of use. He waited, watched, and listened, while this river of half-remembered things went past him. The patterns grew beneath his eyes like music. Too intricate and prolonged to remember with accuracy later, he understood that they were forms of that root-geometry which lies behind all manifested life. The mould was being traced in outline. Life would presently inform it. And a singing rose from the maze of lines whose beauty was like the beauty of the constellations.

This sound was very faint at first, but grew steadily in volume. Although no echoes, properly speaking, were possible, these precipices caught stray notes that trooped in from the further sandy reaches. The figures certainly were chanting, but their chanting was not all he heard. Other sounds came to his ears from far away, running past him through the air from every side, and from incredible distances, all flocking down into the Wadi bed to join the parent note that summoned them. The Desert was giving voice. And memory, lifting her hood yet higher, showed more of her grey, mysterious face that searched his soul with questions. Had he so soon forgotten that strange union of form and sound which once was known to the evocative rituals of olden days?

Henriot tried patiently to disentangle this desert-music that their intoning voices woke, from the humming of the blood in his own veins. But he succeeded only in part. Sand was already in the air. There was reverberation, rhythm, measure; there was almost the breaking of the stream into great syllables. But was it due, this strange reverberation, to the countless particles of sand meeting in midair about him, or—to larger bodies, whose surfaces caught this friction of the sand and threw it back against his ears? The wind, now rising, brought particles that stung his face and hands, and filled his eyes with a minute fine dust that partially veiled the moonlight. But was not something larger, vaster than these particles composed now also on the way?

Movement and sound and flying sand thus merged themselves more and more in a single, whirling torrent. But Henriot sought no commonplace explanation of what he witnessed; and here was the proof that all happened in some vestibule of inner experience where the strain of question and answer had no business. One sitting beside him need not have seen anything at all. His host, for instance, from Hebuan, need not have been aware. Night screened it; Hebuan, as the whole of modern experience, stood in front of the screen. This thing took place behind it. He crouched motionless, watching in some reconstructed ante-chamber of the soul's pre-existence, while the torrent grew into a veritable tempest.

Yet Night remained unshaken; the veil of moonlight did not quiver; the stars dropped their slender golden pillars unobstructed. Calmness reigned everywhere as before. The stupendous representation passed on behind it all.

But the dignity of the little human movements that he watched had become now indescribable. The gestures of the arms and bodies invested themselves with consummate grandeur, as these two strode into the caverns behind manifested life and drew forth symbols that represented vanished Powers. The sound of their chanting voices broke in cadenced fragments against the shores of language. The words Henriot never actually caught, if words they were; yet he understood their purport—these Names of Power to which the type of returning life gave answer as they approached. He remembered fumbling for his drawing materials, with such violence, however, that the pencil snapped in two between his fingers as he touched it. For now, even here, upon the outer fringe of the ceremonial ground, there was a stir of forces that set the very muscles working in him before he had become aware of it...

Then came the moment when his heart leaped against his ribs with a sudden violence that was almost pain, standing a second later still as death. The lines upon the valley floor ceased their maze-like dance. All movement stopped. Sound died away. In the midst of this profound and dreadful silence the sigils lay empty there below him. They waited to be informed. For the moment of entrance had come at last. Life was close.

And he understood why this return of life had all along suggested a Procession and could be no mere momentary flash of vision. From such appalling distance did it sweep down towards the present.

Upon this network, then, of splendid lines, at length held rigid, the entire Desert reared itself with walls of curtained sand, that dwarfed the cliffs, the shouldering hills, the very sky. The Desert stood on end. As once before he had dreamed it from his balcony windows, it rose upright, towering, and close against his face. It built sudden ramparts to the stars that chambered the thing he witnessed behind walls no centuries could ever bring down crumbling into dust.

He himself, in some curious fashion, lay just outside, viewing it apart. As from a pinnacle, he peered within—peered down with straining eyes into the vast picture-gallery Memory threw abruptly open. And the picture spaced its noble outline thus against the very stars. He gazed between columns, that supported the sky itself, like pillars of sand that swept across the field of vanished years. Sand poured and streamed aside, laying bare the Past.

For down the enormous vista into which he gazed, as into an avenue running a million miles towards a tiny point, he saw this moving Thing that came towards him, shaking loose the countless veils of sand the ages had swathed about it. The Ka of buried Egypt wakened out of sleep. She had heard the potent summons of her old, time-honoured ritual. She came. She stretched forth an arm towards the worshippers who evoked her. Out of the Desert, out of the leagues of sand, out of the immeasurable wilderness which was her mummied Form and Body, she rose and came. And this fragment of her he would actually see—this little portion that was obedient to the stammered and broken ceremonial. The partial revelation he would witness—yet so vast, even this little bit of it, that it came as a Procession and a host.

For a moment there was nothing. And then the voice of the woman rose in a resounding cry that filled the Wadi to its furthest precipices, before it died away again to silence. That a human voice could produce such volume, accent, depth, seemed half incredible. The walls of towering sand swallowed it instantly. But the Procession of life, needing a group, a host, an army for its physical expression, reached at that moment the nearer end of the huge avenue. It touched the Present; it entered the world of men.

## X

THE entire range of Henriot's experience, read, imagined, dreamed, then fainted into unreality before the sheer wonder of what he saw. In the brief interval it takes to snap the fingers the climax was thus so hurriedly upon him. And, through it all, he was clearly aware of the pair of little human figures, man and woman, standing erect and commanding at the centre— knew, too, that she directed and controlled, while he in some secondary fashion supported her—and ever watched. But both were dim, dropped somewhere into a lesser scale. It was the knowledge of their presence, however, that alone enabled him to keep his powers in hand at all. But for these two *human* beings there within possible reach, he must have closed his eyes and swooned.

For a tempest that seemed to toss loose stars about the sky swept round about him, pouring up the pillared avenue in front of the procession. A blast of giant energy, of liberty, came through. Forwards and backwards, circling spirally about him like a whirlwind, came this revival of Life that sought to dip itself once more in matter and in form. It came to the accurate outline of its form they had traced for it. He held his mind steady enough to realise that it was akin to what men call a "descent" of some "spiritual movement" that wakens a body of believers into faith—a race, an entire nation; only that he experienced it in this brief, concentrated form before it has scattered down into ten thousand hearts. Here he knew its source and essence, behind the veil. Crudely, unmanageable as yet, he felt it, rushing loose behind appearances. There was this amazing impact of a twisting, swinging force that stormed down as though it would bend and coil the very ribs of the old stubborn hills. It sought to warm them with the stress of its own irresistible life-stream, to beat them into shape, and make pliable their obstinate resistance. Through all things the impulse poured and spread, like fire at white heat.

Yet nothing visible came as yet, no alteration in the actual landscape, no sign of change in things familiar to his eyes, while impetus thus fought against inertia. He perceived nothing formal. Calm and untouched himself, he lay outside the circle of evocation, watching, waiting, scarcely daring to breathe, yet well aware that any minute the scene would transfer itself from memory that was subjective to matter that was objective.

And then, in a flash, the bridge was built, and the transfer was accomplished. How or where he did not see, he could not tell. It was there before he knew it—there before his normal, earthly sight. He saw it, as he saw the hands he was holding stupidly up to shield his face. For this terrific release of force long held back, long stored up, latent for centuries, came pouring down the empty Wadi bed prepared for its reception. Through stones and sand and boulders it came in an impetuous hurricane of power. The liberation of its life appalled him. All that was free, untied, responded instantly like chaff; loose objects fled towards it; there was a yielding in the hills and precipices; and even in the mass of Desert which provided their foundation. The hinges of the Sand went creaking in the night. It shaped for itself a bodily outline.

Yet, most strangely, nothing definitely moved. How could he express the violent contradiction? For the immobility was apparent only—a sham, a counterfeit; while behind it the essential *being* of these things did rush and shift and alter. He saw the two things side by side: the outer immobility the senses commonly agree upon, *and* this amazing flying-out of their inner, invisible substance towards the vortex of attracting life that sucked them in. For stubborn matter turned docile before the stress of this returning life, taught somewhere to be plastic. It was being moulded into an approach to bodily outline. A mobile elasticity invaded rigid substance. The two officiating human beings, safe at the stationary centre, and himself, just outside the circle of operation, alone remained untouched and unaffected. But a few feet in any direction, for any one of them, meant—instantaneous death. They would be absorbed into the vortex, mere corpuscles pressed into the service of this sphere of action of a mighty Body...

How these perceptions reached him with such conviction, Henriot could never say. He knew it, because he *felt* it. Something fell about him from the sky that already paled towards the dawn. The stars themselves, it seemed, contributed some part of the terrific, flowing impulse that conquered matter and shaped itself this physical expression.

Then, before he was able to fashion any preconceived idea of what visible form this potent life might assume, he was aware of further change. It came at the briefest possible interval after the beginning—this certainty that, to and fro about him, as yet however indeterminate, passed Magnitudes that were stupendous as the desert. There was beauty in them too, though a terrible beauty hardly of this earth at all. A fragment of old Egypt had returned—a little portion of that vast Body of Belief that once was Egypt. Evoked by the worship of one human heart, passionately sincere, the Ka of Egypt stepped back to visit the material it once informed—the Sand.

Yet only a portion came. Henriot clearly realised that. It stretched forth an arm. Finding no mass of worshippers through whom it might express itself completely, it pressed inanimate matter thus into its service.

Here was the beginning the woman had spoken of—little opening clue. Entire reconstruction lay perhaps beyond.

And Henriot next realised that these Magnitudes in which this group-energy sought to clothe itself as visible form, were curiously familiar. It was not a new thing that he would see. Booming softly as they dropped downwards through the sky, with a motion the size of them rendered delusive, they trooped up the Avenue towards the central point that summoned them. He realised the giant flock of them—descent of fearful beauty—outlining a type of life denied to the world for ages, countless as this sand that blew against his skin. Careering over the waste of Desert moved the army of dark Splendours, that dwarfed any organic structure called a body men have ever known. He recognised them, cold in him of death, though the outlines reared higher than the pyramids, and towered up to hide whole groups of stars. Yes, he recognised them in their partial revelation, though he never saw the monstrous host complete. But, one of them, he realised, posing its eternal riddle to the sands, had of old been glimpsed sufficiently to seize its form in stone,— yet poorly seized, as a doll may stand for the dignity of a human being or a child's toy represent an engine that draws trains...

And he knelt there on his narrow ledge, the world of men forgotten. The power that caught him was too great a thing for wonder or for fear; he even felt no awe. Sensation of any kind that can be named or realised left him utterly. He forgot himself. He merely watched. The glory numbed him. Block and pencil, as the reason of his presence there at all, no longer existed...

Yet one small link remained that held him to some kind of consciousness of earthly things: he never lost sight of this—that, being just outside the circle of evocation, he was safe, and that the man and woman, being stationary in its untouched centre, were also safe. But—that a movement of six inches in any direction meant for any one of them instant death.

What was it, then, that suddenly strengthened this solitary link so that the chain tautened and he felt the pull of it? Henriot could not say. He came back with the rush of a descending drop to the realisation —dimly, vaguely, as from great distance—that he was with these two, now at this moment, in the Wadi Hof, and that the cold of dawn was in the air about him. The chill breath of the Desert made him shiver.

But at first, so deeply had his soul been dipped in this fragment of ancient worship, he could remember nothing more. Somewhere lay a little spot of streets and houses; its name escaped him. He had once been there; there were many people, but insignificant people. Who were they? And what had he to do with them? All recent memories had been drowned in the tide that flooded him from an immeasurable Past.

And who were they—these two beings, standing on the white floor of sand below him? For a long time he could not recover their names. Yet he remembered them; and, thus robbed of association that names bring, he saw them for an instant naked, and knew that one of them was evil. One of them was vile. Blackness touched the picture there. The man, his name still out of reach, was sinister, impure and dark at the heart. And for this reason the evocation had been partial only. The admixture of an evil motive was the flaw that marred complete success.

The names then flashed upon him—Lady Statham—Richard Vance.

Vance! With a horrid drop from splendour into something mean and sordid, Henriot felt the pain of it. The motive of the man was so insignificant, his purpose so atrocious. More and more, with the name, came back—his first repugnance, fear, suspicion. And human terror caught him. He shrieked. But, as in nightmare, no sound escaped his lips. He tried to move; a wild desire to interfere, to protect, to prevent, flung him forward—close to the dizzy edge of the gulf below. But his muscles refused obedience to the will. The paralysis of common fear rooted him to the rocks.

But the sudden change of focus instantly destroyed the picture; and so vehement was the fall from glory into meanness, that it dislocated the machinery of clairvoyant vision. The inner perception clouded and grew dark. Outer and inner mingled in violent, inextricable confusion. The wrench seemed almost physical. It happened all at once, retreat and continuation for a moment somehow combined. And, if he did not definitely see the awful thing, at least he was aware that it had come to pass. He knew it as positively as though his eye were glued against a magnifying lens in the stillness of some laboratory. He witnessed it.

The supreme moment of evocation was close. Life, through that awful sandy vortex, whirled and raged. Loose particles showered and pelted, caught by the draught of vehement life that moulded the substance of the Desert into imperial outline—when, suddenly, shot the little evil thing across that marred and blasted it.

Into the whirlpool flew forward a particle of material that was a human being. And the Group-Soul caught and used it.

The actual accomplishment Henriot did not claim to see. He was a witness, but a witness who could give no evidence. Whether the woman was pushed of set intention, or whether some detail of sound and pattern was falsely used to effect the terrible result, he was helpless to determine. He pretends no itemised account. She went. In one second, with appalling swiftness, she disappeared, swallowed out of space and time within that awful maw—one little corpuscle among a million through which the Life, now stalking the Desert wastes, moulded itself a troop-like Body. Sand took her.

There followed emptiness—a hush of unutterable silence, stillness, peace. Movement and sound instantly retired whence they came. The avenues of Memory closed; the Splendours all went down into their sandy tombs...

The moon had sunk into the Libyan wilderness; the eastern sky was red. The dawn drew out that wondrous sweetness of the Desert, which is as sister to the sweetness that the moonlight brings. The Desert settled back to sleep, huge, unfathomable, charged to the brim with life that watches, waits, and yet conceals itself behind the ruins of apparent desolation. And the Wadi, empty at his feet, filled slowly with the gentle little winds that bring the sunrise.

Then, across the pale glimmering of sand, Henriot saw a figure moving. It came quickly towards him, yet unsteadily, and with a hurry that was ugly. Vance was on the way to fetch him. And the horror of the man's approach struck him like a hammer in the face. He closed his eyes, sinking back to hide.

But, before he swooned, there reached him the clatter of the murderer's tread as he began to climb over the splintered rocks, and the faint echo of his voice, calling him by name—falsely and in pretence— for help.

HELOUAN.

## The Transfer

THE child first began to cry in the early afternoon—about three o'clock, to be exact. I remember the hour, because I had been listening with secret relief to the sound of the departing carriage. Those wheels fading into distance down the gravel drive with Mrs Frene, and her daughter Gladys to whom I was governess, meant for me some hours' welcome rest, and the June day was oppressively hot. Moreover, there was this excitement in the little country household that had told upon us all, but especially upon myself. This excitement, running delicately behind all the events of the morning, was due to some mystery, and the mystery was of course kept concealed from the governess. I had exhausted myself with guessing and keeping on the watch. For some deep and unexplained anxiety possessed me, so that I kept thinking of my sister's dictum that I was really much too sensitive to make a good governess, and that I should have done far better as a professional clairvoyante.

Mr Frene, senior, "Uncle Frank," was expected for an unusual visit from town about tea-time. That I knew. I also knew that his visit was concerned somehow with the future welfare of little Jamie, Gladys' seven-year-old brother. More than this, indeed, I never knew, and this missing link makes my story in a fashion incoherent—an important bit of the strange puzzle left out. I only gathered that the visit of Uncle Frank was of a condescending nature, that Jamie was told he must be upon his very best behaviour to make a good impression, and that Jamie, who had never seen his uncle, dreaded him horribly already in advance. Then, trailing thinly through the dying crunch of the carriage wheels this sultry afternoon, I heard the curious little wail of the child's crying, with the effect, wholly unaccountable, that every nerve in my body shot its bolt electrically, bringing me to my feet with a tingling of unequivocal alarm. Positively, the water ran into my eyes. I recalled his white distress that morning when told that Uncle Frank was motoring down for tea and that he was to be "very nice indeed" to him. It had gone into me like a knife. All through the day, indeed, had run this nightmare quality of terror and vision.

"The man with the 'normous face?" he had asked in a little voice of awe, and then gone speechless from the room in tears that no amount of soothing management could calm. That was all I saw; and what he meant by "the 'normous face" gave me only a sense of vague presentiment. But it came as anti-climax somehow—a sudden revelation of the mystery and excitement that pulsed beneath the quiet of the stifling summer day. I feared for him. For of all that commonplace household I loved Jamie best, though professionally I had nothing to do with him. He was a high-strung, ultra-sensitive child, and it seemed to me that no one understood him, least of all his honest, tender-hearted parents; so that his little wailing voice brought me from my bed to the window in a moment like a call for help.

The haze of June lay over that big garden like a blanket; the wonderful flowers, which were Mr Frene's delight, hung motionless; the lawns, so soft and thick, cushioned all other sounds; only the limes and huge clumps of guelder roses hummed with bees. Through this muted atmosphere of heat and haze the sound of the child's crying floated faintly to my ears—from a distance. Indeed, I wonder now that I heard it at all, for the next moment I saw him down beyond the garden, standing in his white sailor suit alone, two hundred yards away. He was down by the ugly patch where nothing grew—the Forbidden Corner. A faintness then came over me at once, a faintness as of death, when I saw him *there* of all places—where he never was allowed to go, and where, moreover, he was usually too terrified to go. To see him standing solitary in that singular spot, above all to hear him crying there, bereft me, momentarily of the power to act. Then, before I recover my composure sufficiently to call him in, Mr Frene came round the corner from the Lower Farm with the dogs, and, seeing his son, performed that office for me. In his loud, good-natured, hearty voice he called him, and Jamie turned and ran as though some spell had broken just in time—ran into the open arms of his fond but uncomprehending father, who carried him indoors on his shoulder, while asking "what all this hubbub was about?" And, at their heels, the tail-less sheep-dogs followed, barking loudly, and performing what Jamie called their "Gravel Dance," because they ploughed up the moist, rolled gravel with their feet.

I stepped back swiftly from the window lest I should be seen. Had I witnessed the saving of the child from fire or drowning the relief could hardly have been greater. Only Mr Frene, I felt sure, would not say and do the right thing quite. He would protect the boy from his own vain imaginings, yet not with the explanation that could really heal. They disappeared behind the rose trees, making for the house. I saw no more till later, when Mr Frene, senior, arrived.

To describe the ugly patch as "singular" is hard to justify, perhaps, yet some such word is what the entire family sought, though never—oh, never!—used. To Jamie and myself, though equally we never mentioned it, that treeless, flowerless spot was more than singular. It stood at the far end of the magnificent rose garden, a bald, sore place, where the black earth showed uglily in winter, almost like a piece of dangerous bog, and in summer baked and cracked with fissures where green lizards shot their fire in passing. In contrast to the rich luxuriance of the whole amazing garden it was like a glimpse of death amid life, a centre of disease that cried for healing lest it spread. But it never did spread. Behind it stood the thick wood of silver birches and, glimmering beyond, the orchard meadow, where the lambs played.

The gardeners had a very simple explanation of its barrenness— that the water all drained off it owing to the lie of the slopes immediately about it, holding no remnant to keep the soil alive. I cannot say. It was Jamie—Jamie who felt its spell and haunted it, who spent whole hours there, even while afraid, and for whom it was finally labelled "strictly out of bounds" because it stimulated his already big imagination, not wisely but too darkly—it was Jamie who buried ogres there and heard it crying in an earthy voice, swore that it shook its surface sometimes while he watched it, and secretly gave it food in the form of birds or mice or rabbits he found dead upon his wanderings. And it was Jamie who put so extraordinarily into words the *feeling* that the horrid spot had given me from the moment I first saw it.

"It's bad, Miss Gould," he told me.

"But, Jamie, nothing in Nature is bad—exactly; only different from the rest sometimes."

"Miss Gould, if you please, then it's empty. It's not fed. It's dying because it can't get the food it wants."

And when I stared into the little pale face where the eyes shone so dark and wonderful, seeking within myself for the right thing to say to him, he added, with an emphasis and conviction that made me suddenly turn cold: "Miss Gould"—he always used my name like this in all his sentences—"it's hungry, don't you see? But I know what would make it feel all right."

Only the conviction of an earnest child, perhaps, could have made so outrageous a suggestion worth listening to for an instant; but for me, who felt that things an imaginative child believed were important, it came with a vast disquieting shock of reality. Jamie, in this exaggerated way, had caught at the edge of a shocking fact—a hint of dark, undiscovered truth had leaped into that sensitive imagination. Why there lay horror in the words I cannot say, but I think some power of darkness trooped across the suggestion of that sentence at the end, "I know what would make it feel all right." I remember that I shrank from asking explanation. Small groups of other words, veiled fortunately by his silence, gave life to an unspeakable possibility that hitherto had lain at the back of my own consciousness. The way it sprang to life proves, I think, that my mind already contained it. The blood rushed from my heart as I listened. I remember that my knees shook. Jamie's idea was—had been all along—my own as well.

And now, as I lay down on my bed and thought about it all, I understood why the coming of his uncle involved somehow an experience that wrapped terror at its heart. With a sense of nightmare certainty that left me too weak to resist the preposterous idea, too shocked, indeed, to argue or reason it away, this certainty came with its full, black blast of conviction; and the only way I can put it into words, since nightmare horror really is not properly tellable at all, seems this: that there was something missing in that dying patch of garden; something lacking that it ever searched for; something, once found and taken, that would turn it rich and living as the rest; more—that there *was* some living person who could do this for it. Mr Frene, senior, in a word, "Uncle Frank," was this person who out of his abundant life could supply the lack—unwittingly.

For this connection between the dying, empty patch and the person of this vigorous, wealthy, and successful man had already lodged itself in my subconsciousness before I was aware of it. Clearly it must have lain there all along, though hidden. Jamie's words, his sudden pallor, his vibrating emotion of fearful anticipation had developed the plate, but it was his weeping alone there in the Forbidden Corner that had printed it. The photograph shone framed before me in the air. I hid my eyes. But for the redness—the charm of my face goes to pieces unless my eyes are clear—I could have cried. Jamie's words that morning about the "'normous face" came back upon me like a battering-ram.

Mr Frene, senior, had been so frequently the subject of conversation in the family since I came, I had so often heard him discussed, and had then read so much about him in the papers—his energy, his philanthropy, his success with everything he laid his hand to—that a picture of the man had grown complete within me. I knew him as he was—within; or, as my sister would have said—clairvoyantly. And the only time I saw him (when I took Gladys to a meeting where he was chairman, and later *felt* his atmosphere and presence while for a moment he patronisingly spoke with her) had justified the portrait I had drawn. The rest, you may say, was a woman's wild imagining; but I think rather it was that kind of divining intuition which women share with children. If souls could be made visible, I would stake my life upon the truth and accuracy of my portrait.

For this Mr Frene was a man who drooped alone, but grew vital in a crowd—because he used their vitality. He was a supreme, unconscious artist in the science of taking the fruits of others' work and living—for his own advantage. He vampired, unknowingly no doubt, every one with whom he came in contact; left them exhausted, tired, listless. Others fed him, so that while in a full room he shone, alone by himself and with no life to draw upon he languished and declined. In the man's immediate neighbourhood you felt his presence draining you; he took your ideas, your strength, your very words, and later used them for his own benefit and aggrandisement. Not evilly, of course; the man was good enough; but you felt that he was dangerous owing to the facile way he absorbed into himself all loose vitality that was to be had. His eyes and voice and presence devitalised you. Life, it seemed, not highly organised enough to resist, must shrink from his too near approach and hide away for fear of being appropriated, for fear, that is, of—death.

Jamie, unknowingly, put in the finishing touch to my unconscious portrait. The man carried about with him some silent, compelling trick of drawing out all your reserves—then swiftly pocketing them. At first you would be conscious of taut resistance; this would slowly shade off into weariness; the will would become flaccid; then you either moved away or yielded—agreed to all he said with a sense of weakness pressing ever closer upon the edges of collapse. With a male antagonist it might be different, but even then the effort of resistance would generate force that *he* absorbed and not the other. He never gave out. Some instinct taught him how to protect himself from that. To human beings, I mean, he never gave out. This time it was a very different matter. He had no more chance than a fly before the wheels of a huge—what Jamie used to call—"attraction" engine.

So this was how I saw him—a great human sponge, crammed and soaked with the life, or proceeds of life, absorbed from others—stolen. My idea of a human vampire was satisfied. He went about carrying these accumulations of the life of others. In this sense his "life" was not really his own. For the same reason, I think, it was not so fully under his control as he imagined.

And in another hour this man would be here. I went to the window. My eye wandered to the empty patch, dull black there amid the rich luxuriance of the garden flowers. It struck me as a hideous bit of emptiness yawning to be filled and nourished. The idea of Jamie playing round its bare edge was loathsome. I watched the big summer clouds above, the stillness of the afternoon, the haze. The silence of the overheated garden was oppressive. I had never felt a day so stifling, motionless. It lay there waiting. The household, too, was waiting— waiting for the coming of Mr Frene from London in his big motor-car.

And I shall never forget the sensation of icy shrinking and distress with which I heard the rumble of the car. He had arrived. Tea was all ready on the lawn beneath the lime trees, and Mrs Frene and Gladys, back from their drive, were sitting in wicker chairs. Mr Frene, Junior, was in the hall to meet his brother, but Jamie, as I learned afterwards, had shown such hysterical alarm, offered such bold resistance, that it had been deemed wiser to keep him in his room. Perhaps, after all, his presence might not be necessary. The visit clearly had to do with something on the uglier side of life—money, settlements, or what not; I never knew exactly; only that his parents were anxious, and that Uncle Frank had to be propitiated. It does not matter. That has nothing to do with the affair. What has to do with it—or I should not be telling the story—is that Mrs Frene sent for me to come down "in my nice white dress, if I didn't mind," and that I was terrified, yet pleased, because it meant that a pretty face would be considered a welcome addition to the visitor's landscape. Also, most odd it was, I felt my presence was somehow inevitable, that in some way it was intended that I should witness what I did witness. And the instant I came upon the lawn—I hesitate to set it down, it sounds so foolish, disconnected—I could have sworn, as my eyes met his, that a kind of sudden darkness came, taking the summer brilliance out of everything, and that it was caused by troops of small black horses that raced about us from his person—to attack.

After a first momentary approving glance he took no further notice of me. The tea and talk went smoothly; I helped to pass the plates and cups, filling in pauses with little under-talk to Gladys. Jamie was never mentioned. Outwardly all seemed well, but inwardly everything was awful—skirting the edge of things unspeakable, and so charged with danger that I could not keep my voice from trembling when I spoke.

I watched his hard, bleak face; I noticed how thin he was, and the curious, oily brightness of his steady eyes. They did not glitter, but they drew you with a sort of soft, creamy shine like Eastern eyes. And everything he said or did announced what I may dare to call the *suction* of his presence. His nature achieved this result automatically. He dominated us all, yet so gently that until it was accomplished no one noticed it.

Before five minutes had passed, however, I was aware of one thing only. My mind focussed exclusively upon it, and so vividly that I marvelled the others did not scream, or run, or do something violent to prevent it. And it was this: that, separated merely by some dozen yards or so, this man, vibrating with the acquired vitality of others, stood within easy reach of that spot of yawning emptiness, waiting and eager to be filled. Earth scented her prey.

These two active "centres" were within fighting distance; he so thin, so hard, so keen, yet really spreading large with the loose "surround" of others' life he had appropriated, so practised and triumphant. that other so patient, deep, with so mighty a draw of the whole earth behind it, and—ugh!—so obviously aware that its opportunity at last had come.

I saw it all as plainly as though I watched two great animals prepare for battle, both unconsciously; yet in some inexplicable way I saw it, of course, within me, and not externally. The conflict would be hideously unequal. Each side had already sent out emissaries, how long before I could not tell, for the first evidence *he* gave that something was going wrong with him was when his voice grew suddenly confused, he missed his words, and his lips trembled a moment and turned flabby. The next second his face betrayed that singular and horrid change, growing somehow loose about the bones of the cheek, and larger, so that I remembered Jamie's miserable phrase. The emissaries of the two kingdoms, the human and the vegetable, had met, I make it out, in that very second. For the first time in his long career of battening on others, Mr Frene found himself pitted against a vaster kingdom than he knew and, so finding, shook inwardly in that little part that was his definite actual self. He felt the huge disaster coming.

"Yes, John," he was saying, in his drawling, self-congratulating voice, "Sir George gave me that car—gave it to me as a present. Wasn't it char—?" and then broke off abruptly, stammered, drew breath, stood up, and looked uneasily about him. For a second there was a gaping pause. It was like the click which starts some huge machinery moving— that instant's pause before it actually starts. The whole thing, indeed, then went with the rapidity of machinery running down and beyond control. I thought of a giant dynamo working silently and invisible.

"What's that?" he cried, in a soft voice charged with alarm. "What's that horrid place? And someone's crying there—who is it?"

He pointed to the empty patch. Then, before any one could answer, he started across the lawn towards it, going every minute faster. Before any one could move he stood upon the edge. He leaned over— peering down into it.

It seemed a few hours passed, but really they were seconds, for time is measured by the quality and not the quantity of sensations it contains. I saw it all with merciless, photographic detail, sharply etched amid the general confusion. Each side was intensely active, but only one side, the human, exerted *all* its force—in resistance. The other merely stretched out a feeler, as it were, from its vast, potential strength; no more was necessary. It was such a soft and easy victory. Oh, it was rather pitiful! There was no bluster or great effort, on one side at least. Close by his side I witnessed it, for I, it seemed, alone had moved and followed him. No one else stirred, though Mrs Frene clattered noisily with the cups, making some sudden impulsive gesture with her hands, and Gladys, I remember, gave a cry—it was like a little scream—"Oh, mother, it's the heat, isn't it?" Mr Frene, her father, was speechless, pale as ashes.

But the instant I reached his side, it became clear what had drawn me there thus instinctively. Upon the other side, among the silver birches, stood little Jamie. He was watching. I experienced—for him— one of those moments that shake the heart; a liquid fear ran all over me, the more effective because unintelligible really. Yet I felt that if I could know all, and what lay actually behind, my fear would be more than justified; that the thing *was* awful, full of awe.

And then it happened—a truly wicked sight—like watching a universe in action, yet all contained within a small square foot of space. I think he understood vaguely that if some one could only take his place he might be saved, and that was why, discerning instinctively the easiest substitute within reach, he saw the child and called aloud to him across the empty patch, "James, my boy, come here!"

His voice was like a thin report, but somehow flat and lifeless, as when a rifle misses fire, sharp, yet weak; it had no "crack" in it. It was really supplication. And, with amazement, I heard my own ring out imperious and strong, though I was not conscious of saying it, "Jamie, don't move. Stay where you are!" But Jamie, the little child, obeyed neither of us. Moving up nearer to the edge, he stood there—laughing! I heard that laughter, but could have sworn it did not come from him. The empty, yawning patch gave out that sound.

Mr Frene turned sideways, throwing up his arms. I saw his hard, bleak face grow somehow wider, spread through the air, and downwards. A similar thing, I saw, was happening at the same time to his entire person, for it drew out into the atmosphere in a stream of movement. The face for a second made me think of those toys of green indiarubber that children pull. It grew enormous. But this was an external impression only. What actually happened, I clearly understood, was that all this vitality and life he had transferred from others to himself for years was now in turn being taken from him and transferred—elsewhere.

One moment on the edge he wobbled horribly, then with that queer sideways motion, rapid yet ungainly, he stepped forward into the middle of the patch and fell heavily upon his face. His eyes, as he dropped, faded shockingly, and across the countenance was written plainly what I can only call an expression of destruction. He looked utterly destroyed. I caught a sound—from Jamie?—but this time not of laughter. It was like a gulp; it was deep and muffled and it dipped away into the earth. Again I thought of a troop of small black horses galloping away down a subterranean passage beneath my feet—plunging into the depths—their tramping growing fainter and fainter into buried distance. In my nostrils was a pungent smell of earth.

And then—all passed. I came back into myself. Mr Frene, junior, was lifting his brother's head from the lawn where he had fallen from the heat, close beside the tea-table. He had never really moved from there. And Jamie, I learned afterwards, had been the whole time asleep upon his bed upstairs, worn out with his crying and unreasoning alarm. Gladys came running out with cold water, sponge and towel, brandy too—all kinds of things. "Mother, it *was* the heat, wasn't it?" I heard her whisper, but I did not catch Mrs Frene's reply. From her face it struck me that she was bordering on collapse herself. Then the butler followed, and they just picked him up and carried him into the house. He recovered even before the doctor came.

But the queer thing to me is that I was convinced the others all had seen what I saw, only that no one said a word about it; and to this day no one *has* said a word. And that was, perhaps, the most horrid part of all.

From that day to this I have scarcely heard a mention of Mr Frene, senior. It seemed as if he dropped suddenly out of life. The papers never mentioned him. His activities ceased, as it were. His after-life, at any rate, became singularly ineffective. Certainly he achieved nothing worth public mention. But it may be only that, having left the employ of Mrs Frene, there was no particular occasion for me to hear anything.

The after-life of that empty patch of garden, however, was quite otherwise. Nothing, so far as I know, was done to it by gardeners, or in the way of draining it or bringing in new earth, but even before I left in the following summer it had changed. It lay untouched, full of great, luscious, driving weeds and creepers, very strong, full-fed, and bursting thick with life.

SANDHILLS.

## Clairvoyance

IN the darkest corner, where the firelight could not reach him, he sat listening to the stories. His young hostess occupied the corner on the other side; she was also screened by shadows; and between them stretched the horse-shoe of eager, frightened faces that seemed all eyes. Behind yawned the blackness of the big room, running as it were without a break into the night.

Some one crossed on tiptoe and drew a blind up with a rattle, and at the sound all started: through the window, opened at the top, came a rustle of the poplar leaves that stirred like footsteps in the wind. "There's a strange man walking past the shrubberies," whispered a nervous girl; "I saw him crouch and hide. I saw his eyes!" "Nonsense!" came sharply from a male member of the group; "it's far too dark to see. You heard the wind." For mist had risen from the river just below the lawn, pressing close against the windows of the old house like a soft grey hand, and through it the stir of leaves was faintly audible... Then, while several called for lights, others remembered that the hop-pickers were still about in the lanes, and the tramps this autumn overbold and insolent. All, perhaps, wished secretly for the sun. Only the elderly man in the corner sat quiet and unmoved, contributing nothing. He had told no fearsome story. He had evaded, indeed, many openings expressly made for him, though fully aware that to his well-known interest in psychical things was partly due his presence in the week-end party. "I never have experiences—that way," he said shortly when some one asked him point blank for a tale; "I have no unusual powers." There was perhaps the merest hint of contempt in his tone, but the hostess from her darkened corner quickly and tactfully covered his retreat. And he wondered. For he knew why she invited him. The haunted room, he was well aware, had been specially allotted to him.

And then, most opportunely, the door opened noisily and the host came in. He sniffed at the darkness, rang at once for lamps, puffed at his big curved pipe, and generally, by his mere presence, made the group feel rather foolish. Light streamed past him from the corridor. His white hair shone like silver. And with him came the atmosphere of common sense, of shooting, agriculture, motors, and the rest. Age entered at that door. And his young wife sprang up instantly to greet him, as though his disapproval of this kind of entertainment might need humouring.

It may have been the light—that witchery of half-lights from the fire and the corridor, or it may have been the abrupt entrance of the Practical upon the soft Imaginative that traced the outline with such pitiless, sharp conviction. At any rate, the contrast—for those who had this inner clairvoyant sight all had been prating of so glibly!—was unmistakably revealed. It was poignantly dramatic, pain somewhere in it—naked pain. For, as she paused a moment there beside him in the light, this childless wife of three years' standing, picture of youth and beauty, there stood upon the threshold of that room the presence of a true ghost story.

And most marvellously she changed—her lineaments, her very figure, her whole presentment. Etched against the gloom, the delicate, unmarked face shone suddenly keen and anguished, and a rich maturity, deeper than any mere age, flushed all her little person with its secret grandeur. Lines started into being upon the pale skin of the girlish face, lines of pleading, pity, and love the daylight did not show, and with them an air of magic tenderness that betrayed, though for a second only, the full soft glory of a motherhood denied, yet somehow mysteriously enjoyed. About her slenderness rose all the deep-bosomed sweetness of maternity, a potential mother of the world, and a mother, though she might know no dear fulfilment, who yet yearned to sweep into her immense embrace all the little helpless things that ever lived.

Light, like emotion, can play the strangest tricks. The change pressed almost upon the edge of revelation... Yet, when a moment later lamps were brought, it is doubtful if any but the silent guest who had told no marvellous tale, knew no psychical experience, and disclaimed the smallest clairvoyant faculty, had received and registered the vivid, poignant picture. For an instant it had flashed there, mercilessly clear for all to see who were not blind to subtle spiritual wonder thick with pain. And it was not so much mere picture of youth and age ill-matched, as of youth that yearned with the oldest craving in the world, and of age that had slipped beyond the power of sympathetically divining it... It passed, and all was as before.

The husband laughed with genial good-nature, not one whit annoyed. "They've been frightening you with stories, child," he said in his jolly way, and put a protective arm about her. "Haven't they now? Tell me the truth. Much better," he added, "have joined me instead at billiards, or for a game of Patience, eh?" She looked up shyly into his face, and he kissed her on the forehead. "Perhaps they have—a little, dear," she said, "but now that you've come, I feel all right again." "Another night of this," he added in a graver tone, "and you'd be at your old trick of putting guests to sleep in the haunted room. I was right after all, you see, to make it out of bounds." He glanced fondly, paternally down upon her. Then he went over and poked the fire into a blaze. Some one struck up a waltz on the piano, and couples danced. All trace of nervousness vanished, and the butler presently brought in the tray with drinks and biscuits. And slowly the group dispersed. Candles were lit. They passed down the passage into the big hall, talking in lowered voices of tomorrow's plans. The laughter died away as they went up the stairs to bed, the silent guest and the young wife lingering a moment over the embers.

"You have not, after all then, put me in your haunted room?" he asked quietly. "You mentioned, you remember, in your letter—"

"I admit," she replied at once, her manner gracious beyond her years, her voice quite different, "that I wanted you to sleep there—some one, I mean, who really knows, and is not merely curious. But—forgive my saying so—when I *saw* you"—she laughed very slowly—"and when you told no marvellous story like the others, I somehow felt—"

"But I never *see* anything—" he put in hurriedly.

"You *feel*, though," she interrupted swiftly, the passionate tenderness in her voice but half suppressed. "I can tell it from your—"

"Others, then," he interrupted abruptly, almost bluntly, "have slept there—sat up, rather?"

"Not recently. My husband stopped it." She paused a second, then added, "I had that room—for a year—when first we married."

The other's anguished look flew back upon her little face like a shadow and was gone, while at the sight of it there rose in himself a sudden deep rush of wonderful amazement beckoning almost towards worship. He did not speak, for his voice would tremble.

"I had to give it up," she finished, very low.

"Was it so terrible?" after a pause he ventured.

She bowed her head. "I had to change," she repeated softly.

"And since then—*now*—you see nothing?" he asked.

Her reply was singular. "Because I will not, not because it's gone."... He followed her in silence to the door, and as they passed along the passage, again that curious great pain of emptiness, of loneliness, of yearning rose upon him, as of a sea that never, never can swim beyond the shore to reach the flowers that it loves...

"Hurry up, child, or a ghost will catch you," cried her husband, leaning over the banisters, as the pair moved slowly up the stairs towards him. There was a moment's silence when they met. The guest took his lighted candle and went down the corridor. Good-nights were said again. They moved away, she to her loneliness, he to his unhaunted room. And at his door he turned. At the far end of the passage, silhouetted against the candle-light, he watched them—the fine old man with his silvered hair and heavy shoulders, and the slim young wife with that amazing air as of some great bountiful mother of the world for whom the years yet passed hungry and unharvested. They turned the corner, and he went in and closed his door.

Sleep took him very quickly, and while the mist rose up and veiled the countryside, something else, veiled equally for all other sleepers in that house but two, drew on towards its climax... Some hours later he awoke; the world was still, and it seemed the whole house listened; for with that clear vision which some bring out of sleep, he remembered that there had been no direct denial, and of a sudden realised that this big, gaunt chamber where he lay was after all the haunted room. For him, however, the entire world, not merely separate rooms in it, was ever haunted; and he knew no terror to find the space about him charged with thronging life quite other than his own... He rose and lit the candle, crossed over to the window where the mist shone grey, knowing that no barriers of walls or door or ceiling could keep out this host of Presences that poured so thickly everywhere about him. It was like a wall of being, with peering eyes, small hands stretched out, a thousand pattering wee feet, and tiny voices crying in a chorus very faintly and beseeching... The haunted room! Was it not, rather, a temple vestibule, prepared and sanctified by yearning rites few men might ever guess, for all the childless women of the world? How could she know that he would understand—this woman he had seen but twice in all his life? And how entrust to him so great a mystery that was her secret? Had she so easily divined in him a similar yearning to which, long years ago, death had denied fulfilment? Was she clairvoyant in the true sense, and did all faces bear on them so legibly this great map that sorrow traced?...

And then, with awful suddenness, mere feelings dipped away, and something concrete happened. The handle of the door had faintly rattled. He turned. The round brass knob was slowly moving. And first, at the sight, something of common fear did grip him, as though his heart had missed a beat, but on the instant he heard the voice of his own mother, now long beyond the stars, calling to him to go softly yet with speed. He watched a moment the feeble efforts to undo the door, yet never afterwards could swear that he saw actual movement, for something in him, tragic as blindness, rose through a mist of tears and darkened vision utterly...

He went towards the door. He took the handle very gently, and very softly then he opened it. Beyond was darkness. He saw the empty passage, the edge of the banisters where the great hall yawned below, and, dimly, the outline of the Alpine photograph and the stuffed deer's head upon the wall. And then he dropped upon his knees and opened wide his arms to something that came in upon uncertain, viewless feet. All the young winds and flowers and dews of dawn passed with it... filling him to the brim... covering closely his breast and eyes and lips. There clung to him all the small beginnings of life that cannot stand alone... the little helpless hands and arms that have no confidence... and when the wealth of tears and love that flooded his heart seemed to break upon the frontiers of some mysterious yet impossible fulfilment, he rose and went with curious small steps towards the window to taste the cooling, misty air of that other dark Emptiness that waited so patiently there above the entire world. He drew the sash up. The air felt soft and tender as though there were somewhere children in it too—children of stars and flowers, of mists and wings and music, all that the Universe contains unborn and tiny... And when at length he turned again the door was closed. The room was empty of any life but that which lay so wonderfully blessed within himself. And this, he felt, had marvellously increased and multiplied...

Sleep then came back to him, and in the morning he left the house before the others were astir, pleading some overlooked engagement. For he had seen Ghosts indeed, but yet not ghosts that he could talk about with others round an open fire.

THE LAVENDER ROOM.

## The Golden Fly

IT fell upon him out of a clear sky just when existence seemed on its very best behaviour, and he savagely resented the undeserved affliction of it. Involving him in an atrocious scandal that reflected directly upon his honour, it destroyed in a moment the erection his entire life had so laboriously built up—his reputation. In the eyes of the world he was a broken, discredited man, at the very moment, moreover, when his most cherished ambitions touched fulfilment. And the cruelty of it appalled his sense of justice, for it was impossible to vindicate himself without inculpating others who were dearer to him than life. It seemed more than he could bear; and the grim course he contemplated—decision itself as yet hung darkly waiting in the background—appeared the only way of escape that offered.

He had discussed the matter with friends until his brain whirled. Their sympathy maddened him, with hints of *qui s'excuse s'accuse*, and he turned at last in desperation to something that could not answer back. For the first time in his life he turned to Nature—to that dead, inanimate Nature he had left to poets and rhapsodising women: "I must face it alone," he put it. For the Finger of God was a phrase without meaning to him, and his entire being contained no trace of the religious instinct. He was a business man, honest, selfish, and ambitious; and the collapse of his worldly position was paramount to the collapse of the universe itself—his universe, at any rate. This "crumbling of the universe" was the thought he took out with him. He left the house by the path that led into solitude, and reached the heathery expanse that formed one of the breathing-places of the New Forest. There he flung himself down wearily in the shadow of a little pine-copse. And his crumbled universe lay down with him, for he could not escape it.

Taking the pistol from the hip-pocket where it hurt him, he lay upon his back and watched the clouds. Half stunned, half dazed, he stared into the sky. The perfumed wind played softly on his eyes; he smelt the heather-honey; golden flies hung motionless in the air, like coloured pins fastening the sunshine against the blue curtain of the summer, while dragon-flies, like darting shuttles, wove across its pattern their threads of gleaming bronze. He heard the petulant crying of the peewits, and watched their tumbling flight. Below him tinkled a rivulet, its brown water rippling between banks of peaty earth. Everywhere was singing, peace, and careless unconcern.

And this lordly indifference of Nature calmed and soothed him. Neither human pain nor the injustice of man could shift the key of the water, alter the peewits' cry a single tone, nor influence one fraction of an inch those cloudy frigates of vapour that sailed the sky. The earth bulged sunwards as she had bulged for centuries. The power of her steady gait, superbly calm, breathed everywhere with grandeur— undismayed, unhasting, and supremely confident... And, like the flash of those golden flies, there leaped suddenly upon him this vivid thought: that his world of agony lay neatly buttoned up within the tiny space of his own brain. Outside himself it had no existence at all. His mind contained it—the minute interior he called his heart. From this vaster world about him it lay utterly apart, like deeds in the black boxes of japanned tin he kept at the office, shut off from the universe, huddled in an overcrowded space within his skull.

How this commonplace thought reached him, garbed in such startling novelty, was odd enough; for it seemed as though the fierceness of his pain had burned away something. His thoughts it merely enflamed; but this other thing it consumed. Something that had obscured clear vision shrivelled before it as a piece of paper, eaten up by fire, dwindles down into a thimbleful of unimportant ashes. The thicket of his mind grew half transparent. At the farther end he saw, for the first time—light. The perspective of his inner life, hitherto so enormous, telescoped into the proportions of a miniature. Just as momentous and significant as before, it was somehow abruptly different—seen from another point of view. The suffering had burned up rubbish he himself had piled over the head of a little Fact. Like a point of metal that glows yet will not burn, he discerned in the depths of him the essential shining fact that not all this ruinous conflagration could destroy. And this brilliant, indestructible kernel was—his Innocence. The rest was self-reared rubbish opinion of the world. He had magnified an atom into a universe...

Pain, as it seemed, had cleared a way for the sublimity of Nature to approach him. The calm old Universe rolled past. The deep, majestic Day gave him a push, as though the shoulder of some star had brushed his own. He had thought his feelings were the world: instead, they were merely his way of looking at it. The actual "world" was some glorious, unchanging thing he never saw direct. His attitude of mind was but a peephole into it. The choice of his particular peephole, moreover, lay surely within the power of his individual will. The anguish, centred upon so small a point, had seemed to affect the entire spread universe around him, whereas in reality it affected nothing but his attitude of mind towards it. The truism struck him like a blow between the eyes, that a man is what he thinks or feels himself to be. It leaped the barrier between words and meaning. The intellectual concept became a hard-edged fact, because he realised it—for the first time in his very circumscribed life. And this dreadful pain that had made even suicide seem desirable was entirely a fabrication of his own mind. The universe about him rolled on just the same in the majesty of its eternal purpose. His tiny inner world was clouded, but the glory of this stupendous world about him was undimmed, untroubled, unaffected. Even death itself...

With a swift smash of the hand he crushed the golden fly that settled on his knee. The murder was done impulsively, utterly without intention. He watched the little point of gold quiver for a moment among the hairs of the rough tweed; then lie still for ever... but the scent of heather-honey filled the air as before; the wind passed sighing through the pines; the clouds still sailed their uncharted sea of blue. There lay the whole spread surface of the

Forest in the sun. Only the attitude of the golden fly towards it all was gone. A single, tiny point of view had disappeared. Nature passed on calmly and unhasting; she took no note.

Then, with a rush of awe, another thought flashed through him: Nature *had* taken note. There was a difference everywhere. Not a sparrow falleth, he remembered, without God knowing. God was certainly in Nature somewhere. His clumsy senses could not register this difference, yet it was there. His own small world, fed by these senses, was after all the merest little corner of Existence. To the whole of Existence, that included himself, the golden fly, the sun, and all the stars, he must somehow answer for his crime. It was a wanton interference with a sublime and sovereign Purpose that he now divined for the first time. He looked at the wee point of gold lying still and silent in the forest of hairs. He realised the enormity of his act. It could not have been graver had he put out the sun, or the little, insignificant flame of his own existence. He had done a criminal, evil thing, for he had put an end to a certain point of view; had wiped it out; made it impossible. Had the fly been quicker, less easily overwhelmed, or more tenacious of the scrap of universal life it used, Nature would at this instant be richer for its little contribution to the whole of things—to which he himself also belonged. And wherein, he asked himself, did he differ from that fly in the importance, the significance of his contribution to the universe? The soul... ? He had never given the question a single thought; but if the scrap of life he owned was called a soul, why should that point of golden glory not comprise one too? Its minute size, its trivial purpose, its few hours of apparently futile existence... these formed no true criterion... !

Similarly, the thought rushed over him, a Hand was being stretched out to crush himself. His pain was the shadow of its approach; anger in his heart, the warning. Unless he were quick enough, adroit and skilled enough, he also would be wiped out, while Nature continued her slow, unhasting way without him. His attitude towards the personal pain was really the test of his ability, of his merit—of his right to survive. Pain teaches, pain develops, pain brings growth: he had heard it since his copybook days. But now he realised it, as again thought leaped the barrier between familiar words and meaning. In his attitude of mind to his catastrophe lay his salvation or his... death.

In some such confused and blundering fashion, because along unaccustomed channels, the truth charged into him to overwhelm, yet bringing with it an unwonted sense of joy that seemed to break a crust which long had held back—life. Thus tapped, these sources gushed forth and bubbled over, spread about his being, flooded him with hope and courage, above all with—calmness. Nature held forces just as real and living as human sympathy, and equally able to modify the soul. And Nature was always accessible. A sense of huge companionship, denied him by the littleness of his fellow men, stole sweetly over him. It was amazingly uplifting, yet fear came close behind it, as he realised the presumption of his former attitude of cynical indifference. These Powers were aware of his petty insolence, yet had not crushed him... It was, of course, the awakening of the religious instinct in a man who hitherto had worshipped merely a rather low-grade form of intellect.

And, while the enormous confusion of it shook him, this sense of incommunicable sweetness remained. Bright haunting eyes, with love in them, gazed at him from the blue; and this thing that came so close, stood also far away upon the line of the horizon. It was everywhere. It filled the hollows, but towered over him as well towards the pinnacles of cloud. It was in the sharpness of the peewits' cry, and in the water's murmur. It whispered in the pine-boughs, and blazed in every patch of sunlight. And it was glory, pure and simple. It filled him with a sense of strength for which he could find but one description—Triumph.

And so, first, the anger faded from his mind and crept away. Resentment then slunk after it. Revolt and disappointment also melted, and bitterness gave place to the most marvellous peace the man had ever known. Then came resignation to fill the empty places. Pain, as a means and not an end, had cleared the way, though the accomplishment was like a miracle. But Conversion *is* a miracle. No ordinary pain can bring it. This anguish he understood now in a new relation to life—as something to be taken willingly into himself and dealt with, all regardless of public opinion. What people said and thought was in their world, not in his. It was less than nothing. The pain cultivated dormant tracts. The terror also purged. It disclosed...

He watched the wind, and even the wind brought revelation; for without obstacles in its path it would be silent. He watched the sunshine, and the sunshine taught him too; for without obstacles to fling it back against his eye, he could never see it. He would neither hear the tinkling water nor feel the summer heat unless both one and other overcame some reluctant medium in their pathways. And, similarly with his moral being—his pain resulted from the friction of his personal ambitions against the stress of some noble Power that sought to lift him higher. That Power he could not know direct, but he recognised its strain against him by the resistance it generated in the inertia of his selfishness. His attitude of mind had switched completely round. It was what the preachers termed development through suffering.

Moreover, he had acquired this energy of resistance somehow from the wind and sun and the beauty of a common summer's day. Their peace and strength had passed into himself. Unconsciously on his way home he drew upon it steadily. He tossed the pistol into a pool of water. Nature had healed him; and Nature, should he turn weak again, was always there. It was very wonderful. He wanted to sing...

BREAMORE

## Special Delivery

MEIKLEJOHN, the curate, was walking through the Jura when this thing happened to him. There is only his word to vouch for it, for the inn and its proprietor are now both of the past, and the local record of the occurrence has long since assumed the proportions of a picturesque but inaccurate legend. As a true story, however, it stands out from those of its kidney by the fact that there seems to have been a deliberate intention in it. It saved a life—a life the world had need of. And this singular rescue of a man of value to the best order of things makes one feel that there was some sense, even logic, in the affair.

Moreover, Meiklejohn asserts that it was the only psychic experience he ever knew. Things of the sort were not a "habit" with him. His rescue, thus, was not one of those meaningless interventions that puzzle the man in the street while they exhilarate the psychologist. It was a deliberate and very determined affair.

Meiklejohn found himself that hot August night in one of the valleys that slip like blue shadows hidden among pine-woods between the Swiss frontier and France. He had passed Ste Croix earlier in the day; Les Rasses had been left behind about four o'clock; Buttes, and the Val de Travers, where the cement of many a London street comes from, was his goal. But the light failed long before he reached it, and he stopped at an inn that appeared unexpectedly round a corner of the dusty road, built literally against the great cliffs that formed one wall of the valley. He was so footsore, and his knapsack so heavy, that he turned in without more ado.

Le Guillaume Tell was the name of the inn—dirty white walls, with thin, almost mangy vines scrambling over the door, and the stream brawling beneath shuttered windows with green and white stripes all patched by sun and rain. His room was sevenpence, his dinner of soup, omelette, fruit, cheese, and coffee, a franc. The prices suited his pocket and made him feel comfortable and at home. Immediately behind the hotel—the only house visible, except the sawmill across the road, rose the ever-crumbling ridges and precipices that formed the flanks of Chasseront and ran on past La Sagne towards the grey Aiguilles de Baulmes. He was in the Jura fastnesses where tourists rarely penetrate.

Through the low doorway of the inn he carried with him the strong atmosphere of thoughts that had accompanied him all day— dreams of how he intended to spend his life, plans of sacrifice and effort. For his hopes of great achievement, even then at twenty-five, were a veritable passion in him, and his desire to spend himself for humanity a devouring flame. So occupied, indeed, was his mind with the emotions belonging to this line of thinking, that he hardly noticed the singular, though exceedingly faint, sense of alarm that stirred somewhere in the depths of his being as he passed within that doorway where the drooping vine-leaves clutched at his hat. He remembered it a little later. The sense of danger had been touched in him. He felt at the moment only a hint of discomfort, too vague to claim definite recognition. Yet it was there—the instant he stepped within the threshold—and afterwards he distinctly recalled its sudden and unaccountable advent.

His bedroom, though stuffy, as from windows long unopened, was clean; carpetless, of course, and primitive, with white pine floor and walls, and the short bed, smothered under its duvet, very creaky. And very short! For Meiklejohn was well over six feet.

"I shall have to curl up, as usual, in a knot," was his reflection as he measured the bed with his eye "though tonight I think—after my twenty miles in this air—"

The thought refused to complete itself. He was going to add that he was tired enough to have slept on a stone floor, but for some undefined reason the same sense of alarm that had tapped him on the shoulder as he entered the inn returned now when he contemplated the bed. A sharp repugnance for that bed, as sudden and unaccountable as it was curious, swept into him—and was gone again before he had time to seize it wholly. It was in reality so slight that he dismissed it immediately as the merest fancy; yet, at the same time, he was aware that he would rather have slept on another bed, had there been one in the room—and then the queer feeling that, after all, perhaps, he would *not* sleep there in the end at all. How this idea came to him he never knew. He records it, however, as part of the occurrence.

After eight o'clock a few peasants, and workmen from the sawmill, came in to drink their *demi-litre* of red wine in the common room downstairs, to stare at the unexpected guest, and to smoke their vile tobacco. They were neither picturesque nor amusing—simply dirty and slightly malodorous. At nine o'clock Meiklejohn knocked the ashes from his briar pipe upon the limestone window-ledge, and went upstairs, overpowered with sleep. The sense of alarm had utterly disappeared; his mind was busy once more with his great dreams of the future—dreams that materialised themselves, as all the world knows, in the famous Meiklejohn Institutes...

Berthoud, the proprietor, short and sturdy, with his faded brown coat and no collar, slightly confused with red wine and a "tourist" guest, showed him the way up. For, of course, there was no *femme de chambre*.

"You have the corridor all to yourself" the man said; showed him the best corner of the landing to shout from in case he wanted anything—there being no bell—eyed his boots, knapsack, and flask with considerable curiosity, wished him goodnight, and was gone. He went downstairs with a noise like a horse, thought the curate, as he locked the door after him.

The windows had been open now for a couple of hours, and the room smelt sweet with the odours of sawn wood and shavings, the resinous perfume of the surrounding hosts of pines, and the sharp, delicate touch of a lonely mountain valley where civilisation has not yet tainted the air. Whiffs of coarse tobacco, pungent without being offensive, came invisibly through the cracks of the floor. Primitive and simple it all was—a sort of vigorous "backwoods" atmosphere. Yet, once again, as he turned to examine the room after Berthoud's steps had blundered down below into the passage, something rose faintly within him to set his nerves mysteriously a-quiver.

Out of these perfectly simple conditions, without the least apparent cause, the odd feeling again came over him that he was—in danger.

The curate was not much given to analysis. He was a man of action pure and simple, as a rule. But tonight, in spite of himself, his thoughts went plunging, searching, asking. For this singular message of dread that emanated as it were from the room, or from some article of furniture in the room perhaps—that bed still touched his mind with a peculiar repugnance—demanded somewhat insistently for an explanation. And the only explanation that suggested itself to his unimaginative mind was that the forces of nature hereabouts were overpowering; that, after the slum streets and factory chimneys of the last twelve months, these towering cliffs and smothering pine-forests communicated to his soul a word of grandeur that amounted to awe. Inadequate and far-fetched as the explanation seems, it was the only one that occurred to him; and its value in this remarkable adventure lies in the fact that he connected his sense of danger partly with the bed and partly with the mountains.

"I felt once or twice," he said afterwards, "as though some powerful agency of a spiritual kind were all the time trying to beat into my stupid brain a message of warning." And this way of expressing it is more true and graphic than many paragraphs of attempted analysis.

Meiklejohn hung his clothes by the open window to air, washed, read his Bible, looked several times over his shoulder without apparent cause, and then knelt down to pray. He was a simple and devout soul; his Self lost in the yearning, young but sincere, to live for humanity. He prayed, as usual, with intense earnestness that his life might be preserved for use in the world, when in the middle of his prayer—there came a knocking at the door.

Hastily rising from his knees, he opened. The sound of rushing water filled the corridor. He heard the voices of the workmen below in the drinking-room. But only darkness stood in the passages, filling the house to the very brim. No one was there. He returned to his interrupted devotions.

"I imagined it," he said to himself. He continued his prayers, however, longer than usual. At the back of his thoughts, dim, vague, half-defined only, lay this lurking sense of uneasiness—that he was in danger. He prayed earnestly and simply, as a child might pray, for the preservation of his life...

Again, just as he prepared to get into bed, struggling to make the heaped-up duvet spread all over, came that knocking at the bedroom door. It was soft, wonderfully soft, and something within him thrilled curiously in response. He crossed the floor to open—then hesitated. Suddenly he understood that that knocking at the door was connected with the sense of danger in his heart. In the region of subtle intuitions the two were linked. With this realisation there came over him, he declares, a singular mood in which, as in a revelation, he knew that Nature held forces that might somehow communicate directly and positively with—human beings. This thought rushed upon him out of the night, as it were. It arrested his movements. He stood there upon the bare pine boards, hesitating to open the door.

The delay thus described lasted actually only a few seconds, but in those few seconds these thoughts tore rapidly and like fire through his mind. The beauty of this lost and mysterious valley was certainly in his veins. He felt the strange presence of the encircling forests, soft and splendid, their million branches sighing in the night airs. The crying of the falling water touched him. He longed to transfer their peace and power to the hearts of suffering thousands of men and women and children. The towering precipices that literally dropped their pale walls over the roof of the inn lifted his thoughts to their own wind-swept heights; he longed to convey their message of inflexible strength to the weak-kneed folk in the slums where he worked. He was peculiarly conscious of the presence of these forces of Nature—the irresistible powers that regenerate as easily as they destroy.

All this, and far more, swept his soul like a huge wind as he stood there, waiting to open the door in answer to that mysterious soft knocking.

And there, when at length he opened, stood the figure of a man—staring at him and smiling.

Disappointment seized him instantly. He had expected, almost believed, that he would see something un-ordinary; and instead, there stood a man who had merely mistaken the door of his room, and was now bowing his apology for the interruption. Then, to his amazement, he saw that the man beckoned: the figure was someone who sought to draw him out.

"Come with me," it seemed to say.

But Meiklejohn only realised this afterwards, he says, when it was too late and he had already shut the door in the stranger's face. For the man had withdrawn into the darkness a little, and the curate had taken the movement for a mere acknowledgment of his mistake instead of—as he afterwards felt—a sign that he should follow.

"And the moment the door was shut," he says, "I felt that it would have been better for me to have gone out into the passage to see what he wanted. It came over me that the man had something important to say to me. I had missed it."

For some seconds, it seemed, he resisted the inclination to go after him. He argued with himself; then turned to his bed, pulled back the sheets and heavy duvet, and was met sharply again with the sense of repugnance, almost of fear, as before. It leaped out upon him—as though the drawing back of the blankets had set free some cold blast of wind that struck him across the face and made him shiver.

At the same moment a shadow fell from behind his shoulder and dropped across the pillow and upper half of the bed. It may, of course, have been the magnified shadow of the moth that buzzed about the pale-yellow electric light in the ceiling. He does not pretend to know. It passed swiftly, however, and was gone; and Meiklejohn, feeling less sure of himself than ever before in his life, crossed the floor quickly, almost running, and opened the door to go after the man who had knocked— twice. For in reality less than half a minute had passed since the shutting of the door and its reopening.

But the corridor was empty. He marched down the pine-board floor for some considerable distance. Below he saw the glimmer of the hall, and heard the voices of the peasants and workmen from the sawmill as they still talked and drank their red wine in the public room. That sound of falling water, as before, filled the air. Darkness reigned. But the person—the *messenger*—who had twice knocked at his door was gone utterly... Presently a door opened downstairs, and the peasants clattered out noisily. He turned and went back to bed. The electric light was switched off below. Silence fell. Conquering his strange repugnance, Meiklejohn, with a prayer on his lips, got into bed, and in less than ten minutes was sound asleep.

"I admit," he says, in telling the story, "that what happened afterwards came so swiftly and so confusingly, yet with such a storm of overwhelming conviction of its reality, that its sequence may be somewhat blurred in my memory, while, at the same time, I see it after all these years as though it was a thing of yesterday. But in my sleep, first of all, I again heard that soft, mysterious tapping—not in the course of a dream of any sort, but sudden and alone out of the dark blank of forgetfulness. I tried to wake. At first, however, the bonds of unconsciousness held me tight. I had to struggle in order to return to the waking world. There was a distinct effort before I opened my eyes; and in that slight interval I became aware that the person who had knocked at the door had meanwhile opened it and passed into the room. I had left the lock unturned. The person was close beside me in the darkness—not in utter darkness, however, for a rising three-quarter moon shed its faint silver upon the floor in patches, and, as I sprang swiftly from the bed, I noticed something alive moving towards me across the carpetless boards. Upon the edges of a patch of moonlight, where the fringe of silver and shadow mingled, it stopped. Three feet away from it I, too, stopped, shaking in every muscle. It lay there crouching at my very feet, staring up at me. But was it man or was it animal? For at first I took it certainly for a human being on all fours; but the next moment, with a spasm of genuine terror that half stopped my breath, it was borne in upon me that the creature was—nothing human. Only in this way can I describe it. It was identical with the human figure who had knocked before and beckoned to me to follow, but it was another presentation of that figure.

"And it held (or brought, if you will) some tremendous message for me— some message of tremendous importance, I mean. The first time I had argued, resisted, refused to listen. Now it had returned in a form that ensured obedience. Some quite terrific power emanated from it—a power that I understood instinctively belonged to the mountains and the forests and the untamed elemental forces of Nature. Amazing as it may sound in cold blood, I can only say that I felt as though the towering precipices outside had sent me a direct warning—that my life was in immediate danger.

"For a space that seemed minutes, but was probably less than a few seconds, I stood there trembling on the bare boards, my eyes riveted upon the dark, uncouth shape that covered all the floor beyond. I saw no limbs or features, no suggestion of outline that I could connect with any living form I know, animate or inanimate. Yet it moved and stirred all the time—*whirled within itself*, describes it best; and into my mind sprang a picture of an immense dark wheel, turning, spinning, whizzing so rapidly that it appears motionless, and uttering that low and ominous thunder that fills a great machinery-room of a factory. Then I thought of Ezekiel's vision of the Living Wheels...

"And it must have been at this instant, I think, that the muttering and deep note that issued from it formed itself into words within me. At any rate, I heard a voice that spoke with unmistakable intelligence

"'Come!' it said. 'Come out—at once!' And the sense of power that accompanied the Voice was so splendid that my fear vanished and I obeyed instantly without thinking more. I followed; it led. It altered in shape. The door *was* open. It ran silently in a form that was more like a stream of deep black water than anything else I can think of—out of the room, down the stairs, across the hall, and up to the deep shadows that lay against the door leading into the road. There I lost sight of it."

Meiklejohn's only desire, he says, then was to rush after it—to escape. This he did. He understood that somehow it had passed through the door into the open air. Ten seconds later, perhaps even less, he, too, was in the open air. He acted almost automatically; reason, reflection, logic all swept away. Nowhere, however, in the soft moonlight about him was any sign of the extraordinary apparition that had succeeded in drawing him out of the inn, out of his bedroom, out of his—bed. He stared in a dazed way at everything—just beginning to get control of his faculties a bit—wondering what in the world it all meant. That huge spinning form, he felt convinced, lay hidden somewhere close beside him, waiting for the end. The danger it had enabled him to avoid was close at hand... He *knew* that, he says...

There lay the meadows, touched here and there with wisps of floating mist; the stream roared and tumbled down its rocky bed to his left; across the road the sawmill lifted its skeleton-like outline, moonlight shining on the dew-covered shingles of the roof, its lower part hidden in shadow. The cold air of the valley was exquisitely scented.

To the right, where his eye next wandered, he saw the thick black woods rising round the base of the precipices that soared into the sky, sheeted with silvery moonlight. His gaze ran up them to the far ridges that seemed to push the very stars farther into the heavens. Then, as he saw those stars crowding the night, he staggered suddenly backwards, seizing the wall of the road for support, and catching his breath. For the top of the cliff he fancied, moved. A group of stars was for a fraction of a second—hidden. The earth—the scenery of the valley, at least—turned about him. Something prodigious was happening to the solid structure of the world. The precipices seemed to bend over upon the valley. The far, uppermost ridge of those beetling cliffs shifted downwards. Meiklejohn declares that the way its movement hid momentarily a group of stars was the most startling—for some reason horrible—thing he had ever witnessed.

Then came the roar and crash and thunder as the mass toppled, slid, and finally—took the frightful plunge. How long the forces of rain and frost had been chiselling out the slow detachment of the giant slabs that fell, or whence came the particular extra little push that drove the entire mass out from the parent rock, no one can know. Only one thing is certain: that it was due to no chance, but to the nicely and exactly calculated results of balanced cause and effect. From the beginning of time it had been known—it might have been accurately calculated, rather—that this particular thousand tons of rock would break away from the crumbling tops of the precipices and crash downwards with the roar of many tempests into the lost and mysterious mountain valley where Meiklejohn the curate spent such and such a night of such and such a holiday. It was just as sure as the return of Halley's comet.

"I watched it," he says, "because I couldn't do anything else. I would far rather have run—I was so frightfully close to it all—but I couldn't move a muscle. And in a few seconds it was over. A terrific wind knocked me backwards against the stone wall; there was a vast clattering of smaller stones, set rolling down the neighbouring couloirs; a steady roll of echoes ran thundering up and down the valley; and then all was still again exactly as it had been before. And the curious thing was—ascertained a little later, as you may imagine, and not at once—that the inn, being so closely built up against the cliffs, had almost entirely escaped. The great mass of rock and trees had taken a leap farther out, and filled the meadows, blocked the road, crushed the sawmill like a matchbox, and dammed up the stream; but the inn itself was almost untouched.

"*Almost*—for a single block of limestone, about the size of a grand piano, had dropped straight upon one corner of the roof and smashed its way through my bedroom, carrying everything it contained down to the level of the cellar, so terrific was the momentum of its crushing journey. Not a stick of the furniture was afterwards discoverable—as such. The bed seems to have been caught by the very middle of the fallen mass."

The confusion in Meiklejohn's mind may be imagined—the rush of feeling and emotion that swept over him. Berthoud and the peasants mustered in less than a dozen minutes, talking, crying, praying. Then the stream, dammed up by the accumulation of rock, carried off the debris of the broken roof and walls in less than half an hour. The rock, however, that swept the room and the *empty* bed of Meiklejohn the curate into dust, still lies in the valley where it fell.

"The only other thing that I remember," he says, in telling the story, "is that, as I stood there, shaking with excitement and the painful terror of it all, before Berthoud and the peasants had come to count over their number and learn that no one was missing—while I stood there, leaning against the wall of the road, something rose out of the white dust at my feet, and, with a noise like the whirring of some immense projectile, passed swiftly and invisibly away up into space—so far as I could judge, towards the distant ridges that reared their motionless outline in moonlight beneath the stars."

NOIRVAUX.

## The Destruction of Smith

TEN years ago, in the western States of America, I once met Smith. But he was no ordinary member of the clan: he was Ezekiel B. Smith of Smithville. He *was* Smithville, for he founded it and made it live.

It was in the oil region, where towns spring up on the map in a few days like mushrooms, and may be destroyed again in a single night by fire and earthquake. On a hunting expedition Smith stumbled upon a natural oil well, and instantly staked his claim; a few months later he was rich, grown into affluence as rapidly as that patch of wilderness grew into streets and houses where you could buy anything from an evening's gambling to a tin of Boston baked pork-and-beans. Smith was really a tremendous fellow, a sort of human dynamo of energy and pluck, with rare judgment in his great square head—the kind of judgment that in higher walks of life makes statesmen. His personality cut through the difficulties of life with the clean easy force of putting his whole life into anything he touched. "God's own luck," his comrades called it; but really it was sheer ability and character and personality. The man had power.

From the moment of that "oil find" his rise was very rapid, but while his brains went into a dozen other big enterprises, his heart remained in little Smithville, the flimsy mushroom town he had created. His own life was in it. It was his baby. He spoke tenderly of its hideousness. Smithville was an intimate expression of his very self.

Ezekiel B. Smith I saw once only, for a few minutes; but I have never forgotten him. It was the moment of his death. And we came across him on a shooting trip where the forests melt away towards the vast plains of the Arizona desert. The personality of the man was singularly impressive. I caught myself thinking of a mountain, or of some elemental force of Nature so sure of itself that hurry is never necessary. And his gentleness was like the gentleness of women. Great strength often—the greatest always—has tenderness in it, a depth of tenderness unknown to pettier life.

Our meeting was coincidence, for we were hunting in a region where distances are measured by hours and the chance of running across white men very rare. For many days our nightly camps were pitched in spots of beauty where the loneliness is akin to the loneliness of the Egyptian Desert. On one side the mountain slopes were smothered with dense forest, hiding wee meadows of sweet grass like English lawns; and on the other side, stretching for more miles than a man can count, ran the desolate alkali plains of Arizona where tufts of sage-brush are the only vegetation till you reach the lips of the Colorado Canyons. Our horses were tethered for the night beneath the stars. Two backwoodsmen were cooking dinner. The smell of bacon over a wood fire mingled with the keen and fragrant air—when, suddenly, the horses neighed, signalling the approach of one of their own kind.

Indians, white men—probably another hunting party—were within scenting distance, though it was long before my city ears caught any sound, and still longer before the cause itself entered the circle of our firelight.

I saw a square-faced man, tanned like a redskin, in a hunting shirt and a big sombrero, climb down slowly from his horse and move towards us, keenly searching with his eyes; and at the same moment Hank, looking up from the frying-pan where the bacon and venison spluttered in a pool of pork-fat, exclaimed, "Why, it's Ezekiel B.!" The next words, addressed to Jake, who held the kettle, were below his breath "And if he ain't all broke up! Jest look at the eyes on him!" I saw what he meant—the face of a human being distraught by some extraordinary emotion, a soul in violent distress, yet betrayal well kept under. Once, as a newspaper man, I had seen a murderer walk to the electric chair. The expression was similar. Death was *behind* the eyes, not in them. Smith brought in with him—terror.

In a dozen words we learned he had been hunting for some weeks, but was now heading for Tranter, a "stop-off" station where you could flag the daily train 140 miles south-west. He was making for Smithville, the little town that was the apple of his eye. Something "was wrong" with Smithville. No one asked him what—it is the custom to wait till information is volunteered. But Hank, helping him presently to venison (which he hardly touched), said casually, "Good hunting, Boss, your way?"; and the brief reply told much, and proved how eager he was to relieve his mind by speech. "I'm glad to locate your camp, boys," he said. "That's luck. There's something going wrong"—and a catch came into his voice—"with Smithville." Behind the laconic statement emerged somehow the terror the man experienced. For Smith to confess cowardice and in the same breath admit mere "luck," was equivalent to the hysteria that makes city people laugh or cry. It was genuinely dramatic. I have seen nothing more impressive by way of human tragedy—though hard to explain why—than this square-jawed, dauntless man, sitting there with the firelight on his rugged features, and saying this simple thing. For how in the world could he know it—?

In the pause that followed, his Indians came gliding in, tethered the horses, and sat down without a word to eat what Hank distributed. But nothing was to be read on their impassive faces. Redskins, whatever they may feel, show little. Then Smith gave us another pregnant sentence. "*They* heard it too," he said, in a lower voice, indicating his three men; "they saw it jest as I did." He looked up into the starry sky a second. "It's hard upon our trail right now," he added, as though he expected something to drop upon us from the heavens. And from that moment I swear we all felt creepy. The darkness round our lonely camp hid terror in its folds; the wind that whispered through the dry sage-brush brought whispers and the shuffle of watching figures; and when the Indians went softly out to pitch the tents and get more wood for the fire, I remember feeling glad the duty was not mine. Yet this feeling of uneasiness is something one rarely experiences in the open. It belongs to houses, overwrought imaginations, and the presence of evil men. Nature gives peace and security. That we all felt it proves how real it was. And Smith, who felt it most, of course, had brought it.

"There's something gone wrong with Smithville" was an ominous statement of disaster. He said it just as a man in civilised lands might say, "My wife is dying; a telegram's just come. I must take the train." But how he felt so sure of it, a thousand miles away in this uninhabited corner of the wilderness, made us feel curiously uneasy. For it was an incredible thing—yet true. We all felt *that*. Smith did not imagine things. A sense of gloomy apprehension settled over our lonely camp, as though things were about to happen. Already they stalked across the great black night, watching us with many eyes. The wind had risen, and there were sounds among the trees. I, for one, felt no desire to go to bed. The way Smith sat there, watching the sky and peering into the sheet of darkness that veiled the Desert, set my nerves all jangling. He expected something—but what? It was following him. Across this tractless wilderness, apparently above him against the brilliant stars, Something was "hard upon his trail."

Then, in the middle of painful silences, Smith suddenly turned loquacious—further sign with him of deep mental disturbance. He asked questions like a schoolboy—asked them of me too, as being "an edicated man." But there were such queer things to talk about round an Arizona camp-fire that Hank clearly wondered for his sanity. He knew about the "wilderness madness" that attacks some folks. He let his green cigar go out and flashed me signals to be cautious. He listened intently, with the eyes of a puzzled child, half cynical, half touched with superstitious dread. For, briefly, Smith asked me what I knew about stories of dying men appearing at a distance to those who loved them much. He had read such tales, "heard tell of 'em," but "are they dead true, or are they jest little feery tales?" I satisfied him as best I could with one or two authentic stories. Whether he believed or not I cannot say but his swift mind jumped in a flash to the point. "Then, if that kind o' stuff is true," he asked, simply, "it looks as though a feller had a dooplicate of himself—sperrit maybe—that gits loose and active at the time of death, and heads straight for the party it loves best. Ain't that so, Boss?" I admitted the theory was correct. And then he startled us with a final question that made Hank drop an oath below his breath—sure evidence of uneasy excitement in the old backwoodsman. Smith whispered it, looking over his shoulder into the night: "Ain't it jest possible then," he asked, "seeing that men an' Nature is all made of a piece like, that places too have this dooplicate appearance of theirselves that gits loose when they go under?"

It was difficult, under the circumstances, to explain that such a theory *had* been held to account for visions of scenery people sometimes have, and that a city may have a definite personality made up of all its inhabitants—moods, thoughts, feelings, and passions of the multitude who go to compose its life and atmosphere, and that hence is due the odd changes in a man's individuality when he goes from one city to another. Nor was there any time to do so, for hardly had he asked his singular question when the horses whinnied, the Indians leaped to their feet as if ready for an attack, and Smith himself turned the colour of the ashes that lay in a circle of whitish-grey about the burning wood. There was an expression in his face of death, or, as the Irish peasants say, "destroyed."

"That's Smithville," he cried, springing to his feet, then tottering so that I thought he must fall into the flame; "that's my baby town— got loose and huntin' for me, who made it, and love it better'n anything on Gawd's green earth!" And then he added with a kind of gulp in his throat as of a man who wanted to cry but couldn't "And it's going to bits—it's dying—and I'm not thar to save it—!"

He staggered and I caught his arm. The sound of his frightened, anguished voice, and the shuffling of our many feet among the stones, died away into the night. We all stood, staring. The darkness came up closer. The horses ceased their whinnying. For a moment nothing happened. Then Smith turned slowly round and raised his head towards the stars as though he saw something. "Hear that?" he whispered. "It's coming up close. That's what I've bin hearing now, on and off, two days and nights. Listen!" His whispering voice broke horribly; the man was suffering atrociously. For a moment he became vastly, horribly animated—then stood still as death.

But in the hollow silence, broken only by the sighing of the wind among the spruces, we at first heard nothing. Then, most curiously, something like rapid driven mist came trooping down the sky, and veiled a group of stars. With it, as from an enormous distance, but growing swiftly nearer, came noises that were beyond all question the noises of a city rushing through the heavens. From all sides they came; and with them there shot a reddish, streaked appearance across the misty veil that swung so rapidly and softly between the stars and our eyes. Lurid it was, and in some way terrible. A sense of helpless bewilderment came over me, scattering my faculties as in scenes of fire, when the mind struggles violently to possess itself and act for the best. Hank, holding his rifle ready to shoot, moved stupidly round the group, equally at a loss, and swearing incessantly below his breath. For this overwhelming certainty that Something living had come upon us from the sky possessed us all, and I, personally, felt as if a gigantic Being swept against me through the night, destructive and enveloping, and yet that it was not one, but many. Power of action left me. I could not even observe with accuracy what was going on. I stared, dizzy and bewildered, in all directions; but my power of movement was gone, and my feet refused to stir. Only I remember that the Redskins stood like figures of stone, unmoved.

And the sounds about us grew into a roar. The distant murmur came past us like a sea. There was a babel of shouting. Here, in the deep old wilderness that knew no living human beings for hundreds of leagues, there was a tempest of voices calling, crying, shrieking; men's hoarse clamouring, and the high screaming of women and children. Behind it ran a booming sound like thunder. Yet all of it, while apparently so close above our heads, seemed in some inexplicable way far off in the distance—muted, faint, thinning out among the quiet stars. More like a *memory* of turmoil and tumult it seemed than the actual uproar heard at first hand. And through it ran the crash of big things tumbling, breaking, falling in destruction with an awful detonating thunder of collapse. I thought the hills were toppling down upon us. A shrieking city, it seemed, fled past us through the sky.

How long it lasted it is impossible to say, for my power of measuring time had utterly vanished. A dreadful wild anguish summed up all the feelings I can remember. It seemed I watched, or read, or dreamed some desolating scene of disaster in which human life went overboard wholesale, as though one threw a hatful of insects into a blazing fire. This idea of burning, of thick suffocating smoke and savage flame, coloured the entire experience. And the next thing I knew was that it had passed away as completely as though it had never been at all; the stars shone down from an air of limpid clearness, and—there was a smell of burning leather in my nostrils. I just stepped back in time to save my feet. I had moved in my excitement against the circle of hot ashes. Hank pushed me back roughly with the barrel of his rifle.

But, strangest of all, I understood, as by some flash of divine intuition, the reason of this abrupt cessation of the horrible tumult. The Personality of the town, set free and loosened in the moment of death, had returned to him who gave it birth, who loved it, and of whose life it was actually an expression. The Being of Smithville was literally a projection, an emanation of the dynamic, vital personality of its puissant creator. And, in death, it had returned on him with the shock of an accumulated power impossible for a human being to resist. For years he had provided it with life—but *gradually*. It now rushed back to its source, thus concentrated, in a single terrific moment.

"That's him," I heard a voice saying from a great distance as it seemed. "He's fired his last shot—!" and saw Hank turning the body over with his riflebutt. And, though the face itself was calm beneath the stars, there was an attitude of limbs and body that suggested the bursting of an enormous shell that had twisted every fibre by its awful force yet somehow left the body as a whole intact.

We carried "it" to Tranter, and at the first real station along the line we got the news by telegraph "Smithville wiped out by fire. Burned two days and nights. Loss of life, 3000." And all the way in my dreams I seemed still to hear that curious, dreadful cry of Smithville, the shrieking city rushing headlong through the sky.

HANK'S CAMP.

# The Temptation of the Clay

I

SOME men grow away from places, others grow into them: It is a curious and delicate matter. Before now, a man has been thrown out by his own property, yet his successor made immediately at home there. Once let Imagination dwell upon this psychology of places and it will travel very far. Here lies a great mystery, entangled with the mystery of life itself, delicately baited, too. Only the utterly obtuse, one thinks, can ignore the hint offered by Nature—that there is this very definite relationship existing between places and human beings, and that the aggressive attitude is not always chiefly upon the side of the latter.

So it is that there are spots of country—mere bits of scenery, a valley, plain, or river bank, estate or even garden—that undeniably bid a man stay, and welcome; or for no ascertainable reason reject him, and make him anxious to leave. Campers, looking for a night's resting-place, know this well; and so may owners of estates and houses,—campers on a larger scale, seeking to settle somewhere for the few years of a life-time. Neither one nor other, however, one thinks, unless he be a swift-minded poet with vivid divination, gets quite to the root of the matter.

Very suggestive are the mysterious processes by which such results are sometimes brought about, a certain pathos in them too. For the rejected owner is usually of that hard intellectual type that is utterly insensible to the fairy flails of Beauty, and seeks, therefore, in vain through all his stores of logic for a reasonable cause and effect; whereas the accepted one, exquisitely adjusted though he may be to the seduction of the place that takes him in, yet is unable to tell in words what really happens, or to express a tithe of that sweet marvellous explanation that lies concealed within his heart. The one denies it, the other makes wild, poetic guesses; but neither really knows.

Dick Eliot understood something of the two points of view perhaps, because he experienced both acceptance and rejection; and this story, of how a place first welcomed him, then violently tossed him out again, is as queer a case of such relationship as one may ever hear. But, then, Dick Eliot combined in himself a measure of both types of mind; he was intellectual, and knew that two and two make four, but he was also mystical, and knew that they make five or nothing, or a million— that everything is One, and One is everything. Neither was, perhaps, very strong in him, because life had not provided the opportunity for one or other's exclusive development; but both existed side by side in his general mental composition. And they resulted in a level so delicately poised that the apparent balance yet had instability at its roots.

Leaving England at twenty-two or three—there were misunderstandings with his University, where in classics and philosophy he had promised well; with his step-parents who regarded him as well lost; and in a sense, that yet did not affect his honour, with his country's law—he had since met life in difficult, rough places. He had lived. All manner of experiences had been his; he had known starvation in strange cities, and had more than once been close to death—queer kinds of death. But, also, he had been close to earth, and the earth had wonderfully taught him. The results of this teaching, not recognised at the time, came out later to puzzle and amaze him. For years he dwelt in the wilderness with life reduced to its essentials—the big, crude, thundering facts of it—so that he had come to regard scholarship, once so valued, as over-rated, and action as the sole reality. The poetic, mystical side of him passed into temporary abeyance. Worldly achievement and ambition led him. This, however, was a mood of youth only, a reaction due to the resentment of his exile, and to the grievance he cherished against the academic conventions—so he deemed them—that had cut him off from his inheritance.

At thirty, or thereabouts, he fell in love and married—a vigorous personality of a woman with Red Indian in her blood, picked up in some wild escapade along the frontiers of Arizona and New Mexico; and, within six months of marriage, the death of an aunt had left him unexpected master of this little gem of an estate in the south of England where the following experience took place.

This impulsive action of an aunt whom he had seen but once, due to her wish to spite the other claimants rather than to any pretended love for himself, resulted in a radical change of life. He came home, ignored by his relations, and ignoring them in turn. The former love of books revived; the imaginative point of view re-asserted itself; he saw life from another angle. Action, after all, was but a part of it, another form of play. The mental life was the reality; he studied, meditated, wrote. Once more the deep, poetic mystery of things lit all his thoughts with wonder. Corrected by the hard experiences of his early years, the philosopher and dreamer in him assumed the upper hand, though the speculative dreams he indulged were more sanely regulated than before. The imagination was now more finely tempered.

To look at, he was sometimes obviously forty-five, yet at others could easily have passed for thirty:—a tall, lean figure of a man; spare, as though the wilderness had taken that toll of him which no amount of subsequent easy living could efface. To see him was to think of men toiling in a hard, stern land where all things had to be conquered and nothing yielded of itself, where, moreover, human life was cheap and of small account. He was alert, always in training, cheeks thin, neck sinewy, knees ready instantly to turn a horse by grip alone, the reins unnecessary so that both hands were free to fight. The eyes were keen and dark, moustache clipped very short and partly grizzled; deep furrows marked the jaw and forehead; but the muscular hands were young, the fling of the shoulders young, the toss and set of the big head young as well. And he always dressed in riding breeches, with a strap about the waist instead of braces. You might see him hitch them up as he stepped back to leap the stream, or to take the pine knolls with a run downhill.

Indeed, the imaginative side of him seemed almost incongruous; and that such a figure could conceal a mystical, tenderly poetic side not one man in a thousand need have guessed. But, in spite of these severer traits, the character, you felt, was tender enough upon its under side. It was merely that the control of the body and emotions acquired in the wilds had never been unlearned, and that no amount of softer living could let it be forgotten.

About the rather grim and over-silent mouth, for instance, there were marks like the touches of a flower that sometimes made the sternness seem a clumsy mask. An intuitive woman, or a child, must have found him out at once.

## II

AFTER years spent as he had spent them among the conditions of primitive lands, Dick Eliot came back with his "uncivilised" wife, to find that with the old established values of English "County" existence they had little or nothing in common. Their ostracism by the neighbourhood has no place in this story, except to show how it threw them back intensely into the little property he had inherited. They lived there a dozen years, isolated, childless, knowing that solitude in a crowd which yet is never loneliness.

The "Place," as they always called it, took them, and welcome, to itself. The land, running to several hundred acres, was comparatively worthless, mere jumbled stretch of sand and pines and heathery hills; too remote from any building centre to be easily sold, and of no avail for agricultural purposes. For which, since he had just enough to live on quietly, both were grateful: they could keep it lovely and unspoilt. All round it, however, was an opulent, over-built-upon country that they loathed, since they felt that its quality, once admitted, would cause the Place to wither and die. The gross surfeit of prosperous houses, preserved woods, motoring hotels, and the rest would settle on its virgin face. Builders and business men would commercially appraise it, financiers undress it publicly so that it would know itself naked and ashamed. Deep down its soul would turn weakly and diseased, then disappear, and their own assuredly go with it.

For both had loved the Place at sight. She in particular loved it— with a kind of rude enthusiasm she forced, as it were, upon his gentler character. Its combination of qualities fascinated her—the old-world mellowness with the unkempt, untidy wildness. The way it kept alive that touch of the wilderness she had known from childhood, set in the midst of so much over-civilised country all about, gave her the feeling of having a little, precious secret world entirely to herself. She forced this view with all the vigour of her primitive poetry upon her husband till he accepted it as his own. It became his own; only she realised it more vitally than he did. The contrast laid a spell upon her, and she would not hear of going away. They lived there, in this miniature world, until they knew it with such close intimacy that it became identified with their very selves. She made him see it through her eyes, so that the place was haunted, saturated, invested with their moods of worship, love, and wonder. It became a little mystery-world that their feelings had turned living.

Thus when, after twelve years' happiness together, she died there, he stayed on, sole guardian as it were of all she had loved so dearly. Too vital a man to permit the slightest morbid growth which comes from brooding, he yet lived among fond memories, aware of her presence in every nook and glade, in every tree, her voice in the tinkle of the stream, new values everywhere. Each ridge and valley, made familiar by her step and perfume, strengthened recollection, and more than ever before the Place seemed interwoven with herself and him, subtle expression of vanished joys. The Past stayed on in it; it did not move away; it remained the Present. Her death had doubly consecrated the little estate, making it, so to speak, a sacrament of dear communion. The only change, it seemed, was that he identified it with her being more than with himself or with the two of them. He guarded it unspoilt and sweet because of her who held it once so dear—as another man might have kept a flower she had touched, a picture, or a dress that she had worn. Now it was doubly safe from the damage she had feared—commercial spoliation. "Keep the Place as it is, Dick," she had so often said with a vehemence that belonged to her vigorous type, "I'd hate to see it dirtied!" For her the civilised country round had always been "dirty." And he did so, almost with the feeling that he was keeping her person clean at the same time; for what a man thinks about is real, and he had come to regard the Place and herself as one.

Throwing himself into definite work to occupy his mind, he kept it as the apple of his eye, living in solitude, and cared for only by a mother-ly old housekeeper (years ago his mother's maid) whose services he had by fortunate chance secured. He spent his leisure time in writing —studies of obscure periods in forgotten history that, when published, merely added to the clutter of the world's huge mental lumber-room, to judge by the reviews. Once he made a journey to his haunts of youth, *their* youth, in Arizona, but only to return dissatisfied, with added pain. He settled down finally then, throwing himself with commendable energy into his studies, till the hurrying years brought him thus to forty-five.

Rarely he went to London and pored over musty volumes in the British Museum Reading-room, but after a day or two would hear the murmur of the mill-wheel singing round that portentous, dreary dome, and back he would come again, post-haste. And perhaps he chose his line of study, rather than more imaginative work, because it reasonably absorbed him, while yet it stole no single emotion from his past with her, nor trespassed upon the walking of one dear faint ghost.

### III

AND it was upon this gentle, solitary household that suddenly Mánya Petrovski descended with her presence of wonder and of magic. Out of a clear blue sky she dropped upon him and made herself deliciously at home. Only daughter of his widowed sister, married to a Russian, she was fourteen at the time of her mother's death; and the duty seemed forced upon him with a conviction that admitted of no denial. He had never seen the child in his life, for she was born in the year that he returned to England, family relations simply non-existent; but he had heard of her, partly from Mrs Coove, his housekeeper, and partly from tentative letters his sister wrote from time to time, aiming at reconciliation. He only knew that she was backward to the verge of being stupid, that she "loved Nature and life out of doors," and that she shared with her strange father a certain sulking moodiness that seemed to have been so strong in his own half-civilised Slav temperament. He also remembered that her mother, a curious mixture of puritanism and weakly dread of living, had brought her up strictly in the manufacturing city of the midlands where they dwelt "wealthily," surrounded by an atmosphere of artificiality that he deemed almost criminal. For his sister, fostering old-fashioned religious tendencies, believed that a visible Satan haunted the frontiers of her narrow orthodoxy, and would devour Mánya as soon as look at her once she strayed outside. She too had claimed, he remembered, to love Nature, though her love of it consisted solely in looking cleverly out of windows at passing scenery she need never bother herself to reach. Her husband's violent tempers she had likewise ascribed to his possession by a devil, if not by *the*—her own personal—devil himself. And when this letter, written on her death-bed, came begging him, as the only possible relative, to take charge of the child, he accepted it, as his character was, unflinchingly, yet with the greatest possible reluctance. Significant, too, of his character was the detail that, out of many others surely far more important, first haunted him: "She'll love Nature (by which he meant the Place) in the way her mother did—artificially. We shan't get on a bit!"—thus, instinctively, betraying what lay nearest to his heart.

None the less, he accepted the position without hesitation. There was no money; his sister's property was found to be mortgaged several times above its realisable value, and the child would come to him without a penny. He went headlong at the problem, as at so many other duties that had faced him—puzzling, awkward duties—with a kind of blundering delicacy native to his blood. "Got to be done, no good dreaming about it," he said to himself within a few hours of receiving the letter; and when a little later the telegram came announcing his sister's death, he added shortly with a grim expression, "Here goes, then!" In this plucky, yet not really impulsive decisiveness, the layer of character acquired in Arizona asserted itself. Action ousted dreaming.

And in due course the preparations for the girl's reception were concluded. She would make the journey south alone, and Mrs Coove would meet her. Moreover, evidence to himself at least of true welcome, Mánya should have the bedroom which had been for years unoccupied—his wife's.

For all that, he dreaded her arrival unspeakably. "She'll be bored here. She'll dislike the Place—perhaps hate it. And I shall dislike her too."

## IV

ELIOT ruled his little household well, because he ruled himself. No one, from the tri-weekly gardener to the rough half-breed Westerner who managed the modest stable, felt the least desire to trifle with him. Even Mrs Coove, in the brief morning visits to his study, did not care about asking him to repeat some sentence that she had not quite caught or understood. Yet, in a sense, as with all such men, it was the woman who really managed him. "Mrs" Coove, big, motherly, spinster, divined the child beneath the grim exterior, and simply played with him. She it was who really "ran" the household, relieving him of all domestic worries, and she it was, had he fallen ill— which, even for a day, he never did—who would have nursed him into health again with such tactfully concealed devotion that, while loving the nursing, he would never have guessed the devotion.

So it was largely upon Mrs Coove that he secretly relied to welcome, manage, and look after his little orphaned niece, while, of course, pretending that he did it all himself.

"She'll want a companion, sir, of sorts—if I may make so bold— some one to play with," she told him when he had mentioned that later, of course, he would provide a "governess or something" when he had first "sized up" the child.

He looked hard at her for a moment. He realised her meaning, that the hostile neighbourhood could be relied on to supply nothing of that kind.

"Of course," he said, as though he had thought of it himself.

"She'll love the pony, sir, if she ain't one of the booky sort, which I seem to remember she ain't," added Mrs Coove, looking as usual as though just about to burst into tears. For her motherly face wore a lachrymose expression that was utterly deceptive. Her contempt for books, too, and writing folk was never quite successfully concealed.

In silence he watched the old woman wipe her moist hands upon a black apron, and the perplexities of his new duties grew visibly before his eyes. She had little notion that secretly her master stood a little in awe of her superior domestic knowledge.

"The pony and the woods," he suggested briefly.

"A puppy or a kitten, sir, would help a bit—for indoors, if I may make so bold," the housekeeper ventured, with a passing gulp at her own audacity; "and out of doors, sir, as you say, maybe she'll be 'appy enough. Her pore mother taught—"

The long breath she had taken for this sentence she meant to use to the last gasp if possible. But her master cut her short.

"Miss Mánya arrives at six," he said, turning to his books and papers. "The dog-cart, with you in it, to meet her—please." The "please" was added because he knew her vivid dislike of being too high from the ground, while judging correctly that the pleasure would more than compensate her for this risk of elevation. It was also intended to convey that he appreciated her help, but deplored her wordiness. Laconic even to surliness himself, he disliked long phrases. It was a perpetual wonder to him why even lazy people who detested effort would always use a dozen words where two were more effective.

So Mrs Coove, accustomed to his ways, departed, with a curtsey that more than anything else resembled a sudden collapse of the knees beneath more than they could carry comfortably.

"Thank you, sir; I'll see to it all right," she said, obedient to his glance, beginning the sentence in the room but finishing it in the passage. She looked as though she would weep hopelessly once outside, whereas really she felt beaming pleasure. The compliment of being sent to meet Miss Mánya made her forget her dread of the elevated, swaying dog-cart, as also of the silent half-breed groom who drove it. Full of importance she went off to make preparations.

And later, when Mrs Coove was on her way to the station five miles off, dangerously perched, as it seemed to her, in mid-air, he made his way out slowly into the woods, a vague feeling in him that there was something he must say goodbye to. The Place henceforth, with Mánya in it, would be—not quite the same. What change would come he could not say, but something of the secrecy, the long-loved tender privacy and wonder would depart. Another would share it with him, a trespasser, in a sense an outsider. And, as he roamed the little pine-grown vales, the mossy coverts, and the knee-high bracken, there stole into him this queer sensation that it all was part of a living Something that constituted almost a distinct entity. His wife inspired it, but, also, the Place had a personality of its own, apart from the qualities he had read into it. He realised, for the first time, that it too might take an attitude towards the new arrival. Everywhere, it seemed, there was an air of expectant readiness. It was aware... It might possibly resent it.

And, for moments here and there, as he wandered, rose other ideas in him as well, brought for the first time into existence by the thought of the new arrival. This element, like a sudden shaft of sunlight on a landscape, discovered to him a new aspect of the mental picture. It was vague; yet perplexed him not a little. And it was this: that the thing he loved in all this little property, thinking it always as his own, was in reality what *she* had loved in it, the thing that *she* had made him see through the lens of her own more wild, poetic vision. What he was now saying goodbye to, the thing that the expected intruder might change, or even oust, was after all but a phantom memory—the aspect she had built into it. This curious, painful doubt assailed him for the first time. Was his love and worship of the Place really an individual possession of his own, or had it been all these years but her interpretation of it that he enjoyed vicariously? The thought of Mánya's presence here etched this possibility in sharp relief. Unwelcome, and instantly dismissed, the thought yet obtruded itself—that his feelings had not been quite genuine, quite sincere, and that it was her memory, her so vital vision of the Place he loved rather than the Place itself at first hand.

For the idea that another was on the way to share it stirred the unconscious query: What precisely was it she would share?

And behind it came a still more subtle questioning that he put away almost before it was clearly born: Was he really *quite* content with this unambitious guardianship of the dream-estate, and was the grievance of his exile so completely dead that he would, under all possible conditions, keep its loveliness inviolate and free from spoliation?

The coming of the child, with the new duties involved, and the probable later claims upon his meagre purse, introduced a worldly element that for so long had slept in him. He wondered. The ghosts all walked. But beside them walked other ghosts as well. And this new, strange pain of uncertainty came with them—sinister though exceedingly faint suggestion that he had been worshipping a phantom fastened into his heart by a mind more vigorous than his own.

Ambition, action, practical achievement stirred a little in their sleep.

And on his way back he picked some bits of heather and bracken, a few larch twigs with little cones upon them, and several sprays of pine. These he carried into the house and up into the child's bedroom, where he stuck them about in pots and vases. The flowers Mrs Coove had arranged he tossed away. For flowers in a room, or in a house at all, he never liked; they looked unnatural, artificial. Flowers and food together on a table seemed to him as dreadful as the sickly smelling wreaths people loved to put on coffins. But leaves were different; and earth was best of all. In his own room he had two wide, deep boxes of plain earth, watered daily, renewed from time to time, and more sweetly scented than any flowers in the world.

Opening the windows to let in all the sun and air there was, he glanced round him with critical approval. To most the room must have seemed bare enough, yet he had put extra chairs and tables in it, a sofa too, because he thought the child would like them. Personally, he preferred space about him; his own quarters looked positively unfurnished; rooms were cramped enough as it was, and useless upholstery gave him a feeling of oppression. He still clung to essentials; and an empty room, like earth and sky, was fine and dignified.

But Mánya, he well knew, might feel differently, and he sought to anticipate her wishes as best he might. For Mánya came from a big house where the idea was to conceal every inch of empty space with something valuable and useless; and her playground had been gardens smothered among formal flowerbeds—triangles, crescents, circles, anything that parodied Nature—paths cut cleanly to neat patterns, and plants that acknowledged their shame by growing all exactly alike without a trace of individuality.

He moved to the open window, gazing out across the stretch of hill and heathery valley, thick with stately pines. The wind sighed softly past his ears. He heard the murmur of the droning mill-wheel, the drum and tinkle of falling water mingling with it. And the years that had passed since last he stood and looked forth from this window came up close and peered across his shoulder. The Past rose silently beside him and looked out too... He saw it all through other eyes that once had so large a share in fashioning it.

Again came this singular impression—that, while he waited, the whole Place waited too. It knew that she was coming. Another pair of feet would run upon its face and surface, another voice wake all its little echoes, another mind seek to read its secret and share the mystery of its being.

"If Mánya doesn't like it—!" struck with real pain across his heart. But the thought did not complete itself. Only, into the strong face came a momentary expression of helplessness that sat strangely there. Whether the child would like himself or not seemed a consideration of quite minor importance.

A sound of wheels upon the gravel at the front of the house disturbed his deep reflections, and, shutting the door carefully behind him, he gave one last look round to see that all was right, and then went downstairs to meet her. The sigh that floated through his mind was not allowed to reach the lips but another expression came up into his face. His lips became compressed, and resolution passed into his eyes. It was the look—and how he would have laughed, perhaps, could he have divined it!—the look of set determination that years ago he wore when in some lonely encampment among the Bad Lands something of danger was reported near.

With a sinking heart he went downstairs to meet his duty.

But in the hall, scattering his formal phrases to the winds, a boyish figure, yet with loose flying hair, ran up against him, then stepped sharply back. There was a moment's pitiless examination.

"Uncle Dick!" he heard, cried softly. "Is *that* what you're like? But how wonderful!" And he was aware that a pair of penetrating eyes, set wide apart in a grave but eager face, were mercilessly taking him in. It was he who was being "sized up." No redskin ever made a more rapid and thorough examination, nor, probably, a more accurate one.

"Oh! I *never* thought you would look so kind and splendid!"

"Me!" he gasped, forgetting every single thing he had planned to say in front of this swift-moving creature who attacked him.

She came close up to him, her voice breathless still but if possible softer, eyes shining like two little lamps.

"I expected—from what Mother said—you'd be—just Uncle Richard! And instead it's only Uncle—Uncle Dick!"

Here was unaffected sincerity indeed. He had dreaded—he hardly knew why—some simpering sentence of formality, or even tears at being lonely in a strange house. And, in place of either came this sort of cowboy verdict, straight as a blow from the shoulder. It took his breath away. In his heart something turned very soft and yearning. And yet he—winced.

"Nice drive?" he heard his gruff voice asking. For the life of him he could think of nothing else to say. And the answer came with a little peal of breathless laughter, increasing his amazement and confusion.

"I drove all the way. I made the blackie let me. And the mothery person held on behind like a bolster. It was glorious."

At the same moment two strong, quick arms, thin as a lariat, were round his neck. And he was being kissed—once only, though it felt all over his face. She stood on tiptoe to reach him, pulling his head down towards her lips.

"How are you, Uncle, please?"

"Thanks, Mánya," he said shortly, straightening up in an effort to keep his balance, "all right. Glad you are, too. Mrs Coove, your 'mothery person who held on like a bolster,' will take you upstairs and wash you. Then food—soon as you like."

He had not indulged in such a long sentence for years. It increased his bewilderment to hear it. Something ill-regulated had broken loose.

Mrs Coove, who had watched the scene from the background and doubtless heard the flattering description of herself, moved forward with a mountainous air of possession. Her face as usual seemed to threaten tears, but there was a gleam in her eyes which could only come from the joy of absolute approval. With a movement of her arm that seemed to gather the child in, she went laboriously upstairs. The back of her alone proved to any seeing eye that she had already passed willingly into the state of abject slavery that all instinctive mothers love.

"We shan't be barely five minutes, sir," she called respectfully when halfway up; and the way she glanced down upon her grim master, who stood still with feet wide apart watching them, spoke further her opinion—and her joy at it—that he too was caught within her toils. "She'll manage you, sir, if I may make so bold," was certainly the thought her words did not express.

They vanished round the corner—the heavy tread and the light, pattering step. And he still stood on there, waiting in the hall. A mist rose just before his eyes; he did not see quite clearly. In his heart a surge of strong, deep feeling struggled upwards, but was instantly suppressed. Mánya had said another thing that moved him far more than her childish appreciation of himself, something that stirred him to the depths most strangely.

For, when he asked her how she enjoyed the drive, the girl had replied with undeniable sincerity, looking straight into his eyes:

"The last bit was like a fairy-tale. Uncle, *how* awfully this place must love you!"

She did not say, "How you must love the place!" And—she loathed the "dirty" country all about.

Then, the first rush of excitement over, a sort of shyness, curiously becoming, had settled down all over her like a cloud. It settled down upon himself as well. But—she had said the perfect thing. And his doubts all vanished. It *was*—yes, surely—the Place she loved.

And yet, when all was over, there passed through him an unpleasant afterthought—as though Mánya had applied a test by which already something in himself was found gravely wanting.

## V

WITH its sharp, pine-grown declivities, its tumbling streams, stretches of open heather, and its miniature forests of bracken, the dream-estate was like a liliputian Scotland compressed into a few hundred acres. All was in exquisite proportion.

The old house of rough grey stone, set in one corner, looked out upon a wild, untidy garden that melted unobserved into woods of mystery beyond, and farther off rose sharp against the sky a series of peaked knolls and ridges that in certain lights looked like big hills many miles away. There were diminutive fairy valleys you could cross in twenty minutes; and several rivulets, wandering from the moorlands higher up, formed the single stream that once had worked the Mill.

But the Mill, standing a stone's-throw from the study windows, so that he heard the water singing and gurgling almost among his book-shelves, had for a century ground nothing more substantial than sunshine, air, and shadow. For the gold-dust of the stars is too fine for grinding. But it ground as well the dreams of the lonely occupant of the grey-toned house. And he let it stand there, falling gradually into complete decay, because beneath those crumbling wooden walls—he remembered it as of yesterday—the sudden stroke had come that in a moment, dropping as it seemed out of eternity, had robbed him of his chief possession—fashioner of the greatest dream of all. The splash and murmur of the water, the drone of the creaking wheel in flood time, the white weed that gathered thickly over the pond formed by the ancient dam, and the red-brown tint of walls and rotting roof—all were like the colour of the water's singing, the colour of her memory, and the colour of his thinking too, made sweetly visible.

Indeed, despite his best control, *she* still lurked everywhere, so that he could not recall a single experience of the past years without at the same time some vivid aspect of the scenery, as she saw it, rising up clearly to accompany it. In every corner stood the ghost of a still recoverable mood. Here he had suffered, fought, and prayed; here he had loved and hated; here he had lost and found. All the kaleidoscope aspects of growing older, of hopes and fears and disappointments, were visualised for him in terms of the Place where he had met and dealt with them for his soul's good or ill. But behind them always stood that Figure in Chief; it was she who directed the ghostly band; and she it was who coaxed the romantic scenery thus into the support of all his personal moods, and continued to do so with even greater power after she was gone.

His respect for the Place seemed, therefore, involved with his respect for himself and her. That tumbling stream had an inalienable right of way; that mill of golden-brown claimed ancient lights as truly as any mental palace of thoughts within his mind; and the little dips and rises in the woods were as sacred—so he had always felt—as were those twists and turns of character that he called his views of life and his beliefs. This blending of himself with the Place and her had been very carefully reared. The notion that its foundations were not impregnable for ever was a most disturbing one. That the mere arrival of an intruder could shake it, possibly shatter it, touched sacrilege. And for long he suppressed the outrageous notion so successfully that he almost entirely forgot about it.

This strip of vivid land whereon he dwelt acquired, moreover, a heightened charm from the character of the odious land surrounding it. For on all sides was that type of country best described as over-fed and over-lived-upon. The scenery was choked and smothered unto death; it breathed, if at all, the breath of a fading life pumped through it artificially and with labour. Heavily beneath the skies it lay—acres of inert soil.

There were, indeed, people who admired it, calling it typical of something or other in the south of England; but for him these people, like the land itself, were bourgeois, dull, insipid, and phlegmatic as the back of a sheep. Like rooms in a big club, it was over-furnished with too solid upholstery—thick, fat hedges, formal oak woods, lifeless copses stuck upon slopes from which successful crops had sucked long ago the last vestiges of spontaneous life; and spotted with self-satisfied modern cottages, "improved" beyond redemption, that made him think with laughter of some scattered group of city aldermen. "They're pompous City magnates," he used to tell his wife, "strayed from the safety of Cornhill, and a little frightened by the wind and rain."

Everywhere, amid bushy trees that looked so pampered they were almost sham, stood "country houses," whole crops of them, dozing after heavy meals among gardens of sleek tulip and geraniums. They plastered themselves, with the atmosphere of small Crystal Palaces, upon every available opening, comfortably settled down and weighted with every conceivable modern appliance, and in "Parks" all cut to measure like children's wooden toys. They stood there, heavy and respectable, living close to the ground, and in them, almost without exception, dwelt successful businessmen who owned a "country seat." From his uncivilised, wild-country point of view, they epitomised the soul of the entire scenery about them—something gross and sluggish that involved stagnation. They brooded with an air of vulgar luxury that was too stupid even to be active. Here "resided," in a word, the wealthy.

When he walked or drove through the five miles of opulent ugliness that lay between Mill House and the station, it seemed like crossing an inert stretch of adipose tissue, then lighting suddenly upon a pulsating nerve-centre. To step back into the fresh and hungry beauty of his pine valley, with its tumbling waters and its fragrance of wild loveliness, was an experience he never ceased to take delight in. The air at once turned keen, the trees gave out sharp perfumes, waters rustled, foliage sang. Oh! here was life, activity, and movement. Vital currents flowed through and over it. The grey house among the fir-trees, beckoning to the Mill beyond, was a place where things might happen and pass swiftly. Here was no stagnation possible. Thrills of beauty, denied by that grosser landscape, returned electrically upon the heart. With every breath he drew in wonder and enchantment.

And all this, for some years now, he had enjoyed alone. Rather than diminishing with his middle age, the spell had increased. Then came this sudden question of another's intrusion upon his dream-estate, and he had dreaded painful alteration. The presence of another, most likely stupid, and certainly unsympathetic, must cause a desolating change. Alteration there was bound to be, or at the best a readjustment of values that would steal away the wild and accustomed flavour. He had dreaded the child's arrival unspeakably. It had turned him abruptly timid, and this timidity betrayed the sweetness of the treasure that he guarded. For it came close to fear—the fear men know when they realise an attack they cannot, by any means within their power, hope to defeat.

And alteration, as he apprehended, came; yet not the alteration he had dreaded. Mánya's arrival had been a surprise that was pure joy. Its wonder almost woke suspicion. And the surprise, he found, grew into a series of surprises that at first took his breath away. The alchemy that her little shining presence brought persisted, grew from day to day, till it operated with such augmenting power that it changed himself as well. No stranger fairy-tale was ever written.

## VI

NEXT day he put his work aside and devoted himself whole-heartedly to the lonely child. It was not only duty now. She had stirred his love and pity from the first. They would get on together. Unconsciously, by saying the very thing to win him—"Uncle, *how* the Place must love you!"—she had struck the fundamental tone that made the three of them in harmony, and set the whole place singing. The sense of an intruding trespasser had vanished. The Place accepted her.

It was only later that he realised this completely and in detail, though on looking back he saw clearly that the verdict had been given instantly. For no revision changed it. "I'm all right here with Uncle," was the child's quick intuition, meeting his own halfway:—"We three are all right here together." For she leaped upon his beloved dream-state and made it seem twice as wild and living as before. She delighted in its loneliness and mystery. She clapped her hands and laughed, pointed and asked questions, made her eyes round with wonder, and, in a word, put her own feelings from the start into each nook and corner where he took her. There was no shyness, no confusion; she made herself at home with a little air of possession that, instead of irritating as it might have done, was utterly enchanting. It was like the chorus of approval that increases a man's admiration for the woman he has chosen.

She brought her own interpretations, too, yet without destroying his own.

They even differed from his own, yet only by showing him points and aspects he had not realised. The child saw things most oddly from another point of view. From the very first she began to say astonishing things. They piqued and puzzled him to the end, these things she said. He felt they unravelled something. In his own mind the personality of the Place and the memory of his wife had become confused and jumbled, as it were. Mánya's remarks and questions disentangled something. Her child's divination cleared his perceptions with a singular directness. She had strong in her that divine curiosity of children which is as far removed from mere inquisitiveness as gold-dust from a vulgar-finished ornament. Wonder in her was vital and insatiable, and some of these questions that he could not answer stirred in him, even on that first day of acquaintance, almost the sense of respect.

Morning and afternoon they spent together in visiting every corner of the woods and valleys; no inch was left without inspection; they followed the stream from the moorlands to the Mill, plunged through the bracken, leaped the high tufts of heather, and scrambled together down the precipitous sandpits. She did not jump as well as he did, but showed equal recklessness. And the depths of shadowy pinewood made her hushed and silent like himself. In her childish way she *felt* the wild charm of it all deeply. Not once did she cry "How lovely" or "How wonderful"; but showed her happiness and pleasure by what she did.

"Better than yesterday, eh?" he suggested once, to see what she would answer, yet sure it would be right.

She darted to his side. "That was all stuffed," she said, laconically as himself, and making a wry face. And then she added with a grave expression, half anxious and half solemn, "Fancy, if *that* got in Oh, Uncle!"

"Couldn't," he comforted himself and her, delighted secretly.

But it was on their way home to tea in the dusk, feeling as if they had known one another all their lives, so quickly had friendship been cemented, that she said her first genuinely strange thing. For a long time she had been silent by his side, apparently tired, when suddenly out popped this little criticism that showed her mind was actively working all the time.

"Uncle, you *have* been busy—keeping it so safe. I suppose you did most of it at night."

He started. His own thoughts had been travelling in several directions at once.

"I don't walk in my sleep," he laughed.

"I mean when the stars are shining," she said. She felt it as delicately as that, then! She felt the dream quality in it. "I mean, it loves you best when the sun has set and it comes out of its hole," she added, as he said nothing.

"Mánya, it loves you too—already," he said gently.

Then came the astonishing thing. The voice was curious; the words seemed to come from a long way off, taking time to reach him. They took time to reach her too, as though another had first whispered them. It almost seemed as though she listened while she said them. A sense of the uncanny touched him here in the shadowy dark wood:

"It's a woman, you see, really, and that's why you're so fond of it. That's why it likes me too, and why I can play with it."

The amazing judgment gave him pause at once, for he felt no child ought to know or say such things. It savoured of precociousness, even of morbidity, both of which his soul loathed. But reflection brought clearer judgment. The sentence revealed something he had already been very quick to divine, namely, that while the ordinary mind in her was undeveloped, backward, almost stunted, by her bringing up, another part of her was vividly aware. And this other part was taught of Nature; it was the fairy thing that children had the right to know. She stood close to the earth. Landscape and scenery brought her vivid impressions that fairy-tales, rather stupidly, translate into princes and princesses, ogres, giants, dragons. Mánya, having been denied the fairy books, personified these impressions after her own fashion. What was it after all but the primitive instinct of early races that turned the moods of Nature into beings, calling them gods, or the instinct of a later day that personified the Supreme, calling it God? He himself had "felt" in very imaginative moments that bits of scenery, as with trees and even the heavenly bodies, could actually express such differences of temperament, seem positive or negative, almost male or female. And perhaps, in her original, child's fashion, she felt it too.

Then Mánya interrupted his reflections with a further observation that scattered his philosophising like an explosion. Something, as he heard it, came up close and brushed him. It made him start.

"In some places, you see, Uncle, I feel shy all over. But here I could run about naked. I could undress."

He burst out laughing. Instinctively he felt this was the best thing he could do. A sympathetic answer might have meant too much, yet silence would have made her feel foolish. His laughter turned the idea in her little mind all wholesome and natural.

"Play here to your heart's content, for there's no one to disturb you," he cried. "And when I'm too busy," he added, thinking it a happy inspiration, "Mrs Coove can—"

"Oh," she interrupted like a flash, "but she's too bulgey. She could never jump like you, for one thing."

"True."

"Or play hide-and-seek. She couldn't fit in anywhere. She'd never be able to hide, you see."

And so they reached the house, like two friends who had found suddenly a new delight in life, and sat down to an enormous tea, with jam, buttered muffins, and a stodgy indigestible cake straight from the oven. His tea hitherto had consisted of one cup and two pieces of thin bread and butter. But the appetite of twenty-five had come back again.

A new joy of life had come back with it. After so many years of brooding, dreaming, solitary working, he had grown over solemn, the sense of fun and humour atrophying. He had erected barriers between himself and all his kind, hedged himself in too much. The arrival of this child brought new impetus into the enclosure. Without destroying what imagination had prized so long, she shifted the old values into slightly different keys. Already he caught his thoughts running forward to construct her future—what she might become, how he might help her to develop spiritually and materially—yes, materially as well. His thoughts had hitherto run chiefly backwards.

This need not, indeed could not, involve being unfaithful to the past. But it did mean looking ahead instead of always looking back. It was more wholesome.

Yet what dawned upon him—rather, what chiefly struck him out of his singular observations perhaps, was this: not only that the Place had wholeheartedly accepted her, but that she had instantly established some definite relation with it that was different to his own. It was even deeper, truer, more vital than his own; for it was somehow more natural. It had been discovered, though already there; and it was not, like his own, built up by imaginative emotion. Hence came his notion that she disentangled something; hence the respect he felt for her from the start; hence, too, the original, surprising things she sometimes said.

## VII

FOR several days he watched and studied her, while she turned the Place into a private playground of her own with that air of sweet possession that had charmed him from the first. Backward and undeveloped she undeniably was, but, in view of her stupid, artificial bringing up, he understood this easily. Of books and facts, of knowledge taught in school, she was shockingly ignorant. The wrong part of her had been "forced" at the wrong time; the "play" side had been denied development, and, while gathering force underground, her little brain had learned by heart, but without real comprehension, things that belonged properly to a later stage. For if ever there was one, here was an elemental being, free of the earth, native of open places, called to the wisdom of the woods. It all had been suppressed in her. She now broke out and loose, bewildered, and a little rampant, wild rather, and over joyful. She revelled like an animal in new-found freedom.

In time she sobered. He led her wisely. Yet often she went too fast for him to follow, and slipped beyond his understanding altogether. For there were gaps in her nature, unfilled openings in her mind, loopholes through which she seemed to escape too easily, perhaps too completely, into her playground, certainly too rapidly for him to catch her up. It was then she said these things that so astonished him, making him feel she was somehow an eldritch soul that saw things, Nature especially, from a point of view he had never reached. Her sight of everything was original. A bird's-eye view he could understand; most primitive folk possessed it, and in his wife it had been vividly illuminating. But Mánya had not got this bird's-eye view, the sweeping vision that takes in everything at a single glance from above. Her angle was another one, peculiar to herself. Laughing, he thought of it rather as seeing everything from below—a fish's point of view! Brightness described her best—eyes, skin, teeth, and lips all shone. Yet her manner was subdued, not effervescent, and in it this evidence of depth, a depth he could not always plumb. It was a nature that sparkled, but the sparkle was suppressed; and he loved the sparkle, while loving even more its suppression. It gathered till the point of flame was reached, and it was the possible out-rushing of this potential flame that won his deference, and sometimes stirred his awe. His dread had been considerable, anticipation keen; and the relief was in proportion. Here was a child he could both respect and love; and the sense of responsibility for the little being entrusted to his charge grew very strong indeed.

In due course he supplied a governess, Fräulein Bühlke. She came from the neighbouring town, with her broad, flat German face, framed in flaxen hair that was glossy but not oiled, and smoothed down close to the skull across a shining parting. Mechanically devout, rather fussy, literal in mind, exceedingly worthy and conscientious, her formula was, "You think that would be wise? Then I try it." And the "trying," which the tone suggested would be delicate, was applied with a blundering directness that defeated its own end. Her method was thumping rather than insinuating, and her notion of delicacy was to state her meaning heavily, add to it, "Try to believe that I know best, dear child," and then conscientiously enforce it. Mánya she understood as little as an okapi, but she was kind, affectionate, and patient; and though Eliot always meant to change her, he never did, for the getting of a suitable governess was more than he and Mrs Coove could really manage. "*Der liebe Gote weisst alles*," was the phrase with which she ended all their interviews. And if Mánya's obedience showed a slight contempt, it was a contempt he did not think it wise entirely to check.

For he himself could never scold her. It was impossible. It felt as though he stepped upon a baby. Their relations were those of equals almost, each looking up to the other with respect and wonder. Her schoolroom life became a thing apart. So did the hours in his study. Her walks with the governess and his journeys to the British Museum were mere extensions of the schoolroom and the study. It was when they went out together, roaming about the Place at will, exploring, playing, building fires, and the rest, that their true enjoyment came— enjoyment all the keener because each stuck valiantly to duty first.

Her face, though not exactly pretty, had the charm of some wild intelligence he had never seen before. The nose, slightly tilted, wore a tiny platform at its tip. The mouth was firm, lips exquisitely cut, but it was in the dark, shining eyes that the expression of the soul ran into focus; though at times she knew long periods of silence that seemed almost sullen, when her eyes turned dead and coaly, and she seemed almost gone away from behind them. One day she was old as himself, another a mere baby; something was always escaping the leash and slipping off, then coming back with a rush of some astonishing sentence it had gone to fetch. Her physical appearance sometimes was elusive too, now tall, now short, her little body protean as her little soul.

Like running water she was all over the house, not laughing much, not exactly gay or cheerful either, but somehow charged to the brim with a mysterious spirit of play—grave, earnest play, yet airy with a consummate mischief sometimes that was the despair of Fräulein Bühlke, who wore an expression then as though, after all, there were things God did *not* know. Yes, like running water through the rooms and corridors, and tumbling down the stairs behind the kitten or round the skirts of "bulgey" Mother Coove. Swift and gentle always, yet with force enough to hurt you if you got in her way; almost to sting or slap. Soft, and very girlish to look at, she was really hard as a boy, flexible too as a willow branch, and with a rod of steel laced somewhere invisibly through her tenderness, unsuspected till occasion—rarely—betrayed its presence. It shifted its position too; one never knew where that firmness which is character would crop out and refuse to bend. For then the childishness would vanish. She became imperious as a little natural queen. The half-breed groom had a taste of this latter quality more than once, and afterwards worshipped the ground she walked on. To see them together, she in her dark-grey riding-habit, holding a little whip, and he with his sinister, wild face and half malignant manners, called up some picture of a child and a savage animal she had tamed.

But the thing Mánya chiefly brought into his garden, and so also into the garden of his thoughts, was this new element of Play. She brought with her, not only the child's make-believe, but the child's conviction, earnestness, and sense of reality.

"Tell me *one* thing," she had a way of saying, sure preface to something of significant import that she had to ask, accompanied always by a darker expression in the eyes, puzzled or searching and not on any account to be evaded or lightly answered; "Tell me one thing, Uncle: do these outside things come after us into the house as well?" "Only when we allow them, or invite them in," he replied, taking up her mood as seriously as herself, yet knowing her question to be a feint. She knew the true answer better than himself. She wished to see what he would say. Her sly laughter of approval told him that. "They're already there, though, aren't they?" she whispered, and when he nodded agreement, she added, "Of course; they're everywhere really all the time. They don't move about as we do."

But she had often this singular way of seeing things, and saying them, from the original point of view whence she regarded them—from beneath, as it were, topsy-turvy some might call it, almost a little mad, judged by the sheep-like vision of the majority, yet for herself entirely true, consistent, not imagined merely.

Her literal use of words, too, was sometimes vividly illuminating—as though she saw language *directly*, and robbed of the cloak with which familiar use has smothered it. She undressed phrases, making them shine out alone.

"Moping, child?" he asked once, when one of her silent fits had been somewhat prolonged. "Unhappy?"

"No, Uncle. And I'm *not* moping."

"What is it, then?"

"Fräulein told me I was self-ish, rather."

"That's all right," he said to comfort her. "Be yourself—self-ish—or you're nothing."

She followed her own thought, perhaps not understanding him quite.

"She said I must put my Self out more—for others. Mother used to say it too."

He turned and stared at her. The little face was very grave.

"Eh?" he asked. "Put your Self out?"

Mánya nodded, fixing her eyes, half dreamy, upon his own. She had been far away. Now she was coming back.

"So I'm learning," she said, her voice coming as from a distance. "It's *so* funny. But it's not really difficult—a bit. I could teach you, I think, if you'd promise faithfully to practise regularly."

There was a pause before he asked the next question.

"How d'you do it, child?" came a little gruffly, for he felt queer emotion rising in him.

She shrugged her shoulders.

"Oh, I couldn't tell you *like that*. I could only show you."

There was a touch of weirdness about the child. It stole into him—a faint sense of eeriness, as though she were letting him see through peepholes into that other world she knew so well.

"Well," he asked, more gently, "what happens when you *have* put your Self—er—out? Other things come in, eh?"

"How can I tell?" she answered like a flash. "I'm out."

He stared at her, waiting for more. But nothing followed, and a minute later she was as usual, laughing, her brilliant eyes flashing with mischief, and presently went upstairs to get tidy for their evening meal that was something between an early dinner and high tea. Only at the door she paused a second to fling him another of her characteristic phrases

"I wonder, Uncle. Don't you?" For she certainly knew some natural way, born in her, of moving her Self aside and letting the tide of "bigger things" sweep in and use her. It was her incommunicable secret.

And he did wonder a good deal. Wonder with him had never faded as with most men. It had often puzzled him why this divine curiosity about everything should disappear with the majority after twenty-five, instead, rather, of steadily increasing the more one knows. Familiarity with those few scattered details the world calls knowledge had never dulled its golden edge for him. Only Mánya, and the things she asked and said, gave it a violent new impetus that was like youth returned. And her notion of putting one's Self out in order to let other things come in filled him with about as much wonder as he could comfortably hold just then. He dozed over the fire, thinking deeply, wishing that for a single moment he could stand where this child stood, see things from her point of view, learn the geography of the world she lived in. The source of her inspiration was Nature of course. Yet he too stood close to Nature and was full of sympathetic understanding for her mystery and beauty. Did Mánya then stand nearer than himself? Did she, perhaps, dwell inside it, while he examined from the outside only, a mere onlooker, though an appreciative and loving onlooker?

It came to him that things yielded up to her their essential meaning because she saw them from another side, and he recalled an illuminating line of Alice Meynell about a daisy, and how wonderful it must be to see from "God's side," even of such a simple thing.

Mánya, moreover, saw everything in some amazing fashion as One. The facts of common knowledge men studied so laboriously in isolated groups were but the jewelled facets that hung glittering upon the enormous flanks of this One. The thought flashed through his mind. He remembered another thing she said, and then another; they began to crowd his brain. "I never dream because I know it all awake," she told him once; and only that afternoon, when he asked her why she always stopped and stood straight before him—a habit she had—when he spoke seriously with her, she answered, "Because I want to see you properly. I must be opposite for that! No one can see their own face, or what's next to them, can they?"

Truth, and a philosophical truth! Of no particular importance, maybe, yet strange for a child to have discovered.

Even her ideas of space were singularly original, direct, unhampered by the terms that smother meaning. "Up" and "down" perplexed her; "left" and "right" perpetually deceived her; even "inside" and "outside," when she tried to express them, landed her in a chaos of confusion that to most could have seemed only sheer stupidity. She stood, as it were, in some attitude of naked knowledge behind thought, perception unfettered, untaught, in which she knew that space was only a way of talking about something that no one ever really understands. She saw space, felt it rather, in some absolute sense, not yet "educated" to treat it relatively. She saw everything "round," as though her spatial perceptions were all circles. And circles are infinite, eternal.

With Time, too, it was somewhat similar. "It'll come round again," she said once, when he chided her for having left something undone earlier in the day or, "when I get back to it, Uncle," in reply to his reminding her of a duty for the following day. To the end she was "stupid" about telling the time, and until he cured her of it her invariable answer to his question, "what o'clock it was," would be the literal truth that it was "just now, Uncle," or simply "now," as though she saw things from an absolute, and not a relative point of view. She was always saying things to prove it in this curious manner. And, while it made him sometimes feel uncomfortable in a way he could not quite define, it also increased his attitude of respect towards the secret, mysterious thing she hid so well, though without intending to hide it. She seemed in touch with eternal things—more than other children—not merely with a transient expression of them filtered down for normal human comprehension. Some giant thing she certainly knew. She lived it. Death, for instance, was a conception her mind failed to grasp. She could not realise it. People had "left" or "gone away," perhaps, but somehow for her were always *"there."*

Thus started, his thoughts often travelled far, but always came up with a shock against that big black barrier—the army of the dead. The dead, of course, were always somewhere—if there was survival. But, though he had encountered strange phases of the spiritualistic movement in America, he had known nothing to justify the theory of interference from the other side of that black barrier. The deliverances of the mediums brought no conviction. He sometimes wondered, that was all. And in particular he wondered about that member of the great army who had been for years his close and dear companion. This was natural enough. Could it be that his thought, prolonged and concentrated, formed a prison-house from which escape was difficult? And had his own passionate thinking that ever associated her memory with the Place, detained one soul from farther flight elsewhere? Was this an explanation of that hint Mánya so often brought him—that her presence helped to disentangle, liberate, unravel...? Was the Place haunted in this literal sense?...

### VIII

YET, perhaps, after all, the chief change she introduced was this vital resurrection of his sense of play. For Play is eternal, older than the stars, older even than dreams. She taught him afresh things he had already known, but long forgotten or laid aside. And all she knew came first direct from Nature, large and undiluted.

He learned, for instance, the secret of that deep quiet she possessed even in her wildest moments and how it came from a practice in her mother's house, where all was rush and clamour about worldly "horrid things"—her practice of lying out at night to watch the stars. But not merely to watch them for a minute. She would watch for hours, following the constellations from the moment they loomed above the horizon till they set again at dawn. She saw them move slowly across the entire sky. For "mother hurried and fussed" her so, and by doing this she instinctively drew into her curious wild heart the deep delight of feeling that "there was lots of room really, and no particular hurry about anything." Her inspiration was profound, from ancient sources, natural.

And her "play," for the same reason, was never foolish. It was creative play. It was the faculty by which the poets and dreamers re-create the world, and thus rejuvenate it. Adam knew it when he named the beasts, and Job, when he made rhymes about taking Leviathan with a hook, and sang his little heart-sweet songs about the conies and the hopping hills. In the wise it never dies, for it is most subtly allied to wisdom, and only the dreamless can divorce it quite. It is the natural, untaught poetry of the soul which laughs and weeps with Nature, knowing itself akin, seeing itself in everything and everything in itself. Mánya in some amazing fashion, not yet educated out of her, knew Nature in herself.

She did naughty things too, as he learned from Mrs Coove, when he felt obliged to lecture her, but they were invariably typical and explanatory of her close-to-Nature little being. And he understood what she felt so well that his lectures ended in laughter, with her grave defence "Uncle, you'd have done the same yourself." Once in particular, after a fortnight of parching drought, when the gush of warm rain came with its welcome, drenching soak, and the child ran out upon the balcony in her nightgown to feel it on her body too—how could he prove her wrong, having felt the same delight himself? "I was thirsty and dry all over. I *had* to do it," she explained, puzzled, adding that of course she had changed afterwards and used the rough Turkey towel "just as you do."

But other things he did not understand so well; and one of these was her singular habit of imitating the sounds of Nature, with an accuracy, too, that often deceived even himself. The true sounds of Nature are only two—water and wind, with their many variations. And Mánya, by some trick of tone and breath, could reproduce them marvellously.

"It's the way to get close," she told him when he asked her why, "the way to get inside. If you get the sound exact, you feel the same as they do, and know their things." And the cryptic, yet deeply suggestive explanation contained a significant truth that yet just evaded his comprehension. They often played it together in the woods, though he never approached her own astonishing excellence. This, again, stirred something like awe in him; it was a little eerie, almost uncanny, to hear her "doing trees," or "playing wind and water."

But the strangest of all her odd, original tricks was one that he at length dissuaded her from practising because he felt it stimulated her imagination unwisely, and with too great conviction. It is not easy to describe, and to convey the complete success of the achievement is impossible without seeing the actual results. For she drew invisible things. Her designs, so clumsily done with a butt of pencil, or even the point of her stick in the sand, managed to suggest a meaning that somehow just escaped grasping by the mind. They made him think of puzzle-pictures that intentionally conceal a face or figure. Vague, fluid shapes that never quite achieved an actual form ran through these scattered tracings. She used points in the scenery to indicate an outline of something other than themselves, yet something they contained and clothed. His eye vainly tried to force into view the picture that he felt lay there hiding within these points.

On a large sheet of paper she would draw roughly details of the landscape—tops of trees, the Mill roof, a boulder or a stretch of the stream, for instance—and persuade these points to gather the blank space of paper between them into the semblance, the suggestion rather, of some vague figure, always vast and always very much alive. They marked, within their boundaries, an outline of some form that remained continually elusive. Yet the outline thus framed, whichever way you looked at it, even holding the paper upside down, still remained a figure; a figure, moreover, that moved. For the child had a way of turning the paper round so that the figure had an appearance of moving independently upon itself. The reality of the whole business was more than striking; and it was when she came to giving these figures names that she decided to put a stop to it

One day another curious thing had happened. He had often thought about it since, and wondered whether its explanation lay in mere child's mischief, or in some power of discerning these invisible Presences that she drew.

They were returning together from a scramble in the gravel-pit which they pretended was a secret entrance to the centre of the world; and they were tired. Mánya walked a little in front, as her habit was, so that she could turn and see him "opposite" at a moment's notice when he said an interesting thing. Her red tam-o'-shanter, with the top-knot off, she carried in her hand, swinging it to and fro. From time to time she flicked it out sideways, as though to keep flies away. But there were no flies, for it was chilly and growing dark. The pines were thickly planted here, with sudden open spaces. Their footsteps fell soft and dead upon the needles. And sometimes she flung her arm out with an imperious, sudden gesture of defiance that made him feel suspicious and look over his shoulder. For it was like signing to some one who came close, some one he could not see, but whose presence was very real to her. The unwelcome conviction grew upon him. Some one, in the world she knew apart from him, accompanied them. A few minutes before she had been wild and romping, playing at "mushrooms" with laughter and excitement. She loved doing this—whirling round on her toes till her skirts were horizontal, then sinking with them ballooning round her to the ground, the tam-o'-shanter pulled down over her entire face so that she looked like a giant toadstool with a crimson top. But now she had turned suddenly grave and silent.

"Uncle!" she exclaimed abruptly, turning sharply to face him, and using the hushed tone that was always prelude to some startling question, "tell me *one* thing, please. What would *you* do if—"

She broke off suddenly and sprang swiftly to one side.

"Mánya! if what?" He did not like the movement; it was so obviously done to avoid something that stood in her way—between them—very close. He almost jumped too. "I can't tell you anything while you're darting about like a deer-fly. What d'you want to know?" he added with involuntary sharpness.

She stood facing him with her legs astride the path. She stared straight into his eyes. The dusk played tricks with her height, always delusive. It magnified her. She seemed to stand over him, towering up.

"If some one kept walking close beside you under an umbrella," she whispered earnestly, "so that the face was hidden and you could never see it—what would *you* do?"

"Child! But what a question!" The carelessness in his tone was not quite natural. A shiver ran down his back.

She moved closer, so that he felt her breath and saw the gleam of her big, wide-opened eyes.

"Would you knock up the umbrella with a bang," she whispered, as though afraid she might be overheard, "or just suddenly stoop and look beneath—catching it that way?"

He stepped aside to pass her, but the child stepped with him, barring his movement of escape. She meant to have her answer.

"Take it by surprise like that, I mean. *Would* you, Uncle?"

He stared blankly at her; the conviction in her voice and manner was disquieting.

"Depends what kind of thing," he said, seeing his mistake. He tried to banter, and yet at the same time seem serious. But to joke with Mánya in this mood was never very successful. She resented it. And above all he did not want to lose her confidence.

"Depends," he said slowly, "whether I felt it friendly or unfriendly; but I *think*—er—I should prefer to knock the brolly up."

For a moment she appeared to weigh the wisdom of his judgment, then instantly rejecting it.

"*I* shouldn't!" she answered like a flash. "I should suddenly run up and stoop to see. I should catch it that way!"

And, before he could add a word or make a movement to go on, she darted from beside him with a leap like a deer, flew forwards several yards among the trees, stooped suddenly down, then turned her head and face up sideways as though to peer beneath something that spread close to the ground. Her skirts ballooned about her like the mushroom, one hand supporting her on the earth, while the other, holding the tam-o'-shanter, shaded her eyes.

"Oh! oh!" she cried the next instant, standing bolt upright again, "it's a whole lot! And they've all gone like lightning—gone off there!" She pointed all about her—into the sky, towards the moors, back to the forest, even down into the earth—a curious sweeping gesture; then hid her face behind both hands and came slowly to his side again.

"It wasn't one, Uncle. It was a lot!" she whispered through her fingers. Then she dropped her hands as a new explanation flashed into her. "But p'raps, after all, it was only one! Oh, Uncle, I do believe it *was* only one. Just fancy—how awfully splendid! I wonder!"

Neither the hour nor the place seemed to him suitable for such a discussion. He put his arm round her and hurried out of the wood. He put the woods behind them, like a protective barrier, for his sake as well as hers; that much he clearly realised. He somehow made a shield of them.

In the garden, with the stars peeping through thin clouds, and the lights of the windows beckoning in front, he turned and said laughing, quickening his pace at the same time

"Rabbits, Mánya, rabbits! All the rabbits here use brollies, and the bunnies too." It was the best thing he could think of at the moment. Rather neat he thought it. But her instant answer took the wind out of his sham sails.

"That's just the name for them!" she cried, clapping her hands softly with delight. "Now they needn't hide like that any more. We'll just pretend they're bunnies, and they'll feel disguised enough."

They went into the house, and it was comforting to see the figure of Mother Coove filling the entire hall. At least there was no disguising her. But on the steps Mánya halted a moment and gazed up in his face. She stood in front of him, deaf to Mrs Coove's statements from the rear about wet boots. Her eyes, though shining with excitement, held a puzzled, wild expression.

"Uncle," she whispered, with sly laughter, standing on tiptoe to kiss him, "I wonder—!" then flew upstairs to change before he could find a suitable reply.

But he wondered too, wondered what it was the child had seen. For certainly she had seen something.

Yet the thought that finally stayed with him—as after all the other queer adventures they had together—was this unpleasant one, that his so willing acceptance of the little intruder involved the disapproval, even the resentment, of—another. It haunted him. He never could get quite free of it. Another watched, another listened, another—waited. And Mánya knew.

## IX

AUTUMN passed into winter, and spring at last came round. The dream-estate was a garden of delight and loveliness, fresh green upon the larches and heather all abloom. The routine of the little household was established, and seemed as if it could never have been otherwise. The relationship between the elderly uncle and his little charge was perfect now, like that between a father and his only daughter, spoilt daughter, perhaps a little, who, knowing her power, yet never took advantage of it. He loved her as his own child; and that evasive "something" in her which had won his respect from the first still continued to elude him. He never caught it up. It had increased, too, in the long, dark months. Now, with the lengthening days, it came still more to the front, grown bolder, as though "spring's sweet trouble in the ground" summoned it forth. This sympathy between her being and the Place had strengthened underground. The disentangling had gone on apace. With the first warm softness of the April days he woke abruptly to the fact, and faced it. The older memories had been replaced. It seemed to him almost as though his hold upon the Place had weakened. He loved it still, but loved it in some new way. And his conscience pricked him, for conscience had become identified with the trust of guardianship thus self-imposed. He had let something in, and though it was not the taint of outside country *she* had said would "dirty" it, it yet was alien. It was somehow hostile to the conditions of his original Deed of Trust.

Then, into this little world, dropping like some stray bullet from a distant battle, came with a bang the person of John C. Murdoch. He came for a self-proposed visit of one day, being too "rushed" to stay an hour longer. Chance had put him "on the trail" of his old-time "pard of a hundred camps," and he couldn't miss looking him up, not "for all the money you could shake a stick at." More like a shell than mere bullet he came—explosively and with a kind of tempestuous energy. For his vitality and speed of action were terrific, and he was making money now "dead easy"—so easy, in fact, that it was "like picking it up in the street."

"Then you've done well for yourself since those old days in Arizona," said Eliot, really pleased to see him, for a truer "partner" in difficult times he had never known; "and I'm glad to hear it."

"That's so, Boss"—he had always called the "Englisher" thus because of his refined speech and manners—"God ain't forgot me, and I've got grub-stakes now all over Yurrup. Just raking it in, and if you want a bit, why, name the figger and it's yours." He glanced round at the modest old-fashioned establishment, judging it evidence of unsuccess.

"What line?" asked Eliot, dropping into the long-forgotten lingo.

"Why, patents, bless your heart," was the reply. "They come to me as easy as mother's milk to baby, and if the heart don't wither in me first, I'll patent everything in sight. I'll patent the earth itself before I'm done."

And for a whole hour, smoking one strong green cigar upon another, he gave brief and picturesque descriptions of his various enterprises, with such energy and gusto, moreover, that there woke in Eliot something of the lust of battle he had known in the wild, early days, something of his zest for making a fortune, something too of the old bitter grievance—in a word, the spirit of action, eager strife and keen achievement, which never had quite gone to sleep...

"And now," said Murdoch at length, "tell me about yerself. You look fit and lively. You've had enough of my chin-music. Made yer pile and retired too? Isn't that it? Only you still like things kind o' modest and camp-like. Is that so?"

But Eliot found it difficult to tell. This side of him that life in England had revived, to the almost complete burial of the other, was one that Murdoch would not understand. For one thing, Murdoch had never seen it in his friend; the Arizona days had kept it deeply hidden. He listened with a kind of tolerant pity, while Eliot found himself giving the desired information almost in a tone of apology.

"Every man to his liking," the Westerner cut him short when he had heard less than half of the stammering tale, "and your line ain't mine, I see. I'm no shadow-chaser—never was. You've changed a lot. Why"—looking round at the little pine-clad valley—"I should think you'd rot to death in this place. There's not room to pitch a camp or feed a horse. I'd choke for want of air." And he lit another cigar and spat neatly across ten feet of lawn.

John Casanova Murdoch—in the West he was called "John Cass," or just "John C.," but had resurrected the middle name for the benefit of Yurrup—was a man of parts and character, tried courage, and unfailing in his friendship. "Straight as you make 'em" was the verdict of the primitive country where a man's essential qualities are soon recognised, "and without no frills." And Eliot, whatever he may have thought, felt no resentment. He remembered the rough man's kindness to him when he had been a tenderfoot in more than one awkward place. John C. might "rot to death" in this place, and might think the vulgar country round it "great stuff," but for all that his host liked to see and hear him. He remembered his skill as a mining prospector and an engineer; he was not surprised that he had at last "struck oil."

They talked of many things, but the visitor always brought the conversations round to his two great healthy ambitions, now on the way to full satisfaction: money and power. Upon some chance mention of religion, he waved his hand impatiently with enough vigour to knock a man down, and said, "Religion! Hell! I only discuss facts." And his definition of a "fact" would no doubt have been a dollar bill, a mining "proposition," or a food-problem—some scheme by which John C. could make a bit. Yet though he placed religion among the fantasies, he lived it in his way. He ranked the Pope with Barnum, each of them "biggest in his own line of goods," and "Shakespeare was right enough, but might have made it shorter."

And Eliot, listening, felt the buried portion of his nature waken and revive. It caused him acute discomfort.

"Now show me round the little hole a bit," said Murdoch just before he left. "I'd like to see the damage, just for old times' sake. It won't take above ten minutes if we hustle along."

They hustled along. Eliot led the way with a curious deep uneasiness he could not quite explain. His heart sank within him. Gladly he would have escaped the painful duty, but Murdoch's vigorous energy constrained him. The whole way he felt ashamed, yet would have felt still more ashamed to have refused. He "faced the music" as John Casanova Murdoch phrased it, and while doing so, that other music of his visitor's villainous nasal twang cut across the deep-noted murmur of the wind and water like a buzz-saw with a bit of wire trailing against its teeth.

The entire journey occupied but half an hour, for Eliot made short-cuts, instinctively avoiding certain places, and the whole time Murdoch talked. His business, practical soul expanded with good nature. "The place ain't so bad, if you worked it up a bit," he said, striking a match on the wall of the mill, and spitting into the clear water, "but it's not much bigger than a chicken-run at present. If I was you, Boss, I'd have it cleaned up first." Again he offered a cheque, thinking the unkempt appearance due to want of means. His uninvited opinions were freely offered, as willingly as he would have given money if his old "pard" had needed it; given kindly too, without the least desire to wound. He picked out the prettiest "building sites," and explained where an artificial lake could be made "as easy as rolling off a log." His patent wire would fence the gardens off "and no one ever see it"; and his special concrete paving, from waste material that yielded a hundred per cent profit, would make paths "so neat and pretty you could dance to heaven on 'em." The place might be developed so as to "knock the stuffing" out of the country round about, and the estate become a "puffect picture-book."

"You've got a gold mine here, and God never meant a gold mine to lie unnoticed like a roadside ditch. Only you'll need to gladden it up a bit first. You could make it hum as a picnic or amusement resort for the town people. Take it from me, Boss. It's so."

And the effect upon Eliot as he listened was curious; it was twofold. For while at first the chatter wounded him like insults aimed directly at the dead, at the same time, to his deep disgust, it stirred all his former love of practical, energetic action. The old lust and fever to be up and doing, helping the world go round, making money and worldly position, woke more and more, as Murdoch's vigorous, crude personality stung his will, stung also desires he thought for ever dead. It made him angry to find that they were not dead, and yet he felt that he was feeble not to resent the gross invasion, even cowardly not to resist the coarse attack and kick the vulgar intruder out. It was like a breach of trust to take it all so meekly without protesting, or at least without stating forcibly his position, as though he were not sufficiently sure of himself to protect his memories and his dead. But this was the truth: he was not sure of himself. The blinding light of this simple fellow's mind showed up the hidden inequalities to himself. Another discovered his essential instability to himself. This other side of him had existed all the time; and his attachment to the Place was partly artificial, built up largely by the vigorous assertion of the departed. His love had coloured it wonderfully all these years, but—it was a love that had undergone a change. It had not faded, but grown otherwise. Another kind of love had to some extent replaced and weakened it. He felt mortified, ashamed, but more, he felt uneasy too.

The wrench was pain. "If only she were here and I could explain it to her," ran his thought over and over again, followed by the feeling that perhaps she *was* there, listening to it all—and judging him.

Behind the trees, a little distance away, he saw the flitting figure of Mánya, watching them as they passed noisily along the pathways of her secret playground. Her attitude even at this distance expressed resentment. He imagined her indignant eyes. But, closer than that, another watched and followed, listened and disapproved—that other whom she knew yet never spoke about, who was in league with her, and seemed more and more to him, like a phantom risen from the dead.

With difficulty, and with an uneasiness growing every minute now, he gave his attention to his talkative, well-meaning, though almost offensive guest, at once insufferable yet welcome. One moment he saw him in his camping-kit of twenty years ago, with big sombrero and pistols in his belt, and the next as he was today, reeking of luxury and money, in a London black tail-coat, white Homburg hat, diamonds shining on his fingers and in his gaudy speckled tie, his pointed patent-leather boots gleaming insolently through the bracken and heather.

And through his silence crashed a noise of battle that he thought the entire Place must hear. But clear issue to the battle there was none. The opposing sides were matched with such deadly equality. Which was his real self lay in the balance, until at the last John Casanova unwittingly turned the scales.

It came about so quickly, with such calculated precision, as it were, that Eliot almost felt it had all been prepared beforehand and Murdoch bad come down on purpose. It was like a sudden flank attack that swept him from his last defences. Help that could not reach him in the form of Mánya signalled from the distance with her shining eyes, her red tam-o'-shanter the banner of reinforcements that arrived too late. For John C. stood triumphantly before him, a conqueror in his last dismantled fortress. His face alight with enthusiasm that was all excitement, he held his hands out towards him, cup-wise.

"See here," he said with excitement, but in a hard, dry tone that reminded Eliot of prospecting days in Arizona, "Boss, will you take a look at this, please?"

He had been rooting about in the heather by the edge of the sand-pits. And he thrust his joined hands beneath the other's nose. Something the size of a hen's egg, something that shone a dirty white, lay in them against the thick gold rings. "Didn't I tell you the place was a gol-darned gold mine? But what's the use o' talking? Will you look at this, now?" He repeated it with the air of a man who has suddenly discovered the secret of the world. The voice was quiet with intense excitement kept hard under.

And Eliot obeyed and looked. He saw his visitor, his Bond Street trousers turned up high enough to show the great muscles of his calves, the Homburg hat tilted across one eye, coat-sleeves pulled up and smeared with a whitish mud. There was perspiration on his forehead. It only needed the sombrero and the pistols to complete the picture of twenty years ago when Cass Murdoch, after weeks of heavy labour, found the first gold-dust in his pan. For John C. *had* found gold. It lay, a dirty lump of white earth, in his large spread hands. Those hands were the pan. The breeze that murmured through the pine trees came, sweet and keen, from leagues of open plain and virgin mountains far away... Eliot smelt the wood-fire smoke of camp... heard the crack of the rifle as some one killed the dinner...

"Well, John C.," he gasped, as he dropped back likewise into the vanished pocket of the years, "what's your luck? Out with it, man, out with it!"

"A fortune," replied his visitor. "Put yer finger on it right now, an' don't tell mother or burst out crying unless yer forced to!" High pleasure was in his voice.

He stepped closer, transferring the lump of dirt into the hand his host unconsciously stretched open to receive it. It lay there a moment, looking even dirtier than before against the more delicate skin. Eliot felt it with finger and thumb. It was soft and sticky and a little moist. It stained the flesh.

Then he looked up and stared into his companion's eyes—blankly. A horrible excitement worked underground in him. But he did not even yet understand.

"You've got it," observed John C., with dry finality.

"Got what?" asked Eliot.

"Got it right there in yer westkit pocket," said the other, with an air of supreme satisfaction. His cigar had gone out. He lit it again in leisurely fashion, spat accurately at a distant frond of bracken, eyed the lump of dirt again with inimitable pride, and added, "Got it without asking; the working soft and easy too; water-power on the spot, and the sea all close and handy for shipping it away." He made a gesture to indicate the tumbling stream and the sea-coast a few miles beyond.

Then, seeing that his host still stared with blank incomprehension, holding the little lump at arm's length as though it might bite or burn him, he deigned to explain, but with a note of condescending pity in his voice, as of a man explaining to a stupid child.

"Clay," he said calmly, "and good stuff at that."

"Clay," repeated Eliot, still a little dazed, though light was breaking on him. "Bricks... ?" he asked, with a dull sinking of the heart.

"Bricks, nothing!" snapped the other with impatient scorn, as though his friend were still a tenderfoot in Arizona. "Good, white pottery clay, and soft as a baby's tongue. The best God ever laid down for man. Worth twice its weight in dust. And all to be had for the trouble of shovelling it out. Old pard, you've struck it good and hot this time; and here's my blessing on yer both."

Eliot dropped the lump his fingers held so long and took half-heartedly the giant hand that squeezed his own. Across his brain ran visions of slender vases, exquisite white cups and bowls and pitchers, plates and sweet-rimmed basins, all fashioned in delicate-toned shades of glaze—beautifully finished pottery—"worth twice their weight in dust."

## X

AND half an hour later, when John Casanova Murdoch had boomed away in his luxurious motorcar like a departing thunderstorm, Eliot, coming back by the pinewood that led from the high road, heard a step behind him, and turned to find Mánya's face looking over his very shoulder.

"Uncle, who was that?" There was a touch of indignation in her voice that was almost contempt.

"Man I knew in America—years ago," he said shortly. He still felt dazed, bewildered. But shame and uneasiness came creeping up as well.

"He won't come again, will he?"

"Not again, Mánya."

The child took his arm, apparently only half relieved.

"He was like a bit of the dirty country," she said, and when he interrupted with "Not quite so bad as that, Mánya," she asked abruptly with her usual intuition, "Did he want to buy, or build, or something horrid like that?"

"We haven't met for twenty years," he said evasively. "Used to hunt and camp together in America. He went to the goldfields with me." He was debating all the while whether he should tell her all. He hardly knew what he thought. Like a powerful undertow there drove through the storm of strange emotions the tide of a decision he had already come to. It swept him from all his moorings, though as yet he would not acknowledge it even to himself.

"Uncle," she cried suddenly, stepping across the path, and looking anxiously into his face, "tell me one thing: will anything be different?"

And the simple question, or perhaps the eager, wistful expression in her voice and eyes, showed him the truth that there was no evading. He must tell her sometime. Why not now?

· He decided to make a clean sweep of it.

"Mánya," he began gently, "this Place one day—when I am gone, you know—will be your own. But there'll be no money with it. You'll have very little to live on."

She said nothing, just listening with a little air of boredom, as though she knew this already, yet felt no special interest in it. It belonged to the world of things she could not realise much. She nodded. They still stood there, face to face.

"I've been anxious, child, for a long time about your future," he went on, meeting her dark eyes with a distinct effort, for they seemed to read the shame he felt rising in his heart; "and wondering what I could do to make you safe—"

"I'm safe enough," she interrupted, tossing her hair back and raising her chin a little.

"But when I'm gone," he said gravely, "and Mrs Coove has gone, and there's no one to look after you. Money's your only friend then."

She seemed to reflect. She moved aside, and they walked on slowly towards the house.

"That's a long way off, Uncle. I'm not afraid."

"But it's my duty to provide for you as well as possible," he said firmly.

And then he told her bluntly and in as few words as possible of the discovery of the clay.

The excitement at first in the child was so great that nothing would satisfy her but that they should at once turn back and see the place together. They did so, while he explained how "Mr Murdoch," who was learned in strata, their depth and dip and outcrop, had declared that this deposit of fine white clay was very large. Its spread below the heather-roots might be tremendous. "My aunt," he said, "your great-aunt Julia, lived all her life upon a gold mine here without knowing it, poor as a church mouse."

This particularly thrilled her. "How funny that she never *felt* it!" was her curious verdict. "Was she *very* deaf?"

"Stone deaf, yes," he replied, laughing, "and short-sighted too."

"Ah!" said the child, as though things were thus explained. "But she might have digged!"

She ran among the heather when he showed her the place, found lumps of clay, played ball with them and was wildly delighted. She treated the great discovery as a game; then as a splendid secret "just between us two." Mr Murdoch wouldn't tell, would he? That seemed the only danger that she saw—at first.

But her uncle knew quite well that this excitement was all false; and far from reassuring him, it merely delayed the deeper verdict that was bound to come with full comprehension. All the discovery involved had not reached her brain. As yet she realised only the novelty, the mystery, the wonder. The spot, moreover, where the great deposit showed its lip was beside the loveliest part of all the wood, and just where the child most loved to play.

At last, then, as her body grew tired and the excitement brought the natural physical reaction, he saw the change begin. She paused and looked about her half suspiciously, like an animal that suspects a trap. Her glance ran questioningly to where her uncle leaned, watching her, against a tree. She eyed him. He thought she suddenly looked different, though wherein the difference lay escaped him. He felt as if he were watching a wild animal, only half tamed, that distrusts its owner, and would next deny his mastership and wait its opportunity to spring. The simile, he knew, was exaggerated, but the picture rose within him none the less. Misgiving and uneasiness grew apace.

Abruptly Mánya stopped her wild playing and with the movement of a little panther ran towards him. She took up a position, as usual, directly opposite. With the strange air of dignity that sometimes clothed her, the figure of the child stood there among the darkening trees and asked him questions, keen, searching questions. He was grateful for the shadows, though he felt they did not screen his face from her piercing sight; but it was her imperious manner above all that made his defence seem so clumsily insincere, and the questions a veritable inquisition.

Before the flood of them, as before their pitiless scrutiny, he certainly quailed. Their keen directness convicted him almost of treachery, and he was hard put to it to persuade her and himself that it really was a sense of duty he obeyed in this decision to work the clay. "I'm doing it all for her," he repeated again and again to himself, and loathed, with a dash of terror, that curious sudden drive, as of a blow from outside, that sent his tongue into his cheek. But the terror, he dimly divined, was due to another feeling as well, equally vague yet equally persistent. For it seemed that while she listened to his explanations, another listened in the darkness too. Her resentment and distress he realised vividly; but he felt also the resentment and distress—of another. And more than once, during this strange dialogue in the darkening wood, he knew the horrible sensation that this "other" had come very close, so close as to slip between himself and the child. Almost—that the child was being used as the instrument to express the vehement protest... !

But he faced the music, to use the lingo of John C., and spared himself nothing. He told Mánya, though briefly, that workmen must swarm all through her secret playground, that machinery must grind and boom across the haunted valleys, that the water of her little stream must yield the power to turn great ugly wheels, and that perhaps even a little railway might be built to convey the loads of precious clay down to the sea where steamers would call for them. Acres of trees, too, would be swept away, and heatherland marred and scarred with pits and ditches and quarries. But the benefits in time would all be hers. He put it purposely at its worst, while emphasising as best he could the interest and excitement that must accompany the developments. The dream of many years was nevertheless shattered into bits in half an hour.

The child listened and understood. He was relieved, if puzzled at the same time, that she betrayed no emotion of disappointment or indignation. What she felt she dealt with in her own way—inside. At the stream, however, on her way home, she paused a moment, watching it slip through the darkness underneath the old mill-wheel.

"It won't run any more—for itself," she said in a low, trembling little voice, that was infinitely pathetic.

"No; but it will run for you, Mánya," he answered, though the words had not been addressed really to him; "working away busily for your future."

And then she burst into tears and hid her face against his coat. He found no further thing to say. He walked beside her, feeling like a criminal found out.

But at the end, as they neared the house side by side, she suddenly turned and asked another question that caused him a thrill of vivid surprise and discomfort—so vivid, in fact, that it was fear.

They were standing just beneath *her* bedroom window then. Memory rushed back upon him with overwhelming force, and he glanced up instinctively at the empty panes of glass. It was almost as though he expected to see a face looking reproachfully down upon him. Through him like spears of ice, as he heard the words, there shot again the atrocious sensation that it was not Mánya, the child, who asked the question, but that Other who had recently moved so close. For behind the tone, with no great effort to conceal it either, trailed a new accent that Mánya never used. Greater than resentment, it was anger, and within the anger lay the touch of a yet stronger note—the note of judgment.

"But, tell me one thing, Uncle," she asked in a whispering voice: "will the Place let you?"

## XI

MOTIVE, especially in complex natures, is often beyond reach of accurate discovery, and a mixed motive may prove quite impossible of complete disentanglement. But for the sense of shame that Eliot felt, he might never have discerned that with his genuine desire to provide for Mánya's future there was also involved a secret satisfaction that he himself would profit too. The sight of gold demolishes pretence and artifice; and deep within he felt the old lust of possession and acquisition assert itself. All these years it had been buried, not destroyed. His love of the Place, his worship of Memory, his guardianship of the little dream-estate, compared to the prize of worldly treasure, were on the surface. They were artificial.

This little thing had proved it. The child's tears, her significant question above all, had shown him to himself. If not, whence came this sense of ignominy before her own purer passion, the loss of confidence, this inner quailing before Another who gazed reprovingly, resentfully, upon him from the shadows of the past? That note of menace in Mánya's suggestive question was surely not her own. It haunted him. Day and night he heard it ringing in his brain. This new distrust of himself that he recognised read into it something almost vindictive and revengeful.

But Eliot, for all that, was not the man to give in easily. He resolutely dismissed this birth of morbid fancy. Clinging to the thought that his duty to his niece came first, he resisted the suggestion that imputed a grosser selfishness. Cass Murdoch, too, unwittingly helped; for the side of his character John C.'s visit had revived—the love of fight and energetic action—came valiantly to the rescue. To a great extent he persuaded himself that his motive was—almost entirely—a pure one. Preparations for developing the clay went forward steadily.

Mánya too appeared to help him. She said no more distressing things; she showed keen interest in the coming and going of surveyors, architects, soil experts, and the like. And Murdoch's discovery was no false alarm; the bed of clay was deep and extensive as he prophesied, its quality very fine. Men came with pick and shovel; sample pits were dug; the stuff was tested and judged excellent and the verdict of the manufacturers, to whom "lots" were forwarded on approval, pronounced it admirable for a large and ready market. There was money in it, and the supply would last for years. The papers heralded the fortunate discoverer, and a moderate fortune undeniably was in sight.

The preparations, however, took time, and the finding of the initial capital, which Murdoch readily supplied, also took time, and spring meanwhile slipped into summer before the enterprise was fairly on its feet. Soft winds sighed lazily among the larches, and the scent of flowers pervaded every valley; the pine-trees basked in the sunshine, the pearly water laughed and sang; and at night the moon shot every glade with magic that was like the wings of moths whose flitting scattered everywhere the fine dust of a thousand silvery dreams. The beauty of the little haunted estate leaped into a rich maturity that was utterly enchanting, like wild flowers that are sweetest just before they die.

And over Mánya, too, there passed slowly a mysterious change, for it seemed as if for a time she had been standing still, and now with a sudden leap of beauty passed into the glory of young womanhood. With her short skirts and tumbled hair, her grave and wistful face, swinging idly that red tam-o'-shanter from which she was inseparable, he saw her one evening on the lawn outside his study window, and the change flashed into him across the moonlight with a positive shock. The child had suddenly grown up. A barrier stood between them.

But the barrier was not so sudden as it seemed, for, on looking back, he realised the daily, almost imperceptible manner of its growth. Its complete erection he realised now, but he had been aware of it for a long time—ever since his decision to work the clay, in fact. Here was the proof her deceptive silence had concealed. She had felt it too deeply for words, for arguing, for disappointment volubly expressed; but it had struck into the roots of her little being and had changed her from within outwards. It had aged her. Reality had broken in upon her world of play and dream. He had destroyed her childhood at a single blow. She questioned, doubted, and grew old.

But though everyone grows older in identically this way, by sudden leaps, as it were, due to the forcing impulse of some strong emotion, with Mánya it brought no radical alteration. She deepened rather than definitely changed. The sense of wonder did not fade, but ripened. The crude facts of life could never satisfy a nature such as hers, and though she realised them now for the first time, they could not enter to destroy. They drove her more deeply into herself. That is, she dealt with them.

And the change, though he devoted hours of pondering reflection over it, may be summed up briefly enough in so far as it affected himself. There was a difference in their relationship. He stood away from her, while she, on her side, drew nearer to something else that was not himself. With this elusive and mysterious Thing she lived daily. She took sides with it and with the Place, against himself. It went on largely, he felt, behind his back. She grew more and more identified with some active influence that had always been at work in all the wild gardened loveliness of the property, but was now more active than before. Stirred up and roused it was; he could almost imagine it—aggressive. And Mánya, always knowing it at closer quarters than himself, was now in definite league with it. There was opposition in it, though an opposition as yet inactive.

And in the silent watches of the night sometimes, when imagination wove her pictures all unchecked, he again knew the haunting thought close beside his bed: that the mind and hand of the dead were here at work, using the delicate instrument of this rare, sensitive child to convey protest, resentment, warning. Over the little vales, from all the depth of forest, and above the spread of moorland just beyond, there breathed this atmosphere of disapproval.

Mánya, never telling him much, now told him less than before; for he had forfeited the right to know.

If it made him smile a little to notice that she had made Mother Coove lengthen her dresses, it did not make him smile to learn that she still wore her old shorter ones once the darkness fell, or that she now went out to play in her wild corners of the woods chiefly after dusk. For he saw the significance of this simple manoeuvre, and divined its meaning. She felt shy now in the daylight. This new thing in the spirit of the Place had changed it all. She could not be abandoned as before, go naked and undressed as once she graphically put it. The vulgar influence from outside had come in. It stared offensively. It asked questions, leered, turned everything common and unclean.

And she changed from time to time her playground as the workmen drove her out. She moved from place to place, seeking new corners and going farther into the moors and open spots. She followed the stream, for instance, nearer to its source where its waters still ran unstained. And from the neighbourhood of the sample pits that gaped like open sores amid the beauty, she withheld herself completely. Nothing could persuade her to come near them.

Towards himself especially, her attitude was pregnant with suggestion, and though he made full allowance for the phantoms conscience raises, there always remained the certainty that the child, and another with her, watched him sharply from a distance. She was still affectionate and simple, even with a new touch of resigned docility that was very sweet, as though resolved to respect his older worldly wisdom, yet with an air of pity for his great mistake that was half contempt, half condescension. Her silence about the progress of the work made him feel small. It so mercilessly judged him. And, while the dignity he had always recognised in her increased, it seemed now partly borrowed—his imagination leaned more and more towards this unwelcome explanation—from this invisible Companion who overshadowed her. He felt as though this silence temporarily blocked channels along which something would presently break out with violence and scorn to overwhelm him; till at last he came to regard her as a prisoner regards the foreman of the jury who has formed his verdict and is merely waiting to pronounce it—Guilty. Behind her, as behind the foreman, gathered the composite decision of more than one, and the decision was hostile. It urged her on against him. Opposition accumulated towards positive attack. He dreaded some revelation through the child; and piling guess on guess he felt certain who was this active Influence that sought to use her as its instrument. The dead now, day and night, stood very close beside him.

And meanwhile, things ran far from smoothly with the work itself. Unforeseen difficulties everywhere arose to baffle him. Even Murdoch made oppressive, troublesome conditions about the money that seemed unnecessary, insisting upon details of management with a touch of domineering interference that exasperated. Obstacles rose up automatically, involving, as it were, the very processes of Nature itself. There was a strike that delayed the railway builders for a month, and when they returned the heavy summer rains had washed yards of embankment down again. Soon afterwards a falling tree killed a workman, and there ensued compensation worries that threatened a law-suit. The clay itself, too, played them sudden tricks, proving faulty the maps the surveyors had drawn; its depths and direction were not as supposed, its angle to the lie of the slope deceptive, so that an extra branch of single line for the trucks became essential. And the money was insufficient; further advances became imperative, and, though readily forthcoming, involved more delay. The spirit of lonely peace and beauty departed from the Place, hiding its injured face among the moorland reaches further up. Obstruction, with turmoil and confusion at its back, rose up on every side to baffle him.

Though the advance was steady enough on the whole, and the difficulties were only such as most similar enterprises encounter, Eliot was conscious more and more of this sense of obstacles deliberately interposed. It all seemed so nicely calculated to cause the maximum of trouble and delay. The interference was so cunningly manoeuvred. He brought all his old energy and force to meet them, but there was ever this curious sense of advised and determined opposition that began to sap his confidence.

"More trouble, sir," the foreman said one morning, when Eliot went down to view the work, unaccompanied as usual by Mánya. "There seems no end to it."

"What is it this time?" He abhorred these conversations now. It always seemed that Another stood behind his shoulder, listening.

"The clay has gone," was the curious answer. He said it as though it had gone purposely to spite them like a living thing.

"Gone!" he exclaimed incredulously.

"Sunk away, gone deeper than we expected," was the answer. The man shrugged his shoulders as though something puzzled him. "A kind of subsidence come in the night," he added gloomily.

They stared at one another for a full minute with eyes that screened other meanings. Eliot felt a sort of fury rise within him. Somehow the idea of foul play crossed his mind, though instantly rejected as absurd.

"With this loose sandy bottom, and a steep slope that ain't drained properly, you're never very sure of where you are," said the man at length, feeling his position made some explanation necessary. He seemed to regard the Clay as something ever on the move.

"I see," said Eliot, grateful for a solution that he could apparently accept. They talked of ways and means to circumvent it.

"Queerest job I ever come across, sir," the foreman muttered, as at length Eliot turned away, pretending not to hear it.

And scenes like this were frequent. Another time it was the white weed—with the pretty little flower Mánya loved to twine about her tam-o'-shanter—that had gathered so thickly on the artificial ponds where the water was stored, that it clogged the machinery till the wheels refused to turn; and next, a group of men that quit working without any reasonable excuse—open symptom of a hidden dissatisfaction that had been running underground for weeks. There was something about the job they didn't like. Rumours for a long time had been current—queer, unsubstantiated rumours that those in authority chose to disregard. Superstition hereabouts was rife enough without encouraging it.

Taken altogether, as products of a single hostile influence at work, these difficulties easily assumed in his imaginative mind the importance of a consciously directed opposition. He remembered often now those words of Mánya, the last time she had opened her lips upon the subject. For she had credited the Place with the power of resisting him; only by "the Place" she now meant this mysterious personal influence that she knew behind it.

Yet he persisted in his consciousness of doing right. His duty to the child was clear; her future was in his charge; and the fact that he meant to leave her everything proved that his motive, or part of it at least, was above suspicion. From John C. he also gathered comfort and support. He had only to imagine him standing by his side, repeating that remark about religion, to feel strong again in his determination. Cass Murdoch recognised no mystery or subtlety anywhere. He discussed only facts.

The consciousness that he was partly traitor none the less remained, and with it the feeling that the very Tradition he had nursed and worshipped all these years was up in arms against him. Mánya, standing closer to Nature than himself, had divined this Tradition and, in some fashion curiously her own, had personified it. And this personification linked on with the dead. His love of the Beauty, and his love of a particular memory he had read into the Place, she had most marvellously disentangled. Both were genuine in him; yet he had suffered them in combination to produce a false and artificial Image existing only in his own imagination. There was conflict in his being. His motive was impure.

Behind them stood the giant, naked thing the child divined that was—Reality. She knew it face to face. What was it? The mere definite question which he permitted himself made him sometimes hesitate and wait, not unwilling to call a halt. He was aware that the child stood ever in the background, waiting her time with that sly laughter of superior knowledge. These obstacles and difficulties were sent as warnings; and while he disregarded them of set purpose, something deep within him paused to question—and while it questioned, trembled. For protest, he seemed to discern, had become resentment, resentment grown into resistance; resistance into hostile opposition, and opposition now, with something horribly like anger at its back, was hinting already at a blank refusal that involved almost—revenge.

Hitherto he had been hindered, impeded, thwarted merely; soon he could be deliberately overruled and stopped. Nature, ever defeating an impure motive, would rise up against him and cry finally No.

"But, Uncle, tell me one thing: will the Place let you?" rang now often through his daily thoughts. He heard it more especially at night. At night, too, when sleep refused him, he surprised himself more than once framing sentences of explanation and defence. They rose automatically. They followed him even into his dreams. "My duty to the child is plain. How can I help it? If you were here beside me now, would you not also approve?"

For the idea that *she* was beside him grew curiously persuasive, so that he almost expected to see her in the corridors or on the stairs, standing among the trees or waiting for him by the Mill itself where last she drew the breath of life.

And by way of a climax came then Mánya's request to change her room, and his own decision to move himself into the one she vacated. The reason she gave was that the "trees made such a noise at night" she could not sleep, and since it had three windows, two of which were almost brushed by pine branches, the excuse, though discovered late, seemed natural enough. At any rate he did not press her further. She occupied a room now at the back where a single window gave a view far up into the moors. And, turning out the unnecessary furniture to suit his taste, he moved into the one she had vacated—his wife's.

## XII

SUMMER passed in the leisurely, gorgeous way that sometimes marks its passage into autumn, and the work ploughed forward through the sea of difficulties. The conspiracy of obstacles continued. There was progress on the whole, but a progress that seemed to bring success no nearer. The beds of clay, however, were definitely determined now, and their extent and depth fulfilled the most sanguine expectations. The troubles lay with the railway, the men, water, weather, and a dozen things no one could have foreseen. These seemed far-fetched, and yet were natural enough. And they continued—until Eliot, never a man who yielded easily, began to feel he had undertaken more than he could manage. He weakened. The idea came to him that he would sell his interest and leave the development to others.

To retire from the fight and acknowledge himself defeated was a step he could not lightly take. There was a bitterness in the thought that stung his pride and vanity. There was also the fact that if he held on and first established a paying business, he could obtain far more money—for Mánya. Yet he felt somehow that it was from Mánya herself that the suggestion first had come. For the child gave hints in a hundred different ways that he could not possibly misunderstand. They were indirect, unconsciously given, and they followed invariably upon curious little personal accidents that about this time seemed almost a daily occurrence.

And these little accidents, though perfectly natural taken one by one as they occurred, when regarded all together seemed to compose a formidable whole. They pointed an attack almost. The menace he had imagined was becoming aggressive. Some one who knew his habits was playing him tricks. Some one with intimate knowledge of the way he walked and ran and moved laid traps for him. And at each little "accident" Mánya laughed her strange, sly laughter—precisely as a child who says "I told you so! You brought it on yourself!" She had expected it, perhaps had seen it coming. And now, to avoid more grave disasters, she wanted him—elsewhere. Her deep affection for him, sinner though he was in her eyes, sought to coax him out of the danger zone.

When he slipped in jumping the stream—he, who was sure-footed as a mountain goat!—and turned his ankle; and when the heavy earth, loosened by the rains, rolled down upon him as he climbed the embankment, or when the splinter that entered his hand as he vaulted the fencing near the wharf, led to festering that made him carry his arm in a sling for days—in every case it was the same: the child looked up at him and smiled her curious little smile of one who knew. She was in safety, but he stood in the line of fire. She knew who it was that laid the traps. She saw them being laid. It was always wood, earth, water thus that hurt him and never once an artificial contrivance of man.

"Uncle, it wouldn't happen if you stayed away," was what she said each time, though never phrased the same. And the obvious statement only just covered another meaning that her words contained. She knew worse things would come, and feared for him. "There's no good hiding, Uncle Dick, because it's in the house as well."

He grew to feel unwelcome in his own woods and garden, an intruder in his own moors and valleys, an element the Place rejected and wished elsewhere. The Place had begun to turn him out. And Mánya, this queer mysterious child, in league with the secret Influence at work against him, was being used to point the warnings and convey the messages. Her silent attitude, more even than her actual words, was the messenger. The hints thus brought, moreover, now troubled themselves less and less with disguise. He realised them at last for what they were: and they were beyond equivocation—threatening.

And it was at this point that Eliot made the journey up to London to see Cass Murdoch, and feel his way towards escape. Retirement was the word he used, and the sentence John C. heard in the bar of the big hotel as they discussed clay and cocktails was "sell my interest to more competent hands who will get quicker and bigger results than I can. The work and worry affect my health."

The interview may be easily imagined, for John Casanova Murdoch was more than willing to buy him out, though the conditions, with one exception, have no special interest in this queer history: Eliot was to lease the Place for a period of years. And this meant leaving it.

In the train on his way back his emotions fought one another in a regular pitched battle. He stood in front of himself suddenly revealed— a traitor. It seemed as if for a moment he saw things a little from his niece's inverted point of view, standing outside of Self and looking up. It provided him with unwelcome sensations that escaped analysis. Love and hate are one and the same force, according to the point in the current where one stands; repulsion becomes, from the opposite end, attraction; and a great love may be reversed into a great hate. There is no exact dividing line between heat and cold, no neat frontier where pleasure becomes pain, Just as there is really no such absolute thing as left and right, uphill and downhill, above and below. Mánya stood outside these relative distinctions men have invented for the common purposes of description. He understood at last that the power which had drawn his life into the Place as by a kind of absorption, was now inverted into a process of turning him out again as by a kind of determined elimination.

It was being accomplished, moreover, as he felt and phrased it to himself, from outside; by which perhaps he meant from beyond that fence which men presumptuously assume to contain all the life there is. But the dead stand also beyond that fence. And Mánya, being so obviously in league with this hostile, eliminating Influence stood hand in hand, therefore, with—the dead.

But for him The Dead meant only one.

## XIII

HE walked home from the station, which he reached at nine o'clock. Crossing the zone of the "dirty" country, now successful invader of the dream-estate, he entered his property at length by the upper end of the Piney Valley. A passionate wind was searching the trees for music, and handfuls of rain were flung against the trunks like stones; but, on leaving the road the tempest seemed to pass out towards the sea, leaving an unexpected, sudden hush about his footsteps. The moon peered down through high, scudding clouds. It was partly that the storm was breaking up, and partly that the valley provided shelter; but it gave him the feeling that he had entered a little world prepared for his reception. He was expected, the principal figure in it. Attention everywhere focussed on himself. He felt like a prisoner who comes out of streets indifferent to his presence and enters a Court of Law. This ominous silence preceded the arrival of the Judge.

The path at once dipped downwards into a world of shadows where the splashes of moonlight peered up at him like faces on the ground. He heard the water murmuring out of sight; and it came about his ears like whispering from the body of the Court. There reigned, indeed, the same gentle peace and stillness he had known for years, but somewhere in it a brooding unaccustomed element that was certainly neither peace nor stillness. Something unwonted stirred slowly, very grandly, through the darkness.

He paused a moment to listen; he looked about him; he pushed aside the bracken with his stick, and his eyes glanced up among the lower branches of the trees. And everywhere, it seemed, he encountered other eyes—eyes usually veiled, but now with lifted lids. Then he went on again, faster a little than before. A touch of childhood's terror chilled his blood. And it took at first a childhood's form. He thought of some big, savage animal that lurked in hiding, its presence turning the once friendly wood all otherwise and dreadful. A giant paw filled the little valley to the brim. The stir of the wind was the opening and shutting of its claws. The lips were drawn back to show the gums and teeth. Something opened; there came a rush of air. The awful spring would follow in a moment...

Another hood of memory lifted then and showed him Mánya, as she played about the sand-pits—then paused when the full discovery dawned upon her mind. She had eyed him. She had given him this similar impression of an animal waiting its opportunity to spring. But now it was the Place that waited to spring...

He banished the bizarre, exaggerated picture his imagination conjured up, but could not banish the emotion that produced it. The Place *was* different. Change spread all over it. Potential attack hummed through the very air. Thus might a man feel walking through a hostile crowd. But thus also might he feel in the presence of a friend to whom in a time of confidence he had betrayed himself too lavishly—a friend now turned against him with this added power of knowing all his secrets. His own imagination leaped upon him, calling him coward, traitor, unfaithful steward. Fear made him bitterly regret the familiarity that years of unguarded dreaming had established between himself and—and— His mind hesitated horribly between the choice of pronouns; and when he finally chose the neuter, it seemed that a curious running laughter passed within the sounds of wind and water. It almost was like the mockery of Mánya's laughter taken over by the dying storm.

While he evaded the direct attack, his mind, however, continued searching for the word that should describe accurately, and so limit all this vague, distressing feeling of hostility. But for long he could not find it. The new element that breathed through the sombre intricacies of the glen played with him as it pleased until he could catch it in the proper word, and so imprison it. Branches seemed no longer soft and feathery: they bristled, pointed, stood rigid for a blow. The stream no longer murmured: it laughed and cried aloud. The shadows did not cover smoothly: they concealed; and the whole atmosphere of the Place, instead of welcoming, repelled.

And then, quite suddenly, the word emerged and stood before his face: Disturbance.

Less than disorder, yet more than mere disquietude, this word described the attitude he was conscious of. In its aggressive, threatening, sinister meaning, he accepted it as true.

There was Disturbance. Somewhere in those chains of iron that bind the operations of Nature within invariable, unyielding laws, a link had weakened. Disturbance was the result—but a disturbance that somehow let in purpose. Urging everywhere through the manifestations of Nature in his dream-estate was the drive and stress of purposiveness.

The discovery of the word, moreover, announced the approach, though not yet the actual entrance, of the Judge. There were steps, and the steps were in himself. Some one walked upon his life.

He quickened his pace like a terrified child. With genuine relief at last he reached the house. But even in the friendly building he was aware of this keen discomfort at his heels. It penetrated easily. The Disturbance came in after him into the house itself. Hanging up coat and hat, he then passed into the Study, and the prosaic business of drinking milk and munching water-biscuits scattered the strange illusion for a time. It weakened, at any rate, for it never wholly disappeared. It waited.

The house was silent, every one in bed. He locked the front door carefully, stared at his face a moment in the hat-stand mirror— wondering at a certain change in the expression of the features, though he could not name it—and with his lighted candle went on tiptoe up to bed. But the instant he entered the room he was aware that the feeling of distress had already preceded him. He was forestalled. There was this dark disquiet in the very atmosphere of his bedroom. The Disturbance had established itself in these most private, intimate quarters that once had been his wife's. It was strongest here.

Dismissing a sharp desire to sleep in another room—anywhere but in the place made sacred by long-worshipped memories—he began to undress. He said to himself with a certain vehemence, "I'll ignore the thing." But it was fear that said it. A frightened child without a light might as well determine to ignore the darkness. For this thing was urgent everywhere about him, inside and outside, like the air he breathed. And the next minute, instead of ignoring it, he made an attempt to face it. He would drag the secret out. The fact was, both will and emotions were already in disorder. He knew not how or where to take the thing.

The attempt then showed him another thing. It was no secret. The terror in his heart and conscience made pretence of screening something that he really knew quite well. This aggressive, hostile Presence was a Presence that he recognised, and had recognised all along.

And instinctively he turned to this side and to that, examining the room; for space in this room, he realised, was no longer quite as usual: there was a change in its conditions. Everything contained within it—the very objects between the four walls—were affected. He felt them altered; they had become otherwise. He himself was changed as well, become otherwise. And if anything alive—another person or an animal even—came in, they also, in some undetermined, startling way, would look otherwise than usual. They would look different.

Hurriedly he sought a concrete simile to steady his shaking mind on, and his mind provided this: That, if the temperature were suddenly lowered, the invisible moisture would at once appear, otherwise—frost-crystals on the window-panes, snow, and so forth. The change would not be untrue or even distorted, no falseness in it anywhere, nor exaggeration—only otherwise. And if the presence of the dead, whom he felt so close now in this room, turned visible owing to the changed conditions of the space about him, he would see—but the thought remained unfinished in his mind...

He thrust the terror down into the depths. Yet the idea must have been very insistent in him, for he crossed the floor on tiptoe to lock the door securely, and stood already within easy reach of it, one hand actually stretched out, when there came a faint knocking on the panelling within a few inches of his very face. He saw the handle turn. With suggestive, dreadful stealthiness the door then opened, the merest crack at first, then gradually wider and wider. And the slowness was exasperating. The seconds dragged like hours. Had he not been spellbound he would have violently slammed it to again or torn it instead wide open.

There was just time in his bewildered mind to wonder what form this Presence from the dead would take, when he realised that the figure stood already by his side. She had crossed the threshold. With amazement he saw that it was Mánya.

She came in swiftly. She was on the carpet close against him before he could speak a word or move. And she looked, as he had expected, otherwise: she looked extraordinary. The word came to him in the way she might herself have used it, getting its first meaning out—extra-ordinary.

And her appearance was—might well have been, at least— ludicrous. For she was dressed to go out, but in a fashion that at any other time must have been cause for laughter. Now it stood at the very opposite pole, however. It was superb. Her red tam-o'-shanter was perched carelessly, almost gaily, on her hair, which was already fashioned into plaits for the night, and underneath the garden jacket that he knew so well, he saw white drapery that plainly was her little nightgown. She had pulled her stockings on, but had not fastened them. They hung down, partly showing her skin below the knee. The boots flapped open, with no attempt to button them. Her hurry had been evidently great, and she looked at the first glance like some one surprised by a midnight call of fire.

Yet these details, which he took in at a single glance, stirred no faintest touch of amusement in him, for about her whole presentment was this other nameless quality that showed her to him—utterly otherwise than usual. It made him wince and shudder, yet pause in a wondering amazement too— amazement that barely held back awe. He stared like a man struck suddenly dumb. The phrase the child so often used came back upon him with the force of a shock. The girl had put her Self out. This being that stood just opposite to his face was not Mánya. It was another. It was *the* other!

And both doubt and knowledge dropped down upon him in that fearful moment: knowledge, that it was the Influence she had been so long in league with, and that sought to use her as its instrument of protest; and doubt, as to exactly what—or who—this Influence really was.

For it came to him as being so enormously bigger and vaster than anything his mind could label "the dead." He felt in the presence of a multitude. He had once felt thus when seeing a single Redskin steal like a shadow round the camp, knowing that the night concealed a host of others. About her actual form and body, too, this sense of multitude also spread and trembled, only just concealed: and indescribable utterly. For the edges of the child were ill-defined and misty, so that he could not see exactly where her outline ceased. The candle-light played round and over her as though she filled the room. She might have been all through the air above him, behind as well as opposite, close in front as well. In a sense he felt that she had come to him through the open windows and from the night itself, and not merely along the passage and through the narrow door. She came from the entire Place.

He made a feverish struggling effort to concentrate his mind upon common words. He wanted to move backwards, but his feet refused to stir. The familiar sound of her name he uttered close into her face:—

"Mánya! And at this hour of the night!" he stammered.

His voice was thick and without resonance in his mouth, smothered like a sound in a closed box. And as he heard the name a kind of silent laughter reached him—inaudible really, as though inside him—sly laughter like her own. For the name had lost its known familiarity. It, too, was different and otherwise, though for the life of him he could not seize at first wherein the alteration lay.

She smiled, and her eyes, wide opened, were like stars. The breath came soft and windily between her lips, but no words with it. It was regular, deep, unhurried. There was something in her face that petrified him—something, as it were, non-human. He began to forget who and where he was. Identity slipped from him like a dream.

With another effort, this time a more violent one, he strove to fasten upon things that were close and real in life. He felt the buttons down his coat, fingering them desperately till they hurt his hands and escaped from his slippery moist skin.

"Mánya!" he repeated in a louder voice, while his mind plunged out to seek the child he had always known behind the familiar name.

And this time she answered; but to his horror, the whole room, and even space beyond the actual room, seemed to answer with her. The name was repeated by her lips, yet came from the night beyond the open window too. He had made a question of it. The answer, repeating it, was assent.

"M á n y-a..." he heard all round him, while the head bent gently down and forward.

The shock of it restored to him some power of movement, and he stumbled back a step or two further from her side. It might well have been whimsical and cheap, this artificial play upon a name, but instead of either it was abominably significant. This motionless figure, so close that he could feel her breath upon his face, was positively in some astonishing way more than one. She was many. The laughter that lay behind the trivial little thing was a laughter both grand and terrible. It was the laughter of the sea, of the woods, of sand—a host that no man counteth—the laughter of a multitude.

And he thrust out both his hands automatically lest she should touch him. He shook from head to toe. Contact with her person would break up his being into millions. The sensation of terror was both immense and acute, sweeping him beyond himself. Like her, he was becoming many—becoming hundreds and thousands—sand that none can number.

"Child!" he heard his voice repeating faintly, yet with an emphasis that spaced the words apart with slow distinctness, "what does this mean?" in vain he tried to smother the beseeching note in it that was like a cry for help.

He stepped back another pace. She did not move. Composure then began to come back slowly to him, a little and a little. He remembered who he was, and where he was. He said to himself the commonplace thing: "This is Mánya, my little niece, and she ought to be asleep in bed." It sounded ridiculous even in his mind, but he tried deliberately to think of ordinary things.

And then he said it aloud: "Do you realise where you are and what you are doing, child?" And then he added, gaining courage, a question of authority "Do you realize what time it is?"

Her answer came again without hesitation, as from a long way off: A smile lit up the entire face, gleaming from her skin like moonlight. There were tears, he saw, upon the cheeks. But the face itself was radiant, wonderful.

"The time," she said, peering very softly into his eyes, "is *now*." And she took a slow-gliding step towards him, with a movement that frightened him beyond belief.

But by this time he had himself better in hand. He understood that the child was walking in her sleep. It was her little frame that was being worked and driven by—Another. She was possessed. Something was speaking through the entranced physical body. Her answer regarding time was the answer absolute, not relative, the only true answer that could be given. Other answers would be similar. He understood that here was the long expected revelation, and that he must question her if he wished to hear it. He resolved to do so, but with a cold awe in his heart as though he were about to question—Death.

They both retained their first positions, three feet apart, standing. The candle behind him on the table shed its flickering light across her altered features. Outside he heard the trees shaking and tossing in the gusts of rainy wind.

"Who are you then?" he asked hesitatingly, in a low tone.

There was no reply. But effort, showing that she heard and tried to answer, traced a little frown above the eyebrows; and the eyes looked puzzled for a moment.

"You mean," he whispered, "you cannot tell me?"

The head bowed slowly once by way of assent.

"You cannot find the word, the language?" he helped her. "Is that it?" He still whispered, afraid of his own voice.

"Yes," was the answer, spoken below the breath. Then instantly afterwards, straightening herself up with a vigorous movement that startled him horribly, she made a curious, rushing gesture of the whole body, spreading her arms out through the air about her. "I am—*like that*!" the voice sprang out loud and clear.

She seemed by the gesture to gather space and the night into her wide embrace. She repeated it. The face smiled marvellously. Through this slim body, he realised, there rolled something ancient as the stars. It poured through space against him like a sea. It turned his little ideas of space all—otherwise.

"Tell me where you come from," he asked quickly, eager yet dreading to hear.

"From everywhere," came the answer like a wind.

He paused, breathless with astonishment. He felt himself dwindling. Here was a vaster thing than he had contemplated. It was surely no single discarnate influence that possessed the child!

"And—for whom?" It was whispered as before.

The figure stepped with a single gliding stride towards him, coming so close that he held his ground only by a tremendous effort of the will.

"For you!" The voice came like a clap of wind again, at once soft yet thundering, filling the entire room.

"For me," he faltered. "Your message is for me?"

He felt the assault of strange, violent sensations he had never known before and could not name. A boyhood's dream rushed back upon him for an instant. He recalled his misery and awe when he stood before the Judgment Throne for some unforgivable breach of trust which he could not explain because the dream concealed its nature. Only this was ten times greater, and his guilt beyond redemption.

"And I," he stammered, "who am I?"

Her eyes looked him all over like a stare of the big moon.

"*You*," she answered, without pause or hesitation.

"You do not know my name?" he insisted, still clinging to the clue that her he spoke with must be from the dead.

The little frown came back between the eyes. She nodded darkly.

"*You*," she repeated, giving the answer absolute again, the only really true one.

The girl stood like a statue, serene and solemn. She stared through and beyond him, motionless but for a scarcely perceptible swaying, and calm as a meadow in the dawn. Enormous meanings passed from her eyes across the air, and sank down into him like meanings from a forest or a sea.

From these, he realised, came her stupendous inspiration, and, so realising, he knew at last his deep mistake. For not so do the Dead return. They never, indeed, return, because from the heart that loved them they have never gone away, but only changed their magic intercourse in kind. And, had *she* known, she would have approved the wisdom of his great decision, while clearing his motive of all insincerity at the same time.

It was not *she* who brought the protest and the menace. It was something bigger by far, something awful and untamed. It was the Place itself. And behind the Place stood Nature. It was Nature that possessed the child and used her little lips and hands and body for its thundering message of disapproval.

Mánya was possessed by Nature.

And the shock of the discovery first turned him into stone. His body did not stir the fraction of an inch. In that moment of vivid realisation these two little human figures stood facing one another, motionless as columns; and, while so standing, the One who brought the Message for himself drew closer.

For several minutes he saw absolutely nothing. The approach was too big for any sensory perceptions he could recognise. And then, mercilessly, pitilessly, the power of sight returned.

He knew the touch of a giant, earthy hand was upon his arm. Beside him, in the flickering candle light, stood Nature. He looked into a host of mighty eyes that yet his imagination translated into merely two—eyes set wide apart beneath enormous brows. He met the gaze of the Gigantic, the Patient, the Inexorable that saw him as he was, and judged him where he stood. And a melting ran through his body, as though the bones slipped from their accustomed places, leaving him utterly without support. He swayed, but did not fall. His physical frame stood upright to receive like a blow the revelation that was coming.

And then, with a curious, deep sense of shame, he realised abruptly that his position in regard to her was inappropriate. He, at any rate, had no right to stand. His proper attitude must be a very different one.

He took her by the hand and, bending his head with an air of humble worship, led her slowly across the room. The touch of her was wonderful—like touching wind—all over him. With a reverence he guided her, all unresisting, to a high-backed chair beside the open window. She lowered herself upon it, and sat upright. She stared fixedly before her into space. No clothing in the world could have stolen from her childish face and figure the nameless air of grandeur that she wore. She was august.

And he knelt before her. He raised his folded hands. A moment his eyes rested on the dispassionate little face, then looked beyond her into the night of wind and rain. His gaze returning then sought the eyes again.

And the child, sweet little human interpreter of so vast a Mystery, bent her head downwards and looked into his heart. Wind stirred the hair upon her neck. He saw the bosom gently rise and fall.

"What is it that you have to say to me?" he whispered, like a prayer for mercy. "What is the message that you bring?"

Her lips moved very slightly. The smile broke out again like moonlight across the lowered face. The words dropped through the sky. Very slowly, very distinctly, they fell into his open heart simple as wind or rain.

"Leave—me—as—I—am—and—as—you—found—me. Leave—us—together—as—we—are—and—as—we—were."

## XIV

THERE came then a sudden blast that swept with a shout across the night; and through his mind passed also a tumult like a roaring wind. Both winds, it seemed to him, were in the room at once. He had the sensation of being lifted from the earth. The candle was extinguished. And then the sound and terror dipped away again into silence and into distance whence it came...

He found himself standing stiffly upright, though he had no recollection of rising from his knees. With an abruptness utterly disconcerting he was himself again. No item of memory had faded; he remembered the entire series of events. Only, he was in possession of his normal mind and powers, fear, awe, and wonder all departed. Mánya, who had been walking in her sleep, was sitting close before him in the darkness. He could just distinguish her outline against the open window. But he was master of himself again. Even the wild improbability, the extravagance of his own actions, the very lunacy of the picture that the night now smothered, left him unbewildered. And the calmness that thus followed the complete transition proved to him that all he had witnessed, all that had happened, had been—true. In no single detail was there falseness or distortion due to the excitement of a hysterical mood. It had been right and inevitable.

He lit the candle again quietly, with a hand that did not tremble. He saw

Mánya sitting on the high-backed chair with her head sunk forward on her breast. Gently he raised the face. The eyes were now closed, and the regular, deep breathing showed that the girl was sound asleep—but with the normal sleep of tired childhood. The Immensity to which he had knelt and prayed in her was gone, gone from the room, gone out into the open darkness of the Place. It had visited her, it had used her, it had left her. But at the same time he understood, as by some infallible intuition, that the warning to depart she brought him was not yet complete. It had reached his mind, but not as yet his soul. In its fullness the Notice to Quit could not be delivered between close, narrow walls. Its delivery must be outside.

He looked at the sleeping child in silence for several minutes. She sat there in a semi-collapsed position and in momentary danger of falling from her chair. The lips were parted, the eyes tight shut, the red tam-o'-shanter dropping over one side of the face. Both hands were folded in her lap. By the light of two candles now he watched her, while the perspiration he had not been as yet aware of, dried upon his skin and made him shiver with the cold. And, after long hesitation, he woke her.

With difficulty the girl came to, stared up into his face with a blank expression, rubbed her eyes, and then, with returning consciousness of who and where she was, looked mightily astonished.

"Mánya, child," he began gently, "don't be frightened."

"I'm not," she said at once. "But where am I? Is that you, Uncle?"

"Been walking in your sleep. It's all right. Nothing's happened. Come, I'll see you back to bed again." And he made a gesture as though to take her hand.

But she avoided him. Still looking bewildered and perplexed, she said:

"Oh—I remember now—I wanted to go out and see things. I want to go out still." Then she added quickly as the thought struck her, "But does Fräulein know? You haven't told Fräulein, Uncle, have you? I mean, you won't?"

He shook his head. This was no time for chiding.

"I often go out like this—at night, when you're all asleep. It's the only time now, since—"

He stopped her instantly at that. "You fell asleep while dreaming! Was that it?" He tried to laugh a little, but the laughter would not come.

"I suppose so." She glanced down at her extraordinary garments. But no smile came to the eyes or lips. Then she looked round her, and gazed for a minute through the open window. The rain had ceased, the wind had died away. Moist, fragrant air stole in with many perfumes. "I don't remember quite. I was in bed. I had been asleep already, I think. Then—something woke me." She paused. "There was something crying in the night."

"Something crying in the night?" he repeated quickly, half to himself.

She nodded. "Crying for me," she explained in a tone that sent a shudder all through him before he could prevent it. "So I thought I'd go out and see. Uncle, I *had* to go out," she added earnestly, still whispering, "because they were crying—to get at you. And unless *I* brought them—unless they came through me," she stopped abruptly, her eyes grew moist, she was on the verge of tears—"it would have been so terrible for you, I mean—"

He stiffened as he heard it. He made a violent effort at control, stopping her further explanation.

"And you weren't afraid—to go out like this into the dark?" he asked, more to cover retreat than because he wanted to hear the reply.

"I put myself out for you," she answered simply. "I let them come in. That way you couldn't get hurt. In me they had to come gently. They were an army. Only, nothing out of me could hurt you, Uncle." She suddenly put her arms about his neck and kissed him. "Oh, Uncle Dick, it *was* lucky I was there and ready, wasn't it?"

And Eliot, remembering that great Disturbance in the woods, pressed the child tenderly to himself, praying that she might not understand his heart too well, nor feel the cold that made his entire body tremble like a leaf. He had thought of an angry animal Presence lurking in the darkness. It had been bigger than that, and a thousand times more dangerous!

"You see," she added with a little gasp for breath when he released her, "they waked me up on purpose. I dressed at an awful rate. I got to the door—I remember that perfectly well—and then—" An expression of bewilderment came into her face again.

"Yes," he helped her, "and then—what?"

"Well, I forget exactly; but something stopped me. Something came all round me and took me in their arms. It was like arms of wind. I was lifted up and carried in the air. And after that I forget the rest, forget everything—till now."

She stopped. She took off her tam-o'-shanter and smoothed her untidy hair back from the forehead. And as he looked a moment at her—this little human organism still vibrating with the passage of a universal Power that had obsessed her, making her far more than merely child, yet still leaving in her the sweetness of her simple love— he came to a sudden, bold decision. He would face the thing complete. He would go outside.

"Mánya," he whispered, looking hard at her, "would you like to go out—now—with me? Come, child! Suppose we go together!"

She stared at him, then darted about the room with little springs of excitement. She clapped her hands softly, her eyes alight and shining.

"Uncle Dick! You really mean it? Wouldn't it be grand!"

"Of course, I mean it. See! I'm dressed and ready!" And he pointed to his boots and clothes.

"It's the very best thing we can do, really," she said, trying to speak gravely, but the mischievous element uppermost at the idea of the secret nocturnal Journey. "They'll see that you're not afraid, and you'll be safe then for ever and ever and ever! Hooray!"

She twirled the tam-o'-shanter in the air above her head, skipping in her childish joy.

"And we'll go past Fräulein's door," she insisted mischievously, as he took her outstretched hand and led the way on tiptoe down the dark front stairs.

"Hush!" he whispered gruffly. "Don't talk so loud."

She fastened up her garments, and they moved like shadows through the sleeping house.

## XV

THAT journey he made with this "child of Nature" among the dripping trees and along soaked paths was one that Eliot never forgot. For him its meaning was unmistakable. His early life again supplied a parallel. He had once seen a wretched man marched out of camp with two days' rations to shift for himself in the wilderness as best he might, —a prisoner convicted of treachery, but whose life was spared on the chance that he might redeem it, or die in the attempt. He had seen it done by redskins, he had seen it done by white. And hanging had been better. Yet the crime—stealing a horse, or sneaking another's "grub-stakes"—was one that civilisation punishes with a paltry fine, or condones daily as permissible "business acumen."

In primitive conditions it was a crime against the higher law. It was sinning against Nature. And Nature never is deceived.

Richard Eliot was now being drummed out of camp. And the child who led him, mischief in her eyes and the joy of forbidden pleasure in her heart, was all unconscious of the awful rôle she played. Yet it was she who as well had pleaded for his life and saved him.

Nature turned him out; the Place rejected him and Mánya saw him safely to the confines of that wilderness of houses, ugliness, commercial desolation where he must wander till he re-made his soul or lost it altogether.

They cautiously opened the front door, and the damp air rushed to meet them.

"Hush!" he repeated, closing it carefully behind him. But the child was already upon the lawn. Beyond her, dark blots against the sky, rose the massed outline of the little pointed hills. There were no stars anywhere, though the clouds were breaking into thinning troops; but it was not too dark to see, for a moon watched them somewhere from her place of hiding. The air was warm and very sweet, left breathing by the storm.

"Hush, Mánya!" he whispered again, ill at ease to see her go. She ran back, her feet inaudible upon the thick, wet lawn, and took his hand. "We'll go by the Piney Valley," she said, assuming leadership. And he made no objection, though this was the direction of the sample pits. It led also, he remembered, to the Mill—the spot where she who had left him in charge had gone upon her long long journey.

They went forward side by side. The wind below them hummed gently in the tree-tops, but it did not reach their faces. The whole wet world lay breathing softly about them, exhausted by the tempest. It was very still. It watched them pass. There was no effort to detain them. And in Dick Eliot's heart was a pain that searched him like a pain of death itself.

But his companion, he now clearly realised, was merely the child again—

eerie, wonderful, eldritch, but still the little Mánya that he knew so well. Mischief was in her heart, and the excitement of unlawful adventure in her blood; but nothing more. The vast obsessing Entity that had constituted her judge and executioner was now entirely gone. He was spared the added shame of knowing that she realised what she did.

Sometimes she left his side, to come back presently with a little rush of pleasurable alarm. He was uncertain whether he liked best her going from him or her sudden return. Their tread was now muffled by the needles as they went slowly down the pathways of the Piney Valley. The occasional snapping of small twigs alone betrayed their movements. Heavy branches, soaked like sponges, splashed showers on the ground when their shoulders brushed them in passing, and drops fell of their own weight with mysterious little thuds like footsteps everywhere about them in the woods.

Mánya dived away from his side. She came back sometimes in front of him and sometimes behind. He never quite knew where she was. His mind, indeed, neglected her, for his thoughts were concentrated within himself. Her movements were the movements of a block of shadow, shifting here and there like shadows of trees and clouds in faint moonlight.

"Uncle, tell me one thing," he heard with a start, as she suddenly stood in front of him across the narrow pathway, and so close that he nearly bumped against her. "Isn't there something here that's angry with you? Something you've done wrong to?"

"Hush, child! Don't say such things!" He felt the shiver run through him. He pushed her forward with his hands.

"But they're being said—all round us. Uncle, don't you hear them?" she insisted.

"I've always loved the Place. We've always been happy here together." He whispered it, as though a terror was in him lest it should be overheard and—contradicted.

Her answer flabbergasted him. Her intuitions were so uncannily direct and piercing.

"That's what I meant. You've been unkind. You've hurt it."

"Mánya," he repeated severely, "you must not say such things. And you must not think them."

"I'm so awfully sorry, Uncle Dick," she said softly in the dark, and promptly kissed him. The kiss went like a stab into his heart.

Then she was gone again, and he caught her light footstep several yards in front, as though a shower of drops had fallen on the needles.

"Uncle," came her voice again close beside him. She stood on tiptoe and pulled his ear down to the level of her lips. "Hold my hand tight. We're coming near now." She was curiously excited.

"To the Mill?" he asked, knowing quite well she meant another thing.

"No, to the pits the men dug," she answered, nestling in against him, while his own voice echoed faintly, "Yes, the sample pits." He felt like passing the hostile outposts of the Camp who would shoot him but for the presence of the appointed escort.

A sigh of lonely wind went past them with its shower of drops. And these little hands of wind with their fingers of sweet rain helped forward his expulsion. The empty wilderness beyond lay waiting for his soul. It heard him coming.

And a curious, deep revelation of the child's state of mind then rushed suddenly upon him. He knew that she expected something. And her answer to the question he put explained his own thought to himself.

"What is it you expect, Mánya?" he had asked unwisely.

"Not *expect* exactly, Uncle, for that would be the wrong way. But I *know*."

And several kinds of fear shot through him as he heard it, for the words lifted a veil and let him see into her mind a moment. She had said another of her profoundly mystical truths. Expectation, anticipation, he divined, would provide a mould for what was coming, would give it shape, but yet not quite its natural shape. To anticipate keenly meant to attract too quickly: to force. The expectant desire would coax what was coming into an unnatural form that might be dreadful because not quite true. Let the thing approach in its own way, uninvited by imaginative dread. Let it come upon them as it would, deciding its own shape of arrival. To expect was to invite distortion. This flashed across him behind her simple words.

"You fearful child!" he whispered, forcing an unnatural little laugh.

"The soft, wet, sticky things, half yellow and half white," she began, resenting his laughter, "always moving, and never looking twice the same—"

Then, before he could stop her, she stopped of her own accord.

She clutched his arm. He understood that it was the closeness of the thing that had inspired the atrocious words. She held his arm so tightly that it hurt. They stood in the presence of others than themselves.

Yet these Others had not *come* to them. The movement of approach was not really movement at all. It was a condition in himself that had altered so that he knew. Out here the veil had thinned a little, as it had thinned in the room an hour ago. And he saw space otherwise. This Power that in humanity lies normally inarticulate was breaking through. In the room its language had been a stammer; it was a stammer now. Or, in the terms of sight, it was a little fragment utterly inexplicable by itself, since the entire universe is necessary for its complete expression.

Yet Eliot did perceive the enormous thing behind—the thing to which he had been unfaithful by prostituting his first original love. And the fact that it was interwoven with his ordinary little human feelings at the same time only added to the bewilderment of its stupendous reality.

He saw for a fleeting moment just as Mánya saw—from her immediate point of view.

"It's here," she whispered, in a voice that sounded most oddly everywhere; "it's here, the angry thing you've hurt."

On either side of the path, where the heatherland came close, he saw the openings the men had dug—pale, luminous patches of whitish yellow. Between the bushy tufts they shone faintly gleaming against the night. Perspective, in that instant, became the merest trick of sight, a trivial mental jugglery. That slope of coal-black moor actually was extraordinarily near. The tree-tops were just as well beneath his feet, or he stood among their roots. Either was true. There was neither up nor down. The sky was in his hands, a little thing; or the stars and moon hid washed within the current of his blood. Size was illusion, as relative as time. No object in itself had any "size" at all. He saw her universe, all true, as ever, but from another point of view. And the entire Place ran down here to a concentrated point. The sample pits pressed close against his face.

"The pits," she whispered, with a sound of wind and water in her breath.

So, for a moment, he saw from the point of view whence Mánya always saw. He and the child and the Spirit of the Place stood side by side on that narrow shelf of darkness, sharing a joint and absolute comprehension. Her elemental aspect became his own, for his inner eye was against the peephole through which her Behind-the-Scenes was visible. He realised a new thing, grand as a field of stars.

For the Place here focussed almost into sentiency. Those slow moving forces that stir to growth in crystals, waken and breathe in plants, and first in the animal world know consciousness, here moved vast and inchoate, through the structure of the dream-estate he owned. Yet moved not blind and inarticulate. For the stress of some impulse, normally undivined by men, urged them towards articulate expression. Here was reaction approximate to those reactions of the nervous cells which in their ultimate result men call emotions. And this irresistible correspondence between the two appalled him.

The raw material of definite sensation here poured loose and terrible about him from the ground. In them, moreover, was anger, protest, warning, and a menacing resentment—all directed against his mean, insignificant being. From these sample pits issued the menace and the warning, just as literally as there issued from them also the soft, white clay that would degrade the immemorial beauty he had once thought he loved with a clean, pure love. The pits were wounds. They drew all the feelings of the injured Place into the tenderness of sentient organs.

But behind the threatening anger he recognised a softer passion too. There was a sadness, a deep yearning, and a searching melancholy as well, that seemed to bear witness to his rejection with a sighing as of the sea and wood and hills.

And here, doubtless, came in the interweaving of his own little human emotions. For an overpowering sorrow soaked his heart and mind. The judgment that found him wanting woke all his stores of infinite regret. It would have been better for him had he found that millstone which can save the soul, because it removes temptation.

"It is too late," breathed round him in three weeping voices that passed out between his lips as a single cry together. "It is too late."

Yet nothing happened; that is, he saw nothing—nothing translatable by any words that he could find. Time dwindled and expanded curiously. The past ran on before him, and the future grouped itself behind his back. The seconds and minutes which men tick off from the apparent movement of the sun gave place to some condition within himself where they lay gathered for ever into the circle of the Present. He remembers no actual sequence of acts or movements. Duration drew its horns back into a single point... It is sure, however, that these two human beings marched presently on. They steadily became disentangled from the spot, and somehow or other moved away from the staring pits. For Eliot, looking back, recalls that it felt like walking past the mouths of loaded cannon; also that the pits watched them out of sight as portraits follow a moving figure with their expressionless stare. He thinks that he looked straight before him as he went. He is sure no single word was spoken—until they left the trees behind and emerged into the open. The Mill, the old, familiar building, was the thing that first restored him to a normal world again. He saw its outline, humped and black, shouldering its way against the sky. He heard the water running under the wheel. But even the Mill, like a hooded figure, turned its face away. It expressed the melancholy of a multitude. And the woods were everywhere full of tears.

Mánya, he realised then beside him, was making the humming sound of the water that flowed beneath that motionless wheel. Her voice became the voice of the Place—the undifferentiated sound of Nature. It was the voice of dismissal and farewell. Here was the Gateway through which his soul passed out into the Wilderness.

He involuntarily stooped down to feel her, and she lifted her face up in the darkness and kissed him. But it was across a barrier that she kissed him. He already stood outside.

And half an hour later they were indoors again and the house was still. Mánya slept as soundly as the placid Fräulein Bühlke or the motherly Mrs Coove doubtless also slept.

But he lay battling with strange thoughts for hours. Night and the wind were oddly mingled with them; water, hills, and masses of strong landscape too. They rose before his mind's eye in a giant panorama, endlessly moving past beneath huge skies, and visible against a pale background of luminous, yellowish white. It had strange movements of its own, this yellowish background, like the swaying of a curtain on the stage; and sometimes it surged forwards with a smothering sweep that enveloped everything of beauty he had ever known. It then obliterated the world. Stars were extinguished; scenery turned to soil. The Spectre of the Clay he had invoked possessed the Place.

He lay there frightened in his sleepless bed and saw the dawn—a helpless little mortal, destroyed by his faithlessness and breach of trust. And all night long there lay outside, yet watching him, something else that equally never slept—agile, alert, unconquerable. Only it was no longer *disturbed*. For its purpose was accomplished. It had turned him out.

And it is not necessary to tell how John Casanova Murdoch soon thereafter took the work in hand and developed the Place, as he expressed it, "without a hitch." For John C. had made no promises of love nor had he pretended to establish with Nature that intimate relationship of trust and worship which invokes the spiritual laws. Nature took no note of him, for he worked frankly with her, and his motive, if not exalted, was at least a pure one. And the Clay, as he phrased it a little later in his expressive Western lingo, soon was "paying hand over fist. The money was pouring in—more money than you could shake a stick at!"

SUSSEX.

# Incredible Adventures

by Algernon Blackwood

TO
M. S.—K.

# 'Nothing Happening Here'

an Introduction to
*Incredible Adventures*
by Tim Lebbon

There is a website that claims to tell what religion you are. This is quite a strange claim, not least because if *you* don't know your own beliefs, who does? It presupposes that your dogma ties in with some doctrine already recognised, analysed, acknowledged and packaged. It trivialises the truth. And it reduces one of the most complex, destructive and joyful elements of the human condition to a series of multiple-choice questions and a database designed subjectively by some mysterious computer programmer.

I went to the site and filled in the questionnaire, and apparently I am a neo-Pagan. I can live with that. Whether I can live with it *eternally* remains to be seen.

I wonder, if Algernon Blackwood suddenly appeared among us and had access to the internet, what his results would say (ignoring for a moment the fact that his appearance would be miraculous in itself)! His choices would be interesting to say the least, especially if his return visit allowed him time to look around, evaluate what has happened to the world since his death in 1951, see what we have done. Blackwood was a very spiritual man, and in this cynical time when spiritualism has been usurped by dumbed-down entertainment, a powerful media that tells us how to live, and the Cult of Celebrity, I think he would be very sad.

The stories collected in this volume offer a precious insight into one of the most fascinating writers this country has ever seen. As a man he was intriguing enough: medical student, hotelier, artist's model, reporter, dairy farmer, Golden Dawn member and an undercover agent for the British military intelligence.

As a writer he was extraordinary.

The five stories herein are not easy reading. They're challenging, involving and difficult, and that's not because Blackwood wrote them ninety years ago. It is the way he wrote them and what he was trying to say that makes them so complex and demanding, the effect he endeavoured to convey. His aim was always to do far more than simply tell a story. Blackwood's intention was to grab a reader...and touch them.

Just as in his classic novella *The Willows*, Blackwood uses the powers behind and around us to drive these stories. *The Regeneration of Lord Ernie* tells of a young man devoid of enthusiasm, excitement and character, who is taken on a year-long trip by John Hendricks to try to kick-start his imagination. They travel the globe together, and all along Lord Ernie is uninspired, uncaring and almost lifeless. He has virtually no character, and Hendricks despairs at ever being able to fulfil his commitment to Ernie's father. It takes a visit to the Alps to turn things around... to a place where pagan rituals possess the inhabitants of a small village, either drawing them into the mountains to live essentially a cultish life, or terrifying them where they remain in the village. Here Blackwood explores the links between humans and nature, man and woman and the Earth itself. But this is not necessarily a symbiotic link. The pagans worship and pay homage and perhaps exude some pride in their beliefs...but it is always the Earth that holds the power, complete and mind-blowing in its intensity. Even a century ago humankind was removed enough—perhaps arrogant enough—for Blackwood to write:

'...somewhere in the preposterous superstition there lay a big forgotten truth. He could not believe it, and yet he did believe it. The world had forgotten how to live truly close to Nature.'

In *The Sacrifice* Blackwood again uses the mountains as the setting for his tale. Climbing was a love of his and that shows through in this story, where it is treated as a metaphor for achieving spiritual heights, climbing out of the reservoirs of prescribed beliefs to discover oneself, and the truth. It is a dreamy tale, ambiguous and ambitious and verging on the surreal. Its triumphant ending is truly uplifting, an expression of spiritual freedom for the character Limasson and perhaps for Blackwood himself.

*The Damned* is the most curious tale here. Long, dense, detailed and endlessly philosophical, its true quality and allure lie in the fact that its action is almost entirely emotional and spiritual. As is reiterated time and again in the tale, 'Nothing happened here'. There are no attacks, chases, unspeakable horrors, murders or adventures... indeed, the only adventure here is one of the mind. It's a beautiful piece of writing, a spell rather than a story, and it leaves a powerful trace of itself behind. Yet again Blackwood uses the tale to discuss his own free and wide spiritual beliefs, and the tale itself ends positively when a free-thinking Society enters the story. Their beliefs, that *There is no religion higher than Truth*, refresh the mind after a long tale of darkness, paranoia and hauntings by stale, conflicting creeds. Blackwood again displays his belief that faith is entirely internal and subjective:

'An individual's world is entirely what that individual thinks and believes—interpretation. There is no other. And unless he really thinks and really believes, he has no permanent world at all. I grant that few people think, and fewer still believe, and that most take ready-made suits and make them do. Only the strong make their own things...'

I would love to know what Blackwood would think of our world and society today.

*A Descent into Egypt* is an incredible journey of the mind into a place where the Past holds sway. Blackwood spent some time in Egypt, inspiring several stories, and it is obvious that the place had an incredibly powerful, indelible impression on him. The Egypt written of here is almost alive, more in existence than the petty humans who come and go across its surface while history, the Truth of the land, lies buried beneath millennia of sand and memory.

'Uncouth immensity notes the little human flittings. The days roll by in a tide of golden splendour; one goes helplessly with the flood; but it is an irresistible flood that sweeps backwards and below. The silent-footed natives in their coloured robes move before a curtain, and behind that curtain dwells the soul of ancient Egypt–the Reality, as George Isley called it—watching, with sleepless eyes of grey infinity. Then, sometimes the curtain stirs and lifts an edge; an invisible hand creeps forth; the soul is touched.'

The image of the curtain of reality alluded to here, behind which the Truth lays bare and horrendous, is reminiscent of some of the works of the great Arthur Machen. It would have been curious to have been in the same room as these two great writers: both Golden Dawn members, both concerned with the true power of things beneath the thin veneer of reality, and yet I believe Blackwood was not averse to travelling further to confront these powers, moving a step beyond, actually placing his characters most of the time *behind* this curtain. *A Descent into Egypt* is a haunting, sometimes terrifying treatise on the power of the Past over the petty present.

*Wayfarers* is the shortest tale here, a clever homage to an eternal love that lasts through the ages, ignoring Time, existing in the present as a glorious past, dreamed of and coveted still. Of all the stories herein, Wayfarers is the most traditionally told—there is a beginning, an intriguing and beguiling middle peppered with clues, and then the resolution and twist ending. And even here Blackwood's beliefs shine through: the power of the past; the steering hand of fate; humankind's negligible influence in the scheme of things. And most of all, Love. A love that never dies; one that survives even death.

Algernon Blackwood was brought up by parents who were strict evangelists, and under this cloying atmosphere his daring ideas on theology and spirituality expanded far outside his parent's blinkered teaching. He could never accept that he was 'damned', a concept that many prescribed religions hinge upon, or at least dictate. His refusal to accept any ready-made dogma—evidenced perfectly by the range of ideals and philosophies contained within this volume—made his literary adventures all the more fascinating.

If there's one effect this book is guaranteed to have, it is this: it will open your eyes. And if before you start reading you open your heart and give your perceptions room to expand…you may even see the Truth.

Tim Lebbon<br>
Goytre<br>
June 2002

# The Regeneration of Lord Ernie

I

John Hendricks was bear-leading at the time. He had originally studied for Holy Orders, but had abandoned the Church later for private reasons connected with his faith, and had taken to teaching and tutoring instead. He was an honest, upstanding fellow of five-and-thirty, incorruptible, intelligent in a simple, straightforward way. He played games with his head, more than most Englishmen do, but he went through life without much calculation. He had qualities that made boys like and respect him; he won their confidence. Poor, proud, ambitious, he realised that fate offered him a chance when the Secretary of State for Scotland asked him if he would give up his other pupils for a year and take his son, Lord Ernie, round the world upon an educational trip that might make a man of him. For Lord Ernie was the only son, and the Marquess's influence was naturally great. To have deposited a regenerated Lord Ernie at the castle gates might have guaranteed Hendricks' future. After leaving Eton prematurely the lad had come under Hendricks' charge for a time, and with such excellent results—"I'd simply swear by that chap, you know," the boy used to say—that his father, considerably impressed, and rather as a last resort, had made this proposition. And Hendricks, without much calculation, had accepted it. He liked "Bindy" for himself. It was in his heart to "make a man of him," if possible. They had now been round the world together and had come up from Brindisi to the Italian Lakes, and so into Switzerland. It was middle October. With a week or two to spare they were making leisurely for the ancestral halls in Aberdeenshire.

The nine months' travel, Hendricks realized with keen disappointment, had accomplished, however, very little. The job had been exhausting, and he had conscientiously done his best. Lord Ernie liked him thoroughly, admiring his vigour with a smile of tolerant good-nature through his ceaseless cigarette smoke. They were almost like two boys together. "You *are* a chap and a half, Mr. Hendricks. You really ought to be in the Cabinet with my father." Hendricks would deliver up his useless parcel at the castle gates, pocket the thanks and the hard-earned fee, and go back to his arduous life of teaching and writing in dingy lodgings. It was a pity, even on the lowest grounds. The tutor, truth to tell, felt undeniably depressed. Hopeful by nature, optimistic, too, as men of action usually are, he cast about him, even at the last hour, for something that might stir the boy to life, wake him up, put zest and energy into him. But there was only Paris now between them and the end; and Paris certainly could not be relied upon for help. Bindy's desire for Paris even was not strong enough to count. No desire in him was ever strong. There lay the crux of the problem in a word—Lord Ernie was without desire which is life.

Tall, well-built, handsome, he was yet such a feeble creature, without the energy to be either wild or vicious. Languid, yet certainly not decadent, life ran slowly, flabbily in him. He took to nothing. The first impression he made was fine—then nothing. His only tastes, if tastes they could be called, were out-of-door tastes: he was vaguely interested in flying, yet not enough to master the mechanism of it; he liked motoring at high speed, being driven, not driving himself; and he loved to wander about in woods, making fires like a Red Indian, provided they lit easily, yet even this, not for the poetry of the thing nor for any love of adventure, but just "because." "I like fire, you know; like to watch it burn." Heat seemed to give him curious satisfaction, perhaps because the heat of life, he realized, was deficient in his six-foot body. It was significant, this love of fire in him, though no one could discover why. As a child he had a dangerous delight in fireworks—anything to do with fire. He would watch a candle flame as though he were a fire-worshipper, but had never been known to make a single remark of interest about it. In a wood, as mentioned, the first thing he did was to gather sticks—though the resulting fire was never part of any purpose. He had no purpose. There was no wind or fire of life in the lad at all. The fine body was inert.

Hendricks did wrong, of course, in going where he did—to this little desolate village in the Jura Mountains—though it was the first time all these trying months he had allowed himself a personal desire. But from Domo Dossola the Simplon Express would pass Lausanne, and from Lausanne to the Jura was but a step—all on the way home, moreover. And what prompted him was merely a sentimental desire to revisit the place where ten years before he had fallen violently in love with the pretty daughter of the Pasteur, M. Leysin, in whose house he lodged. He had gone there to learn French. The very slight detour seemed pardonable.

His spiritless charge was easily persuaded.

"We might go home by Pontarlier instead of Bale, and get a glimpse of the Jura," he suggested. "The line slides along its frontiers a bit, and then goes bang across it. We might even stop off a night on the way—if you cared about it. I know a curious old village—Villaret—where I went at your age to pick up French."

"Top-hole," replied Lord Ernie listlessly. "All on the way to Paris, ain't it?"

"Of course. You see there's a fortnight before we need get home."

"So there is, yes. Let's go." He felt it was almost his own idea and that he decided it.

"If you'd really like it."

"Oh, yes! Why not? I'm sick of cities." He flicked some dust off his coat sleeve with an immaculate silk handkerchief, then lit a cigarette. "Just as you like," he added, with a drawl and a smile. "I'm ready for anything." There was no keenness, no personal desire, no choice in reality at all; flabby good-nature merely.

A suggestion was invariably enough, as though the boy had no will of his own, his opposition rarely more than negative sulking that soon flattened out because it was forgotten. Indeed, no sign of positive life lay in him anywhere—no vitality, aggression, coherence of desire and will; vacuous rather than imbecile; unable to go forward upon any definite line of his own, as though all wheels had slipped their cogs; a pasty soul that took good enough impressions, yet never mastered them for permanent use. Nothing stuck. He would never make a politician, much less a statesman. The family title would be borne by a nincompoop. Yet all the machinery was there, one felt—if only it could be driven, made to go. It was sad. Lord Ernie was heir to great estates, with a name and position that might influence thousands.

And Hendricks had been a good selection, with his virility and gentle, understanding firmness. He understood the problem. "You'll do what no one else could," the anxious father told him, "for he worships you, and you can sting without hurting him. You'll put life and interest into him if anybody in this world can. I have great hopes of this tour. I shall always be in your debt, Mr. Hendricks." And Hendricks had accepted the onerous duty in his big, high-minded way. He was conscientious to the backbone. This little side-trip was his sole deflection, if such it can be called even. "Life, light and cheerful influences," had been his instructions; "nothing dull or melancholy; an occasional fling, if he wants it—I'd welcome a fling as a good sign—and as much intercourse with decent people, and stimulating sight-seeing as you can manage—or can stand," the Earl added with a smile. "Only you won't over-tax the lad, will you? Above all, let him think *he* chooses and decides, when possible."

Villaret, however, hardly complied with these conditions; there was melancholy in it; Hendricks' mind—whose reflexes the spongy nature of the empty lad absorbed too easily—would be in a minor key. Yet a night could work no harm. Whence came, he wondered, the fleeting notion that it might do good? Was it, perhaps, that Leysin, the vigorous old Pasteur, might contribute something? Leysin had been a considerable force in his own development, he remembered; they had corresponded a little since; Leysin was out of the common, certainly, restless energy in him as of the sea. Hendricks found difficulty in sorting out his thoughts and motives but Leysin was in them somewhere—this idea that his energetic personality might help. His vitalising effect, at least, would counteract the melancholy.

For Villaret lay huddled upon unstimulating slopes, the robe of gloomy pine-woods sweeping down towards its poverty from bleak heights and desolate gorges. The peasants were morose, ill-living folk. It was a dark untaught corner in a range of otherwise fairy mountains, a backwater the sun had neglected to clean out. Superstitions, Hendricks remembered, of incredible kind still lingered there; a touch of the sinister hovered about the composite mind of its inhabitants. The Pasteur fought strenuously this blackness in their lives and thoughts; in the village itself with more or less success—though even there the drinking and habits of living were utterly unsweetened—but on the heights, among the somewhat arid pastures, the mountain men remained untamed, turbulent, even menacing. Hendricks knew this of old, though he had never understood too well. But he remembered how the English boys at *la cure* were forbidden to climb in certain directions, because the life in these scattered chalets was somehow loose and violent. There was danger there, the danger, however, never definitely stated. Those lonely ridges lay cursed beneath dark skies. He remembered too, the savage dogs, the difficulty of approach, the aggressive attitude towards the plucky Pasteur's visits to these remote upland *paturages*. They did not lie in his parish: Leysin made his occasional visits as man and missionary; for extraordinary rumours, Hendricks recalled, were rife, of some queer worship of their own these lawless peasants kept alive in their distant, windy territory, planted there first, the story had it, by some renegade priest whose name was now forgotten.

Hendricks himself had no personal experiences. He had been too deeply in love to trouble about outside things, however strange. But Marston's case had never quite left his memory—Marston, who climbed up by unlawful ways, stayed away two whole days and nights and came back suddenly with his air of being broken, shattered, appallingly used up, his face so lined and strained it seemed aged by twenty years, and yet with a singular new life in him, so vehement, loud, and reckless, it was like a kind of sober intoxication. He was packed off to England before he could relate anything. But he had suffered shocks. His white, passionate face, his boisterous new vigour, the way M. Leysin screened his view of the heights as he put him personally into the Paris train—almost as though he feared the boy would see the hills and make another dash for them!—made up an unforgettable picture in the mind.

Moreover, between the sodden village and that string of evil chalets that lay in their dark line upon the heights there had been links. Exactly of what nature he never knew, for love made all else uninteresting; only, he remembered swarthy, dark-faced messengers descending into the sleepy hamlet from time to time, big, mountain-limbed fellows with wind in their hair and fire in their eyes; that their visits produced commotion and excitement of difficult kinds; that wild orgies invariably followed in their wake; and that, when the messengers went back, they did not go alone. There was life up there, whereas the village was moribund. And none who went ever cared to return. Cudrefin, the young giant *vigneron*, taken in this way, from the very side of his sweetheart too, came back two years later as a messenger himself. He did not even ask for the girl, who had meanwhile married another. "There's life up there with us," he told the drunken loafers in the "Guillaume Tell," "wind and fire to make you spin to the devil—or to heaven!" He was enthusiasm personified. In the village he had been merely drinking himself stupidly to death. Vaguely, too, Hendricks remembered visits of police from the neighbouring towns, some of them on horseback, all armed, and that once even soldiers accompanied them, and on another occasion a bishop, or whatever the church dignitary was called, had arrived suddenly and promised radical assistance of a spiritual kind that had never materialised—oh, and many other details that now trooped back with suggestions time had certainly not made smaller. For the love had passed along its way and gone, and he was free now to the invasion of other memories, dwarfed at the time by that dominating, sweet passion.

Yet all the tutor wanted now, this chance week in late October, was to see again the corner of the mossy forest where he had known that marvellous thing, first love; renew his link with Leysin who had taught him much; and see if, perchance, this man's stalwart, virile energy might possibly overflow with benefit into his listless charge. The expenses he meant to pay out of his own pocket. Those wild pagans on the heights—even if they still existed— there was no need to mention. Lord Ernie knew little French, and certainly no word of *patois*. For one night, or even two, the risk was negligible.

Was there, indeed, risk at all of any sort? Was not this vague uneasiness he felt merely conscience faintly pricking? He could not feel that he was doing wrong. At worst, the youth might feel depression for a few hours— speedily curable by taking the train.

Something, nevertheless, did gnaw at him in subconscious fashion, producing a sense of apprehension; and he came to the conclusion that this memory of the mountain tribe was the cause of it—a revival of forgotten boyhood's awe. He glanced across at the figure of Bindy lounging upon the hotel lawn in an easy-chair, full in the sunshine, a newspaper at his feet. Reclining there, he looked so big and strong and handsome, yet in reality was but a painted lath without resistance, much less attack, in all his many inches. And suddenly the tutor recalled another thing, the link, however, undiscoverable, and it was this: that the boy's mother, a Canadian, had suffered once severely from a winter in Quebec, where the marquess had first made her acquaintance. Frost had robbed her, if he remembered rightly, of a foot—with the result, at any rate, that she had a wholesome terror of the cold. She sought heat and sun instinctively—fire. Also, that asthma had been her sore affliction—sheer inability to take a full, deep breath. This deficiency of heat and air, therefore, were in her mind. And he knew that Bindy's birth had been an anxious time, the anxiety justified, moreover, since she had yielded up her life for him.

And so the singular thought flashed through him suddenly as he watched the reclining, languid boy, Cudrefin's descriptive phrase oddly singing in his head—

"Heat and fire, fire and wind—why, it's the very thing he lacks! And he's always after them. I wonder—!"

## II

The lumbering yellow *diligence* brought them up from the Lake shore, a long two hours, deposited them at the opening of the village street, and went its grinding, toiling way towards the frontier. They arrived in a blur of rain. It was evening. Lowering clouds drew night before her time upon the world, obscuring the distant summits of the Oberland, but lights twinkled here and there in the nearer landscape, mapping the gloom with signals. The village was very still. Above and below it, however, two big winds were at work, with curious results. For a lower wind from the east in gusty draughts drove the body of the lake into quick white horses which shone like wings against the deep *basses Alpes*, while a westerly current swept the heights immediately above the village. There was this odd division of two weathers, presaging a change. A narrow line of clear bright sky showed up the Jura outline finely towards the north, stars peeping sharply through the pale moist spaces. Hurrying vapours, driven by the upper westerly wind, concealed them thinly. They flashed and vanished. The entire ridge, five thousand feet in the air, had an appearance of moving through the sky. Between these opposing winds at different levels the village itself lay motionless, while the world slid past, as it were, in two directions.

"The earth seems turning round," remarked Lord Ernie. He had been reading a novel all day in train and steamer, and smoking endless cigarettes in the *diligence,* his companion and himself its only occupants. He seemed suddenly to have waked up. "What is it?" he asked with interest.

Hendricks explained the queer effect of the two contrary winds. Columns of peat smoke rose in thin straight lines from the blur of houses, untouched by the careering currents above and below. The winds whirled round them.

Lord Ernie listened attentively to the explanation. "I feel as if I were spinning with it—like a top," he observed, putting his hand to his head a moment. "And what are those lights up there?"

He pointed to the distant ridge, where fires were blazing as though stars had fallen and set fire to the trees. Several were visible, at regular intervals. The sharp summits of the limestone mountains cut hard into the clear spaces of northern sky thousands of feet above.

"Oh, the peasants burning wood and stuff, I suppose," the tutor told him.

The youth turned an instant, standing still to examine them with a shading hand.

"People live up there?" he asked. There was surprise in his voice, and his body stiffened oddly as he spoke.

"In mountain chalets, yes," replied the other a trifle impatiently, noticing his attitude. "Come along now," he added, "let's get to our rooms in the carpenter's house before the rain comes down. You can see the windows twinkling over there," and he pointed to a building near the church. "The storm will catch us." They moved quickly down the deserted street together in the deepening gloom, passing little gardens, doors of open barns, straggling manure heaps, and courtyards of cobbled stones where the occasional figure of a man was seen. But Lord Ernie lingered behind, half loitering. Once or twice, to the other's increasing annoyance, he paused, standing still to watch the heights through openings between the tumble-down old houses. Half a dozen big drops of rain splashed heavily on the road.

"Hurry up!" cried Hendricks, looking back, "or we shall be caught. It's the mountain wind—the *coup de joran.* You can hear it coming!" For the lad was peering across a low wall in an attitude of fixed attention. He made a gesture with one hand, as though he signalled towards the ridges where the fires blazed. Hendricks called pretty sharply to him then. It was possible, of course, that he misinterpreted the movement; it *may* merely have been that he passed his fingers through his hair, across his eyes, or used the palm to focus sight, for his hat was off and the light was quite uncertain. Only Hendricks did not like the lingering or the gesture. He put authority into his tone at once. "Come along, will you; come along, Bindy!" he called.

The answer filled him with amazement.

"All right, all right. I'll follow in a moment. I like this."

The tutor went back a few steps towards him. The tone startled him.

"Like what?" he asked.

And Lord Ernie turned towards him with another face. There was fighting in it. There was resolution.

"This, of course," the boy answered steadily, but with excitement shut down behind, as he waved one arm towards the mountains. "I've dreamed this sort of thing; I've known it somewhere. We've seen nothing like it all our stupid trip." The flash in his brown eyes passed then, as he added more quietly, but with firmness: "Don't wait for me; I'll follow."

Hendricks stood still in his tracks. There was a decision in the voice and manner that arrested him. The confidence, the positive statement, the eager desire, the hint of energy—all this was new. He had never encouraged the boy's habit of vivid dreaming, deeming the narration unwise. It flashed across him suddenly now that the "deficiency" might be only on the surface. Energy and life hid, perhaps, subconsciously in him. Did the dreams betray an activity he knew not how to carry through and correlate with his everyday, external world? And were these dreams evidence of deep, hidden desire—a clue, possibly, to the energy he sought and needed, the exact kind of energy that might set the inert machinery in motion and drive it?

He hesitated an instant, waiting in the road. He was on the verge of understanding something that yet just evaded him. Bindy's childish, instinctive love of fire, his passion for air, for rushing wind, for oceans of limitless—

There came at that moment a deep roaring in the mountains. Far away, but rapidly approaching, the ominous booming of it filled the air. The westerly wind descended by the deep gorges, shaking the forests, shouting as it came. Clouds of white dust spiralled into the sky off the upper roads, spread into sheets like snow, and swept downwards with incredible velocity. The air turned suddenly cooler. More big drops of rain splashed and thudded on the roofs and road. There was a feeling of something violent and instantaneous about to happen, a sense almost of attack. The *joran* tore headlong down into the valley.

"Come on, man," he cried at the top of his voice. "That's the *joran*! I know it of old! It's terrific. Run!" And he caught the lad, still lingering, by the arm.

But Lord Ernie shook himself free with an excitement almost violent.

"I've been up there with those great fires," he shouted. "I know the whole blessed thing. But where was it? Where?" His face was white, eyes shining, manner strangely agitated. "Big, naked fellows who dance like wind, and rushing women of fire, and—"

Two things happened then, interrupting the boy's wild language. The *joran* reached the village and struck it; the houses shook, the trees bent double, and the cloud of limestone dust, painting the darkness white, swept on between Hendricks and the boy with extraordinary force, even separating them. There was a clatter of falling tiles, of banging doors and windows, and then a burst of icy rain that fell like iron shot on everything, raising actual spray. The air was in an instant thick. Everything drove past, roared, trembled. And, secondly—just in that brief instant when man and boy were separated there shot between them with shadowy swiftness the figure of a man, hatless, with flying hair, who vanished with running strides into the darkness of the village street beyond—all so rapidly that sight could focus neither the manner of his coming nor of his going. Hendricks caught a glimpse of a swarthy, elemental type of face, the swing of great shoulders, the leap of big loose limbs—something rushing and elastic in the whole appearance—but nothing he could claim for definite detail. The figure swept through the dust and wind like an animal—and was gone. It was, indeed, only the contrast of Lord Ernie's whitened skin, of his graceful, half-elegant outline, that enabled him to recall the details that he did. The weather-beaten visage seemed to storm away. Bindy's delicate aristocratic face shone so pale and eager. But that a real man had passed was indubitable, for the boy made a flurried movement as though to follow. Hendricks caught his arm with a determined grip and pulled him back.

"Who was that? Who was it?" Lord Ernie cried breathlessly, resisting with all his strength, but vainly.

"Some mountain fellow, of course. Nothing to do with us." And he dragged the boy after him down the road. For a second both seemed to have lost their heads. Hendricks certainly felt a gust of something strike him into momentary consternation that was half alarm.

"From up there, where the fires are?" asked the boy, shouting above the wind and rain.

"Yes, yes, I suppose so. Come along. We shall be soused. Are you mad?" For Bindy still held back with all his weight, trying to turn round and see. Hendricks used more force. There was almost a scuffle in the road.

"All right, I'm coming. I only wanted to look a second. You needn't drag my arm out." He ceased resistance, and they lurched forward together. "But what a chap he was! He went like the wind. Did you see the light streaming out of him—like fire?"

"Like what?" shouted Hendricks, as they dashed now through the driving tempest.

"Fire!" bawled the boy, "It lit me up as he passed—fire that lights but does not burn, and wind that blows the world along—"

"Button your coat and run!" interrupted the other, hurrying his pace, and pulling the lad forcibly after him.

"Don't twist! You're hurting! I can run as well as you!" came back, with an energy Bindy had never shown before in his life. He was breathless, panting, charged with excitement still. "It touched me as he passed—fire that lights but doesn't burn, and wind that blows the heart to flame—let me go, will you? Let go my hand."

He dashed free and away. The torrential rain came down in sheets now from a windless sky, for the *joran* was already miles beyond them, tearing across the angry lake. They reached the carpenter's house, where their lodging was, soaked to the skin. They dried themselves, and ate the light supper of soup and omelette prepared for them—ate it in their dressing-gowns. Lord Ernie went to bed with a hot-water bottle of rough stone. He declared with decision that he felt no chill. His excitement had somewhat passed.

"But I say, Mr. Hendricks," he remarked, as he settled down with his novel and a cigarette, calmed and normal again, "this is a place and a half, isn't it? It stirs me all up. I suppose it's the storm. What do you think?"

"Electrical state of the air, yes," replied the tutor briefly.

Soon afterwards he closed the shutters on the weather side, said goodnight, and went into his own room to unpack. The singular phrase Bindy had used kept singing through his head: "Fire that lights but doesn't burn, and wind that blows the heart to flame"—the first time he had said "blows the world along." Where on earth had the boy got hold of such queer words? He still saw the figure of that wild mountain fellow who had passed between them with the dust and wind and rain. There was confusion in the picture, or rather in his memory of it, perhaps. But it seemed to him, looking back now, that the man in passing had paused a second—the briefest second merely—and had spoken, or, at any rate, had stared closely a moment into Bindy's face, and that some communication had been between them in that moment of elemental violence.

### III

Pasteur Leysin Hendricks remembered very well. Even now in his old age he was a vigorous personality, but in his youth he had been almost revolutionary; wild enough, too, it was rumoured, until he had turned to God of his own accord as offering a larger field for his strenuous vitality. The little man was possessed of tireless life, a born leader of forlorn hopes, attack his métier, and heavy odds the conditions that he loved. Before settling down in this isolated spot—*pasteur de l'eglise independente* in a protestant Canton—he had been a missionary in remote pagan lands. His horizon was a big one, he had seen strange things. An uncouth being, with a large head upon a thin and wiry body supported by steely bowed legs, he had that courage which makes itself known in advance of any proof. Hendricks slipped over to *la cure* about nine o'clock and found him in his study. Lord Ernie was asleep; at least his light was out, no sound or movement audible from his room. The *joran* had swept the heavens of clouds. Stars shone brilliantly. The fires still blazed faintly upon the heights.

The visit was not unexpected, for Hendricks had already sent a message to announce himself, and the moment he sat down, met the Pasteur's eye, heard his voice, and observed his slight imperious gestures, he passed under the influence of a personality stronger than his own. Something in Leysin's atmosphere stretched him, lifting his horizon. He had come chiefly—he now realised it—to borrow help and explanation with regard to Lord Ernie;

the events of two hours before had impressed him more than he quite cared to own, and he wished to talk about it. But, somehow, he found it difficult to state his case; no opening presented itself; or, rather, the Pasteur's mind, intent upon something of his own, was too preoccupied. In reply to a question presently, the tutor gave a brief outline of his present duties, but omitted the scene of excitement in the village street, for as he watched the furrowed face in the light of the study lamp, he realised both anxiety and spiritual high pressure at work below the surface there. He hesitated to intrude his own affairs at first. They discussed, nevertheless, the psychology of the boy, and the unfavourable chances of regeneration, while the old man's face lit up and flashed from time to time, until at length the truth came out, and Hendricks understood his friend's preoccupation.

"What you're attempting with an individual," Leysin exclaimed with ardour, "is precisely what I'm attempting with a crowd. And it's difficult. For poor sinners make poor saints, and the lukewarm I will spue out of my mouth." He made an abrupt, resentful gesture to signify his disgust and weariness, perhaps his contempt as well. "Cut it down! Why cumbereth it the ground?"

"A hard, uncharitable doctrine," began the tutor, realising that he must discuss the Parish before he could introduce Bindy's case effectively. "You mean, of course, that there's no material to work on?"

"No energy to direct," was the emphatic reply. "My sheep here are—real sheep; mere negative, drink-sodden loafers without desire. Hospital cases! I could work with tigers and wild beasts, but who ever trained a slug?"

"Your proper place is on the heights," suggested Hendricks, interrupting at a venture. "There's scope enough up there, or used to be. Have they died out, those wild men of the mountains?" And hit by chance the target in the bull's-eye.

The old man's face turned younger as he answered quickly.

"Men like that," he exclaimed, "do not die off. They breed and multiply." He leaned forward across the table, his manner eager, fervent, almost impetuous with suppressed desire for action. "There's evil thinking up there," he said suggestively, "but, by heaven, it's alive; it's positive, ambitious, constructive. With violent feeling and strong desire to work on, there's hope of some result. Upon vehement impulses like that, pagan or anything else, a man can work with a will. Those are the tigers; down here I have the slugs!"

He shrugged his shoulders and leaned back into his chair. Hendricks watched him, thinking of the stories told about his missionary days among savage and barbarian tribes.

"Born of the vital landscape, I suppose?" he asked. "Wind and frost and blazing sun. Their wild energy, I mean, is due to—"

A gesture from the old man stopped him. "You know who started them upon their wild performances," he said gravely in a lower voice; "you know how that ambitious renegade priest from the Valais chose them for his nucleus, then died before he could lead them out, trained and competent, upon his strange campaign? You heard the story when you were with me as a boy—?"

"I remember Marston," put in the other, uncommonly interested, "Marston—the boy who—" He stopped because he hardly knew how to continue. There was a minute's silence. But it was not an empty silence, though no word broke it. Leysin's face was a study.

"Ah, Marston, yes," he said slowly, without looking up; "you remember him. But that is at my door, too, I suppose. His father was ignorant and obstinate; I might have saved him otherwise." He seemed talking to himself rather than to his listener. Pain showed in the lines about the rugged mouth. "There was no one, you see, who knew how to direct the great life that woke in the lad. He took it back with him, and turned it loose into all manner of useless enterprises, and the doctors mistook his abrupt and fierce ambitions for—for the hysteria which they called the vestibule of lunacy.... Yet small characters may have big ideas.... They didn't understand, of course.... It was sad, sad, sad." He hid his face in his hands a moment.

"Marston went wrong, then, in the end?" for the other's manner suggested disaster of some kind. Hendricks asked it in a whisper. Leysin uncovered his face, looped his neck with one finger, and pointed to the ceiling.

"Hanged himself!" murmured Hendricks, shocked.

The Pasteur nodded, but there was impatience, half anger in his tone.

"They checked it, kept it in. Of course, it tore him!"

The two men looked into each other's eyes for a moment, and something in the younger of them shrank. This was all beyond his ken a little. An odd hint of bleak and cruel reality was in the air, making him shiver along nerves that were normally inactive. The uneasiness he felt about Lord Ernie became alarm. His conscience pricked him.

"More than he could assimilate," continued Leysin. "It broke him. Yet, had outlets been provided, had he been taught how to use it, this elemental energy drawn direct from Nature—" He broke off abruptly, struck perhaps by the expression in his listener's eyes. "It seems incredible, doesn't it, in the twentieth century? I know."

"Evil?" asked Hendricks, stammering rather.

"Why evil?" was the impatient reply. "How can any force be evil? That's merely a question of direction."

"And the priest who discovered these forces and taught their use, then—?"

"Was genuinely spiritual and followed the truth in his own way. He was not necessarily evil." The little Pasteur spoke with vehemence. "You talk like the religion-primers in the kindergarten," he went on. "Listen. This man, sick and weary of his lukewarm flock, sought vital, stalwart systems who might be clean enough to use the elemental powers he had discovered how to attract. Only the bias of the users could make it 'evil' by wrong use. His idea was big and even holy—to train a corps that might regenerate the world. And he chose unreasoning, unintellectual types with a purpose—primitive, giant men who could assimilate the force without risk of being shattered. Under his direction he intended they should prove as effective as the twelve disciples of old who were fisher-folk. And, had he gone on—"

"He, too, failed then?" asked the other, whose tangled thoughts struggled with incredulity and belief as he heard this strange new thing. "He died, you mean?"

"Maison de sante," was the laconic reply, "straight waistcoats, padded cells, and the rest; but still alive, I'm told. It was more than he could manage."

It was a startling story, even in this brief outline, deep suggestion in it. The tutor's sense of being out of his depth increased. After nine months with a lifeless, devitalised human being, this was—well, he seemed to have fallen in his sleep from a comfortable bed into a raging mountain torrent. Strong currents rushed through and over him. The lonely, peaceful village outside, sleeping beneath the stars, heightened the contrast.

"Suppressed or misdirected energy again, I suppose," he said in a low tone, respecting his companion's emotion. "And these mountain mere," he asked abruptly, "do they still keep up their—practices?"

"Their ceremonies, yes," corrected the other, master of himself again. "Turbulent moments of nature, storms and the like, stir them to clumsy rehearsals of once vital rituals—not entirely ineffective, even in their incompleteness, but dangerous for that very reason. This *joran*, for instance, invariably communicates something of its atmospherical energy to themselves. They light their fires as of old. They blunder through what they remember of his ceremonies. With the glasses you may see them in their dozens, men and women, leaping and dancing. It's an amazing sight, great beauty in it, impossible to witness even from a distance without feeling the desire to take part in it. Even my people feel it—the only time they ever get alive,"—he jerked his big head contemptuously towards the street—"or feel desire to act. And some one from the heights—a messenger perhaps—will be down later, this very evening probably, on the hunt—"

"On the hunt?" Hendricks asked it half below his breath. He felt a touch of awe as he heard this experienced, genuinely religious man speak with conviction of such curious things. "On the hunt?" he repeated more eagerly.

"Messengers do come down," was the reply. "A living belief always seeks to increase, to grow, to add to itself. Where there's conviction there's always propaganda."

"Ah, converts—?"

Leysin shrugged his big black shoulders. "Desire to add to their number—desire to save," he said. "The energy they absorb overflows, that's all."

The Englishman debated several questions vaguely in his mind; only his mind, being disturbed, could not hold the balance exactly true. Leysin's influence, as of old, was upon him. A possibility, remote, seductive, dangerous, began to beckon to him, but from somewhere just outside his reasoning mind.

"And they always know when one of their kind is near," the voice slipped in between his tumbling thoughts, "as though they get it instinctively from these universal elements they worship. They select their recruits with marvellous judgment and precision. No messenger ever goes back alone; nor has a recruit ever been known to return to the lazy squalor of the conditions whence he escaped."

The younger man sat upright in his chair, suddenly alert, and the gesture that he made unconsciously might have been read by a keen psychiatrist as evidence of mental self-defence. He felt the forbidden impulse in him gathering force, and tried to call a halt. At any rate, he called upon the other man to be explicit. He enquired point-blank what this religion of the heights might be. What were these elements these people worshipped? In what did their wild ceremonies consist?

And Leysin, breaking bounds, let his speech burst forth in a stream of explanation, learned of actual knowledge, as he claimed, and uttered with a vehement conviction that produced an undeniable effect upon his astonished listener. Told by no dreamer, but by a righteous man who lived, not merely preached his certain faith, Hendricks, before the half was heard, forgot what age and land he dwelt in. Whole blocks of conventional belief crumbled and fell away. Brick walls erected by routine to mark narrow paths of proper conduct—safe, moral, advisable conduct—thawed and vanished. Through the ruins, scrambling at him from huge horizons never recognised before, came all manner of marvellous possibilities. The little confinement of modern thought appalled him suddenly. Leysin spoke slowly, said little, was not even speculative. It was no mere magic of words that made the dim-lit study swim these deep waters beyond the ripple of pert creeds, but rather the overwhelming sense of sure conviction driving behind the statements. The little man had witnessed curious things, yes, in his missionary days, and that he had found truth in them in place of ignorant nonsense was remarkable enough. That silly superstitions prevalent among older nations could be signs really of their former greatness, linked mightily close to natural forces, was a startling notion, but it paved the way in Hendricks' receptive mind just then for the belief that certain so-called elements might be worshipped—known intimately, that is—to the uplifting advantage of the worshippers. And what elements more suitable for adoring imitation than wind and fire? For in a human body the first signs of what men term life are heat which is combustion, and breath which is a measure of wind. Life means fire, drawn first from the sun, and breathing, borrowed from the omnipresent air; there might credibly be ways of assaulting these elements and taking heaven by storm; of seizing from their inexhaustible stores an abnormal measure, of straining this huge raw supply into effective energy for human use—vitality. Living with fire and wind in their most active moments; closely imitating their movements, following in their footsteps, understanding their "laws of being," going *identically* with them—there lay a hint of the method. It was once, when men were primitively close to Nature, instinctual knowledge. The ceremony was the teaching. The Powers of fire, the Principalities of air, existed; and humanity *could* know their qualities by the ritual of imitation, could actually absorb the fierce enthusiasm of flame and the tireless energy of wind. Such transference was conceivable.

Leysin, at any rate, somehow made it so. His description of what he had personally witnessed, both in wilder lands and here in this little mountain range of middle Europe, had a reality in it that was upsetting to the last degree. "There is nothing more difficult to believe," he said, "yet more certainly true, than the effect of these singular elemental rites." He laughed a short dry laugh. "The mediæval superstition that a witch could raise a storm is but a remnant of a once completely efficacious system," he concluded, "though how that strange being, the Valais priest, re-discovered the process and introduced it here, I have never been able to ascertain. That he did so results have proved. At any rate, it lets in life, life moreover in astonishing abundance; though, whether for destruction or regeneration, depends, obviously, upon the use the recipient puts it to. That's where direction comes in."

The beckoning impulse in the tutor's bewildered thoughts drew closer. The moment for communicating it had come at last. Without more ado he took the opening. He told his companion the incident in the village street, the boy's abrupt excitement, his new-found energy, the curious words he used, the independence and vitality of his attitude. He told also of his parentage, of his mother's disabilities, his craving for rushing air in abundance, his love of fire for its own sake, of his magnificent physical machinery, yet of his uselessness.

And Leysin, as he listened, seemed built on wires. Searching questions shot forth like blows into the other's mind. The Pasteur's sudden increase of enthusiasm was infectious. He leaped intuitively to the thing in Hendricks' thought. He understood the beckoning.

The tutor answered the questions as best he could, aware of the end in view with trepidation and a kind of mental breathlessness. Yes, unquestionably, Bindy *had* exchanged communication of some sort with the man, though his excitement had been evident even sooner.

"And you saw this man yourself?" Leysin pressed him.

"Indubitably—a tall and hurrying figure in the dusk."

"He brought energy with him? The boy felt it and responded?"

Hendricks nodded. "Became quite unmanageable for some minutes," he replied.

"He assimilated it though? There was no distress exactly?" Leysin asked sharply.

"None—that I could see. Pleasurable excitement, something aggressive, a rather wild enthusiasm. His will began to act. He used that curious phrase about wind and fire. He turned alive. He wanted to follow the man—"

"And the face—how would you describe it? Did it bring terror, I mean, or confidence?"

"Dark and splendid," answered the other as truthfully as he could. "In a certain sense, rushing, tempestuous, yet stern rather."

"A face like the heights," suggested Leysin impatiently, "a windy, fiery aspect in it, eh?"

"The man swept past like the spirit of a storm in imaginative poetry—" began the tutor, hunting through his thoughts for adequate description, then stopped as he saw that his companion had risen from his chair and begun to pace the floor.

The pasteur paused a moment beside him, hands thrust deep into his pockets, head bent down, and shoulders forward. For twenty seconds he stared into his visitor's face intently, as though he would force into him the thought in his own mind. His features seemed working visibly, yet behind a mask of strong control.

"Don't you see what it is? Don't you see?" he said in a lower, deeper tone. "*They knew.* Even from a distance they were aware of his coming. He is one of themselves." And he straightened up again. "He belongs to them."

"One of them? One of the wind-and-fire lot?" the tutor stammered.

The restless little man returned to his chair opposite, full of suppressed and vigorous movement, as though he were strung on springs.

"He's *of* them," he continued, "but in a peculiar and particular sense. More than merely a possible recruit, his empty organism would provide the very link they need, the perfect conduit." He watched his companion's face with careful keenness. "In the country where I first experienced this marvellous thing," he added significantly, "he would have been set apart as the offering, the sacrifice, as they call it there. The tribe would have chosen him with honour. He would have been the special bait to attract."

"Death?" whispered the other.

But Leysin shook his head. "In the end, perhaps," he replied darkly, "for the vessel might be torn and shattered. But at first charged to the brim and crammed with energy—with transformed vitality they could draw into themselves through him. A monster, if you will, but to them a deity; and superhuman, in our little sense, most certainly."

Then Hendricks faltered inwardly and turned away. No words came to him at the moment. In silence the minds of the two men, one a religious, the other a secular teacher, and each with a burden of responsibility to the race, kept pace together without speech. The religious, however, outstripped the pedagogue. What he next said seemed a little disconnected with what had preceded it, although Hendricks caught the drift easily enough—and shuddered.

"An organism needing heat," observed Leysin calmly, "can absorb without danger what would destroy a normal person. Alcohol, again, neither injures nor intoxicates—up to a given point—the system that really requires it."

The tutor, perplexed and sorely tempted, felt that he drifted with a tide he found it difficult to stem.

"Up to a point," he repeated. "That's true, of course."

"Up to a given point," echoed the other, with significance that made his voice sound solemn. "Then rescue—in the nick of time."

He waited two full minutes and more for an answer; then, as none was audible, he said another thing. His eyes were so intent upon the tutor's that this latter raised his own unwillingly, and understood thus all that lay behind the pregnant little sentence.

"With a number it would not be possible, but with an individual it could be done. Brim the empty vessel first. Then rescue—in the nick of time! Regeneration!"

## IV

In the Englishman's mind there came a crash, as though something fell. There was dust, confusion, noise. Moral platitudes shouted at conventional admonitions. Warnings laughed and copy-book maxims shrivelled up. Above the lot, rising with a touch of grandeur, stood the pulpit figure of the little Pasteur, his big face shining clear through all the turmoil, strength and vision in the flaming eyes—a commanding outline with spiritual audacity in his heart. And Hendricks saw then that the man himself was standing erect in the centre of the room, one finger raised to command attention—listening. Some considerable interval must have passed while he struggled with his inner confusion.

Leysin stood, intently listening, his big head throwing a grotesque shadow on wall and ceiling. "Hark!" he exclaimed, half whispering. "Do you hear that? Listen."

A deep sound, confused and roaring, passed across the night, far away, and slightly booming. It entered the little room so that the air seemed to tremble a moment. To Hendricks it held something ominous.

"The wind," he whispered, as the noise died off into the distance; "yet a moment ago the night was still enough. The stars were shining." There was tense excitement in the room just then. It showed in Leysin's face, which had gone white as a cloth. Hendricks himself felt extraordinarily stirred.

"Not wind, but human voices," the older man said quickly. "It's shouting. Listen!" and his eyes ran round the room, coming to rest finally in a corner where his hat and cloak hung from a nail. A gesture accompanied the look. He wanted to be out. The tutor half rose to take his leave. "You have duties to-night elsewhere," he stammered. "I'm forgetting." His own instinct was to get away himself with Bindy by the first early *diligence*. He was afraid of yielding.

"Hush!" whispered Leysin peremptorily. "Listen!"

He opened the window at the top, and through the crack, where the stars peeped brightly, there came, louder than before, the uproar of human voices floating through the night from far away. The air of the great pine forests came in with it. Hendricks listened intently a moment. He positively jumped to feel a hand upon his arm. Leysin's big head was thrust close up into his face.

"That's the commotion in the village," he whispered. "A messenger has come and gone; someone has gone back with him. To-night I shall be needed—down here, but tomorrow night when the great ritual takes place—up there!"

Hendricks tried to push him away so as not to hear the words; but the little man seemed immovable as a rock. The impulse remained probably in the mind without making the muscles work. For the tutor, sorely tempted, longed to dare, yet faltered in his will.

"—if you felt like taking the risk," the words continued seductively, "we might place the empty vessel near enough to let it fill, then rescue it, charged with energy, in the nick of time." And the Pasteur's eyes were aglow with enthusiasm, his voice even trembling at the thought of high adventure to save another's soul.

"Watch merely?" Hendricks heard his own voice whisper, hardly aware that he was saying it, "without taking part?" He said it thickly, stupidly, a man wavering and unsure of himself. "It would be an experience," he stammered. "I've never—"

"Merely watch, yes; look on; let him see," interrupted the other with eagerness. "We must be very careful. It's worth trying—a last resort."

They still stood close together. Hendricks felt the little man's breath on his face as he peered up at him.

"I admit the chance," he began weakly.

"There is no chance," was the vigorous reply, "there is only Providence. You have been guided."

"But as to risk and failure, what of them? What's involved?" he asked, recklessness increasing in him.

"New wine in old bottles," was the answer. "But here, you tell me, the vessel is not damaged, but merely empty. The machinery is all right. If he merely watches, as from a little distance—"

"Yes, yes, the machinery is there, I agree. The boy has breeding, health, and all the physical qualities—good blood and nerves and muscles. It's only that life refuses to stay and drive them." His heart beat with violence even as he said it; he felt the energy and zeal from the older man pour into him. He was realising in himself on a smaller scale what might take place with the boy in large. But still he shrank. Leysin for the moment said no more. His spiritual discernment was equal to his boldness. Having planted the seed, he left it to grow or die. The decision was not for him.

In the light of the single lamp the two men sat facing each other, listening, waiting, while Leysin talked occasionally, but in the main kept silence. Some time passed, though how long the tutor could not say. In his mind was wild confusion. How could he justify such a mad proposal? Yet how could he refuse the opening, preposterous though it seemed? The enticement was very great; temptation rushed upon him. Striving to recall his normal world, he found it difficult. The face of the old marquess seemed a mere lifeless picture on a wall—it watched but could not interfere. Here was an opportunity to take or leave. He fought the battle in terms of naked souls, while the ordinary four-cornered morality hid its face awhile. He heard himself explaining, delaying, hedging, half-toying with the problem. But the redemption of a soul was at stake, and he tried to forget the environment and conditions of modern thought and belief. Sentences flashed at him out of the battle: "I must take him back worse than when I started, or—what? A violent being like Marston, or a redeemed, converted system with new energy? It's a chance, and my last." Moreover, odd, half-comic detail—there was the support of the Church, of a protestant clergyman whose fundamental beliefs were similar to the evangelical persuasions of the boy's family. Conversion, as demoniacal possession, were both traditions of the blood. After all, the old Marquess might understand and approve. "You took the opening God set in your way in his wisdom. You showed faith and courage. Far be it from me to condemn you." The picture on the wall looked down at him and spoke the words.

The wild hypothesis of the intrepid little missionary-pasteur swept him with an effect like hypnotism. Then, suddenly, something in him seemed to decide finally for itself. He flung himself, morality and all, upon this vigorous other personality. He leaned across the table, his face close to the lamp. His voice shook as he spoke.

"Would you?" he asked—then knew the question foolish, and that such a man would shrink from nothing where the redemption of a soul was at stake; knew also that the question was proof that his own decision was already made.

There was something grotesque almost in the torrent of colloquial French Leysin proceeded to pour forth, while the other sat listening in amazement, half ashamed and half exhilarated. He looked at the stalwart figure, the wiry bowed legs as he paced the floor, the shortness of the coat-sleeves and the absence of shirt-cuffs round the powerful lean wrists. It was a great fighting man he watched, a man afraid of nothing in heaven or earth, prepared to lead a forlorn hope into a hostile unknown land. And the sight, combined with what he heard, set the seal upon his half-hearted decision. He would take the risk and go.

"Pfui!" exclaimed the little Pasteur as though it might have been an oath, his loud whisper breaking through into a guttural sound, "pfui! Bah! Would that my people had machinery like that so that I could use it! I've no material to work on, no force to direct, nothing but heavy, sodden clay. Jelly!" he cried, "negative, useless, lukewarm stuff at best." He lowered his voice suddenly, so as to listen at the same time. "I might as well be a baker kneading dough," he continued. "They drink and yield and drink again; they never attack and drive; they're not worth labouring to save." He struck the wooden table with his fist, making the lamp rattle, while his listener started and drew back. "What good can weak souls, though spotless, be to God? The best have long ago gone up to them," and he jerked his leonine old head towards the mountains. "Where there's *life* there's hope," he stamped his foot as he said it, "but the lukewarm—pfui!—I will spue them out of my mouth!"

He paused by the window a moment, listened attentively, then resumed his pacing to and fro. Clearly, he longed for action. Indifference, half-heartedness had no place in his composition. And Hendricks felt his own slower blood take fire as he listened.

"Ah!" cried Leysin louder, "what a battle I could fight up there for God, could I but live among them, stem the flow of their dark strong vitality, then twist it round and up, up, up!" And he jerked his finger skywards. "It's the great sinners we want, not the meek-faced saints. There's energy enough among those devils to bring a whole Canton to the great Footstool, could I but direct it." He paused a moment, standing over his astonished visitor. "Bring the boy up with you, and let him drink his fill. And pray, pray, I say, that he become a violent sinner first in order that later there shall be something worth offering to God. Over one *sinner* that repenteth—"

A rapid, nervous knocking interrupted the flow of words, and the figure of a woman stood upon the threshold. With the opening of the door came also again the roaring from the night outside. Hendricks saw the tall, somewhat dishevelled outline of the wife—he remembered her vaguely, though she could hardly see him now in his darker corner—and recalled the fact that she had been sent out to Leysin in his missionary days, a worthy, illiterate, but adoring woman. She wore a shawl, her hair was untidy, her eyes fixed and staring. Her husband's sturdy little figure, as he rose, stood level with her chin.

"You hear it, Jules?" she whispered thickly. "The *joran* has brought them down. You'll be needed in the village." She said it anxiously, though Hendricks understood the *patois* with difficulty. They talked excitedly together a moment in the doorway, their outlines blocked against the corridor where a single oil lamp flickered. She warned, urging something; he expostulated. Fragments reached Hendricks in his corner. Clearly the woman worshipped her husband like a king, yet feared for his safety. He, for his part, comforted her, scolded a little, argued, told her to "believe in God and go back to bed."

"They'll take you too; and you'll never return. It's not your parish anyhow..." a touch of anguish in her tone.

But Leysin was impatient to be off. He led her down the passage. "My parish is wherever I can help. I belong to God. Nothing can harm me but to leave undone the work He gives me." The steps went farther away as he guided her to the stairs. Outside the roar of voices rose and fell. Wind brought the drifting sound, wind carried it away. It was like the thunder of the sea.

And the Englishman, using the little scene as a flashlight upon his own attitude, saw it for an instant as God might have seen it. Leysin's point of view was high, scanning a very wide horizon. His eye being single, the whole body was full of light. The risk, it suddenly seemed, was—nothing; to shirk it, indeed, the merest cowardice.

He went up and seized the Pasteur's hand. "To-morrow," he said, a trifle shakily perhaps, yet looking straight into his eyes. "If we stay over—I'll bring the lad with me—provided he comes willingly."

"You will stay over," interrupted the other with decision. "Come to supper at seven. Come in mountain boots. Use persuasion, but not force. He shall see it from a distance—without taking part."

"From a distance—yes," the tutor repeated, "but without taking part."

"I know the signs," the Pasteur broke in significantly. "We can rescue him in the nick of time—charged with energy and life, yet before the danger gets—"

A sudden clangour of bells drowned the whispering voice, cutting the sentence in the middle. It was like an alarm of fire. Leysin sprang sharply round.

"The signal!" he cried; "the signal from the church. Some one's been taken. I must go at once—I shall be needed." He had his hat and cloak on in a moment, was through the passage and into the street, Hendricks following at his heels. The whole place seemed alive. Yet the roadway was deserted, and no lights showed at the windows of the houses. Only from the farther end of the village, where stood the cabaret, came a roar of voices, shouting, crying, singing. The impression was that the population was centred there. Far in the starry sky a line of fires blazed upon the heights, throwing a lurid reflection above the deep black valley. Excitement filled the night.

"But how extraordinary!" exclaimed Hendricks, hurrying to overtake his alert companion; "what life there is about! Everything's on the rush." They went faster, almost running. "I feel the waves of it beating even here." He followed breathlessly.

"A messenger has come—and gone," replied Leysin in a sharp, decided voice. "What you feel here is but the overflow. This is the aftermath. I must work down here with my people—"

"I'll work with you," began the other. But Leysin stopped him.

"Keep yourself for to-morrow night—up there," he said with grave authority, pointing to the fiery line upon the heights, and at the same time quickening his pace along the street. "At the moment," he cried, looking back, "your place is yonder." He jerked his head towards the carpenter's house among the vineyards. The next minute he was gone.

## V

And Hendricks, accredited tutor to a sprig of nobility in the twentieth century, asked himself suddenly how such things could possibly be. The adventure took on abruptly a touch of nightmare. Only the light in the sky above the cabaret windows, and the roar of voices where men drank and sang, brought home the reality of it all. With a shudder of apprehension he glanced at the lurid glare upon the mountains. He was committed now; not because he had merely promised, but because he had definitely made up his mind.

Lighting a match, he saw by his watch that the visit had lasted over two hours. It was after eleven. He hurried, letting himself in with the big house-key, and going on tiptoe up the granite stairs. In his mind rose a picture of the boy as he had known him all these weary, sight-seeing months—the mild brown eyes, the facile indolence, the pliant, watery emotions of the listless creature, but behind him now, like storm clouds, the hopes, desires, fears the Pasteur's talk had conjured up. The yearning to save stirred strongly in his heart, and more and more of the little man's reckless spiritual audacity came with it. His own affection for the lad was genuine, but impatience and adventure pushed eagerly through the tenderness. If only, oh, if only he could put life into that great six-foot, big-boned frame! Some energy as of fire and wind into that inert machinery of mind and body! The idea was utterly incredible, but surely no harm could come of trying the experiment. There *were* the huge and elemental forces, of course, in Nature, and if... A sound in the bedroom, as he crept softly past the door, caught his attention, and he paused a moment to listen. Lord Ernie was not asleep, then, after all. He wondered why the sound got somehow at his heart. There was shuffling behind the door; there was a voice, too—or was it voices? He knocked.

"Who is it?" came at once, in a tone he hardly recognised. And, as he answered, "It's I, Mr. Hendricks; let me in," there followed a renewal of the shuffling, but without the sound of voices, and the door flew open—it was not even locked. Lord Ernie stood before him, dressed to go out. In the faint starlight the tall ungainly figure filled the door-way, erect and huge, the shoulders squared, the trunk no longer drooping. The listlessness was gone. He stood upright, limbs straight and alert; the sagging limp had vanished from the knees. He looked, in this semi-darkness, like another person, almost monstrous. And the tutor drew back instinctively, catching an instant at his breath.

"But, my dear boy! why aren't you asleep?" he stammered. He glanced half nervously about him, "I heard you talking, surely?" He fumbled for a match; but, before he found it, the other had turned on the electric switch. The light flared out. There was no one else in the room. "Is anything wrong with you? What's the matter?"

But the boy answered quietly, though in a deeper voice than Hendricks had ever known in him before "I'm all right; only I couldn't sleep. I've been watching those fires on the mountains. I—I wanted to go out and see."

He still held the field-glasses in his hand, swinging them vigorously by the strap. The room was littered with clothes, just unpacked, the heavy shooting boots in the middle of the floor; and Hendricks, noticing these signs, felt a wave of excitement sweep through him, caught somehow from the presence of the boy. There was a sense of vitality in the room—as though a rush of active movement had just passed through it. Both windows stood wide open, and the roar of voices was clearly audible. Lord Ernie turned his head to listen.

"That's only the village people drinking and shouting," said Hendricks, closely watching each movement that he made. "It's perfectly natural, Bindy, that you feel too excited to sleep. We're in the mountains. The air stimulates tremendously—it makes the heart beat faster." He decided not to press the lad with questions.

"But I never felt like this in the Rockies or the Himalayas," came the swift rejoinder, as he moved to the window and looked out. "There was nothing in India or Japan like that!" He swept his hand towards the wooded heights that towered above the village so close. He talked volubly. "All those things we saw out there were sham—done on purpose for tourists. Up there it's real. I've been watching through the glasses till—I felt I simply must go out and join it. You can see men dancing round the fires, and big, rushing women. Oh, Mr. Hendricks, isn't it all glorious—all too glorious and ripping for words!" And his brown eyes shone like lamps.

"You mean that it's spontaneous, natural?" the other guided him, welcoming the new enthusiasm, yet still bewildered by the startling change. It was not mere nerves he saw. There was nothing morbid in it.

"They're doing it, I mean, because they have to," came the decided answer, "and because they feel it. They're not just copying the world." He put his hand upon the other's arm. There was dry heat in it that Hendricks felt even through his clothes. "And that's what I want," the boy went on, raising his voice, "what I've always wanted without knowing it—real things that can make me alive. I've often had it in my dreams, you know, but now I've found it."

"But I didn't know. You never told me of those dreams."

The boy's cheeks flushed, so that the colour and the fire in his eyes made him positively splendid. He answered slowly, as out of some part he had had hitherto kept deliberately concealed.

"Because I never could get hold of it in words. It sounded so silly even to myself, and I thought Father would train it all away and laugh at it. It's awfully far down in me, but it's so real I knew it must come out one day, and that I should find it. Oh, I say, Mr. Hendricks," and he lowered his voice, leaning out across the window-sill suddenly, *"that* fills me up and feeds me"—he pointed to the heights—"and gives me life. The life I've seen till now was only a kind of show. It starved me. I want to go up there and feel it pouring through my blood." He filled his lungs with the strong mountain air, and paused while he exhaled it slowly, as though tasting it with delight and understanding. Then he burst out again, "I vote we go. Will you come with me? What d'you say. Eh?"

They stared at each other hard a moment. Something as primitive and irresistible as love passed through the air between them. With a great effort the older man kept the balance true.

"Not to-night, not now," he said firmly. "It's too late. To-morrow, if you like—with pleasure."

"But to-morrow *night,*" cried the boy with a rush, "when the fires are blazing and the wind is loose. Not in the stupid daylight."

"All right. Tomorrow night. And my old friend, Monsieur Leysin, shall be our guide. He knows the way, and he knows the people too."

Lord Ernie seized his hands with enthusiasm. His vigour was so disconcerting that it seemed to affect his physical appearance. The body grew almost visibly; his very clothes hung on him differently; he was no longer a nonentity yawning beneath an ancient pedigree and title; he was an aggressive personality. The boy in him rushed into manhood, as it were, while still retaining boyish speech and gesture. It was uncanny. "We'll go more than once, I vote; go again and again. This is a place and a half. It's my place with a vengeance—!"

"Not exactly the kind of place your father would wish you to linger in," his tutor interrupted. "But we might stay a day or two—especially as you like it so."

"It's far better than the towns and the rotten embassies; better than fifty Simlas and Bombays and filthy Cairos," cried the other eagerly. "It's just the thing I need, and when I get home I'll show 'em something. I'll prove it. Why, they simply won't know me!" He laughed, and his face shone with a kind of vivid radiance in the glare of the electric light. The transformation was more than curious. Waiting a moment to see if more would follow, Hendricks moved slowly then towards the door, with the remark that it was advisable now to go to bed since they would be up late the following night—when he noticed for the first time that the pillow and sheets were crumpled and that the bed had already been lain in. The first suspicion flashed back upon him with new certainty.

Lord Ernie was already taking off his heavy coat, preparatory to undressing. He looked up quickly at the altered tone of voice.

"Bindy," the tutor said with a touch of gravity," *you were* alone just now—weren't you—of course?"

The other sat up from stooping over his boots. With his hands resting on the bed behind him, he looked straight into his companion's eyes. Lying was not among his faults. He answered slowly after a decided interval.

"I—I was asleep," he whispered, evidently trying to be accurate, yet hesitating how to describe the thing he had to say, "and had a dream—one of my real, vivid dreams when something happens. Only, this time, it was more real than ever before. It was"—he paused, searching for words, then added—"sweet and awful."

And Hendricks repeated the surprising sentence. "Sweet and awful, Bindy! What in the world do you mean, boy?"

Lord Ernie seemed puzzled himself by the choice of words he used.

"I don't know exactly," he went on honestly, "only I mean that it was awfully real and splendid, a bit of my own life somewhere—somewhere elsewhere it lies hidden away behind a lot of days and months that choke it up. I can never get at it except in woods and places, quite alone, hearing the wind or making fires, or—in sleep." He hid his face in his hands a moment, then looked up with a hint of censure in his eyes. "Why didn't you tell me that such things *were* done? You never told me," he repeated.

"I didn't know it myself until this evening. Leysin—"

"I thought you knew everything," Lord Ernie broke in in that same half-chiding tone.

"Monsieur Leysin told me to-night for the first time," said Hendricks firmly, "that such people and such practices existed. Till now I had never dreamed that such superstitions survived anywhere in the world at all." He resented the reproach. But he was also aware that the boy resented his authority. For the first time his ascendency seemed in question; his voice, his eye, his manner did not quell as formerly. "So you mean, when you say 'sweet and awful,' that it was very real to you?" he asked. He insisted now with purpose. "Is that it, Bindy?"

The other replied eagerly enough. "Yes, that's it, I think—partly. This time it was more than dreaming. It was real. I got there. I remembered. That's what I meant. And after I woke up the thing still went on. The man seemed still in the room beside the bed, calling me to get up and go with him—"

"Man! What man?" The tutor leant upon the back of a chair to steady himself. The wind just then went past the open windows with a singing rush.

"The dark man who passed us in the village, and who pointed to the fires on the heights. He came with the wind, you remember. He pulled my coat."

The boy stood up as he said it. He came across the naked boarding, his step light and dancing. "Fire that heats but does not burn, and wind that blows the heart alight, or something—I forget now exactly. You heard it too." He whispered the words with excitement, raising his arms and knees as in the opening movements of a dance.

Hendricks kept his own excitement down, but with a distinctly conscious effort.

"I heard nothing of the kind," he said calmly. "I was only thinking of getting home dry. You say," he asked with decision, "that you *heard* those words?"

Lord Ernie stood back a little. It was not that he wished to conceal, but that he felt uncertain how to express himself. "In the street," he said, "I heard nothing; the words rose up in my own head, as it were. But in the dream, and afterwards too, when I was wide awake, I heard them out loud, clearly: Fire that heats but does not burn, and wind that blows the heart to flame— that's how it was."

"In French, Bindy? You heard it in French?"

"Oh, it was no language at all. The eyes said it—both times." He spoke as naturally as though it was the Durbah he described again. Only this new aggressive certainty was in his voice and manner. "Mr. Hendricks," he went on eagerly, "you understand what I mean, don't you? When certain people look at one, words start up in the mind as though one heard them spoken. I heard the words in my head, I suppose; only they seemed so familiar, as though I'd known them before—always—"

"Of course, Bindy, I understand. But this man—tell me—did he stay on after you woke up? And how did he go?" He looked round at the barely furnished room for hiding-places. "It was really the dream you carried on after waking, wasn't it?"

Then Bindy laughed, but inwardly, as to himself. There was the faintest possible hint of derision in his voice. "No doubt," he said; "only it was one of my big, real dreams. And how he went I can't explain at all, for I didn't see. You knocked at the door; I turned, and found myself standing in the room, dressed to go out. There was a rush of wind outside the window—and when I looked he was no longer there. The same minute you came in. It was all as quick as that. I suppose I dressed—in my sleep."

They stood for several minutes, staring at each other without speaking. The tutor hesitated between several courses of action, unable, for the life of him, to decide upon any particular one. His instinct on the whole was to stop nothing; but to encourage all possible expression, while keeping rigorous watch and guard. Repression, it seemed to him just then, was the least desirable line to take. Somewhere there was truth in the affair. He felt out of his depth, his authority impaired, and under these temporary disadvantages he might so easily make a grave mistake, injuring instead of helping. While

Lord Ernie finished his undressing he leaned out of the window, taking great draughts of the keen night air, watching the blazing fires and listening to the roar of voices, now dying down into the distance.

And the voice of his thinking whispered to him, "Let it all come out. Repress nothing. Let him have the entire adventure. If it's nonsense it can't injure, and if it's true it's inevitable." He drew his head in and moved towards the door. "Then it's settled," he said quietly, as though nothing unusual had happened; "we'll go up there to-morrow night—with Monsieur Leysin to show us the way. And you'll go to sleep now, won't you? For to-morrow we may be up very late. Promise me, Bindy."

"I'm dead tired," came the answer from the sheets. "I certainly shan't dream any more, if that's what you mean. I promise."

Hendricks turned the light out and went softly from the room. He could always trust the boy.

"Good-night, Bindy," he said.

"Good-night," came the drowsy reply.

Upstairs he lingered a long time over his own undressing, listening, waiting, watching for the least sound below. But nothing happened. Once, for his own peace of mind, he stole stealthily downstairs to the boy's door; then, reassured by the heavy breathing that was distinctly audible, he went up finally and got into bed himself. The night was very still now. It was cool, and the stars were brilliant over lake and forest and mountain. No voices broke the silence. He only heard the tinkle of the little streams beyond the vineyards. And by midnight he was sound asleep.

## VI

And next day broke as soft and brilliant as though October had stolen it from June; the Alps gleamed through an almost summery haze across the lake; the air held no hint of coming winter; and the Jura mountains wore the true blue of memory in Hendricks' mind. Patches of red and yellow splashed the great pine-woods here and there where beech and ash put autumn in the vast dark carpet.

The tutor woke clear-headed and refreshed. All that had happened the night before seemed out of proportion and unreasonable. There had been exaggerated emotion in it: in himself, because he returned to a place still charged with potent memories of youth; and in Lord Ernie, because the lad was overwrought by the electrical disturbance of the atmosphere. The nearness of the ancestral halls, which they both disliked, had emphasised it; the ominous, wild weather had favoured it; and the coincidence of these pagan rites of superstitious peasants had focussed it all into a melodramatic form with an added touch of the supernatural that was highly picturesque and—dangerously suggestive. Hendricks recovered his common sense; judgment asserted itself again.

Yet, for all that, certain things remained authentic. The effect upon the boy was not illusion, nor his words about fire and wind mere meaningless invention. There hid some undivined and significant correspondence between the gaps in his deficient nature and these two turbulent elements. The talk of Leysin, as the conduct of his wife, remained authentic; those facts were too steady to be dismissed, the Pasteur too genuinely in earnest to be catalogued in dream. Neither daylight nor common sense could dissipate their actuality. Truth lay somewhere in it all.

Thus the day, for the tutor, was a battle that shifted with varying fortune between doubt and certainty. In the morning his mind was decided: the wild experiment was unjustifiable; in the afternoon, as the sunshine grew faint and melancholy, it became "interesting, for what harm could come of it?" but towards evening, when shadows lengthened across the purple forests and the trees stood motionless in the calm and windless air, the adventure seemed, as it had seemed the night before, not only justifiable, but right and necessary. It only became inevitable, however, when, after tea together on the balcony, Lord Ernie, mentioning the subject for the first time that day, asked pointedly what time the Pasteur expected them to supper; then, noticing the flush of hesitancy in his companion's eyes, added in his strange deep voice, "You promised we should go." Withdrawal after that was out of the question. To retract would have meant, for one thing, final loss of the boy's confidence—a possibility not to be contemplated for a moment.

Until this moment no word of the preceding night had passed the lips of either. Lord Ernie had been quiet and preoccupied, silent rather, but never listless. He was peaceful, perhaps subdued a little, yet with a suppressed energy in his bearing that Hendricks watched with secret satisfaction. The tutor, closely observant, detected nothing out of gear; life stirred strongly in him; there was purpose, interest, will; there was desire; but there was nothing to cause alarm.

Availing himself then of the lad's absorption in his own affairs, he wandered forth alone upon his sentimental tour of inspection. No ghost of emotion rose to stalk beside him. That early tragedy, he now saw clearly, had been no more than youthful explosion of mere physical passion, wholesome and natural, but due chiefly to propinquity. His thoughts ran idly on; and he was even congratulating himself upon escape and freedom when, abruptly, he remembered a phrase Bindy had used the night before, and stumbled suddenly upon a clue when least expecting it.

He came to a sudden halt. The significance of it crashed through his mind and startled him. "There are big rushing women..." It was the first reference to the other sex, as evidence of their attraction for him, Hendricks had ever known to pass his lips. Hitherto, though twenty years of age, the lad had never spoken of women as though he was aware of their terrible magic. He had not discovered them as females, necessary to every healthy male. It was not purity, of course, but ignorance: he had felt nothing. Something had now awakened sex in him, so that he knew himself a man, and naked. And it had revolutionised the world for him. This new life came from the roots, transforming listless indifference into positive desire; the will woke out of sleep, and all the currents of his system took aggressive form. For all energy, intellectual, emotional, or spiritual, is fundamentally one: it is primarily sexual.

Hendricks paused in his sentimental walk, marvelling that he had not realised sooner this simple truth. It brought a certain logical meaning even into the pagan rites upon the mountains, these ancient rites which symbolised the marriage of the two tremendous elements of wind and fire, heat and air. And the lad's quiet, busy mood that morning confirmed his simple discovery. It involved restraint and purpose. Lord Ernie was alive. Hendricks would take home with him to those ancestral halls a vessel bursting with energy—creative energy. It was admirable that he should witness—from a safe distance—this primitive ceremony of crude pagan origin. It was the very thing. And the tutor hurried back to the house among the vineyards, aware that his responsibility had increased, but persuaded more than ever that his course was justified.

The sky held calm and cloudless through the day, the forests brooding beneath the hazy autumn sunshine. Indications that the second hurricane lay brewing among the heights were not wanting, however, to experienced eyes. Almost a preternatural silence reigned; there was a warm heaviness in the placid atmosphere; the surface of the lake was patched and streaky; the extreme clarity of the air an ominous omen. Distant objects were too close. Towards sunset, moreover, the streaks and patches vanished as though sucked below, while thin strips of tenuous cloud appeared from nowhere above the northern cliffs. They moved with great rapidity at an enormous height, touched with a lurid brilliance as the sun sank out of sight; and when Hendricks strolled over with Lord Ernie to *la cure* for supper there came a sudden rush of heated wind that set the branches sharply rattling, then died away as abruptly as it rose.

They seemed reflected, too, these disturbances, in the human atmospheres about the supper table—there was suppression of various emotions, emotions presaging violence. Lord Ernie was exhilarated, Hendricks uneasy and preoccupied, the Pasteur grave and thoughtful. In Hendricks was another feeling as well—that he had lightly summoned a storm which might carry him off his feet. The boy's excitement increased it, as wind-puffs fan a starting fire. His own judgment had somewhere played him false, betraying him into this incredible adventure. And yet he could not stop it. The Pasteur's influence was over him perhaps. He was ashamed to turn back. He was committed. The unusual circumstances found the weakness in his character.

For somewhere in the preposterous superstition there lay a big forgotten truth. He could not believe it, and yet he did believe it. The world had forgotten how to live truly close to Nature.

A desultory conversation was carried on, chiefly between the two men, while the boy ate hungrily, and Mme. Leysin watched her husband with anxiety as she served the simple meal.

"So you are coming with us, and you like to come?" the Pasteur observed quietly, Hendricks translating.

Lord Ernie replied with a gesture of unmistakable enthusiasm.

"A wild lot of men and women," Leysin went on, keeping his eye hard upon him, "with an interesting worship of their own copied from very ancient times. They live on the heights, and mix little with us valley folk. You shall see their ceremonies tonight."

"They get the wind and fire into themselves, don't they?" asked the boy keenly, and somewhat to the distress of the translator who rendered it, "They get into wind and fire."

"They worship wind and fire," Leysin replied, "and they do it by means of a wonderful dance that somehow imitates the leap of flame and the headlong rush of wind. If you copy the movements and gestures of a person you discover the emotion that causes them. You share it. Their idea is, apparently, that by imitating the movements they invite or attract the force—draw these elemental powers into their systems, so that in the end—"

He stopped suddenly, catching the tutor's eye. Lord Ernie seemed to understand without translation; he had laid down his knife and fork and was leaning forward across the table, listening with deep absorption. His expression was alert with a new intelligence that was almost cunning. An acute sensibility seemed to have awakened in him.

"As with laughing, I suppose?" he said in an undertone to Hendricks quickly. "If you imitate a laughter, you laugh yourself in the end and feel all the jolly excitement of laughter. Is that what he means?"

The tutor nodded with assumed indifference. "Imitation is always infectious," he said lightly; "but, of course, you will not imitate these wild people yourself, Bindy. We'll just look on from a distance."

"From a distance!" repeated the boy, obviously disappointed. "What's the good of that?" A look of obstinacy passed across his altered face. Hendricks met his eyes squarely. "At a circus," he said firmly, "you just watch. You don't imitate the clown, do you?"

"If you look on long enough, you do," was the rather dogged reply.

"Well, take the Russian dancers we saw in Moscow," the other insisted patiently, "you felt the power and beauty without jumping up and whirling in your stall?"

Bindy half glared at him. There was almost contempt in his quiet answer: "But your mind whirled with them. And later your body would too; otherwise it's given you nothing." He paused a second. "I can only get the fun of riding by being on a horse's back and doing his movements exactly with him—not by watching him."

Hendricks smiled and shrugged his shoulders. He did not wish to discourage the enthusiasm lying behind this analysis. The uneasiness in him grew apace. He said something rapidly in French, using an undertone and laughter to confuse the actual words.

"Of course we must not interfere with their ceremonies," put in the Pasteur with decision. "It's sacred to them. We can hide among the trees and watch. You would not leave your seat in church to imitate the priest, would you?" He glanced smilingly at the eager youth before him.

"If he did something real, I would." It was said with a bright flash in the eyes. "Anything real I'd copy like a shot. Only, I never find it."

The reply was disconcerting rather: and Hendricks, as he hurriedly translated, made a clatter with his knife and fork, for something in him rose to meet the truth behind the curious words. From that moment, as though catching a little of the boy's exhilaration, he passed under a kind of spell perhaps. It was, in spite of the exaggeration, oddly stimulating. This dull little meal at the village *cure* masked an accumulating vehemence, eager to break loose. He heard the old father's voice: "Well done, Hendricks! You have accomplished wonders!" He would take back the boy—alive...

Yet all the time there were streaks and patches on his soul as upon the surface of the lake that afternoon. There were signs of terror. He felt himself letting go, an increasing recklessness, a yielding up more and more of his own authority to that of this triumphant boy. Bindy understood the meaning of it all and felt secure; Hendricks faltered, hesitated, stood on the defensive. Yet, ever less and less. Already he accepted the other's guidance. Already Lord Ernie's leadership was in the ascendant. Conviction invariably holds dominion over doubt.

They ate little. It was near the end of the meal when the wind, falling from a clear and starlit sky, struck its first violent blow, dropping with the force of an explosion that shook the wooden house, and passing with a roar towards the distant lake. The oil lamp, suspended from the ceiling, trembled; the Pasteur looked apprehensively at the shuttered windows; and Lord Ernie, with startling abruptness, stood up. His eyes were shining. His voice was brisk, alert, and deep.

"The wind, the wind!" he cried. "Think what it'll be up there! We shall feel it on our bodies!" His enthusiasm was like a rush of air across the table. "And the fire!" he went on. "The flames will lick all over, and tear about the sky. I feel wild and full of them already! How splendid!" And the flame of the little lamp leaped higher in the chimney as he said it.

"The violence of the *coup de joran* is extraordinary," explained Leysin as he got up to turn down the wick, "and the second outburst—" The rest of his sentence was drowned by the noise of Hendricks' voice telling the boy to sit down and finish his supper. And at the same moment the Pasteur's wife came in as though a stroke of wind drove behind her down the passage. The door slammed in the draught. There was a momentary confusion in the room above which her voice rose shrill and frightened.

"The fires are alight, Jules," she whispered in her half intelligible *patois*, "the forest is burning all along the upper ridge." Her face was pale and her speech came stumbling. She lowered her lips to her husband's ear. "They'll be looking out for recruits to-night. Is it necessary, is it right for you to go?"

She glanced uneasily at the English visitors. "You know the danger—"

He stopped her with a gesture. "Those who look on at life accomplish nothing," he answered impatiently. "One must act, always act. Chances are sent to be taken, not stared at." He rose, pushing past her into the passage, and as he did so she gave him one swift comprehensive look of tenderness and admiration, then hurried after him to find his hat and cloak. Willingly she would have kept him at home that night, yet gladly, in another sense, she saw him go. She fumbled in her movements, ready to laugh or cry or pray. Hendricks saw her pain and understood. It was singular how the woman's attitude intensified his own misgivings; her behaviour, the mere expression of her face alone, made the adventure so absolutely real.

Three minutes later they were in the village street. Hendricks and Lord Ernie, the latter impatient in the road beyond, saw her tall figure stoop to embrace him. "I shall pray all night: I shall watch from my window for your return. God, who speaks from the whirlwind, and whose pathway is the fire, will go with you. Remember the younger men; it is ever the younger men that they seek to take...!" Her words were half hysterical. The kiss was given and taken; the open doorway framed her outline a moment; then the buttress of the church blotted her out, and they were off.

## VII

And at once the curious confusion of strong wind was upon them. Gusts howled about the corners of the shuttered houses and tore noisily across the open yards. Dust whirled with the rapidity as of some spectral white machinery. A tile came clattering down about their feet, while overhead the roofs had an air of shifting, toppling, bending. The entire village seemed scooped up and shaken, then dropped upon the earth again in tottering fashion.

"This way," gasped the little Pasteur, blown sideways like a sail, "follow me closely." Almost arm-in-arm at first they hurried down the deserted street, past lampless windows and tight-fastened doors, and soon were beyond the cabaret in that open stretch between the village and the forest where the wind had unobstructed way. Far above them ran the fiery mountain ridge. They saw the glare reflected in the sky as the tempest first swept them all three together, then separated them in the same moment. They seemed to spin or whirl. "It's far worse than I expected," shouted their guide; "here! Give me your hand!" then found, once disentangled from his flapping cloak, that no one stood beside him. For each of them it was a single fight to reach the shelter of the woods, where the actual ascent began. An instant the Pasteur seemed to hesitate. He glanced back at the lighted window of *la cure* across the fields, at the line of fire in the sky, at the figure disappearing in the blackness immediately ahead. "Where's the boy?" he shouted. "Don't let him get too far in front. Keep close. Wait till I come!" They staggered back against each other. "Look how easily he's slipped ahead already!"

"This howling wind—" Hendricks shouted, as they advanced side by side, pushing their shoulders against the storm.

The rest of the sentence vanished into space. Leysin shoved him forward, pointing to where, some twenty yards in front, the figure of Lord Ernie, head down, was battling eagerly with the hurricane. Already he stood near to the shelter of the trees waving his arms with energy towards the summits where the fire blazed. He was calling something at the top of his voice, urging them to hurry. His voice rushed down upon them with a pelt of wind.

"Don't let him get away from us," bawled Leysin, holding his hands cupwise to his mouth. "Keep him in reach. He may see, but must not take part..." A blow full in the face that smote him like the flat of a great sword clapped the sentence short. "That's *your* part. He won't obey me!" Hendricks heard it as they plunged across the windswept reach, panting, struggling, forcing their bodies sideways like two-legged crabs against the terrific force of the descending *joran*. They reached the protection of the forest wall without further attempt at speech. Here there was sudden peace and silence, for the tall, dense trees received the tempest's impact like a cushion, stopping it. They paused a moment to recover breath.

But although the first exhaustion speedily passed, that original confusion of strong wind remained—in Hendricks' mind at least,—for wind violent enough to be battled with has a scattering effect on thought and blows the very blood about. Something in him snapped its cables and blew out to sea. His breath drew in an impetuous quality from the tempest each time he filled his lungs. There was agitation in him that caused an odd exaggeration of the emotions. The boy, as they came up, leaped down from a boulder he had climbed. He opened his arms, making of his cloak a kind of sail that filled and flapped.

"At last!" he cried, impatient, almost vexed. "I thought you were never coming. The wind blew me along. We shall be late—"

The tutor caught his arm with vigour. "You keep by us, Ernest; d'you hear now? No rushing ahead like that. Leysin's the guide, not you." He even shook him. But as he did so he was aware that he himself resisted something that he did not really want to resist, something that urged him forcibly; a little more and he would yield to it with pleasure, with abandon, finally with recklessness. A reaction of panic fear ran over him.

"It was the wind, I tell you," cried the boy, flinging himself free with a hint of insolence in his voice, "for it's alive. I mean to see everything. The wind's our leader and the fire's our guide." He made a movement to start on again.

"You'll obey me," thundered Hendricks, "or else you'll go home. D'you understand?"

With exasperation, yet with uneasy delight, he noted the words Bindy made use of. It was in him that he might almost have uttered them himself. He stepped already into an entirely new world. Exhilaration caught him even now. Putting the brake on was mere pretence. He seized the lad by both shoulders and pushed him to the rear, then placed himself next, so that Leysin moved in front and led the way. The procession started, diving into the comparative shelter of the forest. "Don't let him pass you," he heard in rapid French; "guide him, that's all. The power's already in his blood. Keep yourself in hand as well, and follow me closely." The roar of the storm above them carried the words clean off the world.

Here in the forest they moved, it seemed, along the floor of an ocean whose surface raged with dreadful violence; any moment one or other of them might be caught up to that surface and whirled off to destruction. For the procession was not one with itself. The darkness, the difficulty of hearing what each said, the feeling, too, that each climbed for himself, made everything seem at sixes and sevens. And the tutor, this secret exultation growing in his heart, denied the anxiety that kept it pace, and battled with his turbulent emotions, a divided personality. His power over the boy, he realised, had gravely weakened. A little time ago they had seemed somehow equal. Now, however, a complete reversal of their relative positions had taken place. The boy was sure of himself. While Leysin led at a steady mountaineer's pace on his wiry, short, bowed legs, Hendricks, a yard or two behind him, stumbled a good deal in the darkness, Lord Ernie forever on his heels, eager to push past. But Bindy never stumbled. There was no flagging in his muscles. He moved so lightly and with so sure a tread that he almost seemed to dance, and often he stopped aside to leap a boulder or to run along a fallen trunk. Path there was none. Occasional gusts of wind rushed gustily down into these depths of forest where they moved, and now, from time to time, as they rose nearer to the line of fire on the ridge, an increasing glare lit up the knuckled roots or glimmered on the bramble thickets and heavy beds of moss. It was astonishing how the little Pasteur never missed his way. Periods of thick silence alternated with moments when the storm swept down through gullies among the trees, reverberating like thunder in the hollows.

Slowly they advanced, buffeted, driven, pushed, the wildness of some Walpürgis night growing upon all three. In the tutor's mind was this strange lift of increasing recklessness, the old proportion gone, the spiritual aspect of it troubling him to the point of sheer distress. He followed Leysin as blindly with his body as he followed this new Bindy eagerly with his mind. For this languid boy, now dancing to the tune of flooding life at his very heels, seemed magical in the true sense: energy created as by a wizard out of nothing. From lips that ordinarily sighed in listless boredom poured now a ceaseless stream of questions and ejaculations, ringing with enthusiasm. How long would it take to reach the fiery ridge? Why did they go so slowly? Would they arrive too late? Would their intrusion be welcomed or understood? Already one great change was effected—accepted by Hendricks, too—that the role of mere spectator was impossible. The answers Hendricks gave, indeed, grew more and more encouraging and sympathetic. He, too, was impatient with their leader's crawling pace. Some elemental spell of wind and fire urged him towards the open ridge. The pull became irresistible. He despised the Pasteur's caution, denied his wisdom, wholly rejected now the spirit of compromise and prudence. And once, as the hurricane brought down a flying burst of voices, he caught himself leaping upon a big grey boulder in their path. He leaped at the very moment that the boy behind him leaped, yet hardly realised that he did so; his feet danced without a conscious order from his brain. They met together on the rounded top, stumbled, clutched one another frantically, then slid with waving arms and flying cloaks down the slippery surface of damp moss-laughing wildly.

"Fool!" cried Hendricks, saving himself. "What in the world—?"

"*You* called," laughed Bindy, picking himself up and dropping back to his place in the rear again. "It's the wind, not me; it's in our feet. Half the time you're shouting and jumping yourself!"

And it was a few minutes after this that Lord Ernie suddenly forged ahead. He slipped in front as silently as a shadow before a moving candle in a room. Passing the tutor at a moment when his feet were entangled among roots and stones, he easily overtook the Pasteur and found himself in the lead. He never stumbled; there seemed steel springs in his legs.

From Leysin, too breathless to interfere, came a cry of warning. "Stop him! Take his hand!" his tired voice instantly smothered by the roaring skies. He turned to catch Hendricks by the cloak. "You see *that*!" he shouted in alarm. "For the love of God, don't lose sight of him! He must see, but not take part—remember—!"

And Hendricks yelled after the vanishing figure, "Bindy, go slow, go slow! Keep in touch with us." But he quickened his pace instantly, as though to overtake the boy. He passed his companion the same minute, and was out of sight. "I'll wait for you," came back the boy's shrill answer through the thinning trees. And a flare of light fell with it from the sky, for the final climb of a steep five hundred feet had now begun, and overhead the naked ridge ran east and west with its line of blazing fires. Boulders and rocky ground replaced the pines and spruces.

"But you'll never find the way," shouted Leysin, while a deep trumpeting roar of the storm beyond muffled the remainder of the sentence.

Hendricks heard the next words close beside him from a clump of shadows. He was in touching distance of the excited boy.

"The fires and the singing guide me. Only a fool could miss the way."

"But you *are* a—"

He swallowed the unuttered word. A new, extraordinary respect was suddenly in him. That tall, virile figure, instinct with life, springing so cleverly through the choking darkness, guiding with decision and intelligence, almost infallible—it was no fool that led them thus. He hurried after till his very sinews ached. His eyes, troubled and confused, strained through the trees to find him. But these same trees now fled past him in a torrent.

"Bindy, Bindy!" he cried, at the top of his voice, yet not with the imperious tone the situation called for. The sentence dropped into a lull of wind. Instead of command there was entreaty, almost supplication, in it. "Wait for me, I'm coming. We'll see the glorious thing together!"

And then suddenly the forest lay behind him, with a belt of open pastureland in front below the actual ridge. He felt the first great draught of heat, as a line of furnaces burst their doors with a mighty roar and turned the sky into a blaze of golden daylight. There was a crackling as of musketry. The flare shot up and burned the air about him, and the voices of a multitude, as yet invisible, drove through it like projectiles on the wind. This was the first impression, wholesale and terrific, that met him as he paused an instant on the edge of the sheltering forest and looked forward. Leysin and Lord Ernie seemed to leave his mind, forgotten in this first attack of splendour, but forgotten, as it were, the first with contempt, the latter with an overwhelming regret. For the Pasteur's mistake in that instant seemed obvious. In half measures lay the fatal error, and in compromise the danger. Bindy all along had known the better way and followed it. The lukewarm was the worthless.

"Bindy, boy, where are you? I'm coming..." and stepping on to the grassy strip of ground, soft to his feet, he met a wind that fell upon his body with a shower of blows from all directions at once and beat him to his knees. He dropped, it seemed, into the cover of a sheltering rock, for there followed then a moment of sudden and delicious stillness in which the weary muscles recovered themselves and thought grew slightly steadier. Crouched thus close to the earth he no longer offered a target to the hurricane's attack. He peered upwards, making a screen of his hands.

The ridge, some fifty feet above him, he saw, ran in a generous platform along the mountain crest; it was wide and flat; between the enormous fires of piled-up wood that stretched for half a mile coiled a medley of dense smoke and tearing sparks. No human beings were visible, and yet he was aware of crowding life quite near. On hands and knees, crawling painfully, he then slowly retreated again into the shelter of the forest he had sought to leave. He stood up. The awful blaze was veiled by the roof of branches once more. But, as he rose, seizing a sapling to steady himself by, two hands caught him with violence from behind, and a familiar voice came shouting against his ear. Leysin panting, dishevelled and half broken with the speed, stood beside him.

"The boy! Where is he? We're just in time!" He roared the words to make them carry above the din. "Hurry, hurry! I'll follow... My older legs... See, for the love of God, that he is not taken... I warned you!"

And for a second, as he heard, Hendricks caught at the vanished sense of responsibility again. He saw the face of the old Marquess watching him among the tree trunks. He heard his voice, amazed, reproachful, furious: "It was criminal of you, criminal—"

"Where is the boy—*your* boy?" again broke in the shout of the Pasteur with a slap of hurricane, as he staggered against the tutor, half collapsing, and trying to point the direction. "Watch him, find him for the love of heaven before it is too late—before they see him...!"

The tutor's normal and responsible self dived out of sight again as he heard the cry of weakness and alarm. It seemed the wind got under him, lifting him bodily from his feet. He did not pause to think. Like a man midway in a whirling prizefight, he felt dazed but confident, only conscious of one thing—that he must hold out to the end, take part in all the splendid fighting—*win*. The lust of the arena, the pride of youth and battle, the impetuous recklessness of the charge in primitive war caught at his heart, brimming it with headlong courage. To play the game for all it might be worth seemed shouted everywhere about him, as the abandon of wind and fire rushed through him like a storm. He felt lifted above all possibility of little failure. The Marquess with his conventional traditions, the Pasteur with his considerations of half-way safety, both vanished utterly; safety, indeed, both for himself and for the boy in his charge lay in unconditional surrender. This was no time for little thought-out actions. It was all or nothing!

"God bless the whirlwind and the fire!" he shouted, opening wide his arms.

But his voice was inaudible amid the uproar, and the forward movement of his body remained at first only in the brain. He turned to push the old man aside, even to strike him down if necessary. "Lukewarm yourself and a coward!" rose in his throat, yet found no utterance, for in that moment a tall, slim figure, swift as a shadow, steady as a hawk, shot hard across the open space between the forest and the ridge. In the direction of the blazing platform it disappeared against a curtain of thick smoke, emerged for one second in a storm of light, then vanished finally behind a ruin of loose rocks. And Hendricks, his eyes wounded by heat and wind, his muscles paralysed, understood that the boy deliberately invited capture. The multitude that hid behind the smoke and fire, feeding the blazing heaps with eager hands, had become aware of him, and presently would appear to claim him. They would take him to themselves. Already answering flares ran east and west along the desolate ridge.

"I'll join you! I'm coming! Wait for me!" he tried to cry. The uproar smothered it.

### VIII

And this uproar, he now perceived, was composed entirely of wind and fire. Here, on the roof of the hills beneath a starry sky, these two great elements expressed their nature with unhampered freedom, for there was neither rain to modify the one, nor solid obstacle to check the other. Their voices merged in a single sound—the hollow boom of wind and the deep, resounding clap of flame. The splitting crackle of burning branches imitated the high, shrill whistle of the tearing gusts that, javelin-like, flew to and fro in darts of swifter sound. But one shout rose from the summit, no human cry distinguishable in it, nor amid the thousand lines of skeleton wood that pierced the golden background was any human outline visible. Fire and wind encouraged one another to madness, manifesting in prodigious splendour by themselves.

Then, suddenly, before a gigantic canter of the wind, the driving smoke rolled upwards like a curtain, and the flames, ceasing their wild flapping, soared steadily in gothic windows of living gold towards the stars. In towering rows between columns of black night they transformed the empty space between them into a colossal temple aisle. They tapered aloft symmetrically into vanishing crests. And Hendricks stood upright. Rising so that his shoulders topped the edge of the boulder, and utterly contemptuous of

Leysin's hand that sought with violence to drag him into shelter, he gazed as one who sees a vision. For at first he could only stand and stare, aware of sensation but not of thought. An enormous, overpowering conviction blew his whole being to white heat. Here was a supply of elemental power that human beings—empty, needy, starved, deficient human beings—could use. His love for the boy leaped headlong at the skirts of this terrific salvation. A majestic possibility stormed through him.

Yet it was no nightmare wonder that met his staring and half-shielded eyes, although some touch of awful dream seemed in it, set, moreover, to a scale that scantier minds might deem distortion. The heat from some thirty fires, placed at regular intervals, made midnight quiver with immense vibrations. Of varying, yet calculated size, these towering heaps emitted notes of measured and alternating depth, until the roar along the entire line produced a definite scale almost of melody, the near ones shrilly singing, those more distant booming with mountainous pedal notes. The consonance was monstrous, yet conformed to some magnificent diapason. This chord of firemusic paced the starlit sky, directed, but never overmastered, by the wind that measured it somehow into meaning. Repeated in quick succession, the notes now crashing in a mass, now singing alone in solitary beauty, the effect suggested an idea of ordered sequence, of gigantic rhythm. It seemed, indeed, as though some controlling agency, mastering excess, coerced both raging elements to express through this stupendous dance some definite idea. Here, as it were, was the alphabet of some natural, undifferentiated language, a language of sight and sound, predating speech, symbolical in the ultimate, deific sense. Some Lord of Fire and some Lord of Air were in command. Harnessed and regulated, these formless cohorts of energy that men call stupidly mere flame and wind, obeyed a higher power that had invoked them, yet a power that, by understanding their laws of being, held him most admirably in control.

This, at least, seems a hint of the explanation that flashed into Hendricks as he stared in amazed bewilderment from the shelter of the nearest boulder. He read a sentence in some natural, forgotten script. He watched a primitive ritual that once invoked the gods. He was aware of rhythm, and he was aware of system, though as yet he did not see the hand that wrote this marvellous sentence on the night. For still the human element remained invisible. He only realized—in dim, blundering fashion—that he witnessed a revelation of those two powers which, in large, lie at the foundations of the Universe, and, in little, are the basic essentials of human existence—the powers behind heat and air. Fragments of that talk with Leysin stammered back across his mind, like letters in some stupendous word he dared not reconstruct entire. He shuddered and grew wise. Realms of forgotten being opened their doors before his dazzled sight. Vision fluttered into far, piercing vistas of ancient wonder, haunting and half-remembered, then lost its way in blindness that was pain. For a moment, it seemed, he was aware of majestic Presences behind the turmoil, shadowy but mighty, charged with a vague potentiality as of immense algebraical formulæ, symbolical and beyond full comprehension, yet willing and able to be used for practical results. He *felt* the elements as nerves of a living Universe... Yet thinking was not really in him anywhere; feeling was all he knew. The world he moved in, as the script he read, belonged to conditions too utterly remote for reason to recover a single clue to their intelligible reconstruction. Glory, clean and strong as of primitive star-worship, passed between what he saw and all that he had ever known before. The curtain of conventional belief was rent in twain. The terrific thing was true...

For an unmeasured interval the tutor, oblivious of time and actual place, stood on the brink of this majestic pageant, staring with breathless awe, while the swaying of the entire scenery increased like the sway of an ocean lifted to the sky by many winds. Then, suddenly, in one of those temporary lulls that passed between the beat of the great notes, his searching eyes discovered a new thing. The focus of his sight was altered, and he realised at last the source of the directing and the controlling power. Behind the fires and beyond the smoke he recognised the disc-like, shining ovals that upon this little earth stand in the image of the one, eternal Likeness. He saw the human faces, symbols of spiritual dominion over all lesser orders, each one possessed of belief, intelligence and will. Singly so feeble, together so invincible, this assemblage, unscorched by the fire and by the wind unmoved, seemed to him impressive beyond all possible words. And a further inkling of the truth flashed on him as he stared: that a group of humans, a crowd, combining upon a given object with concentrated purpose, possessed of that terrific power, certain faith, may know in themselves the energy to move great mountains, and therefore that lesser energy to guide the fluid forces of the elements. And a sense of cosmic exultation leaped into his being. For a moment he knew a touch of almost frenzy. Proud joy rose in him like a splendour of omnipotence. Humanity, it seemed to him, here came into a grand but long neglected corner of its kingdom as originally planned by Heaven. Into the hands of a weakling and deficient boy the guidance had been given.

Motionless beneath the stars, lit by the glare till they shone like idols of yellow stone, and magnified by the sheets of flying, intolerable light the wind chased to and fro, these rows of faces appeared at first as a single line of undifferentiated fire against the background of the night. The eyes were all cast down in prayer, each mind focussed steadily upon one clear idea—the control and assimilation of two elemental powers. The crowd was one; feeling was one; desire, command and certain faith were one. The controlling power that resulted was irresistible.

Then came a remarkable, concerted movement. With one accord the eyes all opened, blazing with reflected fire. A hundred human countenances rose in a single shining line. The men stood upright. Swarthy faces, tanned by sun and wind, heads uncovered, hair and beards tossing in the air, turned all one way. Mouths opened too. There came a roar that even the hurricane could not drown—a word of command, it seemed, that sprang into the pulses of the dancing elements and reduced their turmoil to a wave of steadier movement. And at the same moment a hundred bodies, naked above the waist, arms outstretched and hands with the palms held upwards, swayed forwards through the smoke and fire. They came towards the spot, where, half concealed from view, the tutor crouched and watched.

And Hendricks, thinking himself discovered, first quailed, then rose to meet them. No power to resist was in him. It was, rather, willing response that he experienced. He stepped out from the shelter of the boulder and entered the brilliant glare. Hatless himself, shoulders squared, cloak flying in the wind, he took three strides towards the advancing battalion—then, undecided, paused. For the line, he saw, disregarded him as though he were not there at all. It was not *him* the worshippers sought. The entire troop swept past to a point some fifty feet below where the end of the ridge broke out of the thinning trees. Beautiful as a curving wave of flame, the figures streamed across the narrow, open space with a drilled precision as of some battle line, and Hendricks, with a sense of wild, secret triumph saw them pause at the brink of the platformed ridge, form up their serried ranks yet closer, then open two hundred arms to welcome some one whom the darkness should immediately deliver. Simultaneously, from the covering trees, the tall, slim shadow of Lord Ernie darted out into the light.

"Magnificent!" cried Hendricks, but his voice was smothered instantly in a mightier sound, and his movement forward seemed ineffective stumbling. The hundred voices thundered out a single note. Like a deer the boy leaped; like a tongue of flame he flew to join his own; and instantly was surrounded, borne shoulder high upon those upturned palms, swept back in triumph towards the procession of enormous fires. Wrapped by smoke and sparks, lifted by wind, he became part of the monstrous rhythm that turned that mountain ridge alive. He stood upright upon the platform of interlacing arms; he swayed with their movements as a thing of wind and fire that flew. The shining faces vanished then, turned all towards the blazing piles so that the boy had the appearance of standing on a wall of living black. His outline was visible a moment against the sky, firelight between his wide-stretched legs, streaming from his hair and horizontal arms, issuing almost, as it seemed, from his very body. The next second he leaped to the ground, ran forward—appallingly close—between two heaped-up fires, flung both hands heavenwards, and—knelt.

And Hendricks, sympathetically following the boy's performance as though his own mind and body took part in it, experienced then a singular result: it seemed the heart in him began to roar. This was no rustle of excited blood that the little cavern of his skull increased, but a deeper sound that proclaimed the kinship of his entire being with the ritual. His own nature had begun to answer. From that moment he perceived the spectacle, not with the senses of sight and hearing, separately, but with his entire body— synthetically. He became a part of this assembly that was itself one single instrument: a cosmic sounding-board for the rhythmical expression of impersonal Nature Powers. Leysin, he dimly realised, fixed in his churchy tenets, remained outside, apart, and compromising; Hendricks accepted and went with. All little customary feelings dipped utterly away, lost, false, denied, even as a unit in a crowd loses its normal characteristics in the greater mood that sways the whole. The fire no longer burned him, for he was the fire; nor did he stagger against the furious wind, because the wind was in his heart. He moved all over, alive in every point and corner. With his skin he breathed, his bones and tissue ran with glorious heat. He cried aloud. He praised. "I am the whirlwind and I am the fire! Fire that lights but does not burn, and wind that blows the hearts to flame!" His body sang it, or rather the elements sang it through his body; for the sound of his voice was not audible, and it was wind and fire that thundered forth his feeling in their crashing rhythm.

## IX

And so it was that he no longer saw this thing pictorially, nor in the little detached reports the individual senses brought, but knew it in himself complete, as a man knows love and passion. Memory afterwards translated these vast central feelings into pictures, but the pictures touched reality without containing it. Like a vision it happened all at once, as a room or landscape happens, and what happens all at once, coming through a synthesis of the senses, is not properly describable later. To instantaneous knowledge mere sequence is a falsehood. The sequence first comes in with the telling afterwards. That kneeling form, he understood, was the empty vessel to which conventional life had hitherto denied the heat and air it craved. The breath of life now poured at full tide into it, the fire of deity lit its heart of touchwood, wind blew into desire; and later flame would burst forth in action, consuming opposition. He must let it fill to the brim. It was not salvation, but creation. Then thought went out, extinguished by a puff of something greater...

For beyond the smoke and sparks, beyond the space the men had occupied, a new and gentler movement, lyrical with bird-like beauty, ran suddenly along the ridge. What Hendricks had taken for branches heaped in rows for the burning, stirred marvellously throughout their whole collective mass, stirred sweetly, too, and with an exquisite loveliness. The entire line rose gracefully into the air with a whirr as of sweeping birds. There was a soft and undulating motion as though a draught of flowing wind turned faintly visible, yet with an increasing brilliance, like shining lilies of flame that now flocked forward in a troop, bending deliciously all one way. And in the same second these tall lilies of fire revealed themselves as figures, naked above the waist, hair streaming on the wind, eyes alight and bare arms waving. Above the men's deep pedal bass their voices rose with clear, shrill sweetness on the storm. The band swept forwards swift as wind towards the kneeling boy. The long line curved about him foldingly. The women took him as the south wind takes a bird.

There may have been—indeed, there was—an interval, for Hendricks caught, again and again repeated, the boy's great cry of passionate delight above the tumult. Ringing and virile it rose to heaven, clear as a fine-wrought bell. And instantaneously the knitted figures of flame disentangled themselves again, the mass unfolded like an opening flower, and, as by a military word of command, dissolved itself once more into a long thin line of running fire. The women advanced, and the waiting men flowed forward in a stream to meet them. This interweaving of the figures was as easily accomplished as the mingling of light and heavy threads upon some living loom. Hands joining hands, all singing, these naked worshippers of fire and wind passed in and out among the blazing piles with a headlong precision that was torrential and yet orderly. The speed increased; the faces flashed and vanished, then flashed and passed again; each woman between two men, each man between two women, and Lord Ernie, radiantly alive, between two girls of rich, o'erflowing beauty. Their movements were undulating, like the undulations of fire, yet with sudden, unexpected upward leaps as when fire is partnered abruptly by a cantering wind. For the women were fire, and the men were wind. The imitative dance was in full swing. The marvellous wind and fire ritual unrolled its old-world magic.

It was awe-inspiring certainly, but for Hendricks, as he watched, the terror of big conflagrations was wholly absent: rather, he felt the sense of deep security that rhythmic movement causes. Bathed in a sea of elemental power, he burned to share the pagan splendour and the rush of primitive delight. It seemed he had a cosmic body in which new centres stirred to life, linking him on to this source of natural forces. Through these centres he drew the chaotic energy into nerves and blood and muscle, into the very substance of his thought, indeed, transmuting them into the magic of the will. Abundant and inexhaustible vigour filled the air, pouring freely into whatever empty receptacle lay at hand. Sheets of flame, whole separate fragments of it, torn at the edges, raced, loudly, hungrily flapping on vehement gusts of wind; curved as they flew; leaped, twisted, flashed and vanished. And the figures closely copied them. The women tossed their bodies aloft, then dipped suddenly to the earth, invisible, till the rushing men urged them into view again with wild impetuous swing, so that the entire line stretched and contracted like an immense elastic band of life, now knotted, now dissolved.

Yet, while of raging and terrific beauty, there was never that mad abandon which is disorder; but rather a kind of sacred natural revel that prohibited mere licence. There was even a singular austerity in it that betrayed a definite ritual and not mere reckless pageantry. No walls could possibly have contained it. In cathedral, temple, or measured space, however grand, it could only have seemed exaggerated and apostate; here, beneath the open sky, it was beautiful and true. For overhead the stars burned clear and steady, the constellations watching it from their immovable towers—a representation of their own leisured and hierarchic dance in swifter miniature. And indeed this relationship it bore to a universal rhythm was the key, it seemed, to its deep significance; for the close imitation of natural movements seduced the colossal powers of fire and wind to swell human emotions till they became mould and vessel for this elemental manifestation in men and women. Golden yellow in the blaze, the limbs of the women flashed and passed; their hair flew dark a moment across gleaming breasts; and their waving arms tossed in ever-shifting patterns through the driving smoke. The fires boiled and roared, scattering torrents of showering sparks like stars; and amid it all the slim, white shoulders of the boy, his clothes torn from him, his eyes ablaze, and his lips opened to the singing as though he had known it always, drove to and fro on the crest of the ritual like some flying figure of wind and fire incarnate.

All of which, instantaneously yet in sequence, Hendricks witnessed, painted upon the wild night sky. A volcanic energy poured through him too. He knew a golden enthusiasm of immeasurable strength, of unconquerable hope, of irresistible delight. Wind set his feet to dancing, and fire swept across his face without a trace of burning.

Nature was part of him. He had stepped inside. No obstacle existed that could withstand for a single second the torrential energy that fired his heart and blood. There was lightning in his veins. He could sweep aside life's difficult barriers with the ease of a tornado, and shake the rubbish of doubt and care from the years with earthquake shocks. Empires he could mould, and play with nations, drive men and women before him like a flock of sheep, shatter convention, and dislocate the machinery time has foisted upon natural energies. He knew in himself the omnipotence of the lesser elemental deities. Yet, as sympathetic observer, he can but have felt a tithe of what Lord Ernie felt.

"We are the whirlwind and we are the fire!" he cried aloud with the rushing worshippers. "We are unconquerable and immense! We destroy the lukewarm and absorb the weak! For we can make evil into good by bending it all one way!..."

The roar swept thunderingly past him, catching at his voice and body. He felt himself snatched forward by the wind. The fire licked sweetly at him. It was the final abandonment. He plunged recklessly towards the surge of dancers...

## X

What stopped him he did not know. Some hard and steely thing pricked sharply into him. An opposing power, fierce as a sword, stabbed at his heart—and he heard a little sound quite close beside him, a sound that pierced the babel, reaching his consciousness as from far away.

"Keep still! Cling tight to this old rock! Hold yourself in, or else they'll have you too!"

It was as if some insect scratched within his ear. His arm, that same instant, was violently seized. He came down with a crash. He had been half in the air. He had been dancing.

"Turn your eyes away, away! Take hold of this big tree!" The voice cried furiously, but with a petty human passion in it that marred the world. There was an intolerable revulsion in him as he heard it. He felt himself dragged forcibly backwards. He lost his balance, stumbling among loose stones.

"Loose me! Let me go!" he shouted, struggling like a wild animal, yet vainly, against the inflexible grip that held him. "I am one with the fire that lights but does not burn. I am the wind that blows the worlds along. Damnation take you... Let me free!"

Confusion caught him, smothering speech and blinding sight. He fell backwards, away from the heat and wind. He was furious, but furious with he knew not whom or what. The interference had destroyed the rhythm, broken it into fragments. Violent impulses clashed through him without the will to choose or guide them. For power had deserted him and flowed elsewhere. He stood no longer in the stream of energy. He was emptied. And at first he could not tell whether his instinct was to return himself, to rescue his precious boy, or—to crush the interfering object out of existence with what was left to him of raging anger. He turned, stood up, and flung the Pasteur aside with violence. He raised his feet to stamp and kill... when a phrase with meaning darted suddenly across his wild confusion and recalled him to some fragment of truer responsibility and life.

"...There'll be only violence in him—reckless violence instead of strength—destructive. Save him before it is too late!"

"It *is* too late," he roared in answer. "What devil hinders me?"

But his roar was feeble, and his ironed boots refused the stamping. Power slipped wholly out of him. The rhythm poured past, instead of through him. Interference had destroyed the circuit. More glimmerings of responsibility came back. He stooped like a drunken man and helped the other to his feet. The rapidity of the change was curious, proving that the spell had been put upon him from without. It was not, as with the boy, mere development of pre-existing tendencies.

"Help me," he implored suddenly instead, "help me! There has been madness in me. For God's sake, help me to get him out!" It seemed the face of the old Marquess, stern and terrible, broke an instant through the smoky air, black with reproach and anger. And, with a violent effort of the will, Hendricks turned round to face the elemental orgy, bent on rescue. But this time the heat was intolerable and drove him back. The hair, hitherto untouched, now singed upon his head. Fire licked his very breath away. He bent double, covering his face with arms and cloak.

"Pray!" shouted Leysin, dropping to his knees. "It is the only way. My God is higher than this. Pray, pray!"

And, automatically, Hendricks fell upon his knees beside him, though to pray he knew not how. For no real faith was in him as in the other, and his eye was far from single. The fast fading grandeur of what he had experienced still left its pagan tumult in his blood. The pretence of prayer could only have been blasphemy. He watched instead, letting the other invoke his mighty Deity alone, that Deity he had served, unflinchingly all his life with faith and fasting, and with belief beyond assault.

It was an impressive picture, fraught with passionate drama. On his knees behind a sheltering boulder, a blackened pine-tree tossing scorched branches above his head, this righteous man prayed to his God, sure of his triumphant answer. Hendricks watched with an admiration that made him realise his own insignificance. The eyes were closed, the leonine big head set firm upon the diminutive body, the face now lit by flame, now veiled by smoke, the strong hands clasped together and upraised. He envied him. He recognised, too, that the elements themselves, with all their chaos of might and terror, were after all but servants of the Vastness which dips the butterflies in colour and puts down upon the breasts of little robins. And, because the Pasteur's life had been always prayer in action, his little human will invoked the Will of Greatness, merged with it, used it, and directed it steadily against the commotion of these unleashed elements. Certain of himself and of his God, the Pasteur never doubted. His prayer set instantly in action those forces which balance suns and keep the stars afloat.

Thus, trembling with terror that made him wholly ineffective, Hendricks watched, and, as he watched, became aware of the amazing change. For it seemed as if a stream of power, steady and in opposition to the tumult, now poured audaciously against the elemental rhythm, altering its direction, modifying gradually its stupendous impetus. There were pauses in the huge vibrations: they wavered, broke, and fled. They knew confusion, as when the prow of a steel-nosed vessel drives against the tide. The tide is vaster, but the steel is—different. The whole sky shivered, as this new entering force, so small, so soft, yet of such incalculable energy, began at once its overmastering effect. Signs of violence or rout, or of anything disordered, had no part in it; excess before it slipped into willing harness; there was light that sponged away all glare, as when morning sunshine cleans a forest of its shadows. Some little whispering power sang marvellously as of old across the desolate big mountains, "Peace! Be still!" turning the monstrous turbulence into obedient sweetness. And upon his face and hands Hendricks felt faint, delicate touches of some refreshing softness that he could not understand.

Yet not instantly was this harmony restored; at first there was the stress of vehement opposition. The night of wind and fire drove roaring through the sky. There were bursts of triumphant tumult, but convulsion in them and no true steadiness as before. The human figures hitherto had danced with that fluid appearance which belongs to fire, and with that instantaneous rush which is of wind, the men increasing the women, and the women answering with joy; limbs and faces had melted into each other till the circular ritual looked like a glowing wheel of flame rotating audibly. But slowly now the speed of the wheel decreased; the single utterance was marred by the crying of many voices, all at different pitch, discordant, inharmonious, dismayed. The fires somehow dwindled; there came pauses in the wind; and Hendricks became aware of a curious hissing noise, as more and more of these odd soft touches found his face and hands. Here and there, he saw, a figure stumbled, fell, then gathered itself clumsily together again with a frightened shout, breaking violently out of the circle. More and more these figures blundered and dropped out; and although they returned again, so that the dance apparently increased, these were but moments in the final violence of the dispersing hurricane. The rejected ones dashed back wildly into the wrong places; men and women no longer stood alternate, but in groups together, falsely related. The entire movement was dislocated; the ceremony grew rapidly incoherent; meaning forsook it. The composite instrument that had transmuted the elemental forces into human, emotional storage was imperfect, broken, out of tune. The disarray turned rout.

And then it was, while Leysin continued without ceasing his burning and successful prayer, that his companion, conscious of returning harmony, rose to his feet, aware suddenly that he could also help. A portion of the powers he had absorbed still worked in him, but in a new direction. He felt confident and unafraid. He did not stumble. With unerring tread he advanced towards the lessening fires, feeling as he did so the cold soft touches multiply with a rush upon his skin. From all sides they came by hundreds, like messengers of help.

"Ernest!" he cried aloud, and his voice, though little raised, carried resonantly above the dying turmoil; "Ernest! Come back to us. Your father calls you!"

And from threescore faces hurrying in confusion through the smoke, one paused and turned. It stood apart, hovering as though in air, while the mob of disordered figures rushed in a body along the ridge. Plunging like frightened cattle below the farther edge, then vanishing into thick darkness, they left behind them this one solitary face. A final dying flame licked out at it; a rush of smoke drove past to hide it; there was a high, wild scream—and the figure shot forward with a headlong leap and fell with a crash at Hendricks' feet. Lord Ernie, blackened by smoke and scorched by fire, lay safe outside the danger zone.

And Hendricks knelt beside him. Remorse and shame made him powerless to do more as he pulled the torn clothing over the neck and chest and heard his own heart begging for forgiveness. He realised his own weakness and faithlessness. A great temptation had found him wanting...

It was owing to Leysin that the rescue was complete. The Pasteur was instantly by his side.

"Saved as by water," he cried, as he folded his cloak about the prostrate body, and then raised the head and shoulders; "saved by His ministers of rain. For His miracles are love, and work through natural laws."

He made a sign to Hendricks. Carrying the boy between them, they scrambled down the slope into the shelter of the trees below. The cold, soft touches were then explained. The *joran* had dropped as suddenly as it rose, and the torrential rain that invariably follows now poured in rivers from the sky. Water, drenching the fires and padding the savage wind, had stopped the dancers midway in their frenzied ritual. It was the element they dreaded, for it was hostile. Rain soused the mountain ridge, extinguishing the last embers of the numerous fires. It rushed in rivulets between their feet. The heated earth gave out a hissing steam, and the only sound in the spaces where wind and fire had boomed and thundered a little while before was now the splash of water and the drip of quenching drops.

In the cover of the sheltering trees the body stirred, lifted its head, and sat up slowly. The eyes opened.

"I'm cold. I'm frightened," whispered a shivering voice. "Where am I?"

Only the pelt and thud of the rain sounded behind the quavering words.

"Where are the others? Have I been away? Hendricks—Mr. Hendricks—is that you—?"

He stared about him, his face now a mere luminous disc in the thick darkness. No breath of wind was loose. They spoke to him till he answered with assurance, groping to find their hands with his own, his words confused and strange with hidden meaning for a time. "I'm all right now," he kept repeating. "I know exactly. It was one of my big dreams... I suppose I fell asleep... and the rain woke me. Great heavens! What a night to be out." And then he clambered vigorously to his feet with a sudden movement of great energy again, saying that hunger was in him and he must eat. There was no complaint of heat or cold, of burning or of bruises. The boy recovered marvellously. In ten minutes, breaking away from all support, he led, as they descended through the dripping forest in the gloom and chill of very early morning. It was the others who called to him for guidance in the tangled woods. Lord Ernie was in the lead. Throughout the difficult woods he was ever in front, and singing:

"Fire that lights but does not burn! And wind that blows the heart to flame! They both are in me now for ever and ever! Oh, praise the Lord of Fire and the Lord of Wind...!"

And this voice, now near, now distant, sounding through the dripping forest on their homeward journey, was an experience weird and unforgettable for those other two. Leysin, it seemed, had one sentence only which he kept repeating to himself—"Heaven grant he may direct it all for good. For they have filled him to the brim, and he is become an instrument of power."

But Hendricks, though he understood the risk, felt only confidence. Lord Ernie's regeneration had begun.

Soaked and bedraggled, all three, they reached the village about two o'clock. The boy, utterly unmanageable, said an emphatic No to spirits, soup, or medical appliances. His skin, indeed, showed no signs of burning, nor was there the smallest symptom of cold or fever in him. "I'm a perfect furnace," he laughed; "I feel health and strength personified." And the brightness of his eyes, his radiant colour, the vigour of his voice and manner—both in some way astonishing—made all pretence of assistance unnecessary and absurd. "It's like a new birth," he cried to Hendricks, as he almost cantered beside him down the road to their house, "and, by Jove, I'll wake 'em up at home and make the world go round. I know a hundred schemes. I tell you, sir, I'm simply bursting! For the first time I'm alive!"

And an hour later, when the tutor peeped in upon him, the boy was calmly sleeping. The candle light, shaded carefully with one hand, fell upon the face. There were new lines and a new expression in it. Will and purpose showed in the stern set of the lips and jaw. It was the face of a man, and of a man one would not lightly trifle with. Purpose, will, and power were established on their thrones. To such a man the entire world might one day bow the head. "If only it will last," thought Hendricks, as, shaken, bewildered, and more than a little awed, he tiptoed out of the room again and went to bed. But through his dreams, sheeted in flame and veiled in angry smoke, the face of the old Marquess glowered upon him from a heavy sky above ancestral towers.

## XI

From the obituary notices of the 9th Marquess of Oakham the following selections have their interest: He succeeded to his father, then in the Cabinet as Minister for Foreign Affairs, at the age of twenty-one. His career was brief but singular, the early magnificence of the younger Pitt offering a standard of comparison, though by no means a parallel, to his short record of astonishing achievement. His effect upon the world, first as Chief of the Government Labour Department and subsequently as Home Secretary, and Minister of War, is described as shattering, even cataclysmic. His public life lasted five years. He died at the age of twenty-nine. His personality was revolutionary and overwhelming. For, judging by these extracts, he was a "Napoleonic figure whose personal influence combined the impetus of Mirabeau and the dominance of Alexander. His authority held an incalculable element, precisely described as uncanny. His spirit was puissant, elemental, his activity irresistible." Yet, according to another journal, "he was, properly speaking, neither intellectual, astute, nor diplomatic, and possessed as little subtlety as might be expected of a miner whose psychology was called upon to explain the Trinity. In no sense was he Statesman, and even less strategist, yet his name swept Europe, changed the map of the Nearer East, its mere whisper among the Chancelleries convulsing men's counsels with an influence almost menacing."

His enthusiasm appears to have been amazing. "Some stupendous and untiring energy drove through him, paralysing attack, and rendering the bitterest and most skilful opposition nugatory. His hand was imperious, upsetting with a touch the chessboards set by the most able statecraft, and his voice was heard with a kind of reverence in every capital."

The brevity of his astonishing career called for universal comment, as did the hypnotising effect of his singular ascendancy. "In five short years of power he achieved his sway. He rushed upon the world, he shook it, he retired," as one journal picturesquely phrased it. "The manner of his ending, moreover—a stroke of lightning,—seemed in keeping with his life. There was neither lingering, delay, nor warning. Of distinguished stock, noble, yet ordinary enough in all but name, his power is unexplained by heredity; his family furnished no approach to greatness, as history supplied no parallel to his dynamic intensity. Nor, we are informed, among his near of kin, does any inherit his volcanic energy."

The world, however, was apparently well relieved of his tumultuous presence, for his influence was generally surveyed as "destructive rather than constructive." He was unmarried, and the title went to a nephew.

The cheaper journals abounded, of course, in details of his personal and private life that were freely copied into the foreign press, and supply curious material for the student of human nature and the psychologist. The amazing revelations no doubt were picturesquely exaggerated, yet the substratum of truth in them all was generally admitted. No contradictions, at any rate, appeared. They read like the story of some primitive, wild giant let loose upon the world—primitive, because his specific brain power was admittedly of no high order; wild, because he was in favour of fierce, spontaneous action, and his mere presence, on occasions, could stir a nation, not alone a crowd, to vehement, terrific methods. His energy seemed inexhaustible, his fire inextinguishable.

Legends were rife, even before he died, among the peasantry of his Scotch estates, that he was in league with the devil. His habit of keeping enormous fires in his private rooms, fires that burned day and night from January to December, and in open hearths widened to thrice their natural size, stimulated the growth of this particular myth among those of his personal environment. All manner of stories raged. But it was his strange custom out-of-doors that provided the diabolical suggestion. For, "behind a specially walled-in space on an open ridge, denuded of pines, in a distant part of the estate, a series of gigantic heaps of wood, all ready to ignite, were—it was said—kept in a state of constant preparedness. And on stormy nights, especially when winds were high, and invariably at the period of the equinoctial tempests, his lordship would himself light these tremendous bonfires, and spend the nocturnal hours in their blazing presence, communing, the stories variously relate, with the witches at their Sabbath, or with hordes of fire-spirits, who emerged from the Bottomless Pit in order to feed his soul with their unquenchable supplies. From these nightly orgies, it seems clear, at any rate, he returned at dawn with a splendour of energy that no one could resist, and with a mien whose grandeur invited worship rather than inspired alarm."

His biography, it was further stated, would be written by Sir John Hendricks, Bt., who began life as Private Secretary to his father, the 8th Marquess, but whose rapid rise to position was due to his intimate association as trusted friend and adviser to the subject of these obituary notices. The biography, however, had not appeared, within five years of Lord Oakham's sudden death, and curiosity is only further stimulated by the suggestive whisper that it never will, and never can appear.

# The Sacrifice

### I

Limasson was a religious man, though of what depth and quality were unknown, since no trial of ultimate severity had yet tested him. An adherent of no particular creed, he yet had his gods; and his self-discipline was probably more rigorous than his friends conjectured. He was so reserved. Few guessed, perhaps, the desires conquered, the passions regulated, the inner tendencies trained and schooled—not by denying their expression, but by transmuting them alchemically into nobler channels. He had in him the makings of an enthusiastic devotee, and might have become such but for two limitations that prevented. He loved his wealth, labouring to increase it to the neglect of other interests; and, secondly, instead of following up one steady line of search, he scattered himself upon many picturesque theories, like an actor who wants to play all parts rather than concentrate on one. And the more picturesque the part, the more he was attracted. Thus, though he did his duty unshrinkingly and with a touch of love, he accused himself sometimes of merely gratifying a sensuous taste in spiritual sensations. There was this unbalance in him that argued want of depth.

As for his gods—in the end he discovered their reality by first doubting, then denying their existence.

It was this denial and doubt that restored them to their thrones, converting his dilettante skirmishes into genuine, deep belief; and the proof came to him one summer in early June when he was making ready to leave town for his annual month among the mountains.

With Limasson mountains, in some inexplicable sense, were a passion almost, and climbing so deep a pleasure that the ordinary scrambler hardly understood it. Grave as a kind of worship it was to him; the preparations for an ascent, the ascent itself in particular, involved a concentration that seemed symbolical as of a ritual. He not only loved the heights, the massive grandeur, the splendour of vast proportions blocked in space, but loved them with a respect that held a touch of awe. The emotion mountains stirred in him, one might say, was of that profound, incalculable kind that held kinship with his religious feelings, half realised though these were. His gods had their invisible thrones somewhere among the grim, forbidding heights. He prepared himself for this annual mountaineering with the same earnestness that a holy man might approach a solemn festival of his church.

And the impetus of his mind was running with big momentum in this direction, when there fell upon him, almost on the eve of starting, a swift series of disasters that shook his being to its last foundations, and left him stunned among the ruins. To describe these is unnecessary. People said, "One thing after another like that! What appalling luck! Poor wretch!" then wondered, with the curiosity of children, how in the world he would take it. Due to no apparent fault of his own, these disasters were so sudden that life seemed in a moment shattered, and his interest in existence almost ceased. People shook their heads and thought of the emergency exit. But Limasson was too vital a man to dream of annihilation. Upon him it had a different effect—he turned and questioned what he called his gods. They did not answer or explain. For the first time in his life he doubted. A hair's breadth beyond lay definite denial.

The ruin in which he sat, however, was not material; no man of his age, possessed of courage and a working scheme of life, would permit disaster of a material order to overwhelm him. It was collapse of a mental, spiritual kind, an assault upon the roots of character and temperament. Moral duties laid suddenly upon him threatened to crush. His *personal* existence was assailed, and apparently must end. He must spend the remainder of his life caring for others who were nothing to him. No outlet showed, no way of escape, so diabolically complete was the combination of events that rushed his inner trenches. His faith was shaken. A man can but endure so much, and remain human. For him the saturation point seemed reached. He experienced the spiritual equivalent of that physical numbness which supervenes when pain has touched the limit of endurance. He laughed, grew callous, then mocked his silent gods.

It is said that upon this state of blank negation there follows sometimes a condition of lucidity which mirrors with crystal clearness the forces driving behind life at a given moment, a kind of clairvoyance that brings explanation and therefore peace. Limasson looked for this in vain. There was the doubt that questioned, there was the sneer that mocked the silence into which his questions fell; but there was neither answer nor explanation, and certainly not peace. There was no relief. In this tumult of revolt he did none of the things his friends suggested or expected. He merely followed the line of least resistance. He yielded to the impetus that was upon him when the catastrophe came. To their indignant amazement he went out to his mountains.

All marvelled that at such a time he could adopt so trivial a line of action, neglecting duties that seemed paramount; they disapproved. Yet in reality he was taking no definite action at all, but merely drifting with the momentum that had been acquired just before. He was bewildered with so much pain, confused with suffering, stunned with the crash that flung him helpless amid undeserved calamity. He turned to the mountains as a child to its mother, instinctively. Mountains had never failed to bring him consolation, comfort, peace. Their grandeur restored proportion whenever disorder threatened life. No calculation, properly speaking, was in his move at all; but a blind desire for a violent physical reaction such as climbing brings. And the instinct was more wholesome than he knew.

In the high upland valley among lonely peaks whither Limasson then went, he found in some measure the proportion he had lost. He studiously avoided thinking; he lived in his muscles recklessly. The region with its little Inn was familiar to him; peak after peak he attacked, sometimes with, but more often without a guide, until his reputation as a sane climber, a laurelled member of all the foreign Alpine Clubs, was seriously in danger. That he overdid it physically is beyond question, but that the mountains breathed into him some portion of their enormous calm and deep endurance is also true. His gods, meanwhile, he neglected utterly for the first time in his life. If he thought of them at all, it was as tinsel figures imagination had created, figures upon a stage that merely decorated life for those whom pretty pictures pleased. Only—he had left the theatre and their make-believe no longer hypnotised his mind. He realised their impotence and disowned them. This attitude, however, was subconscious; he lent to it no substance, either of thought or speech. He ignored rather than challenged their existence.

And it was somewhat in this frame of mind—thinking little, feeling even less—that he came out into the hotel vestibule after dinner one evening, and took mechanically the bundle of letters the porter handed to him. They had no possible interest for him; in a corner where the big steam-heater mitigated the chilliness of the hall, he idly sorted them. The score or so of other guests, chiefly expert climbing men, were trailing out in twos and threes from the dining-room; but he felt as little interest in them as in his letters: no conversation could alter facts, no written phrases change his circumstances. At random, then, he opened a business letter with a typewritten address—it would probably be impersonal, less of a mockery, therefore, than the others with their tiresome sham condolences. And, in a sense, it was impersonal; sympathy from a solicitor's office is mere formula, a few extra ticks upon the universal keyboard of a Remington. But as he read it, Limasson made a discovery that startled him into acute and bitter sensation. He had imagined the limit of bearable suffering and disaster already reached. Now, in a few dozen words, his error was proved convincingly. The fresh blow was dislocating.

This culminating news of additional catastrophe disclosed within him entirely new reaches of pain, of biting, resentful fury. Limasson experienced a momentary stopping of the heart as he took it in, a dizziness, a violent sensation of revolt whose impotence induced almost physical nausea. He felt like—death.

"Must I suffer all things?" flashed through his arrested intelligence in letters of fire.

There was a sullen rage in him, a dazed bewilderment, but no positive suffering as yet. His emotion was too sickening to include the smaller pains of disappointment; it was primitive, blind anger that he knew. He read the letter calmly, even to the neat paragraph of machine-made sympathy at the last, then placed it in his inner pocket. No outward sign of disturbance was upon him; his breath came slowly; he reached over to the table for a match, holding it at arm's length lest the sulphur fumes should sting his nostrils.

And in that moment he made his second discovery. The fact that further suffering was still possible included also the fact that some touch of resignation had been left in him, and therefore some vestige of belief as well. Now, as he felt the crackling sheet of stiff paper in his pocket, watched the sulphur die, and saw the wood ignite, this remnant faded utterly away. Like the blackened end of the match, it shrivelled and dropped off. It vanished. Savagely, yet with an external calmness that enabled him to light his pipe with untrembling hand, he addressed his futile deities. And once more in fiery letters there flashed across the darkness of his passionate thought:

"Even this you demand of me—this cruel, ultimate sacrifice?"

And he rejected them, bag and baggage; for they were a mockery and a lie. With contempt he repudiated them for ever. The stage of doubt had passed. He denied his gods. Yet, with a smile upon his lips; for what were they after all but the puppets his religious fancy had imagined? They never had existed. Was it, then, merely the picturesque, sensational aspect of his devotional temperament that had created them? That side of his nature, in any case, was dead now, killed by a single devastating blow. The gods went with it.

Surveying what remained of his life, it seemed to him like a city that an earthquake has reduced to ruins. The inhabitants think no worse thing could happen. Then comes the fire.

Two lines of thought, it seems, then developed parallel in him and simultaneously, for while underneath he stormed against this culminating blow, his upper mind dealt calmly with the project of a great expedition he would make at dawn. He had engaged no guide. As an experienced mountaineer, he knew the district well; his name was tolerably familiar, and in half an hour he could have settled all details, and retired to bed with instructions to be called at two. But, instead, he sat there waiting, unable to stir, a human volcano that any moment might break forth into violence. He smoked his pipe as quietly as though nothing had happened, while through the blazing depths of him ran ever this one self-repeating statement: "Even this you demand of me, this cruel, ultimate sacrifice!..." His self-control, dynamically estimated, just then must have been very great and, thus repressed, the store of potential energy accumulated enormously.

With thought concentrated largely upon this final blow, Limasson had not noticed the people who streamed out of the *salle à manger* and scattered themselves in groups about the hall. Some individual, now and again, approached his chair with the idea of conversation, then, seeing his absorption, turned away. Even when a climber whom he slightly knew reached across him with a word of apology for the matches, Limasson made no response, for he did not see him. He noticed nothing. In particular he did not notice two men who, from an opposite corner, had for some time been observing him. He now looked up—by chance?—and was vaguely aware that they were discussing him. He met their eyes across the hall, and started.

For at first he thought he knew them. Possibly he had seen them about in the hotel—they seemed familiar—yet he certainly had never spoken with them. Aware of his mistake, he turned his glance elsewhere, though still vividly conscious of their attention. One was a clergyman or a priest; his face wore an air of gravity touched by sadness, a sternness about the lips counteracted by a kindling beauty in the eyes that betrayed enthusiasm nobly regulated. There was a suggestion of stateliness in the man that made the impression very sharp. His clothing emphasised it. He wore a dark tweed suit that was strict in its simplicity. There was austerity in him somewhere.

His companion, perhaps by contrast, seemed inconsiderable in his conventional evening dress. A good deal younger than his friend, his hair, always a tell-tale detail, was a trifle long; the thin fingers that flourished a cigarette wore rings; the face, though picturesque, was flippant, and his entire attitude conveyed a certain insignificance. Gesture, that faultless language which challenges counterfeit, betrayed unbalance somewhere. The impression he produced, however, was shadowy compared to the sharpness of the other. "Theatrical" was the word in Limasson's mind, as he turned his glance elsewhere. But as he looked away he fidgeted. The interior darkness caused by the dreadful letter rose about him. It engulfed him. Dizziness came with it...

Far away the blackness was fringed with light, and through this light, stepping with speed and carelessness as from gigantic distance, the two men, suddenly grown large, came at him. Limasson, in self-protection, turned to meet them. Conversation he did not desire. Somehow he had expected this attack.

Yet the instant they began to speak—it was the priest who opened fire—it was all so natural and easy that he almost welcomed the diversion. A phrase by way of introduction—and he was speaking of the summits. Something in Limasson's mind turned over. The man was a serious climber, one of his own species. The sufferer felt a certain relief as he heard the invitation, and realised, though dully, the compliment involved.

"If you felt inclined to join us—if you would honour us with your company," the man was saying quietly, adding something then about "your great experience" and "invaluable advice and judgment."

Limasson looked up, trying hard to concentrate and understand.

"The Tour du Néant?" he repeated, mentioning the peak proposed. Rarely attempted, never conquered, and with an ominous record of disaster, it happened to be the very summit he had meant to attack himself next day.

"You have engaged guides?" He knew the question foolish.

"No guide will try it," the priest answered, smiling, while his companion added with a flourish, "but we—we need no guide—if *you* will come."

"You are unattached, I believe? You are alone?" the priest enquired, moving a little in front of his friend, as though to keep him in the background.

"Yes," replied Limasson. "I am quite alone." He was listening attentively, but with only part of his mind. He realised the flattery of the invitation. Yet it was like flattery addressed to some one else. He felt himself so indifferent, so—dead. These men wanted his skilful body, his experienced mind; and it was his body and mind that talked with them, and finally agreed to go. Many a time expeditions had been planned in just this way, but to-night he felt there was a difference. Mind and body signed the agreement, but his soul, listening elsewhere and looking on, was silent. With his rejected gods it had left him, though hovering close still. It did not interfere; it did not warn; it even approved; it sang to him from great distance that this expedition cloaked another. He was bewildered by the clashing of his higher and his lower mind.

"At one in the morning, then, if that will suit you..." the older man concluded.

"I'll see to the provisions," exclaimed the younger enthusiastically, "and I shall take my telephoto for the summit. The porters can come as far as the Great Tower. We're over six thousand feet here already, you see, so..." and his voice died away in the distance as his companion led him off.

Limasson saw him go with relief. But for the other man he would have declined the invitation. At heart he was indifferent enough. What decided him really was the coincidence that the Tour du Néant was the very peak he had intended to attack himself *alone,* and the curious feeling that this expedition cloaked another somehow—almost that these men had a hidden motive. But he dismissed the idea—it was not worth thinking about. A moment later he followed them to bed. So careless was he of the affairs of the world, so dead to mundane interests, that he tore up his other letters and tossed them into a corner of the room—unread.

## II

Once in his chilly bedroom he realised that his upper mind had permitted him to do a foolish thing; he had drifted like a schoolboy into an unwise situation. He had pledged himself to an expedition with two strangers, an expedition for which normally he would have chosen his companions with the utmost caution. Moreover, he was guide; they looked to him for safety, while yet it was they who had arranged and planned it. But who were these men with whom he proposed to run grave bodily risks?

He knew them as little as they knew him. Whence came, he wondered, the curious idea that this climb was really planned by another who was no one of them?

The thought slipped idly across his mind; going out by one door, it came back, however, quickly by another. He did not think about it more than to note its passage through the disorder that passed with him just then for thinking. Indeed, there was nothing in the whole world for which he cared a single brass farthing. As he undressed for bed, he said to himself: "I shall be called at one... but why am I going with these two on this wild plan? ... And who made the plan?..."

It seemed to have settled itself. It came about so naturally and easily, so quickly. He probed no deeper. He didn't care. And for the first time he omitted the little ritual, half prayer, half adoration, it had always been his custom to offer to his deities upon retiring to rest. He no longer recognised them.

How utterly broken his life was! How blank and terrible and lonely! He felt cold, and piled his overcoats upon the bed, as though his mental isolation involved a physical effect as well. Switching off the light by the door, he was in the act of crossing the floor in the darkness when a sound beneath the window caught his ear. Outside there were voices talking. The roar of falling water made them indistinct, yet he was sure they were voices, and that one of them he knew. He stopped still to listen. He heard his own name uttered—"John Limasson." They ceased. He stood a moment shivering on the boards, then crawled into bed beneath the heavy clothing. But in the act of settling down, they began again. He raised himself again hurriedly to listen. What little wind there was passed in that moment down the valley, carrying off the roar of falling water, and into the moment's space of silence dropped fragments of definite sentences. "They are close, you say—close down upon the world?" It was the voice of the priest surely.

"For days they have been passing," was the answer—a rough, deep tone that might have been a peasant's, and a kind of fear in it, "for all my flocks are scattered."

"The signs are sure? You know them?"

"Tumult," was the answer in much lower tones. "There has been tumult in the mountains..."

There was a break then as though the voices sank too low to be heard. Two broken fragments came next, end of a question—beginning of an answer.

"...the opportunity of a life-time?"

"...if he goes of his own free will, success is sure. For acceptance is..."

And the wind, returning, bore back the sound of the falling water, so that Limasson heard no more...

An indefinable emotion stirred in him as he turned over to sleep. He stuffed his ears lest he should hear more. He was aware of a sinking of the heart that was inexplicable. What in the world were they talking about, these two? What was the meaning of these disjointed phrases? There lay behind them a grave significance almost solemn. That "tumult in the mountains" was somehow ominous, its suggestion terrible and mighty. He felt disturbed, uncomfortable, the first emotion that had stirred in him for days. The numbness melted before its faint awakening. Conscience was in it—he felt vague prickings—but it was deeper far than conscience. Somewhere out of sight, in a region life had as yet not plumbed, the words sank down and vibrated like pedal notes. They rumbled away into the night of undecipherable things. And, though explanation failed him, he felt they had reference somehow to the morrow's expedition: how, what, wherefore, he knew not; his name had been spoken—then these curious sentences; that was all. Yet to-morrow's expedition, what was it but an expedition of impersonal kind, not even planned by himself? Merely his own plan taken and altered by others—made over? His personal business, his personal life, were not really in it at all.

The thought startled him a moment. He had no personal life...!

Struggling with sleep, his brain played the endless game of disentanglement without winning a single point, while the under-mind in him looked on and smiled—because it *knew*. Then, suddenly, a great peace fell over him. Exhaustion brought it perhaps. He fell asleep; and next moment, it seemed, he was aware of a thundering at the door and an unwelcome growling voice, "'s *ist bald ein Uhr, Herr! Aufstehen!*"

Rising at such an hour, unless the heart be in it, is a sordid and depressing business; Limasson dressed without enthusiasm, conscious that thought and feeling were exactly where he had left them on going to sleep. The same confusion and bewilderment were in him; also the same deep solemn emotion stirred by the whispering voices. Only long habit enabled him to attend to detail, and ensured that nothing was forgotten. He felt heavy and oppressed, a kind of anxiety about him; the routine of preparation he followed gravely, utterly untouched by the customary joy; it was mechanical. Yet through it ran the old familiar sense of ritual, due to the practice of so many years, that cleansing of mind and body for a big Ascent—like initiatory rites that once had been as important to him as those of some priest who approached the worship of his deity in the temples of ancient time. He performed the ceremony with the same care as though no ghost of vanished faith still watched him, beckoning from the air as formerly... His knapsack carefully packed, he took his ice-axe from beside the bed, turned out the light, and went down the creaking wooden stairs in stockinged feet, lest his heavy boots should waken the other sleepers. And in his head still rang the phrase he had fallen asleep on—as though just uttered:

"The signs are sure; for days they have been passing—close down upon the world. The flocks are scattered. There has been tumult—tumult in the mountains." The other fragments he had forgotten. But who were "they"? And why did the word bring a chill of awe into his blood?

And as the words rolled through him Limasson felt tumult in his thoughts and feelings too. There had been tumult in his life, and all his joys were scattered—joys that hitherto had fed his days. The signs were sure. Something was close down upon his little world—passing—sweeping. He felt a touch of terror.

Outside in the fresh darkness of very early morning the strangers stood waiting for him. Rather, they seemed to arrive in the same instant as himself, equally punctual. The clock in the church tower sounded one. They exchanged low greetings, remarked that the weather promised to hold good, and started off in single file over soaking meadows towards the first belt of forest. The porter—mere peasant, unfamiliar of face and not connected with the hotel—led the way with a hurricane lantern. The air was marvellously sweet and fragrant. In the sky overhead the stars shone in their thousands. Only the noise of falling water from the heights and the regular thud of their heavy boots broke the stillness. And, black against the sky, towered the enormous pyramid of the Tour du Néant they meant to conquer.

Perhaps the most delightful portion of a big ascent is the beginning in the scented darkness while the thrill of possible conquest lies still far off. The hours stretch themselves queerly; last night's sunset might be days ago; sunrise and the brilliance coming seem in another week, part of dim futurity like children's holidays. It is difficult to realise that this biting cold before the dawn, and the blazing heat to come, both belong to the same to-day.

There were no sounds as they toiled slowly up the zigzag path through the first fifteen hundred feet of pinewoods; no one spoke; the clink of nails and ice-axe points against the stones was all they heard. For the roar of water was felt rather than heard; it beat against the ears and the skin of the whole body at once. The deeper notes were below them now in the sleeping valley; the shriller ones sounded far above, where streams just born out of ponderous snow-beds tinkled sharply...

The change came delicately. The stars turned a shade less brilliant, a softness in them as of human eyes that say farewell. Between the highest branches the sky grew visible. A sighing air smoothed all their crests one way; moss, earth, and open spaces brought keen perfumes; and the little human procession, leaving the forest, stepped out into the vastness of the world above the tree-line. They paused while the porter stooped to put his lantern out. In the eastern sky was colour. The peaks and crags rushed closer.

Was it the Dawn? Limasson turned his eyes from the height of sky where the summits pierced a path for the coming day, to the faces of his companions, pale and wan in the early twilight. How small, how insignificant they seemed amid this hungry emptiness of desolation. The stupendous cliffs fled past them, led by headstrong peaks crowned with eternal snows. Thin lines of cloud, trailing half way up precipice and ridge, seemed like the swish of movement—as though he caught the earth turning as she raced through space. The four of them, timid riders on the gigantic saddle, clung for their lives against her titan ribs, while currents of some majestic life swept up at them from every side. He drew deep draughts of the rarefied air into his lungs. It was very cold. Avoiding the pallid, insignificant faces of his companions, he pretended interest in the porter's operations; he stared fixedly on the ground. It seemed twenty minutes before the flame was extinguished, and the lantern fastened to the pack behind. This Dawn was unlike any he had seen before.

For, in reality, all the while, Limasson was trying to bring order out of the extraordinary thoughts and feelings that had possessed him during the slow forest ascent, and the task was not crowned with much success. The Plan, made by others, had taken charge of him, he felt; and he had thrown the reins of personal will and interest loosely upon its steady gait. He had abandoned himself carelessly to what might come. Knowing that he was leader of the expedition, he yet had suffered the porter to go first, taking his own place as it was appointed to him, behind the younger man, but before the priest. In this order, they had plodded, as only experienced climbers plod, for hours without a rest, until half way up a change had taken place. He had wished it, and instantly it was effected. The priest moved past him, while his companion dropped to the rear—the companion who forever stumbled in his speed, whereas the older man climbed surely, confidently. And thereafter

Limasson walked more easily—as though the relative positions of the three were of importance somehow. The steep ascent of smothering darkness through the woods became less arduous. He was glad to have the younger man behind him.

For the impression had strengthened as they climbed in silence that this ascent pertained to some significant Ceremony, and the idea had grown insistently, almost stealthily, upon him. The movements of himself and his companions, especially the positions each occupied relatively to the other, established some kind of intimacy that resembled speech, suggesting even question and answer. And the entire performance, while occupying hours by his watch, it seemed to him more than once, had been in reality briefer than the flash of a passing thought, so that he saw it within himself—pictorially. He thought of a picture worked in colours upon a strip of elastic. Some one pulled the strip, and the picture stretched. Or some one released it again, and the picture flew back, reduced to a mere stationary speck. All happened in a single speck of time.

And the little change of position, apparently so trivial, gave point to this singular notion working in his under-mind—that this ascent was a ritual and a ceremony as in older days, its significance approaching revelation, however, for the first time—now. Without language, this stole over him; no words could quite describe it. For it came to him that these three formed a unit, himself being in some fashion yet the acknowledged principal, the leader. The labouring porter had no place in it, for this first toiling through the darkness was a preparation, and when the actual climb began, he would disappear, while Limasson himself went first. This idea that they took part together in a Ceremony established itself firmly in him, with the added wonder that, though so often done, he performed it now for the first time with full comprehension, knowledge, truth. Empty of personal desire, indifferent to an ascent that formerly would have thrilled his heart with ambition and delight, he understood that climbing had ever been a ritual for his soul and of his soul, and that power must result from its sincere accomplishment. It was a symbolical ascent.

In words this did not come to him. He felt it, never criticising. That is, he neither rejected nor accepted. It stole most sweetly, grandly, over him. It floated into him while he climbed, yet so convincingly that he had felt his relative position must be changed. The younger man held too prominent a post, or at least a wrong one—in advance. Then, after the change, effected mysteriously as though all recognised it, this line of certainty increased, and there came upon him the big, strange knowledge that all of life is a Ceremony on a giant scale, and that by performing the movements accurately, with sincere fidelity, there may come—knowledge. There was gravity in him from that moment.

This ran in his mind with certainty. Though his thought assumed no form of little phrases, his brain yet furnished detailed statements that clinched the marvellous thing with simile and incident which daily life might apprehend: That knowledge arises from action; that to do the thing invites the teaching and explains it. Action, moreover, is symbolical; a group of men, a family, an entire nation, engaged in those daily movements which are the working out of their destiny, perform a Ceremony which is in direct relation somewhere to the pattern of greater happenings which are the teachings of the Gods. Let the body imitate, reproduce—in a bedroom, in a wood—anywhere—the movements of the stars, and the meaning of those stars shall sink down into the heart. The movements constitute a script, a language. To mimic the gestures of a stranger is to understand his mood, his point of view—to establish a grave and solemn intimacy. Temples are everywhere, for the entire earth is a temple, and the body, House of Royalty, is the biggest temple of them all. To ascertain the pattern its movements trace in daily life, could be to determine the relation of that particular ceremony to the Cosmos, and so learn power. The entire system of Pythagoras, he realised, could be taught without a single word—by movements; and in everyday life even the commonest act and vulgarest movement are part of some big Ceremony—a message from the Gods. Ceremony, in a word, is three-dimensional language, and action, therefore, is the language of the Gods. The Gods he had denied were speaking to him... passing with tumult close across his broken life... Their passage it was, indeed, that had caused the breaking!

In this cryptic, condensed fashion the great fact came over him—that he and these other two, here and now, took part in some great Ceremony of whose ultimate object as yet he was in ignorance. The impact with which it dropped upon his mind was tremendous. He realised it most fully when he stepped from the darkness of the forest and entered the expanse of glimmering, early light; up till this moment his mind was being prepared only, whereas now he knew. The innate desire to worship which all along had been his, the momentum his religious temperament had acquired during forty years, the yearning to have proof, in a word, that the Gods he once acknowledged were really true, swept back upon him with that violent reaction which denial had aroused.

He wavered where he stood....

Looking about him, then, while the others rearranged burdens the returning porter now discarded, he perceived the astonishing beauty of the time and place, feeling it soak into him as by the very pores of his skin. From all sides this beauty rushed upon him. Some radiant, winged sense of wonder sped past him through the silent air. A thrill of ecstasy ran down every nerve. The hair of his head stood up. It was far from unfamiliar to him, this sight of the upper mountain world awakening from its sleep of the summer night, but never before had he stood shuddering thus at its exquisite cold glory, nor felt its significance as now, so mysteriously *within himself.* Some transcendent power that held sublimity was passing across this huge desolate plateau, far more majestic than the mere sunrise among mountains he had so often witnessed. There was Movement. He understood why he had seen his companions insignificant. Again he shivered and looked about him, touched by a solemnity that held deep awe.

Personal life, indeed, was wrecked, destroyed, but something greater was on the way. His fragile alliance with a spiritual world was strengthened. He realised his own past insolence. He became afraid.

### III

The treeless plateau, littered with enormous boulders, stretched for miles to right and left, grey in the dusk of very early morning. Behind him dropped thick guardian pinewoods into the sleeping valley that still detained the darkness of the night. Here and there lay patches of deep snow, gleaming faintly through thin rising mist; singing streams of icy water spread everywhere among the stones, soaking the coarse rough grass that was the only sign of vegetation. No life was visible; nothing stirred; nor anywhere was movement, but of the quiet trailing mist and of his own breath that drifted past his face like smoke. Yet through the splendid stillness there was movement; that sense of absolute movement which results in stillness—it was owing to the stillness that he became aware of it—so vast, indeed, that only immobility could express it. Thus, on the calmest day in summer, may the headlong rushing of the earth through space seem more real than when the tempest shakes the trees and water on its surface; or great machinery turn with such vertiginous velocity that it appears steady to the deceived function of the eye. For it was not through the eye that this solemn Movement made itself known, but rather through a massive sensation that owned his entire body as its organ. Within the league-long amphitheatre of enormous peaks and precipices that enclosed the plateau, piling themselves upon the horizon, Limasson felt the outline of a Ceremony extended. The pulses of its grandeur poured into him where he stood. Its vast design was knowable because they themselves had traced—were even then tracing—its earthly counterpart in little. And the awe in him increased.

"This light is false. We have an hour yet before the true dawn," he heard the younger man say lightly. "The summits still are ghostly. Let us enjoy the sensation, and see what we can make of it."

And Limasson, looking up startled from his reverie, saw that the far-away heights and towers indeed were heavy with shadow, faint still with the light of stars. It seemed to him they bowed their awful heads and that their stupendous shoulders lowered. They drew together, shutting out the world.

"True," said his companion, "and the upper snows still wear the spectral shine of night. But let us now move faster, for we travel very light. The sensations you propose will but delay and weaken us."

He handed a share of the burdens to his companion and to Limasson. Slowly they all moved forward, and the mountains shut them in.

And two things Limasson noted then, as he shouldered his heavier pack and led the way: first, that he suddenly knew their destination though its purpose still lay hidden; and, secondly, that the porter's leaving before the ascent proper began signified finally that ordinary climbing was not their real objective. Also—the dawn was a lifting of inner veils from off his mind, rather than a brightening of the visible earth due to the nearing sun. Thick darkness, indeed, draped this enormous, lonely amphitheatre where they moved.

"You lead us well," said the priest, a few feet behind him, as he picked his way unfalteringly among the boulders and the streams.

"Strange that I do so," replied Limasson, in a low tone, "for the way is new to me, and the darkness grows instead of lessening." The language seemed hardly of his choosing. He spoke and walked as in a dream.

Far in the rear the voice of the younger man called plaintively after them: "You go so fast, I can't keep up with you," and again he stumbled and dropped his ice-axe among the rocks. He seemed for ever stooping to drink the icy water, or clambering off the trail to test the patches of snow as to quality and depth. "You're missing all the excitement," he cried repeatedly. "There are a hundred pleasures and sensations by the way."

They paused a moment for him to overtake them; he came up panting and exhausted, making remarks about the fading stars, the wind upon the heights, new routes he longed to try up dangerous couloirs, about everything, it seemed, except the work in hand. There was eagerness in him, the kind of excitement that saps energy and wastes the nervous force, threatening a probable collapse before the arduous object is attained.

"Keep to the thing in hand," replied the priest sternly. "We are not really going fast; it is you who are scattering yourself to no purpose. It wears us all. We must husband our resources," and he pointed significantly to the pyramid of the Tour du Néant that gleamed above them at an incredible altitude.

"We are here to amuse ourselves; life is a pleasure, a sensation, or it is nothing," grumbled his companion; but there was a gravity in the tone of the older man that discouraged argument and made resistance difficult. The other arranged his pack for the tenth time, twisting his axe through an ingenious scheme of straps and string, and fell silently into line behind his leaders. Limasson moved on again... and the darkness at length began to lift. Far overhead, at first, the snowy summits shone with a hue less spectral; a delicate pink spread softly from the east; there was a freshening of the chilly wind; then suddenly the highest peak that topped the others by a thousand feet of soaring rock, stepped sharply into sight, half golden and half rose. At the same instant, the vast Movement of the entire scene slowed down; there came one or two terrific gusts of wind in quick succession; a roar like an avalanche of falling stones boomed distantly—and Limasson stopped dead and held his breath.

For something blocked the way before him, something he knew he could not pass. Gigantic and unformed, it seemed part of the architecture of the desolate waste about him, while yet it bulked there, enormous in the trembling dawn, as belonging neither to plain nor mountain. Suddenly it was there, where a moment before had been mere emptiness of air. Its massive outline shifted into visibility as though it had risen from the ground. He stood stock still. A cold that was not of this world turned him rigid in his tracks. A few yards behind him the priest had halted too. Further in the rear they heard the stumbling tread of the younger man, and the faint calling of his voice—a feeble, broken sound as of a man whom sudden fear distressed to helplessness.

"We're off the track, and I've lost my way," the words came on the still air. "My axe is gone... let us put on the rope!... Hark! Do you hear that roar?" And then a sound as though he came slowly groping on his hands and knees.

"You have exhausted yourself too soon," the priest answered sternly. "Stay where you are and rest, for we go no further. This is the place we sought."

There was in his tone a kind of ultimate solemnity that for a moment turned Limasson's attention from the great obstacle that blocked his further way. The darkness lifted veil by veil, not gradually, but by a series of leaps as when some one inexpertly turns a wick. He perceived then that not a single Grandeur loomed in front, but that others of similar kind, some huger than the first, stood all about him, forming an enclosing circle that hemmed him in.

Then, with a start, he recovered himself. Equilibrium and common sense returned. The trick that sight had played upon him, assisted by the rarefied atmosphere of the heights and by the witchery of dawn, was no uncommon one, after all. The long straining of the eyes to pick the way in an uncertain light so easily deceives perspective. Delusion ever follows abrupt change of focus. These shadowy encircling forms were but the rampart of still distant precipices whose giant walls framed the tremendous amphitheatre to the sky.

Their closeness was a mere gesture of the dusk and distance.

The shock of the discovery produced an instant's unsteadiness in him that brought bewilderment. He straightened up, raised his head, and looked about him. The cliffs, it seemed to him, shifted back instantly to their accustomed places; as though after all they *had* been close; there was a reeling among the topmost crags; they balanced fearfully, then stood still against a sky already faintly crimson. The roar he heard, that might well have seemed the tumult of their hurrying speed, was in reality but the wind of dawn that rushed against their ribs, beating the echoes out with angry wings. And the lines of trailing mist, streaking the air like proofs of rapid motion, merely coiled and floated in the empty spaces.

He turned to the priest, who had moved up beside him.

"How strange," he said, "is this beginning of new light! My sight went all astray for a passing moment. I thought the mountains stood right across my path. And when I looked up just now it seemed they all ran back." His voice was small and lost in the great listening air.

The man looked fixedly at him. He had removed his slouch hat, hot with the long ascent, and as he answered, a long thin shadow flitted across his features. A breadth of darkness dropped about them. It was as though a mask were forming. The face that now was covered had been—naked. He was so long in answering that Limasson heard his mind sharpening the sentence like a pencil.

He spoke very slowly: "*They* move perhaps even as Their powers move, and

Their minutes are our years. Their passage ever is in tumult. There is disorder then among the affairs of men; there is confusion in their minds. There may be ruin and disaster, but out of the wreckage shall issue strong, fresh growth. For like a sea, They pass."

There was in his mien a grandeur that seemed borrowed marvellously from the mountains. His voice was grave and deep; he made no sign or gesture; and in his manner was a curious steadiness that breathed through the language a kind of sacred prophecy.

Long, thundering gusts of wind passed distantly across the precipices as he spoke. The same moment, expecting apparently no rejoinder to his strange utterance, he stooped and began to unpack his knapsack. The change from the sacerdotal language to this commonplace and practical detail was singularly bewildering.

"It is the time to rest," he added, "and the time to eat. Let us prepare." And he drew out several small packets and laid them in a row upon the ground. Awe deepened over Limasson as he watched, and with it a great wonder too. For the words seemed ominous, as though this man, upon the floor of some vast Temple, said: "Let us prepare a sacrifice...!" There flashed into him, out of depths that had hitherto concealed it, a lightning clue that hinted at explanation of the entire strange proceeding—of the abrupt meeting with the strangers, the impulsive acceptance of their project for the great ascent, their grave behaviour as though it were a Ceremonial of immense design, his change of position, the bewildering tricks of sight, and the solemn language, finally, of the older man that corroborated what he himself had deemed at first illusion. In a flying second of time this all swept through him—and with it the sharp desire to turn aside, retreat, to run away.

Noting the movement, or perhaps divining the emotion prompting it, the priest looked up quickly. In his tone was, a coldness that seemed as though this scene of wintry desolation uttered words:

"You have come too far to think of turning back. It is not possible. You stand now at the gates of birth—and death. All that might hinder, you have so bravely cast aside. Be brave now to the end."

And, as Limasson heard the words, there dropped suddenly into him a new and awful insight into humanity, a power that unerringly discovered the spiritual necessities of others, and therefore of himself. With a shock he realised that the younger man who had accompanied them with increasing difficulty as they climbed higher and higher—was but a shadow of reality. Like the porter, he was but an encumbrance who impeded progress. And he turned his eyes to search the desolate landscape.

"You will not find him," said his companion, "for he is gone. Never, unless you weakly call, shall you see him again, nor desire to hear his voice." And Limasson realised that in his heart he had all the while disapproved of the man, disliked him for his theatrical fondness of sensation and effect, more, that he had even hated and despised him. Starvation might crawl upon him where he had fallen and eat his life away before he would stir a finger to save him. It was with the older man he now had dreadful business in hand.

"I am glad," he answered, "for in the end he must have proved my death—our death!"

And they drew closer round the little circle of food the priest had laid upon the rocky ground, an intimate understanding linking them together in a sympathy that completed Limasson's bewilderment.

There was bread, he saw, and there was salt; there was also a little flask of deep red wine. In the centre of the circle was a miniature fire of sticks the priest had collected from the bushes of wild rhododendron. The smoke rose upwards in a thin blue line. It did not even quiver, so profound was the surrounding stillness of the mountain air, but far away among the precipices ran the boom of falling water, and behind it again, the muffled roar as of peaks and snow-fields that swept with a rolling thunder through the heavens.

"They are passing," the priest said in a low voice, "and They know that you are here. You have now the opportunity of a lifetime; for, if you yield acceptance of your own free will, success is sure. You stand before the gates of birth and death. They offer you life."

"Yet... I denied Them!" He murmured it below his breath.

"Denial is evocation. You called to them, and They have come. The sacrifice of your little personal life is all They ask. Be brave—and yield it."

He took the bread as he spoke, and, breaking it in three pieces, he placed one before Limasson, one before himself, and the third he laid upon the flame which first blackened and then consumed it.

"Eat it and understand," he said, "for it is the nourishment that shall revive your fading life." Next, with the salt, he did the same. Then, raising the flask of wine, he put it to his lips, offering it afterwards to his companion. When both had drunk there still remained the greater part of the contents. He lifted the vessel with both hands reverently towards the sky. He stood upright.

"The blood of your personal life I offer to Them in your name. By the renunciation which seems to you as death shall you pass through the gates of birth to the life of freedom beyond. For the ultimate sacrifice that They ask of you is—this."

And bending low before the distant heights, he poured the wine upon the rocky ground.

For a period of time Limasson found no means of measuring, so terrible were the emotions in his heart, the priest remained in this attitude of worship and obeisance. The tumult in the mountains ceased. An absolute hush dropped down upon the world. There seemed a pause in the inner history of the universe itself. All waited—till he rose again. And, when he did so, the mask that had for hours now been spreading across his features, was accomplished. The eyes gazed sternly down into his own. Limasson looked—and recognised. He stood face to face with the man whom he knew best of all others in the world... himself.

There had been death. There had also been that recovery of splendour which is birth and resurrection.

And the sun that moment, with the sudden surprise that mountains only know, rushed clear above the heights, bathing the landscape and the standing figure with a stainless glory. Into the vast Temple where he knelt, as into that greater inner Temple which is mankind's true House of Royalty, there poured the completing Presence which is—Light.

"For in this way, and in this way only, shall you pass from death to life," sang a chanting voice he recognised also now for the first time as indubitably his own.

It was marvellous. But the birth of light is ever marvellous. It was anguish; but the pangs of resurrection since time began have been accomplished by the sweetness of fierce pain. For the majority still lie in the pre-natal stage, unborn, unconscious of a definite spiritual existence. In the womb they grope and stifle, depending ever upon another. Denial is ever the call to life, a protest against continued darkness for deliverance. Yet birth is the ruin of all that has hitherto been depended on. There comes then that standing alone which at first seems desolate isolation. The tumult of destruction precedes release.

Limasson rose to his feet, stood with difficulty upright, looked about him from the figure so close now at his side to the snowy summit of that Tour du Néant he would never climb. The roar and thunder of *Their* passage was resumed. It seemed the mountains reeled.

"They are passing," sang the voice that was beside him and within him too, "but They have known you, and your offering is accepted. When They come close upon the world there is ever wreckage and disaster in the affairs of men. They bring disorder and confusion into the mind, a confusion that seems final, a disorder that seems to threaten death. For there is tumult in Their Presence, and apparent chaos that seems the abandonment of order. Out of this vast ruin, then, there issues life in new design. The dislocation is its entrance, the dishevelment its strength. There has been birth..."

The sunlight dazzled his eyes. That distant roar, like a wind, came close and swept his face. An icy air, as from a passing star, breathed over him.

"Are you prepared?" he heard.

He knelt again. Without a sign of hesitation or reluctance, he bared his chest to the sun and wind. The flash came swiftly, instantly, descending into his heart with unerring aim. He saw the gleam in the air, he felt the fiery impact of the blow, he even saw the stream gush forth and sink into the rocky ground, far redder than the wine...

He gasped for breath a moment, staggered, reeled, collapsed... and within the moment, so quickly did all happen, he was aware of hands that supported him and helped him to his feet. But he was too weak to stand. They carried him up to bed. The porter, and the man who had reached across him for the matches five minutes before, intending conversation, stood, one at his feet and the other at his head. As he passed through the vestibule of the hotel, he saw the people staring, and in his hand he crumpled up the unopened letters he had received so short a time ago.

"I really think—I can manage alone," he thanked them. "If you will set me down, I can walk. I felt dizzy for a moment."

"The heat in the hall—" the gentleman began, in a quiet, sympathetic voice.

They left him standing on the stairs, watching a moment to see that he had quite recovered. Limasson walked up the two flights to his room without faltering. The momentary dizziness had passed. He felt quite himself again, strong, confident, able to stand alone, able to move forward, able to *climb*.

## The Damned

### I

"I'm over forty, Frances, and rather set in my ways," I said good-naturedly, ready to yield if she insisted that our going together on the visit involved her happiness. "My work is rather heavy just now too, as you know. The question is, *could* I work there—with a lot of unassorted people in the house?"

"Mabel doesn't mention any other people, Bill," was my sister's rejoinder. "I gather she's alone—as well as lonely."

By the way she looked sideways out of the window at nothing, it was obvious she was disappointed, but to my surprise she did not urge the point; and as I glanced at Mrs. Franklyn's invitation lying upon her sloping lap the neat, childish handwriting conjured up a mental picture of the banker's widow, with her timid, insignificant personality, her pale grey eyes and her expression as of a backward child. I thought, too, of the roomy country mansion her late husband had altered to suit his particular needs, and of my visit to it a few years ago when its barren spaciousness suggested a wing of Kensington Museum fitted up temporarily as a place to eat and sleep in. Comparing it mentally with the poky Chelsea flat where I and my sister kept impecunious house, I realised other points as well. Unworthy details flashed across me to entice: the fine library, the organ, the quiet work-room I should have, perfect service, the delicious cup of early tea, and hot baths at any moment of the day—without a geyser!

"It's a longish visit, a month—isn't it?" I hedged, smiling at the details that seduced me, and ashamed of my man's selfishness, yet knowing that Frances expected it of me. "There *are* points about it, I admit. If you're set on my going with you, I could manage it all right."

I spoke at length in this way because my sister made no answer. I saw her tired eyes gazing into the dreariness of Oakley Street and felt a pang strike through me. After a pause, in which again she said no word, I added: "So, when you write the letter, you might hint, perhaps, that I usually work all the morning, and—er—am not a very lively visitor! Then she'll understand, you see." And I half-rose to return to my diminutive study, where I was slaving, just then, at an absorbing article on Comparative Æsthetic Values in the Blind and Deaf.

But Frances did not move. She kept her grey eyes upon Oakley Street where the evening mist from the river drew mournful perspectives into view. It was late October. We heard the omnibuses thundering across the bridge. The monotony of that broad, characterless street seemed more than usually depressing. Even in June sunshine it was dead, but with autumn its melancholy soaked into every house between King's Road and the Embankment. It washed thought into the past, instead of inviting it hopefully towards the future. For me, its easy width was an avenue through which nameless slums across the river sent creeping messages of depression, and I always regarded it as Winter's main entrance into London—fog, slush, gloom trooped down it every November, waving their forbidding banners till March came to rout them. Its one claim upon my love was that the south wind swept sometimes unobstructed up it, soft with suggestions of the sea. These lugubrious thoughts I naturally kept to myself, though I never ceased to regret the little flat whose cheapness had seduced us. Now, as I watched my sister's impassive face, I realised that perhaps she, too, felt as I felt, yet, brave woman, without betraying it.

"And, look here, Fanny," I said, putting a hand upon her shoulder as I crossed the room, "it would be the very thing for you. You're worn out with catering and housekeeping. Mabel is your oldest friend, besides, and you've hardly seen her since *he* died—"

"She's been abroad for a year, Bill, and only just came back," my sister interposed. "She came back rather unexpectedly, though I never thought she would go *there* to live—" She stopped abruptly. Clearly, she was only speaking half her mind. "Probably," she went on, "Mabel wants to pick up old links again."

"Naturally," I put in, "yourself chief among them." The veiled reference to the house I let pass. It involved discussing the dead man for one thing.

"I feel I ought to go anyhow," she resumed, "and of course it would be jollier if you came too. You'd get in such a muddle here by yourself, and eat wrong things, and forget to air the rooms, and—oh, everything!" She looked up, laughing. "Only," she added, "there's the British Museum—?"

"But there's a big library there," I answered, "and all the books of reference I could possibly want. It was of you I was thinking. You could take up your painting again; you always sell half of what you paint. It would be a splendid rest, too, and Sussex is a jolly country to walk in. By all means, Fanny, I advise—"

Our eyes met, as I stammered in my attempts to avoid expressing the thought that hid in both our minds. My sister had a weakness for dabbling in the various "new" theories of the day, and Mabel, who before her marriage had belonged to foolish societies for investigating the future life to the neglect of the present one, had fostered this undesirable tendency. Her amiable, impressionable temperament was open to every psychic wind that blew. I deplored, detested the whole business. But even more than this I abhorred the later influence that Mr. Franklyn had steeped his wife in, capturing her body and soul in his sombre doctrines. I had dreaded lest my sister also might be caught.

"Now that she is alone again—"

I stopped short. Our eyes now made pretence impossible, for the truth had slipped out inevitably, stupidly, although unexpressed in definite language. We laughed, turning our faces a moment to look at other things in the room. Frances picked up a book and examined its cover as though she had made an important discovery, while I took my case out and lit a cigarette I did not want to smoke. We left the matter there. I went out of the room before further explanation could cause tension. Disagreements grow into discord from such tiny things—wrong adjectives, or a chance inflection of the voice. Frances had a right to her views of life as much as I had. At least, I reflected comfortably, we had separated upon an agreement this time, recognised mutually, though not actually stated.

And this point of meeting was, oddly enough, our way of regarding some one who was dead. For we had both disliked the husband with a great dislike, and during his three years' married life had only been to the house once—for a week-end visit; arriving late on Saturday, we had left after an early breakfast on Monday morning. Ascribing my sister's dislike to a natural jealousy at losing her old friend, I said merely that he displeased me. Yet we both knew that the real emotion lay much deeper. Frances, loyal, honourable creature, had kept silence; and beyond saying that house and grounds—he altered one and laid out the other—distressed her as an expression of his personality somehow ("distressed" was the word she used), no further explanation had passed her lips.

Our dislike of his personality was easily accounted for—up to a point, since both of us shared the artist's point of view that a creed, cut to measure and carefully dried, was an ugly thing, and that a dogma to which believers must subscribe or perish everlastingly was a barbarism resting upon cruelty. But while my own dislike was purely due to an abstract worship of Beauty, my sister's had another twist in it, for with her "new" tendencies, she believed that all religions were an aspect of truth and that no one, even the lowest wretch, could escape "heaven" in the long run.

Samuel Franklyn, the rich banker, was a man universally respected and admired, and the marriage, though Mabel was fifteen years his junior, won general applause; his bride was an heiress in her own right—breweries—and the story of her conversion at a revivalist meeting where Samuel Franklyn had spoken fervidly of heaven, and terrifyingly of sin, hell and damnation, even contained a touch of genuine romance. She was a brand snatched from the burning; his detailed eloquence had frightened her into heaven; salvation came in the nick of time; his words had plucked her from the edge of that lake of fire and brimstone where their worm dieth not and the fire is not quenched. She regarded him as a hero, sighed her relief upon his saintly shoulder, and accepted the peace he offered her with a grateful resignation.

For her husband was a "religious man" who successfully combined great riches with the glamour of winning souls. He was a portly figure, though tall, with masterful, big hands, the fingers rather thick and red; and his dignity, that just escaped being pompous, held in it something that was implacable. A convinced assurance, almost remorseless, gleamed in his eyes when he preached especially, and his threats of hell fire must have scared souls stronger than the timid, receptive Mabel whom he married. He clad himself in long frock-coats that buttoned unevenly, big square boots, and trousers that invariably bagged at the knee and were a little short; he wore low collars, spats occasionally, and a tall black hat that was not of silk. His voice was alternately hard and unctuous; and he regarded theatres, ball-rooms and race-courses as the vestibule of that brimstone lake of whose geography he was as positive as of his great banking offices in the City. A philanthropist up to the hilt, however, no one ever doubted his complete sincerity; his convictions were ingrained, his faith borne out by his life—as witness his name upon so many admirable Societies, as treasurer, patron, or heading the donation list. He bulked large in the world of doing good, a broad and stately stone in the rampart against evil. And his heart was genuinely kind and soft for others—who believed as he did.

Yet in spite of this true sympathy with suffering and his desire to help, he was narrow as a telegraph wire and unbending as a church pillar; he was intensely selfish; intolerant as an officer of the Inquisition, his bourgeois soul constructed a revolting scheme of heaven that was reproduced in miniature in all he did and planned. Faith was the *sine qua non* of salvation, and by "faith" he meant belief in his own particular view of things—"which faith, except every one do keep whole and undefiled, without doubt he shall perish everlastingly." All the world but his own small, exclusive sect must be damned eternally—a pity, but alas, inevitable. *He* was right.

Yet he prayed without ceasing, and gave heavily to the poor—the only thing he could not give being big ideas to his provincial and suburban deity. Pettier than an insect, and more obstinate than a mule, he had also the superior, sleek humility of a "chosen one." He was churchwarden, too. He read the Lessons in a "place of worship," either chilly or overheated, where neither organ, vestments, nor lighted candles were permitted, but where the odour of hairwash on the boys' heads in the back rows pervaded the entire building.

This portrait of the banker, who accumulated riches both on earth and in heaven, may possibly be overdrawn, however, because Frances and I were "artistic temperaments" that viewed the type with a dislike and distrust amounting to contempt. The majority considered Samuel Franklyn a worthy man and a good citizen. The majority, doubtless, held the saner view. A few years more, and he certainly would have been made a baronet. He relieved much suffering in the world, as assuredly as he caused many souls the agonies of torturing fear by his emphasis upon damnation. Had there been one point of beauty in him, we might have been more lenient; only we found it not, and, I admit, took little pains to search. I shall never forget the look of dour forgiveness with which he heard our excuses for missing Morning Prayers that Sunday morning of our single visit to The Towers. My sister learned that a change was made soon afterwards, prayers being "conducted" after breakfast instead of before.

The Towers stood solemnly upon a Sussex hill amid park-like modern grounds, but the house cannot better be described—it would be so wearisome for one thing—than by saying that it was a cross between an overgrown, pretentious Norwood villa and one of those saturnine Institutes for cripples the train passes as it slinks ashamed through South London into Surrey. It was "wealthily" furnished and at first sight imposing, but on closer acquaintance revealed a meagre personality, barren and austere. One looked for Rules and Regulations on the walls, all signed By Order. The place was a prison that shut out "the world." There was, of course, no billiard-room, no smoking-room, no room for play of any kind, and the great hall at the back, once a chapel which might have been used for dancing, theatricals, or other innocent amusements, was consecrated in his day to meetings of various kinds, chiefly brigades, temperance or missionary societies. There was a harmonium at one end—on the level floor—a raised dais or platform at the other, and a gallery above for the servants, gardeners and coachmen. It was heated with hot-water pipes, and hung with Doré's pictures, though these latter were soon removed and stored out of sight in the attics as being too unspiritual. In polished, shiny wood, it was a representation in miniature of that poky exclusive Heaven he took about with him, externalising it in all he did and planned, even in the grounds about the house.

Changes in The Towers, Frances told me, had been made during Mabel's year of widowhood abroad—an organ put into the big hall, the library made liveable and recatalogued—when it was permissible to suppose she had found her soul again and returned to her normal, healthy views of life, which included enjoyment and play, literature, music and the arts, without, however, a touch of that trivial thoughtlessness usually termed worldliness. Mrs. Franklyn, as I remembered her, was a quiet little woman, shallow, perhaps, and easily influenced, but sincere as a dog and thorough in her faithful friendships. Her tastes at heart were catholic, and that heart was simple and unimaginative. That she took up with the various movements of the day was sign merely that she was searching in her limited way for a belief that should bring her peace. She was, in fact, a very ordinary woman, her calibre a little less than that of Frances. I knew they used to discuss all kinds of theories together, but as these discussions never resulted in action, I had come to regard her as harmless. Still, I was not sorry when she married, and I did not welcome now a renewal of the former intimacy. The philanthropist had given her no children, or she would have made a good and sensible mother. No doubt she would marry again.

"Mabel mentions that she's been alone at The Towers since the end of August," Frances told me at tea-time; "and I'm sure she feels out of it and lonely. It would be a kindness to go. Besides, I always liked her."

I agreed. I had recovered from my attack of selfishness. I expressed my pleasure.

"You've written to accept," I said, half statement and half question.

Frances nodded. "I thank for you," she added quietly, "explaining that you were not free at the moment, but that later, if not inconvenient, you might come down for a bit and join me."

I stared. Frances sometimes had this independent way of deciding things. I was convicted, and punished into the bargain.

Of course there followed argument and explanation, as between brother and sister who were affectionate, but the recording of our talk could be of little interest. It was arranged thus, Frances and I both satisfied. Two days later she departed for The Towers, leaving me alone in the flat with everything planned for my comfort and good behaviour—she was rather a tyrant in her quiet way—and her last words as I saw her off from Charing Cross rang in my head for a long time after she was gone:

"I'll write and let you know, Bill. Eat properly, mind, and let me know if anything goes wrong." She waved her small gloved hand, nodded her head till the feather brushed the window, and was gone.

II

After the note announcing her safe arrival a week of silence passed, and then a letter came; there were various suggestions for my welfare, and the rest was the usual rambling information and description Frances loved, generously italicised.

"...and we are quite alone," she went on in her enormous handwriting that seemed such a waste of space and labour, "though some others are coming presently, I believe. You could work here to your heart's content. Mabel *quite* understands, and says she would love to have you when you feel free to come. She has changed a bit—back to her old natural self: she never mentions *him*. The place has changed too in certain ways: it has more cheerfulness, I think. *She* has put it in, this cheerfulness, spaded it in, if you know what I mean; but it lies about uneasily and is not natural—quite. The organ is a beauty. She must be very rich now, but she's as gentle and sweet as ever. Do you know, Bill, I think he must have *frightened* her into marrying him. I get the impression she was afraid of him." This last sentence was inked out, but I read it through the scratching; the letters being too big to hide. "He had an inflexible will beneath all that oily kindness which passed for spiritual. He was a real personality, I mean. I'm sure he'd have sent you and me cheerfully to the stake in another century—*for our own good*. Isn't it odd she never speaks of him, even to me?" This, again, was stroked through, though without the intention to obliterate—merely because it was repetition, probably. "The only reminder of him in the house now is a big copy of the presentation portrait that stands on the stairs of the Multitechnic Institute at Peckham—you know—that life-size one with his fat hand sprinkled with rings resting on a thick Bible and the other slipped between the buttons of a tight frock-coat. It hangs in the dining-room and rather dominates our meals. I wish Mabel would take it down. I think she'd like to, if she *dared*. There's not a single photograph of him anywhere, even in her own room. Mrs. Marsh is here—you remember her, *his* housekeeper, the wife of the man who got penal servitude for killing a baby or something,—*you* said she robbed him and justified her stealing because the story of the unjust steward was in the Bible! How we laughed over that! *She's* just the same, too, gliding about all over the house and turning up when least expected."

Other reminiscences filled the next two sides of the letter, and ran, without a trace of punctuation, into instructions about a Salamander stove for heating my work-room in the flat; these were followed by things I was to tell the cook, and by requests for several articles she had forgotten and would like sent after her, two of them blouses, with descriptions so lengthy and contradictory that I sighed as I read them—"unless you come down soon, in which case perhaps you wouldn't mind bringing them; *not* the mauve one I wear in the evening sometimes, but the pale blue one with lace round the collar and the crinkly front. They're in the cupboard—or the drawer, I'm not sure which—of my bedroom. Ask *Annie* if you're in doubt. Thanks most *awfully*. Send a telegram, remember, and we'll meet you in the motor *any time*. I don't quite know if I shall stay the whole month—*alone*. It all depends..." And she closed the letter, the italicised words increasing recklessly towards the end, with a repetition that Mabel would love to have me "for myself," as also to have a "man in the house," and that I only had to telegraph the day and the train... This letter, coming by the second post, interrupted me in a moment of absorbing work, and, having read it through to make sure there was nothing requiring instant attention, I threw it aside and went on with my notes and reading. Within five minutes, however, it was back at me again. That restless thing called "between the lines" fluttered about my mind. My interest in the Balkan States—political article that had been "ordered"—faded. Somewhere, somehow I felt disquieted, disturbed. At first I persisted in my work, forcing myself to concentrate, but soon found that a layer of new impressions floated between the article and my attention. It was like a shadow, though a shadow that dissolved upon inspection. Once or twice I glanced up, expecting to find some one in the room, that the door had opened unobserved and Annie was waiting for instructions. I heard the 'buses thundering across the bridge. I was aware of Oakley Street. Montenegro and the blue Adriatic melted into the October haze along that depressing Embankment that aped a river bank, and sentences from the letter flashed before my eyes and stung me. Picking it up and reading it through more carefully, I rang the bell and told Annie to find the blouses and pack them for the post, showing her finally the written description, and resenting the superior smile with which she at once interrupted, "*I* know them, sir," and disappeared.

But it was not the blouses: it was that exasperating thing "between the lines" that put an end to my work with its elusive teasing nuisance. The first sharp impression is alone of value in such a case, for once analysis begins the imagination constructs all kinds of false interpretation. The more I thought, the more I grew fuddled. The letter, it seemed to me, wanted to say another thing; instead the eight sheets *conveyed* it merely. It came to the edge of disclosure, then halted. There was something on the writer's mind, and I felt uneasy. Studying the sentences brought, however, no revelation, but increased confusion only; for while the uneasiness remained, the first clear hint had vanished. In the end I closed my books and went out to look up another matter at the British Museum Library. Perhaps I should discover it that way—by turning the mind in a totally new direction. I lunched at the Express Dairy in Oxford Street close by, and telephoned to Annie that I would be home to tea at five.

And at tea, tired physically and mentally after breathing the exhausted air of the Rotunda for five hours, my mind suddenly delivered up its original impression, vivid and clear-cut; no proof accompanied the revelation; it was mere presentiment, but convincing. Frances was disturbed in her mind, her orderly, sensible, housekeeping mind; she was uneasy, even perhaps afraid; something in the house distressed her, and she had need of me. Unless I went down, her time of rest and change, her quite necessary holiday, in fact, would be spoilt. She was too unselfish to say this, but it ran everywhere between the lines. I saw it clearly now. Mrs. Franklyn, moreover—and that meant Frances, too—would like a "man in the house." It was a disagreeable phrase, a suggestive way of hinting something she dared not state definitely. The two women in that great, lonely barrack of a house were afraid.

My sense of duty, affection, unselfishness, whatever the composite emotion may be termed, was stirred; also my vanity. I acted quickly, lest reflection should warp clear, decent judgment. "Annie," I said, when she answered the bell, "you need not send those blouses by the post. I'll take them down to-morrow when I go. I shall be away a week or two, possibly longer." And, having looked up a train, I hastened out to telegraph before I could change my fickle mind.

But no desire came that night to change my mind. I was doing the right, the necessary thing. I was even in something of a hurry to get down to The Towers as soon as possible. I chose an early afternoon train.

### III

A telegram had told me to come to a town ten miles from the house, so I was saved the crawling train to the local station, and travelled down by an express. As soon as we left London the fog cleared off, and an autumn sun, though without heat in it, painted the landscape with golden browns and yellows. My spirits rose as I lay back in the luxurious motor and sped between the woods and hedges. Oddly enough, my anxiety of overnight had disappeared. It was due, no doubt, to that exaggeration of detail which reflection in loneliness brings. Frances and I had not been separated for over a year, and her letters from The Towers told so little. It had seemed unnatural to be deprived of those intimate particulars of mood and feeling I was accustomed to. We had such confidence in one another, and our affection was so deep. Though she was but five years younger than myself, I regarded her as a child. My attitude was fatherly. In return, she certainly mothered me with a solicitude that never cloyed. I felt no desire to marry while she was still alive. She painted in water-colours with a reasonable success, and kept house for me; I wrote, reviewed books and lectured on æsthetics; we were a humdrum couple of quasi-artists, well satisfied with life, and all I feared for her was that she might become a suffragette or be taken captive by one of these wild theories that caught her imagination sometimes, and that Mabel, for one, had fostered. As for myself, no doubt she deemed me a trifle solid or stolid—I forget which word she preferred—but on the whole there was just sufficient difference of opinion to make intercourse suggestive without monotony, and certainly without quarrelling. Drawing in deep draughts of the stinging autumn air, I felt happy and exhilarated. It was like going for a holiday, with comfort at the end of the journey instead of bargaining for centimes.

But my heart sank noticeably the moment the house came into view. The long drive, lined with hostile monkey trees and formal wellingtonias that were solemn and sedate, was mere extension of the miniature approach to a thousand semi-detached suburban "residences"; and the appearance of The Towers, as we turned the corner with a rush, suggested a commonplace climax to a story that had begun interestingly, almost thrillingly. A villa had escaped from the shadow of the Crystal Palace, thumped its way down by night, grown suddenly monstrous in a shower of rich rain, and settled itself insolently to stay. Ivy climbed about the opulent red-brick walls, but climbed neatly and with disfiguring effect, sham as on a prison or—the simile made me smile—an orphan asylum. There was no hint of the comely roughness of untidy ivy on a ruin. Clipped, trained and precise it was, as on a brand-new protestant church. I swear there was not a bird's nest nor a single earwig in it anywhere. About the porch it was particularly thick, smothering a seventeenth-century lamp with a contrast that was quite horrible. Extensive glasshouses spread away on the further side of the house; the numerous towers to which the building owed its name seemed made to hold school bells; and the window-sills thick with potted flowers, made me think of the desolate suburbs of Brighton or Bexhill. In a commanding position upon the crest of a hill, it overlooked miles of undulating, wooded country southwards to the Downs, but behind it, to the north, thick banks of ilex, holly, and privet protected it from the cleaner and more stimulating winds. Hence, though highly placed, it was shut in. Three years had passed since I last set eyes upon it, but the unsightly memory I had retained was justified by the reality. The place was deplorable.

It is my habit to express my opinions audibly sometimes, when impressions are strong enough to warrant it; but now I only sighed "Oh, dear," as I extricated my legs from many rugs and went into the house. A tall parlourmaid, with the bearing of a grenadier, received me, and standing behind her was Mrs. Marsh, the housekeeper, whom I remembered because her untidy back hair had suggested to me that it had been burnt. I went at once to my room, my hostess already dressing for dinner, but Frances came in to see me just as I was struggling with my black tie that had got tangled like a bootlace. She fastened it for me in a neat, effective bow, and while I held my chin up, for the operation, staring blankly at the ceiling, the impression came—I wondered, was it her touch that caused it?—that something in her trembled. Shrinking perhaps is the truer word. Nothing in her face or manner betrayed it, nor in her pleasant, easy talk while she tidied my things and scolded my slovenly packing, as her habit was, questioning me about the servants at the flat. The blouses, though right, were crumpled, and my scolding was deserved. There was no impatience even. Yet somehow or other the suggestion of a shrinking reserve and holding back reached my mind. She had been lonely, of course, but it was more than that; she was glad that I had come, yet for some reason unstated she could have wished that I had stayed away. We discussed the news that had accumulated during our brief separation, and in doing so the impression, at best exceedingly slight, was forgotten. My chamber was large and beautifully furnished; the hall and dining-room of our flat would have gone into it with a good remainder; yet it was not a place I could settle down in for work. It conveyed the idea of impermanence, making me feel transient as in a hotel bedroom. This, of course, was the fact. But some rooms convey a settled, lasting hospitality even in a hotel; this one did not; and as I was accustomed to work in the room I slept in, at least when visiting, a slight frown must have crept between my eyes.

"Mabel has fitted a work-room for you just out of the library," said the clairvoyant Frances. "No one will disturb you there, and you'll have fifteen thousand books all catalogued within easy reach. There's a private staircase, too. You can breakfast in your room and slip down in your dressing-gown if you want to." She laughed. My spirits took a turn upwards as absurdly as they had gone down.

"And how are *you*?" I asked, giving her a belated kiss. "It's jolly to be together again. I did feel rather lost without you, I'll admit."

"That's natural," she laughed. "I'm so glad!"

She looked well and had country colour in her cheeks. She informed me that she was eating and sleeping well, going out for little walks with Mabel, painting bits of scenery again, and enjoying a complete change and rest; and yet, for all her brave description, the words somehow did not quite ring true. Those last words in particular did not ring true. There lay in her manner, just out of sight, I felt, this suggestion of the exact reverse—of unrest, shrinking, almost of anxiety. Certain small strings in her seemed overtight. "Keyed-up" was the slang expression that crossed my mind. I looked rather searchingly into her face as she was telling me this.

"Only—the evenings," she added, noticing my query, yet rather avoiding my eyes, "the evenings are—well, rather heavy sometimes, and I find it difficult to keep awake."

"The strong air after London makes you drowsy," I suggested, "and you like to get early to bed." Frances turned and looked at me for a moment steadily. "On the contrary, Bill, I dislike going to bed—here. And Mabel goes so early." She said it lightly enough, fingering the disorder upon my dressing table in such a stupid way that I saw her mind was working in another direction altogether. She looked up suddenly with a kind of nervousness from the brush and scissors. "Billy," she said abruptly, lowering her voice, "isn't it odd, but I *hate* sleeping alone here? I can't make it out quite; I've never felt such a thing before in my life. Do you—think it's all nonsense?" And she laughed, with her lips but not with her eyes; there was a note of defiance in her I failed to understand.

"Nothing a nature like yours feels strongly is nonsense, Frances," I replied soothingly.

But I, too, answered with my lips only, for another part of my mind was working elsewhere, and among uncomfortable things. A touch of bewilderment passed over me. I was not certain how best to continue. If I laughed she would tell me no more, yet if I took her too seriously the strings would tighten further. Instinctively, then, this flashed rapidly across me: that something of what she felt, I had also felt, though interpreting it differently. Vague it was, as the coming of rain or storm that announce themselves hours in advance with their hint of faint, unsettling excitement in the air. I had been but a short hour in the house,—big, comfortable, luxurious house,—but had experienced this sense of being unsettled, unfixed, fluctuating—a kind of impermanence that transient lodgers in hotels must feel, but that a guest in a friend's home ought not to feel, be the visit short or long. To Frances, an impressionable woman, the feeling had come in the terms of alarm. She disliked sleeping alone, while yet she longed to sleep. The precise idea in my mind evaded capture, merely brushing through me, three-quarters out of sight; I realised only that we both felt the same thing, and that neither of us could get at it clearly. Degrees of unrest we felt, but the actual thing did not disclose itself. It did not happen.

I felt strangely at sea for a moment. Frances would interpret hesitation as endorsement, and encouragement might be the last thing that could help her.

"Sleeping in a strange house," I answered at length, "is often difficult at first, and one feels lonely. After fifteen months in our tiny flat one feels lost and uncared for in a big house. It's an uncomfortable feeling—I know it well. And this *is* a barrack, isn't it? The masses of furniture only make it worse. One feels in storage somewhere underground—the furniture doesn't furnish. One must never yield to fancies, though—"

Frances looked away towards the windows; she seemed disappointed a little.

"After our thickly-populated Chelsea," I went on quickly, "it seems isolated here."

But she did not turn back, and clearly I was saying the wrong thing. A wave of pity rushed suddenly over me. Was she really frightened, perhaps? She was imaginative, I knew, but never moody; common sense was strong in her, though she had her times of hypersensitiveness. I caught the echo of some unreasoning, big alarm in her. She stood there, gazing across my balcony towards the sea of wooded country that spread dim and vague in the obscurity of the dusk. The deepening shadows entered the room, I fancied, from the grounds below. Following her abstracted gaze a moment, I experienced a curious sharp desire to leave, to escape. Out yonder was wind and space and freedom. This enormous building was oppressive, silent, still. Great catacombs occurred to me, things beneath the ground, imprisonment and capture. I believe I even shuddered a little.

I touched her shoulder. She turned round slowly, and we looked with a certain deliberation into each other's eyes.

"Fanny," I asked, more gravely than I intended, "You are not frightened, are you? Nothing has happened, has it?"

She replied with emphasis. "Of course not! How could it—I mean, why should I?" She stammered, as though the wrong sentence flustered her a second. "It's simply—that I have this ter—this dislike of sleeping alone."

Naturally, my first thought was how easy it would be to cut our visit short. But I did not say this. Had it been a true solution, Frances would have said it for me long ago.

"Wouldn't Mabel double-up with you?" I said instead, "or give you an adjoining room, so that you could leave the door between you open? There's space enough, Heaven knows."

And then, as the gong sounded in the hall below for dinner, she said, as with an effort, this thing: "Mabel did ask me—on the third night—after I had told her. But I declined."

"You'd rather be alone than with her?" I asked, with a certain relief.

Her reply was so gravely given, a child would have known there was more behind it: "Not that; but that she did not really want it."

I had a moment's intuition and acted on it impulsively. "She feels it too, perhaps, but wishes to face it by herself—and get over it?"

My sister bowed her head, and the gesture made me realise of a sudden how grave and solemn our talk had grown, as though some portentous thing were under discussion. It had come of itself—indefinite as a gradual change of temperature. Yet neither of us knew its nature, for apparently neither of us could state it plainly. Nothing happened, even in our words.

"That was my impression," she said, "—that if she yields to it she encourages it. And a habit forms so easily. Just think," she added, with a faint smile that was the first sign of lightness she had yet betrayed, "what a nuisance it would be—everywhere—if everybody was afraid of being alone—like that."

I snatched readily at the chance. We laughed a little, though it was a quiet kind of laughter that seemed wrong. I took her arm and led her towards the door.

"Disastrous, in fact," I agreed.

She raised her voice to its normal pitch again, as I had done. "No doubt it will pass," she said, "now that you have come. Of course, it's chiefly my imagination." Her tone was lighter, though nothing could convince me that the matter itself was light—just then. "And in any case," tightening her grip on my arm as we passed into the bright enormous corridor and caught sight of Mrs. Franklyn waiting in the cheerless hall below, "I'm very glad you're here, Bill, and Mabel, I know, is too."

"If it doesn't pass," I just had time to whisper with a feeble attempt at jollity, "I'll come at night and snore outside your door. After that you'll be so glad to get rid of me that you won't mind being alone."

"That's a bargain," said Frances.

I shook my hostess by the hand, made a banal remark about the long interval since last we met, and walked behind them into the great dining-room, dimly lit by candles, wondering in my heart how long my sister and I should stay, and why in the world we had ever left our cosy little flat to enter this desolation of riches and false luxury at all. The unsightly picture of the late Samuel Franklyn, Esq., stared down upon me from the further end of the room above the mighty mantelpiece. He looked, I thought, like some pompous Heavenly Butler who denied to all the world, and to us in particular, the right of entry without presentation cards signed by his hand as proof that we belonged to his own exclusive set. The majority, to his deep grief, and in spite of all his prayers on their behalf, must burn and "perish everlastingly."

## IV

With the instinct of the healthy bachelor I always try to make myself a nest in the place I live in, be it for long or short. Whether visiting, in lodging-house, or in hotel, the first essential is this nest—one's own things built into the walls as a bird builds in its feathers. It may look desolate and uncomfortable enough to others, because the central detail is neither bed nor wardrobe, sofa nor arm-chair, but a good solid writing-table that does not wriggle, and that has wide elbow-room. And The Towers is vividly described for me by the single fact that I could not "nest" there. I took several days to discover this, but the first impression of impermanence was truer than I knew. The feathers of the mind refused here to lie one way. They ruffled, pointed and grew wild.

Luxurious furniture does not mean comfort; I might as well have tried to settle down in the sofa and arm-chair department of a big shop. My bedroom was easily managed; it was the private work-room, prepared especially for my reception, that made me feel alien and outcast. Externally, it was all one could desire: an ante-chamber to the great library, with not one, but two generous oak tables, to say nothing of smaller ones against the walls with capacious drawers. There were reading-desks, mechanical devices for holding books, perfect light, quiet as in a church, and no approach but across the huge adjoining room. Yet it did not invite.

"I hope you'll be able to work here," said my little hostess the next morning, as she took me in—her only visit to it while I stayed in the house—and showed me the ten-volume Catalogue. "It's absolutely quiet and no one will disturb you."

"If you can't, Bill, you're not much good," laughed Frances, who was on her arm. "Even I could write in a study like this!"

I glanced with pleasure at the ample tables, the sheets of thick blotting-paper, the rulers, sealing-wax, paper-knives, and all the other immaculate paraphernalia. "It's perfect," I answered, with a secret thrill, yet feeling a little foolish. This was for Gibbon or Carlyle, rather than for my pot-boiling insignificancies. "If I can't write masterpieces here, it's certainly not *your* fault," and I turned with gratitude to Mrs. Franklyn. She was looking straight at me, and there was a question in her small pale eyes I did not understand. Was she noting the effect upon me, I wondered?

"You'll write here—perhaps a story about the house," she said; "Thompson will bring you anything you want; you only have to ring." She pointed to the electric bell on the central table, the wire running neatly down the leg. "No one has ever worked here before, and the library has been hardly used since it was put in. So there's no previous atmosphere to affect your imagination—er—adversely."

We laughed. "Bill isn't that sort," said my sister; while I wished they would go out and leave me to arrange my little nest and set to work. I thought, of course, it was the huge listening library that made me feel so inconsiderable—the fifteen thousand silent, staring books, the solemn aisles, the deep, eloquent shelves. But when the women had gone and I was alone, the beginning of the truth crept over me, and I felt that first hint of disconsolateness which later became an imperative No. The mind shut down, images ceased to rise and flow. I read, made copious notes, but I wrote no single line at The Towers. Nothing completed itself there. Nothing happened.

The morning sunshine poured into the library through ten long narrow windows; birds were singing; the autumn air, rich with a faint aroma of November melancholy that stung the imagination pleasantly, filled my antechamber. I looked out upon the undulating wooded landscape, hemmed in by the sweep of distant Downs, and I tasted a whiff of the sea. Rooks cawed as they floated above the elms, and there were lazy cows in the nearer meadows. A dozen times I tried to make my nest and settle down to work, and a dozen times, like a turning fastidious dog upon a hearth-rug, I rearranged my chair and books and papers. The temptation of the Catalogue and shelves, of course, was accountable for much, yet not, I felt, for all. That was a manageable seduction. My work, moreover, was not of the creative kind that requires absolute absorption; it was the mere readable presentation of data I had accumulated. My note-books were charged with facts ready to tabulate—facts, too, that interested me keenly. A mere effort of the will was necessary, and concentration of no difficult kind. Yet, somehow, it seemed beyond me: something for ever pushed the facts into disorder... and in the end I sat in the sunshine, dipping into a dozen books selected from the shelves outside, vexed with myself and only half-enjoying it. I felt restless. I wanted to be elsewhere.

And even while I read, attention wandered. Frances, Mabel, her late husband, the house and grounds, each in turn and sometimes all together, rose uninvited into the stream of thought, hindering any consecutive flow of work. In disconnected fashion came these pictures that interrupted concentration, yet presenting themselves as broken fragments of a bigger thing my mind already groped for unconsciously. They fluttered round this hidden thing of which they were aspects, fugitive interpretations, no one of them bringing complete revelation. There was no adjective, such as pleasant or unpleasant, that I could attach to what I felt, beyond that the result was unsettling. Vague as the atmosphere of a dream, it yet persisted, and I could not dissipate it. Isolated words or phrases in the lines I read sent questions scouring across my mind, sure sign that the deeper part of me was restless and ill at ease.

Rather trivial questions, too—half-foolish interrogations, as of a puzzled or curious child: Why was my sister afraid to sleep alone, and why did her friend feel a similar repugnance, yet seek to conquer it? Why was the solid luxury of the house without comfort, its shelter without the sense of permanence? Why had Mrs. Franklyn asked us to come, artists, unbelieving vagabonds, types at the furthest possible remove from the saved sheep of her husband's household? Had a reaction set in against the hysteria of her conversion? I had seen no signs of religious fervour in her; her atmosphere was that of an ordinary, high-minded woman, yet a woman of the world. Lifeless, though, a little, perhaps, now that I came to think about it: she had made no definite impression upon me of any kind. And my thoughts ran vaguely after this fragile clue.

Closing my book, I let them run. For, with this chance reflection came the discovery that I could not *see* her clearly—could not feel her soul, her personality. Her face, her small pale eyes, her dress and body and walk, all these stood before me like a photograph; but her Self evaded me. She seemed not there, lifeless, empty, a shadow—nothing. The picture was disagreeable, and I put it by. Instantly she melted out, as though light thought had conjured up a phantom that had no real existence. And at that very moment, singularly enough, my eye caught sight of her moving past the window, going silently along the gravel path. I watched her, a sudden new sensation gripping me. "There goes a prisoner," my thought instantly ran, "one who wishes to escape, but cannot."

What brought the outlandish notion, heaven only knows. The house was of her own choice, she was twice an heiress, and the world lay open at her feet. Yet she stayed—unhappy, frightened, caught. All this flashed over me, and made a sharp impression even before I had time to dismiss it as absurd. But a moment later explanation offered itself, though it seemed as far-fetched as the original impression. My mind, being logical, was obliged to provide something, apparently. For Mrs. Franklyn, while dressed to go out, with thick walking-boots, a pointed stick, and a motor-cap tied on with a veil as for the windy lanes, was obviously content to go no further than the little garden paths. The costume was a sham and a pretence. It was this, and her lithe, quick movements that suggested a caged creature—a creature tamed by fear and cruelty that cloaked themselves in kindness—pacing up and down, unable to realise why it got no further, but always met the same bars in exactly the same place. The mind in her was barred.

I watched her go along the paths and down the steps from one terrace to another, until the laurels hid her altogether; and into this mere imagining of a moment came a hint of something slightly disagreeable, for which my mind, search as it would, found no explanation at all. I remembered then certain other little things. They dropped into the picture of their own accord.

In a mind not deliberately hunting for clues, pieces of a puzzle sometimes come together in this way, bringing revelation, so that for a second there flashed across me, vanishing instantly again before I could consider it, a large, distressing thought that I can only describe vaguely as a Shadow. Dark and ugly, oppressive certainly it might be described, with something torn and dreadful about the edges that suggested pain and strife and terror. The interior of a prison with two rows of occupied condemned cells, seen years ago in New York, sprang to memory after it—the connection between the two impossible to surmise even. But the "certain other little things" mentioned above were these: that Mrs. Franklyn, in last night's dinner talk, had always referred to "this house," but never called it "home"; and had emphasised unnecessarily, for a well-bred woman, our "great kindness" in coming down to stay so long with her. Another time, in answer to my futile compliment about the "stately rooms," she said quietly, "It is an enormous house for so small a party; but I stay here very little, and only till I get it straight again." The three of us were going up the great staircase to bed as this was said, and, not knowing quite her meaning, I dropped the subject. It edged delicate ground, I felt. Frances added no word of her own. It now occurred to me abruptly that "stay" was the word made use of, when "live" would have been more natural. How insignificant to recall! Yet why did they suggest themselves just at this moment? ... And, on going to Frances's room to make sure she was not nervous or lonely, I realised abruptly, that Mrs. Franklyn, of course, had talked with *her* in a confidential sense that I, as a mere visiting brother, could not share. Frances had told me nothing. I might easily have wormed it out of her, had I not felt that for us to discuss further our hostess and her house merely because we were under the roof together, was not quite nice or loyal.

"I'll call you, Bill, if I'm scared," she had laughed as we parted, my room being just across the big corridor from her own. I had fallen asleep, thinking what in the world was meant by "getting it straight again."

And now in my ante-chamber to the library, on the second morning, sitting among piles of foolscap and sheets of spotless blotting-paper, all useless to me, these slight hints came back and helped to frame the big, vague Shadow I have mentioned. Up to the neck in this Shadow, almost drowned, yet just treading water, stood the figure of my hostess in her walking costume. Frances and I seemed swimming to her aid. The Shadow was large enough to include both house and grounds, but further than that I could not see... Dismissing it, I fell to reading my purloined book again. Before I turned another page, however, another startling detail leaped out at me: the figure of Mrs. Franklyn in the Shadow was not living. It floated helplessly, like a doll or puppet that has no life in it. It was both pathetic and dreadful.

Any one who sits in reverie thus, of course, may see similar ridiculous pictures when the will no longer guides construction. The incongruities of dreams are thus explained. I merely record the picture as it came. That it remained by me for several days, just as vivid dreams do, is neither here nor there. I did not allow myself to dwell upon it. The curious thing, perhaps, is that from this moment I date my inclination, though not yet my desire, to leave. I purposely say "to leave." I cannot quite remember when the word changed to that aggressive, frantic thing which is escape.

## V

We were left delightfully to ourselves in this pretentious country mansion with the soul of a villa. Frances took up her painting again, and, the weather being propitious, spent hours out of doors, sketching flowers, trees and nooks of woodland, garden, even the house itself where bits of it peered suggestively across the orchards. Mrs. Franklyn seemed always busy about something or other, and never interfered with us except to propose motoring, tea in another part of the lawn, and so forth. She flitted everywhere, preoccupied, yet apparently doing nothing. The house engulfed her rather. No visitors called. For one thing, she was not supposed to be back from abroad yet; and for another, I think, the neighbourhood—her husband's neighbourhood—was puzzled by her sudden cessation from good works. Brigades and temperance societies did not ask to hold their meetings in the big hall, and the vicar arranged the school-treats in another's field without explanation. The full-length portrait in the dining-room, and the presence of the housekeeper with the "burnt" back-hair, indeed, were the only reminders of the man who once had lived here. Mrs. Marsh retained her place in silence, well-paid sinecure as it doubtless was, yet with no hint of that suppressed disapproval one might have expected from her. Indeed, there was nothing positive to disapprove, since nothing "worldly" entered grounds or building. In her master's lifetime she had been another "brand snatched from the burning," and it had then been her custom to give vociferous "testimony" at the revival meetings where he adorned the platform and led in streams of prayer. I saw her sometimes on the stairs, hovering, wandering, half-watching and half-listening, and the idea came to me once that this woman somehow formed a link with the departed influence of her bigoted employer. She, alone among us, *belonged* to the house, and looked at home there. When I saw her talking—oh, with such correct and respectful mien—to Mrs. Franklyn, I had the feeling that for all her unaggressive attitude, she yet exerted some influence that sought to make her mistress stay in the building for ever—live there. She would prevent her escape, prevent her "getting it straight again," thwart somehow her will to freedom, if she could. The idea in me was of the most fleeting kind. But another time, when I came down late at night to get a book from the library ante-chamber, and found her sitting in the hall—alone—the impression left upon me was the reverse of fleeting. I can never forget the vivid, disagreeable effect it produced upon me. What was she doing there at half-past eleven at night, all alone in the darkness? She was sitting upright, stiff, in a big chair below the clock. It gave me a turn. It was so incongruous and odd. She rose quietly as I turned the corner of the stairs, and asked me respectfully, her eyes cast down as usual, whether I had finished with the library, so that she might lock up. There was no more to it than that; but the picture stayed with me—unpleasantly.

These various impressions came to me at odd moments, of course, and not in a single sequence as I now relate them. I was hard at work before three days were past, not writing, as explained, but reading, making notes, and gathering material from the library for future use. It was in chance moments that these curious flashes came, catching me unawares with a touch of surprise that sometimes made me start. For they proved that my under-mind was still conscious of the Shadow, and that far away out of sight lay the cause of it that left me with a vague unrest, unsettled, seeking to "nest" in a place that did not want me. Only when this deeper part knows harmony, perhaps, can good brain work result, and my inability to write was thus explained. Certainly, I was always seeking for something here I could not find—an explanation that continually evaded me. Nothing but these trivial hints offered themselves. Lumped together, however, they had the effect of defining the Shadow a little. I became more and more aware of its very real existence. And, if I have made little mention of Frances and my hostess in this connection, it is because they contributed at first little or nothing towards the discovery of what this story tries to tell. Our life was wholly external, normal, quiet, and uneventful; conversation banal—Mrs. Franklyn's conversation in particular. They said nothing that suggested revelation. Both were in this Shadow, and both knew that they were in it, but neither betrayed by word or act a hint of interpretation. They talked privately, no doubt, but of that I can report no details.

And so it was that, after ten days of a very commonplace visit, I found myself looking straight into the face of a Strangeness that defied capture at close quarters. "There's something here that never happens," were the words that rose in my mind, "and that's why none of us can speak of it." And as I looked out of the window and watched the vulgar blackbirds, with toes turned in, boring out their worms, I realised sharply that even they, as indeed everything large and small in the house and grounds, shared this strangeness, and was twisted out of normal appearance because of it. Life, as expressed in the entire place, was crumpled, dwarfed, emasculated. God's meanings here were crippled, His love of joy was stunted. Nothing in the garden danced or sang. There was hate in it. "The Shadow," my thought hurried on to completion, "is a manifestation of hate; and hate is the Devil." And then I sat back frightened in my chair, for I knew that I had partly found the truth.

Leaving my books, I went out into the open. The sky was overcast, yet the day by no means gloomy, for a soft, diffused light oozed through the clouds and turned all things warm and almost summery. But I saw the grounds now in their nakedness because I understood. Hate means strife, and the two together weave the robe that terror wears. Having no so-called religious beliefs myself, nor belonging to any set of dogmas called a creed, I could stand outside these feelings and observe. Yet they soaked into me sufficiently for me to grasp sympathetically what others, with more cabined souls (I flattered myself), might feel. That picture in the dining-room stalked everywhere, hid behind every tree, peered down upon me from the peaked ugliness of the bourgeois towers, and left the impress of its powerful hand upon every bed of flowers. "You must not do this, you must not do that," went past me through the air. "You must not leave these narrow paths," said the rigid iron railings of black. "You shall not walk here," was written on the lawns. "Keep to the steps," "Don't pick the flowers; make no noise of laughter, singing, dancing," was placarded all over the rose-garden, and "Trespassers will be—not prosecuted but—*destroyed*" hung from the crest of monkey-tree and holly. Guarding the ends of each artificial terrace stood gaunt, implacable policemen, warders, gaolers. "Come with us," they chanted, "or be damned eternally."

I remember feeling quite pleased with myself that I had discovered this obvious explanation of the prison-feeling the place breathed out. That the posthumous influence of heavy old Samuel Franklyn might be an inadequate solution did not occur to me. By "getting the place straight again," his widow, of course, meant forgetting the glamour of fear and foreboding his depressing creed had temporarily forced upon her; and Frances, delicately-minded being, did not speak of it because it was the influence of the man her friend had loved. I felt lighter; a load was lifted from me. "To trace the unfamiliar to the familiar," came back a sentence I had read somewhere, "is to understand." It was a real relief. I could talk with Frances now, even with my hostess, no danger of treading clumsily. For the key was in my hands. I might even help to dissipate the Shadow, "to get it straight again." It seemed, perhaps, our long invitation was explained!

I went into the house laughing—at myself a little. "Perhaps after all the artist's outlook, with no hard and fast dogmas, is as narrow as the others! How small humanity is! And why is there no possible and true combination of *all* outlooks?"

The feeling of "unsettling" was very strong in me just then, in spite of my big discovery which was to clear everything up. And at that moment I ran into Frances on the stairs, with a portfolio of sketches under her arm.

It came across me then abruptly that, although she had worked a great deal since we came, she had shown me nothing. It struck me suddenly as odd, unnatural. The way she tried to pass me now confirmed my new-born suspicion that—well, that her results were hardly what they ought to be.

"Stand and deliver!" I laughed, stepping in front of her. "I've seen nothing you've done since you've been here, and as a rule you show me all your things. I believe they are atrocious and degrading!" Then my laughter froze.

She made a sly gesture to slip past me, and I almost decided to let her go, for the expression that flashed across her face shocked me. She looked uncomfortable and ashamed; the colour came and went a moment in her cheeks, making me think of a child detected in some secret naughtiness. It was almost fear.

"It's because they're not finished then?" I said, dropping the tone of banter, "or because they're too good for me to understand?" For my criticism of painting, she told me, was crude and ignorant sometimes. "But you'll let me see them later, won't you?"

Frances, however, did not take the way of escape I offered. She changed her mind. She drew the portfolio from beneath her arm instead. "You can see them if you *really* want to, Bill," she said quietly, and her tone reminded me of a nurse who says to a boy just grown out of childhood, "you are old enough now to look upon horror and ugliness—only I don't advise it."

"I do want to," I said, and made to go downstairs with her. But, instead, she said in the same low voice as before, "Come up to my room, we shall be undisturbed there." So I guessed that she had been on her way to show the paintings to our hostess, but did not care for us all three to see them together. My mind worked furiously.

"Mabel asked me to do them," she explained, in a tone of submissive horror, once the door was shut, "in fact, she begged it of me. You know how persistent she is in her quiet way. I—er—had to."

She flushed and opened the portfolio on the little table by the window, standing behind me as I turned the sketches over—sketches of the grounds and trees and garden. In the first moment of inspection, however, I did not take in clearly why my sister's sense of modesty had been offended. For my attention flashed a second elsewhere. Another bit of the puzzle had dropped into place, defining still further the nature of what I called "the Shadow." Mrs. Franklyn, I now remembered, had suggested to me in the library that I might perhaps write something about the place, and I had taken it for one of her banal sentences and paid no further attention. I realized now that it was said in earnest. She wanted our interpretations, as expressed in our respective "talents," painting and writing. Her invitation *was* explained. She left us to ourselves on purpose.

"I should like to tear them up," Frances was whispering behind me with a shudder, "only I promised—" She hesitated a moment.

"Promised not to?" I asked, with a queer feeling of distress, my eyes glued to the papers.

"Promised always to show them to her first," she finished so low I barely caught it.

I have no intuitive, immediate grasp of the value of paintings; results come to me slowly, and though every one believes his own judgment to be good, I dare not claim that mine is worth more than that of any other layman. Frances had too often convicted me of gross ignorance and error. I can only say that I examined these sketches with a feeling of amazement that contained revulsion, if not actually horror and disgust. They were outrageous. I felt hot for my sister, and it was a relief to know she had moved across the room on some pretence or other, and did not examine them with me. Her talent, of course, is mediocre, yet she has her moments of inspiration—moments, that is to say, when a view of Beauty not normally her own flames divinely through her. And these interpretations struck me forcibly as being thus "inspired,"—not her own. They were uncommonly well done; they were also atrocious. The meaning in them, however, was never more than hinted. There the unholy skill and power came in; they suggested so abominably, leaving most to the imagination. To find such significance in a bourgeois villa garden, and to interpret it with such delicate yet legible certainty, was a kind of symbolism that was sinister, even diabolical. The delicacy was her own, but the point of view was another's. And the word that rose in my mind was not the gross description of "impure," but the more fundamental qualification—"un-pure."

In silence I turned the sketches over one by one, as a boy hurries through the pages of an evil book lest he be caught.

"What does Mabel do with them?" I asked presently, in a low tone, as I neared the end. "Does she keep them?"

"She makes notes about them in a book and then destroys them," was the reply from the end of the room. I heard a sigh of relief. "I'm glad you've seen them, Bill. I wanted you to—but was afraid to show them. You understand?"

"I understand," was my reply, though it was not a question intended to be answered. All I understood really was that Mabel's mind was as sweet and pure as my sister's, and that she had some good reason for what she did. She destroyed the sketches, but first made notes! It was an interpretation of the place she sought. Brother-like, I felt resentment, though, that Frances should waste her time and talent, when she might be doing work that she could sell. Naturally, I felt other things as well...

"Mabel pays me five guineas for each one," I heard. "Absolutely insists."

I stared at her stupidly a moment, bereft of speech or wit.

"I must either accept, or go away," she went on calmly, but a little white. "I've tried everything. There was a scene the third day I was here—when I showed her my first result. I wanted to write to you, but hesitated—"

"It's unintentional, then, on your part—forgive my asking it, Frances, dear?" I blundered, hardly knowing what to think or say. "Between the lines" of her letter came back to me. "I mean, you make the sketches in your ordinary way and—the result comes out of itself, so to speak?"

She nodded, throwing her hands out like a Frenchman. "We needn't keep the money for ourselves, Bill. We can give it away, but—I must either accept or leave," and she repeated the shrugging gesture. She sat down on the chair facing me, staring helplessly at the carpet.

"You say there was a scene?" I went on presently. "She insisted?"

"She begged me to continue," my sister replied very quietly. "She thinks—that is, she has an idea or theory that there's something about the place—something she can't get at quite." Frances stammered badly. She knew I did not encourage her wild theories.

"Something she feels, yes," I helped her, more than curious.

"Oh, you know what I mean, Bill," she said desperately. "That the place is saturated with some influence that she is herself too positive or too stupid to interpret. She's trying to make herself negative and receptive, as she calls it, but can't, of course, succeed. Haven't you noticed how dull and impersonal and insipid she seems, as though she had no personality? She thinks impressions will come to her that way. But they don't—"

"Naturally."

"So she's trying me—us—what she calls the sensitive and impressionable artistic temperament. She says that until she is sure exactly what this influence is, she can't fight it, turn it out, 'get the house straight,' as she phrases it."

Remembering my own singular impressions, I felt more lenient than I might otherwise have done. I tried to keep impatience out of my voice.

"And this influence, what—whose is it?"

We used the pronoun that followed in the same breath, for I answered my own question at the same moment as she did:

"*His.*" Our heads nodded involuntarily towards the floor, the dining-room being directly underneath. And my heart sank, my curiosity died away on the instant, I felt bored. A commonplace haunted house was the last thing in the world to amuse or interest me. The mere thought exasperated, with its suggestions of imagination, overwrought nerves, hysteria, and the rest. Mingled with my other feelings was certainly disappointment. To see a figure or feel a "presence," and report from day to day strange incidents to each other would be a form of weariness I could never tolerate.

"But really, Frances," I said firmly, after a moment's pause, "it's too far-fetched, this explanation. A curse, you know, belongs to the ghost stories of early Victorian days." And only my positive conviction that there *was* something after all worth discovering, and that it most certainly was *not* this, prevented my suggesting that we terminate our visit forthwith, or as soon as we decently could. "This is not a haunted house, whatever it is," I concluded somewhat vehemently, bringing my hand down upon her odious portfolio.

My sister's reply revived my curiosity sharply.

"I was waiting for you to say that. Mabel says exactly the same. *He* is in it—but it's something more than that alone, something far bigger and more complicated." Her sentence seemed to indicate the sketches, and though I caught the inference I did not take it up, having no desire to discuss them with her just then, indeed, if ever.

I merely stared at her and listened. Questions, I felt sure, would be of little use. It was better she should say her thought in her own way.

"He is one influence, the most recent," she went on slowly, and always very calmly, "but there are others—deeper layers, as it were—underneath. If his were the only one, something would happen. But nothing ever does happen. The others hinder and prevent—as though each were struggling to predominate."

I had felt it already myself. The idea was rather horrible. I shivered.

"That's what is so ugly about it—that nothing ever happens," she said. "There is this endless anticipation—always on the dry edge of a result that never materializes. It is torture. Mabel is at her wits' ends, you see. And when she begged me—what I felt about my sketches—I mean—" She stammered badly as before.

I stopped her. I had judged too hastily. That queer symbolism in her paintings, pagan and yet not innocent, was, I understood, the result of mixture. I did not pretend to understand, but at least I could be patient. I consequently held my peace. We did talk on a little longer, but it was more general talk that avoided successfully our hostess, the paintings, wild theories, and *him*—

until at length the emotion Frances had hitherto so successfully kept under burst vehemently forth again. It had hidden between her calm sentences, as it had hidden between the lines of her letter. It swept her now from head to foot, packed tight in the thing she then said.

"Then, Bill, if it is not an ordinary haunted house," she asked, *"what is it?"*

The words were commonplace enough. The emotion was in the tone of her voice that trembled; in the gesture she made, leaning forward and clasping both hands upon her knees, and in the slight blanching of her cheeks as her brave eyes asked the question and searched my own with anxiety that bordered upon panic. In that moment she put herself under my protection. I winced.

"And why," she added, lowering her voice to a still and furtive whisper, "does nothing ever happen? If only,"—this with great emphasis—"something *would* happen—break this awful tension—bring relief. It's the waiting I cannot stand." And she shivered all over as she said it, a touch of wildness in her eyes.

I would have given much to have made a true and satisfactory answer. My mind searched frantically for a moment, but in vain. There lay no sufficient answer in me. I felt what she felt, though with differences. No conclusive explanation lay within reach. Nothing happened. Eager as I was to shoot the entire business into the rubbish heap where ignorance and superstition discharge their poisonous weeds, I could not honestly accomplish this. To treat Frances as a child, and merely "explain away" would be to strain her confidence in my protection, so affectionately claimed. It would further be dishonest to myself—weak, besides—to deny that I had also felt the strain and tension even as she did. While my mind continued searching, I returned her stare in silence; and Frances then, with more honesty and insight than my own, gave suddenly the answer herself—an answer whose truth and adequacy, so far as they went, I could not readily gainsay:

"I think, Bill, because it is too big to happen here—to happen anywhere, indeed, all at once—and too awful!"

To have tossed the sentence aside as nonsense, argued it away, proved that it was really meaningless, would have been easy—at any other time or in any other place; and, had the past week brought me none of the vivid impressions it had brought me, this is doubtless what I should have done. My narrowness again was proved. We understand in others only what we have in ourselves. But her explanation, in a measure, I knew was true. It hinted at the strife and struggle that my notion of a Shadow had seemed to cover thinly.

"Perhaps," I murmured lamely, waiting in vain for her to say more. "But you said just now that you felt the thing was 'in layers,' as it were. Do you mean each one—each influence—fighting for the upper hand?"

I used her phraseology to conceal my own poverty. Terminology, after all, was nothing, provided we could reach the idea itself.

Her eyes said yes. She had her clear conception, arrived at independently, as was her way. And, unlike her sex, she kept it clear, unsmothered by too many words.

"One set of influences gets at me, another gets at you. It's according to our temperaments, I think." She glanced significantly at the vile portfolio. "Sometimes they are mixed—and therefore false. There has always been in me, more than in you, the pagan thing, perhaps, though never, thank God, like *that*."

The frank confession of course invited my own, as it was meant to do. Yet it was difficult to find the words.

"What I have felt in this place, Frances, I honestly can hardly tell you, because—er—my impressions have not arranged themselves in any definite form I can describe. The strife, the agony of vainly-sought escape, and the unrest—a sort of prison atmosphere—this I have felt at different times and with varying degrees of strength. But I find, as yet, no final label to attach. I couldn't say pagan, Christian, or anything like that, I mean, as you do. As with the blind and deaf, you may have an intensification of certain senses denied to me, or even another sense altogether in embryo—"

"Perhaps," she stopped me, anxious to keep to the point, "you feel it as Mabel does. She feels the whole thing *complete*."

"That also is possible," I said very slowly. I was thinking behind my words. Her odd remark that it was "big and awful" came back upon me as true. A vast sensation of distress and discomfort swept me suddenly. Pity was in it, and a fierce contempt, a savage, bitter anger as well. Fury against some sham authority was part of it.

"Frances," I said, caught unawares, and dropping all pretence, "what in the world can it be?" I looked hard at her. For some minutes neither of us spoke.

"Have *you* felt no desire to interpret it?" she asked presently.

"Mabel did suggest my writing something about the house," was my reply, "but I've felt nothing imperative. That sort of writing is not my line, you know. My own feeling," I added, noticing that she waited for more, "is the impulse to explain, discover, get it out of me somehow, and so get rid of it. Not by writing, though—as yet." And again I repeated my former question: "What in the world do you think it is?" My voice had become involuntarily hushed. There was awe in it.

Her answer, given with slow emphasis, brought back all my reserve: the phraseology provoked me rather:—

"Whatever it is, Bill, it is not of God."

I got up to go downstairs. I believe I shrugged my shoulders. "Would you like to leave, Frances? Shall we go back to town?" I suggested this at the door, and hearing no immediate reply, I turned back to look. Frances was sitting with her head bowed over and buried in her hands. The attitude horribly suggested tears. No woman, I realised, can keep back the pressure of strong emotion as long as Frances had done, without ending in a fluid collapse. I waited a moment uneasily, longing to comfort, yet afraid to act—and in this way discovered the existence of the appalling emotion in myself, hitherto but half guessed. At all costs a scene must be prevented: it would involve such exaggeration and overstatement. Brutally, such is the weakness of the ordinary man, I turned the handle to go out, but my sister then raised her head. The sunlight caught her face, framed untidily in its auburn hair, and I saw her wonderful expression with a start. Pity, tenderness and sympathy shone in it like a flame. It was undeniable. There shone through all her features the imperishable love and yearning to sacrifice self for others which I have seen in only one type of human being. It was the great mother look.

"We must stay by Mabel and help her get it straight," she whispered, making the decision for us both.

I murmured agreement. Abashed and half ashamed, I stole softly from the room and went out into the grounds. And the first thing clearly realised when alone was this: that the long scene between us was without definite result. The exchange of confidence was really nothing but hints and vague suggestion. We had decided to stay, but it was a negative decision not to leave rather than a positive action. All our words and questions, our guesses, inferences, explanations, our most subtle allusions and insinuations, even the odious paintings themselves, were without definite result. Nothing had happened.

## VI

And instinctively, once alone, I made for the places where she had painted her extraordinary pictures; I tried to see what she had seen. Perhaps, now that she had opened my mind to another view, I should be sensitive to some similar interpretation—and possibly by way of literary expression. If I were to write about the place, I asked myself, how should I treat it? I deliberately invited an interpretation in the way that came easiest to me—writing.

But in this case there came no such revelation. Looking closely at the trees and flowers, the bits of lawn and terrace, the rose-garden and corner of the house where the flaming creeper hung so thickly, I discovered nothing of the odious, unpure thing her colour and grouping had unconsciously revealed. At first, that is, I discovered nothing. The reality stood there, commonplace and ugly, side by side with her distorted version of it that lay in my mind. It seemed incredible. I tried to force it, but in vain. My imagination, ploughed less deeply than hers, or to another pattern, grew different seed. Where I saw the gross soul of an overgrown suburban garden, inspired by the spirit of a vulgar, rich revivalist who loved to preach damnation, she saw this rush of pagan liberty and joy, this strange licence of primitive flesh which, tainted by the other, produced the adulterated, vile result.

Certain things, however, gradually then became apparent, forcing themselves upon me, willy nilly. They came slowly, but overwhelmingly. Not that facts had changed, or natural details altered in the grounds—this was impossible—but that I noticed for the first time various aspects I had not noticed before—trivial enough, yet for me, just then, significant. Some I remembered from previous days; others I saw now as I wandered to and fro, uneasy, uncomfortable,—almost, it seemed, watched by some one who took note of my impressions. The details were so foolish, the total result so formidable. I was half aware that others tried hard to make me see. It was deliberate. My sister's phrase, "one layer got at me, another gets at you," flashed, undesired, upon me.

For I saw, as with the eyes of a child, what I can only call a goblin garden—house, grounds, trees, and flowers belonged to a goblin world that children enter through the pages of their fairy tales. And what made me first aware of it was the whisper of the wind behind me, so that I turned with a sudden start, feeling that something had moved closer. An old ash tree, ugly and ungainly, had been artificially trained to form an arbour at one end of the terrace that was a tennis lawn, and the leaves of it now went rustling together, swishing as they rose and fell. I looked at the ash tree, and felt as though I had passed that moment between doors into this goblin garden that crouched behind the real one. Below, at a deeper layer perhaps, lay hidden the one my sister had entered.

To deal with my own, however, I call it goblin, because an odd aspect of the quaint in it yet never quite achieved the picturesque. Grotesque, probably, is the truer word, for everywhere I noticed, and for the first time, this slight alteration of the natural due either to the exaggeration of some detail, or to its suppression, generally, I think, to the latter. Life everywhere appeared to me as blocked from the full delivery of its sweet and lovely message. Some counter influence stopped it—suppression; or sent it awry—exaggeration. The house itself, mere expression, of course, of a narrow, limited mind, was 'sheer ugliness; it required no further explanation. With the grounds and garden, so far as shape and general plan were concerned, this was also true; but that trees and flowers and other natural details should share the same deficiency perplexed my logical soul, and even dismayed it. I stood and stared, then moved about, and stood and stared again. Everywhere was this mockery of a sinister, unfinished aspect. I sought in vain to recover my normal point of view. My mind had found this goblin garden and wandered to and fro in it, unable to escape.

The change was in myself, of course, and so trivial were the details which illustrated it, that they sound absurd, thus mentioned one by one. For me, they proved it, is all I can affirm. The goblin touch lay plainly everywhere: in the forms of the trees, planted at neat intervals along the lawns; in this twisted ash that rustled just behind me; in the shadow of the gloomy Wellingtonias, whose sweeping skirts obscured the grass; but especially, I noticed, in the tops and crests of them. For here, the delicate, graceful curves of last year's growth seemed to shrink back into themselves. None of them pointed upwards. Their life had failed and turned aside just when it should have become triumphant. The character of a tree reveals itself chiefly at the extremities, and it was precisely here that they all drooped and achieved this hint of goblin distortion—in the growth, that is, of the last few years. What ought to have been fairy, joyful, natural, was instead uncomely to the verge of the grotesque. Spontaneous expression was arrested. My mind perceived a goblin garden, and was caught in it. The place grimaced at me.

With the flowers it was similar, though far more difficult to detect in detail for description. I saw the smaller vegetable growth as impish, half-malicious. Even the terraces sloped ill, as though their ends had sagged since they had been so lavishly constructed; their varying angles gave a queerly bewildering aspect to their sequence that was unpleasant to the eye. One might wander among their deceptive lengths and get lost—lost among open terraces!—with the house quite close at hand. Unhomely seemed the entire garden, unable to give repose, restlessness in it everywhere, almost strife, and discord certainly.

Moreover, the garden grew into the house, the house into the garden, and in both was this idea of resistance to the natural—the spirit that says No to joy. All over it I was aware of the effort to achieve another end, the struggle to burst forth and escape into free, spontaneous expression that should be happy and natural, yet the effort for ever frustrated by the weight of this dark shadow that rendered it abortive. Life crawled aside into a channel that was a cul-de-sac, then turned horribly upon itself. Instead of blossom and fruit, there were weeds. This approach of life I was conscious of—then dismal failure. There was no fulfilment. Nothing happened.

And so, through this singular mood, I came a little nearer to understand the unpure thing that had stammered out into expression through my sister's talent. For the unpure is merely negative; it has no existence; it is but the cramped expression of what is true, stammering its way brokenly over false boundaries that seek to limit and confine. Great, full expression of anything is pure, whereas here was only the incomplete, unfinished, and therefore ugly. There was strife and pain and desire to escape. I found myself shrinking from house and grounds as one shrinks from the touch of the mentally arrested, those in whom life has turned awry. There was almost mutilation in it.

Past items, too, now flocked to confirm this feeling that I walked, liberty captured and half-maimed, in a monstrous garden. I remembered days of rain that refreshed the countryside, but left these grounds, cracked with the summer heat, unsatisfied and thirsty; and how the big winds, that cleaned the woods and fields elsewhere, crawled here with difficulty through the dense foliage that protected The Towers from the North and West and East. They were ineffective, sluggish currents. There was no real wind. Nothing happened. I began to realize—far more clearly than in my sister's fanciful explanation about "layers"—that here were many contrary influences at work, mutually destructive of one another. House and grounds were not haunted merely; they were the arena of past thinking and feeling, perhaps of terrible, impure beliefs, each striving to suppress the others, yet no one of them achieving supremacy because no one of them was strong enough, no one of them was true. Each, moreover, tried to win me over, though only one was able to reach my mind at all. For some obscure reason—possibly because my temperament had a natural bias towards the grotesque—it was the goblin layer. With me, it was the line of least resistance...

In my own thoughts this "goblin garden" revealed, of course, merely my personal interpretation. I felt now objectively what long ago my mind had felt subjectively. My work, essential sign of spontaneous life with me, had stopped dead; production had become impossible. I stood now considerably closer to the cause of this sterility. The Cause, rather, turned bolder, had stepped insolently nearer. Nothing happened anywhere; house, garden, mind alike were barren, abortive, torn by the strife of frustrate impulse, ugly, hateful, sinful. Yet behind it all was still the desire of life—desire to escape— accomplish. Hope—an intolerable hope—I became startlingly aware— crowned torture.

And, realising this, though in some part of me where Reason lost her hold, there rose upon me then another and a darker thing that caught me by the throat and made me shrink with a sense of revulsion that touched actual loathing. I knew instantly whence it came, this wave of abhorrence and disgust, for even while I saw red and felt revolt rise in me, it seemed that I grew partially aware of the layer next below the goblin. I perceived the existence of this deeper stratum. One opened the way for the other, as it were. There were so many, yet all inter-related; to admit one was to clear the way for all. If I lingered I should be caught—horribly. They struggled with such violence for supremacy among themselves, however, that this latest uprising was instantly smothered and crushed back, though not before a glimpse had been revealed to me, and the redness in my thoughts transferred itself to colour my surroundings thickly and appallingly—with blood. This lurid aspect drenched the garden, smeared the terraces, lent to the very soil a tinge as of sacrificial rites, that choked the breath in me, while it seemed to fix me to the earth my feet so longed to leave. It was so revolting that at the same time I felt a dreadful curiosity as of fascination—I wished to stay. Between these contrary impulses I think I actually reeled a moment, transfixed by a fascination of the Awful. Through the lighter goblin veil I felt myself sinking down, down, down into this turgid layer that was so much more violent and so much more ancient. The upper layer, indeed, seemed fairy by comparison with this terror born of the lust for blood, thick with the anguish of human sacrificial victims.

*Upper!* Then I was already sinking; my feet were caught; I was actually in it! What atavistic strain, hidden deep within me, had been touched into vile response, giving this flash of intuitive comprehension, I cannot say. The coatings laid on by civilisation are probably thin enough in all of us. I made a supreme effort. The sun and wind came back. I could almost swear I opened my eyes. Something very atrocious surged back into the depths, carrying with it a thought of tangled woods, of big stones standing in a circle, motionless white figures, the one form bound with ropes, and the ghastly gleam of the knife. Like smoke upon a battlefield, it rolled away...

I was standing on the gravel path below the second terrace when the familiar goblin garden danced back again, doubly grotesque now, doubly mocking, yet, by way of contrast, almost welcome. My glimpse into the depths was momentary, it seems, and had passed utterly away. The common world rushed back with a sense of glad relief, yet ominous now for ever, I felt, for the knowledge of what its past had built upon. In street, in theatre, in the festivities of friends, in music-room or playing-field, even indeed in church—how could the memory of what I had seen and felt not leave its hideous trace? The very structure of my Thought, it seemed to me, was stained. What has been thought by others can never be obliterated until...

With a start my reverie broke and fled, scattered by a violent sound that I recognised for the first time in my life as wholly desirable. The returning motor meant that my hostess was back. Yet, so urgent had been my temporary obsession, that my first presentation of her was—well, not as I knew her now. Floating along with a face of anguished torture I saw Mabel, a mere effigy captured by others' thinking, pass down into those depths of fire and blood that only just had closed beneath my feet. She dipped away. She vanished, her fading eyes turned to the last towards some saviour who had failed her. And that strange intolerable hope was in her face.

The mystery of the place was pretty thick about me just then. It was the fall of dusk, and the ghost of slanting sunshine was as unreal as though badly painted. The garden stood at attention all about me. I cannot explain it, but I can tell it, I think, exactly as it happened, for it remains vivid in me for ever—that, for the first time, something *almost happened*, myself apparently the combining link through which it pressed towards delivery:

I had already turned towards the house. In my mind were pictures—not actual thoughts—of the motor, tea on the verandah, my sister, Mabel—when there came behind me this tumultuous, awful rush—as I left the garden. The ugliness, the pain, the striving to escape, the whole negative and suppressed agony that was the Place, focussed that second into a concentrated effort to produce a result. It was a blinding tempest of long frustrate desire that heaved at me, surging appallingly behind me like an anguished mob. I was in the act of crossing the frontier into my normal self again, when it came, catching fearfully at my skirts. I might use an entire dictionary of descriptive adjectives yet come no nearer to it than this—the conception of a huge assemblage determined to escape with me, or to snatch me back among themselves. My legs trembled for an instant, and I caught my breath—then turned and ran as fast as possible up the ugly terraces.

At the same instant, as though the clanging of an iron gate cut short the unfinished phrase, I *thought* the beginning of an awful thing:

"The Damned..."

Like this it rushed after me from that goblin garden that had sought to keep me:

"The Damned!"

For there was sound in it. I know full well it was subjective, not actually heard at all; yet somehow sound was in it—a great volume, roaring and booming thunderously, far away, and below me. The sentence dipped back into the depths that gave it birth, unfinished. Its completion was prevented. As usual, nothing happened. But it drove behind me like a hurricane as I ran towards the house, and the sound of it I can only liken to those terrible undertones you may hear standing beside Niagara. They lie behind the mere crash of the falling flood, within it somehow, not audible to all—felt rather than definitely heard.

It seemed to echo back from the surface of those sagging terraces as I flew across their sloping ends, for it was somehow underneath them. It was in the rustle of the wind that stirred the skirts of the drooping Wellingtonias. The beds of formal flowers passed it on to the creepers, red as blood, that crept over the unsightly building. Into the structure of the vulgar and forbidding house it sank away; The Towers took it home. The uncomely doors and windows seemed almost like mouths that had uttered the words themselves, and on the upper floors at that very moment I saw two maids in the act of closing them again.

And on the verandah, as I arrived breathless, and shaken in my soul, Frances and Mabel, standing by the tea-table, looked up to greet me. In the faces of both were clearly legible the signs of shock. They watched me coming, yet so full of their own distress that they hardly noticed the state in which I came. In the face of my hostess, however, I read another and a bigger thing than in the face of Frances. Mabel *knew*. She had experienced what I had experienced. She had heard that awful sentence I had heard, but heard it not for the first time; heard it, moreover, I verily believe, complete and to its dreadful end.

"Bill, did you hear that curious noise just now?" Frances asked it sharply before I could say a word. Her manner was confused; she looked straight at me; and there was a tremor in her voice she could not hide.

"There's wind about," I said, "wind in the trees and sweeping round the walls. It's risen rather suddenly." My voice faltered rather.

"No. It wasn't wind," she insisted, with a significance meant for me alone, but badly hidden. "It was more like distant thunder, we thought. How you ran too!" she added. "What a pace you came across the terraces!"

I knew instantly from the way she said it that they both had already heard the sound before and were anxious to know if I had heard it, and how. My interpretation was what they sought.

"It was a curiously deep sound, I admit. It may have been big guns at sea," I suggested, "forts or cruisers practising. The coast isn't so very far, and with the wind in the right direction—"

The expression on Mabel's face stopped me dead.

"Like huge doors closing," she said softly in her colourless voice, "enormous metal doors shutting against a mass of people clamouring to get out." The gravity, the note of hopelessness in her tones, was shocking.

Frances had gone into the house the instant Mabel began to speak. "I'm cold," she had said; "I think I'll get a shawl." Mabel and I were alone. I believe it was the first time we had been really alone since I arrived. She looked up from the teacups, fixing her pallid eyes on mine. She had made a question of the sentence.

"You hear it like that?" I asked innocently. I purposely used the present tense.

She changed her stare from one eye to the other; it was absolutely expressionless. My sister's step sounded on the floor of the room behind us.

"If only—" Mabel began, then stopped, and my own feelings leaping out instinctively completed the sentence I felt was in her mind:

"—something would happen."

She instantly corrected me. I had caught her thought, yet somehow phrased it wrongly.

"We could escape!" She lowered her tone a little, saying it hurriedly. The "we" amazed and horrified me; but something in her voice and manner struck me utterly dumb. There was ice and terror in it. It was a dying woman speaking—a lost and hopeless soul.

In that atrocious moment I hardly noticed what was said exactly, but I remember that my sister returned with a grey shawl about her shoulders, and that Mabel said, in her ordinary voice again, "It is chilly, yes; let's have tea inside," and that two maids, one of them the grenadier, speedily carried the loaded trays into the morning-room and put a match to the logs in the great open fireplace. It was, after all, foolish to risk the sharp evening air, for dusk was falling steadily, and even the sunshine of the day just fading could not turn autumn into summer. I was the last to come in. Just as I left the verandah a large black bird swooped down in front of me past the pillars; it dropped from overhead, swerved abruptly to one side as it caught sight of me, and flapped heavily towards the shrubberies on the left of the terraces, where it disappeared into the gloom. It flew very low, very close. And it startled me, I think because in some way it seemed like my Shadow materialized—as though the dark horror that was rising everywhere from house and garden, then settling back so thickly yet so imperceptibly upon us all, were incarnated in that whirring creature that passed between the daylight and the coming night.

I stood a moment, wondering if it would appear again, before I followed the others indoors, and as I was in the act of closing the windows after me, I caught a glimpse of a figure on the lawn. It was some distance away, on the other side of the shrubberies, in fact where the bird had vanished. But, in spite of the twilight that half magnified, half obscured it, the identity was unmistakable. I knew the housekeeper's stiff walk too well to be deceived. "Mrs. Marsh taking the air," I said to myself. I felt the necessity of saying it, and I wondered why she was doing so at this particular hour. If I had other thoughts they were so vague, and so quickly and utterly suppressed, that I cannot recall them sufficiently to relate them here.

And, once indoors, it was to be expected that there would come explanation, discussion, conversation, at any rate, regarding the singular noise and its cause, some uttered evidence of the mood that had been strong enough to drive us all inside. Yet there was none. Each of us purposely, and with various skill, ignored it. We talked little, and when we did it was of anything in the world but that. Personally, I experienced a touch of that same bewilderment which had come over me during my first talk with Frances on the evening of my arrival, for I recall now the acute tension, and the hope, yet dread, that one or other of us must sooner or later introduce the subject. It did not happen, however; no reference was made to it even remotely. It was the presence of Mabel, I felt positive, that prohibited. As soon might we have discussed Death in the bedroom of a dying woman.

The only scrap of conversation I remember, where all was ordinary and commonplace, was when Mabel spoke casually to the grenadier asking why Mrs. Marsh had omitted to do something or other—what it was I forget—and that the maid replied respectfully that "Mrs. Marsh was very sorry, but her 'and still pained her." I enquired, though so casually that I scarcely know what prompted the words, whether she had injured herself severely, and the reply, "She upset a lamp and burnt herself," was said in a tone that made me feel my curiosity was indiscreet, "but she always has an excuse for not doing things she ought to do." The little bit of conversation remained with me, and I remember particularly the quick way Frances interrupted and turned the talk upon the delinquencies of servants in general, telling incidents of her own at our flat with a volubility that perhaps seemed forced, and that certainly did not encourage general talk as it may have been intended to do. We lapsed into silence immediately she finished.

But for all our care and all our calculated silence, each knew that something had, in these last moments, come very close; it had brushed us in passing; it had retired; and I am inclined to think now that the large dark thing I saw, riding the dusk, probably bird of prey, was in some sense a symbol of it in my mind—that actually there had been no bird at all, I mean, but that my mood of apprehension and dismay had formed the vivid picture in my thoughts. It had swept past us, it had retreated, but it was now, at this moment, in hiding very close. And it was watching us.

Perhaps, too, it was mere coincidence that I encountered Mrs. Marsh, his housekeeper, several times that evening in the short interval between tea and dinner, and that on each occasion the sight of this gaunt, half-saturnine woman fed my prejudice against her. Once, on my way to the telephone, I ran into her just where the passage is somewhat jammed by a square table carrying the Chinese gong, a grandfather's clock and a box of croquet mallets. We both gave way, then both advanced, then again gave way—simultaneously. It seemed impossible to pass. We stepped with decision to the same side, finally colliding in the middle, while saying those futile little things, half apology, half excuse, that are inevitable at such times. In the end she stood upright against the wall for me to pass, taking her place against the very door I wished to open. It was ludicrous.

"Excuse me—I was just going in—to telephone," I explained. And she sidled off, murmuring apologies, but opening the door for me while she did so. Our hands met a moment on the handle. There was a second's awkwardness—it was so stupid. I remembered her injury, and by way of something to say, I enquired after it. She thanked me; it was entirely healed now, but it might have been much worse; and there was something about the "mercy of the Lord" that I didn't quite catch. While telephoning, however—a London call, and my attention focussed on it—I realised sharply that this was the first time I had spoken with her; also, that I had—touched her.

It happened to be a Sunday, and the lines were clear. I got my connection quickly, and the incident was forgotten while my thoughts went up to London. On my way upstairs, then, the woman came back into my mind, so that I recalled other things about her—how she seemed all over the house, in unlikely places often; how I had caught her sitting in the hall alone that night; how she was for ever coming and going with her lugubrious visage and that untidy hair at the back that had made me laugh three years ago with the idea that it looked singed or burnt; and how the impression on my first arrival at The Towers was that this woman somehow kept alive, though its evidence was outwardly suppressed, the influence of her late employer and of his sombre teachings. Somewhere with her was associated the idea of punishment, vindictiveness, revenge. I remembered again suddenly my odd notion that she sought to keep her present mistress here, a prisoner in this bleak and comfortless house, and that really, in spite of her obsequious silence, she was intensely opposed to the change of thought that had reclaimed Mabel to a happier view of life.

All this in a passing second flashed in review before me, and I discovered, or at any rate reconstructed, the real Mrs. Marsh. She was decidedly in the Shadow. More, she stood in the forefront of it, stealthily leading an assault, as it were, against The Towers and its occupants, as though, consciously or unconsciously, she laboured incessantly to this hateful end.

I can only judge that some state of nervousness in me permitted the series of insignificant thoughts to assume this dramatic shape, and that what had gone before prepared the way and led her up at the head of so formidable a procession. I relate it exactly as it came to me. My nerves were doubtless somewhat on edge by now. Otherwise I should hardly have been a prey to the exaggeration at all. I seemed open to so many strange impressions.

Nothing else, perhaps, can explain my ridiculous conversation with her, when, for the third time that evening, I came suddenly upon the woman halfway down the stairs, standing by an open window as if in the act of listening. She was dressed in black, a black shawl over her square shoulders and black gloves on her big, broad hands. Two black objects, prayer-books apparently, she clasped, and on her head she wore a bonnet with shaking beads of jet. At first I did not know her, as I came running down upon her from the landing; it was only when she stood aside to let me pass that I saw her profile against the tapestry and recognised Mrs. Marsh. And to catch her on the front stairs, dressed like this, struck me as incongruous—impertinent. I paused in my dangerous descent. Through the opened window came the sound of bells—church bells—a sound more depressing to me than superstition, and as nauseating. Though the action was ill-judged, I obeyed the sudden prompting—was it a secret desire to attack, perhaps?—and spoke to her.

"Been to church, I suppose, Mrs. Marsh?" I said. "Or just going, perhaps?"

Her face, as she looked up a second to reply, was like an iron doll that moved its lips and turned its eyes, but made no other imitation of life at all.

"Some of us still goes, sir," she said unctuously. It was respectful enough, yet the implied judgment of the rest of the world made me almost angry. A deferential insolence lay behind the affected meekness.

"For those who believe no doubt it *is* helpful," I smiled. "True religion brings peace and happiness, I'm sure—joy, Mrs. Marsh, JOY!" I found keen satisfaction in the emphasis.

She looked at me like a knife. I cannot describe the implacable thing that shone in her fixed, stern eyes, nor the shadow of felt darkness that stole across her face. She glittered. I felt hate in her. I knew—she knew too—who was in the thoughts of us both at that moment.

She replied softly, never forgetting her place for an instant:

"There is joy, sir—in 'eaven—over one sinner that repenteth, and in church there goes up prayer to Gawd for those 'oo—well, for the others, sir, 'oo—"

She cut short her sentence thus. The gloom about her as she said it was like the gloom about a hearse, a tomb, a darkness of great hopeless dungeons. My tongue ran on of itself with a kind of bitter satisfaction:

"We must believe there are no others, Mrs. Marsh. Salvation, you know, would be such a failure if there were. No merciful, all-foreseeing God could ever have devised such a fearful plan—"

Her voice, interrupting me, seemed to rise out of the bowels of the earth:

"They rejected the salvation when it was hoffered to them, sir, on earth."

"But you wouldn't have them tortured for ever because of one mistake in ignorance," I said, fixing her with my eye. "Come now, would you, Mrs. Marsh? No God worth worshipping could permit such cruelty. Think a moment what it means."

She stared at me, a curious expression in her stupid eyes. It seemed to me as though the "woman" in her revolted, while yet she dared not suffer her grim belief to trip. That is, she would willingly have had it otherwise but for a terror that prevented.

"We may pray for them, sir, and we do—we *may* 'ope." She dropped her eyes to the carpet.

"Good, good!" I put in cheerfully, sorry now that I had spoken at all. "That's more hopeful, at any rate, isn't it?"

She murmured something about Abraham's bosom, and the "time of salvation not being for ever," as I tried to pass her. Then a half gesture that she made stopped me. There was something more she wished to say—to ask. She looked up furtively. In her eyes I saw the "woman" peering out through fear.

"Per'aps, sir," she faltered, as though lightning must strike her dead, "per'aps, would you think, a drop of cold water, given in His name, might moisten—?"

But I stopped her, for the foolish talk had lasted long enough.

"Of course," I exclaimed, "of course. For God is love, remember, and love means charity, tolerance, sympathy, and sparing others pain," and I hurried past her, determined to end the outrageous conversation for which yet I knew myself entirely to blame. Behind me, she stood stock-still for several minutes, half bewildered, half alarmed, as I suspected. I caught the fragment of another sentence, one word of it, rather—"punishment"—but the rest escaped me. Her arrogance and condescending tolerance exasperated me, while I was at the same time secretly pleased that I might have touched some string of remorse or sympathy in her after all. Her belief was iron; she dared not let it go; yet somewhere underneath there lurked the germ of a wholesome revulsion. She would help "them"—if she dared. Her question proved it.

Half-ashamed of myself, I turned and crossed the hall quickly lest I should be tempted to say more, and in me was a disagreeable sensation as though I had just left the Incurable Ward of some great hospital. A reaction caught me as of nausea. Ugh! I wanted such people cleansed by fire. They seemed to me as centres of contamination whose vicious thoughts flowed out to stain God's glorious world. I saw myself, Frances, Mabel too especially, on the rack, while that odious figure of cruelty and darkness stood over us and ordered the awful handles turned in order that we might be "saved"—forced, that is, to think and believe exactly as *she* thought and believed.

I found relief for my somewhat childish indignation by letting myself loose upon the organ then. The flood of Bach and Beethoven brought back the sense of proportion. It proved, however, at the same time that there *had* been this growth of distortion in me, and that it had been provided apparently by my closer contact—for the first time—with that funereal personality, the woman who, like her master, believed that all holding views of God that differed from her own, must be damned eternally. It gave me, moreover, some faint clue perhaps, though a clue I was unequal to following up, to the nature of the strife and terror and frustrate influence in the house. That housekeeper had to do with it. She kept it alive. Her thought was like a spell she waved above her mistress's head.

## VII

That night I was wakened by a hurried tapping at my door, and before I could answer, Frances stood beside my bed. She had switched on the light as she came in. Her hair fell straggling over her dressing-gown. Her face was deathly pale, its expression so distraught it was almost haggard. The eyes were very wide. She looked almost like another woman.

She was whispering at a great pace: "Bill, Bill, wake up, quick!"

"I *am* awake. What is it?" I whispered too. I was startled.

"Listen!" was all she said. Her eyes stared into vacancy.

There was not a sound in the great house. The wind had dropped, and all was still. Only the tapping seemed to continue endlessly in my brain. The clock on the mantelpiece pointed to half-past two. "I heard nothing, Frances. What is it?" I rubbed my eyes; I had been very deeply asleep.

"Listen!" she repeated very softly, holding up one finger and turning her eyes towards the door she had left ajar. Her usual calmness had deserted her. She was in the grip of some distressing terror.

For a full minute we held our breath and listened. Then her eyes rolled round again and met my own, and her skin went even whiter than before.

"It woke me," she said beneath her breath, and moving a step nearer to my bed. "It was the Noise." Even her whisper trembled.

"The Noise!" The word repeated itself dully of its own accord. I would rather it had been anything in the world but that—earthquake, foreign cannon, collapse of the house above our heads! "The noise, Frances! Are you *sure?*" I was playing really for a little time.

"It was like thunder. At first I thought it was thunder. But a minute later it came again—from underground. It's appalling." She muttered the words, her voice not properly under control.

There was a pause of perhaps a minute, and then we both spoke at once. We said foolish, obvious things that neither of us believed in for a second. The roof had fallen in, there were burglars downstairs, the safes had been blown open. It was to comfort each other as children do that we said these things; also it was to gain further time.

"There's some one in the house, of course," I heard my voice say finally, as I sprang out of bed and hurried into dressing-gown and slippers. "Don't be alarmed. I'll go down and see," and from the drawer I took a pistol it was my habit to carry everywhere with me. I loaded it carefully while Frances stood stock-still beside the bed and watched. I moved towards the open door.

"You stay here, Frances," I whispered, the beating of my heart making the words uneven, "while I go down and make a search. Lock yourself in, girl. Nothing can happen to you. It was downstairs, you said?"

"Underneath," she answered faintly, pointing through the floor.

She moved suddenly between me and the door. "Listen! Hark!" she said, the eyes in her face quite fixed; "it's coming again," and she turned her head to catch the slightest sound. I stood there watching her, and while I watched her, shook. But nothing stirred. From the halls below rose only the whirr and quiet ticking of the numerous clocks. The blind by the open window behind us flapped out a little into the room as the draught caught it.

"I'll come with you, Bill—to the next floor," she broke the silence. "Then I'll stay with Mabel—till you come up again." The blind sank down with a long sigh as she said it.

The question jumped to my lips before I could repress it:

"Mabel is awake. She heard it too?"

I hardly know why horror caught me at her answer. All was so vague and terrible as we stood there playing the great game of this sinister house where nothing ever happened.

"We met in the passage. She was on her way to me."

What shook in me, shook inwardly. Frances, I mean, did not see it. I had the feeling just then that the Noise was upon us, that any second it would boom and roar about our ears. But the deep silence held. I only heard my sister's little whisper coming across the room in answer to my question:

"Then what is Mabel doing now?"

And her reply proved that she was yielding at last beneath the dreadful tension, for she spoke at once, unable longer to keep up the pretence. With a kind of relief, as it were, she said it out, looking helplessly at me like a child:

"She is weeping and gna—"

My expression must have stopped her. I believe I clapped both hands upon her mouth, though when I realised things clearly again, I found they were covering my own ears instead. It was a moment of unutterable horror. The revulsion I felt was actually physical. It would have given me pleasure to fire off all the five chambers of my pistol into the air above my head; the sound—a definite, wholesome sound that explained itself—would have been a positive relief. Other feelings, though, were in me too, all over me, rushing to and fro. It was vain to seek their disentanglement; it was impossible. I confess that I experienced, among them, a touch of paralysing fear—though for a moment only; it passed as sharply as it came, leaving me with a violent flush of blood to the face such as bursts of anger bring, followed abruptly by an icy perspiration over the entire body. Yet I may honestly avow that it was not ordinary personal fear I felt, nor any common dread of physical injury. It was, rather, a vast, impersonal shrinking—a sympathetic shrinking—from the agony and terror that countless others, somewhere, somehow, felt for themselves. The first sensation of a prison overwhelmed me in that instant, of bitter strife and frenzied suffering, and the fiery torture of the yearning to escape that was yet hopelessly uttered... It was of incredible power. It was real. The vain, intolerable hope swept over me.

I mastered myself, though hardly knowing how, and took my sister's hand. It was as cold as ice, as I led her firmly to the door and out into the passage. Apparently she noticed nothing of my so near collapse, for I caught her whisper as we went. "You *are* brave, Bill; splendidly brave."

The upper corridors of the great sleeping house were brightly lit; on her way to me she had turned on every electric switch her hand could reach; and as we passed the final flight of stairs to the floor below, I heard a door shut softly and knew that Mabel had been listening—waiting for us. I led my sister up to it. She knocked, and the door was opened cautiously an inch or so. The room was pitch black. I caught no glimpse of Mabel standing there. Frances turned to me with a hurried whisper, "Billy, you *will* be careful, won't you?" and went in. I just had time to answer that I would not be long, and Frances to reply, "You'll find us here—" when the door closed and cut her sentence short before its end.

But it was not alone the closing door that took the final words. Frances—by the way she disappeared I knew it—had made a swift and violent movement into the darkness that was as though she sprang. She leaped upon that other woman who stood back among the shadows, for, simultaneously with the clipping of the sentence, another sound was also stopped—stifled, smothered, choked back lest I should also hear it. Yet not in time. I heard it—a hard and horrible sound that explained both the leap and the abrupt cessation of the whispered words.

I stood irresolute a moment. It was as though all the bones had been withdrawn from my body, so that I must sink and fall. That sound plucked them out, and plucked out my self-possession with them. I am not sure that it was a sound I had ever heard before, though children, I half remembered, made it sometimes in blind rages when they knew not what they did. In a grown-up person certainly I had never known it. I associated it with animals rather—horribly. In the history of the world, no doubt, it has been common enough, alas, but fortunately to-day there can be but few who know it, or would recognise it even when heard. The bones shot back into my body the same instant, but red-hot and burning; the brief instant of irresolution passed; I was torn between the desire to break down the door and enter, and to run—run for my life from a thing I dared not face.

Out of the horrid tumult, then, I adopted neither course. Without reflection, certainly without analysis of what was best to do for my sister, myself or Mabel, I took up my action where it had been interrupted. I turned from the awful door and moved slowly towards the head of the stairs. But that dreadful little sound came with me. I believe my own teeth chattered. It seemed all over the house—in the empty halls that opened into the long passages towards the music-room, and even in the grounds outside the building. From the lawns and barren garden, from the ugly terraces themselves, it rose into the night, and behind it came a curious driving sound, incomplete, unfinished, as of wailing for deliverance, the wailing of desperate souls in anguish, the dull and dry beseeching of hopeless spirits in prison.

That I could have taken the little sound from the bedroom where I actually heard it, and spread it thus over the entire house and grounds, is evidence, perhaps, of the state my nerves were in. The wailing assuredly was in my mind alone. But the longer I hesitated, the more difficult became my task, and, gathering up my dressing-gown, lest I should trip in the darkness, I passed slowly down the staircase into the hall below. I carried neither candle or matches; every switch in room and corridor was known to me. The covering of darkness was indeed rather comforting than otherwise, for if it prevented seeing, it also prevented being seen. The heavy pistol, knocking against my thigh as I moved, made me feel I was carrying a child's toy, foolishly. I experienced in every nerve that primitive vast dread which is the Thrill of darkness. Merely the child in me was comforted by that pistol.

The night was not entirely black; the iron bars across the glass front door were visible, and, equally, I discerned the big, stiff wooden chairs in the hall, the gaping fireplace, the upright pillars supporting the staircase, the round table in the centre with its books and flower-vases, and the basket that held visitors' cards. There, too, was the stick and umbrella-stand and the shelf with railway guides, directory, and telegraph forms. Clocks ticked everywhere with sounds like quiet footfalls. Light fell here and there in patches from the floor above. I stood a moment in the hall, letting my eyes grow more accustomed to the gloom, while deciding on a plan of search. I made out the ivy trailing outside over one of the big windows... and then the tall clock by the front door made a grating noise deep down inside its body—it was the Presentation clock, large and hideous, given by the congregation of his church—and, dreading the booming strike it seemed to threaten, I made a quick decision. If others beside myself were about in the night, the sound of that striking might cover their approach.

So I tiptoed to the right, where the passage led towards the dining-room. In the other direction were the morning- and drawing-room, both little used, and various other rooms beyond that had been his, generally now kept locked. I thought of my sister, waiting upstairs with that frightened woman for my return. I went quickly, yet stealthily.

And, to my surprise, the door of the dining-room was open. It had been opened. I paused on the threshold, staring about me. I think I fully expected to see a figure blocked in the shadows against the heavy sideboard, or looming on the other side beneath his portrait. But the room was empty; I *felt* it empty. Through the wide bow-windows that gave on to the verandah came an uncertain glimmer that even shone reflected in the polished surface of the dinner-table, and again I perceived the stiff outline of chairs, waiting tenantless all round it, two larger ones with high carved backs at either end. The monkey-trees on the upper terrace, too, were visible outside against the sky, and the solemn crests of the Wellingtonias on the terraces below. The enormous clock on the mantelpiece ticked very slowly, as though its machinery were running down, and I made out the pale round patch that was its face. Resisting my first inclination to turn the lights up—my hand had gone so far as to finger the friendly knob—I crossed the room so carefully that no single board creaked, nor a single chair, as I rested a hand upon its back, moved on the parquet flooring. I turned neither to the right or left, nor did I once look back.

I went towards the long corridor, filled with priceless *objets d'art*, that led through various antechambers into the spacious music-room, and only at the mouth of this corridor did I next halt a moment in uncertainty. For this long corridor, lit faintly by high windows on the left from the verandah, was very narrow, owing to the mass of shelves and fancy tables it contained. It was not that I feared to knock over precious things as I went, but that, because of its ungenerous width, there would be no room to pass another person—if I met one. And the certainty had suddenly come upon me that somewhere in this corridor another person at this actual moment stood. Here, somehow, amid all this dead atmosphere of furniture, and impersonal emptiness, lay the hint of a living human presence; and with such conviction did it come upon me, that my hand instinctively gripped the pistol in my pocket before I could even think. Either some one had passed along this corridor just before me, or some one lay waiting at its further end—withdrawn or flattened into one of the little recesses, to let me pass. It was the person who had opened the door. And the blood ran from my heart as I realised it.

It was not courage that sent me on, but rather a strong impulsion from behind that made it impossible to retreat: the feeling that a throng pressed at my back, drawing nearer and nearer; that I was already half surrounded, swept, dragged, coaxed into a vast prison-house where there was wailing and gnashing of teeth, where their worm dieth not and their fire is not quenched. I can neither explain nor justify the storm of irrational emotion that swept me as I stood in that moment, staring down the length of the silent corridor towards the music-room at the far end, I can only repeat that no personal bravery sent me down it, but that the negative emotion of fear was swamped in this vast sea of pity and commiseration for others that surged upon me.

My senses, at least, were no whit confused; if anything, my brain registered impressions with keener accuracy than usual. I noticed, for instance, that the two swinging doors of baize that cut the corridor into definite lengths, making little rooms of the spaces between them, were both wide open—in the dim light no mean achievement. Also that the fronds of a palm plant, some ten feet in front of me, still stirred gently from the air of some one who had recently gone past them. The long green leaves waved to and fro like hands. Then I went stealthily forward down the narrow space, proud even that I had this command of myself, and so carefully that my feet made no sound upon the Japanese matting on the floor.

It was a journey that seemed timeless. I have no idea how fast or slow I went, but I remember that I deliberately examined articles on each side of me, peering with particular closeness into the recesses of wall and window. I passed the first baize doors, and the passage beyond them widened out to hold shelves of books; there were sofas and small reading-tables against the wall. It narrowed again presently, as I entered the second stretch. The windows here were higher and smaller, and marble statuettes of classical subjects lined the walls, watching me like figures of the dead. Their white and shining faces saw me, yet made no sign. I passed next between the second baize doors. They, too, had been fastened back with hooks against the wall. Thus all doors were open—had been recently opened.

And so, at length, I found myself in the final widening of the corridor which formed an antechamber to the music-room itself. It had been used formerly to hold the overflow of meetings. No door separated it from the great hall beyond, but heavy curtains hung usually to close it off, and these curtains were invariably drawn. They now stood wide. And here—I can merely state the impression that came upon me—I knew myself at last surrounded. The throng that pressed behind me, also surged in front: facing me in the big room, and waiting for my entry, stood a multitude; on either side of me, in the very air above my head, the vast assemblage paused upon my coming. The pause, however, was momentary, for instantly the deep, tumultuous movement was resumed that yet was silent as a cavern underground. I felt the agony that was in it, the passionate striving, the awful struggle to escape. The semi-darkness held beseeching faces that fought to press themselves upon my vision, yearning yet hopeless eyes, lips scorched and dry, mouths that opened to implore but found no craved delivery in actual words, and a fury of misery and hate that made the life in me stop dead, frozen by the horror of vain pity. That intolerable, vain Hope was everywhere.

And the multitude, it came to me, was not a single multitude, but many; for, as soon as one huge division pressed too close upon the edge of escape, it was dragged back by another and prevented. The wild host was divided against itself. Here dwelt the Shadow I had "imagined" weeks ago, and in it struggled armies of lost souls as in the depths of some bottomless pit whence there is no escape. The layers mingled, fighting against themselves in endless torture. It was in this great Shadow I had clairvoyantly seen Mabel, but about its fearful mouth, I now was certain, hovered another figure of darkness, a figure who sought to keep it in existence, since to her thought were due those lampless depths of woe without escape... Towards me the multitudes now surged.

It was a sound and a movement that brought me back into myself. The great clock at the further end of the room just then struck the hour of three. That was the sound. And the movement—? I was aware that a figure was passing across the distant centre of the floor. Instantly I dropped back into the arena of my little human terror. My hand again clutched stupidly at the pistol butt. I drew back into the folds of the heavy curtain. And the figure advanced.

I remember every detail. At first it seemed to me enormous—this advancing shadow—far beyond human scale; but as it came nearer, I measured it, though not consciously, by the organ pipes that gleamed in faint colours, just above its gradual soft approach. It passed them, already half-way across the great room. I saw then that its stature was that of ordinary men. The prolonged booming of the clock died away. I heard the footfall, shuffling upon the polished boards. I heard another sound—a voice, low and monotonous, droning as in prayer. The figure was speaking. It was a woman. And she carried in both hands before her a small object that faintly shimmered—a glass of water. And then I recognised her.

There was still an instant's time before she reached me, and I made use of it. I shrank back, flattening myself against the wall. Her voice ceased a moment, as she turned and carefully drew the curtains together behind her, closing them with one hand. Oblivious of my presence, though she actually touched my dressing-gown with the hand that pulled the cords, she resumed her dreadful, solemn march, disappearing at length down the long vista of the corridor like a shadow. But as she passed me, her voice began again, so that I heard each word distinctly as she uttered it, her head aloft, her figure upright, as though she moved at the head of a procession:

"A drop of cold water, given in His name, shall moisten their burning tongues."

It was repeated monotonously over and over again, droning down into the distance as she went, until at length both voice and figure faded into the shadows at the further end.

For a time, I have no means of measuring precisely, I stood in that dark corner, pressing my back against the wall, and would have drawn the curtains down to hide me had I dared to stretch an arm out. The dread that presently the woman would return passed gradually away. I realised that the air had emptied, the crowd her presence had stirred into activity had retreated; I was alone in the gloomy under-spaces of the odious building... Then I remembered suddenly again the terrified women waiting for me on that upper landing; and realised that my skin was wet and freezing cold after a profuse perspiration. I prepared to retrace my steps. I remember the effort it cost me to leave the support of the wall and covering darkness of my corner, and step out into the grey light of the corridor. At first I sidled, then, finding this mode of walking impossible, turned my face boldly and walked quickly, regardless that my dressing-gown set the precious objects shaking as I passed. A wind that sighed mournfully against the high, small windows seemed to have got inside the corridor as well; it felt so cold; and every moment I dreaded to see the outline of the woman's figure as she waited in recess or angle against the wall for me to pass.

Was there another thing I dreaded even more? I cannot say. I only know that the first baize doors had swung-to behind me, and the second ones were close at hand, when the great dim thunder caught me, pouring up with prodigious volume so that it seemed to roll out from another world. It shook the very bowels of the building. I was closer to it than that other time, when it had followed me from the goblin garden. There was strength and hardness in it, as of metal reverberation. Some touch of numbness, almost of paralysis, must surely have been upon me that I felt no actual terror, for I remember even turning and standing still to hear it better.

"That is the Noise," my thought ran stupidly, and I think I whispered it aloud; *"the Doors are closing."* The wind outside against the windows was audible, so it cannot have been really loud, yet to me it was the biggest, deepest sound I have ever heard, but so far away, with such awful remoteness in it, that I had to doubt my own ears at the same time. It seemed underground—the rumbling of earthquake gates that shut remorselessly within the rocky Earth—stupendous, ultimate thunder. *They* were shut off from help again. The doors had closed.

I felt a storm of pity, an agony of bitter, futile hate sweep through me. My memory of the figure changed then. The Woman with the glass of cooling water had stepped down from Heaven; but the Man—or was it Men?—who smeared this terrible layer of belief and Thought upon the world!...

I crossed the dining-room—it was fancy, of course, that held my eyes from glancing at the portrait for fear I should see it smiling approval—and so finally reached the hall, where the light from the floor above seemed now quite bright in comparison. All the doors I closed carefully behind me; but first I had to open them. The woman had closed every one. Up the stairs, then, I actually ran, two steps at a time. My sister was standing outside Mabel's door.

By her face I knew that she had also heard. There was no need to ask. I quickly made my mind up. "There's nothing," I said, and detailed briefly my tour of search. "All is quiet and undisturbed downstairs." May God forgive me!

She beckoned to me, closing the door softly behind her. My heart beat violently a moment, then stood still.

"Mabel," she said aloud.

It was like the sentence of a judge, that one short word.

I tried to push past her and go in, but she stopped me with her arm. She was wholly mistress of herself, I saw.

"Hush!" she said in a lower voice. "I've got her round again with brandy. She's sleeping quietly now. We won't disturb her."

She drew me further out into the landing, and as she did so, the clock in the hall below struck half-past three. I had stood, then, thirty minutes in the corridor below. "You've been such a long time," she said simply. "I feared for you," and she took my hand in her own that was cold and clammy.

## VIII

And then, while that dreadful house stood listening about us in the early hours of this chill morning upon the edge of winter, she told me, with laconic brevity, things about Mabel that I heard as from a distance. There was nothing so unusual or tremendous in the short recital, nothing indeed I might not have already guessed for myself. It was the time and scene, the inference, too, that made it so afflicting: the idea that Mabel believed herself so utterly and hopelessly lost—beyond recovery *damned*.

That she had loved him with so passionate a devotion that she had given her soul into his keeping, this certainly I had not divined—probably because I had never thought about it one way or the other. He had "converted" her, I knew, but that she had subscribed whole-heartedly to that most cruel and ugly of his dogmas—this was new to me, and came with a certain shock as I heard it. In love, of course, the weaker nature is receptive to all manner of suggestion. This man had "suggested" his pet brimstone lake so vividly that she had listened and believed. He had frightened her into heaven; and his heaven, a definite locality in the skies, had its foretaste here on earth in miniature—The Towers, house and garden. Into his dolorous scheme of a handful saved and millions damned, his enclosure, as it were, of sheep and goats, he had swept her before she was aware of it. Her mind no longer was her own. And it was Mrs. Marsh who kept the thought-stream open, though tempered, as she deemed, that touch of craven, superstitious mercy.

But what I found it difficult to understand, and still more difficult to accept, was that, during her year abroad, she had been so haunted with a secret dread of that hideous after-death that she had finally revolted and tried to recover that clearer state of mind she had enjoyed before the religious bully had stunned her—yet had tried in vain. She had returned to The Towers to find her soul again, only to realise that it was lost eternally. The cleaner state of mind lay then beyond recovery. In the reaction that followed the removal of his terrible "suggestion," she felt the crumbling of all that he had taught her, but searched in vain for the peace and beauty his teachings had destroyed. Nothing came to replace these. She was empty, desolate, hopeless; craving her former joy and carelessness, she found only hate and diabolical calculation. This man, whom she had loved to the point of losing her soul for him, had bequeathed to her one black and fiery thing—the terror of the damned. His thinking wrapped her in this iron garment that held her fast.

All this Frances told me, far more briefly than I have here repeated it. In her eyes and gestures and laconic sentences lay the conviction of great beating issues and of menacing drama my own description fails to recapture. It was all so incongruous and remote from the world I lived in that more than once a smile, though a smile of pity, fluttered to my lips; but a glimpse of my face in the mirror showed rather the leer of a grimace. There was no real laughter anywhere that night. The entire adventure seemed so incredible, here, in this twentieth century—but yet delusion, that feeble word, did not occur once in the comments my mind suggested though did not utter. I remembered that forbidding Shadow too; my sister's water-colours; the vanished personality of our hostess; the inexplicable, thundering Noise, and the figure of Mrs. Marsh in her midnight ritual that was so childish yet so horrible. I shivered in spite of my own "emancipated" cast of mind.

"There *is* no Mabel," were the words with which my sister sent another shower of ice down my spine. "He has killed her in his lake of fire and brimstone."

I stared at her blankly, as in a nightmare where nothing true or possible ever happened.

"He killed her in his lake of fire and brimstone," she repeated more faintly.

A desperate effort was in me to say the strong, sensible thing which should destroy the oppressive horror that grew so stiflingly about us both, but again the mirror drew the attempted smile into the merest grin, betraying the distortion that was everywhere in the place.

"You mean," I stammered beneath my breath, "that her faith has gone, but that the terror has remained?" I asked it, dully groping. I moved out of the line of the reflection in the glass.

She bowed her head as though beneath a weight; her skin was the pallor of grey ashes.

"You mean," I said louder, "that she has lost her—mind?"

"She is terror incarnate," was the whispered answer. "Mabel has lost her soul. Her soul is—there!" She pointed horribly below. "She is seeking it...?"

The word "soul" stung me into something of my normal self again.

"But her terror, poor thing, is not—cannot be—transferable to *us*!" I exclaimed more vehemently.

"It certainly is not convertible into feelings, sights and—even sounds!"

She interrupted me quickly, almost impatiently, speaking with that conviction by which she conquered me so easily that night.

"It is her terror that has revived 'the Others.' It has brought her into touch with them. They are loose and driving after her. Her efforts at resistance have given them also hope—that escape, after all, *is* possible. Day and night they strive."

"Escape! Others!" The anger first rising in me dropped of its own accord at the moment of birth. It shrank into a shuddering beyond my control. In that moment, I think, I would have believed in the possibility of anything and everything she might tell me. To argue or contradict seemed equally futile.

"His strong belief, as also the beliefs of others who have preceded him," she replied, so sure of herself that I actually turned to look over my shoulder, "have left their shadow like a thick deposit over the house and grounds. To them, poor souls imprisoned by thought, it was hopeless as granite walls—until her resistance, her effort to dissipate it—let in light. Now, in their thousands, they are flocking to this little light, seeking escape. Her own escape, don't you see, may release them all!"

It took my breath away. Had his predecessors, former occupants of this house, also preached damnation of all the world but their own exclusive sect? Was this the explanation of her obscure talk of "layers," each striving against the other for domination? And if men are spirits, and these spirits survive, could strong Thought thus determine their condition even afterwards?

So many questions flooded into me that I selected no one of them, but stared in uncomfortable silence, bewildered, out of my depth, and acutely, painfully distressed. There was so odd a mixture of possible truth and incredible, unacceptable explanation in it all; so much confirmed, yet so much left darker than before. What she said did, indeed, offer a quasi-interpretation of my own series of abominable sensations—strife, agony, pity, hate, escape—but so far-fetched that only the deep conviction in her voice and attitude made it tolerable for a second even. I found myself in a curious state of mind. I could neither think clearly nor say a word to refute her amazing statements, whispered there beside me in the shivering hours of the early morning with only a wall between ourselves and—Mabel. Close behind her words I remember this singular thing, however—that an atmosphere as of the Inquisition seemed to rise and stir about the room, beating awful wings of black above my head.

Abruptly, then, a moment's common-sense returned to me. I faced her.

"And the Noise?" I said aloud, more firmly, "the roar of the closing doors? We have *all* heard that! Is that subjective too?"

Frances looked sideways about her in a queer fashion that made my flesh creep again. I spoke brusquely, almost angrily. I repeated the question, and waited with anxiety for her reply.

"What noise?" she asked, with the frank expression of an innocent child. "What closing doors?"

But her face turned from grey to white, and I saw that drops of perspiration glistened on her forehead. She caught at the back of a chair to steady herself, then glanced about her again with that sidelong look that made my blood run cold. I understood suddenly then. She did not take in what I said. I knew now. She was listening—for something else.

And the discovery revived in me a far stronger emotion than any mere desire for immediate explanation. Not only did I not insist upon an answer, but I was actually terrified lest she *would* answer. More, I felt in me a terror lest I should be moved to describe my own experiences below-stairs, thus increasing their reality and so the reality of all. She might even explain them too!

Still listening intently, she raised her head and looked me in the eyes. Her lips opened to speak. The words came to me from a great distance, it seemed, and her voice had a sound like a stone that drops into a deep well, its fate though hidden, known.

"We are in it with her, too, Bill. We are in it with her. Our interpretations vary—because we are—in parts of it only. Mabel is in it—*all*."

The desire for violence came over me. If only she would say a definite thing in plain King's English! If only I could find it in me to give utterance to what shouted so loud within me! If only—the same old cry—something would happen! For all this elliptic talk that dazed my mind left obscurity everywhere. Her atrocious meaning, none the less, flashed through me, though vanishing before it wholly divulged itself.

It brought a certain reaction with it. I found my tongue. Whether I actually believed what I said is more than I can swear to; that it seemed to me wise at the moment is all I remember. My mind was in a state of obscure perception less than that of normal consciousness.

"Yes, Frances, I believe that what you say is the truth, and that we are in it with her"—I meant to say it with loud, hostile emphasis, but instead I whispered it lest she should hear the trembling of my voice—"and for that reason, my dear sister, we leave to-morrow, you and I—to-day, rather, since it is long past midnight—we leave this house of the damned. We go back to London."

Frances looked up, her face distraught almost beyond recognition. But it was not my words that caused the tumult in her heart. It was a sound—the sound she had been listening for—so faint I barely caught it myself, and had she not pointed I could never have known the direction whence it came. Small and terrible it rose again in the stillness of the night, the sound of gnashing teeth. And behind it came another—the tread of stealthy footsteps. Both were just outside the door.

The room swung round me for a second. My first instinct to prevent my sister going out—she had dashed past me frantically to the door—gave place to another when I saw the expression in her eyes. I followed her lead instead; it was surer than my own. The pistol in my pocket swung uselessly against my thigh. I was flustered beyond belief and ashamed that I was so.

"Keep close to me, Frances," I said huskily, as the door swung wide and a shaft of light fell upon a figure moving rapidly. Mabel was going down the corridor. Beyond her, in the shadows on the staircase, a second figure stood beckoning, scarcely visible.

"Before they get her! Quick!" was screamed into my ears, and our arms were about her in the same moment. It was a horrible scene. Not that Mabel struggled in the least, but that she collapsed as we caught her and fell with her dead weight, as of a corpse, limp, against us. And her teeth began again.

They continued, even beneath the hand that Frances clapped upon her lips...

We carried her back into her own bedroom, where she lay down peacefully enough. It was so soon over... The rapidity of the whole thing robbed it of reality almost. It had the swiftness of something remembered rather than of something witnessed. She slept again so quickly that it was almost as if we had caught her sleep-walking. I cannot say. I asked no questions at the time; I have asked none since; and my help was needed as little as the protection of my pistol. Frances was strangely competent and collected... I lingered for some time uselessly by the door, till at length, looking up with a sigh, she made a sign for me to go.

"I shall wait in your room next door," I whispered, "till you come." But, though going out, I waited in the corridor instead, so as to hear the faintest call for help. In that dark corridor upstairs I waited, but not long. It may have been fifteen minutes when Frances reappeared, locking the door softly behind her. Leaning over the banisters, I saw her.

"I'll go in again about six o'clock," she whispered, "as soon as it gets light. She is sound asleep now. Please don't wait. If anything happens I'll call—you might leave your door ajar, perhaps." And she came up, looking like a ghost.

But I saw her first safely into bed, and the rest of the night I spent in an armchair close to my opened door, listening for the slightest sound. Soon after five o'clock I heard Frances fumbling with the key, and, peering over the railing again, I waited till she reappeared and went back into her own room. She closed her door. Evidently she was satisfied that all was well.

Then, and then only, did I go to bed myself, but not to sleep. I could not get the scene out of my mind, especially that odious detail of it which I hoped and believed my sister had not seen—the still, dark figure of the housekeeper waiting on the stairs below—waiting, of course, for Mabel.

## IX

It seems I became a mere spectator after that; my sister's lead was so assured for one thing, and for another, the responsibility of leaving Mabel alone—Frances laid it bodily upon my shoulders—was a little more than I cared about. Moreover, when we all three met later in the day, things went on so exactly as before, so absolutely without friction or distress, that to present a sudden, obvious excuse for cutting our visit short seemed ill judged. And on the lowest grounds it would have been desertion. At any rate, it was beyond my powers, and Frances was quite firm that *she* must stay. We therefore did stay. Things that happen in the night always seem exaggerated and distorted when the sun shines brightly next morning; no one can reconstruct the terror of a nightmare afterwards, nor comprehend why it seemed so overwhelming at the time.

I slept till ten o'clock, and when I rang for breakfast, a note from my sister lay upon the tray, its message of counsel couched in a calm and comforting strain. Mabel, she assured me, was herself again and remembered nothing of what had happened; there was no need of any violent measures; I was to treat her exactly as if I knew nothing. "And, if you don't mind, Bill, let us leave the matter unmentioned between ourselves as well. Discussion exaggerates; such things are best not talked about. I'm sorry I disturbed you so unnecessarily; I was stupidly excited. Please forget all the things I said at the moment." She had written "nonsense" first instead of "things," then scratched it out. She wished to convey that hysteria had been abroad in the night, and I readily gulped the explanation down, though it could not satisfy me in the smallest degree.

There was another week of our visit still, and we stayed it out to the end without disaster. My desire to leave at times became that frantic thing, desire to escape; but I controlled it, kept silent, watched and wondered. Nothing happened. As before, and everywhere, there was no sequence of development, no connection between cause and effect; and climax, none whatever. The thing swayed up and down, backwards and forwards like a great loose curtain in the wind, and I could only vaguely surmise what caused the draught or why there was a curtain at all. A novelist might mould the queer material into coherent sequence that would be interesting but could not be true. It remains, therefore, not a story but a history. Nothing happened.

Perhaps my intense dislike of the fall of darkness was due wholly to my stirred imagination, and perhaps my anger when I learned that Frances now occupied a bed in our hostess's room was unreasonable. Nerves were unquestionably on edge. I was for ever on the look-out for some event that should make escape imperative, but yet that never presented itself. I slept lightly, left my door ajar to catch the slightest sound, even made stealthy tours of the house below-stairs while everybody dreamed in their beds. But I discovered nothing; the doors were always locked; I neither saw the housekeeper again in unreasonable times and places, nor heard a footstep in the passages and halls. The Noise was never once repeated. That horrible, ultimate thunder, my intensest dread of all, lay withdrawn into the abyss whence it had twice arisen. And though in my thoughts it was sternly denied existence, the great black reason for the fact afflicted me unbelievably. Since Mabel's fruitless effort to escape, the Doors kept closed remorselessly. She had failed; *they* gave up hope. For this was the explanation that haunted the region of my mind where feelings stir and hint before they clothe themselves in actual language. Only I firmly kept it there; it never knew expression.

But, if my ears were open, my eyes were opened too, and it were idle to pretend that I did not notice a hundred details that were capable of sinister interpretation had I been weak enough to yield. Some protective barrier had fallen into ruins round me, so that Terror stalked behind the general collapse, feeling for me through all the gaping fissures. Much of this, I admit, must have been merely the elaboration of those sensations I had first vaguely felt, before subsequent events and my talks with Frances had dramatised them into living thoughts. I therefore leave them unmentioned in this history, just as my mind left them unmentioned in that interminable final week.

Our life went on precisely as before—Mabel unreal and outwardly so still; Frances, secretive, anxious, tactful to the point of slyness, and keen to save to the point of self-forgetfulness. There were the same stupid meals, the same wearisome long evenings, the stifling ugliness of house and grounds, the Shadow settling in so thickly that it seemed almost a visible, tangible thing. I came to feel the only friendly things in all this hostile, cruel place were the robins that hopped boldly over the monstrous terraces and even up to the windows of the unsightly house itself. The robins alone knew joy; they danced, believing no evil thing was possible in all God's radiant world. They believed in everybody; *their* god's plan of life had no room in it for hell, damnation and lakes of brimstone. I came to love the little birds. Had Samuel Franklyn known them, he might have preached a different sermon, bequeathing love in place of terror!...

Most of my time I spent writing; but it was a pretence at best, and rather a dangerous one besides. For it stirred the mind to production, with the result that other things came pouring in as well. With reading it was the same. In the end I found an aggressive, deliberate resistance to be the only way of feasible defence. To walk far afield was out of the question, for it meant leaving my sister too long alone, so that my exercise was confined to nearer home. My saunters in the grounds, however, never surprised the goblin garden again. It was close at hand, but I seemed unable to get wholly into it. Too many things assailed my mind for any one to hold exclusive possession, perhaps.

Indeed, all the interpretations, all the "layers," to use my sister's phrase, slipped in by turns and lodged there for a time. They came day and night, and though my reason denied them entrance they held their own as by a kind of squatters' right. They stirred moods already in me, that is, and did not introduce entirely new ones; for every mind conceals ancestral deposits that have been cultivated in turn along the whole line of its descent. Any day a chance shower may cause this one or that to blossom. Thus it came to me, at any rate. After darkness the Inquisition paced the empty corridors and set up ghastly apparatus in the dismal halls; and once, in the library, there swept over me that easy and delicious conviction that by confessing my wickedness I could resume it later, since Confession is expression, and expression brings relief and leaves one ready to accumulate again. And in such mood I felt bitter and unforgiving towards all others who thought differently. Another time it was a Pagan thing that assaulted me—so trivial yet oh, so significant at the time—when I dreamed that a herd of centaurs rolled up with a great stamping of hoofs round the house to destroy it, and then woke to hear the horses tramping across the field below the lawns; they neighed ominously and their noisy panting was audible as if it were just outside my windows.

But the tree episode, I think, was the most curious of all—except, perhaps, the incident with the children which I shall mention in a moment—for its closeness to reality was so unforgettable. Outside the east window of my room stood a giant Wellingtonia on the lawn, its head rising level with the upper sash. It grew some twenty feet away, planted on the highest terrace, and

I often saw it when closing my curtains for the night, noticing how it drew its heavy skirts about it, and how the light from other windows threw glimmering streaks and patches that turned it into the semblance of a towering, solemn image. It stood there then so strikingly, somehow like a great old-world idol, that it claimed attention. Its appearance was curiously formidable. Its branches rustled without visibly moving and it had a certain portentous, forbidding air, so grand and dark and monstrous in the night that I was always glad when my curtains shut it out. Yet, once in bed, I had never thought about it one way or the other, and by day had certainly never sought it out.

One night, then, as I went to bed and closed this window against a cutting easterly wind, I saw—that there were two of these trees. A brother Wellingtonia rose mysteriously beside it, equally huge, equally towering, equally monstrous. The menacing pair of them faced me there upon the lawn. But in this new arrival lay a strange suggestion that frightened me before I could argue it away. Exact counterpart of its giant companion, it revealed also that gross, odious quality that all my sister's paintings held. I got the odd impression that the rest of these trees, stretching away dimly in a troop over the further lawns, were similar, and that, led by this enormous pair, they had all moved boldly closer to my windows. At the same moment a blind was drawn down over an upper room; the second tree disappeared into the surrounding darkness. It was, of course, this chance light that had brought it into the field of vision, but when the black shutter dropped over it, hiding it from view, the manner of its vanishing produced the queer effect that it had slipped into its companion—almost that it had been an emanation of the one I so disliked, and not really a tree at all! In this way the garden turned vehicle for expressing what lay behind it all!...

The behaviour of the doors, the little, ordinary doors, seemed scarcely worth mention at all, their queer way of opening and shutting of their own accord; for this was accountable in a hundred natural ways, and to tell the truth, I never caught one in the act of moving. Indeed, only after frequent repetitions, did the detail force itself upon me, when, having noticed one, I noticed all. It produced, however, the unpleasant impression of a continual coming and going in the house, as though, screened cleverly and purposely from actual sight, some one in the building held constant invisible intercourse with others.

Upon detailed descriptions of these uncertain incidents I do not venture, individually so trivial, but taken all together so impressive and so insolent. But the episode of the children, mentioned above, was different. And I give it because it showed how vividly the intuitive child-mind received the impression—one impression, at any rate—of what was in the air. It may be told in a very few words. I believe they were the coachman's children, and that the man had been in Mr. Franklyn's service; but of neither point am I quite positive. I heard screaming in the rose-garden that runs along the stable walls—it was one afternoon not far from the tea-hour—and on hurrying up I found a little girl of nine or ten fastened with ropes to a rustic seat, and two other children—boys, one about twelve and one much younger—

gathering sticks beneath the climbing rose-trees. The girl was white and frightened, but the others were laughing and talking among themselves so busily while they picked that they did not notice my abrupt arrival. Some game, I understood, was in progress, but a game that had become too serious for the happiness of the prisoner, for there was a fear in the girl's eyes that was a very genuine fear indeed. I unfastened her at once; the ropes were so loosely and clumsily knotted that they had not hurt her skin; it was not that which made her pale. She collapsed a moment upon the bench, then picked up her tiny skirts and dived away at full speed into the safety of the stable-yard. There was no response to my brief comforting, but she ran as though for her life, and I divined that some horrid boys' cruelty had been afoot. It was probably mere thoughtlessness, as cruelty with children usually is, but something in me decided to discover exactly what it was.

And the boys, not one whit alarmed at my intervention, merely laughed shyly when I explained that their prisoner had escaped, and told me frankly what their "gime" had been. There was no vestige of shame in them, nor any idea, of course, that they aped a monstrous reality. That it was mere pretence was neither here nor there. To them, though make-believe, it was a make-believe of something that was right and natural and in no sense cruel. Grown-ups did it too. It was necessary for her good.

"We were going to burn her up, sir," the older one informed me, answering my "Why?" with the explanation, "Because she wouldn't believe what we wanted 'er to believe."

And, game though it was, the feeling of reality about the little episode was so arresting, so terrific in some way, that only with difficulty did I confine my admonitions on this occasion to mere words. The boys slunk off, frightened in their turn, yet not, I felt, convinced that they had erred in principle. It was their inheritance. They had breathed it in with the atmosphere of their bringing-up. They would renew the salutary torture when they could—till she "believed" as they did.

I went back into the house, afflicted with a passion of mingled pity and distress impossible to describe, yet on my short way across the garden was attacked by other moods in turn, each more real and bitter than its predecessor. I received the whole series, as it were, at once. I felt like a diver rising to the surface through layers of water at different temperatures, though here the natural order was reversed, and the cooler strata were uppermost, the heated ones below. Thus, I was caught by the goblin touch of the willows that fringed the field; by the sensuous curving of the twisted ash that formed a gateway to the little grove of sapling oaks where fauns and satyrs lurked to play in the moonlight before Pagan altars; and by the cloaking darkness, next, of the copse of stunted pines, close gathered each to each, where hooded figures stalked behind an awful cross. The episode with the children seemed to have opened me like a knife. The whole Place rushed at me.

I suspect this synthesis of many moods produced in me that climax of loathing and disgust which made me feel the limit of bearable emotion had been reached, so that I made straight to find Frances in order to convince her that at any rate I must leave. For, although this was our last day in the house, and we had arranged to go next day, the dread was in me that she would still find some persuasive reason for staying on. And an unexpected incident then made my dread unnecessary. The front door was open and a cab stood in the drive; a tall, elderly man was gravely talking in the hall with the parlour-maid we called the Grenadier. He held a piece of paper in his hand. "I have called to see the house," I heard him say, as I ran up the stairs to Frances, who was peering like an inquisitive child over the banisters...

"Yes," she told me, with a sigh, I know not whether of resignation or relief, "the house is to be let or sold. Mabel has decided. Some Society or other, I believe—"

I was overjoyed: this made our leaving right and possible. "You never told me, Frances!"

"Mabel only heard of it a few days ago. She told me herself this morning. It is a chance, she says. Alone she cannot get it 'straight.'"

"Defeat?" I asked, watching her closely.

"She thinks she has found a way out. It's not a family, you see, it's a Society, a sort of Community—they go in for thought—"

"A Community!" I gasped. "You mean religious?"

She shook her head. "Not exactly," she said, smiling, "but some kind of association of men and women who want a headquarters in the country—a place where they can write and meditate—*think*—mature their plans and all the rest—I don't know exactly what."

"Utopian dreamers?" I asked, yet feeling an immense relief come over me as I heard. But I asked in ignorance, not cynically. Frances would know. She knew all this kind of thing.

"No, not that exactly," she smiled. "Their teachings are grand and simple—old as the world too, really—the basis of every religion before men's mind perverted them with their manufactured creeds—"

Footsteps on the stairs, and the sound of voices, interrupted our odd impromptu conversation, as the Grenadier came up, followed by the tall, grave gentleman who was being shown over the house. My sister drew me along the corridor towards her room, where she went in and closed the door behind me, yet not before I had stolen a good look at the caller—long enough, at least, for his face and general appearance to have made a definite impression on me. For something strong and peaceful emanated from his presence; he moved with such quiet dignity; the glance of his eyes was so steady and reassuring, that my mind labelled him instantly as a type of man one would turn to in an emergency and not be disappointed. I had seen him but for a passing moment, but I had seen him twice, and the way he walked down the passage, looking competently about him, conveyed the same impression as when I saw him standing at the door—fearless, tolerant, wise. "A sincere and kindly character," I judged instantly, "a man whom some big kind of love has trained in sweetness towards the world; no hate in him anywhere." A great deal, no doubt, to read in so brief a glance! Yet his voice confirmed my intuition, a deep and very gentle voice, great firmness in it too.

"Have I become suddenly sensitive to people's atmospheres in this extraordinary fashion?" I asked myself, smiling, as I stood in the room and heard the door close behind me. "Have I developed some clairvoyant faculty here?" At any other time I should have mocked.

And I sat down and faced my sister, feeling strangely comforted and at peace for the first time since I had stepped beneath The Towers' roof a month ago. Frances, I then saw, was smiling a little as she watched me.

"You know him?" I asked.

"You felt it too?" was her question in reply. "No," she added, "I don't know him—beyond the fact that he is a leader in the Movement and has devoted years and money to its objects. Mabel felt the same thing in him that you have felt—and jumped at it."

"But you've seen him before?" I urged, for the certainty was in me that he was no stranger to her. She shook her head. "He called one day early this week, when you were out. Mabel saw him. I believe"—she hesitated a moment, as though expecting me to stop her with my usual impatience of such subjects—"I believe he has explained everything to her—the beliefs he embodies, she declares, are her salvation—might be, rather, if she could adopt them."

"Conversion again?" For I remembered her riches, and how gladly a Society would gobble them. "The layers I told you about," she continued calmly, shrugging her shoulders slightly—"the deposits that are left behind by strong thinking and real belief—but especially by ugly, hateful belief, because, you see—unfortunately there's more vital passion in that sort—"

"Frances, I don't understand a bit," I said out loud, but said it a little humbly, for the impression the man had left was still strong upon me and I was grateful for the steady sense of peace and comfort he had somehow introduced. The horrors had been so dreadful. My nerves, doubtless, were more than a little overstrained. Absurd as it must sound, I classed him in my mind with the robins, the happy, confiding robins, who believed in everybody and thought no evil! I laughed a moment at my ridiculous idea, and my sister, encouraged by this sign of patience in me, continued more fluently:

"Of course you don't understand, Bill. Why should you? You've never thought about such things. Needing no creed yourself, you think all creeds are rubbish."

"I'm open to conviction—I'm tolerant," I interrupted.

"You're as narrow as Sam Franklyn, and as crammed with prejudice," she answered, knowing that she had me at her mercy.

"Then, pray, what may be his, or his Society's beliefs?" I asked, feeling no desire to argue, "and how are they going to prove your Mabel's salvation? Can they bring beauty into all this aggressive hate and ugliness?"

"Certain hope and peace," she said, "that peace which is understanding, and that understanding which explains *all* creeds and therefore tolerates them."

"Toleration! The one word a religious man loathes above all others! His pet word is damnation—"

"Tolerates them," she repeated patiently, unperturbed by my explosion, "because it includes them all."

"Fine, if true," I admitted, "very fine. But how, pray, does it include them all?"

"Because the key-word, the motto, of their Society is, 'There is no religion higher than Truth,' and it has no single dogma of any kind. Above all," she went on, "because it claims that no individual can be 'lost.' It teaches universal salvation. To damn outsiders is uncivilised, childish, impure. Some take longer than others—it's according to the way they think and live—but all find peace, through development, in the end. What the creeds call a hopeless soul, it regards as a soul having further to go. There is no damnation—"

"Well, well," I exclaimed, feeling that she rode her hobby-horse too wildly, too roughly over me, "but what is the bearing of all this upon this dreadful place, and upon Mabel? I'll admit that there is this atmosphere—this—er—inexplicable horror in the house and grounds, and that if not of damnation exactly, it is certainly damnable. I'm not too prejudiced to deny that, for I've felt it myself."

To my relief she was brief. She made her statement, leaving me to take it or reject it as I would. "The thought and belief its former occupants—have left behind. For there has been coincidence here, a coincidence that must be rare. The site on which this modern house now stands was Roman, before that early Britain, with burial mounds, before that again, Druid—the Druid stones still lie in that copse below the field, the Tumuli among the ilexes behind the drive. The older building Sam Franklyn altered and practically pulled down was a monastery; he changed the chapel into a meeting hall, which is now the music room; but, before he came here, the house was occupied by Manetti, a violent Catholic without tolerance or vision; and in the interval between these two, Julius Weinbaum had it, Hebrew of most rigid orthodox type imaginable—so they all have left their—"

"Even so," I repeated, yet interested to hear the rest, "what of it?"

"Simply this," said Frances with conviction, "that each in turn has left his layer of concentrated thinking and belief behind him; because each believed intensely, absolutely, beyond the least weakening of any doubt—the kind of strong belief and thinking that is rare anywhere to-day, the kind that wills, impregnates objects, saturates the atmosphere, haunts, in a word. And each, believing he was utterly and finally right, damned with equally positive conviction the rest of the world. One and all preached that implicitly if not explicitly. It's the root of every creed. Last of the bigoted, grim series came Samuel Franklyn."

I listened in amazement that increased as she went on. Up to this point her explanation was so admirable. It was, indeed, a pretty study in psychology if it were true.

"Then why does nothing ever happen?" I enquired mildly. "A place so thickly haunted ought to produce a crop of no ordinary results!"

"There lies the proof," she went on, in a lowered voice, "the proof of the horror and the ugly reality. The thought and belief of each occupant in turn kept all the others under. They gave no sign of life at the time. But the results of thinking never die. They crop out again the moment there's an opening. And, with the return of Mabel in her negative state, believing nothing positive herself, the place for the first time found itself free to reproduce its buried stores. Damnation, hell-fire, and the rest—the most permanent and vital thought of all those creeds, since it was applied to the majority of the world—broke loose again, for there was no restraint to hold it back. Each sought to obtain its former supremacy. None conquered. There results a pandemonium of hate and fear, of striving to escape, of agonised, bitter warring to find safety, peace—salvation. The place is saturated by that appalling stream of thinking—the terror of the damned. It concentrated upon Mabel, whose negative attitude furnished the channel of deliverance. You and I, according to our sympathy with her, were similarly involved. Nothing happened, because no one layer could ever gain the supremacy."

I was so interested—I dare not say amused—that I stared in silence while she paused a moment, afraid that she would draw rein and end the fairy tale too soon.

"The beliefs of this man, of his Society rather, vigorously thought and therefore vigorously given out here, will put the whole place straight. It will act as a solvent. These vitriolic layers actively denied, will fuse and disappear in the stream of gentle, tolerant sympathy which is love. For each member, worthy of the name, loves the world, and all creeds go into the melting pot; Mabel, too, if she joins them out of real conviction, will find salvation—"

"Thinking, I know, is of the first importance," I objected, "but don't you, perhaps, exaggerate the power of feeling and emotion which in religion are *au fond* always hysterical?"

"What *is* the world," she told me, "but thinking and feeling? An individual's world is entirely what that individual thinks and believes—interpretation. There is no other. And unless he really thinks and really believes, he has no permanent world at all. I grant that few people think, and still fewer believe, and that most take ready-made suits and make them do. Only the strong make their own things; the lesser fry, Mabel among them, are merely swept up into what has been manufactured for them. They get along somehow. You and I have made for ourselves, Mabel has not. She is a nonentity, and when her belief is taken from her, she goes with it."

It was not in me just then to criticise the evasion, or pick out the sophistry from the truth. I merely waited for her to continue.

"None of us have Truth, my dear Frances," I ventured presently, seeing that she kept silent. "Precisely," she answered, "but most of us have beliefs. And what one believes and thinks affects the world at large. Consider the legacy of hatred and cruelty involved in the doctrines men have built into their creeds where the *sine quâ non* of salvation is absolute acceptance of one particular set of views or else perishing everlastingly—for only by repudiating history can they disavow it—"

"You're not quite accurate," I put in. "Not all the creeds teach damnation, do they? Franklyn did, of course; but the others are a bit modernised now surely?"

"Trying to get out of it," she admitted, "perhaps they are, but damnation of unbelievers—of most of the world, that is—is their rather favourite idea if you talk with them."

"I never have."

She smiled. "But I have," she said significantly, "so, if you consider what the various occupants of this house have so strongly held and thought and believed, you need not be surprised that the influence they have left behind them should be a dark and dreadful legacy. For thought, you know, does leave—"

The opening of the door, to my great relief, interrupted her, as the Grenadier led in the visitor to see the room. He bowed to both of us with a brief word of apology, looked round him, and withdrew, and with his departure the conversation between us came naturally to an end. I followed him out.

Neither of us in any case, I think, cared to argue further.

And, so far as I am aware, the curious history of The Towers ends here, too. There was no climax in the story sense. Nothing ever really happened. We left next morning for London. I only know that the Society in question took the house and have since occupied it to their entire satisfaction, and that Mabel, who became a member shortly afterwards, now stays there frequently when in need of repose from the arduous and unselfish labours she took upon herself under its ægis. She dined with us only the other night, here in our tiny Chelsea flat, and a jollier, saner, more interesting and happy guest I could hardly wish for. She was vital—in the best sense; the lay-figure had come to life. I found it difficult to believe she was the same woman whose fearful effigy had floated down those dreary corridors and almost disappeared in the depths of that atrocious Shadow.

What her beliefs were now I was wise enough to leave unquestioned, and Frances, to my great relief, kept the conversation well away from such inappropriate topics. It was clear, however, that the woman had in herself some secret source of joy, that she was now an aggressive, positive force, sure of herself, and apparently afraid of nothing in heaven or hell. She radiated something very like hope and courage about her, and talked as though the world were a glorious place and everybody in it kind and beautiful. Her optimism was certainly infectious.

The Towers were mentioned only in passing. The name of Marsh came up—not *the* Marsh, it so happened, but a name in some book that was being discussed—and I was unable to restrain myself. Curiosity was too strong. I threw out a casual enquiry Mabel could leave unanswered if she wished. But there was no desire to avoid it. Her reply was frank and smiling.

"Would you believe it? She married," Mabel told me, though obviously surprised that I remembered the housekeeper at all; "and is happy as the day is long. She's found her right niche in life. A sergeant—"

"The army!" I ejaculated.

"Salvation Army," she explained merrily.

Frances exchanged a glance with me. I laughed too, for the information took me by surprise. I cannot say why exactly, but I expected at least to hear that the woman had met some dreadful end, not impossibly by burning.

"And The Towers, now called the Rest House," Mabel chattered on, "seems to me the most peaceful and delightful spot in England—"

"Really," I said politely.

"When I lived there in the old days—while you were there, perhaps, though I won't be sure," Mabel went on, "the story got abroad that it was haunted. Wasn't it odd? A less likely place for a ghost I've never seen. Why, it had no atmosphere at all." She said this to Frances, glancing up at me with a smile that apparently had no hidden meaning. "Did *you* notice anything queer about it when you were there?" This was plainly addressed to me.

"I found it—er—difficult to settle down to anything," I said, after an instant's hesitation. "I couldn't work there—"

"But I thought you wrote that wonderful book on the Deaf and Blind while you stayed with me," she asked innocently.

I stammered a little. "Oh, no, not then. I only made a few notes—er—at The Towers. My mind, oddly enough, refused to produce at all down there. But—why do you ask? Did anything—was anything *supposed* to happen there?"

She looked searchingly into my eyes a moment before she answered.

"Not that I know of," she said simply.

## A Descent into Egypt

### I

He was an accomplished, versatile man whom some called brilliant. Behind his talents lay a wealth of material that right selection could have lifted into genuine distinction. He did too many things, however, to excel in one, for a restless curiosity kept him ever on the move. George Isley was an able man. His short career in diplomacy proved it; yet, when he abandoned this for travel and exploration, no one thought it a pity. He would do big things in any line. He was merely finding himself.

Among the rolling stones of humanity a few acquire moss of considerable value. They are not necessarily shiftless; they travel light; the comfortable pockets in the game of life that attract the majority are too small to retain them; they are in and out again in a moment. The world says, "What a pity! They stick to nothing!" but the fact is that, like questing wild birds, they seek the nest they need. It is a question of values. They judge swiftly, change their line of flight, are gone, not even hearing the comment that they might have "retired with a pension."

And to this homeless, questing type George Isley certainly belonged. He was by no means shiftless. He merely sought with insatiable yearning that soft particular nest where he could settle down in permanently. And to an accompaniment of sighs and regrets from his friends he found it; he found it, however, not in the present, but by retiring from the world "without a pension," unclothed with honours and distinctions. He withdrew from the present and slipped softly back into a mighty Past where he belonged. Why; how; obeying what strange instincts—this remains unknown, deep secret of an inner life that found no resting-place in modern things. Such instincts are not disclosable in twentieth-century language, nor are the details of such a journey properly describable at all. Except by the few—poets, prophets, psychiatrists and the like—such experiences are dismissed with the neat museum label—"queer."

So, equally, must the recorder of this experience share the honour of that little label—he who by chance witnessed certain external and visible signs of this inner and spiritual journey. There remains, nevertheless, the amazing reality of the experience; and to the recorder alone was some clue of interpretation possible, perhaps, because in himself also lay the lure, though less imperative, of a similar journey. At any rate the interpretation may be offered to the handful who realize that trains and motors are not the only means of travel left to our progressive race.

In his younger days I knew George Isley intimately. I know him now. But the George Isley I knew of old, the arresting personality with whom I travelled, climbed, explored, is no longer with us. He is not here. He disappeared—gradually—into the past. There is no George Isley. And that such an individuality could vanish, while still his outer semblance walks the familiar streets, normal apparently, and not yet fifty in the number of his years, seems a tale, though difficult, well worth the telling. For I witnessed the slow submergence. It was very gradual. I cannot pretend to understand the entire significance of it. There was something questionable and sinister in the business that offered hints of astonishing possibilities. Were there a corps of spiritual police, the matter might be partially cleared up, but since none of the churches have yet organised anything effective of this sort, one can only fall back upon variants of the blessed "Mesopotamia," and whisper of derangement, and the like. Such labels, of course, explain as little as most other *clichés* in life. That well-groomed, soldierly figure strolling down Piccadilly, watching the Races, dining out—there is no derangement there. The face is not melancholy, the eye not wild; the gestures are quiet and the speech controlled. Yet the eye is empty, the face expressionless. Vacancy reigns there, provocative and significant. If not unduly noticeable, it is because the majority in life neither expect, nor offer, more.

At closer quarters you may think questioning things, or you may think—nothing; probably the latter. You may wonder why something continually expected does not make its appearance; and you may watch for the evidence of "personality" the general presentment of the man has led you to expect. Disappointed, therefore, you may certainly be; but I defy you to discover the smallest hint of mental disorder, and of derangement or nervous affliction, absolutely nothing. Before long, perhaps, you may feel you are talking with a dummy, some well-trained automaton, a nonentity devoid of spontaneous life; and afterwards you may find that memory fades rapidly away, as though no impression of any kind has really been made at all. All this, yes; but nothing pathological. A few may be stimulated by this startling discrepancy between promise and performance, but most, accustomed to accept face values, would say, "a pleasant fellow, but nothing in him much..." and an hour later forgot him altogether.

For the truth is as you, perhaps, divined. You have been sitting beside no one, you have been talking to, looking at, listening to—no one. The intercourse has conveyed nothing that can waken human response in you, good, bad or indifferent. There is no George Isley. And the discovery, if you make it, will not even cause you to creep with the uncanniness of the experience, because the exterior is so wholly pleasing. George Isley to-day is a picture with no meaning in it that charms merely by the harmonious colouring of an inoffensive subject. He moves undiscovered in the little world of society to which he was born, secure in the groove first habit has made comfortably automatic for him. No one guesses; none, that is, but the few who knew him intimately in early life. And his wandering existence has scattered these; they have forgotten what he was. So perfect, indeed, is he in the manners of the commonplace fashionable man, that no woman in his "set" is aware that he differs from the type she is accustomed to. He turns a compliment with the accepted language of her text-book, motors, golfs and gambles in the regulation manner of his particular world. He is an admirable, perfect automaton. He is nothing. He is a human shell.

II

The name of George Isley had been before the public for some years when, after a considerable interval, we met again in a hotel in Egypt, I for my health, he for I knew not what—at first. But I soon discovered: archæology and excavation had taken hold of him, though he had gone so quietly about it that no one seemed to have heard. I was not sure that he was glad to see me, for he had first withdrawn, annoyed, it seemed, at being discovered, but later, as though after consideration, had made tentative advances. He welcomed me with a curious gesture of the entire body that seemed to shake himself free from something that had made him forget my identity. There was pathos somewhere in his attitude, almost as though he asked for sympathy. "I've been out here, off and on, for the last three years," he told me, after describing something of what he had been doing. "I find it the most repaying hobby in the world. It leads to a reconstruction—an imaginative reconstruction, of course, I mean—of an enormous thing the world had entirely lost. A very gorgeous, stimulating hobby, believe me, and a very entic—" he quickly changed the word—"exacting one indeed."

I remember looking him up and down with astonishment. There was a change in him, a lack; a note was missing in his enthusiasm, a colour in the voice, a quality in his manner. The ingredients were not mixed quite as of old. I did not bother him with questions, but I noted thus at the very first a subtle alteration. Another facet of the man presented itself. Something that had been independent and aggressive was replaced by a certain emptiness that invited sympathy. Even in his physical appearance the change was manifested—this odd suggestion of lessening. I looked again more closely. Lessening was the word. He had somehow dwindled. It was startling, vaguely unpleasant too.

The entire subject, as usual, was at his fingertips; he knew all the important men; and had spent money freely on his hobby. I laughed, reminding him of his remark that Egypt had no attractions for him, owing to the organised advertisement of its somewhat theatrical charms. Admitting his error with a gesture, he brushed the objection easily aside. His manner, and a certain glow that rose about his atmosphere as he answered, increased my first astonishment. His voice was significant and suggestive. "Come out with me," he said in a low tone, "and see how little the tourists matter, how inappreciable the excavation is compared to what remains to be done, how gigantic"—he emphasised the word impressively—"the scope for discovery remains." He made a movement with his head and shoulders that conveyed a sense of the prodigious, for he was of massive build, his cast of features stern, and his eyes, set deep into the face, shone past me with a sombre gleam in them I did not quite account for. It was the voice, however, that brought the mystery in. It vibrated somewhere below the actual sound of it. "Egypt," he continued—and so gravely that at first I made the mistake of thinking he chose the curious words on purpose to produce a theatrical effect—"that has enriched her blood with the pageant of so many civilisations, that has devoured Persians, Greeks and Romans, Saracens and Mamelukes, a dozen conquests and invasions besides,—what can mere tourists or explorers matter to her? The excavators scratch their skin and dig up mummies; and as for tourists!"—he laughed contemptuously—"flies that settle for a moment on her covered face, to vanish at the first signs of heat! Egypt is not even aware of them. The real Egypt lies underground in darkness. Tourists must have light, to be seen as well as to see. And the diggers—!"

He paused, smiling with something between pity and contempt I did not quite appreciate, for, personally, I felt a great respect for the tireless excavators. And then he added, with a touch of feeling in his tone as though he had a grievance against them, and had not also "dug" himself, "Men who uncover the dead, restore the temples, and reconstruct a skeleton, thinking they have read its beating heart..." He shrugged his great shoulders, and the rest of the sentence may have been but the protest of a man in defence of his own hobby, but that there seemed an undue earnestness and gravity about it that made me wonder more than ever. He went on to speak of the strangeness of the land as a mere ribbon of vegetation along the ancient river, the rest all ruins, desert, sun-drenched wilderness of death, yet so breakingly alive with wonder, power and a certain disquieting sense of deathlessness. There seemed, for him, a revelation of unusual spiritual kind in this land where the Past survived so potently. He spoke almost as though it obliterated the Present.

Indeed, the hint of something solemn behind his words made it difficult for me to keep up the conversation, and the pause that presently came I filled in with some word of questioning surprise, which yet, I think, was chiefly in concurrence. I was aware of some big belief in him, some enveloping emotion that escaped my grasp. Yet, though I did not understand, his great mood swept me... His voice lowered, then, as he went on to mention temples, tombs and deities, details of his own discoveries and of their affect upon him, but to this I listened with half an ear, because in the unusual language he had first made use of I detected this other thing that stirred my curiosity more—stirred it uncomfortably.

"Then the spell," I asked, remembering the effect of Egypt upon myself two years before, "has worked upon you as upon most others, only with greater power?"

He looked hard at me a moment, signs of trouble showing themselves faintly in his rugged, interesting face. I think he wanted to say more than he could bring himself to confess. He hesitated.

"I'm only glad," he replied after a pause, "it didn't get hold of me earlier in life. It would have absorbed me. I should have lost all other interests. Now,"—that curious look of helplessness, of asking sympathy, flitted like a shadow through his eyes—"now that I'm on the decline... it matters less."

On the decline! I cannot imagine by what blundering I missed this chance he never offered again; somehow or other the singular phrase passed unnoticed at the moment, and only came upon me with its full significance later when it was too awkward to refer to it. He tested my readiness to help, to sympathise, to share his inner life. I missed the clue. For, at the moment, a more practical consideration interested me in his language. Being of those who regretted that he had not excelled by devoting his powers to a single object, I shrugged my shoulders. He caught my meaning instantly. Oh, he was glad to talk. He felt the possibility of my sympathy underneath, I think.

"No, no, you take me wrongly there," he said with gravity. "What I mean—and I ought to know if any one does!—is that while most countries give, others take away. Egypt changes you. No one can live here and remain exactly what he was before."

This puzzled me. It startled, too, again. His manner was so earnest. "And Egypt, you mean, is one of the countries that takes away?" I asked. The strange idea unsettled my thoughts a little.

"First takes away from you," he replied, "but in the end takes you away. Some lands enrich you," he went on, seeing that I listened, "while others impoverish. From India, Greece, Italy, all ancient lands, you return with memories you can use. From Egypt you return with—nothing. Its splendour stupefies; it's useless. There is a change in your inmost being, an emptiness, an unaccountable yearning, but you find nothing that can fill the lack you're conscious of. Nothing comes to replace what has gone. You have been drained."

I stared; but I nodded a general acquiescence. Of a sensitive, artistic temperament this was certainly true, though by no means the superficial and generally accepted verdict. The majority imagine that Egypt has filled them to the brim. I took his deeper reading of the facts. I was aware of an odd fascination in his idea.

"Modern Egypt," he continued, "is, after all, but a trick of civilisation," and there was a kind of breathlessness in his measured tone, "but ancient Egypt lies waiting, hiding, underneath. Though dead, she is amazingly alive. And you feel her touching you. She takes from you. She enriches herself. You return from Egypt—less than you were before."

What came over my mind is hard to say. Some touch of visionary imagination burned its flaming path across my mind. I thought of some old Grecian hero speaking of his delicious battle with the gods—battle in which he knew he must be worsted, but yet in which he delighted because at death his spirit would join their glorious company beyond this world. I was aware, that is to say, of resignation as well as resistance in him. He already felt the effortless peace which follows upon long, unequal battling, as of a man who has fought the rapids with a strain beyond his strength, then sinks back and goes with the awful mass of water smoothly and indifferently—over the quiet fall.

Yet, it was not so much his words which clothed picturesquely an undeniable truth, as the force of conviction that drove behind them, shrouding my mind with mystery and darkness. His eyes, so steadily holding mine, were lit, I admit, yet they were calm and sane as those of a doctor discussing the symptoms of that daily battle to which we all finally succumb. This analogy occurred to me.

"There *is*"—I stammered a little, faltering in my speech—"an incalculable element in the country somewhere, I confess. You put it—rather strongly, though, don't you?"

He answered quietly, moving his eyes from my face towards the window that framed the serene and exquisite sky towards the Nile.

"The real, invisible Egypt," he murmured, "I do find rather—strong. I find it difficult to deal with. You see," and he turned towards me, smiling like a tired child, "I think the truth is that Egypt deals with me."

"It draws—" I began, then started as he interrupted me at once.

"Into the Past." He uttered the little word in a way beyond me to describe. There came a flood of glory with it, a sense of peace and beauty, of battles over and of rest attained. No saint could have brimmed "Heaven" with as much passionately enticing meaning. He went willingly, prolonging the struggle merely to enjoy the greater relief and joy of the consummation.

For again he spoke as though a struggle were in progress in his being. I got the impression that he somewhere wanted help. I understood the pathetic quality I had vaguely discerned already. His character naturally was so strong and independent. It now seemed weaker, as though certain fibres had been drawn out. And I understood then that the spell of Egypt, so lightly chattered about in its sensational aspect, so rarely known in its naked power, the nameless, creeping influence that begins deep below the surface and thence sends delicate tendrils outwards, was in his blood. I, in my untaught ignorance, had felt it too; it is undeniable; one is aware of unaccountable, queer things in Egypt; even the utterly prosaic feel them. Dead Egypt is marvellously alive...

I glanced past him out of the big windows where the desert glimmered in its featureless expanse of yellow leagues, two monstrous pyramids signalling from across the Nile, and for a moment—inexplicably, it seemed to me afterwards—I lost sight of my companion's stalwart figure that was yet so close before my eyes. He had risen from his chair; he was standing near me; yet my sight missed him altogether. Something, dim as a shadow, faint as a breath of air, rose up and bore my thoughts away, obliterating vision too. I forgot for a moment who I was; identity slipped from me. Thought, sight, feeling, all sank away into the emptiness of those sun-baked sands, sank, as it were, into nothingness, caught away from the Present, enticed, absorbed... And when I looked back again to answer him, or rather to ask what his curious words could mean—he was no longer there. More than surprised—for there was something of shock in the disappearance—I turned to search. I had not seen him go. He had stolen from my side so softly, slipped away silently, mysteriously, and—so easily. I remember that a faint shiver ran down my back as I realised that I was alone.

Was it that, momentarily, I had caught a reflex of his state of mind? Had my sympathy induced in myself an echo of what he experienced in full—a going backwards, a loss of present vigour, the enticing, subtle draw of those immeasurable sands that hide the living dead from the interruptions of the careless living...?

I sat down to reflect and, incidentally, to watch the magnificence of the sunset; and the thing he had said returned upon me with insistent power, ringing like distant bells within my mind. His talk of the tombs and temples passed, but this remained. It stimulated oddly. His talk, I remembered, had always excited curiosity in this way. Some countries give, while others take away. What did he mean precisely? What had Egypt taken away from him? And I realised more definitely that something in him *was* missing, something he possessed in former years that was now no longer there. He had grown shadowy already in my thoughts. The mind searched keenly, but in vain... and after some time I left my chair and moved over to another window, aware that a vague discomfort stirred within me that involved uneasiness—for him. I felt pity. But behind the pity was an eager, absorbing curiosity as well. He seemed receding curiously into misty distance, and the strong desire leaped in me to overtake, to travel with him into some vanished splendour that he had re-discovered. The feeling was a most remarkable one, for it included yearning—the yearning for some nameless, forgotten loveliness the world has lost. It was in me too.

At the approach of twilight the mind loves to harbour shadows. The room, empty of guests, was dark behind me; darkness, too, was creeping across the desert like a veil, deepening the serenity of its grim, unfeatured face. It turned pale with distance; the whole great sheet of it went rustling into night. The first stars peeped and twinkled, hanging loosely in the air as though they could be plucked like golden berries; and the sun was already below the Lybian horizon, where gold and crimson faded through violet into blue. I stood watching this mysterious Egyptian dusk, while an eerie glamour seemed to bring the incredible within uneasy reach of the half-faltering senses... And suddenly the truth dropped into me. Over George Isley, over his mind and energies, over his thoughts and over his emotions too, a kind of darkness was also slowly creeping. Something in him had dimmed, yet not with age; it had gone out. Some inner night, stealing over the Present, obliterated it. And yet he looked towards the dawn. Like the Egyptian monuments his eyes turned—eastwards.

And so it came to me that what he had lost was personal ambition. He was glad, he said, that these Egyptian studies had not caught him earlier in life; the language he made use of was peculiar: "Now I am on the decline it matters less." A slight foundation, no doubt, to build conviction on, and yet I felt sure that I was partly right. He was fascinated, but fascinated against his will. The Present in him battled against the Past. Still fighting, he had yet lost hope. The desire *not* to change was now no longer in him...

I turned away from the window so as not to see that grey, encroaching desert, for the discovery produced a certain agitation in me. Egypt seemed suddenly a living entity of enormous power. She stirred about me. She was stirring now. This flat and motionless land pretending it had no movement, was actually busy with a million gestures that came creeping round the heart. She was reducing him. Already from the complex texture of his personality she had drawn one vital thread that in its relation to the general woof was of central importance—ambition. The mind chose the simile; but in my heart where thought fluttered in singular distress, another suggested itself as truer. "Thread" changed to "artery." I turned quickly and went up to my room where I could be alone. The idea was somewhere ghastly.

### III

Yet, while dressing for dinner, the idea exfoliated as only a living thing exfoliates. I saw in George Isley this great question mark that had not been there formerly. All have, of course, some question mark, and carry it about, though with most it rarely becomes visible until the end. With him it was plainly visible in his atmosphere at the hey-day of his life. He wore it like a fine curved scimitar above his head. So full of life, he yet seemed willingly dead. For, though imagination sought every possible explanation, I got no further than the somewhat negative result—that a certain energy, wholly unconnected with mere physical health, had been withdrawn. It was more than ambition, I think, for it included intention, desire, self-confidence as well. It was life itself. He was no longer in the Present. He was no longer *here*.

"Some countries give while others take away... I find Egypt difficult to deal with. I find it..." and then that simple, uncomplex adjective—"strong." In memory and experience the entire globe was mapped for him; it remained for Egypt, then, to teach him this marvellous new thing. But not Egypt of to-day; it was vanished Egypt that had robbed him of his strength. He had described it as underground, hidden, waiting... I was again aware of a faint shuddering—as though something crept secretly from my inmost heart to share the experience with him, and as though my sympathy involved a willing consent that this should be so. With sympathy there must always be a shedding of the personal self; each time I felt this sympathy, it seemed that something left me. I thought in circles, arriving at no definite point where I could rest and say "that's it; I understand." The giving attitude of a country was easily comprehensible; but this idea of robbery, of deprivation baffled me. An obscure alarm took hold of me—for myself as well as for him.

At dinner, where he invited me to his table, the impression passed off a good deal, however, and I convicted myself of a woman's exaggeration; yet, as we talked of many a day's adventure together in other lands, it struck me that we oddly left the present out. We ignored to-day. His thoughts, as it were, went most easily backwards. And each adventure led, as by its own natural weight and impetus, towards one thing—the enormous glory of a vanished age. Ancient Egypt was "home" in this mysterious game life played with death. The specific gravity of his being, to say nothing for the moment of my own, had shifted lower, further off, backwards and below, or as he put it—underground. The sinking sensation I experienced was of a literal kind...

And so I found myself wondering what had led him to this particular hotel. I had come out with an affected organ the specialist promised me would heal in the marvellous air of Heolouan, but it was queer that my companion also should have chosen it. Its clientele was mostly invalid, German and Russian invalid at that. The Management set its face against the lighter, gayer side of life that hotels in Egypt usually encourage eagerly. It was a true rest-house, a place of repose and leisure, a place where one could remain undiscovered and unknown. No English patronised it. One might easily— the idea came unbidden, suddenly—hide in it.

"Then you're doing nothing just now," I asked, "in the way of digging? No big expeditions or excavating at the moment?"

"I'm recuperating," he answered carelessly. "I've had two years up at the Valley of the Kings, and overdid it rather. But I'm by way of working at a little thing near here across the Nile." And he pointed in the direction of Sakkhara, where the huge Memphian cemetery stretches underground from the Dachûr Pyramids to the Gizeh monsters, four miles lower down. "There's a matter of a hundred years in that alone!"

"You must have accumulated a mass of interesting material. I suppose later you'll make use of it—a book or—"

His expression stopped me—that strange look in the eyes that had stirred my first uneasiness. It was as if something struggled up a moment, looked bleakly out upon the present, then sank away again.

"More," he answered listlessly, "than I can ever use. It's much more likely to use me." He said it hurriedly, looking over his shoulder as though some one might be listening, then smiled significantly, bringing his eyes back upon my own again. I told him that he was far too modest. "If all the excavators thought like that," I added, "we ignorant ones should suffer." I laughed, but the laughter was only on my lips.

He shook his head indifferently. "They do their best; they do wonders," he replied, making an indescribable gesture as though he withdrew willingly from the topic altogether, yet could not quite achieve it. "I know their books; I know the writers too of various nationalities." He paused a moment, and his eyes turned grave. "I cannot understand quite—how they do it," he added half below his breath.

"The labour, you mean? The strain of the climate, and so forth?" I said this purposely, for I knew quite well he meant another thing. The way he looked into my face, however, disturbed me so that I believe I visibly started. Something very deep in me sat up alertly listening, almost on guard. "I mean," he replied, "that they must have uncommon powers of resistance."

There! He had used the very word that had been hiding in me! "It puzzles me," he went on, "for, with one exception, they are not unusual men. In the way of gifts—oh, yes. It's in the way of resistance and protection that I mean. Self-protection," he added with emphasis.

It was the way he said resistance and self-protection that sent a touch of cold through me: I learned later that he himself had made surprising discoveries in these two years, penetrating closer to the secret life of ancient sacerdotal Egypt than any of his predecessors or co-labourers—then, inexplicably, had ceased. But this was told to me afterwards and by others. At the moment I was only conscious of this odd embarrassment. I did not understand, yet felt that he touched upon something intimately personal to himself. He paused, expecting me to speak.

"Egypt, perhaps, merely pours through them," I ventured. "They give out mechanically, hardly realising how much they give. They report facts devoid of interpretation. Whereas with you it's the actual spirit of the past that is discovered and laid bare. You live it. You feel old Egypt and disclose her. That divining faculty was always yours—uncannily, I used to think."

The flash of his sombre eyes betrayed that my aim was singularly good. It seemed a third had silently joined our little table in the corner. Something intruded, evoked by the power of what our conversation skirted but ever left unmentioned. It was huge and shadowy; it was also watchful. Egypt came gliding, floating up beside us. I saw her reflected in his face and gaze. The desert slipped in through walls and ceiling, rising from beneath our feet, settling about us, listening, peering, waiting. The strange obsession was sudden and complete. The gigantic scale of her swam in among the very pillars, arches, and windows of that modern dining-room. I felt against my skin the touch of chilly air that sunlight never reaches, stealing from beneath the granite monoliths. Behind it came the stifling breath of the heated tombs, of the Serapeum, of the chambers and corridors in the pyramids. There was a rustling as of myriad footsteps far away, and as of sand the busy winds go shifting through the ages. And in startling contrast to this impression of prodigious size, Isley himself wore suddenly an air of strangely dwindling. For a second he shrank visibly before my very eyes. He was receding. His outline seemed to retreat and lessen, as though he stood to the waist in what appeared like flowing mist, only his head and shoulders still above the ground. Far, far away I saw him.

It was a vivid inner picture that I somehow transferred objectively. It was a dramatised sensation, of course. His former phrase "now that I am declining" flashed back upon me with sharp discomfort. Again, perhaps, his state of mind was reflected into me by some emotional telepathy. I waited, conscious of an almost sensible oppression that would not lift. It seemed an age before he spoke, and when he did there was the tremor of feeling in his voice he sought nevertheless to repress. I kept my eyes on the table for some reason. But I listened intently.

"It's you that have the divining faculty, not I," he said, an odd note of distance even in his tone, yet a resonance as though it rose up between reverberating walls. "There *is*, I believe, something here that resents too close inquiry, or rather that resists discovery—almost—takes offence."

I looked up quickly, then looked down again. It was such a startling thing to hear on the lips of a modern Englishman. He spoke lightly, but the expression of his face belied the careless tone. There was no mockery in those earnest eyes, and in the hushed voice was a little creeping sound that gave me once again the touch of goose-flesh. The only word I can find is subterranean: all that was mental in him had sunk, so that he seemed speaking underground, head and shoulders alone visible. The effect was almost ghastly.

"Such extraordinary obstacles are put in one's way," he went on, "when the prying gets too close to the—reality; physical, external obstacles, I mean. Either that, or—the mind loses its assimilative faculties. One or other happens—" his voice died down into a whisper—"and discovery ceases of its own accord."

The same minute, then, he suddenly raised himself like a man emerging from a tomb; he leaned across the table; he made an effort of some violent internal kind, on the verge, I fully believe, of a pregnant personal statement. There was confession in his attitude; I think he was about to speak of his work at Thebes and the reason for its abrupt cessation. For I had the feeling of one about to hear a weighty secret, the responsibility unwelcome. This uncomfortable emotion rose in me, as I raised my eyes to his somewhat unwillingly, only to find that I was wholly at fault. It was not me he was looking at. He was staring past me in the direction of the wide, unshuttered windows. The expression of yearning was visible in his eyes again. Something had stopped his utterance.

And instinctively I turned and saw what he saw. So far as external details were concerned, at least, I saw it.

Across the glare and glitter of the uncompromising modern dining-room, past crowded tables, and over the heads of Germans feeding unpicturesquely, I saw—the moon. Her reddish disc, hanging unreal and enormous, lifted the spread sheet of desert till it floated off the surface of the world. The great window faced the east, where the Arabian desert breaks into a ruin of gorges, cliffs, and flat-topped ridges; it looked unfriendly, ominous, with danger in it; unlike the serener sand-dunes of the Lybian desert, there lay both menace and seduction behind its flood of shadows. And the moonlight emphasised this aspect: its ghostly desolation, its cruelty, its bleak hostility, turning it murderous. For no river sweetens this Arabian desert; instead of sandy softness, it has fangs of limestone rock, sharp and aggressive. Across it, just visible in the moonlight as a thread of paler grey, the old camel-trail to Suez beckoned faintly. And it was this that he was looking at so intently.

It was, I know, a theatrical stage-like glimpse, yet in it a seductiveness most potent. "Come out," it seemed to whisper, "and taste my awful beauty. Come out and lose yourself, and die. Come out and follow my moonlit trail into the Past... where there is peace and immobility and silence. My kingdom is unchanging underground. Come down, come softly, come through sandy corridors below this tinsel of your modern world. Come back, come down into my golden past..."

A poignant desire stole through my heart on moonlit feet; I was personally conscious of a keen yearning to slip away in unresisting obedience. For it was uncommonly impressive, this sudden, haunting glimpse of the world outside. The hairy foreigners, uncouthly garbed, all busily eating in full electric light, provided a sensational contrast of emphatically distressing kind. A touch of what is called unearthly hovered about that distance through the window. There was weirdness in it. Egypt looked in upon us. Egypt watched and listened, beckoning through the moonlit windows of the heart to come and find her. Mind and imagination might flounder as they pleased, but something of this kind happened undeniably, whether expression in language fails to hold the truth or not. And George Isley, aware of being seen, looked straight into the awful visage—fascinated.

Over the bronze of his skin there stole a shade of grey. My own feeling of enticement grew—the desire to go out into the moonlight, to leave my kind and wander blindly through the desert, to see the gorges in their shining silver, and taste the keenness of the cool, sharp air. Further than this with me it did not go, but that my companion felt the bigger, deeper draw behind this surface glamour, I have no reasonable doubt. For a moment, indeed, I thought he meant to leave the table; he had half risen in his chair; it seemed he struggled and resisted—and then his big frame subsided again; he sat back; he looked, in the attitude his body took, less impressive, smaller, actually shrunken into the proportions of some minuter scale. It was as though something in that second had been drawn out of him, decreasing even his physical appearance. The voice, when he spoke presently with a touch of resignation, held a lifeless quality as though deprived of virile timbre.

"It's always there," he whispered, half collapsing back into his chair, "it's always watching, waiting, listening. Almost like a monster of the fables, isn't it? It makes no movement of its own, you see. It's far too strong for that. It just hangs there, half in the air and half upon the earth—a gigantic web. Its prey flies into it. That's Egypt all over. D'you feel like that too, or does it seem to you just imaginative rubbish? To me it seems that she just waits her time; she gets you quicker that way; in the end you're bound to go."

"There's power certainly," I said after a moment's pause to collect my wits, my distress increased by the morbidness of his simile. "For some minds there may be a kind of terror too—for weak temperaments that are all imagination." My thoughts were scattered, and I could not readily find good words. "There is startling grandeur in a sight like that, for instance," and I pointed to the window. "You feel drawn—as if you simply *had* to go." My mind still buzzed with his curious words, "In the end you're bound to go." It betrayed his heart and soul. "I suppose a fly does feel drawn," I added, "or a moth to the destroying flame. Or is it just unconscious on their part?"

He jerked his big head significantly. "Well, well," he answered, "but the fly isn't necessarily weak, or the moth misguided. Over-adventurous, perhaps, yet both obedient to the laws of their respective beings. They get warnings too—only, when the moth wants to know too much, the fire stops it. Both flame and spider enrich themselves by understanding the natures of their prey; and fly and moth return again and again until this is accomplished."

Yet George Isley was as sane as the head waiter who, noticing our interest in the window, came up just then and enquired whether we felt a draught and would prefer it closed. Isley, I realised, was struggling to express a passionate state of soul for which, owing to its rarity, no adequate expression lies at hand. There is a language of the mind, but there is none as yet of the spirit. I felt ill at ease. All this was so foreign to the wholesome, strenuous personality of the man as I remembered it.

"But, my dear fellow," I stammered, "aren't you giving poor old Egypt a bad name she hardly deserves? I feel only the amazing strength and beauty of it; awe, if you like, but none of this resentment you so mysteriously hint at."

"You understand, for all that," he answered quietly; and again he seemed on the verge of some significant confession that might ease his soul. My uncomfortable emotion grew. Certainly he was at high pressure somewhere. "And, if necessary, you could help. Your sympathy, I mean, is a help already." He said it half to himself and in a suddenly lowered tone again.

"A help!" I gasped. "My sympathy! Of course, if—"

"A witness," he murmured, not looking at me, "some one who understands, yet does not think me mad."

There was such appeal in his voice that I felt ready and eager to do anything to help him. Our eyes met, and my own tried to express this willingness in me; but what I said I hardly know, for a cloud of confusion was on my mind, and my speech went fumbling like a schoolboy's. I was more than disconcerted. Through this bewilderment, then, I just caught the tail-end of another sentence in which the words "relief it is to have... some one to hold to... when the disappearance comes..." sounded like voices heard in dream. But I missed the complete phrase and shrank from asking him to repeat it.

Some sympathetic answer struggled to my lips, though what it was I know not. The thing I murmured, however, seemed apparently well chosen. He leaned across and laid his big hand a moment on my own with eloquent pressure. It was cold as ice. A look of gratitude passed over his sunburned features. He sighed. And we left the table then and passed into the inner smoking-rooms for coffee—a room whose windows gave upon columned terraces that allowed no view of the encircling desert. He led the conversation into channels less personal and, thank heaven, less intensely emotional and mysterious. What we talked about I now forget; it was interesting but in another key altogether. His old charm and power worked; the respect I had always felt for his character and gifts returned in force, but it was the pity I now experienced that remained chiefly in my mind. For this change in him became more and more noticeable. He was less impressive, less convincing, less suggestive. His talk, though so knowledgeable, lacked that spiritual quality that drives home. He was uncannily less *real*. And I went up to bed, uneasy and disturbed. "It is not age," I said to myself, "and assuredly it is not death he fears, although he spoke of disappearance. It is mental—in the deepest sense. It is what religious people would call soul. Something is happening to his soul."

## IV

And this word "soul" remained with me to the end. Egypt was taking his soul away into the Past. What was of value in him went willingly; the rest, some lesser aspect of his mind and character, resisted, holding to the present. A struggle, therefore, was involved. But this was being gradually obliterated too.

How I arrived gaily at this monstrous conclusion seems to me now a mystery; but the truth is that from a conversation one brings away a general idea that is larger than the words actually heard and spoken. I have reported, naturally, but a fragment of what passed between us in language, and of what was suggested—by gesture, expression, silence—merely perhaps a hint. I can only assert that this troubling verdict remained a conviction in my mind. It came upstairs with me; it watched and listened by my side. That mysterious Third evoked in our conversation was bigger than either of us separately; it might be called the spirit of ancient Egypt, or it might be called with equal generalisation, the Past. This Third, at any rate, stood by me, whispering this astounding thing. I went out on to my little balcony to smoke a pipe and enjoy the comforting presence of the stars before turning in. It came out with me. It was everywhere. I heard the barking of dogs, the monotonous beating of a distant drum towards Bedraschien, the sing-song voices of the natives in their booths and down the dim-lit streets. I was aware of this invisible Third behind all these familiar sounds. The enormous night-sky, drowned in stars, conveyed it too. It was in the breath of chilly wind that whispered round the walls, and it brooded everywhere above the sleepless desert. I was alone as little as though George Isley stood beside me in person—and at that moment a moving figure caught my eye below. My window was on the sixth storey, but there was no mistaking the tall and soldierly bearing of the man who was strolling past the hotel. George Isley was going slowly out into the desert.

There was actually nothing unusual in the sight. It was only ten o'clock; but for doctor's orders I might have been doing the same myself. Yet, as I leaned over the dizzy ledge and watched him, a chill struck through me, and a feeling nothing could justify, nor pages of writing describe, rose up and mastered me. His words at dinner came back with curious force. Egypt lay round him, motionless, a vast grey web. His feet were caught in it. It quivered. The silvery meshes in the moonlight announced the fact from Memphis up to Thebes, across the Nile, from underground Sakkhâra to the Valley of the Kings. A tremor ran over the entire desert, and again, as in the dining-room, the leagues of sand went rustling. It seemed to me that I caught him in the act of disappearing.

I realised in that moment the haunting power of this mysterious still atmosphere which is Egypt, and some magical emanation of its mighty past broke over me suddenly like a wave. Perhaps in that moment I felt what he himself felt; the withdrawing suction of the huge spent wave swept something out of me into the past with it. An indescribable yearning drew something living from my heart, something that longed with a kind of burning, searching sweetness for a glory of spiritual passion that was gone. The pain and happiness of it were more poignant than may be told, and my present personality—some vital portion of it, at any rate—wilted before the power of its enticement.

I stood there, motionless as stone, and stared. Erect and steady, knowing resistance vain, eager to go yet striving to remain, and half with an air of floating off the ground, he went towards the pale grey thread which was the track to Suez and the far Red Sea. There came upon me this strange, deep sense of pity, pathos, sympathy that was beyond all explanation, and mysterious as a pain in dreams. For a sense of his awful loneliness stole into me, a loneliness nothing on this earth could possibly relieve. Robbed of the Present, he sought this chimera of his soul, an unreal Past. Not even the calm majesty of this exquisite Egyptian night could soothe the dream away; the peace and silence were marvellous, the sweet perfume of the desert air intoxicating; but all these intensified it only.

And though at a loss to explain my own emotion, its poignancy was so real that a sigh escaped me and I felt that tears lay not too far away. I watched him, yet felt I had no right to watch. Softly I drew back from the window with the sensation of eaves-dropping upon his privacy; but before I did so I had seen his outline melt away into the dim world of sand that began at the very walls of the hotel. He wore a cloak of green that reached down almost to his heels, and its colour blended with the silvery surface of the desert's dark sea-tint. This sheen first draped and then concealed him. It covered him with a fold of its mysterious garment that, without seam or binding, veiled Egypt for a thousand leagues. The desert took him. Egypt caught him in her web. He was gone.

Sleep for me just then seemed out of the question. The change in him made me feel less sure of myself. To see him thus invertebrate shocked me. I was aware that I had nerves.

For a long time I sat smoking by the window, my body weary, but my imagination irritatingly stimulated. The big sign-lights of the hotel went out; window after window closed below me; the electric standards in the streets were already extinguished; and Helouan looked like a child's white blocks scattered in ruin upon the nursery carpet. It seemed so wee upon the vast expanse. It lay in a twinkling pattern, like a cluster of glow-worms dropped into a negligible crease of the tremendous desert. It peeped up at the stars, a little frightened.

The night was very still. There hung an enormous brooding beauty everywhere, a hint of the sinister in it that only the brilliance of the blazing stars relieved. Nothing really slept. Grouped here and there at intervals about this dun-coloured world stood the everlasting watchers in solemn, tireless guardianship—the soaring pyramids, the Sphinx, the grim Colossi, the empty temples, the long-deserted tombs. The mind was aware of them, stationed like sentries through the night. "This is Egypt; you are actually in Egypt," whispered the silence. "Eight thousand years of history lie fluttering outside your window. *She* lies there underground, sleepless, mighty, deathless, not to be trifled with. Beware! Or she will change you too!"

My imagination offered this hint: Egypt *is* difficult to realise. It remains outside the mind, a fabulous, half-legendary idea. So many enormous elements together refuse to be assimilated; the heart pauses, asking for time and breath; the senses reel a little, and in the end a mental torpor akin to stupefaction creeps upon the brain. With a sigh the struggle is abandoned and the mind surrenders to Egypt on her own terms. Alone the diggers and archæologists, confined to definite facts, offer successful resistance. My friend's use of the words "resistance" and "protection" became clearer to me. While logic halted, intuition fluttered round this clue to the solution of the influences at work. George Isley realised Egypt more than most—but as she had been.

And I recalled its first effect upon myself, and how my mind had been unable to cope with the memory of it afterwards. There had come to its summons a colossal medley, a gigantic, coloured blur that merely bewildered. Only lesser points lodged comfortably in the heart. I saw a chaotic vision: sands drenched in dazzling light, vast granite aisles, stupendous figures that stared unblinking at the sun, a shining river and a shadowy desert, both endless as the sky, mountainous pyramids and gigantic monoliths, armies of heads, of paws, of faces—all set to a scale of size that was prodigious. The items stunned; the composite effect was too unwieldy to be grasped. Something that blazed with splendour rolled before the eyes, too close to be seen distinctly—at the same time very distant—unrealised.

Then, with the passing of the weeks, it slowly stirred to life. It had attacked unseen; its grip was quite tremendous; yet it could neither be told, nor painted, nor described. It flamed up unexpectedly—in the foggy London streets, at the Club, in the theatre. A sound recalled the street-cries of the Arabs, a breath of scented air brought back the heated sand beyond the palm groves. Up rose the huge Egyptian glamour, transforming common things; it had lain buried all this time in deep recesses of the heart that are inaccessible to ordinary daily life. And there hid in it something of uneasiness that was inexplicable; awe, a hint of cold eternity, a touch of something unchanging and terrific, something sublime made lovely yet unearthly with shadowy time and distance. The melancholy of the Nile and the grandeur of a hundred battered temples dropped some unutterable beauty upon the heart. Up swept the desert air, the luminous pale shadows, the naked desolation that yet brims with sharp vitality. An Arab on his donkey tripped in colour across the mind, melting off into tiny perspective, strangely vivid. A string of camels stood in silhouette against the crimson sky. Great winds, great blazing spaces, great solemn nights, great days of golden splendour rose from the pavement or the theatre-stall, and London, dim-lit England, the whole of modern life, indeed, seemed suddenly reduced to a paltry insignificance that produced an aching longing for the pageantry of those millions of vanished souls. Egypt rolled through the heart for a moment—and was gone.

I remembered that some such fantastic experience had been mine. Put it as one may, the fact remains that for certain temperaments Egypt can rob the Present of some thread of interest that was formerly there. The memory became for me an integral part of personality; something in me yearned for its curious and awful beauty. He who has drunk of the Nile shall return to drink of it again... And if for myself this was possible, what might not happen to a character of George Isley's type? Some glimmer of comprehension came to me. The ancient, buried, hidden Egypt had cast her net about his soul. Grown shadowy in the present, his life was being transferred into some golden, reconstructed Past, where it was real. Some countries give, while others take away. And George Isley was worth robbing...

Disturbed by these singular reflections, I moved away from the open window, closing it. But the closing did not exclude the presence of the Third. The biting night air followed me in. I drew the mosquito curtains round the bed, but the light I left still burning; and, lying there, I jotted down upon a scrap of paper this curious impression as best I could, only to find that it escaped easily between the words. Such visionary and spiritual perceptions are too elusive to be trapped in language. Reading it over after an interval of years, it is difficult to recall with what intense meaning, what uncanny emotion, I wrote those faded lines in pencil. Their rhetoric seems cheap, their content much exaggerated; yet at the time truth burned in every syllable. Egypt, which since time began has suffered robbery with violence at the hands of all the world, now takes her vengeance, choosing her individual prey. Her time has come. Behind a modern mask she lies in wait, intensely active, sure of her hidden power. Prostitute of dead empires, she lies now at peace beneath the same old stars, her loveliness unimpaired, bejewelled with the beaten gold of ages, her breasts uncovered, and her grand limbs flashing in the sun. Her shoulders of alabaster are lifted above the sand-drifts; she surveys the little figures of to-day. She takes her choice...

That night I did not dream, but neither did the whole of me lie down in sleep. During the long dark hours I was aware of that picture endlessly repeating itself, the picture of George Isley stealing out into the moonlight desert. The night so swiftly dropped her hood about him; so mysteriously he merged into the unchanging thing which cloaks the past. It lifted. Some huge shadowy hand, gloved softly yet of granite, stretched over the leagues to take him. He disappeared.

They say the desert is motionless and has no gestures! That night I saw it moving, hurrying. It went tearing after him. You understand my meaning? No! Well, when excited it produces this strange impression, and the terrible moment is—when you surrender helplessly—you desire it shall swallow you. You let it come. George Isley spoke of a web. It is, at any rate, some central power that conceals itself behind the surface glamour folk call the spell of Egypt. Its home is not apparent. It dwells with ancient Egypt—underground. Behind the stillness of hot windless days, behind the peace of calm, gigantic nights, it lurks unrealised, monstrous and irresistible. My mind grasped it as little as the fact that our solar system with all its retinue of satellites and planets rushes annually many million miles towards a star in Hercules, while yet that constellation appears no closer than it did six thousand years ago. But the clue dropped into me. George Isley, with his entire retinue of thought and life and feeling, was being similarly drawn. And I, a minor satellite, had become aware of the horrifying pull. It was magnificent... And I fell asleep on the crest of this enormous wave.

## V

The next few days passed idly; weeks passed too, I think; hidden away in this cosmopolitan hotel we lived apart, unnoticed. There was the feeling that time went what pace it pleased, now fast, now slow, now standing still. The similarity of the brilliant days, set between wondrous dawns and sunsets, left the impression that it was really one long, endless day without divisions. The mind's machinery of measurement suffered dislocation. Time went backwards; dates were forgotten; the month, the time of year, the century itself went down into undifferentiated life.

The Present certainly slipped away curiously. Newspapers and politics became unimportant, news uninteresting, English life so remote as to be unreal, European affairs shadowy. The stream of life ran in another direction altogether—backwards. The names and faces of friends appeared through mist. People arrived as though dropped from the skies. They suddenly were there; one saw them in the dining-room, as though they had just slipped in from an outer world that once was real—somewhere. Of course, a steamer sailed four times a week, and the journey took five days, but these things were merely known, not realised. The fact that here it was summer, whereas over there winter reigned, helped to make the distance not quite thinkable. We looked at the desert and made plans. "We will do this, we will do that; we must go there, we'll visit such and such a place..." yet nothing happened. It always was to-morrow or yesterday, and we shared the discovery of Alice that there was no real "to-day." For our thinking made everything happen. That was enough. It *had* happened. It was the reality of dreams. Egypt was a dream-world that made the heart live backwards.

It came about, thus, that for the next few weeks I watched a fading life, myself alert and sympathetic, yet unable somehow to intrude and help. Noticing various little things by which George Isley betrayed the progress of the unequal struggle, I found my assistance negatived by the fact that I was in similar case myself. What he experienced in large and finally, I, too, experienced in little and for the moment. For I seemed also caught upon the fringe of the invisible web. My feelings were entangled sufficiently for me to understand... And the decline of his being was terrible to watch. His character went with it; I saw his talents fade, his personality dwindle, his very soul dissolve before the insidious and invading influence. He hardly struggled. I thought of those abominable insects that paralyse the motor systems of their victims and then devour them at their leisure—alive. The incredible adventure was literally true, but, being spiritual, may not be told in the terms of a detective story. This version must remain an individual rendering—an aspect of *one* possible version. All who know the real Egypt, that Egypt which has nothing to do with dams and Nationalists and the external welfare of the falaheen, will understand. The pilfering of her ancient dead she suffers still; she, in revenge, preys at her leisure on the living.

The occasions when he betrayed himself were ordinary enough; it was the glimpse they afforded of what was in progress beneath his calm exterior that made them interesting. Once, I remember, we had lunched together at Mena, and, after visiting certain excavations beyond the Gizeh pyramids, we made our way homewards by way of the Sphinx. It was dusk, and the main army of tourists had retired, though some few dozen sight-seers still moved about to the cries of donkey-boys and baksheesh. The vast head and shoulders suddenly emerged, riding undrowned above the sea of sand. Dark and monstrous in the fading light, it loomed, as ever, a being of non-human lineage; no amount of familiarity could depreciate its grandeur, its impressive setting, the lost expression of the countenance that is too huge to focus as a face. A thousand visits leaves its power undiminished. It has intruded upon our earth from some uncommon world. George Isley and myself both turned aside to acknowledge the presence of this alien, uncomfortable thing. We did not linger, but we slackened pace. It was the obvious, inevitable thing to do. He pointed then, with a suddenness that made me start. He indicated the tourists standing round.

"See," he said, in a lowered tone, "day and night you'll always find a crowd obedient to that thing. But notice their behaviour. People don't do that before any other ruin in the world I've ever seen." He referred to the attempts of individuals to creep away alone and stare into the stupendous visage by themselves. At different points in the deep sandy basin were men and women, standing solitary, lying, crouching, apart from the main company where the dragomen mouthed their exposition with impertinent glibness.

"The desire to be alone," he went on, half to himself, as we paused a moment, "the sense of worship which insists on privacy."

It *was* significant, for no amount of advertising could dwarf the impressiveness of the inscrutable visage into whose eyes of stone the silent humans gazed. Not even the red-coat, standing inside one gigantic ear, could introduce the commonplace. But my companion's words let another thing into the spectacle, a less exalted thing, dropping a hint of horror about that sandy cup: It became easy, for a moment, to imagine these tourists worshipping—against their will; to picture the monster noticing that they were there; that it might slowly turn its awful head; that the sand might visibly trickle from a stirring paw; that, in a word, they might be taken—changed.

"Come," he whispered in a dropping tone, interrupting my fancies as though he half-divined them, "it is getting late, and to be alone with the thing is intolerable to me just now. But you notice, don't you," he added, as he took my arm to hurry me away, "how little the tourists matter? Instead of injuring the effect, they increase it. It uses *them*."

And again a slight sensation of chill, communicated possibly by his nervous touch, or possibly by his earnest way of saying these curious words, passed through me. Some part of me remained behind in that hollow trough of sand, prostrate before an immensity that symbolised the past. A curious, wild yearning caught me momentarily, an intense desire to understand exactly why that terror stood there, its actual meaning long ago to the hearts that set it waiting for the sun, what definite rôle it played, what souls it stirred and why, in that system of towering belief and faith whose indestructible emblem it still remained. The past stood grouped so solemnly about its menacing presentment. I was distinctly aware of this spiritual suction backwards that my companion yielded to so gladly, yet against his normal, modern self. For it made the past appear magnificently desirable, and loosened all the rivets of the present. It bodied forth three main ingredients of this deep Egyptian spell—size, mystery, and immobility.

Yet, to my relief, the cheaper aspect of this Egyptian glamour left him cold. He remained unmoved by the commonplace mysterious; he told no mummy stories, nor ever hinted at the supernatural quality that leaps to the mind of the majority. There was no play in him. The influence was grave and vital. And, although I knew he held strong views with regard to the impiety of disturbing the dead, he never in my hearing attached any possible revengeful character to the energy of an outraged past. The current tales of this description he ignored; they were for superstitious minds or children; the deities that claimed his soul were of a grander order altogether. He lived, if it may be so expressed, already in a world his heart had reconstructed or remembered; it drew him in another direction altogether; with the modern, sensational view of life his spirit held no traffic any longer; he was living backwards. I saw his figure receding mournfully, yet never sentimentally, into the spacious, golden atmosphere of recaptured days. The enormous soul of buried Egypt drew him down. The dwindling of his physical appearance was, of course, a mental interpretation of my own; but another, stranger interpretation of a spiritual kind moved parallel with it—marvellous and horrible. For, as he diminished outwardly and in his modern, present aspect, he grew within—gigantic. The size of Egypt entered into him. Huge proportions now began to accompany any presentment of his personality to my inner vision. He towered. These two qualities of the land already obsessed him—magnitude and immobility.

And that awe which modern life ignores contemptuously woke in my heart. I almost feared his presence at certain times. For one aspect of the Egyptian spell is explained by sheer size and bulk. Disdainful of mere speed to-day, the heart is still uncomfortable with magnitude; and in Egypt there is size that may easily appall, for every detail shunts it laboriously upon the mind. It elbows out the present. The desert's vastness is not made comprehensible by mileage, and the sources of the Nile are so distant that they exist less on the map than in the imagination. The effort to realise suffers paralysis; they might equally be in the moon or Saturn. The undecorated magnificence of the desert remains unknown, just as the proportions of pyramid and temple, of pylons and Colossi approach the edge of the mind yet never enter in. All stand outside, clothed in this prodigious measurement of the past. And the old beliefs not only share this titanic effect upon the consciousness, but carry it stages further. The entire scale haunts with uncomfortable immensity, so that the majority run back with relief to the measurable details of a more manageable scale. Express trains, flying machines, Atlantic liners—these produce no unpleasant stretching of the faculties compared to the influence of the Karnak pylons, the pyramids, or the interior of the Serapeum.

Close behind this magnitude, moreover, steps the monstrous. It is revealed not in sand and stone alone, in queer effects of light and shadow, of glittering sunsets and of magical dusks, but in the very aspect of the bird and animal life. The heavy-headed buffaloes betray it equally with the vultures, the myriad kites, the grotesqueness of the mouthing camels. The rude, enormous scenery has it everywhere. There is nothing lyrical in this land of passionate mirages. Uncouth immensity notes the little human flittings. The days roll by in a tide of golden splendour; one goes helplessly with the flood; but it is an irresistible flood that sweeps backwards and below. The silent-footed natives in their coloured robes move before a curtain, and behind that curtain dwells the soul of ancient Egypt—the Reality, as George Isley called it—watching, with sleepless eyes of grey infinity. Then, sometimes the curtain stirs and lifts an edge; an invisible hand creeps forth; the soul is touched. And some one disappears.

## VI

The process of disintegration must have been at work a long time before I appeared upon the scene; the changes went forward with such rapidity.

It was his third year in Egypt, two of which had been spent without interruption in company with an Egyptologist named Moleson, in the neighbourhood of Thebes. I soon discovered that this region was for him the centre of attraction, or as he put it, of the web. Not Luxor, of course, nor the images of reconstructed Karnak; but that stretch of grim, forbidding mountains where royalty, earthly and spiritual, sought eternal peace for the physical remains. There amid surroundings of superb desolation, great priests and mighty kings had thought themselves secure from sacrilegious touch. In caverns underground they kept their faithful tryst with centuries, guarded by the silence of magnificent gloom. There they waited, communing with passing ages in their sleep, till Ra, their glad divinity, should summon them to the fulfillment of their ancient dream. And there, in the Valley of the Tombs of the Kings, their dream was shattered, their lovely prophecies derided, and their glory dimmed by the impious desecration of the curious.

That George Isley and his companion had spent their time, not merely digging and deciphering like their practical confrères, but engaged in some strange experiments of recovery and reconstruction, was matter for open comment among the fraternity. That incredible things had happened there was the big story of two Egyptian seasons at least. I heard this later only—tales of utterly incredible kind, that the desolate vale of rock was seen repeopled on moonlit nights, that the smoke of unaccustomed fires rose to cap the flat-topped peaks, that the pageantry of some forgotten worship had been seen to issue from the openings of these hills, and that sounds of chanting, sonorous and marvellously sweet, had been heard to echo from those bleak, repellent precipices. The tales apparently were grossly exaggerated; wandering Bedouins brought them in; the guides and dragomen repeated them with mysterious additions; till they filtered down through the native servants in the hotels and reached the tourists with highly picturesque embroidery. They reached the authorities too. The only accurate fact I gathered at the time, however, was that they had abruptly ceased. George Isley and Moleson, moreover, had parted company. And Moleson, I heard, was the originator of the business. He was, at this time, unknown to me; his arresting book on "A Modern Reconstruction of Sun-worship in Ancient Egypt" being my only link with his unusual mind. Apparently he regarded the sun as the deity of the scientific religion of the future which would replace the various anthropomorphic gods of childish creeds. He discussed the possibility of the zodiacal signs being some kind of Celestial Intelligences. Belief blazed on every page. Men's life is heat, derived solely from the sun, and men were, therefore, part of the sun in the sense that a Christian is part of his personal deity. And absorption was the end. His description of "sun-worship ceremonials" conveyed an amazing reality and beauty. This singular book, however, was all I knew of him until he came to visit us in Helouan, though I easily discerned that his influence somehow was the original cause of the change in my companion.

At Thebes, then, was the active centre of the influence that drew my friend away from modern things. It was there, I easily guessed, that "obstacles" had been placed in the way of these men's too close enquiry. In that haunted and oppressive valley, where profane and reverent come to actual grips, where modern curiosity is most busily organised, and even tourists are aware of a masked hostility that dogs the prying of the least imaginative mind—there, in the neighbourhood of the hundred-gated city, had Egypt set the headquarters of her irreconcilable enmity. And it was there, amid the ruins of her loveliest past, that George Isley had spent his years of magical reconstruction and met the influence that now dominated his entire life.

And though no definite avowal of the struggle betrayed itself in speech between us, I remember fragments of conversation, even at this stage, that proved his willing surrender of the present. We spoke of fear once, though with the indirectness of connection I have mentioned. I urged that the mind, once it is forewarned, can remain master of itself and prevent a thing from happening.

"But that does not make the thing unreal," he objected.

"The mind can deny it," I said. "It then becomes unreal."

He shook his head. "One does not deny an unreality. Denial is a childish act of self-protection against something you expect to happen." He caught my eye a moment. "You deny what you are afraid of," he said. "Fear invites." And he smiled uneasily. "You know it must get you in the end." And, both of us being aware secretly to what our talk referred, it seemed bold-blooded and improper; for actually we discussed the psychology of his disappearance. Yet, while I disliked it, there was a fascination about the subject that compelled attraction... "Once fear gets in," he added presently, "confidence is undermined, the structure of life is threatened, and you—go gladly. The foundation of everything is belief. A man is what he believes about himself; and in Egypt you can believe things that elsewhere you would not even think about. It attacks the essentials." He sighed, yet with a curious pleasure; and a smile of resignation and relief passed over his rugged features and was gone again. The luxury of abandonment lay already in him.

"But even belief," I protested, "must be founded on some experience or other." It seemed ghastly to speak of his spiritual malady behind the mask of indirect allusion. My excuse was that he so obviously talked willingly.

He agreed instantly. "Experience of one kind or another," he said darkly, "there always is. Talk with the men who live out here; ask any one who thinks, or who has the imagination which divines. You'll get only one reply, phrase it how they may. Even the tourists and the little commonplace officials feel it. And it's not the climate, it's not nerves, it's not any definite tendency that they can name or lay their finger on. Nor is it mere orientalising of the mind. It's something that first takes you from your common life, and that later takes common life from you. You willingly resign an unremunerative Present. There are no half-measures either—once the gates are open."

There was so much undeniable truth in this that I found no corrective by way of strong rejoinder. All my attempts, indeed, were futile in this way. He meant to go; my words could not stop him. He wanted a witness,—he dreaded the loneliness of going—but he brooked no interference. The contradictory position involved a perplexing state of heart and mind in both of us. The atmosphere of this majestic land, to-day so trifling, yesterday so immense, most certainly induced a lifting of the spiritual horizon that revealed amazing possibilities.

### VII

It was in the windless days of a perfect December that Moleson, the Egyptologist, found us out and paid a flying visit to Helouan. His duties took him up and down the land, but his time seemed largely at his own disposal. He lingered on. His coming introduced a new element I was not quite able to estimate; though, speaking generally, the effect of his presence upon my companion was to emphasise the latter's alteration. It underlined the change, and drew attention to it. The new arrival, I gathered, was not altogether welcome. "I should never have expected to find you *here*," laughed Moleson when they met, and whether he referred to Helouan or to the hotel was not quite clear. I got the impression he meant both; I remembered my fancy that it was a good hotel to hide in. George Isley had betrayed a slight involuntary start when the visiting card was brought to him at tea-time. I think he had wished to escape from his former co-worker. Moleson had found him out. "I heard you had a friend with you and were contemplating further exper—work," he added. He changed the word "experiment" quickly to the other.

"The former, as you see, is true, but not the latter," replied my companion dryly, and in his manner was a touch of opposition that might have been hostility. Their intimacy, I saw, was close and of old standing. In all they said and did and looked, there was an undercurrent of other meaning that just escaped me. They were up to something—they *had* been up to something; but Isley would have withdrawn if he could!

Moleson was an ambitious and energetic personality, absorbed in his profession, alive to the poetical as well as to the practical value of archæology, and he made at first a wholly delightful impression upon me. An instinctive flair for his subject had early in life brought him success and a measure of fame as well. His knowledge was accurate and scholarly, his mind saturated in the lore of a vanished civilisation. Behind an exterior that was quietly careless, I divined a passionate and complex nature, and I watched him with interest as the man for whom the olden sun-worship of unscientific days held some beauty of reality and truth. Much in his strange book that had bewildered me now seemed intelligible when I saw the author. I cannot explain this more closely. Something about him somehow made it possible. Though modern to the finger-tips and thoroughly equipped with all the tendencies of the day, there seemed to hide in him another self that held aloof with a dignified detachment from the interests in which his "educated" mind was centred. He read living secrets beneath museum labels, I might put it. He stepped out of the days of the Pharoahs if ever man did, and I realised early in our acquaintance that this was the man who had exceptional powers of "resistance and self-protection," and was, in his particular branch of work, "unusual." In manner he was light and gay, his sense of humour strong, with a way of treating everything as though laughter was the sanest attitude towards life. There is, however, the laughter that hides—other things. Moleson, as I gathered from many clues of talk and manner and silence, was a deep and singular being. His experiences in Egypt if any, he had survived admirably. There were at least two Molesons. I felt him more than double—multiple.

In appearance tall, thin and fleshless, with a dried-up skin and features withered as a mummy's, he said laughingly that Nature had picked him physically for his "job"; and, indeed, one could see him worming his way down narrow tunnels into the sandy tombs, and writhing along sunless passages of suffocating heat without too much personal inconvenience. Something sinuous, almost fluid in his mind expressed itself in his body too. He might go in any direction without causing surprise. He might go backwards or forwards. He might go in two directions at once.

And my first impression of the man deepened before many days were past. There was irresponsibility in him, insincerity somewhere, almost want of heart. His morality was certainly not to-day's, and the mind in him was slippery. I think the modern world, to which he was unattached, confused and irritated him. A sense of insecurity came with him. His interest in George Isley was the interest in a psychological "specimen." I remembered how in his book he described the selection of individuals for certain functions of that marvellous worship, and the odd idea flashed through me—well, that Isley exactly suited some purpose of his re-creating energies. The man was keenly observant from top to toe, but not with his sight alone; he seemed to be aware of motives and emotions before he noticed the acts or gestures that these caused. I felt that he took me in as well. Certainly he eyed me up and down by means of this inner observation that seemed automatic with him.

Moleson was not staying in our hotel; he had chosen one where social life was more abundant; but he came up frequently to lunch and dine, and sometimes spent the evening in Isley's rooms, amusing us with his skill upon the piano, singing Arab songs, and chanting phrases from the ancient Egyptian rituals to rhythms of his own invention. The old Egyptian music, both in harmony and melody, was far more developed than I had realised, the use of sound having been of radical importance in their ceremonies. The chanting in particular he did with extraordinary effect, though whether its success lay in his sonorous voice, his peculiar increasing of the vowel sounds, or to anything deeper, I cannot pretend to say. The result at any rate was of a unique description. It brought buried Egypt to the surface; the gigantic Presence entered sensibly into the room. It came, huge and gorgeous, rolling upon the mind the instant he began, and something in it was both terrible and oppressive. The repose of eternity lay in the sound. Invariably, after a few moments of that transforming music, I saw the Valley of the Kings, the deserted temples, titanic faces of stone, great effigies coifed with zodiacal signs, but above all—the twin Colossi.

I mentioned this latter detail.

"Curious *you* should feel that too—curious you should say it, I mean," Moleson replied, not looking at me, yet with an air as if I had said something he expected. "To me the Memnon figures express Egypt better than all the other monuments put together. Like the desert, they are featureless. They sum her up, as it were, yet leave the message unuttered. For, you see, they cannot." He laughed a little in his throat. "They have neither eyes nor lips nor nose; their features are gone."

"Yet they tell the secret—to those who care to listen," put in Isley in a scarcely noticeable voice. "Just because they have no words. They still sing at dawn," he added in a louder, almost a challenging tone. It startled me.

Moleson turned round at him, opened his lips to speak, hesitated, stopped. He said nothing for a moment. I cannot describe what it was in the lightning glance they exchanged that put me on the alert for something other than was obvious. My nerves quivered suddenly, and a breath of colder air stole in among us. Moleson swung round to me again. "I almost think," he said, laughing when I complimented him upon the music, "that I must have been a priest of Aton-Ra in an earlier existence, for all this comes to my finger-tips as if it were instinctive knowledge. Plotinus, remember, lived a few miles away at Alexandria with his great idea that knowledge is recollection," he said, with a kind of cynical amusement. "In those days, at any rate," he added more significantly, "worship was real and ceremonials actually expressed great ideas and teaching. There was power in them." Two of the Molesons spoke in that contradictory utterance.

I saw that Isley was fidgeting where he sat, betraying by certain gestures that uneasiness was in him. He hid his face a moment in his hands; he sighed; he made a movement—as though to prevent something coming. But Moleson resisted his attempt to change the conversation, though the key shifted a little of its own accord. There were numerous occasions like this when I was aware that both men skirted something that had happened, something that Moleson wished to resume, but that Isley seemed anxious to postpone.

I found myself studying Moleson's personality, yet never getting beyond a certain point. Shrewd, subtle, with an acute rather than a large intelligence, he was cynical as well as insincere, and yet I cannot describe by what means I arrived at two other conclusions as well about him; first, that this insincerity and want of heart had not been so always; and secondly, that he sought social diversion with deliberate and un-ordinary purpose. I could well believe that the first was Egypt's mark upon him, and the second an effort at resistance and self-protection.

"If it wasn't for the gaiety," he remarked once in a flippant way that thinly hid significance, "a man out here would go under in a year. Social life gets rather reckless—exaggerated—people do things they would never dream of doing at home. Perhaps you've noticed it," he added, looking suddenly at me; "Cairo and the rest—they plunge at it as though driven—a sort of excess about it somewhere." I nodded agreement. The way he said it was unpleasant rather. "It's an antidote," he said, a sub-acid flavour in his tone. "I used to loathe society myself. But now I find gaiety—a certain irresponsible excitement—of importance. Egypt gets on the nerves after a bit. The moral fibre fails. The will grows weak." And he glanced covertly at Isley as with a desire to point his meaning. "It's the clash between the ugly present and the majestic past, perhaps." He smiled.

Isley shrugged his shoulders, making no reply; and the other went on to tell stories of friends and acquaintances whom Egypt had adversely affected: Barton, the Oxford man, school teacher, who had insisted on living in a tent until the Government relieved him of his job. He took to his tent, roamed the desert, drawn irresistibly, practical considerations of the present of no avail. This yearning took him, though he could never define the exact attraction. In the end his mental balance was disturbed. "But now he's all right again; I saw him in London only this year; he can't say what he felt or why he did it. Only—he's different." Of John Lattin, too, he spoke, whom agoraphobia caught so terribly in Upper Egypt; of Malahide, upon whom some fascination of the Nile induced suicidal mania and attempts at drowning; of Jim Moleson, a cousin (who had camped at Thebes with himself and Isley), whom megalomania of a most singular type attacked suddenly in a sandy waste—all radically cured as soon as they left Egypt, yet, one and all, changed and made otherwise in their very souls.

He talked in a loose, disjointed way, and though much he said was fantastic, as if meant to challenge opposition, there was impressiveness about it somewhere, due, I think, to a kind of cumulative emotion he produced.

"The monuments do not impress merely by their bulk, but by their majestic symmetry," I remember him saying. "Look at the choice of form alone—the pyramids, for instance. No other shape was possible: dome, square, spires, all would have been hideously inadequate. The wedge-shaped mass, immense foundations and pointed apex were the *mot juste* in outline. Do you think people without greatness in themselves chose that form? There was no unbalance in the minds that conceived the harmonious and magnificent structures of the temples. There was stately grandeur in their consciousness that could only be born of truth and knowledge. The power in their images is a direct expression of eternal and essential things they knew."

We listened in silence. He was off upon his hobby. But behind the careless tone and laughing questions, there was this, lurking passionateness that made me feel uncomfortable. He was edging up, I felt, towards some climax that meant life and death to himself and Isley. I could not fathom it. My sympathy let me in a little, yet not enough to understand completely. Isley, I saw, was also uneasy, though for reasons that equally evaded me.

"One can almost believe," he continued, "that something still hangs about in the atmosphere from those olden times." He half-closed his eyes, but I caught the gleam in them. "It affects the mind through the imagination. With some it changes the point of view. It takes the soul back with it to former, quite different conditions, that must have been almost another kind of consciousness."

He paused an instant and looked up at us. "The *intensity* of belief in those days," he resumed, since neither of us accepted the challenge, "was amazing—something quite unknown anywhere in the world to-day. It was so sure, so positive; no mere speculative theories, I mean; as though something in the climate, the exact position beneath the stars, the 'attitude' of this particular stretch of earth in relation to the sun—thinned the veil between humanity—and other things. Their hierarchies of gods, you know, were not mere idols; animals, birds, monsters, and what-not, all typified spiritual forces and powers that influenced their daily life. But the strong thing is—they *knew*. People who were scientific as they were did not swallow foolish superstitions. They made colours that could last six thousand years, even in the open air; and without instruments they measured accurately—an enormously difficult and involved calculation—the precession of the equinoxes. You've been to Denderah?"—he suddenly glanced again at me. "No! Well, the minds that realised the zodiacal signs could hardly believe, you know, that Hathor was a cow!"

Isley coughed. He was about to interrupt, but before he could find words, Moleson was off again, some new quality in his tone and manner that was almost aggressive. The hints he offered seemed more than hints. There was a strange conviction in his heart. I think he was skirting a bigger thing that he and his companion knew, yet that his real object was to see in how far I was open to attack—how far my sympathy might be with them. I became aware that he and George Isley shared this bigger thing. It was based, I felt, on some certain knowledge that experiment had brought them.

"Think of the grand teaching of Aknahton, that young Pharaoh who regenerated the entire land and brought it to its immense prosperity. He taught the worship of the sun, but not of the visible sun. The deity had neither form nor shape. The great disk of glory was but the manifestation, each beneficent ray ending in a hand that blessed the world. It was a god of everlasting energy, love and power, yet men could know it at first hand in their daily lives, worshipping it at dawn and sunset with passionate devotion. No anthropomorphic idol masqueraded in *that!*"

An extraordinary glow was about him as he said it. The same minute he lowered his voice, shifting the key perceptibly. He kept looking up at me through half-closed eyelids.

"And another thing they wonderfully knew," he almost whispered, "was that, with the precession of their deity across the equinoctial changes, there came new powers down into the world of men. Each cycle—each zodiacal sign—brought its special powers which they quickly typified in the monstrous effigies we label to-day in our dull museums. Each sign took some two thousand years to traverse. Each sign, moreover, involved a change in human consciousness. There was this relation between the heavens and the human heart. All that they knew. While the sun crawled through the sign of Taurus, it was the Bull they worshipped; with Aries, it was the ram that coifed their granite symbols. Then came, as you remember, with Pisces the great New Arrival, when already they sank from their grand zenith, and the Fish was taken as the emblem of the changing powers which the Christ embodied. For the human soul, they held, echoed the changes in the immense journey of the original deity, who is its source, across the Zodiac, and the truth of 'As above, so Below,' remains the key to all manifested life. And to-day the sun, just entering Aquarius, new powers are close upon the world. The old—that which has been for two thousand years—again is crumbling, passing, dying. New powers and a new consciousness are knocking at our doors. It is a time of change. It is also"—he leaned forward so that his eyes came close before me—"the time to make the change. The soul can choose its own conditions. It can—"

A sudden crash smothered the rest of the sentence. A chair had fallen with a clatter upon the wooden floor where the carpet left it bare. Whether Isley in rising had stumbled against it, or whether he had purposely knocked it over, I could not say. I only knew that he had abruptly risen and as abruptly sat down again. A curious feeling came to me that the sign was somehow prearranged. It was so sudden. His voice, too, was forced, I thought.

"Yes, but we can do without all that, Moleson," he interrupted, with acute abruptness. "Suppose we have a tune instead."

## VIII

It was after dinner in his private room, and he had sat very silent in his corner until this sudden outburst. Moleson got up quietly without a word and moved over to the piano. I saw—or was it imagination merely?—a new expression slide upon his withered face. He meant mischief somewhere.

From that instant—from the moment he rose and walked over the thick carpet—he fascinated me. The atmosphere his talk and stories had brought remained. His lean fingers ran over the keys, and at first he played fragments from popular musical comedies that were pleasant enough, but made no demand upon the attention. I heard them without listening. I was thinking of another thing—his walk. For the way he moved across those few feet of carpet had power in it. He looked different; he seemed another man; he was changed. I saw him curiously—as I sometimes now saw Isley too—bigger. In some manner that was both enchanting and oppressive, his presence from that moment drew my imagination as by an air of authority it held.

I left my seat in the far corner and dropped into a chair beside the window, nearer to the piano. Isley, I then noticed, had also turned to watch him. But it was George Isley not quite as he was now. I felt rather than saw the change. Both men had subtly altered. They seemed extended, their outlines shadowy.

Isley, alert and anxious, glanced up at the player, his mind of earlier years—for the expression of his face was plain—following the light music, yet with difficulty that involved effort, almost struggle. "Play that again, will you?" I heard him say from time to time. He was trying to take hold of it, to climb back to a condition where that music had linked him to the present, to seize a mental structure that was gone, to grip hold tightly of it—only to find that it was too far forgotten and too fragile. It would not bear him. I am sure of it, and I can swear I divined his mood. He fought to realise himself as he had been, but in vain. In his dim corner opposite I watched him closely. The big black Blüthner blocked itself between us. Above it swayed the outline, lean and half shadowy, of Moleson as he played. A faint whisper floated through the room. "You are in Egypt." Nowhere else could this queer feeling of presentiment, of anticipation, have gained a footing so easily. I was aware of intense emotion in all three of us. The least reminder of To-day seemed ugly. I longed for some ancient forgotten splendour that was lost.

The scene fixed my attention very steadily, for I was aware of something deliberate and calculated on Moleson's part. The thing was well considered in his mind, intention only half concealed. It was Egypt he interpreted by sound, expressing what in him was true, then observing its effect, as he led us cleverly towards—the past. Beginning with the present, he played persuasively, with penetration, with insistent meaning, too. He had that touch which conjured up real atmosphere, and, at first, that atmosphere termed modern. He rendered vividly the note of London, passing from the jingles of musical comedy, nervous rag-times and sensuous Tango dances, into the higher strains of concert rooms and "cultured" circles. Yet not too abruptly. Most dexterously he shifted the level, and with it our emotion. I recognised, as in a parody, various ultra-modern thrills: the tumult of Strauss, the pagan sweetness of primitive Debussy, the weirdness and ecstasy of metaphysical Scriabin. The composite note of To-day in both extremes, he brought into this private sitting-room of the desert hotel, while George Isley, listening keenly, fidgeted in his chair.

"'Après-midi d'un Faune,'" said Moleson dreamily, answering the question as to what he played. "Debussy's, you know. And the thing before it was from 'Til Eulenspiegel'—Strauss, of course."

He drawled, swaying slowly with the rhythm, and leaving pauses between the words. His attention was not wholly on his listener, and in the voice was a quality that increased my uneasy apprehension. I felt distress for Isley somewhere. Something, it seemed, was coming; Moleson brought it. Unconsciously in his walk, it now appeared consciously in his music; and it came from what was underground in him. A charm, a subtle change, stole oddly over the room. It stole over my heart as well. Some power of estimating left me, as though my mind were slipping backwards and losing familiar, common standards.

"The true modern note in it, isn't there?" he drawled; "cleverness, I think—intellectual—surface ingenuity—no depth or permanence—just the sensational brilliance of To-day." He turned and stared at me fixedly an instant. "Nothing *everlasting,*" he added impressively. "It tells everything it knows—because it's small enough—"

And the room turned pettier as he said it; another, bigger shadow draped its little walls. Through the open windows came a stealthy gesture of eternity. The atmosphere stretched visibly. Moleson was playing a marvellous fragment from Scriabin's "Prometheus." It sounded thin and shallow. This modern music, all of it, was out of place and trivial. It was almost ridiculous. The scale of our emotion changed insensibly into a deeper thing that has no name in dictionaries, being of another age. And I glanced at the windows where stone columns framed dim sections of great Egypt listening outside. There was no moon; only deep draughts of stars blazed, hanging in the sky. I thought with awe of the mysterious knowledge that vanished people had of these stars, and of the Sun's huge journey through the Zodiac...

And, with astonishing suddenness as of dream, there rose a pictured image against that starlit sky. Lifted into the air, between heaven and earth, I saw float swiftly past a panorama of the stately temples, led by Denderah, Edfu, Abou Simbel. It paused, it hovered, it disappeared. Leaving incalculable solemnity behind it in the air, it vanished, and to see so vast a thing move at that easy yet unhasting speed unhinged some sense of measurement in me. It was, of course, I assured myself, mere memory objectified owing to something that the music summoned, yet the apprehension rose in me that the whole of Egypt presently would stream past in similar fashion—Egypt as she was in the zenith of her unrecoverable past. Behind the tinkling of the modern piano passed the rustling of a multitude, the tramping of countless feet on sand... It was singularly vivid. It arrested in me something that normally went flowing... And when I turned my head towards the room to call attention to my strange experience, the eyes of Moleson, I saw, were laid upon my own. He stared at me. The light in them transfixed me, and I understood that the illusion was due in some manner to his evocation. Isley rose at the same moment from his chair. The thing I had vaguely been expecting had shifted closer. And the same moment the musician abruptly changed his key.

"You may like this better," he murmured, half to himself, but in tones he somehow made echoing. "It's more suited to the place." There was a resonance in the voice as though it emerged from hollows underground. "The other seems almost sacrilegious—here." And his voice drawled off in the rhythm of slower modulations that he played. It had grown muffled. There was an impression, too, that he did not strike the piano, but that the music issued from himself.

"Place! What place?" asked Isley quickly. His head turned sharply as he spoke. His tone, in its remoteness, made me tremble.

The musician laughed to himself. "I meant that this hotel seems really an impertinence," he murmured, leaning down upon the notes he played upon so softly and so well; "and that it's but the thinnest kind of pretence—when you come to think of it. We are in the desert really. The Colossi are outside, and all the emptied temples. Or ought to be," he added, raising his tone abruptly with a glance at me.

He straightened up and stared out into the starry sky past George Isley's shoulders.

"That," he exclaimed, with betraying vehemence, "is where we are and what we play to!" His voice suddenly increased; there was a roar in it. "That," he repeated, "is the thing that takes our hearts away." The volume of intonation was astonishing.

For the way he uttered the monosyllable suddenly revealed the man beneath the outer sheath of cynicism and laughter, explained his heartlessness, his secret stream of life. He, too, was soul and body in the past. "That" revealed more than pages of descriptive phrases. His heart lived in the temple aisles, his mind unearthed forgotten knowledge; his soul had clothed itself anew in the seductive glory of antiquity: he dwelt with a quickening magic of existence in the reconstructed splendour of what most term only ruins. He and George Isley together had revivified a power that enticed them backwards; but whereas the latter struggled still, the former had already made his permanent home there. The faculty in me that saw the vision of streaming temples saw also this—remorselessly definite. Moleson himself sat naked at that piano. I saw him clearly then. He no longer masqueraded behind his sneers and laughter. He, too, had long ago surrendered, lost himself, gone out, and from the place his soul now dwelt in he watched George Isley sinking down to join him. He lived in ancient, subterranean Egypt. This great hotel stood precariously on the merest upper crust of desert. A thousand tombs, a hundred temples lay outside, within reach almost of our very voices. Moleson was merged with "that."

This intuition flashed upon me like the picture in the sky; and both were true.

And, meanwhile, this other thing he played had a surge of power in it impossible to describe. It was sombre, huge and solemn. It conveyed the power that his walk conveyed. There was distance in it, but a distance not of space alone. A remoteness of time breathed through it with that strange sadness and melancholy yearning that enormous interval brings. It marched, but very far away; it held refrains that assumed the rhythms of a multitude the centuries muted; it sang, but the singing was underground in passages that fine sand muffled. Lost, wandering winds sighed through it, booming. The contrast, after the modern, cheaper music, was dislocating. Yet the change had been quite naturally effected.

"It would sound empty and monotonous elsewhere—in London, for instance," I heard Moleson drawling, as he swayed to and fro, "but here it is big and splendid—true. You hear what I mean," he added gravely. "You understand?"

"What is it?" asked Isley thickly, before I could say a word. "I forget exactly. It has tears in it more than I can bear." The end of his sentence died away in his throat.

Moleson did not look at him as he answered. He looked at me.

"You surely ought to know," he replied, the voice rising and falling as though the rhythm forced it. You have heard it all before—that chant from the ritual we—"

Isley sprang up and stopped him. I did not hear the sentence complete. An extraordinary thought blazed into me that the voices of both men were not quite their own. I fancied—wild, impossible as it sounds—that I heard the twin Colossi singing to each other in the dawn. Stupendous ideas sprang past me, leaping. It seemed as though eternal symbols of the cosmos, discovered and worshipped in this ancient land, leaped into awful life. My consciousness became enveloping. I had the distressing feeling that ages slipped out of place and took me with them; they dominated me; they rushed me off my feet like water. I was drawn backwards. I, too, was changing—being changed.

"I remember," said Isley softly, a reverence of worship in his voice. But there was anguish in it too, and pity; he let the present go completely from him; the last strands severed with a wrench of pain. I imagined I heard his soul pass weeping far away—below.

"I'll sing it," murmured Moleson, "for the voice is necessary. The sound and rhythm are utterly divine!"

## IX

And forthwith his voice began a series of long-drawn cadences that seemed somehow the root-sounds of every tongue that ever was. A spell came over me I could touch and feel. A web encompassed me; my arms and feet became entangled; a veil of fine threads wove across my eyes. The enthralling' power of the rhythm produced some magical movement in the soul. I was aware of life everywhere about me, far and near, in the dwellings of the dead, as also in the corridors of the iron hills. Thebes stood erect, and Memphis teemed upon the river banks. For the modern world fell, swaying, at this sound that restored the past, and in this past both men before me lived and had their being. The storm of present life passed o'er their heads, while they dwelt underground, obliterated, gone. Upon the wave of sound they went down into their recovered kingdom.

I shivered, moved vigorously, half rose up, then instantly sank back again, resigned and helpless. For I entered by their side, it seemed, the conditions of their strange captivity. My thoughts, my feelings, my point of view were transplanted to another centre. Consciousness shifted in me. I saw things from another's point of view—antiquity's.

The present forgotten but the past supreme, I lost Reality. Our room became a pin-point picture seen in a drop of water, while this subterranean world, replacing it, turned immense. My heart took on the gigantic, leisured stride of what had been. Proportions grew; size captured me; and magnitude, turned monstrous, swept mere measurement away. Some hand of golden sunshine picked me up and set me in the quivering web beside those other two. I heard the rustle of the settling threads; I heard the shuffling of the feet in sand; I heard the whispers in the dwellings of the dead. Behind the monotony of this sacerdotal music I heard them in their dim carved chambers. The ancient galleries were awake. The Life of unremembered ages stirred in multitudes about me.

The reality of so incredible an experience evaporates through the stream of language. I can only affirm this singular proof—that the deepest, most satisfying knowledge the Present could offer seemed insignificant beside some stalwart majesty of the Past that utterly usurped it. This modern room, holding a piano and two figures of To-day, appeared as a paltry miniature pinned against a vast transparent curtain, whose foreground was thick with symbols of temple, sphinx, and pyramid, but whose background of stupendous hanging grey slid off towards a splendour where the cities of the Dead shook off their sand and thronged space to its ultimate horizons... The stars, the entire universe, vibrating and alive, became involved in it. Long periods of time slipped past me. I seemed living ages ago... I was living backwards...

The size and eternity of Egypt took me easily. There was an overwhelming grandeur in it that elbowed out all present standards. The whole place towered and stood up. The desert reared, the very horizons lifted; majestic figures of granite rose above the hotel, great faces hovered and drove past; huge arms reached up to pluck the stars and set them in the ceilings of the labyrinthine tombs. The colossal meaning of the ancient land emerged through all its ruined details... reconstructed—burningly alive...

It became at length unbearable. I longed for the droning sounds to cease, for the rhythm to lessen its prodigious sweep. My heart cried out for the gold of the sunlight on the desert, for the sweet air by the river's banks, for the violet lights upon the hills at dawn. And I resisted, I made an effort to return.

"Your chant is horrible. For God's sake, let's have an Arab song—or the music of To-day!"

The effort was intense, the result was—nothing. I swear I used these words. I heard the actual sound of my voice, if no one else did, for I remember that it was pitiful in the way great space devoured it, making of its appreciable volume the merest whisper as of some bird or insect cry. But the figure that I took for Moleson instead of answer or acknowledgment, merely grew and grew as things grow in a fairy tale. I hardly know; I certainly cannot say. That dwindling part of me which offered comments on the entire occurrence noted this extraordinary effect as though it happened naturally—that Moleson himself was marvellously increasing.

The entire spell became operative all at once. I experienced both the delight of complete abandonment and the terror of letting go what *had* seemed real. I understood Moleson's sham laughter, and the subtle resignation of George Isley. And an amazing thought flashed birdlike across my changing consciousness—that this resurrection into the Past, this rebirth of the spirit which they sought, involved taking upon themselves the guise of these ancient symbols each in turn. As the embryo assumes each evolutionary stage below it before the human semblance is attained, so the souls of those two adventurers took upon themselves the various emblems of that intense belief. The devout worshipper takes on the qualities of his deity. They wore the entire series of the old-world gods so potently that I perceived them, and even objectified them by my senses. The present was their prenatal stage; to enter the past they were being born again.

But it was not Moleson's semblance alone that took on this awful change. Both faces, scaled to the measure of Egypt's outstanding quality of size, became in this little modern room distressingly immense. Distorting mirrors can suggest no simile, for the symmetry of proportion was not injured. I lost their human physiognomies. I saw their thoughts, their feelings, their augmented, altered hearts, the thing that Egypt put there while she stole their love from modern life. There grew an awful stateliness upon them that was huge, mysterious, and motionless as stone.

For Moleson's narrow face at first turned hawk-like in the semblance of the sinister deity, Horus, only stretched to tower above the toy-scaled piano; it was keen and sly and monstrous after prey, while a swiftness of the sunrise leaped from both the brilliant eyes. George Isley, equally immense of outline, was in general presentment more magnificent, a breadth of the Sphinx about his spreading shoulders, and in his countenance an inscrutable power of calm temple images. These were the first signs of obsession; but others followed. In rapid series, like lantern-slides upon a screen, the ancient symbols flashed one after another across these two extended human faces and were gone. Disentanglement became impossible. The successive signatures seemed almost superimposed as in a composite photograph, each appearing and vanished before recognition was even possible, while I interpreted the inner alchemy by means of outer tokens familiar to my senses. Egypt, possessing them, expressed herself thus marvellously in their physical aspect, using the symbols of her intense, regenerative power...

The changes merged with such swiftness into one another that I did not seize the half of them—till, finally, the procession culminated in a single one that remained fixed awfully upon them both. The entire series merged. I was aware of this single masterful image which summed up all the others in sublime repose. The gigantic thing rose up in this incredible statue form. The spirit of Egypt synthesised in this monstrous symbol, obliterated them both. I saw the seated figures of the grim Colossi, dipped in sand, night over them, waiting for the dawn...

## X

I made a violent effort, then, at self-assertion—an effort to focus my mind upon the present. And, searching for Moleson and George Isley, its nearest details, I was aware that I could not find them. The familiar figures of my two companions were not discoverable.

I saw it as plainly as I also saw that ludicrous, wee piano—for a moment. But the moment remained; the Eternity of Egypt stayed. For that lonely and terrific pair had stooped their shoulders and bowed their awful heads. They were in the room. They imaged forth the power of the everlasting Past through the little structures of two human worshippers. Room, walls, and ceiling fled away. Sand and the open sky replaced them.

The two of them rose side by side before my bursting eyes. I knew not where to look. Like some child who confronts its giants upon the nursery floor, I turned to stone, unable to think or move. I stared. Sight wrenched itself to find the men familiar to it, but found instead this symbolising vision. I could not see them properly. Their faces were spread with hugeness, their features lost in some uncommon magnitude, their shoulders, necks, and arms grown vast upon the air. As with the desert, there was physiognomy yet no personal expression, the human thing all drowned within the mass of battered stone. I discovered neither cheeks nor mouth nor jaw, but ruined eyes and lips of broken granite. Huge, motionless, mysterious, Egypt informed them and took them to herself. And between us, curiously presented in some false perspective, I saw the little symbol of To-day—the Blüthner piano. It was appalling. I knew a second of majestic horror. I blenched. Hot and cold gushed through me. Strength left me, power of speech and movement, too, as in a moment of complete paralysis.

The spell, moreover, was not within the room alone; it was outside and everywhere. The Past stood massed about the very walls of the hotel. Distance, as well as time, stepped nearer. That chanting summoned the gigantic items in all their ancient splendour. The shadowy concourse grouped itself upon the sand about us, and I was aware that the great army shifted noiselessly into place; that pyramids soared and towered; that deities of stone stood by; that temples ranged themselves in reconstructed beauty, grave as the night of time whence they emerged; and that the outline of the Sphinx, motionless but aggressive, piled its dim bulk upon the atmosphere. Immensity answered to immensity... There were vast intervals of time and there were reaches of enormous distance, yet all happened in a moment, and all happened within a little space. It was now and here. Eternity whispered in every second as in every grain of sand. Yet, while aware of so many stupendous details all at once, I was really aware of one thing only—that the spirit of ancient Egypt faced me in these two terrific figures, and that my consciousness, stretched painfully yet gloriously, included all, as She also unquestionably included them—and me.

For it seemed I shared the likeness of my two companions. Some lesser symbol, though of similar kind, obsessed me too. I tried to move, but my feet were set in stone; my arms lay fixed; my body was embedded in the rock. Sand beat sharply upon my outer surface, urged upwards in little flurries by a chilly wind. There was nothing felt: I *heard* the rattle of the scattering grains against my hardened body...

And we waited for the dawn; for the resurrection of that unchanging deity who was the source and inspiration of all our glorious life... The air grew keen and fresh. In the distance a line of sky turned from pink to violet and gold; a delicate rose next flushed the desert; a few pale stars hung fainting overhead; and the wind that brought the sunrise was already stirring. The whole land paused upon the coming of its mighty God...

Into the pause there rose a curious sound for which we had been waiting. For it came familiarly, as though expected. I could have sworn at first that it was George Isley who sang, answering his companion. There beat behind its great volume the same note and rhythm, only so prodigiously increased that, while Moleson's chant had waked it, it now was independent and apart. The resonant vibrations of what he sang had reached down into the places where it slept. *They* uttered synchronously. Egypt spoke. There was in it the deep muttering as of a thousand drums, as though the desert uttered in prodigious syllables. I listened while my heart of stone stood still. There were two voices in the sky. *They* spoke tremendously with each other in the dawn:

"So easily we still remain possessors of the land... While the centuries roar past us and are gone."

Soft with power the syllables rolled forth, yet with a booming depth as though caverns underground produced them.

"Our silence is disturbed. Pass on with the multitude towards the East... Still in the dawn we sing the old-world wisdom... They shall hear our speech, yet shall not hear it with their ears of flesh. At dawn our words go forth, searching the distances of sand and time across the sunlight... At dusk they return, as upon eagles' wings, entering again our lips of stone... Each century one syllable, yet no sentence yet complete. While our lips are broken with the utterance..."

It seemed that hours and months and years went past me while I listened in my sandy bed. The fragments died far away, then sounded very close again. It was as though mountain peaks sang to one another above clouds. Wind caught the muffled roar away. Wind brought it back... Then, in a hollow pause that lasted years, conveying marvellously the passage of long periods, I heard the utterance more clearly. The leisured roll of the great voice swept through me like a flood:

"We wait and watch and listen in our loneliness. We do not close our eyes. The moon and stars sail past us, and our river finds the sea. We bring Eternity upon your broken lives... We see you build your little lines of steel across our territory behind the thin white smoke. We hear the whistle of your messengers of iron through the air... The nations rise and pass. The empires flutter westwards and are gone... The sun grows older and the stars turn pale... Winds shift the line of the horizons, and our River moves its bed. But we, everlasting and unchangeable, remain. Of water, sand and fire is our essential being, yet built within the universal air... There is no pause in life, there is no break in death. The changes bring no end. The sun returns... There is eternal resurrection... But our kingdom is underground in shadow, unrealised of your little day... Come, come! The temples still are crowded, and our Desert blesses you. Our River takes your feet. Our sand shall purify, and the fire of our God shall burn you sweetly into wisdom... Come, then, and worship, for the time draws near. It is the dawn..."

The voices died down into depths that the sand of ages muffled, while the flaming dawn of the East rushed up the sky. Sunrise, the great symbol of life's endless resurrection, was at hand. About me, in immense but shadowy array, stood the whole of ancient Egypt, hanging breathlessly upon the moment of adoration. No longer stern and terrible in the splendour of their long neglect, the effigies rose erect with passionate glory, a forest of stately stone. Their granite lips were parted and their ancient eyes were wide. All faced the east. And the sun drew nearer to the rim of the attentive Desert.

## XI

Emotion there seemed none, in the sense that *I* knew feeling. I knew, if anything, the ultimate secrets of two primitive sensations—joy and awe... The dawn grew swiftly brighter. There was gold, as though the sands of Nubia spilt their brilliance on each shining detail; there was glory, as though the retreating tide of stars spilt their light foam upon the world; and there was passion, as though the beliefs of all the edges floated back with abandonment into the—Sun. Ruined Egypt merged into a single temple of elemental vastness whose floor was the empty desert, but whose walls rose to the stars.

Abruptly, then, chanting and rhythm ceased; they dipped below. Sand muffled them. And the Sun looked down upon its ancient world...

A radiant warmth poured through me. I found that I could move my limbs again. A sense of triumphant life ran through my stony frame. For one passing second I heard the shower of gritty particles upon my surface like sand blown upwards by a gust of wind, but this time I could *feel* the sting of it upon my skin. It passed. The drenching heat bathed me from head to foot, while stony insensibility gave place with returning consciousness to flesh and blood. The sun had risen... I was alive, but I was—changed.

It seemed I opened my eyes. An immense relief was in me. I turned; I drew a deep, refreshing breath; I stretched one leg upon a thick, green carpet. Something had left me; another thing had returned. I sat up, conscious of welcome release, of freedom, of escape.

There was some violent, disorganising break. I found myself; I found Moleson; I found George Isley, too. He had got shifted in that room without my being aware of it. Isley had risen. He came upon me like a blow. I saw him move his arms. Fire flashed from below his hands; and I realized then that he was turning on the electric lights. They emerged from different points along the walls, in the alcove, beneath the ceiling, by the writing-table; and one had just that minute blazed into my eyes from a bracket close above me. I was back again in the Present among modern things.

But, while most of the details presented themselves gradually to my recovered senses, Isley returned with this curious effect of speed and distance—like a blow upon the mind. From great height and from prodigious size—he dropped. I seemed to find him rushing at me. Moleson was simply "there"; there was no speed or sudden change in him as with the other. Motionless at the piano, his long thin hands lay down upon the keys yet did not strike them. But Isley came back like lightning into the little room, signs of the monstrous obsession still about his altering features. There was battle and worship mingled in his deep-set eyes. His mouth, though set, was smiling. With a shudder I positively saw the vastness slipping from his face as shadows from a stretch of broken cliff. There was this awful mingling of proportions. The colossal power that had resumed his being drew slowly inwards. There was collapse in him. And upon the sun-burned cheek of his rugged face I saw a tear.

Poignant revulsion caught me then for a moment. The present showed itself in rags. The reduction of scale was painful. I yearned for the splendour that was gone, yet still seemed so hauntingly almost within reach. The cheapness of the hotel room, the glaring ugliness of its tinsel decoration, the baseness of ideals where utility instead of beauty, gain instead of worship, governed life—this, with the dwindled aspect of my companions to the insignificance of marionettes, brought a hungry pain that was at first intolerable. In the glare of light I noticed the small round face of the portable clock upon the mantelpiece, showing half-past eleven. *Moleson had been* two hours at the piano. And this measuring faculty of my mind completed the disillusionment. I was, indeed, back among present things. The mechanical spirit of To-day imprisoned me again.

For a considerable interval we neither moved nor spoke; the sudden change left the emotions in confusion; we had leaped from a height, from the top of the pyramid, from a star—and the crash of landing scattered thought. I stole a glance at Isley, wondering vaguely why he was there at all; the look of resignation had replaced the power in his face; the tear was brushed away. There was no struggle in him now, no sign of resistance; there was abandonment only; he seemed insignificant. The real George Isley was elsewhere: he himself had not returned.

By jerks, as it were, and by awkward stages, then, we all three came back to common things again. I found that we were talking ordinarily, asking each other questions, answering, lighting cigarettes, and all the rest. Moleson played some commonplace chords upon the piano, while he leaned back listlessly in his chair, putting in sentences now and again and chatting idly to whichever of us would listen. And Isley came slowly across the room towards me, holding out cigarettes. His dark brown face had shadows on it. He looked exhausted, worn, like some soldier broken in the wars.

"You liked it?" I heard his thin voice asking. There was no interest, no expression; it was not the real Isley who spoke; it was the little part of him that had come back. He smiled like a marvellous automaton.

Mechanically I took the cigarette he offered me, thinking confusedly what answer I could make.

"It's irresistible," I murmured; "I understand that it's easier to go."

"Sweeter as well," he whispered with a sigh, "and very wonderful!"

### XII

The hand that lit my cigarette, I saw, was trembling. A desire to do something violent woke in me suddenly—to move energetically, to push or drive something away.

"What was it?" I asked abruptly, in a louder, half-challenging voice, intended for the man at the piano. "Such a performance—upon others—without first asking their permission—seems to me unpermissible—it's—"

And it was Moleson who replied. He ignored the end of my sentence as though he had not heard it. He strolled over to our side, taking a cigarette and pressing it carefully into shape between his long thin fingers.

"You may well ask," he answered quietly; "but it's not so easy to tell. We discovered it"—he nodded towards Isley—"two years ago in the 'Valley.' It lay beside a Priest, a very important personage, apparently, and was part of the Ritual he used in the worship of the sun. In the Museum now—you can see it any day at the Boulak—it is simply labeled 'Hymn to Ra.' The period was Aknahton's."

"The words, yes," put in Isley, who was listening closely.

"The words?" repeated Moleson in a curious tone. "There *are* no words. It's all really a manipulation of the vowel sounds. And the rhythm, or chanting, or whatever you like to call it, I—I invented myself. The Egyptians did not write their music, you see." He suddenly searched my face a moment with questioning eyes. "Any words you heard," he said, "or thought you heard, were merely your own interpretation."

I stared at him, making no rejoinder.

"They made use of what they called a 'root-language' in their rituals," he went on, "and it consisted entirely of vowel sounds. There were no consonants. For vowel sounds, you see, run on for ever without end or beginning, whereas consonants interrupt their flow and break it up and limit it. A consonant has no sound of its own at all. Real language is continuous."

We stood a moment, smoking in silence. I understood then that this thing Moleson had done was based on definite knowledge. He had rendered some fragment of an ancient Ritual he and Isley had unearthed together, and while he knew its effect upon the latter, he chanced it on myself. Not otherwise, I feel, could it have influenced me in the extraordinary way it did. In the faith and poetry of a nation lies its soul-life, and the gigantic faith of Egypt blazed behind the rhythm of that long, monotonous chant. There was blood and heart and nerves in it. Millions had heard it sung; millions had wept and prayed and yearned; it was ensouled by the passion of that marvellous civilisation that loved the godhead of the Sun, and that now hid, waiting but still alive, below the ground. The majestic faith of ancient Egypt poured up with it—that tremendous, burning elaboration of the after-life and of Eternity that was the pivot of those spacious days. For centuries vast multitudes, led by their royal priests, had uttered this very form and ritual— believed it, lived it, felt it. The rising of the sun remained its climax. Its spiritual power still clung to the great ruined symbols. The faith of a buried civilisation had burned back into the present and into our hearts as well.

And a curious respect for the man who was able to produce this effect upon two modern minds crept over me, and mingled with the repulsion that I felt. I looked furtively at his withered, dried-up features. He wore some vague and shadowy impress still of what had just been in him. There was a stony appearance in his shrunken cheeks. He looked smaller. I saw him lessened. I thought of him as he had been so short a time before, imprisoned in his great stone captors that had obsessed him...

"There's tremendous power in it,—an awful power," I stammered, more to break the oppressive pause than for any desire in me to speak with him. "It brings back Egypt in some extraordinary way—ancient Egypt, I mean— brings it close—into the heart." My words ran on of their own accord almost. I spoke with a hush, unwittingly. There was awe in me. Isley had moved away towards the window, leaving me face to face with this strange incarnation of another age.

"It must," he replied, deep light still glowing in his eyes, "for the soul of the old days is in it. No one, I think, can hear it and remain the same. It expresses, you see, the essential passion and beauty of that gorgeous worship, that splendid faith, that reasonable and intelligent worship of the sun, the only scientific belief the world has ever known. Its popular form, of course, was largely superstitious, but the sacerdotal form—the form used by the priests, that is—who understood the relationship between colour, sound and symbol, was—"

He broke off suddenly, as though he had been speaking to himself. We sat down. George Isley leaned out of the window with his back to us, watching the desert in the moonless night.

"You have tried its effect before upon—others?" I asked point-blank.

"Upon myself," he answered shortly.

"Upon others?" I insisted.

He hesitated an instant.

"Upon one other—yes," he admitted.

"Intentionally?" And something quivered in me as I asked it.

He shrugged his shoulders slightly. "I'm merely a speculative archæologist," he smiled, "and—and an imaginative Egyptologist. My bounden duty is to reconstruct the past so that it lives for others."

An impulse rose in me to take him by the throat.

"You know perfectly well, of course, the magical effect it's sure—likely, at least—to have?"

He stared steadily at me through the cigarette smoke. To this day I cannot think exactly what it was in this man that made me shudder.

"I'm sure of nothing," he replied smoothly, "but I consider it quite legitimate to try. Magical—the word you used—has no meaning for me. If such a thing exists, it is merely scientific—undiscovered or forgotten knowledge." An insolent, aggressive light shone in his eyes as he spoke; his manner was almost truculent. "You refer, I take it, to—our friend—rather than to yourself?"

And with difficulty I met his singular stare. From his whole person something still emanated that was forbidding, yet overmasteringly persuasive. It brought back the notion of that invisible Web, that dim gauze curtain, that motionless Influence lying waiting at the centre for its prey, those monstrous and mysterious Items standing, alert, and watchful, through the centuries. "You mean," he added lower, "his altered attitude to life—his going?"

To hear him use the words, the very phrase, struck me with sudden chill. Before I could answer, however, and certainly before I could master the touch of horror that rushed over me, I heard him continuing in a whisper. It seemed again that he spoke to himself as much as he spoke to me.

"The soul, I suppose, has the right to choose its own conditions and surroundings. To pass elsewhere involves translation, not extinction." He smoked a moment in silence, then said another curious thing, looking up into my face with an expression of intense earnestness. Something genuine in him again replaced the pose of cynicism. "The soul is eternal and can take its place anywhere, regardless of mere duration. What is there in the vulgar and superficial Present that should hold it so exclusively; and where can it find to-day the belief, the faith, the beauty that are the very essence of its life—where in the rush and scatter of this tawdry age can it make its home? Shall it flutter for ever in a valley of dry bones, when a living Past lies ready and waiting with loveliness, strength, and glory?" He moved closer; he touched my arm; I felt his breath upon my face. "Come with us," he whispered awfully; "come back with us! Withdraw your life from the rubbish of this futile ugliness! Come back and worship with us in the spirit of the Past. Take up the old, old splendour, the glory, the immense conceptions, the wondrous certainty, the ineffable knowledge of essentials. It all lies about you still; it's calling, ever calling; it's very close; it draws you day and night—calling, calling, calling..."

His voice died off curiously into distance on the word; I can hear it to this day, and the soft, droning quality in the intense yet fading tone: "Calling, calling, calling." But his eyes turned wicked. I felt the sinister power of the man. I was aware of madness in his thought, and mind. The Past he sought to glorify I saw black, as with the forbidding Egyptian darkness of a plague. It was not beauty but Death that I heard calling, calling, calling.

"It's real," he went on, hardly aware that I shrank, "and not a dream. These ruined symbols still remain in touch with that which was. They are potent to-day as they were six thousand years ago. The amazing life of those days brims behind them. They are not mere masses of oppressive stone; they express in visible form great powers that still are—*knowable.*" He lowered his head, peered up into my face, and whispered. Something secret passed into his eyes.

"I saw you change," came the words below his breath, "as you saw the change in us. But only worship can produce that change. The soul assumes the qualities of the deity it worships. The powers of its deity possess it and transform it into its own likeness. You also felt it. *You* also were possessed. I saw the stone-faced deity upon your own."

I seemed to shake myself as a dog shakes water from its body. I stood up. I remember that I stretched my hands out as though to push him from me and expel some creeping influence from my mind. I remember another thing as well. But for the reality of the sequel, and but for the matter-of-fact result still facing me to-day in the disappearance of George Isley—the loss to the present time of all George Isley *was*—I might have found subject for laughter in what I saw. Comedy was in it certainly. Yet it was both ghastly and terrific. Deep horror crept below the aspect of the ludicrous, for the apparent mimicry cloaked truth. It was appalling because it was real.

In the large mirror that reflected the room behind me I saw myself and Moleson; I saw Isley too in the background by the open window. And the attitude of all three was the attitude of hieroglyphics come to life. My arms indeed were stretched, but not stretched, as I had thought, in mere selfdefence. They were stretched—unnaturally. The forearms made those strange obtuse angles that the old carved granite wears, the palms of the hands held upwards, the heads thrown back, the legs advanced, the bodies stiffened into postures that expressed forgotten, ancient minds. The physical conformation of all three was monstrous; and yet reverence and truth dictated even the uncouthness of the gestures. Something in all three of us inspired the forms our bodies had assumed. Our attitudes expressed buried yearnings, emotions, tendencies—whatever they may be termed—that the spirit of the Past evoked.

I saw the reflected picture but for a moment. I dropped my arms, aware of foolishness in my way of standing. Moleson moved forward with his long, significant stride, and at the same instant Isley came up quickly and joined us from his place by the open window. We looked into each other's faces without a word. There was this little pause that lasted perhaps ten seconds. But in that pause I felt the entire world slide past me. I heard the centuries rush by at headlong speed. The present dipped away. Existence was no longer in a line that stretched two ways; it was a circle in which ourselves, together with Past and Future, stood motionless at the centre, all details equally accessible at once. The three of us were falling, falling backwards...

"Come!" said the voice of Moleson solemnly, but with the sweetness as of a child anticipating joy, "Come! Let us go together, for the boat of Ra has crossed the Underworld. The darkness has been conquered. Let us go out together and find the dawn. Listen! It is calling, calling, calling..."

## XIII

I was aware of rushing, but it was the soul in me that rushed. It experienced dizzy, unutterable alterations. Thousands of emotions, intense and varied, poured through me at lightning speed, each satisfyingly known, yet gone before its name appeared. The life of many centuries tore headlong back with me, and, as in drowning, this epitome of existence shot in a few seconds the steep slopes the Past had so laboriously built up. The changes flashed and passed. I wept and prayed and worshipped; I loved and suffered; I battled, lost and won. Down the gigantic scale of ages that telescoped thus into a few brief moments, the soul in me went sliding backwards towards a motionless, reposeful Past.

I remember foolish details that interrupted the immense descent—I put on coat and hat; I remember some one's words, strangely sounding as when some bird wakes up and sings at midnight—"We'll take the little door; the front one's locked by now"; and I have a vague recollection of the outline of the great hotel, with its colonnades and terraces, fading behind me through the air. But these details merely flickered and disappeared, as though I fell earthwards from a star and passed feathers or blown leaves upon the way. There was no friction as my soul dropped backwards into time; the flight was easy and silent as a dream. I felt myself sucked down into gulfs whose emptiness offered no resistance... until at last the appalling speed decreased of its own accord, and the dizzy flight became a kind of gentle floating. It changed imperceptibly into a gliding motion, as though the angle altered. My feet, quite naturally, were on the ground, moving through something soft that clung to them and rustled while it clung.

I looked up and saw the bright armies of the stars. In front of me I recognised the flat-topped, shadowy ridges; on both sides lay the open expanses of familiar wilderness; and beside me, one on either hand, moved two figures who were my companions. We were in the desert, but it was the desert of thousands of years ago. My companions, moreover, though familiar to some part of me, seemed strangers or half known. Their names I strove in vain to capture; Mosely, Ilson, sounded in my head, mingled together falsely. And when I stole a glance at them, I saw dark lines of mannikins unfilled with substance, and was aware of the grotesque gestures of living hieroglyphics. It seemed for an instant that their arms were bound behind their backs impossibly, and that their heads turned sharply across their lineal shoulders.

But for a moment only; for at a second glance I saw them solid and compact; their names came back to me; our arms were linked together as we walked. We had already covered a great distance, for my limbs were aching and my breath was short. The air was cold, the silence absolute. It seemed, in this faint light, that the desert flowed beneath our feet, rather than that we advanced by taking steps. Cliffs with hooded tops moved past us, boulders glided, mounds of sand slid by. And then I heard a voice upon my left that was surely Moleson speaking:

"Towards Enet our feet are set," he half sang, half murmured, "towards Enet-te-ntore. There, in the House of Birth, we shall dedicate our hearts and lives anew."

And the language, no less than the musical intonation of his voice, enraptured me. For I understood he spoke of Denderah, in whose majestic temple recent hands had painted with deathless colours the symbols of our cosmic relationships with the zodiacal signs. And Denderah was our great seat of worship of the goddess Hathor, the Egyptian Aphrodite, bringer of love and joy. The falcon-headed Horus was her husband, from whom, in his home at Edfu, we imbibed swift kinds of power. And—it was the time of the New Year, the great feast when the forces of the living earth turn upwards into happy growth.

We were on foot across the desert towards Denderah, and this sand we trod was the sand of thousands of years ago.

The paralysis of time and distance involved some amazing lightness of the spirit that, I suppose, touched ecstasy. There was intoxication in the soul. I was not divided from the stars, nor separate from this desert that rushed with us. The unhampered wind blew freshly from my nerves and skin, and the Nile, glimmering faintly on our right, lay with its lapping waves in both my hands. I knew the life of Egypt, for it was in me, over me, round me. I was a part of it. We went happily, like birds to meet the sunrise. There were no pits of measured time and interval that could detain us. We flowed, yet were at rest; we were endlessly alive; present and future alike were inconceivable; we were in the Kingdom of the Past.

The Pyramids were just a-building, and the army of Obelisks looked about them, proud of their first balance; Thebes swung her hundred gates upon the world. New, shining Memphis glittered with myriad reflections into waters that the tears of Isis sweetened, and the cliffs of Abou Simbel were still innocent of their gigantic progeny. Alone, the Sphinx, linking timelessness with time, brooded unguessed and underived upon an alien world. We marched within antiquity towards Denderah...

How long we marched, how fast, how far we went, I can remember as little as the marvellous speech that passed across me while my two companions spoke together. I only remember that suddenly a wave of pain disturbed my wondrous happiness and caused my calm, which had seemed beyond all reach of break, to fall away. I heard their voices abruptly with a kind of terror. A sensation of fear, of loss, of nightmare bewilderment came over me like cold wind. What *they* lived naturally, true to their inmost hearts, *I* lived merely by means of a temperamental sympathy. And the stage had come at which my powers failed. Exhaustion overtook me. I wilted. The strain—the abnormal backwards stretch of consciousness that was put upon me by another—gave way and broke. I heard their voices faint and horrible. My joy was extinguished. A glare of horror fell upon the desert and the stars seemed evil. An anguishing desire for the safe and wholesome Present usurped all this mad yearning to obtain the Past. My feet fell out of step. The rushing of the desert paused. I unlinked my arms. We stopped all three.

The actual spot is to this day well known to me. I found it afterwards, I even photographed it. It lies actually not far from Helouan—a few miles at most beyond the Solitary Palm, where slopes of undulating sand mark the opening of a strange, enticing valley called the Wadi Gerraui. And it is enticing because it beckons and leads on. Here, amid torn gorges of a limestone wilderness, there is suddenly soft yellow sand that flows and draws the feet onward. It slips away with one too easily; always the next ridge and basin must be seen, each time a little further. It has the quality of decoying. The cliffs say, No; but this streaming sand invites. In its flowing curves of gold there is enchantment.

And it was here upon its very lips we stopped, the rhythm of our steps broken, our hearts no longer one. My temporary rapture vanished. I was aware of fear. For the Present rushed upon me with attack in it, and I felt that my mind was arrested close upon the edge of madness. Something cleared and lifted in my brain.

The soul, indeed, could "choose its dwelling-place"; but to live elsewhere completely was the choice of madness, and to live divorced from all the sweet wholesome business of To-day involved an exile that was worse than madness. It was death. My heart burned for George Isley. I remembered the tear upon his cheek. The agony of his struggle I shared suddenly with him. Yet with him was the reality, with me a sympathetic reflection merely. *He* was already too far gone to fight...

I shall never forget the desolation of that strange scene beneath the morning stars. The desert lay down and watched us. We stood upon the brink of a little broken ridge, looking into the valley of golden sand. This sand gleamed soft and wonderful in the starlight some twenty feet below. The descent was easy—but I would not move. I refused to advance another step. I saw my companions in the mysterious half-light beside me peering over the edge, Moleson in front a little.

And I turned to him, sure of the part I meant to play, yet conscious painfully of my helplessness. My personality seemed a straw in mid-stream that spun in a futile effort to arrest the flood that bore it. There was vivid human conflict in the moment's silence. It was an eddy that paused in the great body of the tide. And then I spoke. Oh, I was ashamed of the insignificance of my voice and the weakness of my little personality.

"Moleson, we go no further with you. We have already come too far. We now turn back."

Behind my words were a paltry thirty years. His answer drove sixty centuries against me. For his voice was like the wind that passed whispering down the stream of yellow sand below us. He smiled.

"Our feet are set towards Enet-te-more. There is no turning back. Listen! It is calling, calling, calling!"

"We will go home," I cried, in a tone I vainly strove to make imperative.

"Our home is there," he sang, pointing with one long thin arm towards the brightening east, "for the Temple calls us and the River takes our feet. We shall be in the House of Birth to meet the sunrise—"

"You lie," I cried again, "you speak the lies of madness, and this Past you seek is the House of Death. It is the kingdom of the underworld."

The words tore wildly, impotently out of me. I seized George Isley's arm.

"Come back with me," I pleaded vehemently, my heart aching with a nameless pain for him. "We'll retrace our steps. Come home with me! Come back! Listen! The Present calls you sweetly!"

His arm slipped horribly out of my grasp that had seemed to hold it so tightly. Moleson, already below us in the yellow sand, looked small with distance. He was gliding rapidly further with uncanny swiftness. The diminution of his form was ghastly. It was like a doll's. And his voice rose up, faint as with the distance of great gulfs of space.

"Calling... calling... You hear it for ever calling..."

It died away with the wind along that sandy valley, and the Past swept in a flood across the brightening sky. I swayed as though a storm was at my back. I reeled. Almost I went too—over the crumbling edge into the sand.

"Come back with me! Come home!" I cried more faintly. "The Present alone is real. There is work, ambition, duty. There is beauty, too—the beauty of good living! And there is love! There is—a woman... calling, calling...!"

That other voice took up the word below me. I heard the faint refrain sing down the sandy walls. The wild, sweet pang in it was marvellous.

"Our feet are set for Enet-te-ntore. It is calling, calling...!"

My voice fell into nothingness. George Isley was below me now, his outline tiny against the sheet of yellow sand. And the sand was moving. The desert rushed again. The human figures receded swiftly into the Past they had reconstructed with the creative yearning of their souls.

I stood alone upon the edge of crumbling limestone, helplessly watching them. It was amazing what I witnessed, while the shafts of crimson dawn rose up the sky. The enormous desert turned alive to the horizon with gold and blue and silver. The purple shadows melted into grey. The flat-topped ridges shone. Huge messengers of light flashed everywhere at once. The radiance of sunrise dazzled my outer sight.

But if my eyes were blinded, my inner sight was focussed the more clearly upon what followed. I witnessed the disappearance of George Isley. There was a dreadful magic in the picture. The pair of them, small and distant below me in that little sandy hollow, stood out sharply defined as in a miniature. I saw their outlines neat and terrible like some ghastly inset against the enormous scenery. Though so close to me in actual space, they were centuries away in time. And a dim, vast shadow was about them that was not mere shadow of the ridges. It encompassed them; it moved, crawling over the sand, obliterating them. Within it, like insects lost in amber, they became visibly imprisoned, dwindled in size, borne deep away, absorbed.

And then I recognised the outline. Once more, but this time recumbent and spread flat upon the desert's face, I knew the monstrous shapes of the twin obsessing symbols. The spirit of ancient Egypt lay over all the land, tremendous in the dawn. The sunrise summoned her. She lay prostrate before the deity. The shadows of the towering Colossi lay prostrate too. The little humans, with their worshipping and conquered hearts, lay deep within them.

George Isley I saw clearest. The distinctness, the reality were appalling. He was naked, robbed, undressed. I saw him a skeleton, picked clean to the very bones as by an acid. His life lay hid in the being of that mighty Past. Egypt had absorbed him. He was gone...

I closed my eyes, but I could not keep them closed. They opened of their own accord. The three of us were nearing the great hotel that rose yellow, with shuttered windows, in the early sunshine. A wind blew briskly from the north across the Mokattam Hills. There were soft cannon-ball clouds dotted about the sky, and across the Nile, where the mist lay in a line of white, I saw the tops of the Pyramids gleaming like mountain peaks of gold. A string of camels, laden with white stone, went past us. I heard the crying of the natives in the streets of Helouan, and as we went up the steps the donkeys arrived and camped in the sandy road beside their *bersim* till the tourists claimed them.

"Good morning," cried Abdullah, the man who owned them. "You all go Sakkhârah to-day, or Memphis? Beat'ful day to-day, and vair good donkeys!"

Moleson went up to his room without a word, and Isley did the same. I thought he staggered a moment as he turned the passage corner from my sight. His face wore a look of vacancy that some call peace. There was radiance in it. It made me shudder. Aching in mind and body, and no word spoken, I followed their example. I went upstairs to bed, and slept a dreamless sleep till after sunset...

## XIV

And I woke with a lost, unhappy feeling that a withdrawing tide had left me on the shore, alone and desolate. My first instinct was for my friend, George Isley. And I noticed a square, white envelope with my name upon it in his writing.

Before I opened it I knew quite well what words would be inside:

"We are going up to Thebes," the note informed me simply. "We leave by the night train. If you care to—" But the last four words were scratched out again, though not so thickly that I could not read them. Then came the address of the Egyptologist's house and the signature, very firmly traced, "Yours ever, GEORGE ISLEY." I glanced at my watch and saw that it was after seven o'clock. The night train left at half-past six. They had already started...

The pain of feeling forsaken, left behind, was deep and bitter, for myself; but what I felt for him, old friend and comrade, was even more intense, since it was hopeless. Fear and conventional emotion had stopped me at the very gates of an amazing possibility—some state of consciousness that, *realizing* the Past, might doff the Present, and by slipping out of Time, experience Eternity. That was the seduction I had escaped by the uninspired resistance of my pettier soul. Yet he, my friend, yielding in order to conquer, had obtained an awful prize—ah, I understood the picture's other side as well, with an unutterable poignancy of pity—the prize of immobility which is sheer stagnation, the imagined bliss which is a false escape, the dream of finding beauty away from present things. From that dream the awakening must be rude indeed. Clutching at vanished stars, he had clutched the oldest illusion in the world. To me it seemed the negation of life that had betrayed him. The pity of it burned me like a flame.

But I did not "care to follow" him and his companion. I waited at Helouan for his return, filling the empty days with yet emptier explanations. I felt as a man who sees what he loves sinking down into clear, deep water, still within visible reach, yet gone beyond recovery. Moleson had taken him back to Thebes; and Egypt, monstrous effigy of the Past, had caught her prey.

The rest, moreover, is easily told. Moleson I never saw again. To this day I have never seen him, though his subsequent books are known to me, with the banal fact that he is numbered with those energetic and deluded enthusiasts who start a new religion, obtain notoriety, a few hysterical followers and—oblivion.

George Isley, however, returned to Helouan after a fortnight's absence. I saw him, knew him, talked and had my meals with him. We even did slight expeditions together. He was gentle and delightful as a woman who has loved a wonderful ideal and attained to it—in memory. All roughness was gone out of him; he was smooth and polished as a crystal surface that reflects whatever is near enough to ask a picture. Yet his appearance shocked me inexpressibly: there was nothing in him—*nothing.* It was the representation of George Isley that came back from Thebes; the outer simulacra; the shell that walks the London streets to-day. I met no vestige of the man I used to know. George Isley had disappeared.

With this marvellous automaton I lived another month. The horror of him kept me company in the hotel where he moved among the cosmopolitan humanity as a ghost that visits the sunlight yet has its home elsewhere.

This empty image of George Isley lived with me in our Helouan hotel until the winds of early March informed his physical frame that discomfort was in the air, and that he might as well move elsewhere—elsewhere happening to be northwards.

And he left just as he stayed—automatically. His brain obeyed the conventional stimuli to which his nerves, and consequently his muscles, were accustomed. It sounds so foolish. But he took his ticket automatically; he gave the natural and adequate reasons automatically; he chose his ship and landing-place in the same way that ordinary people chose these things; he said good-bye like any other man who leaves casual acquaintances and "hopes" to meet them again; he lived, that is to say, entirely in his brain. His heart, his emotions, his temperament and personality, that nameless sum-total for which the great sympathetic nervous system is accountable—all this, his soul, had gone elsewhere. This once vigorous, gifted being had become a normal, comfortable man that everybody could understand—a commonplace nonentity. He was precisely what the majority expected him to be—ordinary; a good fellow; a man of the world; he was "delightful." He merely reflected daily life without partaking of it. To the majority it was hardly noticeable; "very pleasant" was a general verdict. His ambition, his restlessness, his zeal had gone; that tireless zest whose driving power is yearning had taken flight, leaving behind it physical energy without spiritual desire. His soul had found its nest and flown to it. He lived in the chimera of the Past, serene, indifferent, detached. I saw him immense, a shadowy, majestic figure, standing—ah, not moving!—in a repose that was satisfying because it could not change. The size, the mystery, the immobility that caged him in seemed to me—terrible. For I dared not intrude upon his awful privacy, and intimacy between us there was none. Of his experiences at Thebes I asked no single question—it was somehow not possible or legitimate; he, equally, vouchsafed no word of explanation—it was uncommunicable to a dweller in the Present. Between us was this barrier we both respected. He peered at modern life, incurious, listless, apathetic, through a dim, gauze curtain. He was behind it.

People round us were going to Sakkhâra and the Pyramids, to see the Sphinx by moonlight, to dream at Edfu and at Denderah. Others described their journeys to Assouan, Khartoum and Abou Simbel, and gave details of their encampments in the desert. Wind, wind, wind! The winds of Egypt blew and sang and sighed. From the White Nile came the travellers, and from the Blue Nile, from the Fayum, and from nameless excavations without end. They talked and wrote their books. They had the magpie knowledge of the present. The Egyptologists, big and little, read the writing on the wall and put the hieroglyphs and papyri into modern language. Alone George Isley *knew* the secret. He lived it.

And the high passionate calm, the lofty beauty, the glamour and enchantment that are the spell of this thrice-haunted land, were in my soul as well—sufficiently for me to interpret his condition. I could not leave, yet having left I could not stay away. I yearned for the Egypt that he knew. No word I uttered; speech could not approach it. We wandered by the Nile together, and through the groves of palms that once were Memphis. The sandy wastes beyond the Pyramids knew our footsteps; the Mokattam Ridges, purple at evening and golden in the dawn, held our passing shadows as we silently went by. At no single dawn or sunset was he to be found indoors, and it became my habit to accompany him—the joy of worship in his soul was marvellous. The great, still skies of Egypt watched us, the hanging stars, the gigantic dome of blue; we felt together that burning southern wind; the golden sweetness of the sun lay in our blood as we saw the great boats take the northern breeze upstream. Immensity was everywhere and this golden magic of the sun...

But it was in the Desert especially, where only sun and wind observe the faint signalling of Time, where space is nothing because it is not divided, and where no detail reminds the heart that the world is called To-Day—it was in the desert this curtain hung most visibly between us, he on that side, I on this. It was transparent. He was with a multitude no man can number. Towering to the moon, yet spreading backwards towards his burning source of life, drawn out by the sun and by the crystal air into some vast interior magnitude, the spirit of George Isley hung beside me, close yet far away, in the haze of olden days.

And, sometimes, he moved. I was aware of gestures. His head was raised to listen. One arm swung shadowy across the sea of broken ridges. From leagues away a line of sand rose slowly. There was a rustling. Another—an enormous—arm emerged to meet his own, and two stupendous figures drew together. Poised above Time, yet throned upon the centuries, They knew eternity. So easily they remained possessors of the land. Facing the east, they waited for the dawn. And their marvellously forgotten singing poured across the world....

# Wayfarers

I missed the train at Evain, and, after infinite trouble, discovered a motor that would take me, ice-axe and all, to Geneva. By hurrying, the connection might be just possible. I telegraphed to Haddon to meet me at the station, and lay back comfortably, dreaming of the precipices of Haute Savoie. We made good time; the roads were excellent, traffic of the slightest, when—crash! There was an instant's excruciating pain, the sun went out like a snuffed candle, and I fell into something as soft as a bed of flowers and as yielding to my weight as warm water...

It was *very* warm. There was a perfume of flowers. My eyes opened, focussed vividly upon a detailed picture for a moment, then closed again. There was no context—at least, none that I could recall—for the scene, though familiar as home, brought nothing that I definitely remembered. Broken away from any sequence, unattached to any past, unaware even of my own identity, I simply saw this picture as a camera snaps it off from the world, a scene apart, with meaning only for those who knew the context:

The warm, soft thing I lay in was a bed—big, deep, comfortable; and the perfume came from flowers that stood beside it on a little table. It was in a stately, ancient chamber, with lofty ceiling and immense open fireplace of stone; old-fashioned pictures—familiar portraits and engravings I knew intimately—hung upon the walls; the floor was bare, with dignified, carved furniture of oak and mahogany, huge chairs and massive cupboards. And there were latticed windows set within deep embrasures of grey stone, where clambering roses patterned the sunshine that cast their moving shadows on the polished boards. With the perfume of the flowers there mingled, too, that delicate, elusive odour of age—of wood, of musty tapestries in spacious halls and corridors, and of chambers long unopened to the sun and air.

By the door that stood ajar far away at the end of the room—very far away it seemed—an old lady, wearing a little cap of silk embroidery, was whispering to a man of stern, uncompromising figure, who, as he listened, bent down to her with a grave and even solemn face. A wide stone corridor was just visible through the crack of the open door behind her.

The picture flashed, and vanished. The numerous details I took in because they were well known to me already. That I could not supply the context was merely a trick of the mind, the kind of trick that dreams play. Darkness swamped vision again. I sank back into the warm, soft, comfortable bed of delicious oblivion. There was not the slightest desire to know; sleep and soft forgetfulness were all I craved.

But a little later—or was it a very great deal later?—when I opened my eyes again, there was a thin trail of memory. I remembered my name and age. I remembered vaguely, as though from some unpleasant dream, that I was on the way to meet a climbing friend in the Alps of Haute Savoie, and that there was need to hurry and be very active. Something had gone wrong, it seemed. There had been a stupid, violent disaster, pain in it somewhere, an accident. Where were my belongings? Where, for instance, was my precious ice-axe—tried old instrument on which my life and safety depended? A rush of jumbled questions poured across my mind. The effort to sort them hurt atrociously...

A figure stood beside my bed. It was the same old lady I had seen a moment ago—or was it a month ago, even last year perhaps? And this time she was alone. Yet, though familiar to me as my own right hand, I could not for the life of me attract her name. Searching for it brought the pain again. Instead, I asked an easier question; it seemed the most important somehow, though a feeling of shame came with it, as though I knew I was talking nonsense:

"My ice-axe—is it safe? It should have stood any ordinary strain. It's ash..." My voice failed absurdly, caught away by a whisper half-way down my throat. What *was* I talking about? There was vile confusion somewhere.

She smiled tenderly, sweetly, as she placed her small, cool hand upon my forehead. Her touch calmed me as it always did, and the pain retreated a little.

"All your things are safe," she answered, in a voice so soft beneath the distant ceiling it was like a bird's note singing in the sky. "And *you* are also safe. There is no danger now. The bullet has been taken out and all is going well. Only you must be patient, and lie very still, and rest." And then she added the morsel of delicious comfort she knew quite well I waited for: "Marion is near you all day long, and most of the night besides. She rarely leaves you. She is in and out all day."

I stared, thirsting for more. Memory put certain pieces in their place again. I heard them click together as they joined. But they only tried to join. There were several pieces missing. They must have been lost in the disaster. The pattern was too ridiculous.

"I ought to tel—telegraph—" I began, seizing at a fragment that poked its end up, then plunged out of sight again before I could read more of it. The pieces fell apart; they would not hold together without these missing fragments. Anger flamed up in me.

"They're badly made," I said, with a petulance I was secretly ashamed of; "you have chosen the wrong pieces! I'm not a child—to be treated—" A shock of heat tore through me, led by a point of iron, with blasting pain.

"Sleep, my poor dear Félix, sleep," she murmured soothingly, while her tiny hand stroked my forehead, just in time to prevent that pointed, hot thing entering my heart. "Sleep again now, and a little later you shall tell me their names, and I will send on horseback quickly—"

"Telegraph—" I tried to say, but the word went lost before I could pronounce it. It was a nonsense word, caught up from dreams. Thought fluttered and went out.

"I will send," she whispered, "in the quickest possible way. You shall explain to Marion. Sleep first a little longer; promise me to lie quite still and sleep. When you wake again, she will come to you at once."

She sat down gently on the edge of the enormous bed, so that I saw her outline against the window where the roses clambered to come in. She bent over me—or was it a rose that bent in the wind across the stone embrasure? I saw her clear blue eyes—or was it two raindrops upon a withered roseleaf that mirrored the summer sky?

"Thank you," my voice murmured with intense relief, as everything sank away and the old-world garden seemed to enter by the latticed windows. For there was a power in her way that made obedience sweet, and her little hand, besides, cushioned the attack of that cruel iron point so that I hardly felt its entrance. Before the fierce heat could reach me, darkness again put out the world...

Then, after a prodigious interval, my eyes once more opened to the stately, old-world chamber that I knew so well; and this time I found myself alone. In my brain was a stinging, splitting sensation, as though Memory shook her pieces together with angry violence, pieces, moreover, made of clashing metal. A degrading nausea almost vanquished me. Against my feet was a heated metal body, too heavy for me to move, and bandages were tight round my neck and the back of my head. Dimly, it came back to me that hands had been about me hours ago, soft, ministering hands that I loved. Their perfume lingered still. Faces and names fled in swift procession past me, yet without my making any attempt to bid them stay. I asked myself no questions. Effort of any sort was utterly beyond me. I lay and watched and waited, helpless and strangely weak.

One or two things alone were clear. They came, too, without the effort to think them:

There had been a disaster; they had carried me into the nearest house; and—the mountain heights, so keenly longed for, were suddenly denied me. I was being cared for by kind people somewhere far from the world's high routes. They were familiar people, yet for the moment I had lost the name. But it was the bitterness of losing my holiday climbing that chiefly savaged me, so that strong desire returned upon itself unfulfilled. And, knowing the danger of frustrated yearnings, and the curious states of mind they may engender, my trembling brain registered a decision automatically:

"Keep careful watch upon yourself," it whispered.

For I saw the peaks that towered above the world, and felt the wind rise from the hidden valleys. The perfume of lonely ridges came to me, and I saw the snow against the blue-black sky. Yet I could not reach them. I lay, instead, broken and useless upon my back, in a soft, deep, comfortable bed. And I loathed the thought. A dull and evil fury rose within me. Where was Haddon? He would get me out of it if any one could. And where was my dear, old trusted ice-axe? Above all, who were these gentle, old-world people who cared for me?...And, with this last thought, came some fairy touch of sweetness so delicious that I was conscious of sudden resignation—more, even of delight and joy.

This joy and anger ran races for possession of my mind, and I knew not which to follow: both seemed real, and both seemed true. The cruel confusion was an added torture. Two sets of places and people seemed to mingle.

"Keep a careful watch upon yourself," repeated the automatic caution.

Then, with returning, blissful darkness, came another thing—a tiny point of wonder, where light entered in. I thought of a woman...It was a vehement, commanding thought; and though at first it was very close and real—as much of To-day as Haddon and my precious ice-axe—the next second it was leagues away in another world somewhere. Yet, before the confusion twisted it all askew, I knew her; I remembered clearly even where she lived; that I knew her husband, too—had stayed with them in—in Scotland—yes, in Scotland. Yet no word in this life had ever crossed my lips, for she was not free to come. Neither of us, with eyes or lips or gesture, had ever betrayed a hint to the other of our deeply hidden secret. And, although for me she was *the* woman, my great yearning—long, long ago it was, in early youth—had been sternly put aside and buried with all the vigour nature gave me. Her husband was my friend as well.

Only, now, the shock had somehow strained the prison bars, and the yearning escaped for a moment full-edged, and vehement with passion long denied. The inhibition was destroyed. The knowledge swept deliciously upon me that we had the right to be together, because we always *were* together. I had the right to ask for her.

My mind was certainly a mere field of confused, ungoverned images. No thinking was possible, for it hurt too vilely. But this one memory stood out with violence. I distinctly remember that I called to her to come, and that she had the right to come because my need was so peremptory. To the one most loved of all this life had brought me, yet to whom I had never spoken because she was in another's keeping, I called for help, and called, I verily believe, aloud:

"Please come!" Then, close upon its heels, the automatic warning again: "Keep close watch upon yourself...!"

It was as though one great yearning had loosed the other that was even greater, and had set it free.

Disappearing consciousness then followed the cry for an incalculable distance. Down into subterraneans within myself that were positively frightening it plunged away. But the cry was real; the yearning appeal held authority in it as of command. Love gave the right, supplied the power as well. For it seemed to me a tiny answer came, but from so far away that it was scarcely audible. And names were nowhere in it, either in answer or appeal.

"I am always here. I have never, never left you!"

The unconsciousness that followed was not complete, apparently. There was a memory of effort in it, of struggle, and, as it were, of searching. Some one was trying to get at me. I tossed in a troubled sea upon a piece of wreckage that another swimmer also fought to reach. Huge waves of transparent green now brought this figure nearer, now concealed it, but it came steadily on, holding out a rope. My exhaustion was too great for me to respond, yet this swimmer swept up nearer, brought by enormous rollers that threatened to engulf us both. The rope was for my safety, too. I saw hands outstretched. In the deep water I saw the outline of the body, and once I even saw the face. But for a second, merely. The wave that bore it crashed with a horrible roar that smothered us both and swept me from my piece of wreckage. In the violent flood of water the rope whipped against my feeble hands. I grasped it. A sense of divine security at once came over me—an intolerable sweetness of utter bliss and comfort, then blackness and suffocation as of the grave. The white-hot point of iron struck me. It beat audibly against my heart. I heard the knocking. The pain brought me up to the surface, and the knocking of my dreams was in reality a knocking on the door. Some one was gently tapping.

Such was the confusion of images in my pain-wracked mind, that I expected to see the old lady enter, bringing ropes and ice-axes, and followed by Haddon, my mountaineering friend; for I thought that I had fallen down a deep crevasse and had waited hours for help in the cold, blue darkness of the ice. I was too weak to answer, and the knocking for that matter was not repeated. I did not even hear the opening of the door, so softly did she move into the room. I only knew that before I actually saw her, this wave of intolerable sweetness drenched me once again with bliss and peace and comfort, my pain retreated, and I closed my eyes, knowing I should feel that cool and soothing hand upon my forehead.

The same minute I did feel it. There was a perfume of old gardens in the air. I opened my eyes to look the gratitude I could not utter, and saw, close against me—not the old lady, but the young and lovely face my worship had long made familiar. With lips that smiled their yearning and eyes of brown that held tears of sympathy, she sat down beside me on the bed. The warmth and fragrance of her atmosphere enveloped me. I sank away into a garden where spring melts magically into summer. Her arms were round my neck. Her face dropped down, so that I felt her hair upon my cheek and eyes. And then, whispering my name twice over, she kissed me on the lips.

"Marion," I murmured.

"Hush! Mother sends you this," she answered softly. "You are to take it all; she made it with her own hands. But *I* bring it to you. You must be quite obedient, please."

She tried to rise, but I held her against my breast. "Kiss me again and I'll promise obedience always," I strove to say. But my voice refused so long a sentence, and anyhow her lips were on my own before I could have finished it. Slowly, very carefully, she disentangled herself, and my arms sank back upon the coverlet. I sighed in happiness. A moment longer she stood beside my bed, gazing down with love and deep anxiety into my face.

"And when all is eaten, all, mind, *all*," she smiled, "you are to sleep until the doctor comes this afternoon. You are much better. Soon you shall get up. Only, remember," shaking her finger with a sweet pretence of looking stern, "I shall exact complete obedience. You must yield your will utterly to mine. You are in my heart, and my heart must be kept very warm and happy."

Her eyes were tender as her mother's, and I loved the authority and strength that were so real in her. I remembered how it was this strength that had sealed the contract her beauty first drew up for me to sign. She bent down once more to arrange my pillows.

"What happened to—to the motor?" I asked hesitatingly, for my thoughts *would* not regulate themselves. The mind presented such incongruous fragments.

"The—what?" she asked, evidently puzzled. The word seemed strange to her. "What is that?" she repeated, anxiety in her eyes.

I made an effort to tell her, but I could not. Explanation was suddenly impossible. The whole idea dived away out of sight. It utterly evaded me. I had again invented a word that was without meaning. I was talking nonsense. In its place my dream came up. I tried to tell her how I had dreamed of climbing dangerous heights with a stranger, and had spoken another language with him than my own—English, was it?—at any rate, not my native French.

"Darling," she whispered close into my ear, "the bad dreams will not come back. You are safe here, quite safe." She put her little hand like a flower on my forehead and drew it softly down the cheek. "Your wound is already healing. They took the bullet out four days ago. I have got it," she added with a touch of shy embarrassment, and kissed me tenderly upon my eyes.

"How long have you been away from me?" I asked, feeling exhaustion coming back.

"Never once for more than ten minutes," was the reply. "I watched with you all night. Only this morning, while mother took my place, I slept a little. But, hush!" she said, with dear authority again; "you are not to talk so much. You must eat what I have brought, then sleep again. You must rest and sleep. Good-bye, good-bye, my love. I shall come back in an hour, and I shall always be within reach of your dear voice."

Her tall, slim figure, dressed in the grey I loved, crossed silently to the door. She gave me one more look—there was all the tenderness of passionate love in it—and then was gone.

I followed instructions meekly, and when a delicious sleep stole over me soon afterwards, I had forgotten utterly the ugly dream that I was climbing dangerous heights with another man, forgotten as well everything else, except that it seemed so many days since my love had come to me, and that my bullet wound would after all be healed in time for our wedding on the day so long, so eagerly waited for.

And when, several hours later, her mother came in with the doctor—his face less grave and solemn this time—the news that I might get up next day and lie a little in the garden, did more to heal me than a thousand bandages or twice that quantity of medical instructions.

I watched them as they stood a moment by the open door. They went out very slowly together, speaking in whispers. But the only thing I caught was the mother's voice, talking brokenly of the great wars. Napoleon, the doctor was saying in a low, hushed tone, was in full retreat from Moscow, though the news had only just come through. They passed into the corridor then, and there was a sound of weeping as the old lady murmured something about her son and the cruelty of Heaven. "Both will be taken from me," she was sobbing softly, while he stooped to comfort her; "one in marriage, and the other in death." They closed the door then, and I heard no more.

## I

Convalescence seemed to follow very quickly then, for I was utterly obedient as I had promised, and never spoke of what could excite me to my own detriment—the wars and my own unfortunate part in them. We talked instead of our love, our already too-long engagement, and of the sweet dream of happiness that life held waiting for us in the future. And, indeed, I was sufficiently weary of the world to prefer repose to much activity, for my body was almost incessantly in pain, and this old garden where we lay between high walls of stone, aloof from the busy world and very peaceful, was far more to my taste just then than wars and fighting.

The orchards were in blossom, and the winds of spring showered their rain of petals upon the long, new grass. We lay, half in sunshine, half in shade, beneath the poplars that lined the avenue towards the lake, and behind us rose the ancient grey-stone towers where the jackdaws nested in the ivy and the pigeons cooed and fluttered from the woods beyond.

There was loveliness everywhere, but there was sadness too, for though we both knew that the wars had taken her brother whence there is no return, and that only her aged, failing mother's life stood between ourselves and the stately property, there hid a sadness yet deeper than either of these thoughts in both our hearts. And it was, I think, the sadness that comes with spring. For spring, with her lavish, short-lived promises of eternal beauty is ever a symbol of passing human happiness, incomplete and always unfulfilled. Promises made on earth are playthings, after all, for children. Even while we make them so solemnly, we seem to know they are not meant to hold. They are made, as spring is made, with a glory of soft, radiant blossoms that pass away before there is time to realise them. And yet they come again with the return of spring, as unashamed and glorious as if Time had utterly forgotten.

And this sadness was in her too. I mean it was part of her and she was part of it. Not that our love could change to pass or die, but that its sweet, so long-desired accomplishment must hold away, and, like the spring, must melt and vanish before it had been fully known. I did not speak of it. I well understood that the depression of a broken body can influence the spirit with its poisonous melancholy, but it must have betrayed itself in my words and gestures, even in my manner too. At any rate, she was aware of it. I think, if truth be told, she felt it too. It seemed so painfully inevitable.

My recovery, meanwhile, was rapid, and from spending an hour or two in the garden, I soon came to spend the entire day. For the spring came on with a rush, and the warmth increased deliciously. While the cuckoos called to one another in the great beech-woods behind the château, we sat and talked and sometimes had our simple meals or coffee there together, and I particularly recall the occasion when solid food was first permitted me and she gave me a delicate young *bondelle*, fresh caught that very morning in the lake. There were leaves of sweet, crisp lettuce with it, and she picked the bones out for me with her own white hands.

The day was radiant, with a sky of cloudless blue, soft airs stirred the poplar crests; the little waves fell on the pebbly beach not fifty metres away, and the orchard floor was carpeted with flowers that seemed to have caught from heaven's stars the patterns of their yellow blossoms. The bees droned peacefully among the fruit trees; the air was full of musical deep hummings. My former vigour stirred delightfully in my blood, and I knew no pain, beyond occasional dull twinges in the head that came with a rush of temporary darkness over my mind. The scar was healed, however, and the hair had grown over it again. This temporary darkness alarmed her more than it alarmed me. There were grave complications, apparently, that I did not know of.

But the deep-lying sadness in me seemed independent of the glorious weather, due to causes so intangible, so far off, that I never could dispel them by arguing them away. For I could not discover what they actually were. There was a vague, distressing sense of restlessness that I ought to have been elsewhere and otherwise, that we were together for a few days only, and that these few days I had snatched unlawfully from stern, imperative duties. These duties were immediate, but neglected. In a sense, I had no right to this spring-tide of bliss her presence brought me. I was playing truant somehow, somewhere. It was *not* my absence from the regiment; that I know. It was infinitely deeper, set to some enormous scale that vaguely frightened me, while it deepened the sweetness of the stolen joy.

Like a child, I sought to pin the sunny hours against the sky and make them stay. They passed with such a mocking swiftness, snatched momentarily from some big oblivion. The twilights swallowed our days together before they had been properly tasted, and on looking back, each afternoon of happiness seemed to have been a mere moment in a flying dream. And I must have somehow betrayed the aching mood, for Marion turned of a sudden and gazed into my face with yearning and anxiety in the sweet brown eyes.

"What is it, dearest?" I asked, "and why do your eyes bring questions?"

"You sighed," she answered, smiling a little sadly; "and sighed so deeply. You are in pain again. The darkness, perhaps, is over you?" And her hand stole out to meet my own. "You are in pain?"

"Not physical pain," I said, "and not *the* darkness either. I see *you* clearly," and would have told her more, as I carried her soft fingers to my lips, had I not divined from the expression in her eyes that she read my heart and knew all my strange, mysterious forebodings in herself.

"I know," she whispered before I could find speech, "for I feel it too. It is the shadow of separation that oppresses you—yet of no common, measurable separation you can understand. Is it not that?"

Leaning over then, I took her close into my arms, since words in that moment were mere foolishness. I held her so that she could not get away; but even while I did so it was like trying to hold the spring, or fasten the flying hour with a fierce desire. All slipped from me, and my arms caught at the sunshine and the wind.

"We have both felt it all these weeks," she said bravely, as soon as I had released her, "and we both have struggled to conceal it. But now"—she hesitated for a second, and with so exquisite a tenderness that I would have caught her to me again but for my anxiety to hear her further words—"now that you are well, we may speak plainly to each other, and so lessen our pain by sharing it." And then she added, still more softly: "You feel there is 'something' that shall take you from me—yet what it is you cannot discover nor divine. Tell me, Félix—all your thought, that I in turn may tell you mine."

Her voice floated about me in the sunny air. I stared at her, striving to focus the dear face more clearly for my sight. A shower of apple blossoms fell about us, and her words seemed floating past me like those passing petals of white. They drifted away. I followed them with difficulty and confusion. With the wind, I fancied, a veil of indefinable change slipped across her face and eyes.

"Yet nothing that could alter feeling," I answered; for she had expressed my own thought completely. "Nor anything that either of us can control. Only—perhaps, that everything must fade and pass away, just as this glory of the spring must fade and pass away—"

"Yet leaving its sweetness in us," she caught me up passionately, "and to come again, my beloved, to come again in every subsequent life, each time with an added sweetness in it, too!" Her little face showed suddenly the courage of a lion in its eyes. Her heart was ever braver than my own, a vigorous, fighting soul. She spoke of lives, I prattled of days and hours merely.

A touch of shame stole over me. But that delicate, swift change in her spread, too. With a thrill of ominous warning I noticed how it rose and grew about her. From within, outwards, it seemed to pass—like a shadow of great blue distance. Shadow was somewhere in it, so that she dimmed a little before my very eyes. The dreadful yearning searched and shook me, for I could not understand it, try as I would. She seemed going from me—drifting like her words and like the apple blossoms.

"But when we shall no longer be here to know it," I made answer quickly, yet as calmly as I could, "and when we shall have passed to some other place—to other conditions—where we shall not recognise the joy and wonder. When barriers of mist shall have rolled between us—our love and passion so made-over that we shall not know each other"—the words rushed out feverishly, half beyond control—"and perhaps shall not even dare to speak to each other of our deep desire—"

I broke off abruptly, conscious that I was speaking out of some unfamiliar place where I floundered, helpless among strange conditions. I was saying things I hardly understood myself. Her bigger, deeper mood spoke through me, perhaps.

Her darling face came back again; she moved close within reach once more.

"Hush, hush!" she whispered, terror and love both battling in her eyes. "It is the truth, perhaps, but you must not say such things. To speak them brings them closer. A chain is about our hearts, a chain of fashioning lives without number, but do not seek to draw upon it with anxiety or fear. To do so can only cause the pain of wrong entanglement, and interrupt the natural running of the iron links." And she placed her hand swiftly upon my mouth, as though divining that the bleak attack of anguish was again upon me with its throbbing rush of darkness.

But for once I was disobedient and resisted. The physical pain, I realised vividly, was linked closely with this spiritual torture. One caused the other somehow. The disordered brain received, though brokenly, some hints of darker and unusual knowledge. It had stammered forth in me, but through her it flowed easily and clear. I saw the change move more swiftly then across her face. Some ancient look passed into both her eyes.

And it was inevitable; I must speak out, regardless of mere bodily well-being.

"We shall have to face them some day," I cried, although the effort hurt abominably, "then why not now?" And I drew her hand down and kissed it passionately over and over again. "We are not children, to hide our faces among shadows and pretend we are invisible. At least we have the Present—the Moment that is here and now. We stand side by side in the heart of this deep spring day. This sunshine and these flowers, this wind across the lake, this sky of blue and this singing of the birds—all, all are ours *now*. Let us use the moment that Time gives, and so strengthen the chain you speak of that shall bring us again together times without number. We shall then, perhaps, remember. Oh, my heart, think what that would mean—to remember!"

Exhaustion caught me, and I sank back among my cushions. But Marion rose up suddenly and stood beside me. And as she did so, another Sky dropped softly down upon us both, and I smelt again the incense of old, old gardens that brought long-forgotten perfumes, incredibly sweet, but with it an ache of far-off, passionate remembrance that was pain. This great ache of distance swept over me like a wave.

I know not what grand change then was wrought upon her beauty, so that I saw her defiant and erect, commanding Fate because she understood it. She towered over me, but it was her soul that towered. The rush of internal darkness in me blotted out all else. The familiar, present sky grew dim, the sunshine faded, the lake and flowers and poplars dipped away. Conditions a thousand times more vivid took their place. She stood out, clear and shining in the glory of an undressed soul, brave and confident with an eternal love that separation strengthened but could never, never change. The deep sadness I abruptly realised, was very little removed from joy—because, somehow, it was the condition of joy. I could not explain it more than that.

And her voice, when she spoke, was firm with a note of steel in it; intense, yet devoid of the wasting anger that passion brings. She was determined beyond Death itself, upon a foundation sure and lasting as the stars. The heart in her was calm, because she *knew*. She was magnificent.

"We are together—always," she said, her voice rich with the knowledge of some unfathomable experience, "for separation is temporary merely, forging new links in the ancient chain of lives that binds our hearts eternally together." She looked like one who has conquered the adversity Time brings, by accepting it. "You speak of the Present as though our souls were already fitted now to bid it stay, needing no further fashioning. Looking only to the Future, you forget our ample Past that has made us what we are. Yet our Past is here and now, beside us at this very moment. Into the hollow cups of weeks and months, of years and centuries, Time pours its flood beneath our eyes. Time is our school room... Are you so soon afraid? Does not separation achieve that which companionship never could accomplish? And how shall we dare eternity together if we cannot be strong in separation first?"

I listened while a flood of memories broke up through film upon film and layer upon layer that had long covered them.

"This Present that we seem to hold between our hands," she went on in that earnest, distant voice, "*is* our moment of sweet remembrance that you speak of, of renewal, perhaps, too, of reconciliation—a fleeting instant when we may kiss again and say goodbye, but with strengthened hope and courage revived. But we may not stay together finally—we *cannot*—until long discipline and pain shall have perfected sympathy and schooled our love by searching, difficult tests, that it may last for ever."

I stretched my arms out dumbly to take her in. Her face shone down upon me, bathed in an older, fiercer sunlight. The change in her seemed in an instant then complete. Some big, soft wind blew both of us ten thousand miles away. The centuries gathered us back together.

"Look, rather, to the Past," she whispered grandly, "where first we knew the sweet opening of our love. Remember, if you can, how the pain and separation have made it so worth while to continue. And be braver thence."

She turned her eyes more fully upon my own, so that their light persuaded me utterly away with her. An immense new happiness broke over me. I listened, and with the stirrings of an ampler courage. It seemed I followed her down an interminable vista of remembrance till I was happy with her among the flowers and fields of our earliest pre-existence.

Her voice came to me with the singing of birds and the hum of summer insects.

"Have you so soon forgotten," she sighed, "when we knew together the perfume of the hanging Babylonian Gardens, or when the Hesperides were so soft to us in the dawn of the world? And do you not remember," with a little rise of passion in her voice, "the sweet plantations of Chaldea, and how we tasted the odour of many a drooping flower in the gardens of Alcinous and Adonis, when the bees of olden time picked out the honey for our eating? It is the fragrance of those first hours we knew together that still lies in our hearts to-day, sweetening our love to this apparent suddenness. Hence comes the full, deep happiness we gather so easily To-day... The breast of every ancient forest is torn with storms and lightning... that's why it is so soft and full of little gardens. You have forgotten too easily the glades of Lebanon, where we whispered our earliest secrets while the big winds drove their chariots down those earlier skies..."

There rose an indescribable tempest of remembrance in my heart as I strove to bring the pictures into focus; but words failed me, and the hand I eagerly stretched out to touch her own, met only sunshine and the rain of apple blossoms.

"The myrrh and frankincense," she continued, in a sighing voice that seemed to come with the wind from invisible caverns in the sky, "the grapes and pomegranates—have they all passed from you, with the train of apes and peacocks, the tigers and the ibis, and the hordes of dark-faced slaves? And this little sun that plays so lightly here upon our woods of beech and pine—does it bring back nothing of the old-time scorching when the olive slopes, the figs and ripening cornfields heard our vows and watched our love mature?... Our spread encampment in the Desert—do not these sands upon our little beach revive its lonely majesty for you, and have you forgotten the gleaming towers of Semiramis... or, in Sardis, those strange lilies that first tempted our souls to their divine disclosure...?"

Conscious of a violent struggle between pain and joy, both too deep for me to understand, I rose to seize her in my arms. But the effort dimmed the flying pictures. The wind that bore her voice down the stupendous vista fled back into the caverns whence it came. And the pain caught me in a vice of agony so searching that I could not move a muscle. My tongue lay dry against my lips. I could not frame a word of any sentence...

Her voice presently came back to me, but fainter, like a whisper from the stars. The light dimmed everywhere; I saw no more the vivid, shining scenery she had summoned. A mournful dusk instead crept down upon the world she had momentarily revived.

"...we may not stay together," I heard her little whisper, "until long discipline shall have perfected sympathy, and schooled our love to last. For this love of ours is for ever, and the pain that tries it is the furnace that fashions precious stones..."

Again I stretched my arms out. Her face shone a moment longer in that forgotten fiercer sunlight, then faded very swiftly. The change, like a veil, passed over it. From the place of prodigious distance where she had been, she swept down towards me with such dizzy speed. As she was To-day I saw her again, more and more.

"Pain and separation, then, are welcome," I tried to stammer, "and we will desire them"—but my thought got no further into expression than the first two words. Aching blotted out coherent utterance.

She bent down very close against my face. Her fragrance was about my lips. But her voice ran off like a faint thrill of music, far, far away. I caught the final words, dying away as wind dies in high branches of a wood. And they reached me this time through the droning of bees and of waves that murmured close at hand upon the shore.

"...for our love is of the soul, and our souls are moulded in Eternity. It is not yet, it is not now, our perfect consummation. Nor shall our next time of meeting know it. We shall not even speak... For I shall not be free..." was what I heard. She paused.

"You mean we shall not know each other?" I cried, in an anguish of spirit that mastered the lesser physical pain.

I barely caught her answer:

"My discipline then will be in another's keeping—yet only that I may come back to you... more perfect... in the end..."

The bees and waves then cushioned her whisper with their humming. The trail of a deeper silence led them far away. The rush of temporary darkness passed and lifted. I opened my eyes. My love sat close beside me in the shadow of the poplars. One hand held both my own, while with the other she arranged my pillows and stroked my aching head. The world dropped back into a tiny scale once more.

"You have had the pain again," Marion murmured anxiously, "but it is better now. It is passing." She kissed my cheek. "You must come in..."

But I would not let her go. I held her to me with all the strength that was in me. "I had it, but it's gone again. An awful darkness came with it," I whispered in the little ear that was so close against my mouth. "I've been dreaming," I told her, as memory dipped away, "dreaming of you and me—together somewhere—in old gardens, or forests—where the sun was—"

But she would not let me finish. I think, in any case, I could not have said more, for thought evaded me, and any language of coherent description was in the same instant beyond my power. Exhaustion came upon me, that vile, compelling nausea with it.

"The sun here is too strong for you, dear love," I heard her saying, "and you must rest more. We have been doing too much these last few days. You must have more repose." She rose to help me move indoors.

"I have been unconscious, then?" I asked, in the feeble whisper that was all I could manage.

"For a little while. You slept, while I watched over you."

"But I was away from you! Oh, how could you let me sleep, when our time together is so short?"

She soothed me instantly in the way she knew we both loved so. I clung to her until she released herself again.

"Not away from me," she smiled, "for I was with you in your dreaming."

"Of course, of course you were"; but already I knew not exactly why I said it, nor caught the deep meaning that struggled up into my words from such unfathomable distance.

"Come," she added, with her sweet authority again, "we must go in now. Give me your arm, and I will send out for the cushions. Lean on me. I am going to put you back to bed."

"But I shall sleep again," I said petulantly, "and we shall be separated."

"We shall dream together," she replied, as she helped me slowly and painfully towards the old grey walls of the Château.

## II

Half an hour later I slept deeply, peacefully, upon my bed in the big stately chamber where the roses watched beside the latticed windows.

And to say I dreamed again is not correct, for it can only be expressed by saying that I saw and knew. The figures round the bed were actual, and in life. Nothing could be more real than the whisper of the doctor's voice—that solemn, grave-faced man who was so tall—as he said, sternly yet brokenly, to some one: "You must say good-bye; and you had better say it *now*." Nor could anything be more definite and sure, more charged with the actuality of living, than the figure of Marion, as she stooped over me to obey the terrible command. For I saw her face float down towards me like a star, and a shower of pale spring blossoms rained upon me with her hair. The perfume of old, old gardens rose about me as she slipped to her knees beside the bed and kissed my lips—so softly it was like the breath of wind from lake and orchard, and so lingeringly it was as though the blossoms lay upon my mouth and grew into flowers that she planted there.

"Good-bye, my love; be brave. It is only separation."

"It is death," I tried to say, but could only feebly stir my lips against her own.

I drew her breath of flowers into my mouth... and there came then the darkness which is final.

The voices grew louder. I heard a man struggling with an unfamiliar language. Turning restlessly, I opened my eyes—upon a little, stuffy room, with white walls whereon no pictures hung. It was very hot. A woman was standing beside the bed, and the bed was very short. I stretched, and my feet kicked against the boarding at the end.

"Yes, he *is* awake," the woman said in French. "Will you come in? The doctor said you might see him when he woke. I think he'll know you." She spoke in French. I just knew enough to understand.

And of course I knew him. It was Haddon. I heard him thanking her for all her kindness, as he blundered in. His French, if anything, was worse than my own. I felt inclined to laugh. I did laugh. "By Jove! Old man, this is bad luck, isn't it? You've had a narrow shave. This good lady telegraphed—"

"Have you got my ice-axe? Is it all right?" I asked. I remembered clearly the motor accident— everything.

"The ice-axe is right enough," he laughed, looking cheerfully at the woman, "but what about yourself? Feel bad still? Any pain, I mean?"

"Oh, I feel all right," I answered, searching for the pain of broken bones, but finding none. "What happened? I was stunned, I suppose?"

"Bit stunned, yes," said Haddon. "You got a nasty knock on the head, it seems. The point of the axe ran into you, or something."

"Was that all?"

He nodded. "But I'm afraid it's knocked our climbing on the head. Shocking bad luck, isn't it?"

"I telegraphed last night," the kind woman was explaining.

"But I couldn't get here till this morning," Haddon said. "The telegram didn't find me till midnight, you see." And he turned to thank the woman in his voluble, dreadful French. She kept a little pension on the shores of the lake. It was the nearest house, and they had carried me in there and got the doctor to me all within the hour. It proved slight enough, apart from the shock. It was not even concussion. I had merely been stunned. Sleep had cured me, as it seemed.

"Jolly little place," said Haddon, as he moved me that afternoon to Geneva, whence, after a few days' rest, we went on into the Alps of Haute Savoie, "and lucky the old body was so kind and quick. Odd, wasn't it?" He glanced at me.

Something in his voice betrayed he hid another thought. I saw nothing "odd" in it at all, only very tiresome. "What's its name?" I asked, taking a shot at a venture.

He hesitated a second. Haddon, the climber, was not skilled in the delicacies of tact.

"Don't know its present name," he answered, looking away from me across the lake, "but it stands on the site of an old château—destroyed a hundred years ago—the Château de Bellerive."

And then I understood my old friend's absurd confusion. For Bellerive chanced also to be the name of a married woman I knew in Scotland—at least, it was her maiden name, and she was of French extraction.

THE END

## The Best in Mystery & Noir Fiction Past & Present

1-933586-26-5 **Benjamin Appel** Sweet Money Girl / Life and Death of a Tough Guy $21.95
1-933586-03-6 **Malcolm Braly** Shake Him Till He Rattles / It's Cold Out There $19.95
1-933586-10-9 **Gil Brewer** Wild to Possess / A Taste for Sin $19.95
1-933586-20-6 **Gil Brewer** A Devil for O'Shaugnessy / The Three-Way Split $14.95
1-933586-24-9 **W. R. Burnett** It's Always Four O'Clock / Iron Man $19.95
1-933586-31-1 **Catherine Butzen** Thief of Midnight $15.95
1-933586-38-9 **James Hadley Chase** Come Easy--Go Easy / In a Vain Shadow $19.95
0-9667848-0-4 **Storm Constantine** Oracle Lips (limited hb) $45.00
1-933586-30-3 **Jada M. Davis** One for Hell $19.95
1-933586-43-5 **Bruce Elliot** One is a Lonely Number /
              **Elliott Chaze** Black Wings Has My Angel $19.95
1-933586-34-6 **Don Elliott** Gang Girl / Sex Bum $19.95
1-933586-12-5 **A. S. Fleischman** Look Behind You Lady / The Venetian Blonde $19.95
1-933568-28-1 **A. S. Fleischman** Danger in Paradise / Malay Woman $19.95
1-933586-35-4 **Orrie Hitt** The Cheaters / Dial "M" for Man $19.95
0-9667848-7-1 **Elisabeth Sanxay Holding** Lady Killer / Miasma $19.95
0-9667848-9-8 **Elisabeth Sanxay Holding** The Death Wish / Net of Cobwebs $19.95
0-9749438-5-1 **Elisabeth Sanxay Holding** Strange Crime in Bermuda / Too Many Bottles $19.95
1-933586-16-8 **Elisabeth Sanxay Holding** The Old Battle Ax / Dark Power $19.95
1-933586-17-6 **Russell James** Underground / Collected Stories $14.95
0-9749438-8-6 **Day Keene** Framed in Guilt / My Flesh is Sweet $19.95
1-933586-33-8 **Day Keene** Dead Dolls Don't Talk / Hunt the Killer / Too Hot to Hold $23.95
1-933586-21-4 **Mercedes Lambert** Dogtown / Soultown $14.95
1-933586-14-1 **Dan Marlowe/Fletcher Flora/Charles Runyon** Trio of Gold Medals $15.95
1-933586-07-9 **Ed by McCarthy & Gorman** Invasion of the Body Snatchers: A Tribute $19.95
1-933586-09-5 **Margaret Millar** An Air That Kills / Do Evil in Return $19.95
1-933586-23-0 **Wade Miller** The Killer / Devil on Two Sticks $17.95
1-933586-27-3 **E. Phillips Oppenheim** The Amazing Judgment / Mr. Laxworthy's Adventures $19.95
0-9749438-3-5 **Vin Packer** Something in the Shadows / Intimate Victims $19.95
1-933586-05-2 **Vin Packer** Whisper His Sin / The Evil Friendship $19.95
1-933586-18-4 **Richard Powell** A Shot in the Dark / Shell Game $14.95
1-933586-19-2 **Bill Pronzini** Snowbound / Games $14.95
0-9667848-8-x **Peter Rabe** The Box / Journey Into Terror $21.95
0-9749438-4-3 **Peter Rabe** Murder Me for Nickels / Benny Muscles In $19.95
1-933586-00-1 **Peter Rabe** Blood on the Desert / A House in Naples $21.95
1-933586-11-7 **Peter Rabe** My Lovely Executioner / Agreement to Kill $19.95
1-933586-22-2 **Peter Rabe** Anatomy of a Killer / A Shroud for Jesso $14.95
1-933586-32-x **Peter Rabe** The Silent Wall / The Return of Marvin Palaver $19.95
0-9749438-2-7 **Douglas Sanderson** Pure Sweet Hell / Catch a Fallen Starlet $19.95
1-933586-06-0 **Douglas Sanderson** The Deadly Dames / A Dum-Dum for the President $19.95
1-933586-29-X **Charlie Stella** Johnny Porno $15.95
1-933586-39-7 **Charlie Stella** Rough Riders $15.95
1-933586-08-7 **Harry Whittington** A Night for Screaming / Any Woman He Wanted $19.95
1-933586-25-7 **Harry Whittington** To Find Cora / Like Mink Like Murder / Body and Passion $23.95
 1-933586-36-2 **Harry Whittington** Rapture Alley / Winter Girl / Strictly for the Boys $23.95

www.ingramcontent.com/pod-product-compliance
Lightning Source LLC
LaVergne TN
LVHW011926070526
838202LV00054B/4511